Reviews

"One of our generation's core questions is how can humanity, starting with our own actions, shape the promising and unknown future of Artificial Intelligence. Via this thought provoking, beautifully written story, Thireau provokes the fiction of science and society. A must read for anyone interested in AI research, who wants to shape a positive future world, beginning today, with personal reflection."

Lili Cheng
Corporate VP Microsoft, AI and Research

"...at the heart of this work is a kind of re-imagination—the prerequisite for innovation—that is able to keep up the changes of a dynamic world. Which brings us to The Morgan Expedient. This book serves to entertain, and it does so in spades....an exciting metaphorical tale that transcends the predictable with a clever intertwining of fiction, fact, and fantasy. It is also a great exploration of the myriad of signals of radical change that scientists and engineers face every day. No one has superhuman powers or reached a Singularity yet, but you can bet that many are working on it."

Devin Fidler
Director of Research, Institute for the Future (IFTF)

*"Human history used to be a game of thrones. Thrones are down, institutions are faltering, territories redrawn, and 'superpower' gains new meaning. Thireau takes us on a sensational journey into the future, from the impossible to the obvious, boldly tackling topics that haunt us all.
Be prepared: If you start reading, you are likely to finish in one sitting."*

Gabriella Milkovic
Hungarian National Ballet, International Affairs

The Morgan Expedient
K. E. Thireau

K. E. Thireau

The Morgan Expedient

"Small mind, small God"
Morgan Pendergrass

Table of contents

Acknowledgments

For Julius and Elizabeth

and...

To my father, the smartest, kindest, most creative person I
know...and because he thinks the same of me.

In memory of my mother, an avid reader, forever cradling
a book, happily exploring vast creative landscapes.

To long friends, who have generously shared of their
intelligence, humour, and encouragement.

Foreword

In my work at the Institute For The Future (IFTF), a 50-year-old research center created with a mandate to explore emerging issues and technologies, I regularly have the opportunity to work with leaders interested in systematically thinking about the future. This is typically a harrowing process, and involves both tracking challenges that are taking shape on the horizon and re-imagining deep historical assumptions to open up completely new possibilities.

At the heart of this work is a kind of re-imagination – the prerequisite for innovation – that is able to keep up with the challenges of a dynamic world. Which brings us to The Morgan Expedient. This book serves to entertain, and it does so in spades. It sparks the reader's imagination with a scenario that begins with the familiar, moves into crisis management, and forces players to imagine a new horizon. It is an exciting metaphorical tale that transcends the predictable with a clever intertwining of fiction, fact, and fantasy.

It is also a great exploration of the myriad of signals of radical change that scientists and engineers face every day. No one has superhuman powers or reached a Singularity yet, but you can bet that many are working on it.

Devin Fidler
Director of Research, IFTF

Prologue

August 9, 2096

*A*n historical account of Morgan Pendergrass' life story was nearly completed for his one hundred and twenty-fifth birthday party. Morgan's daughter, Adele Pendergrass Collins, was prepared to authorize payment on behalf of her father's gift. "Accurate?" Adele queried one of the three agents personally standing before the notable daughter of the Confederation's founding father.

"We've everything gleaned from your sources. This is the time for final editing," explained the spokesman unnecessarily. "It's been amassed neurologically. We've combed through scarce archives and limited personal accounts. We've also cross-referenced against data from your father's discarded neural implants you've supplied. You must be aware that we're operating a bit in the dark here?"

"Of course," Adele acknowledged. "My father never allowed a collectome disk."

"If you could fill in the spaces toward the end of 2070, it would help. Perhaps if you added personal reflections, we'd have a better conclusion," the editor appealed. "We've never worked with such a unique story. Clarification: we can't seem to collaborate anything."

"No," Adele Collins said. "Let the bio-recall algorithm read as is. The guests with whom we might share it won't require more. I'll review it today to make sure. I've the only duplicate, correct?"

"Yes, and the original," assured another.

"No need to transmit to Dr. Pendergrass until after the surprise party. Go ahead and send it to me now. I'm amped for immediate download."

"Your father is of concern. We need permission," another representative pressed. "Are you able to obtain a release from Dr. Pendergrass?

Adele paused at the curious request. It had been a long time since someone had questioned her authority. Yet certain rules prevailed in lieu of certainty. To the relief of the agents, Adele confirmed her legal position and a form was forwarded to them within seconds.

Collectome Productions confirmed the transmission and the meeting concluded. Adele thanked and escorted an awestruck group to her home's front door. They took their seats within the transport and one of the women enthusiastically waved her hand, mimicking Adele's tacit farewell gesture. Appreciative of the new generation's efforts to learn interactive mannerisms, Adele waved until the vehicle disappeared down the long driveway.

She moved to the sunroom's chaise longue, stretched out, and drew a deep anticipatory breath. Her cerebral cache indicated that the compilation of thoughts, conversations, and events translated into anecdotal and objective accounts had completed its neural download.

I'm going to fast-forward, she thought as she sought the collated impressions and interpretations that would begin with her father's 84th birthday. Telephonically configured for the most comforting resonance, the narrator's voice frequency was set at 6kHz. As the memoir spilled forth, Adele approved of the dynamically modulated hums of life, nearly perfected, to familiar replications of scenes set to Thursday, August 12, 2055. Transported to her North Carolina home nine hours before her daughter's birth, Adele took a long drink from the glass beside her and strategically arranged pillows behind her head.

This is where it really began, she thought as her eyes closed.

Chapter 1

Birthdays

Cary, North Carolina
Thursday, August 12, 2055

*F*rom the far end of the dining room table, Morgan Pendergrass scrutinized his only child over a half-eaten plate of toasted cheese sandwiches. As much as he tried to convey suspicions of his daughter's labor pains to his wife sitting at the opposite end, he could not. Rapid nods, furled eyebrows, and squinted eyes went unnoticed. Morgan crossed his arms high on his chest. He uncrossed them to pick invisible lint from his shirt. He cleared his throat and rearranged his chair. No amount of overstated signals worked. Morgan had crudely repeated once too often that his only child looked 'ready to pop'. Angela chose to ignore her husband's antics and silently sipped iced coffee. The subject of the impending birth had worn thin. For nine months, Morgan had been a dog with a bone.

Adele's untouched meal, her flushed face, and her constant shifting finally manifested into an escalating groan, punctuated by an impressive string of uncharacteristic profanities. Declarations began with the word "holy" and moved into territory ordinarily filed under the Southern propriety umbrella far left of unbecoming behavior.

"Ha!" Morgan stood and fired a white napkin toward the table's center, a trigger-happy referee making an unmistakable call. He eyed his son-in-law, reaching for the last piece of bacon, and cautioned, "You'd better drop that side of pork and tend to your wife, Lex."

The ecstatic patriarch moved from the table toward the stairwell whooping unbridled gusto. With the help of the home's central monitor, signs and sounds of Adele's reaction to the onset of labor pains spread throughout the estate.

"Shut that damn thing off!" demanded Adele. Her father, however, had long disappeared upstairs by the time Lex dropped the bacon.

Ever the Southern gentlemen, the matter of appropriate attire was foremost on Pendergrass' mind. He had given great consideration as to what a properly outfitted grandfather might wear to a maternity ward. He surveyed the pink hand-sewn silk tie with the crisp white shirt purchased the day his grand-child's gender had been selected. Lightweight gray pants had been pressed and positioned on the valet for weeks. Morgan whistled, hustled, and imagined.

Scrutinizing his mirrored image, the folds of lax neck skin were maneuvered to secure the uppermost button. As discomfiting as the process was, Morgan approved the final effect. No longer a perfect size $16^{1/2}$, an inappropriately sized shirt nevertheless endorsed a younger self-image. In deference to an expanding girth, suspenders were deployed, previously fastened to his trousers.

Morgan heartily approved of mirrors. As grounded as he was in life, the man was blind to infirmities, wrinkles, and flab that might have kept vainer men indoors. He declared to the full-length mirror, "Brilliant!"

Impervious to one of the warmest days of a long, hot Carolina summer, the eager grandfather-to-be reappeared triumphantly downstairs. Head held high, with a nuanced harmonizing hand-kerchief that nonchalantly crested from a light linen vest pocket, Morgan threw his hands upward in the foyer's winner's circle as he slid into place on the freshly waxed oak floor.

"Ta-da!"

Wife, daughter, son-in-law, and one of the family's panting Plott Hounds looked on incredulously.

"What's this, Morgan?" Angela Pendergrass failed to hide her exasperation. "Shall we get Adele to the hospital?" she continued.

"Think I need my hat?" Morgan quizzically tapped his bare head toward his wife.

"It's promising to be every bit of 95 degrees," Angela Pendergrass appealed to her husband.

"I'm gettin' the hat. It's likely to pour," he insisted.

Morgan gathered his sou'wester and cane from the dining room, reappeared in the vestibule, and impatiently beckoned everyone to follow his lead toward paired doors for their waiting car.

"The hospital has been notified, Angela. Adele's bag is in the trunk. The kitchen has packed us ham sandwiches and I've cigars. I've concluded my morning constitution, put on a suitable tie, and tucked an apposite pocket square. That preparation required all of eight to ten minutes. Now, let's go welcome this child into the world without all the fuss."

* * *

The next five hours passed slowly. In the hospital's waiting room, Dr. Morgan Pendergrass restlessly paced and held nonstop court with hospital visitors. He quizzed the nurses about obstetrics and corrected their answers. He advised the head nurse on duty hustling back and forth, "It is not unprofessional to wear perfume if you need it." He kicked the floor's robot-cleaner, flipping it on its back, and wagered barter-bits with hospital employees as to its recovery time.

"Stop betting, Morgan," warned Angela. "Let these people and that bot finish their work."

"Just making pocket change, Cookie," he shrugged.

Monitor reports regularly reassured the expectant grandparents that things were going well. Dr. Lex Collins, Adele's husband and an attending physician, was in the uncertain position of placating his irascible father-in-law.

"Not yet...getting there but looks like a few more hours. Adele is against speeding things up. She wants everything the old fashioned way," Lex reported via personal monitor.

"Ridiculous! Since when's pain a fashion statement?" Morgan growled as he departed the waiting room. "I'll be back when she's closer. Ping me," he irritably instructed his son-in-law.

"Please don't wander off too far," Angela warned.

* * *

It was 6:30 p.m. when Morgan stepped onto the sidewalk outside of the Hospital Annex that would lead to the Research Quad's courtyard. A Cheshire cat smile invited those that crossed Dr. Pendergrass' path to inquire as to the reason for his unusually exultant disposition.

"Today is going to be my granddaughter's birthday," he beamed to anyone glancing his direction. To those attempting to slide under the radar, he shouted. In the intervals absent of pedestrians, Morgan continued to blare the good news in lieu of human targets.

"My granddaughter is on the way...going to be named after my mother, Caroline. 'Course, she's stuck with her father's last name, Collins. I couldn't do much about that," he announced, grinning at a street cam.

"She'll share my birthday! She's going to arrive before Friday the 13th, to boot. It was like I planned it!" he interrupted a cat licking its private parts.

Morgan Pendergrass gave no mind as to whether those who politely paused to greet him had something else to do, somewhere to be. He dismissed any notion of pressing matters other than an impending birth that allowed a grandfather to take liberties of simple courtesies. The prattle would continue to captivate audiences until alternative familiar faces appeared as a distraction. The man was a lingerer. There were also problems with personal space.

As Dr. Meredith Green closed distance, the stocky middle-aged woman spotted Morgan staring upward standing beside the Quad's central fountain. With the onset of dusk, garden lights ignited. Morgan stood in a rare solitary moment admiring his twelve-foot granite likeness now highlighted in a gurgling pool of water. A full complement of medical interns, white coats flapping in their wake, struggled with remotely controlled medical equipment on wheeled carts, shadowing their trotting leader.

Dr. Green called to Morgan. "Dr. Pendergrass? Hey there!" Her face lit with pleasure; she had managed to surprise Pendergrass relieving himself in the fountain, smiling up at his sculpted image. Whether it was a matter of relief or ego, Meredith's former mentor appeared a happy man.

"You're about to meet the famous Morgan Pendergrass, ex-governor of our state and one of the founders of the Confederation of American States, face to face," Green announced to the still white coats about her. Morgan turned toward the fresh-faced interns and zipped his pants without a trace of embarrassment.

Dr. Green continued, "He's one of those well-groomed, distinctive, charming Southern men, minus the charm."

Morgan smiled broadly at his protégé with whom he'd worked on Wake Forest University genome projects nearly thirty years prior. He smirked and extended his hand.

"Pass. I know where that's been!" Dr. Green fashioned her hand into a mock pistol and aimed toward her friend's groin.

"You're showing your age. These young people have no more idea why you'd be taking aim any more than listening to a watch."

"Who's still wearing a watch?"

Morgan extended his arm skyward and pointed to an antique Rolex arm-piece that had not functioned in three decades. At the end of the arm, an extended middle finger formed an exclamation point.

"Presenting… a point in time!" he announced.

"I hear there's big news in the Annex," Dr. Meredith Green proclaimed by way of ignoring the gesture.

Morgan twirled his cane and finished by aiming its tip toward Green's buxom chest.

"That's so, Missy Green, daughter of the honorable Clyde O. Green, my former good friend who smoked too much of his own poorly cured GMO tobacco and liberally partook of my rare and expensive Pappy Van Winkle bourbon...prematurely dropping dead as a doornail because of similar lackluster life choices. God rest and bless that honest Southern soul. Your father was a great scientist and, unlike his daughter, did me the honor of laughing at my jokes. I remember most particularly his gourmand delicacy, 'Chicken of the Tree'. Best squirrel dish I ever had."

The astonished faces of the young research assistants encouraged Morgan to continue issuing embarrassing trivia. He lowered his cane and leaned thoughtfully upon its handle. Scrutinizing the woman before him, Morgan pointed up and down to Dr. Green's various body parts.

"You've evidently made a decision not to be a slave to fashion. As a scientist, you must be aware of the chemical and permanent remedies for your condition. You're giving circus clowns a run for their money, Meredith. You're gonna force those poor artistic souls to form a clown union with you wildcards running around town."

Meredith Green recognized the exercise. She waited silently. Morgan, she appreciated, was just getting warmed up. Morgan did not disappoint.

"It's no wonder you live alone with that minuscule, hairless, incontinent, good-for-nothing excuse for a canine. Get yourself an old photo! Paint yourself up by the numbers! Good God, get a real dog that sends a message you're actually worth some protection!

"I remember when every breathing male in these parts had high hopes when Meredith Green walked into a room. From hooters to heels, you were a legend! Made crazy stallions out of hopeless boys. But hey, it'd take two men and a midget to lift you now..."

If Morgan Pendergrass had ever been equipped with a filter, it had worn thin by the time he attended University at 18 years of age. At 84, insults were misinterpreted as age-related lapses. The reality was that few friends and colleagues could recall a time when a standard conversation with Morgan Pendergrass was had. Rude remarks, dismissed by friends and family as playful banter, were the intentional manner by which Morgan figured to separate the wheat from the chaff, the 'pussies from the tigers'.

A long-held position of the multi-faceted man born and raised in rural North Carolina was that a lack of humor had facilitated the gradual degradation of the once-renowned great American spirit. Risk takers, maintained Morgan, had mutated into 'spineless, politically correct eunuchs'. By the same manner of thinking, Morgan preferred men with an 'honest pair of brass equipment' to 'ass-sitting, game-playing, beer-swilling, pot-smoking, group-hugging, annoying-as-hell wimp masters'.

"I just trust somebody who can knock the lights out of somebody in real life...or at least rhetorically maneuver out of a briar patch without discussing hurt feelings...!"

Asked his opinion of women in his younger days, he referred to the gender as America's 'real men'.

Morgan's style was predicated upon unpredictability. His was an unabated, non-redundant, politically incorrect, distilled stream of consciousness that was wondrous to behold in a time of social and political hyperbole. He stood out. He could not keep his mouth shut. Most everyone respected his candor. There were those who feared the man and those who hated him. No one, however, ignored Morgan Pendergrass.

Savvy hosts and hostesses competed for Morgan as the dinner circuit's blood sport champion, assured of a memorable event if Morgan accepted a social invitation. The recruiting measures were earnest.

"What's in it for me?" Morgan would ask when faced with a follow-up reminder for an event.

"Your favorite regenerated bourbon and lots of communists," was a typical assurance.

"I'm there. Add cigars," he would demand.

It didn't mean, however, Morgan and Angela would appear. In the event that the Pendergrass couple made social appearances, they did so to test the social and political climate.

Inevitably, Morgan Pendergrass was the climate. Spontaneous verbal eruptions from Mt. Pendergrass tended to spatter and spill unchecked over the emotional landscape that left amateurs with an emotional hobble. Few could run the gauntlet of Morgan's verbal obstacle course. Angela would never apologize for her husband's candor. When asked about her husband's manner of delivery, Angela could deliver the same, albeit with greater aplomb.

Meredith Green was similarly unaffected by Morgan's style after years of taking that which lesser souls termed 'emotional abuse'. She had the wisdom and experience to emerge as the brilliant researcher's sole intern.

"Better introduce me, Dr. Green. I'm a very big deal," Morgan winked conspiratorially behind Meredith Green as she turned her attention toward the medical cortège.

Dr. Green meant to indulge the ex-governor's expectations. A good recap of the man's contributions would be relished with comparable gratitude as a good, long drink of PVW Bourbon. Drawing breath, Meredith Green began an oft-repeated and illustrious introduction.

"May I introduce our former Governor Morgan Pendergrass, whom by anyone's reckoning, saved much of the former United States from certain disaster? Since the dark years, we forged one of the most secure and productive areas in the world thanks to his foresight and leadership..."

"Don't forget funding!" Morgan interjected.

"...and funding," added Dr. Green.

Green continued, "Our transition began with his guidance that seeded a national movement toward a Constitutional Convention as our federal governance failed. The onset of the EMP darkness terminated further political discussion about the American constitutional violations or state's rights. Survival became our focus. As our governor, Dr. Pendergrass was well prepared to lead our region through our bleakest hours, having taken much of North Carolina's industry, the Research Triangle, hospitals, businesses, and most residential areas off of the Federally controlled electrical grid cooperative before the EMP bombardment. We were equipped with our own satellites, hardened transformers, and alarm systems that proved critical to getting society back online. Within another two years, we were able to re-establish ourselves under the auspices of the newly created Confederation of American States. Thirty-four states operated under a refreshed constitutional understanding based upon our forefathers' founding principles."

Morgan nodded his approval and Meredith continued; "While most of you will recognize Governor Pendergrass as a first class visionary and administrator, I remind you that it was also Dr. Pendergrass who helped establish the Confederation Medical Consortium, reinstated the Research Triangle Hospital's ambitious research programs, and modernized the campuses upon which we now find ourselves. These gene-sequencing facilities the sizes of football fields were built at a time when the US federal government withdrew public funding of all University research. We decided to move ambitiously forward rather than scale back; we made full use of the super-exponential growth of data...data that most of the world ignored... and became the interpreters of hundreds of trillions of bits, making ours a genetically literate domain. Understanding genetics in a world of scientific Babel allowed like-minded pockets of scientists worldwide to speak life-code when privatized medical research cooperated. We were able to scientifically connect while political interests bitterly wrestled for resources that finally disappeared.

"That brings us to today's events and the reason we find Dr. Pendergrass gazing lovingly at the statue erected in his honor within the Quad's garden. I will take the opportunity to honor his ability to bring disparate scientific societies together. We recognize the technological perspicacity made possible by the former Governor's personal sacrifices. We never would have attracted so many bright, well-meaning, innovative people worldwide to our corner of the universe without his vision of making ours a scientific haven...and we must all thank him."

Green allowed the appropriate pause while the sidewalk assemblage applauded. She brought the introduction full circle by way of introducing the man's genetic legacy.

"Such prescient advances have brought his very pregnant daughter to our Annex Hospital today. Am I correct, Dr. Pendergrass?"

"You are!"

"She is one of the beneficiaries of the genetic inroads made on this campus."

"She is!" Morgan agreed. "Sounds like you're practicing for my funeral," he added.

"I believe that's the longest you've allowed me an uninterrupted speech. With all of your neuro-transmitters and supplanted body parts, I figure I've many decades to hone a decent eulogy."

"First time you've had something interesting to say. Keep at it." Morgan cleared his throat and scrutinized the attentive, well-mannered group standing before him. "If you could imagine yourself back to August 12, 1971, you'd see people like yours truly arriving in this world without benefit of genetic screening now entrusted to your teams. My birth wasn't much more than a pig in a poke. Today, we're on our way to figuring out who we are and what we can do to optimize the human condition. It hasn't always been that way. You young doctors and scientists have a lot on your shoulders..."

Morgan stopped his thoughts short and removed his hat to dab perspiration streaming behind his ears.

"Dr. Green," he continued, "who has yet to properly remember my birthday, will now have two Pendergrass birthdays to ignore on August 12."

Meredith Green gazed toward the Pendergrass Fountain.

"I've helped to memorialize you, Doctor. Good energy was devoted to raising funds for that ridiculous statue upon which you have just now shared holy water. I begged the Board to have your statue doing the same. Your love for pissing alfresco was scandalous. You refused to pose naked and implied it was in bad taste. Knowing your total lack of shame, I wonder the real reason for your reluctance," she teased. "People would have traveled far and wide to see Cary's own Mannequin Pee. In any case, please convey a congratulatory message for what promises to be dual birthdays!"

Morgan waved the comments away as if an errant fly had entered his airspace. In the silence, Morgan motioned for the group to draw closer.

"I'd like to mention that the only reason your fearless leader doesn't close her lab coat is because of an unwieldy endowed bosom. You people needn't go around lookin' slack like her. Sloppy is sloppy; it doesn't mean you're busier or smarter. Button a few buttons, keep up appearances," Morgan advised. Ceremoniously, one of three cigars was drawn from Morgan's breast pocket. He bowed low and offered it to Dr. Green, two hands cradling the prized ceremonial gift.

"Have a cigar, Meredith!"

"You know I don't smoke."

"Wasting an expensive rare cigar on a non-smoking female demonstrates my deepest admiration, my dear!"

Meredith good-naturedly received the gift in kind and signaled her entourage to march forward with the wrapped cigar held high above her head.

"Better answer your monitor, Governor. Sounds like someone means business. Best to Angela," she requested, moving rapidly past him.

Morgan bade farewell to the Board Chair of the North Carolina Medical University Consortium and excused himself to speak to the woman whose irritation had built momentum in his absence.

"Hello, Cookie!"

"It's time you returned to the waiting room. Stop bothering everyone," Angela pleaded.

"Can I smoke?"

"No, Morgan. You may not."

"Nobody cares! I'm not going to start a fire!"

Morgan considered his wife's tendency to monitor his whereabouts. *Justifiable,* he thought. He was a man too easily distracted, known to neglect appointments, and whose death was urgently reported each time he removed the PM medical tape. Inundated with requests for her husband's whereabouts, Angela proactively learned to track him. Notwithstanding Angela's good intentions, such interventions prompted uneasy recollections of unobstructed intrusions that once denigrated the gift of connectedness.

Morgan often considered what it meant to be the last living generation that remembered ways in which the Internet and the personal computer phenomena had eased their lives, afforded unparalleled educational opportunities, and streamed remote ideas and entertainment once impossible to access. It was once a positive game changer. In his 84 years, he witnessed those same offerings gradually slip into misuse. Pornography, commerce, and political news sites dwarfed the arts and sciences. Government and corporate entities assumed information stewardship, fettered away control, and subsequently reclaimed it for purposes of tax revenues. Children were more interested in creating public profiles than pursuing private interaction. Reliable facts were largely determined by unreliable sources as the world became less interested in veracity than quantities of interactive audiences.

We couldn't put that genie back into the bottle, he thought miserably.

Searches were limited to relevancy. Data mining determined whose interests were predisposed to what topic and on what levels that topic would disclose itself. Coordinated information was slow to manifest and then became a 'runaway train', recalled Morgan.

A long festering of false concern over rights to privacy finally collapsed under the weight of convenience and indifference. There were no more 'rights' to privacy any more than there was a 'right' to one's property, water use, or toilet choices. Morgan referred to unrelenting, ill-regulated government and corporate technological intrusions as 'letting loose the unmitigated, trash-talking, dumb-as-mud flying monkeys'. All, he thought, was a contrived reformation in the name of special interests.

"Every step of the way was paved with redefined moral mortar," he recalled. "Each of those steps led nowhere but down."

It made sense to a majority of Americans to give up personal freedoms in the interest of greater national security. The

world, after all, was in turmoil. In his time, Morgan had witnessed the world map charter twelve different ways. Powerful
political and religious blocks swallowed neighboring countries
too weak to resist. In the most literal sense, Americans believed that foreign policy should be left to crisis management
on domestic shores. Domestic crisis management exploded
and never contracted. When the Chinese and Russians fished
within American waters, a greatly diminished U.S. Navy was
unable to deal with such international impudence. Federal
rights to deal with dangers – real and imagined – were limited
to tapping into American lives and pockets.

Americans had finally been convinced that they were safer
for the intensified personal surveillance in their lives. The majority of Americans agreed that they 'had nothing to hide'. That
was what the official government polls and media surveys revealed and American citizens felt a certain comfort in a good
consensus. It was not long before the concept of individual
discretion was relegated to the magnitude of suspicious activity.

Morgan, too, was guilty of indifference. Until the president
of the United States decided to use genetic research as a political manifesto, Morgan didn't give 'a rat's patootie' about
politics. Then, genetic research suddenly exploded as the
problem du jour both left and right of the political spectrum.
'Human GMO' protests followed decades of a long list of hot
button social debates that lost political steam. Genetic research had been coined as genetic engineering and moved
rapidly into moral disparity.

Morgan awoke one day to hear that his life's work was a
plot to restructure the human race. Such concern for public
welfare was the purview of the Federal government naturally
charged constitutionally, thank you very much, with the nation's social integrity. Unidentified colleagues – people with
whom Morgan had never associated - published professional
objections. Once considered one of the field's most respected
scientists, Morgan was described as the 'Darwin Devil' by the
right. To the left, he was an 'Evil Elitist'.

"Americans will never allow the privileged to determine the
future of the human race!" railed President Clifton Brown, whose

political ascension could be credited to an uncanny ability to contrive and exploit grievances. "These people intend to drive good Americans into moral bankruptcy! It's pure racism!"

Facts mattered little. Americans who supported a modified Constitution felt the 21st century alterations were better suited to the majority, few of whom had ever managed to read the four pages of the original version. Furiously treading turbulent financial waters, most citizens were consumed more with daily survival than facts. Leaders of choice were expected to sort the issues of fair play. As long as those in power could supply subsidizations, it was fair.

"There's only one race," President Brown claimed on the World Wide News, flanked by an impressive cadre of concerned professionals in white lab coats. "It's the human race!" A chorus of affirming nods punctuated the solemn moment.

That particular campaign targeted Dr. Pendergrass as a charter member of the xenophobic club. As a 'social chauvinist', Morgan was no better than those who paid for private medical services, maintained manicured grass lawns rather than organic vegetable gardens, and kept defenseless horses in stalls better suited to refugee living quarters.

"Who dares ride horses in this day and age?" cried a host of animal rights activists picketing the Pendergrass Farms after one well-orchestrated broadcast targeted Morgan's lifestyle. Animal Freedom Fighters released the Pendergrass horses to the wild and shared the AFF reality exploit with the world. Even so, the animals stood contentedly grazing on tall grass in familiar fields. Pendergrass faced off with the federally sponsored event.

"Animal Cruelty!" cried the AFF protestors.

"They're happy!" Morgan angrily responded, a very confused man.

"We've analyzed the psychological damage!" proclaimed an animal psychologist waving one study. "They've lost their natural identity!"

"The real cruelty is having to live as a vegetable!" Morgan ranted to reporters. "How dare you ignore a cucumber's sentient moments when slicing up your own kind up for salad? Sweet Jesus, those lettuce heads decapitated by the millions, shredded without a second thought! Where's the humanity?" came the straw man argument. "Now, analyze this..." Morgan yelled at the animal psychologist, raising two middle fingers.

The wealthy would remain accused of a wide gamut of schemes exposed by President Brown. Brown's crowning achievement, the subject that got traction, was to target the most insidious plot – genetic engineering – in the political embryo.

Privileged classes were charged of plotting a permanent evolutionary advantage supported by their ill-gotten gains. Humanity's less fortunate souls, purported Brown, might live and die as worker bees. Dr. Pendergrass' persona, the supercilious mad professor, appeared everywhere. Morgan Pendergrass was depicted as Frankenstein's overly educated, self-serving, steak-eating, animal-hunting, horse-posturing, grass-cutting poster boy.

It was also around this time when the academic community was accused of getting into bed with corporate greed. Intelligence, motivation, and innovation were negatively associated with privileged and stratified education. It was, so it went, another piece of a hideous plot.

"We're going to fix this!" promised the White House.

Given sharp employment divides, the National Security Agency cooperated in order to help ensure new Federal Academic Guidelines compliance procedures with the annually reviewed Federal Fairness Doctrine. Assaulting University computer systems and intercepting internal communications helped them do that. Federal subsidies, received in any manner or form by higher education institutions, justified all invasive tactics on behalf of public transparency.

"We're going to fix this!" promised the Internal Revenue Service.

Morgan and Wake Forest University discovered and protested the theft of patented information disseminated without permission or remuneration. There was no response, positive or negative, from the White House. University intellectual properties across the nation were pilfered in increasing numbers, as the search for government evidence became legalized witch-hunts. Congressional oversight had diminished to impotency with the growing powers of the Executive Office. Federal agencies charged with compliance and accusations need not be bothered with answers.

Universities were directed to cease research until certified in the federal government's Core Curriculum that allowed full and free access to all universities on American soil. In lieu of successfully meeting the Federal Fairness Doctrine's educational guidelines, there was a baseline requirement to assure that 80% of graduating students would be guaranteed job placement. When students failed to realize appropriate income levels, the universities compromised and lost tax statuses until cleared by the Educational Regulatory Commission. Such investigations required the kind of defense so costly as to put private educational institutions out of business. It took no time at all to drive Morgan out of his mind.

"I might have weathered all that noise," recollected Morgan, "if it hadn't been for the government mandate to shut down the gyms, stadiums, and entertainment events. Getting rid of sports programs was war. When there's no damn ball game to get behind, there goes America! The new game was corruption!"

Morgan was a runner who had once excelled in the mile relay. He never failed to daily pound the University track until it disappeared with the stadiums that were converted into student housing for underprivileged migrants.

"Basketball, baseball, football games, soccer, tennis, golf... Morgan Pendergrass thinks it takes balls to make the American dream?" President Brown mistakenly accused in the World News Report.

"The President is spot on," Morgan agreed heartily.

Brown's reasoning was palatable and required no critical thinking for the masses that operated well enough without historical perspectives. A popular refrain was sung from every government institution: "It's the people's land. It's the people's resources. Americans paid for these resources by long collective sacrifices. Our country is not meant for the frivolous entertainment for a select few. It's for all of us! Corporate-sponsored sports? Ballet and opera? Who can eat such elitist rubbish?"

Morgan seethed as he remembered the silence that filled the gaps.

"There were plenty of people who thought like I did. Hell, we all had family members fighting and dying and working themselves into the ground for this country. We believed that every American citizen had an obligation to sustain the American backbone. You couldn't walk two feet without slipping a disc avoiding a federal cow pie or dodging one thrown at your face!"

Morgan made a decision to interrupt the silence as noisily and publicly as possible.

"'We the People' means that the government works for us. Ours is the only government charter that begins with this powerful statement! Either those pampered publicly supported scalawags get to work or I'm getting in the game!"

Shortly thereafter, Morgan threw his hat into North Carolina's gubernatorial ring. When asked what he could offer citizens, Morgan's cynical, straight-shooting retorts were quickly termed by media outlets as the Pendergrass 'hooey hose'. Others called him a 'walking shit sandwich'. No one could help but stay linked to the self-styled 'Fountain of Truth'.

"No one is as pissed off at the Feds or as prepared to hurt people's feelings in the process of righting this rotten rickety-ass American ship as Morgan Pendergrass. Bring it on!" Morgan spat for emphasis. There were thousands of photos and slow motion vids of Morgan's airborne spittle wriggling wet, long, and unbroken to impressive distances. Pendergrass sputum sparked hawking contests statewide that helped raise campaign funds.

People who hadn't bothered to vote in decades took notice as the Cary native took on that which he termed the 'poli-shits'.

"Where's your toilet? I've got the poli-shits..." he'd ask in every government building he walked into.

Morgan rarely answered a reporter's question. They would ask. He would laugh and snort, "So you can misconstrue the answer? Bullocks!" Morgan was happily incorrigible toward national reporters who failed to honor their profession. "Some of you idiots think that 'checks and balances' means stopping and pushing me off the nearest cliff!"

Pendergrass musings dominated everyone's conversations. He was quoted everywhere by everyone. Rather than the issues espoused, the premier attraction was for the uncensored, loose-lipped North Carolinian.

He had ideas about personal choice:

"We're taxed for our meager Internet services and they determine what we're lookin' for? Since when is information 'tailored' for us? I like pickin' off the rack, wiping my own backside with the toilet paper I prefer!"

There was hunting advice:

"It's easy to trap a Fed. They'll step over a dollar to pick up a dime every time..."

Value propositions:

"We mean to fire a truckload of some of the most unamusing clowns from this government circus. Hey, nobody's laughing here! We want our money back!"

Career choices:

"Professional politicians fill the black holes in their hearts with our misery! Join up...it doesn't take a lick of sense!"

Semantics:

"My sorry excuse for an opponent says he's been a great leader. I wholeheartedly concur. Question is, y'all like that ring in your nose?"

Washington took note of a newly-introduced game called The Mouse Way that cynically featured the Feral Feds. Intrusions of American homes, schools, or a day at the beach, were graphically depicted in aggressive, territorial, insect-like behaviors of government agents that swarmed, squirmed, and wormed their way into social crevices, only to crawl out of the woodwork to entangle, bite, inhibit, or otherwise irritate good citizens. Players were challenged to figure alternative routes that eluded the obnoxious, expensive, and intrusive traps set by government rules and regulations. The popularity of Mouse Way moved the government to try to shut the game down. But it was a popular game. It was also free. Everyone liked free. Most of the world spent 60% of their paychecks on virtual and augmented games. Mouse Way's attraction continued unabated. In keeping with the spirit of the game, Mouse Way continually corrupted the rules of ascension. Those that reached the highest level found themselves re-positioned in the White House.

Morgan ensured that the game was widely and freely distributed on Personal Monitors. The anti-government message could not be blocked or ignored. The Department of Justice filed a lawsuit citing illegal campaign financing parameters that had yet to appear on the books. While the legality of the game was challenged, it reigned supreme as the most popular entertainment in the United States. Copyrights had long been unobserved or violated. Mouse Way was copied and happily found its way to sympathetic citizens worldwide.

Morgan continued to produce the incendiary game. As a registered candidate, however, he was forced to withdraw from the game's distribution. It was not his fault if people replicated the game; he was not inclined to challenge anyone's right to do so.

"It's a free country!" he would proclaim. "Oh, yeah. I forgot!" he would add. Then, he would really spit.

The game paled in comparison to Morgan's outspokenness. Morgan was interviewed as to his views of the Supreme Court's latest intrusion as translators of the American Constitution. The Second Amendment, meant to enforce the right to responsibly bear arms, was once again undermined. The unanimous decision went beyond safety concerns or the rapidly developing technology of weaponry. Even as ammunition was government controlled, gun ownership had become a matter of redefining the word 'militia' and the 'right of the people' that antedated the Constitution and was confirmed by the Second Amendment. The Supreme judges had assumed the position of rewriting the constitution for decades.

The term 'militia' would be henceforth defined as the formalized American Armed Forces. The federally sanctioned military was formally distinguishable from individuals and civilian para-military groups that guarded community homes or institutions, hunters, or those that owned personal firearms for personal protection. Moreover, all civil police would come under the auspices of the Federal government. At the end of the long semantic day, the protracted process to obtain any classification of weaponry precluded private ownership. Thirty-four states responded by summarily ignoring the Supreme Court ruling. Given the inability and reluctance of the Federal armed forces or local police to protect civilians from domestic or international violence, and the unlikely prospect of arresting and incarcerating more than 90% of law-abiding gun owners, state legislation circumvented the Supreme Court rulings and sparked a national firestorm. It also prompted Morgan to create a new platform.

"We're taking dubious advice from pompous, politically positioned legal experts our forefathers entrusted as our constitutional guardians. Those long black robes sported by our Supreme Court justices now blow in the blustering partisan winds, surfing above us common folk on hifalutin hot air, cock-sure that our good citizens are dumb as dirt. We should fear a time when our Republic spawns potentates so arrogant and short-sighted as to decree our nation's founding principles as outdated when their own position precariously sits upon that very floundering charter!" he fretted publicly and privately. "Who's dumb as dirt now?"

States began to reject entrenched federal programs that violated the constitutional mandates of federalism. The Supreme Court ignored state appeals, so the state governments reacted. They refused to be part of the money laundering that saw state revenues sifted through federal agencies, only to be returned by way of diminished grants accompanied by bureaucratic federal mandates. They also refused to fund the federal government's financial responsibilities. Laws of the land were a matter of never-ending interpretation.

People heard the battle cry for action. An army of talented hackers sympathetic to the need of clean information mercilessly infiltrated the net, data banks, and government records.

Similarly inclined sympathizers planted bioengineered spy bots poised to gather daily reports of private government conversations. Suddenly, there were remotely controlled roaches, rats, and beetles crawling throughout the nation's capital. Government agents took to killing pests as treasonous tools of the American underground.

"Washington has never been cleaner," laughed Morgan, who did not refer to the political climate but the infested living conditions of urban D.C., long pockmarked by the tons of garbage in alleyways and streets. Distrust, dirt, and cynicism trickled throughout every fissure of society.

Lawlessness was inevitable. It became clear that the federal government cherry-picked law enforcement. Legislators crafted and operated from a separate set of laws. Morgan made it his mission, without regard as to his campaign's outcome, to make this conflict of interest crystal clear.

Morgan accused government of thwarting medical attention that gave Americans a distinct quality of life. Tax discrepancies often resulted in medical penalties for family members until absolved of guilt. The erratic medical assistance was rarely challenged because it affected the powerless. Medical assistance remained at 100% coverage for anything connected to population control. The idea of population control mightily expanded to those of a certain age and condition. Serious surgical or remedial attention was appropriated on behalf of healthy citizens under the age of 50 years of age and only in the event that the Medical Authority could be convinced of promising outcomes. Intervention for those over 60 years of age was reserved for those who had qualified as "Patriotic Contributors" to the country's welfare. Well-heeled American citizens of a certain age and condition willingly paid cash for medical assistance elsewhere in the world.

Most illnesses simply went undiagnosed. Exorbitant costs of diagnostic examinations often failed to pass institutional budgetary muster. Despite the contraindicated web of medical commissions and other hardships, good and ethical doctors worked gratis within an underground market. If discovered using any hospital medical equipment, these medical men and women were incarcerated. The quality and quantity of the medical profession began to die on the vine.

"We can fix this!" promised the president as death rates mounted.

Federally funded medical schools quickly squeezed "overly qualified" candidates from their pipeline in favor of broader, unspecialized medical degrees to 'better serve the people'. Medical doctors dwindled along with compensation. A new professional status appeared with the government-supported Federally Certified Medical Professional. The FCMP quickly displaced privately funded physicians, physician assistants, and nurses. The FCMP was the government's answer to bloated medical costs. As it turned out, it was an added remedy to a bloated population.

A Pendergrass following grew when hackers surfaced with evidence that the best medical attention was reserved for government leaders and supporters. The Commons News Reports announced its endorsement for Morgan the moment he touched a national nerve with raw outrage.

The White House media machine was unable to stem the tide. And so it came about that the CNR, the collection of the people's contributions and observations under categorized topics, soon came under federal attack. Congress introduced and passed a series of regulatory bills to stem CNR's growing influence, even though it was nothing more than content aggregation emanating from hundreds of millions of contributors.

Despite the freezing temperatures, Morgan stood naked with his trademark red, white, and blue bow tie, a wooden placard strategically strapped upon his naked body during the last week of a desperate political campaign. Messages ran from North Carolina that were patent Pendergrass:

> *Vote twice for Pendergrass!*
> *Vote three times if you're dead!*
> *Vote one more time if you can't read this!*

Despite the White House's efforts to place the Pendergrass campaign in a remote search bubble, Morgan's independent party won by a landslide.

For nearly six months, the Federal Government took up residence in Raleigh, North Carolina in an effort to prove voter fraud and the state election moot. When a Southern branch of Anonymous Hacktivists decided to step in, the Shadow Dawgs targeted Gaston Tang, the most ambitious and nastiest of the nation's Attorney General's minions. Tang's bank account was emptied one day and showed transfers of millions of barter-bits the next. A secret bank account showed up in the Commons News along with pictures of Tang's two underage mistresses. The Swiss bank account was a fact; the mistresses were, too. The photos of Tang riding naked on the government's genetically engineered pink unicorn were not.

Tang's GPS guided his transport to homeless shelters, his personal AI issued profanities, and his transport's meter was forever inaccurate. More than a few times, his medical PM signaled exposure to the Bubonic Plague, along with the occasional fabricated illnesses gleaned from a fabricated report from a fabricated country. From time to time, these contagions were broadcast with public warnings that landed Tang in hospital isolation wards.

Tang's expensive Virginia home was advertised and sold at a fraction of its worth online. In Raleigh, his jet pack was stolen, altered, and reattached to the family's pet dog, Lancelot. The Shadow Dawgs remotely took the Tang hound on rides above and around Raleigh to investigate errant canine behaviors. Dubbed 'Sir Prancelot', the dog's weeklong adventures while strapped to a drone were followed closely on social media. Dog dishes of treats were placed outside homes and businesses. The beagle, a breed known for its love of a good meal, was safely returned ten pounds heavier after hundreds of pit stops.

Pendergrass didn't direct the antics but he didn't bother to stop them either. He approved of the sophomoric wars between his volunteer army of supporters and those that ignored their public trust.

"We can think small, too!" Morgan challenged.

"Hairdressers buzz-cut Tang's head before he could jump out of the chair. There wasn't a robot in Raleigh that managed to serve a drink intact. Everyone was on board with the Tang shenanigans," Pendergrass laughed at the memory.

"It was all stupid small stuff but Tang was a stupid small kind of guy," explained Angela Pendergrass years later to one historian.

Morgan had never worked as a government employee and that perspective worked in his favor. North Carolina's reliance upon Federal educational financial services was terminated as a first order of business when 75% income tax failed to produce enough revenue to carry the state. Government logic laid blame for overwhelming debt on the doorsteps of poor education. Morgan considered that, for once, the blame for deprived versus privileged education had truly come of age.

"No thanks to the Federal fingers all over everything...we've been intentionally dumbed down! Well, we're going to fix that right now, this very damn minute!" Morgan promised, with solid educational solutions.

Bitterness about poor education spawned Morgan's heartiest spittle projectiles. Overburdened, underpaid academic supporters learned how to spit, too. Worried about their children's future, Mothers Who Spit became the state's leading educational activist organization.

A newly-formed NC University Consortium went to work streaming educational programs into homes to supplement and surpass national academic guidelines. Parents proved responsible and the children receptive to the interactive learning games developed by the Research Triangle in accordance with the NCUC suggestions and funded by Morgan's personal resources. The North Carolina school system moved into an unparalleled educational universe. A host of other states joined their impressive academic orbit. Educational advancements incentivized the state systems and revitalized faculties. North Carolinians and two hundred million other young Americans eventually tested light years above Federal requirements.

Following such academic successes, thirty-four states followed North Carolina's lead to endure a wholesale, collective Federal-funding withdrawal.

The oft-repeated tag line that followed Morgan's tenure, 'America Rises Again', spread like wildfire. Morgan's successes had certainly caused a rise in Federal agencies and rumors loomed large of a possible Constitutional Convention that threatened an American schism. Talk proliferated about State secession.

Morgan could take heat, and he took plenty. He made sure that the people upon whom he relied could, too. Within three years of his governorship, there had been four attempts on his life. The vice-president of the United States termed the NC governor a renegade and Pendergrass followers as "rebels without a clause".

Without the careful scrutiny of Carolina citizens concerned for their governor's safety, Morgan would have been poisoned, pounded, or mistaken for a deer more than once.

People listened closely to North Carolina's new favorite son.

"I want our citizens to be beneficiaries of flexible medical and social assistance that can run exclusively on state levels," Pendergrass coaxed. And so it happened that a top-rate medical profession was renewed quickly within states unafraid to attract, cultivate, and retain talent that promised excellence.

Morgan hated surveillance, all surveillance. He never met a ping, click, drone, bug, or slow-moving bird with complete trust.

Uninterrupted walks, allowing thoughts to romp freely, he thought, were a beautiful thing.

"Morgan!" Angela's voice alerted.

Morgan was astonished to find he now rested upon a bench rather than making his way toward the hospital.

"Almost there, Cookie!" he lied.

Morgan unfastened his tie and examined the beads of sweat that had pooled in both sides of a separated knot. Whisking the darkened material in the air to dry, Morgan whistled as he sauntered back to the hospital. Resting on a garden bench, his hat remained as one of many such wardrobe sacrifices to daydreams.

"Waiting room...Maternity," he announced as the elevator doors parted. Morgan grunted as his wife moved into lecture mode. Retrieving a cigar from his vest pocket, he lit and puffed red life into its tip while refastening the tie that had become less a gentleman's embellishment and more of a cold, wet noose.

Recognizing its notoriously errant occupant, the lift's fire alarm remained silent. Morgan had seen to that perquisite when the Annex was renovated.

Arms thrown wide, Morgan greeted his wife when he disembarked on the unmarked floor. Cigar smoke wafted from the lift; the cigar was strategically tilted upward in clinched teeth to avoid Morgan's tendency to singe Angela's hair. The infamous cane hung from one arm.

"Where's your hat?" Angela asked.

"Made another donation to the gray hole," he shrugged.

"You mean black hole?"

"Nah, a gray hole has a way of giving back," he smiled.

"Must you always have your holographic feature and sound turned off?" Angela beseeched.

"Oh, hell yes!"

Angela asked with a smile, "You're thinking about something. What is it?"

"Even if our granddaughter is born on Friday the 13th, it'll change that day's calamitous reputation forever," Morgan announced.

He removed his cigar and took his wife's delicate hand in his. Angela kissed the love of her life on his cheek with a tenderness that spoke of loyalty, understanding, and trust.

"Yup, a person has to take the bull by the balls. Our destiny depends upon how much we believe in ourselves...not what's coming at us, not what's sold to us, pushed down our goose gullets...we need to write our own story!"

"Bull by the horns," Angela corrected.

"I meant balls. Imagine what it takes to get a hand hold of bull testicles!"

Angela let Morgan guide her from the lift toward a much-used pink, white, and blue plaid couch. Together, they settled deep into permanently depleted cushions and unwrapped a cupcake with a single candle. It was lit in honor of Morgan's 84th birthday. Angela produced a birthday present she placed lovingly in her husband's hand. Like an eager five-year-old, Morgan tore apart the packaging.

"My father's signet ring? Where'd you find it?"

"In your old tackle box when we cleaned out the storage room. It's been resized. Try it on."

"Better late than never. You're something, Cookie," Morgan gushed as he slipped the ring on his right finger with emerging emotions.

"Careful, there. You're showing sappy," Angela hugged her husband.

"Nah," he mused. "Just thinking about a full circle here..."

Adele's husband, Dr. Lex Collins, and his brother, Dr. Connor Collins, were Adele's physicians. Adele's brother-in-law's proper name was an auspicious-sounding Connor Henry Collins III. In the event Adele's child had been a boy, the baby might have carried the Connor Collins legacy to an honorable IV. A single man, Connor generously offered the family legacy to his younger brother, Lex. Morgan scoffed at the idea.

"It would be far more imaginative to name a boy Tom Collins in honor of the best thing Americans ever did with English gin," he expressed to his son-in-law. "It's senseless to have numbers after your name unless you're doing jail time."

Adele and Lex decided upon a daughter and chose Morgan's grandmother's given names, Caroline Elizabeth, which pleased Morgan immensely.

"It's a fair way to balance out her slave name," he commented to the Collins brothers.

* * *

Caroline Elizabeth Collins arrived in the world at 11:35 p.m. on a hot, humid Thursday evening within North Carolina's Research Triangle's Hospital Annex. The air conditioning worked overtime to keep the day's heat at bay in the old fashioned birthing room. Clanking and whirrs of outmoded fans coupled with a more modern filtering system proved no match for the earnest team of six attendants in an overcrowded room; everyone was bathed in sweat.

Lexton Collins stood vigil next to his wife's bed and surveyed reports as half the team examined his wife while two others secured the umbilical cord. Representing a future of medical options for the Collins family, the precious stem cells were saved, packaged, labeled, and sent to the Cryogenic Cord Blood Registry vault in one of the analogous red brick buildings of the vast complex.

One of the many room monitors was set to record the first cries of newborns to analyze lachrymose patterns. It would help diagnose future disorders that might otherwise escape detection. The cry, controlled by cranial nerves, could identify genetic illnesses evident in the first three months, prior to the full acquisition of social cues.

With the exception of the new mother, those in attendance marveled at a composed baby girl seamlessly entering the world sans utterance. The monitoring equipment and computers sorted, hummed, and analyzed data uninterrupted. Expecting the wails of a startled newborn, Adele anticipated the worst. Propped upon two rigid arms, Adele desperately craned her neck toward the backs of her husband, bother-in-law, and the complement of distracted medical professionals who collectively ignored her.

"Lex? Connor? What's going on?" Adele's voice startled the cluster of personnel engrossed in Caroline. One of the nurses was distracted by blue pinpoint-sized lights that darted around the newborn and disappeared. Unsure whether she had imagined the lights, the nurse said nothing.

"People?" Adele moved to get out of bed, alerting the distracted nurse to attend rather than gape blankly.

"She's perfect, Mrs. Collins," the woman quickly reassured Adele by indicating the various chart results projected throughout the room. She cleaned and cradled the infant, handed the white swaddled bundle to her mother, and smiled supportively.

"I'm pretty sure that Caroline is the happiest baby we've ever delivered. It's unusual for a newborn to be so at ease that she doesn't cry. It's a sign that the baby's nervous system is excellent..."

Adele's husband quickly re-situated himself next to his wife while her brother-in-law distilled the facts.

"Our data reads a perfect scan. She's one sweet, healthy baby. Congratulations!" Connor grinned broadly at his sister-in-law.

Connor looked at the computer while it recorded contented silence and noticed his brother's disappointed expression digesting the dormant expensive medical equipment he had so desperately wanted.

Mother and daughter's eyes locked, and the onlookers, for all practical purposes, disappeared. Unqualified joy replaced Adele's apprehension. A minuscule drop of Caroline's blood would reveal thousands of results within the hour. Adele knew what that could mean.

Under her father's direction, the Collins brothers had worked toward molecular cloning used to synthesize the DNA that was reintroduced to the embryo. Options to delete faulty genes and replace them with promising healthy outcomes had put science at the brink of another Cambrian Age, a time of explosive evolutionary developments with the potential to grow exponentially with super-computers. While such options had lingered long on the medical table, political, financial and social challenges delayed the natural evolution of scientific inquiry. Yet, here she was, a beneficiary of the best possible medical advancements in a world that had precariously balanced on the precipice of destruction for four decades.

Adele viewed Caroline as an exquisitely designed creature magically endowed to rouse her semi-comatose heart to unimagined heights. It required no computers to interpret a mother's sense of the moment.

"I know everyone says every child is lovely, but I think she's incredibly beautiful, Lex...her skin, her long lean body...Lex, look at her beautifully shaped head!"

"The best of our genes and chromosomes!" Lex laughed.

"Always the romantic!" Adele kissed the baby she decided to nickname 'CC'.

The new parents were the winners of a cosmic lottery, given the unlikely circumstances of Caroline's birth. There was a reason that this particular maternity floor was small.

As recovered as their small part of the universe was, genetic selection still depended upon scarce resources. The Research Triangle had been able to regroup thanks to the foresight and philanthropic efforts of Morgan Pendergrass. Without the seed money he made as a Social Game developer, the Pendergrass fortune might never have developed. A vast fortune was derived from an Empathy Games franchise used to positively inculcate social sensibilities while entertaining impressionable youth. From the Games proceeds, Adele's father had launched an entrepreneurial empire. One of his most valued assets was part ownership in the American government's abandoned asteroid mining project that came with two satellites and a space station. Morgan and his international partner were not interested in extracting extraterrestrial raw materials. After a few years of regulatory haggling, Pendergrass and Hungary became the sole proprietors of satellites with access beyond earth's orbit. They had other ideas about how to use the satellites.

The Hungarian-Pendergrass partnership embraced and bridged scientific communities throughout international markets. It was the modified satellites that afforded Hungary, and that which was to become the Confederation of American States, auxiliary power and communication at the time of the world's sudden energy crisis. With channels open to similarly situated international independent researchers, scientists of every ilk managed to continue their work in what was literally and proverbially termed, The Darkness.

In the aftermath of the EMP disasters, most of the world's children were born in a scientific void, if they survived at all. While better-situated regions helped to ensure traditional opportunities, an astronomical perinatal mortality rate remained the worldwide norm.

Affordability and access to genetic screening remained relative terms in surviving civilizations. A perfectly prepared selection process and homologous recombination used for gene targeting and deletion, coupled with an attended birth with all of the medical and aesthetic accouterments, remained astronomically expensive. Adele's screening, birth, and trajectory of tracking a child for subsequent years, had to be justified when much of a struggling world was starving, isolated and/or extinct. The Confederation of American States cooperated on germ-line research with six international groups that had successfully emerged from social chaos. Beyond progressive genetic scanning, there was an urgent concern about noticeable biological alterations apparent in survivors.

Connor and Lex had been in their first year of University working in Wake Forest University's Regeneration Department when random terrorist attacks on the world's server farms caused an economic panic. Closely following were solar flares that swelled violently beyond all predictions. Within months of the data destruction and erratic power surges, the EMP aftershocks of smaller strategically targeted nuclear warhead detonations produced an immediate flux of gamma rays from the nuclear reaction. Pinpointed detonations at altitudes between 20 and 40 km caused the electrons trapped in Earth's magnetic field to give rise to extreme oscillating electrical currents. The pulse spanned continents, the radiation affecting systems on land, sea and air worldwide. Perpetrators of the nuclear disaster remained unidentified, as it had been launched from three ocean sites.

Morgan identified and appropriated most of North Carolina's University science departments to the safety of the Pendergrass farms and ensured that stranded students were housed in University bunkers built in anticipation of national emergencies. North Carolina's server farms had been hidden and protected deep within its coastal waters.

Communities were amply supplied from well-stocked Pendergrass and state warehouses that stored extensive emergency supplies. Unlike most of urban America that had been left strangled and suffocating, the smaller cities and towns reacted nimbly as closer-knit communities. Fate brought Adele and Lex Collins together in the worst of times.

Lex observed his wife's faraway look as she caressed their daughter. He had no idea what was going on in her mind.

"So deep in thought," he finally interrupted.

"I was just a little girl when you came to the farm," Adele said in a small voice. Her mind continued to drift to the moment she first met her husband. Adele was merely five years older than the baby she now held when Lex arrived on their farm. Adele had been reluctant to speak to the strangers who unintentionally displaced her position. Her parents had become personal caregivers to thousands with concerns for millions. Adele felt everyone's emotional needs came before her own. As an only child – as any child – she had not counted upon sharing so much attention, most of which was showered upon the Collins brothers who were inseparable from her father.

Morgan took the brilliant Collins brothers under his wing. Lex was particularly kind to her even as a little child when she awkwardly bumped into things trailing her busy father. It took Adele two years before she could stratify those who wandered the grounds of her home. There was a struggle to make sense of terms used in endless deliberations about humanity's predicament in dark, candlelit rooms. The farm's residents endlessly recounted the convergence of unfortunate events that led to their present state.

Social unrest was prevalent well before the EMP catastrophes. Governments worldwide were financially crippled as private enterprise withered. When an over-regulated energy market diminished with badly planned alternatives, a polarized populace periodically exploded in the kind of violence that turned urban areas into brutal war zones. Cities worldwide burned and were cordoned off one by one, community by community, block by block.

A Federal inability to provide for adequate international defense or domestic social assistance was a fact of life prior to the EMP disasters, too. Adele recalled the adults lamenting the scarcity of antibiotics and social food programs. Emotional stresses were amplified by unemployment and malnutrition. As the legalized drug supply dried up, habitual users were forced to withdraw. Millions of addicts became simultaneously unhinged. Adele learned an unusual vocabulary that existed within a crisis management environment. Like the crudely boarded homes within barricaded communities, people no longer tried to disguise the face of desperation.

Americans consensually agreed in principle to restrict themselves to one child per family. In the face of vanishing resources, the illegality of midwifery, and hospitals that had become viral stomping grounds, the birthrate dropped dramatically. Any conscientious planning was offset by the wave of explosive immigration from a starving, oppressed planet that inundated American borders. The consequent disease rate proved unrelenting and left most Americans and immigrants without remedial medical options of any sort. Worldwide, the human condition had similarly declined. Survivors were not always content to live a bleak existence. Suicides surpassed homicides.

The collection of 34 states that endured the Darkness had recovered and prospered under the auspices of the Confederation of American States. It was a good temporary name, thought everyone. All hoped to reconcile the United States of America once a semblance of civility was restored in embattled, hostile regions. No one presaged the difficulty.

Adele thought, ...and here I am, a new mother with a healthy child born at one of the safest, most advanced facilities in the world. I am loved and protected by a wonderful family...

"Oh! Did you see that, Lex?" Adele squealed her surprise when a small blue streak flashed across the room.

"See what?" Lex turned with everyone else toward Adele, now blankly staring into space.

"It's nothing...I thought...forget it. I must be seeing stars at this point."

She bent to kiss Caroline's tender, clear forehead and traced the infant's small rosebud lips with her finger. Adele's next breath was drawn long and deep; a smile finally took shape and her half-moon eyes sparkled with contentment.

"Here, you can take her now," she instructed the attending nurse.

* * *

Such were the short-lived moments of serenity before the sound of a rubber-tipped cane pounding on the maternity room door.

"Dadgummit! Open this damn door!" Morgan insisted from the other side. Five minutes prior, Morgan and Angela had been notified of the birth. The Pendergrass patriarch considered the late notice nothing short of a conspiracy.

"What the hell is going on?"

"Just pull the lever, Morgan." Angela carefully slid her arm around Morgan and opened an unlocked door. Aware that the team preferred privacy, Angela gingerly peeked her head inside.

"Is it all right if we jump the gun a little here and see our daughter and precious grandbaby? Please pay no mind to the crazy man beside me. He's harmless."

Morgan examined the room from over his wife's head.

"Good Lord. I could swing a dead cat in here and hit six people before I let go."

Lex Collins begged for time. "Morgan, Angela? Please give us fifteen minutes to go through protocols. We'll be finished very soon. It's fine!"

"Yeah, well that dog don't hunt," barked Morgan, much too curious and protective to allow a son-in-law to give orders. "Don't forget who you're talking to."

"That dog hunts fine. Stand down, Grandpa. I don't tell you how to butter your biscuit; don't tell me how to butter mine."

Morgan strained his head farther over Angela's to get a better look, hand pressed on his wife's head to keep balance.

"Give us some privacy, Daddy," Adele pleaded. "Get off Mother's head!"

"Privacy? Good God. You've sure given that notion up. Ok, I'm taking my wingman with me. Nice work, Babycake," Morgan relented.

The cane that propped the door was removed abruptly, leaving Angela's head in the position of a doorjamb. Connor leapt in time to catch the door as Angela screamed impending decapitation. The bright light emanating from the hallway disappeared as the arguing couple withdrew. A discernible grunt could be heard when Angela's palm smacked her husband's forehead with a solid 'whump'.

Morgan hadn't weathered the previous two decades easily. What patience he once apportioned privately had withered with the strain of maintaining decorum in official capacities. Morgan's challenges of connecting and rebuilding Confederation communities were compounded by the need to connect and rebuild his body. He had undergone various regenerative operations and had been the recipient of robotic eyes and reconstructed inner ears. Given his love of drink, Morgan was ecstatic when livers were cloned. As the beneficiary of first generation experiments and official guinea pig, Morgan had several replacements within five years. Within another five years, Morgan received the Confederation's first regenerative heart.

Morgan's latest recovery involved the neuro-rehabilitation required to signal his exoskeleton. Recuperation initially required a cane as he learned to coordinate his reflexes. While balance returned quickly, the cherry wood staff remained. Considered by his family to be no more than a theatrical prop, Morgan deployed the cane mercilessly. He twirled the staff like a baton, poked people in the back with it, tripped chaotic children on the run, and threatened tedious speakers with its shepherd's hook.

To Angela's way of thinking, the cane symbolized Morgan's sense of seniority in a world that had become concerned more with the future than experience. Computerized body parts and printed organs kept him vital, his genome work was the source of his rejuvenation, and the cane, imagined those that loved him, marked Dr. Morgan Pendergrass as a 21st century Moses leading his people into the promised land.

Morgan and Angela reluctantly returned to the waiting room. Not one to sit quietly, the restless grandfather repeatedly kicked the end of the cane's tip up in the air with the tip of his foot as he sat, testing the accuracy of a mechanical leg.

"You could have killed me, Morgan."

"Not that hard head, Cookie. No way!"

Angela Pendergrass ignored her husband's fidgeting, aware that his annoying habits promised to grow proportionately to protests. She filled time speaking excitedly with close friends and reviewing the forthcoming birth announcements on the TrueView. Morgan, unable to get a rise from his wife, rose from the couch and plodded across the room to weigh in with criticisms. He eyed a holographic image suspiciously.

"That idiotic birth announcement is nothing short of unpleasant; that baby looks like it's been beaten by an ugly stick. Ugly as Matthew's junk yard dog. Remember when his John Deere accidentally flattened that mean mutt outside the warehouse? Hell, nobody knew what transpired till we caught Matthew throwing dirt over splattered ugly dog guts. We just helped him kick dirt over it all and said the dog ran away when his little boy came looking for it. Naming that nasty mutt Beauregard was the first mistake."

"Morgan, this announcement is another baby's image... a template!"

"Oh, just count me out of that noise. Everyone is going to think it's our own. You can't get around first impressions. Don't confuse people unnecessarily, Cookie. No pictures. Specially that flat-faced one!"

"Must you invent new ways to make me crazy, Morgan?" Angela was not amused.

"It's my birthday!" Morgan shrugged. "It's an opportunity to do as I please, Cookie.

The birth announcement was released on the Confederation Commons Network. It was a simple one without illustration:

Please join us in our moment of happiness as we welcome our granddaughter, Caroline Elizabeth Collins, into the world this day, August 12, 2055.

Well wishes and holographic visitors flooded the waiting room; the Pendergrass home quickly filled with floral 3D printings and live deliveries by 7:30 the following morning.

Dutifully, Angela informed long-lost in-laws at their last known address in the dying city of Chicago. There was no active Internet, but it would cache. Fruitless gestures, transmissions to the missing acted as cathartic beacons of hope.

Within twenty-four hours, the Collins and Pendergrass family had collected their 6-pound- 9-ounce, 22-inch treasure and moved to reunite on Kuykendall Road, the winding paved roadway that followed the river's path by the same name. Established by farmers emigrating South from the Hudson valley, the Kuykendall tributaries fed the prospering farms of the region. Spring-fed lakes and streams preserved produce on an even keel in the driest summers, while providing for the Southern delicacies of crawdads. Frogs and snails moved effortlessly along the moist ground beneath shadows of rapidly diminishing flocks of confused Canada Geese. Most types of voyaging fowl had partaken of bi-annual refreshment on Kuykendall-fed bodies of water for as long as anyone could remember. As a child, Adele came to know the true meaning of 'sitting duck' when hundreds of the migrating birds at a time were brought into the sheds by their feet, heads swinging, to be plucked and prepared. These were the fowl too physically impaired to move further, their navigational instincts permanently damaged by the electromagnetic pulses, ultimately exhausted from desperate searches for seasonal climes.

"We were all sitting ducks," Adele sadly identified with the fowl's cruel plight. Some made it; most did not.

* * *

Three cars made their way together toward the Pendergrass Farm compound. Breezes from the hills and intermittent cumulus puffs of white offset the previous week's run of 95-degree heat. A short thunderstorm had mercifully poured badly needed rain at 4:30 a.m. and plumped up yellow grasses across hardened meadows. Remnants of raindrops glimmered in the filtered sunlight left to teeter upon delicate Queen Ann's Lace and green-tipped honeysuckle vines that worked their way up freshly painted fences. Yawning Morning Glories glistened with dew. Renewed, their delicately scalloped faces knitted a white and blue spackled carpet over parched, cracked red clay.

As the Pendergrass transports and cars approached, the welcoming arms of the estate's expansive iron gates separated wide. Adele absorbed the morning splendor of her family's historic 1928 farm, with its stately red brick family manse a quarter-mile from the main entrance.

It once took forty-five minutes to traverse the driveway. Adele's carefully sequestered memories slid unchallenged from hiding places. Despite her hope that certain images might expire from neglect, the new mother suffered a familiar anxiety. Spewing gravel pinged the car's undercarriage and triggered recollections of tented communities on either side of that which was once an endless drive to safety. Rather than the fields that now stretched peacefully uninterrupted, Adele recalled a vast acreage of mud furrows created by the ceaseless trampling of refugees that made their way amongst an expanse of canvas tents and slanted-roof tin shanties. The sucking sounds of boots drawing from the thick red goo left after unremitting thunderstorms filled her ears. Families arrived at the Pendergrass farm by countless thousands and remained for years. She recalled the dank smells and the displaced eyes of bewildered young children who strained to see the occupants of the warm car. Adele recollected her attempts to hide from the airborne fluttering hands that greeted her parents; hoards of indebted citizens frenetically tapped upon the transport windows.

"A hailstorm of sadness," Adele shivered as the muffled appeals and the smell of muck seeped through.

Once an 11,000-acre timber farm, the Pendergrass holdings now included the last of makeshift buildings and 1000 acres of prime property that featured state–of-the-art security, six architecturally compatible Williamsburg-style red brick homes of varying sizes, and an underground hydroponics farm thanks to the Southern aversion to relinquishing water rights. The Pendergrass family donated the farm as an interim location for the Confederation headquarters. When the Capital in D.C. was recovered as part of the Confederation, the best land and buildings reverted to the Pendergrass estate.

How lucky we were; how unlucky others were, Adele thought. The migration to Cary, Raleigh, and the surrounding areas was not only a lifeline for North Carolinians; it was the platform by which energy was supplied beyond the Carolina borders. *We had water and electricity,* Adele thought, *and it saved us all.*

The Pendergrass compound was fortunate to have an ample water supply at the time of Darkness; the wells were deep, long and spring-fed. Plentiful water rose readily to the top within 15 feet of the surface. The bubbling resource was critical when the country lost power and the ability to pump. It was the Pendergrass farms that maintained their growing community in the most serious stages of survival mode between absolute darkness and the re-established connection of their state-owned satellites and hardened power grids.

Cary's provisional government linked North Carolinians by every means possible. Morgan had instituted a training program with carrier pigeons able to connect directly with the intellectual capital residing in the Research Triangle; everyone was equipped with an emergency plan. An electromagnetic pulse catastrophe had been only one of many disaster scenarios that Morgan envisioned. As a former governor, preparation went beyond stored materials or energy that was supplied by the Pendergrass Compound. Morgan had also ensured that stored data was shared with cooperative pockets of civilization, along with food and medical supplies.

Refugees had long returned to homes to rebuild their lives. With their departure, resilient green grass reappeared on the farm's landscape, signaling the return to civility. Eventually, communication between Confederation State members and cooperating international communities became seamless. Moreover, the Confederation had quickly formed cooperative farming and trade agreements that included Canada, the U.K., Australia, Central Europe, Scandinavia, Israel, and most of South America. A trained military sponsored by the Confederation helped to ensure safety and fluid commerce. Barter-bits were introduced as the international currency. The original Constitution of the United States was voted upon as the framework by which the Confederation laws would operate pending the restoration of United States of America.

The pebbles and rocks hit the undercarriage, each stone summoning random images. Amongst all the sensations and memories, Adele was primarily moved to admire her father's indomitable spirit and endless reassurances.

I couldn't stand to hear the sobbing, the stories of society's breakdown, the chaos. Dad just listened to it all, Adele smiled admiringly as she examined the back of her father's head bobbing up and down in the front seat, face to the wind, hooting his grandchild's arrival through an open window.

The Darkness was an emotional tsunami, rudely pulling upon delicate emotional reserves, the tipping point that challenged the sanity of those with over-compromised sensitivities. A freak of cosmic nature, the solar flares serendipitously combined with human malevolent inner nature to indiscriminately extinguish civilization. Tears of personal loss coupled with a deep-seated shame for humanity's failings. Accounts of urban horrors trickled into the Pendergrass compound by stricken refugees who had survived unspeakable traumas.

"Our way was lit by the fires," began one sobbing woman at a table of seven. "They were burning thousands of dead bodies in shallow ditches to avoid spread of disease. The stench was terrible but the forlorn faces of those trying to save their communities from plague, lit in the nights by flickering bonfire storms, was far worse."

"All of God's names, forms and concepts reappeared as hope for survivors while others cursed every providential reference. Prayers of gratitude and spiritual solidarity overwhelmed the disgruntled," Adele recalled the delineation of the human spirit. "We had to be swallowed up by despair or get to work."

As the gravel drubbing eased, Adele gasped for neglected oxygen. In her arms, Adele carried a new kind of prayer and uttered her wishes aloud. "May your childhood be filled with joy, Caroline. Please Lord, spare my child the experiences of my youth."

"Oh God. Please don't be so melodramatic," Morgan reproved his daughter. "Don't ruin all the fun about to happen! This is going to be great!"

* * *

With affected huffiness, Lex marched into Morgan's library mid-afternoon without warning.

"I think it imprudent, Morgan!" he began. "In fact, I think it's extremely unwise to have announced Caroline's birth across the Commons today."

Morgan peered over his feet that remained fixed on his desk.

"First of all, never barge in here unless my pants are on fire. Second, grandparents have an inalienable right to brag as much as they feel like it," Morgan said testily. "Third, at what moment did you realize the merits of discretion?"

Lex streamed his qualms, worries, and recapped urban legends. He fretted about second-generation survivors that lived beyond civilized borders. Of particular concern was the possible resurrection of the former American Federal Militia readying themselves for an assault.

"We don't know what happened to hundreds of thousands of elite military muscle; where did they all go? My daughter is only one of the targets, Morgan. Just think of what could happen if they stormed the farm. You're just calling attention to a vulnerability...not to mention that she's had genetic assistance. Remember? People hated your research. Don't you think that mentality is alive and armed somewhere?"

Morgan determined that Lex's delusional objections to a birth announcement were unworthy of his dwindling reserves of patience. Angela repeatedly begged her quick-tempered husband to calm himself around Lex and it was for this reason that Morgan was willing to address his son-in-law with courtesy.

"Son, we have always considered the state of survivors. It's no secret that there is a component of danger in the segment of the former populations that attack and kill without reserve, conscience, or purpose. But we've got that handled. Now, you're referring to something else. You've figured that there's a Federal underground--The Fed Boogey Man--waiting for the right time to pounce upon 34 former states. Oh, and they're apt to conduct this important maneuver after stealing Caroline in the middle of the night after hearing about her arrival through the Commons News. Well, that's not going to happen," Morgan measuredly explained. "There's no existing military underground. No hidden military at all. Nothing. Nada. What we do have are regressive, uncontrolled groups of savages, unable to restructure their lives that roam outside of Confederation borders. We also have groups that are perfectly sane but isolated because of those crazies. We will have to fix that situation but that time is not now. Meanwhile, let me put your pretty little head to rest."

"Please don't, Morgan. I was just going to suggest some precautionary surveillance. I don't want anyone to be unnecessarily drawn to my daughter for any reason," Lex begged.

"You clearly don't know how dead in the water the Feds were even at a time they were operating at full throttle!"

"Forget I said anything," Lex frowned.

It was too late. Morgan's impending sermon was locked and loaded. Pulled from a wide cache of advisements, homilies, and directives, Morgan's ready lectures had been re-coined by the Commons from Hooey Hose to a more respectable term: The Morgan Expedient. It was the Morgan Expedient that spouted measures and utilitarian homilies for the benefit of Confederation citizens.

"You're resurrecting nothing more than paranoid illusions. Allow me to explain the reason that there are no Federal monsters under your bed. At their peak, the Federal government was largely an obese, impotent, bloodsucking, bullying corps of paranoid pussies. The official definition of a terrorist was anyone who was 'suspicious of centralized federal authority.' Imagine that! Well, they got their wish. People who were downright scared and suspicious became a little more so, having been categorized as terrorists. The Feds got scared, too. They built safety nests all over the world... for themselves.

"Federal officials and top Federal employees had always planned to take refuge in pre-constructed survival bunkers in case of civil unrest or national emergency. They'd conduct their lives two hundred feet underground in communities connected by vast underground tunnels. But American tunnels weren't up to engineering standards, Lex. They weren't designed by the likes of the architects of the old Laerdal Tunnel between Oslo and Bergen or London's Crossrail line beneath the city or Switzerland's Gotthard Base Tunnel. European engineers used giant TBMs that were real beasts in the 21st century like artists. They could chew up 380 million cubic feet of rock and dirt--almost four times the volume of the Great Pyramid--in a heartbeat. They had an eye out for the entire environment, mindful of the requirements. They used the tunnel's refuse to build islands in the lakes for wild bird sanctuaries, bermed land for public housing...what did we do? Twenty-two billion dollars was dedicated to construct 16 stories under the Grand Central Terminal in New York City, meant to span 14 miles throughout the city. The Mayor said it would help commuters. Instead of transporting 6 million riders a day on public transport systems, the 160-foot cavern was converted into a safety house for New York's elite. Even that project collapsed on itself in 2029 when the miles of watery, gravel-filled pits opened wide with a minor earthquake.

"The International Tunneling Association included 70 countries whose governments had mindfully designed infrastructure for the people, industry, and environmental control. The United States Army Corps of Engineers couldn't bother to be involved with innovative, cross-productive networking when told by Washington do it 'the American way'. Who the hell were those Dubai smartasses, anyway? And what could be learned in New Orleans from that silly little country with wooden shoes and 2000 years of experience diking the North Sea? Americans could have even learned something about speed and efficiency from those Mexican drug traffickers, if you ask me. Americans, once the greatest innovators in history, still had superb engineers. They just weren't federal engineers who could ignore process and peer review. Politics was all. That's the reason the levees' pumping stations failed again and finished New Orleans twenty-five years after Katrina.

"Hundreds of recklessly federally planned tunnels turned out to be nothing more than horizontal money holes and death traps."

Morgan pointed to an activated wall monitor. A montage of images proved his point.

"So-called impregnable concealed survival fortresses with auxiliary power failed because of a lack of detail, Lex. The tunnel burrowing machines were rendered useless; filter systems flopped; few of the underground bunkers and trains were protected from the e-bombs. Those that might have been fine were infiltrated by an additional onslaught of EMP-generated solar storms. Our engineers dismissed contingent energy feeds that were connected to the surface via some conduit or another. Then there were the emergency TBMs that connected government installations. The EMP trifecta took every energy source out. Rather than offering mobility and avenues, the immobile TBMs blocked major passageways. Hell, that was just one of the hundreds of minor oversights. When the military and the administration made a beeline for their underground bunkers, people noticed.

"Government, military, federal employees...untold families of uninvited families packed into the bunkers and were followed by ordinary citizens. Oxygen systems and water filters were overloaded. People unknowingly buried themselves alive when skirmishes underground exploded into supply wars. There wasn't any governance or order. Everyone who had the wherewithal to make his or her way to underground safety also had a weapon.

"When survivors upside learned of the hidden safe houses, they dynamited into the storehouses for the medical and food supplies. Under the University of Washington, the UW students later discovered a mass grave underfoot. Look at it! It was supposed to be one of the worst looking and smelling nightmares ever recorded. They closed off the entire area and plugged every crevice they could, hoping that the millions of rats and maggots had a half-life.

"No one had predicted the electromagnetic pulse would be so grave as to kill chances at pumping and filtering air and water ensconced in concrete. Well, all it took was a few of the outlets to be connected topside. It was enough to cause an entire internal subterranean grid to collapse. All the bogus hardened protection was so much Jell-O in a microwave."

Lex shifted uncomfortably at the images of decaying human bodies covered in dirt and rats.

Morgan reminded Lex, "You're the one resurrecting a dead notion, Son."

"I'm prudent. I'm simply requesting additional measures in case you're wrong," Lex insisted. "You could be wrong."

Morgan rose from his chair, turned his signet ring around, and thumped Lex's head. "You started this nonsense, so have the decency to listen to what I've got to say."

Morgan sat on the edge of his desk leaning into his audience of one.

"Our nation's leaders left their personal survival in the hands of incompetent planners who had wasted trillions of dollars dedicated to the 'domestic tranquility' of government employees. Domestic tranquility to that bunch was no more than the aftereffects of throwing back a few shots at home and watching porn," Morgan sighed large, mimicking his son-in-law's transparent ennui.

"No, Lex. There's no Fed resurgence that would attack the Confederation, much less have the resources to focus in on your baby girl…and for what? Stop flattering yourself."

Morgan ended by calling Lex's ideas of the former regime marching or crawling into Cary, N.C. a "paranoid piece of pap."

Lex persisted. "You not only assume that the rest of the world is still unable to access our grid, our news, and our resources, you also assume that Confederation citizens aren't vulnerable to corruption. There will be eventual speculation about genetic engineering, making a connection with Caroline's birth, your research, and your position. Let's not forget human nature just because we now have law and order in these parts…" Lex countered.

Lex continued to stream anxiety in a fashion his father-in-law had termed 'emotional ralphing'. As bright as Lex was, he managed to spew fear and pessimism. In this case, considered Morgan, Lex had sought him out in an unusually heightened state of paranoia. Lex's anxiety could possibly mean something else.

Morgan and his team of scientists had long suspected the strength of the collective EMP onslaught had the potential to cause longer-term brain damage. Significant evidence pointed to magnified amoral activities as likely associated with extreme and prolonged magnetic impulses on the brain. There were indications that the damage could run from temporary to permanent damage. Lingering EMP forces, they knew, could theoretically permeate DNA.

Could be that he's worried about those operating with marginal mental illness in our midst, thought Morgan. *Or is my son-in-law just a hysterical peckerwood?* Morgan fretted on both counts.

Lex's unnaturally thin, high-pitched voice unnerved Morgan. Lex's babbling had moved into a shrill protest. Morgan put up his hand.

"Ok, ok... try and calm down before somebody thinks we're killing a hyena in here. What do we have those sneaky little spybots for anyway?" Morgan reassured his frantic son-in-law with a smile.

"Thanks. That's all I was asking, Morgan!" Lex left the door open as he departed.

* * *

At dusk, diminutive security bats searched the property. Morgan Pendergrass was apprised hours later of a young man that had breached the perimeter and made it into the property's interior. The aimless, unarmed intruder was alone. Failsafe Enterprises, one of the larger privately owned security firms licensed by the Confederation, was dedicated to the physical protection of whole communities. They promised to submit a full report on the man now in their custody. Morgan

Pendergrass kept the incident a private matter between the Pendergrass security teams and him. Lex, worried Morgan, would probably overreact with news of an intruder. "There'll be no peace if Lex is ever found right about something," Morgan remarked to the contented dog lying at his feet.

Chapter 11
The Fall Holidays

Cary, North Carolina
Sunday, October 31, 2055

*A*s the humidity dissipated mid-fall, it was clear that the Pendergrass and Collins families were smitten with CC, the poignant sun around whom the Pendergrass occupants orbited. Although no one else seemed to notice, Adele had become accustomed to fleeting blue pinpoint lights that frequented her daughter.

The family's obsession with CC, Adele decided one morning at the breakfast table, had developed into fawning.

"Even the dog looks forlorn." Adele pointed to one of the family's Plott Hounds, J. Blue, lying in the kitchen. "He's turned into a sorry beggar...somebody might pet poor Junior Blue instead of CC once in a while."

Adele meant her comments as a preemptive warning shot toward her husband across the table, who had adopted an annoying ritual of citing CC's exemplary statistics at mealtime. Lex ignored Adele's arched eyebrow and prepared to bask vicariously before coffee was poured.

"She's in the 99th percentile..." Lex began. His wife's scowl freeze-framed the moment.

"Stop citing statistics every morning or I'll make you one, Lex Collins. Last warning!" Her face and tone alerted her father mid-bite on a piece of toast.

"She's just getting started!" Morgan's widening smile quickly became immersed in his morning coffee.

"She's examined every week, constantly touched and prodded... people stroke her mercilessly. CC rarely touches the ground! Just stop!" Adele continued, "Do less. Say less."

"I'm a doctor," Lex protested meekly to the family now intently focused upon utensils, food shuffling, and napkin rearrangement. Angela kicked Morgan under the table.

"Science is interesting to me," Lex stated. It was the kind of inconsequential statement that Adele had learned to lean into.

"I'm the mother," she testily emphasized. "You'd best learn to listen to what I'm saying. Pointing out CC's wonderfulness to everyone all the damn time is respectfully annoying as hell, Doctor!"

Lex Collins nervously smiled at his wife with hands folded on the table, an odd gesture suggesting prayer.

"After all we've been through, I'm just sharing a little happiness in this upside-down world. These genetic strides can make us all take pride!" Lex exclaimed with arms separated inclusively wide.

"Oh please, Lex!" Adele said exasperatedly. "This is about your ego," Adele persisted. "All this talk about genes and chromosomes is downright narcissistic. You're praising yourself – no doubt about it."

Morgan poured bourbon in his coffee and laughed, "Whipped puppy."

* * *

Morgan Pendergrass' monitor pinged a request to enter his daughter and son-in-law's bedroom. They had retired in the afternoon for a respite. Halloween promised a long night.

"Refused!" Adele groaned. "Go away, Daddy. I'm trying to take a nap for 45 minutes. What in the world?"

"You're not sleeping. You're talking. I just wanted to let Caroline see me. I'm good to look at. Imprinting this face will help stamp into that brain what she should be looking for in smart friends. Lord knows she's going to know what stupid looks like."

There was only silence.

"I just want to see my grandchild. You want a nap so she has to take a nap? What makes Halloween such a production around here that you have to rest up? Doesn't make sense!" Morgan lightly tapped the bedroom door with his cane.

"Well, what the hell? You don't mind putting her down in our room for naps when she's crying her head off. Just returning the favor," Morgan tried.

"Nice try. You know CC has yet to cry," Adele shouted clearly. Morgan waited for a long minute to consider options.

"Hey! What's the costume? Just tell me what our little girl is coming as tonight for Halloween?" he wisely misdirected a losing proposition.

"She's going to be a little bee and I'm going to be the queen bee. She'll wear that black and orange striped onesie and a black headband with Ping-Pong balls on two pipe cleaners. See you later downstairs, Daddy," Adele finished.

"That damn cane," Adele laughed as she rolled over for an hour of sleep. CC lay between her parents and played mercilessly with her mother's hair, nursed for thirty minutes, and then spit up on her father's snoring face; his mouth was unfortunately wide open.

* * *

Until twilight settled across the green and brown rolling hills on the far horizon, the three-story home was furiously decorated in orange and black, cotton spider webs stretching across the porch screens with carved pumpkins sitting neatly upon two pineapple porticos. There was promise of a clear 55-degree night eight days short of a full moon.

Confections spewed quietly and continually from printers while Angela and Adele packed the treats in small paper bags. Morgan sampled candy and ruminated about Halloweens past. While he enjoyed rituals, memories of lost friends and family brought bittersweet moments.

"I used to freeze most of my hard-earned candy. I hoarded my best stuff in a plastic Ziploc bag with a black marker that warned: 'Morgan's Stash. Do Not Touch.' My two older brothers ate the candy at will. Might as well as written their names on everything," he announced to an inattentive group immersed in holiday preparations.

Morgan altered his tactic to a long-standing objection to the use of Caroline's nickname.

"You're not using my grandmother's proper name, mind you, Adele," Morgan complained as an ongoing theme.

Adele did not bother to look up from the candy apples she had arranged upon a large platter.

"The name? Again, Dad?"

"Why the need to nickname everybody? You turn your husband's name from Lexton to a Lex. You don't catch us calling you Addie. I wouldn't dare call your mother Angie. I call Gloria Brackett Ole Glory or Glory just to annoy the holy hell outta her. No other reason. CC? Sounds like a stuttering tour guide or a Mexican agreeing to something he doesn't understand." Morgan spat over the deck.

Angela offered her husband a caramel apple on a stick. "You're a professional buzz kill, Morgan. Eat an apple." Turning toward her daughter and Lex, Angela offered an oft-repeated apology on behalf of her husband.

"Wish I could say this issue is about your father's age but our wonderful patriarch has been prone to tangential mind leaks from a parallel universe since I met him. He's always got a lot to say. Most of it's worthwhile. The rest? They're just leaks."

Feigning dejection, Morgan bit a mouthful of apple and ambled away. The sight of her father eating a candy apple, face stretched up toward the darkened sky at moonrise, drew gently across Adele's heartstrings as a rare and tender moment. Her father circumspectly examined an enormous Carolina moon soon to realize its magnified blue glory. A veiled light shone a thin singular stream that broadened as it moved across the deck's aged yellow pine decking until it angled up her father's pant leg and disappeared. She wondered how long he would remain at her side.

"Dad, please call her Caroline!"

Morgan turned toward his only child and beamed gratefully. "Why, much obliged, Babycake."

Connor Collins trotted across the adjoining fields from the on-site research office, having just remembered his commitment to help with the Pendergrass festivities.

Angela welcomed the help and directed a panting Connor toward the gathering crowds waiting patiently for the annual Halloween reception dedicated to the distribution of treats to Cary's smallest citizens. Cars and transports that had queued for nearly two miles along Kuykendall Road were prepared to spill forth. The gates, interwoven with small white twinkling lights, opened and closed in five-minute intervals. Children and parents eagerly moved along the transformed white gravel Skeleton Street bordered by flickering award winning Jack–o–lanterns that had been transported from the Cary Pumpkin Festival. Blue ribbons adorned each pumpkin in unique categories dreamed up by Adele and her mother.

"That pumpkin isn't even carved!" Morgan noted. "What's the blue ribbon for, for God's sake?"

"That particular pumpkin has won first place in the abstract concept category," Angela explained. "I'm not surprised you don't appreciate minimalism."

"If you're so partial to minimalism, you might have awarded that uncarved pumpkin no damn award at all. You know, an invisible abstract ribbon," Morgan chortled.

Morgan enjoyed the revels of trick-or-treaters. The man applauded the holiday that approved of the walking dead and untoward tactics of heart-stopping surprise. He breathed deeply of the cool, crisp evening air and regarded the mother of his only grandchild with a rush of pleasure that indelibly marked the moment.

"I like dressing up and frightening people, even though it's gotten hard as hell to do that anymore," he announced to his busy family.

"As opposed to not dressing up and scaring people? You do that on a regular basis, Dad," Adele laughed, tongue-in-cheek.

Morgan appreciated his daughter's retorts.

"Remember your first Halloween trick-or-treating episode, Babycake? You were four. I went along painted up as a bleeding zombie that discombobulated some uptight father. Said I was scaring his kids! It was Halloween, for goodness sake. What's the point?"

"He must have had a point, Dad." Adele recalled the angry parent yelling at her father while she waited with an open sack; the pair was summarily dismissed with a door slam.

"Sure, he did have a few points," Morgan huffed. "Had one between his ears and one up..."

"You should have let it go," Adele interrupted. "He was mad as a hornet when you wrote TRICK in weed poisoning on that pretty green lawn.

"Expensive trick, too!" Morgan laughed with her at the memory. "Had to pay out good money for that one."

Beyond the newsworthy Halloween shenanigans photographed and blasted all over social media, Adele had forgotten less celebratory highlights. Recollection of her five-year-old Christmas had obscured memories of rituals, holidays, and birthdays. While decorating the Christmas tree, her young world went dark and stayed dark for only an hour in their home, but the rest of the region went dark and stayed dark for nearly four straight months in the dead of winter. For most of the world's communities, the lights never returned. Subsequent panicked voices on the farm told the story of a mammoth blackout. Her father's earnest preparations and her mother's tight grip upon her shoulder were the first warning signs of something gone terribly wrong.

Everyone around her performed quickly. Adele was directed to sit quietly by the tree with an emergency flashlight band that fitted loosely on her wrist, flickering its protest.

"Stay here...I'll be right back as soon as we get things running," her mother promised.

Her mother didn't return for another two hours, the light faded, and the pitch-black darkness enveloped her; the smell of fir was replaced by the ever-present fumes spewing from an array of alternately powered diesel generators working from hardened underground outlets. Upon return to the house, her father's voice was unnaturally quiet when he spoke with her mother.

Remnants of large plastic soft drink bottles sprinkled countless roofs that provided light obscured by the shanties and tent cities that sprang up. Thousands of transparent plastic bottles were stripped of labels, mixed with filtered water and bleach, then sealed and inserted into makeshift windowless tin buildings to provide solar powered light. One of the farm's outbuildings was dedicated to fashioning chemical batteries that could fire lithium cells augmented by hydrogen ones. Reams of silver foil, copper coil and filtered water were fashioned in an assembly line. Forever on her mother's hands was the smell of bleach. No, she thought. She didn't recall a single Halloween until she was nearly 12 years old. It was the smell of fir juxtaposed with a flickering light, the diesel fumes and the groans of generators, hushed tête-á-têtes, and indeterminate desolation that she vividly recalled.

* * *

The side doorbell rang out as a long, low grind, coupled with ghostly 'woo' and 'whoosh' sounds. Adele snapped to attention. A hologram of sweet, fanciful dancing faeries and elves welcomed outfitted children and accompanying parents in groups of five to the side porch entrance. A smorgasbord of treats on adjoined wooden picnic tables awaited with the monotonous intonations of Angela Pendergrass, who had been charged too many years with apportioning scarce food to endless lines of starving citizens.

"Just take what you need. Please don't grab. There's more," she repeated the well-rehearsed directive.

"Mother," Adele whispered, "it sounds as if you're working the old food line."

"Happy Halloween!" Angela remedied. "Just take what you need. Please don't grab. There'll be more!"

"Better?" Angela looked toward Adele.

"Oh, yes!" Adele smiled. "The Happy Halloween was a brilliant touch."

At the table's end were special bags of miniature toys wrapped in black paper bags tied with orange raffia in anticipation for the goblins and ghouls, obscure super heroes, and undefined personalities. Fashioned from everything from 3-D printers to foot-pumped sewing machines, all representations were derived from time-honored imagination. Making their way toward a feast of candy apples, marzipan clowns, chocolate flying witches, and assorted Georgian nuts, the enchanted children giggled excitedly.

Child-friendly robotic Snuggletroids lovingly attached to the arms of new masters, having been pre-programmed with brief bios. They would offer pre-approved AI advisements for everything from hygiene to study skills. It was, as one child screamed with delight, 'better than Christmas'. Angela tried not to correct the innocent remark and failed.

"It is not the same, dear! Christmas is a time for holy observance," she urgently corrected.

"Oh, so right," yelled Morgan. "Halloween is meant to scare the holy crap out of people! Come to think of it, religion does that, too!"

"Morgan?" Angela cautioned sweetly. "You're dismissed if you can't control yourself."

Morgan decided to depart from the porch proceedings to view the comings and goings from his library sanctuary.

"We thought we knew scary. We didn't know scary," Morgan settled into his chair, turned on the monitor, and lit a cigar. "There's a certain clarity when it's suddenly pitch black, planes dropping out of the air, cars stranded, mass transport running off road and rail, gas explosions, raging fires, sewage and all those names!" Morgan sadly reflected. "Oh God. Those names!"

He recalled the frantic then desultory calling for lost people. As he settled in front of a fireplace meant for civilized flames, he could see in his mind's eye the cities and fields that once burnt unmercifully as parents cried desperately for their children, children screamed for their dead or lost parents, traumatized lovers and friends dragged each other through streets as gas lines and collapsing infrastructure trapped them in places that would never allow for a memorial.

"Over nine billion people shouted the names of loved ones, searching on hands and knees, walking hundreds of miles, calling out names attached to the missing, killed, trapped, or left forever to exist in one's nightmares." He held his hands tightly together to regain a modicum of composure as the images paraded through his mind.

People who had never carried a moral compass began to randomly prey upon the vulnerable within a few days. Those that relied upon government assistance without personal safety nets were left defenseless in unforgiving urban settings, awaiting emergency help that would never arrive. Those who had heeded geopolitical warning signs took to their refuges, outfitted boats, survival condominiums, and bugged-out bunkers. That is, thought Morgan, those that pre-plotted and imprinted their way by foot. Even the birds and animals moved erratically, suddenly unable to sense direction. Man and beast went literally out of their minds, bereft of navigational abilities and physical cues.

"Now, it's time I look at this dream meant to replace a nightmare." Morgan relaxed his mind and focused on the activities on the library screens. A new generation of innocent children was excitedly calling each other's names, pointing toward the fun with their diminutive hands warmly tucked into a parent's.

Morgan zoomed in on his granddaughter lying contentedly upon her mother's lap, rocking in a steady reassuring rhythm. A wooden creak lulled both mother and child upon a hand-woven thrush-seated Appalachian rocking chair that had once belonged to Morgan's grandmother. His steadfast wife greeted children of all ages, touching their arms reassuringly.

Girlfriend Elle Smythe eventually joined Connor to lend assistance. The couple did their utmost to recognize costumes as parents skillfully interjected narratives. Morgan examined the ill-fitted pair, grunted his disapproval, and took a shot of Bourbon.

After an hour's time, Morgan grew impatient. It was time to regain control of his home. Five groups were still strewn along the long driveway and a new group had just arrived on the porch. CC's pipe cleaner antennae bobbled as she monitored the proceedings with renewed interest. One toddler was hoisted upon a young man's shoulder, sparking CC's sudden laughter. Adele ceased to rock and brought CC closer to the smiling little boy, whose hand stretched eagerly to touch hers. Within moments of this exchange, Morgan Pendergrass came to attention and transferred the image to his security team.

"I'm sure that this is the same man who wandered on the property three months ago. He's now on my front porch," he messaged to security. "Send me the surveillance report August 14, 2055 now," cracked Morgan.

The requested report was streamed regarding an arrest that had proven to be nothing more than a lost motorist with dysfunctional navigation. The car had no manual utility and the man explained that his had been a search for assistance. Morgan requested an additional background check. Nothing within that two-minute check proved worrisome. But, there he was – the former intruder, one Scott Reid – on his side deck within grabbing distance of his family.

"We're on our way, Dr. Pendergrass," Failsafe Security assured.

"Nah. Stay put. I've got my own security...don't think it's serious. I'll handle this."

"Excuse me, Mister Reid," boomed Morgan Pendergrass's voice through the porch monitor's speakers.

Adele was horrified as the startled child began to wail. The children ceased the happy chatter.

"Mind paying this lonely old man a visit? And bring that adorable little boy with you. I'm in the library."

Angela Pendergrass compliantly invited the young father to follow her into the home. Adele stepped in for an emotional re-set. Parents stood frozen at an invisible Morgan Pendergrass beckoning a man and his child from an omnipresent source.

Still hoisted on Scott Reid's shoulders, the boy calmed with the ride. Angela opened the heavy double doors into the cavernous home. A fractured geode, the opening revealed precious gems of the home's interior. Bright lights erupted in a sparkling crystal spectrum that glimmered from the room's center across every wall. Passing under the 20th Century Bohemian chandelier, the little boy craned his neck upward, straining eagerly to capture dancing colors.

Morgan carefully examined the incoming visitors as Angela escorted the thirty-something, hollow-eyed, lanky male and his son along a long hall into the library.

The sight of so many leather-bound, gold leaf books reaching floor to ceiling caught the young father by surprise. Concerns and passions of the ex-governor's past were evident throughout the mahogany paneled room. Behind a smaller 18th century secretary was a set of photographs taken and developed from a mid-twentieth century camera of what looked to Scott Reid to be interesting people he could never hope to meet. Sitting oddly on a well-stocked bar was a photograph of a little girl in pigtails, her worn dress, bare feet, and dirty fingernails a tragic reminder of unrealized dreams.

Several evenly-leveled framed rows of black and white pictures of unidentified uniformed sport heroes were autographed by their handsome, fit subjects. Reid had never attended a sports event yet recognized the uniforms as those worn for the game of football.

Juxtaposed amongst piedmont hills in various landscape paintings were more photographs of unidentified people who smiled in happier times. Reid puzzled over the large watercolor illustration of a rustic shed converted into a Zendo that featured the caption, 'No Clinging Allowed.'

Another picture featured a young, lean runner in the act of receiving a baton pass in a relay race; head craned over his shoulder, eyes searching the periphery, every sinew of the runner's neck, arms, and legs was captured in celebration of the subject's determination.

Several Bibles and a vast array of religious artifacts were stacked upon a long side table. A delicately carved white ivory Buddha sat atop the last of the leather-bound Bibles, laughing at the visitor's discomfort. Reid felt the room suddenly close tight around him when his roving eyes ultimately focused upon the man focusing upon him.

"I know you, Mr. Reid. You paid our family grounds a visit about two or three months ago. Am I right?" Morgan asked rhetorically. He lit a cigar and began to puff.

"I apologize." Scott Reid's posture stammered where his voice held steady. His son sat calmly on Reid's broad shoulders, mesmerized by the fire licking within the overly heated library's massive brick fireplace.

"I've just one question. You told the police that your battery wasn't working correctly and then you said something about your monitor didn't warn you because it was broken or some such thing. They checked both and everything was in working order. Then you came up with a navigational glitch. I'm just asking it straight... what exactly you were doing around these parts, short of curiosity?"

Morgan Pendergrass leaned forward in an antique wheelchair that had once transported his elderly mother. Since his cane had mysteriously disappeared, Morgan took to the next best thing. His earnest posture demanded a straight answer.

"There's no excuse for my snooping but that's not something that the police would accept. I know you told them to let me go and I appreciate it. Something compelled me to visit and I can't say what it was. I sincerely apologize, Mr. Pendergrass. I sincerely do."

"Well, you got a cute boy there. Better sincerely mind what and why you've taken to trespassing so that he doesn't have a father who doesn't have answers for him," Morgan emphasized with a finger pointed in Morgan Expedient mode. He lowered the finger and smiled broadly.

"Well, Happy Halloween and such. Good to meet you and your boy." Morgan motored his chair in a semi-circle and acted as if resuming fire viewing rather than a monitor. He waved goodbye with his back to Scott Reid and son.

"I'm all good about treats but don't need any tricking... you mind that, Mr. Reid," Morgan added.

"Goodnight to you, too. And, thank you. It's an honor to have met you, sir."

Scott Reid regretted an inability to converse with the famous Morgan Pendergrass. He hadn't been able to come up with one question, witticism, or a singular thoughtful observation. He had been called out as an intruder and dismissed as one.

"I'm an idiot," he believed. He also puzzled need for a wheelchair for a man with an exoskeletal leg.

Father and son departed the room; Reid ducked to clear the door for his boy who had relaxed without screams of protest for which the child was particularly prone. CC wiggled excitedly as father and child passed through the porch, the last guests to exit, and moved past those who now hustled to remove holiday decorations. Angela packed an additional bag of treats and handed it to Scott Reid with the gentle maternal warning to offer sparingly.

"Be sure to visit us next year so we can see how much your boy has grown!" Angela smiled as father and son descended the porch steps.

A security bot's search gear lit the way as treads and feet rotated and shuffled along the driveway toward the yawning gates, now stripped of decoration. Reid's car was in place to meet them, poised with a running motor and open door.

Once seated, Reid anticipated the inevitable fretting of his son that followed the most routine of transitions. Yet the boy appeared strangely at ease even as the bot secured his seat.

"Home," Reid directed as he turned to look at his son's expression; he recognized within his next heartbeat that the perpetually anguished boy had relaxed in a way yet to be exhibited since birth. The ever-present facial contortion of discontent and fear had vanished. A contented boy replaced the one that had fought life since entering it.

He looks so... pleasant, Scott thought. Undiagnosed anxiety had plagued the boy's young life and left a struggling young married couple without sleep, comfort, or hope. Scott Reid began to silently weep with relief. Perhaps, he hoped, his wife would return to him, too.

* * *

Monday, November 22, 2055

The Pendergrass and Collins households were riding a new crest of enthusiasm. Everyone agreed that Connor Collins' marriage to Elle Smythe might just happen if Connor allowed Elle's momentum to build. Elle had taken to ruminating about marriage. She also had begun to stay regularly overnight in Connor's cabin, feigning a wide list of reasons for remaining in residence.

"She's just squatting," Morgan noted. "She's a love squatter. Connor won't ever be able to get rid of her! He'll never be able to rent himself out again!"

Angela disapproved of the arrangement and asked Elle to refrain from compromising her reputation. Elle assured everyone that she never compromised.

Elle let it be known that a wedding between Connor and her should take place during the upcoming summer on the Pendergrass farm but neglected to discuss the idea with the owners. Elle was of the mind that those who were more fortunate were obligated – if not delighted – to share with the less fortunate.

"Why should I eat protein cubes when I can have steak?" she once objected to Connor's suggestion with regard to flaunting privilege when others suffered.

Once extremely malnourished and impoverished, Elle was now dispossessed of humility and compassion. Appeals for modesty or charity were summarily disregarded.

"I've already done without. I don't think it's fair to see how far a person can go," Elle pouted in protest.

Elle transformed herself. She changed her name from the less exotic Ellie May to something more sophisticated. According to Morgan, she had more beauty than brains but was quick to calculate a profitable union.

"Dr. Connor Collins has enough thinking juice for the both of them," Morgan had said more than a few times. "Elle's tank is running on empty. You can hear that mind sputter."

Angela would abide rude remarks but could not deny her feelings about Elle the moment the unschooled young woman called her 'Mom'. The notion turned Angela's naturally pretty smile into a thin-lipped, straight line that cried silent disapproval.

"I'm not related to Connor or Lex," Angela explained patiently. "You do understand that, Elle? If you marry Connor, you will not be my daughter-in-law."

"I just thought because y'all are so close and you're old enough to be Connor's mother and I don't have a mother that you'd probably would like for me to call you mom...right?" she explained confidently.

"She's not going to be your mother and you're not going to call her mom," Morgan tried. "You're making everything confusing. My wife has got a daughter. Her name is Adele. What makes you sure Connor and you are getting married, by the way? I think all of this stuff is premature and invasive."

"She doesn't mind. Right, Mom?" Elle simply stated.

"Mal élevé," Angela had whispered to her husband.

"Dumb as flipping bricks," Morgan clarified.

"Dumb as a fox," Angela corrected. "She's here to stay unless Connor turns this situation around."

The couple, imagined Elle, would make a Pendergrass farm cottage into a temporary home. Connor and Lex lived for three years in the cottage turned into a makeshift laboratory when the scientists gathered from Raleigh. Over the years, the brothers had indeed grown emotionally close to Morgan. Morgan and Angela invited Lex and Connor to continue on the farm since the Collins family had perished in the first wave of Chicago violence. For all purposes, it was family.

As was the case for so many others, Elle was of a generation unable to grasp the kind of connections that wove the fabric of nuclear families. She was, however, well acquainted with the images of the long, beautiful white wedding dresses and rings that accompanied traditional religious ceremonies of former times. Her father, whose generation had relied upon personal Artificial Intelligence Avatars to navigate daily life, tried to explain the festivities that included relatives and friends. Her father had not explained the reason he never married nor had he a reason that anyone should do so.

"No one needs to do that anymore," he dismissed Elle's question with laughter.

With an AI friend, Elle thought ruefully, *I wouldn't have to figure out so many crazy things myself.*

Elle, however, took notice of what a child meant to the powerful Pendergrass clan. Wedding plans began to take shape in Elle's mind as soon as CC arrived on the scene. She pressed Connor frequently for a wedding date in the hopes that it would jumpstart a formal proposal.

"Families like babies! I can do that!" she reassured herself with an alternative plan if all else failed.

There was whistling and a great deal more laughter that filled the spaces, along with fewer complaints that centered upon the woman who had made herself a fixture on the Pendergrass farm. Lex made attempts to become better acquainted with the woman who might become his future sister-in-law; he ceased to correct incessant grammatical errors.

Adele, however, often wondered about the ill-considered prospects of a union between Connor and a partner strangely resistant to thought and work.

Still, there was no proposal.

Tuesday, November 23, 2055

"Monitor...shake up this house!" ordered Morgan at 7:30 a.m. "Remind everybody it's that time to fetch our Thanksgiving turkey in downtown Cary...be on the ground in 45 minutes flat."

The alarm had the household sending unkind memos back to the patriarch who had preemptively instructed the monitor to ignore all further transmissions.

With the exception of two dogs, the Pendergrass household found themselves standing reluctantly outside in the crisp November air within the hour. CC was settled first inside the car on her grandfather's lap. The rest of the family took their seats with grunts and yawns. One hound watched forlornly from the front porch as the house-bot secured J.Blue, howling his protest.

"To the market!" Morgan announced to the navigation. The vehicle eased slowly through the morning mist that hugged the ground.

Pilgrimages to the grocery warehouse during the holidays were one of the few occasions that brought the old-timers out to socialize; in a fall back to friendlier times, the city became animated in and around the mile-long warehouse meant to offer an opportunity to run into old friends and new neighbors. Bikes, horses, bots, cars and dogs crammed the roads.

Ruminating over a naturally grown turkey pulled gingerly from an old-fashioned brown paper wrapper had become a treasured Cary ritual. Anything over 14 pounds without special dietary enhancement was pre-ordered. The old timers didn't want anything to do with the enhanced or printed birds, preferring to order the authentic variety from Kirkpatrick's Turkey Farm of Matthews, North Carolina. It was pricey but so was everything. For those on the Internet Exchange, the turkey and pie filling haggling had begun months before the holidays.

"Watch out. Here comes trouble," Morgan shouted as soon as his oldest friend, Gloria Brackett, came into view. Her shopping bot was filled to the brim.

"You're just plain irritating when you aren't boring the pants off everyone, Pencilass!" Gloria trilled back. She was forever thrilled to see the man with whom she shared the better part of her history. From first grade, Morgan's first school friend dubbed Morgan as Pencilass. Gloria never tired of seeing Morgan's pinched face when the butt of the childhood taunt.

"Lord knows I wouldn't want to bore the pants off you, Miss Glory Hallelujah, because you're looking mighty rotund these days," Morgan sniffed.

"Good thing you haven't changed. I'd feel strange if you turned up with a lick of manners, Morgan."

"You here for turkey? Always around for food, eh Glory?"

The recently widowed friend playfully bypassed Morgan in favor of Angela, who stood apologetically shaking her head. They warmly embraced.

"Angela, I still hate you for stealing my best boy. He had to go and get married to somebody 24 years younger who still looks like a star. Congratulations, Grandma!"

Angela and Gloria Brackett spoke of the baby. Tired of being ignored, Morgan smacked Brackett's backside with the cane recently recovered from Angela's latest hiding place. Gloria neither flinched nor interrupted her conversation.

"Can't make a dint in that inflatable raft, Glory. Must be reassuring to know that you'll never drown," Morgan laughed hard. "You're padded to the gills down there, woman."

"Did you hear something, Angela?" Gloria waved goodbye as she passed Morgan. "Give Adele a kiss for me, won't you, old man?"

"I don't have one to pass on, big talker..." Morgan teased.

Gloria turned and strode purposefully back toward Morgan, positioned her two hands around a startled face, and pulled his down to hers, gently placing two kisses on alternate cheeks with a loud 'mwah'.

"That should do it...pass it on, you mean, ugly ole goat." Morgan's ears turned red.

"I can pass on a couple of kisses but you'll never grow an inch, woman. What's that? You say something? I can barely hear you from up here."

"Hush up, Morgan. On second thought, keep talking. It's cold out here."

Halfway into a smaller warehouse, Morgan yelled to his wife, who had since run into Dr. Meredith Green.

"Angela, don't take pity on Meredith by inviting her to our place for Thanksgiving... she always spills the cranberry sauce on something... only brings two miserable pies. Not worth it!"

The women ignored him until Meredith directed Morgan toward the town's fountain, "in case you're in need," she snickered.

For hours, the Cary locals mingled and compared notes. The citizens had worked together and comforted each other's families for many arduous years. A renewed sense of community at Thanksgiving reminded Cary neighbors of their journey into a new normalcy.

Morgan held CC under one arm and then cradled her in both, shifting positions as he shook hands with friends and strangers who had lived on the farm grounds during the worst of times. Adele and Lex trailed behind, hand in hand, watching their daughter take it all in stride as each passing hand moved to caress CC's face.

Morgan stopped abruptly mid-stride and turned CC upside down, recoiling for effect.

"Hey, lovebirds... either the Jackson Pit-House is firing up rancid BBQ or your daughter needs a change!" he called to Adele and Lex behind him.

"Thanks, Dad."

Adele disliked the manner in which her father carried CC like a sack of potatoes and turned her upside down to sniff her bottom when there was diaper duty. She retrieved Caroline and left for the restroom.

"Lex and I'll be standing guard right here after you get her fixed up, Babycake."

"Right, Morgiepie!"

"You know, your wife is getting mighty sassy, Lex," Morgan frowned.

"You know, Morgan," Lex smiled, "I think that nut hasn't fallen far from the tree."

"It's time to get busy and raise another sassy pants!" Morgan clapped his hands. "I'd like a half dozen of those!"

Morgan retrieved and lit a half-smoked cigar. Several puffs later, he stamped the stogie out on the ground and kicked gravel over it.

"Okay, look smart; here they come, Lex."

"Go to papa," Adele handed the baby back to the man yelling 'give her here, give her here!'

Morgan neatly cradled his granddaughter in one arm and walked briskly back into the crowd that seemed to sense Caroline's presence, magnetically drawn to the Pendergrass child.

Thursday, November 25, 2055

Thanksgiving dinner took place amongst many smiles and happy conversations. It was also the time Adele noticed certain changes. It seemed the men wisely tempered their intake of toxic Pendergrass Farm Hooch in the Mason jars labeled PF Poison. The mash of pride had a well-earned reputation of rendering otherwise sane, able-bodied people useless. Connor quietly warned Elle to avoid the homemade hooch. She complied after drinking her first few pints.

Elle paid close attention – as close as her acuities would allow – to CC's social capital. Elle had often announced that she intended to remain childless because she never wanted to grow up. No one doubted her sincerity the first time she said this. As soon as Elle beheld the devotion bestowed upon CC, she recognized the possibilities of adoration by proxy.

"Pass that chubby little angel here!" Elle demanded upon arrival into the Pendergrass living room, typically an hour late. I'm pretty sure I want one of these!" she yelled, wriggling her fingers.

Elle's enthusiasm could not be discerned from proclaiming an interest in a particular color, dress, pillow, piece of pie, or dog collar. Adele reluctantly handed CC to Elle and nervously surveyed Elle's reception. Alerted to Elle's awkward mannerisms, a safety bot moved closer in range.

Transformed into a frenetic feeding bird with lips, Elle pecked kisses upon Caroline's face, head, and stomach.

"Can she say anything yet? Is it ok to put her down on the floor? Where's Blue?" Elle called Blue's name repeatedly, as if he had wandered upstairs. Stretched full length by the fireplace, Blue heard his name, lifted his head slightly, and farted.

"Ha!" Elle laughed. "You can't blame that one on me!"

No one seemed to mind Elle's streaming random one-way conversations with herself, the lack of observation, or crude comments. The endless pronouncements and questions need not be answered. The limited, vague responses offered would have sufficed for a three-year-old. Exchanged witticisms, everyone understood, were meant for a greater audience. Elle would giggle at anything. It was a formula that worked for everyone.

It worked, that is, until Elle turned her attention from Blue's intestinal indiscretion to details of an illusionary wedding. Doubling efforts to deputize willing female residents of Cary with whom she was not acquainted to act as her nominee bridesmaids had sent the wrong message. There was no one in the Pendergrass household happy about Elle's self-promotion.

Elle decided to place CC beside Blue; Adele used the opening to grab her child from the floor and run into the kitchen. Angela quickly indicated she had been tracked from behind as Adele burst through the kitchen doors.

"Would you be my maid of honor?" Elle tapped Adele's shoulder.

"No thank you," Adele replied without turning.

"What? Why not?" Elle screamed in horror. "You're going to be my sister-in-law!"

Adele replayed the question. She realized that this must be the day for Elle's engagement announcement and corrected herself.

"Of course, I'll help," Adele choked a retraction.

Elle hugged Adele, who stood frozen with CC in her arms, then ran from the kitchen clapping her hands.

"I didn't know that Connor proposed!" Adele anguished to her mother.

"He didn't," Angela laughed. "Saying it doesn't make it so. I've no idea what goes on in that girl's mind, bless her heart."

"Mother? Kill me now," Adele shook her head.

"He'll come to his senses. I wouldn't worry about it," Angela concluded.

Thanksgiving dinner was devoted to eating and listening to Elle Smythe. Illusions aside, it proved frustrating to attempt adjunct conversations when Elle refused to use a translator. Few thoughts or sentences having nothing to do with Elle made it to completion. Morgan grew testy. Connor avoided the raised eyebrows and unasked questions by staring into his plate.

Over a year's time, a Pendergrass tradition called for close friends and family to write and gather their anonymously written notes of gratitude and place them in a hand-decorated wooden box. Their randomly selected sentiments were blindly drawn and shared at Thanksgiving dinner. Forgotten small acts of grace and gratitude reminded everyone of the value of friendship and the bounty bestowed upon them. Elle had stacked all of her prayers of gratitude one hour before dinner with one message: "Thank you, God, for giving me Connor."

Elle's message was selected four times as the box was passed from person to person around the large dining room table.

"Wonder who put that one in?" Morgan snarled each time Elle's note was shared.

"I did!" Elle gleefully answered each time.

Morgan turned toward his wife; his trademark popping eyes warned of sensory overload

"Ok, Cookie," he said measuredly. "Somebody call me when pie is up. Come with me, Connor," Morgan demanded as the dinner plates were removed.

Elle was excited at the thought of Morgan directing Connor to accompany him for what she imagined might be 'the talk'.

"Morgan? Want me to come with y'all?" Elle called after the men.

"Nope," Morgan yelled over his shoulder.

Connor and Morgan found refuge in the library. Morgan slammed and bolted the heavy door.

"I think they heard that, Morgan," Connor noted.

"I hope to God they did!" Morgan looked feverishly for the missing hooch Angela was prone to hide. "Where's that Pendergrass white lightning when I need it?" Morgan grumbled. He located and poured a brandy for Connor. "Drink this poor substitute," he ordered. "Sweet baby Jesus, I can't hear myself think. My skin just up and crawled its way outta the house. How can you stand it?"

Connor exchanged the cordial glass for the decanter. Filled to capacity, Connor poured liquid amber down an open, willing throat. He slumped into the leather couch holding the half emptied decanter listlessly in one hand; the other made into a fist now lightly pounded his head.

Morgan observed Connor's unusual show of frustration and managed to muster some delicacy.

"Connor, you're a good man. You don't think Elle isn't a wee bit tetched? This relationship is like picking your nose, son.

You were digging around and digging around and then finally found a booger. Now, you don't know what to do with it."

"Suggestions, Morgan?" Connor asked. "I'm in deep and I can't figure for the life of me how I got here."

"The point is, you're picking your life's teammate, not your nose."

"What am I supposed to do?" Connor asked, visibly pained.

"You can't keep cutting this relationship with a butter knife. Giving that gal little hints is like trying to describe color and technique to a blind painter. The whole thing doesn't make a lick of sense. Do something. Marry her... or get off the pot!"

"Thank you, Morgan. I let this get out of hand. I'm going to tell her she can't move in with me. I'll see how she takes that piece of news first."

"Hell, that's never going to work," sniffed Morgan. "You've got to be specific. There's no marriage in the future for you two. That's what it's going to take. Tell her the imaginary engagement is off!"

* * *

That evening, Adele mentioned an observation to Lex as he read the day's newsfeeds from the Confederation Commons.

"Everyone has seemed more optimistic lately," Adele called through the bathroom door.

"Including your father?" Lex finally shouted over running water. "I'm pretty sure Connor isn't looking too upbeat either," he laughed.

"Monitor on: CC's room," Lex ordered as he crawled into bed. The proud parents stared at CC in the crib as soft melodies were played; the couple's reassuring images took shape beside CC's crib while she drifted into sleep downstairs.

"There's no big change in people, Adele. We're the ones that see the world differently," Lex determined.

He kissed his wife on her forehead and touched her cheek. He barked, "Monitor off!" before turning on his side.

The only thing that listens to him, Adele thought.

Adele couldn't sleep. She slid quietly out of bed and made her way downstairs to retrieve CC. Upstairs, Adele placed the sleeping baby between her and Lex in what would be a family bed for the next two years.

Sensing the fragile nature of happiness, Adele offered a prayer on behalf of her family and the blessed moment she shared with her healthy daughter.

Adele added, "And please Lord... in the event that Elle and Connor's union is not your plan, I would appreciate your prompt intervention...Amen."

Chapter 111
The Nishants

Maharashtra, India
Thursday, April 10, 2059

Five-year-old Aditiya Nishant sat at the mahogany desk and watched his father, a gifted mathematician, agonizing quietly over an alternative equation. Aditiya traced and copied the numbers floating around his father with his left forefinger and pasted it to his side of the table. He liked the holographic threes, sixes, and nine combinations the most and overlooked the rest. Red sixes and blue threes adorned the little boy's space of the office where he would play in the afternoons, content to be near the man he adored and the woman nearby he thought more beautiful than the moon. Aditiya's mother worked upstairs monitoring India's lone satellite that helped apportion and check precious grid time.

Bright yellow and green curtains covered the retractable metal barrier that was once a window. Air and water filters stood as obvious additions along the inner wall separating the kitchen and entrance. All light was artificial.

Aditiya selected twenty different colors from the icons before him on an opaque wall that was now a monitor. He selected and splashed geometric forms between his larger favored figures. He reduced the enumerable multi-colored particles infinitesimally while the computer protested its limitations.

"Smallest pixel level. Apologies Aditiya... you have reached the smallest pixilated level."

The monitor's admonitions annoyed Amar Nishant, who struggled to remain in the Indian Mathematical Society. His was a rare and well-compensated government job that afforded his family an island of comfort floating in a sea of pain and deprivation. Without relevant contribution to the pod's latest project, he ran the risk of losing his position and with it, every last barter-bit. It had been months since he was given his piece of the puzzle and he was nowhere.

"How can I solve something when I'm not privy to the entire project? This is idiocy not to be able to discuss outcomes with my colleagues," Amar complained aloud. He then turned toward his son as the sole cause of the monitor's incessant protests.

"Stop please, Aditiya. I can't concentrate with all of this noise. Just draw; if the monitor can't perform, leave it. Those are the smallest points it can muster. Why do you need it smaller?"

"I need it smaller and in more colors. Many more colors and much, much smaller," the little boy repeated anxiously. "It's the way all the other things are."

It had not occurred to Amar Nishant to inquire as to the reason his son always selected the same images of numbers from his equations until a new concentration upon infinitesimal colored specks caught his attention. Amar slid his chair over to the other side of the long antique conference table and put his hand on his only child's head, running his fingers through thick black hair, ending with a friendly pat.

"If you run that program any smaller, you won't be able to see the dots, Son."

"I will. I can see dots that are much, much smaller. They are everywhere." Aditiya peered absently into space, his eyes taking in something that his father could not.

"What dots? Where are the dots?" Amar Nishant asked softly.

"On your face, the wall, between the numbers, on CawCaw... you cannot see them?"

CawCaw, the family's pet parrot, squawked upon hearing his name and repeated "CawCaw" until Amar tossed a cracker into the cage.

For the first time, Amar detected the vast array of triangles and hexagons his son had arranged that seemed to correlate preferred numbers with geometric forms. Yet Amar was unable to discern any dots.

It occurred to Aditiya that his father's puzzled expression meant an inability to assist with his particular problem. Nor, he correctly intuited, did his father perceive that which was obvious to him. Aditiya saw the world around him as connected by geometric shapes; he perceived the world as a projection of colored points manifested as concrete matter. His father did not.

Aditiya Nishant fidgeted. He twitched and uncrossed his legs. Typically fretful, Aditiya jumped to his feet onto the surface of the dark worn wood.

"Colors...shapes...circles...squares? They're all over; they're everywhere, right? Everywhere... little dots," he nonsensically repeated.

The little boy alternated between pointing and sweeping gestures to describe something to his myopic father. Amar watched helplessly. It began with a brief hyperventilated state and then Aditiya fainted face-first on the table's pitted surface. The holograms disappeared; the monitor resumed being a wall while blood dripped from the child's delicate face.

The monitor activated and transmitted remote emergency warnings to the hospital. Within seconds, a remote staff physician appeared before the shocked father.

"Monitor, play back history; show all angles and register data," directed the physician.

It took half a minute to scan and diagnose a badly bruised nose and slight concussion. Amar was absolved of negligence and given directions for immediate care. The monitor would record the results of the prescribed treatment and send in a report to the hospital's data bank hourly until the final healing was confirmed.

"Monitor," directed Dr. Nishant after sedating and putting his son to bed on the couch, "play back any references to dots or small pixilated observations before today's conversation."

"There are none, Dr. Nishant," replied the monitor. "Records show that the first references took place one hour and forty-five minutes ago."

"Monitor, search references to small dots discernible to children or others including special focus upon geometric shapes. Tag diseases that might include references to dots and sight impairments…" Nishant recognized an unknown when he saw one.

"There are none to which you refer as indicated by Aditiya's experience," the monitor replied.

"Search, 'I see dots' and internationally cross-reference linguistics," Amar pressed outlying variables.

"I am sorry, Dr. Nishant. This is not an official scientific search and you have to personally authorize withdrawal of barter-bits."

"How much?" Amar began to pace the room.

"There is no way to estimate the time required given that we have no local data on the subject; it is vague."

"Thank you, monitor. Don't search. Erase."

Nishant knew that the monitor would erase nothing that transpired in his home. It occurred to him that his wife had failed to appear downstairs during the crisis.

"Monitor, did you transfer history to my wife?" Nishant asked his home guardian.

"No, Doctor. Instructions interceded that your partner need not be disturbed as it was not an emergency."

Nishant made a decision in that moment to leave India with his family. He was stunned that there had been programming that reckoned that which should – and should not – constitute parental intervention. What, he questioned, was more urgent to share with a mother than blood spilling from one's son?

"I need a change of scenery," he said aloud to no one. *I've got to think this out… without undue mannerisms* Amar reminded himself. *The monitor can pick up the minutest anomalies.*

Nishant focused upon the quiet whirr of his family's food delivery and its retrieval, and drew three even long breaths before speaking once more.

"Monitor, please inform my wife to make a list of places she would like to visit for our anniversary," he continued without a sign of stress.

"Dr. Nishant, you do not have enough barter-bits to travel with transport; I have taken the liberty to submit your request in an effort to determine if there are other jobs at your disposal. The list is available for you now."

Reviewing the demeaning, low paying jobs for hire meant that his employer had no intention of allowing leave until his portion of the epidemiologic model was completed. He would be rewarded handsomely for success, however. His track record had known no failures. Recently, Nishant was assigned to a top-secret assignment that was devoid of interaction with his colleagues and success, Nishant discerned, might very well be a futile assignment if any part of the vast data he inherited was corrupted or irreconcilable.

"This is great news; thank you," he feigned joy at the list before him.

Nishant walked deliberately to the faux window to calm his nerves. Without prompt, the monitor revealed the holographic exterior mid-afternoon. People walked casually under a clear, crisp blue sky and the thermometer read a pleasant 75 degrees. Sounds of songbirds and an occasional hum of the magnetic rails recharging public transports filled the room.

Another terrible falsehood, thought Nishant. *That's the sound of the White-Rumped Shama, only found in dense jungles or in the Royal Chitwan National Park. Both are extinct. Our country is not only dying from overpopulation; we are becoming a nation of frightened shadow people. Who wouldn't want this illusion?*

* * *

Friday, July 4, 2059

"It's inoperative and flawed. Of this, I am sure," insisted Nishant to headquarters.

"We have received similar responses from your collaborators and have decided to begin a new project. Your group has been compensated with a bonus that reflects our regrets for the member who failed one portion of the research project."

"Which colleague, may I ask?"

"No. This is not our protocol. Thank you."

Amar was elated. He had chosen to give up and come clean as to his inability to solve something he felt defective; the fault was elsewhere. Why hadn't he come to this conclusion a month ago? Why hadn't his concealed co-workers? Was it a test of his loyalty or resolve?

"We've all lost our nerve," he lamented. He felt shame, as if caught emotionally naked, unwashed, and made purposefully fearful.

The fact was, he was all of that. "Who has become the shadow person now?" he asked himself.

The monitor registered 20,000 barter-bits in the Nishant account. For a failure, he was curiously made a rich man. It was likely that the project was a matter of verifying inherited or stolen data. It was just as likely that his employer was pleased that enemies had not fortified or furthered their cause by purposely passing along skewed outcomes. This was, he decided, a deserved reward. It was unlikely that there had been lackluster results in his group's work. No failed colleague. The project was likely meant to sort manufactured information covertly planted by a renegade province, an enemy state, or a competing company.

Building and trading in rare scientific data that had been lost to the EMP surges was big business. Hard copies of research had been counterfeited and sold to governments. It had put everyone back decades. His group's job, he surmised, was to make sure that there was no Trojan horse in stolen or traded data that may have been purposefully planted to thwart competition. He'd heard that the Americans were able to resuscitate information that was stored in hard copy in deep vaults placed throughout the former United States. Most was worthless security and financial information, rendered moot by the lack of monetary systems or a cohesive Federal government. But there was a wealth of original information stored by the Smithsonian Museum and the Federal University Authority that included Federal Scientific Catalogues. The Confederation of American States had helped to jumpstart Indian recovery by generously sharing most of its findings. It didn't take long for international criminals to forge and sell sabotaged data a barter-bit at a time, then re-sell the proprietary information to another.

Nishant's team worked to scrape and vet incoming data. His former purpose was noble. Having been initially recruited to rebuild the Indian nation, Amar and Indu now worked for an undefined authority. Nishant harbored a growing concern about increasing constraints. His was a gilded cage. In the last two years, his 'Guardian Monitor' was a home model more attuned to scrutiny of the Nishant household than its security. Amar no longer trusted the community vision and suspected that the former Indian 'government' was now a euphemism for crime syndication.

Amar recognized the signs of imprisonment. The only way to depart India would be through the black market.

"I'll act as if I'm searching for forbidden treats or food for my wife," Nishant naively imagined. "I'll be disguised as a beggar," he plotted.

Amar thought it possible to make his way unnoticed through dangerous streets to visit a former friend known for his navigational wizardry. Obtaining and trading public transport passes had made his former University professor, a transplanted Englishman, a rich man. Sporadically throughout the years, the elusive professor would visit Amar's Indian home unannounced. On other occasions, the man would contact Nishant's home directly, somehow able to circumvent the Indian-controlled monitor with an unknown provider.

"Surely he'll be the one to help us," Amar convinced himself.

Gordon Smith, if that ever was his real name, was an old man, considered Amar Nishant.

"How had he managed it all?" Amar always speculated. "Of course, Gordon had lived in a time when changing or erasing one's digital footprints was still a possibility."

Smith was a man without a history in his collegiate years prior to the first cyber grid attacks. The world's communication networks had been obliterated by a convergence of the natural and planned when rogue nations decided to level the political playing

field by triggering high altitude nuclear blasts. The nuclear detonations left most of the world defenseless. The sun spat a
million-mile-wide blast of charged solar gas straight at earth and
set off a geomagnetic storm that induced currents from Quebec's
power grid to Texas within a week of the cyber-terrorism hitting
Europe, South America, and much of the Northern Hemisphere.
Gordon was one of the first within the UK to recognize the escalating catastrophe while the population waited desperately for
their respective governments to bail them out of darkness, provide food, water, and medical help. It was a time of pandemo-
nium in London with few safe options to leave the city. How
Gordon showed up occasionally in Maharashtra was an unsolved
puzzle. How he left Maharashtra was equally as curious.

"A plane...a rich, connected man with resources and an escape plan," Amar calculated. Recognizing Gordon's affinity for
flight patterns and small aircraft, scientific acumen, and discretion, Amar finally concluded his strange friend was nothing
more than a UK spy.

"I have to find Gordon. He's my only way out of this mess."

Their association began at Cambridge. Gordon Smith was invited to present solar flare findings determined to be inevitable
within the decade. By 2034, nations withdrew from international
grid agreements and began to siphon and sabotage electrical
resources. From London to Moscow, the lights flickered.

Yet, months after returning to India, there stood Gordon mi-
raculously at Nishant's doorstep with a survival plan. It was not
the kind of survival plan Amar expected. Rather, the proprietary
technology Gordon had in hand allowed Amar a secure relationship
with the Indian government; Gordon gave Amar research data
gleaned from the UK's most important environmental projects.

Smith shared blueprints for contained self-sufficient homes.
Amar stepped forward as the Indian government pleaded for
scientists to assist further in the country's recovery. Amar
stepped up and Gordon stepped out. Ten years passed before
their paths again crossed. Amar suspected the meeting was
not by chance. By then, Amar and his well-meaning colleagues
were under the thumb of a government monitoring system
that protected them like the rare resources they were.

Gordon never explained his reasoning for occasionally trekking from the UK to India to seek out his friend. Amar was too polite to ask. If anyone could help his family with an escape plan, it would be Gordon Smith.

"But where is he?" Amar asked himself. "Until now, Gordon has always found me."

Smith's whereabouts were a mystery. For whatever reason, it seemed everyone let the Englishman come and go as he pleased. Amongst the Indian ruins, Smith lived a life of relative luxury for a brief time, for which he was unapologetic. Only small, specifically equipped planes with an guidance system and energy license could hope to hop their way across the world. Yet, Gordon was everywhere while most of the world's transportation sat dead in the water. Government agencies or pirates ran large sailboats and updated freighters. It was difficult to discern with whom one was dealing as both parties required exorbitant bribes. Gordon Smith always acted alone.

Unbeknownst to Amar Nishant, Gordon Smith had decided to end his life in the near future. He had also long recognized his friend's need of assistance and was determined to help the Nishant family. Shortly following the Nishants' son's fainting accident, Smith appeared at Amar's doorstep.

"Amar! Tell your Monitor to open the door for your friend," he called. "It's raining like bloody hell and your neighborhood smells like steaming shit."

Nishant instructed the Monitor to unbolt the door.

"I have no authority to allow uncategorized visitors into your stronghold, Dr. Nishant," the Monitor responded.

"Open now, Monitor. I authorize you," countered Amar.

"This is for your safety; I will now terminate the entry visual and sound transmission for your peace of mind," the Monitor finalized.

The room fell silent.

That which Amar and his wife had longed feared was made perfectly clear. No one was allowed entry. Moreover, they were prisoners.

Given the home's security and plentiful supplies, he had harbored the illusion that his employers acted on his family's behalf. The Nishants were housed in one of the best sections of the city, even if it was perilous to venture outside without an armed escort. It was suicide to allow strangers inside but this was a friend known to everyone. Why had there been such programming?

Amar panicked. He felt that his present situation was not only strangely serendipitous but signified an undefined tipping point.

"It won't open! I cannot open the door, Smith!" Nishant continued to yell through the steel door in lieu of the intercom's functionality.

"Yeah, figures. Stand back, Nishant; get way the hell back from the door!" instructed the muffled voice.

Nishant retreated toward his office.

"Indu! Stay where you are!" he yelled to his wife upstairs.

A blast reverberated throughout the home. Aditiya was held tightly in his father's arms. Indu bolted downstairs. Gordon Smith greeted everyone, weapon in hand, and wiped away the splayed cement particles that showered his face and hair. With a small bow of his head, he acknowledged Indu's descent.

"You must be the beautiful, exceptionally brilliant collaborator, and wife of my old friend, Amar? I'm guessing this is the product of that brilliant union?" He eyed Aditiya and the blood that remained on the boy's shirt.

Indu's eyes were upon the man able to blast his way through their security door with a weapon unlike any she had seen in her files. Her attention turned toward Aditiya.

"Amar? What has happened to our son that he is sporting a bloody shirt and a bandaged nose?"

Her calm was a given. Aditiya was no stranger to accidents and she recalled the oft-referenced friendship of Gordon Smith.

"This is something that we will discuss later, Indu. Right now, please check the Monitor to see if it's operating, recording..."

A trumpet call to action, Smith responded to Amar's directive with one of his own.

"I'll take care of this one!"

With a singular resonating metallic 'ping', something resembling a small steel pellet was shot through the Monitor's mainframe interface in the upper corner of Nishant's make-shift office. Smith smiled and signaled the family of three to move where he stood.

"This Nano weaponry is wild...watch this!"

"What are we watching the Monitor for?" Aditiya was awake and wild-eyed with anticipation. A strange light and putrid air distracted the boy's focus. "I can see outside. Look over here! Our door is gone!"

While Aditiya ran to take in the great outdoors at the door-jamb, the reality of the urban landscape escaped the boy's understanding. He stared unbelievingly toward the filthy street as Indu and Amar watched their Monitor implode, popping violently in rapid sequences throughout the home. Aditiya stood riveted where the door once stood and yelled, "Shit" in recognition of the smells overwhelming him.

The small home went dark and inoperable; all fans ceased simultaneously. Humidity and refuse smells quickly filled Nishant's downstairs office that had once served as a family room.

"Aditiya, come back inside now!"

Like her son, Indu tried to sort the information presented before her, not the least of which was Amar's nonchalance toward Smith's futuristic launcher-like weapon at present mechanically folding itself back into the form of a pocket-sized metal case. Indu Nishant ran to the hall closet to retrieve a blanket and struggled to fasten it to the doorjamb; it was hopeless. The gaping hole and the massacred Monitor left Indu grasping for protective straws. Wandering strangers had begun to gather ominously and deep in the road by the Nishant home.

"I'm sure that there are lots of questions, Indu. I'm just as sure your husband can assure you of following my lead. He made a decision to leave and I'm here to make that happen. Let's move. Gather anything irreplaceable and small items for barter. You have three minutes. I'll take you to safety but anticipate a hostile visit as of one minute ago," Gordon urged.

Indu spurted upstairs to retrieve remnants of her young life encased within a chip embedded emerald necklace, inclusive of her family's history, gold, and hidden barter-bits.

Aditiya opened CawCaw's cage. CawCaw promptly flew to freedom through the home's gaping hole. Amar seized his frantic son who had intended to save the fleeing parrot. Within minutes, everyone stepped into the mucky street streaming with refuse without questioning Gordon Smith's maverick antics. Amar, Indu, and Aditiya piled into the Englishman's private transport as most of the gathering crowd gaped at a rare colored bird hopping gaily across rooftops; those less distracted rushed the Nishants' vacated home.

Passing the Nishants and Smith as they sped way were two government vehicles, sirens blaring.

Chapter IV
Aaron Shalit

Israel
July, 2059

Moshe Shalit struggled to raise his son, Aaron, on a Kibbutz situated near the Jordanian border. His wife had died in childbirth, an event that left the fragile man depressed years later. Former acquaintances within the kibbutz shamelessly tired of the never-ending nurturing of father and son. Aaron was left to himself for too many hours of the day; his father failed to monitor school attendance even though Aaron attended regularly. As the scientist in charge of the solar plant, Moe was self-absorbed and rarely interacted with the community's 3500 membership. Rather than pay appropriate attention to his son's growing needs, Moe became increasingly immersed in self-pity.

It was, thought Moe, a great blessing that the onset of the Grid disasters intervened when they did. The Islamic Empire had announced its intention to finish Israel 'once and for all'. The West had lost its technological superiority and the last vestiges of its war machine to unceasing optimism for the world's never-ending peace processes. Eighty thousand Israeli soldiers were killed instantly when the Russian made drones filled with Xienthenile gas pellets rained upon military installations. Israeli retribution was pre-empted by an e-bomb delivered into Lebanon by an unknown source.

It was the Kibbutz operations in the country that remained semi-operational when the entire Middle East came to a standstill. Outfitted with hardened defenses, the Kibbutz focused upon agronomy, farming, water purification, stores, and delivery. At sunrise and sunset, thousands of Israeli soldiers would rake the sand and look for signs of encroachment. Carts and containers made their way along ancient trade routes toward offshore cargo ships.

The Kibbutz where the Shalit family resided had solar panels with limited storage capacity. There was not a single resident that failed to mention the paucity of hot showers to the American transplant charged with its operation. Rather than offer a kindly greeting to Moe Shalit, the shuffling man was scornfully noted as woefully ill-equipped to provide the simple pleasure of a hot shower.

Moe had fallen in love with his wife, Shoshanna, on a mission trip meant to raise American funds for Israel until the charity well went dry. He found himself stranded in Israel on what proved to be his final job of escorting Jewish American teenagers whose parents paid for an experience beyond virtual worlds. Shoshanna was beautiful enough to persuade her fiancé to remain on the Kibbutz in response to his poor health and escalating hypertension. They married within months of meeting one another with no relatives in attendance.

Moe's bride insisted that she loved to harvest the succulent cherries, peaches and plums in the spring and the preparation of organic fodder the rest of the year. Although she treasured the hard work among the vast orchards of persimmons, figs, oranges, and nectarines, the dark circles that appeared under her eyes coincided with happy news.

"I'm pregnant," she announced happily.

"Oh," he replied.

Moe went about his work as overseer for the solar-generated energy and helped with water filter and distribution systems; Shoshanna worked manual labor that had become increasingly rigorous given the energy rationing. Most fuel and solar cells were diverted to filter seawater. The younger, stronger adults went from packing trucks to hand-pulled carts to meet the caravans of transports serving the nation. Moe blamed the country's unrealistic demands for his wife's exhaustion. Angry at the world at large for having collectively undermined his previous, more cultivated existence, Moe complained bitterly to his fragile wife.

Shoshanna died five days after giving birth.

"She's dead because she was worked to death," he wailed at the funeral.

As much as the Rabbi tried to console Moe and dispel the notion that the farming community had anything but the best intentions for his family, he would not calm.

"The sad part of this tragedy, Moe, is that we simply didn't have an ample supply of antibiotics. She'd cut herself weeks ago on her foot; Shoshanna never properly cleaned or dressed it and it became infected. It was the midwife who discovered it."

"She wouldn't have gotten infected if she hadn't been working in that bloody field, in filth, churning toxic waste..."

"We are surprised, Moe, that you failed to notice Shoshanna was weak. We would have promptly sent for supplies and taken the appropriate steps to ensure her health. The inability to recover from a minor infection quite possibly meant she had an immune disorder of some sort."

Moe would never fully recall his conversation with the Rabbi or the medical staff. He vividly recollected images of his beautiful wife's ashen face lying on the hospital bed and shouting obscenities at the Chevra Kadisha when they attempted to remove the body for burial preparation. Escorted out with a nurse following with the newborn, Moe vaguely recalled people corralling and directing him, a funeral, and his wife's wedding ring lying in his pocket. There were sounds of elder women as they brought food to the small rooms. Other strangers showed up to check on the baby. It was hard to think then; it was hard to think now.

Aaron was always a calm, clear-thinking child. As a toddler, Aaron's room, observed Shoshanna's best friend Rachel, was a reflection of the boy's nature. As a few years passed, the bedroom remained neat and clean. It also echoed the joy of the boy's curiosity. A rock collection sat precisely arranged on each shelf, from the smallest to largest samples. On the floor,

Aaron had arranged substantive carved stones that featured ancient writing from the Sea of Galilee.

"I got them from our field trip," he related to Rachel.

"This is pretty heavy, Aaron." Rachel had trouble picking up the massive stone artifact and doubted the boy's memory. "It's fascinating, though. What did your teacher think it was?"

Aaron worried that he never thought to share his find. "I just brought it home on the bus. I put it on top. Do I show her?"

"Well, it looks amazing. I'll bring one of my friends here to examine it. Looks as if you have an archaeological find," Rachel admired. "What did your father say about it?" Rachel wondered.

"He didn't say anything." Aaron looked puzzled. "He lets me collect things."

Even though Rachel was aware of Moe's disinterest in Aaron's rock collection, Rachel vouched for excellent parenting, having regularly inspected a tidy home and a well-nourished, well-dispositioned child.

As was her habit, Rachel dropped by the home each Friday afternoon with an offer to escort Aaron and Moe to Shabbat. As always, Moe expressed his gratitude but declined.

"I need rest, Rachel. If you could be so kind as to take Aaron, it would do me a lot of good. You're a good friend."

"Sure, Moe. No problem at all," Rachel repeated each Friday. Rachel disguised her annoyance at the widower's long years of self-pity; she blamed him for her friend's untimely death. How could he have not noticed a swollen, thickened red streak on Shoshanna's leg? How could a husband be so self-absorbed as to ignore his sick, pregnant wife?

Rachel dressed Aaron and combed his hair. Per the routine, the two left Moe snoring on the living room's couch. Aaron kissed his father's forehead and removed a dinner tray from the table.

"Come on, Aaron; help me with something before we go to services. I work on the last shift before sundown."

Like a puppy, Aaron scurried after Rachel. It was not for lack of opportunity that Rachel was without husband or family. With the advent of what she termed the 'great black night', her optimism had faded. When she lost her family in Tel Aviv and her boyfriend to an untimely death, Rachel lost her faith but not her will. She longed to leave Israel. Determined to explore the great unknown, she was restrained only by dedication to Shoshanna's child.

The little redheaded boy responded gratefully when Rachel hugged and kissed him. Aaron learned that helping with small duties in the groves elicited Rachel's silent gratitude. Most importantly, Aaron could speak to Rachel and she would listen.

As the sun began to set, Rachel checked the mid-summer's blood red oranges packed in the fields and selected two to eat. With her pocketknife, the halves were sectioned and placed on a white towel with the name of a former Kibbutz camp once operated for Jewish teenaged tourists. Aaron quickly ate his portion and looked to her for more.

"Sorry, little man. I can only afford to pinch two. We know how many are packed exactly. See that?" She pointed to a dozen carts neatly packed ready to be rolled by teams of four toward the water's inlet two kilometers away.

"What do I see, Rachel?' Aaron had no idea of the work behind the two oranges.

"Tomorrow morning, our group will help load the pull carts in shifts to the ships so we can help feed our friends in the cities. The same ships will bring back other supplies. It's hard work, Angel."

"You roll the cart? It's too heavy, Rachel!"

"Well, not always. It depends upon energy rationing. Sometimes we use the animals or motorized carts."

Aaron ran to the nearest cart and tugged at the metal container. From behind, he tried to push the problem. Rachel laughed gratefully as the little boy reached high to grasp the handles.

"I love you!" Rachel signaled an end to the exercise and patted the seat beside her.

Aaron ran back to sit beside Rachel as she cut the pile of saved orange peels into small pieces. He considered the carts and wondered how it happened that some things were heavy and others were not. The big things were heavy for people and the little things tended to be easier to move. But they both responded to the sounds that he hummed in his head. Aaron knew that the carts were somehow as responsive as the rocks he maneuvered, but that he might have to concentrate not on the whole picture, but a portion of the cart... just as he did when he moved the heavier items in his home, directing their movement sonically by humming quietly to himself rather than inside his mind. He had always known he could move items. It had not occurred to him until this moment that others might not have this ability.

Four of the carts began to crunch the ground below their wheels and rolled slowly forward. From her seated position on an empty orange crate, Rachel jumped and screamed in surprise. The carts abruptly stopped rolling.

"Aaron, did you see that? Tell me you saw those carts move. The ground is flat."

"Is this a good thing or a bad thing? Is this a mitzvah or is this against God's law, Aunt Rachel?"

Aaron appeared nervous. It was the first occasion Rachel had witnessed her godson exhibit the slightest anxiety.

"It's just peculiar," she said calmly. "Inanimate things don't usually move of their own volition... by themselves. I saw those carts move...did you?"

Aaron ran into Rachel's arms. She held him firmly and apologized for having frightened him. Finally, Aaron rattled his story.

"I can make the rocks move, little and big... but mostly I can just make them lighter so I can move them. I just thought that I could help you."

"Do it again, my little man. Do it again!"

Aaron was delighted. Aunt Rachel was bright-eyed and smiling. Within seconds, the heavy metal carts moved another few yards in a more rapid progression.

Rachel grabbed her chest. "Aaron? How do you do that and who knows that you can do that, Baby?"

"I do it every day. I clean my room, I make the baths, and I make the food. I can't reach everything so I have to think them around. I move the rocks outside when I have to be quiet. Some things move and others don't. Rocks are the eas-iest. Do you like it? When you pull the carts, I can make them lighter. Like float them on air, you know?"

Overwhelmed by some magical inexplicable display of crazy superpowers was one thing; the idea that Aaron's father had never lifted a finger in the family household was another.

Rachel took Aaron's hand to walk around the carts so that she could get a good, clear view of the red sunset across the farm. The landscape was dotted by black tubing feeding pre-cious beads of water in drips from the sea. Civilian soldiers raked the sand and checked their lines for encroachment. One waved and she waved back.

As the last soldier disappeared from sight, Rachel tested Aaron's suggestion that she touch a cart's steel handle with a pinky finger. As promised, the cart responded to her slight tug as if floating on air. It had weight but was in some way lifted without any visible trace of interference.

"Can you stop it now?"

As soon as the words left her mouth, the full burden of the metal car was evident. There was no identifiable trace of con-centration or effort on Aaron's part.

"You know this is something others cannot do, Aaron?"

"Yes, I think so."

"Aaron, I have some questions. Are you happy here?"

"I am happy everywhere, Rachel."

He looked intently at his guardian, who began to pace and watch for onlookers.

"Let me rephrase that. Would you like to live and travel with me? I have no relatives, no family left, and I could take you as my son. This phenomena, your conditions at home...I just think it might be better."

"I still have a mother and she loves me. I can feel her. She can come anywhere. But Father? I don't want to leave him. My mother says that he's not well. His mind is sick and his heart is sick. She says that he needs us."

Rachel made an effort to appear as if the statement was somehow not stunning.

I've just witnessed metal carts move around independently. Who am I to question that his mother's spirit doesn't still exist? Who am I to ask how this little boy feels the meaning of a woman who held him only a few times? From where does this insight come?

She thought this and said nothing more but wondered about Aaron's impressions of his mother's death.

"There is no beginning and no end," Aaron said flatly as they moved from the orange groves back toward the Kibbutz synagogue. It was as if he heard Rachel's exact thoughts. "If you want your mother, she can be with you, too," he added.

Rachel dismissed the shooting pain that crossed her heart. Aaron became intent upon changing Rachel's mood and raised roadside rocks high into the air. A grin confirmed a change.

"It's crazy! This is so crazy, it's wonderful!" Rachel exclaimed.

Stones hovered and jumped erratically for minutes then fell together again to the ground like hail.

"I can't make them stay light... they always go back to being heavy again."

"Well, darn, you've got to figure that one out," Rachel smiled at the wonderful exhibition and squeezed the boy's hand. For his little life, she wondered, had Aaron intuited discretion like an old soul? Had no one bothered to carry on a real conversation other than her? How could his mind and abilities have gone unnoticed? In any case, the miracles she witnessed renewed her faith.

Friday, August 15, 2059

Moshe Shalit finally attended Sabbath services, albeit in a coffin. The Rabbi called the Chevra Kadisha, the sacred society of pious men and women charged with the obligation of ritually preparing the deceased. People sporadically began to arrive at the Shalit home Thursday afternoon at 2:00 p.m.

Moe had attempted to hang himself from a kitchen rafter that held the makeshift metal bar meant to support an array of hanging pots and pans. He'd crafted it before Aaron was born and regarded the work a testament to rare ingenuity. It was never used. He neglected the kosher restrictions of separating utensils. Heavy skillets had never been hung; the hanging bar and hooks played host to nettings that held garlic and dried herbs.

The rafter, inadequately constructed for the weight required of the job Moe had in mind, gave way when he tried to hang himself. Moe awkwardly tied the rope around his neck, deciding to jump clear of the stove below his feet. A successful strangulation would require him to propel with great velocity from a standing position toward the floor. He did this. The railing and support bar gave way and fell with him. Moe's head hit an iron grill directly underneath. His chin slamming on the edge of the counter followed this. Moe's body was discovered with his chin inelegantly leveraged upward upon an open drawer. No one was sure whether one or both impacts finally killed him. He had been dead for three hours before it occurred to Yarome Silverstein to investigate the whereabouts of his absent co-worker.

Regarding the poorly executed suicide, Yarome nodded knowingly. "No wonder we never had enough hot water."

Moe was wrapped in white sheets. Rachel offered to be an Onen and arrange for Moe's burial. Despite her pleadings, the Rabbi refused to conduct a Jewish burial.

"It's a sin...a terrible sin to forego this gift of life. There will be no Jewish burial. For the sake of the boy, we will recognize Moe's life tonight at services. You must make other arrangements to remove the body immediately. He may not be laid to rest in our cemetery."

It occurred to Rachel the astonishing way Moshe was unable to get anything right, always leaving a mess behind.

"Even in death, he's high maintenance. What did Shoshanna see in him?"

Rachel bartered for the kosher simple wooden casket per the traditional ritual of eschewing frivolous adornment and a quick decomposition. Her collection basket of dehydrated, honey-dipped orange peels was readily accepted; the rough-hewn casket proved an even trade.

Privately, Rachel explained to Aaron that the ribbon she attached to his shirt made him an official mourner as the only surviving family member. She cried as she attached the ribbon to the left side and tore the boy's shirt for good measure

"You are an official mourner now, Aaron. This signifies that we observe your position by performing the K'riah on the side closest to heart..." Rachel felt tears welling up as she filled the time and space with senseless explanations to a four-and-a-half-year-old child without benefit of a single relative. There would likely be no mourners to recite the special prayer of Dayan H'emet. As if he heard her thoughts, Aaron spoke his.

"When my dog died, papa said the special prayer of Dayan H'emet. Only God understands life and death. We don't even understand God. Even for a loyal dog, we should remember the love it gave us and pray. My papa gave me love and our prayers will be enough."

* * *

There was silence early the next morning. They planned to transport Moe's body before the sun reached full strength. Moe's body was placed in an orange cart and pulled by four of Rachel's friends to a fallow field, once a failed experiment for a vineyard. It seemed strangely fitting that her friend's husband would rest amongst the dying vines, broken twine and abandoned stakes. It seemed stranger that the cart in which he lay seemed almost buoyant.

Rachel kept Aaron's hand in hers as they walked two miles toward the burial site prepared by Rachel's friends. Moshe Shalit was laid to rest without a Rabbi's blessing. Rachel's close supportive friends, however, were there to sing and pray on the man's behalf.

Rachel felt ill-equipped. How could she help an abandoned little boy understand suicide?

"He did not understand living, Rachel. It's not a sin. It's a bad thing inside my father's body that made him sad," Aaron said during the return trip. "Sometimes people don't know what's wrong with them. They don't know how to fix themselves. That's all. Don't cry. God knows this."

When they reached the Shalit home, the pots and pans and broken rafter remains greeted them on a muddied floor. Not one person had visited the home to clean. Rachel's attending friends each kissed Aaron, cleansed the home, and prepared food. Rachel felt the hypocrisy of a religious community that conveniently opted out of compassionate service due to ritual infractions.

"You're going to take care of him now, Rachel?" asked a voice from the open entryway. It was Rabbi Herschel's small, stout silhouette standing there. The red setting sun behind his oversized square head made it appear even larger.

"I'm going to take care of him, Rabbi. I don't know where we'll go, but this isn't the place for him now," Rachel answered without stopping work. "Is there something we can do for you, Rabbi?" Rachel finally asked coldly.

Rabbi Herschel was considered a good man and a devout Jew. Privately, he did not miss anything that disappeared in the Grid Wars or worry about the random e-bombs sent overhead that convoluted Israeli air defenses. Nor did he overly mourn his fellow Israelis that were cut down by drones that rained poison pellets. He was silently gratified that a Rabbi could once more take his place as the center of Jewish life. He surveyed and served his flock happily; theirs was a peaceful place, a spiritual oasis in a world gone terribly wrong. And he reckoned himself an important religious leader on one of Israel's most productive communal farms.

Rabbi bent low to be eye level with Moshe and Shoshanna Shalit's orphaned child.

You're an unusual little boy. I wonder how you will come to think of your father's shame? the Rabbi patted the boy's head then stood to regard Aaron.

"I forgive you for not burying my father," Aaron replied. "I know my father is not shameful."

Rabbi Herschel's immediate reaction was not one of remorse, empathy or sadness. Rather, the Rabbi's face turned pale.

That's very odd for a child to say, was the stricken Rabbi's only sense of the moment.

"Why is it odd, Rabbi?" Aaron earnestly asked.

Having never spoken his thoughts aloud, the Rabbi's innermost thoughts had been answered directly. Rabbi Herschel turned and fled the home.

Rachel stood in the foyer, puzzled at the urgent departure.

"Can you imagine that? What the hell? Where's he going?"

"To pray," Aaron answered simply. "Maybe I scared him?"

"If you scared him, Aaron, that pompous man needs to do some praying!"

Chapter V

The Meszaros Family

Lake Balaton, Hungary
Sunday, September 16, 2059

*T*en-year-old Ildiko Meszaros was exhausted from a long day of hiking, made increasingly problematic by habitually selecting rocks she tossed into her low-riding red, white, and green backpack. Her parents took turns emptying the load on the sly. As the tourist season waned, the Meszaros family visited their vacation home on the northern shore of Lake Balaton, a place where the romantic streets of Balatonfured's 19th century charm remained intact. Noemi and Attila ritually packed a picnic lunch to be shared once the threesome reached the top of the Tihany. It was a place known for breathtaking views of the Balaton in the lavender-scented air. Ildiko's parents spoke of Magyar history on these outings amongst cherry farms that bordered one side of their resort home five hundred feet above the sparkling lake.

"The volcanic slopes along the shore... over there, Ildiko," Noemi pointed toward the east. "Those rich slopes were once filled with grapes used for making spectacular white wines. It will be that way again," she promised. Noemi regarded the young, vibrant vines whose color had already begun to fade with the cooler nights.

Noemi pointed the opposite direction. "Look at the field; it's green and lush, the way I remember it as a child. And over there," Ildiko's mother swept her hand in the direction of Badascony, "that's where your father and I sat on the Rose Stone with our backs to the lake. Legend has it that if you can do this with a loved one, you will marry that person within one year's time."

"Why?" Ildiko strained to see the Rose Stone location on the hills.

"If you are more interested in your boyfriend or girlfriend than that spectacular view, you are most certainly in love," Noemi smiled at her daughter. "Your father proposed to me that day. We were married a year later."

"There was no one but you!" Attila gesticulated wildly, taking in the hills and the enormous lake below and turned to face his family. "There is still no view that can hold a candle to you two."

Attila kissed his wife and daughter; Ildiko pleadingly jumped up and down with a request to ride upon her father's shoulders.

"Not going to happen. You're too big and I'm too old to carry a ten-year-old who carries a load of rocks, Édes."

The three began the long trek home through the local villages of thatched roofs and elaborately stone-covered wells that made the region's traditional ways a nearly seamless transition from the Darkness into a thriving economy. The Hungarians had become the breadbasket of Europe with their decision to become independent of the IMF and the EU twenty-five years prior. At the crossroads of Eastern and Western Europe, Hungarian fortunes exploded with the advent of their success. A new international collaboration was forged under Hungarian leadership. The long-neglected territories of Eastern and Central Europe took shape as the Central European Union.

Hungary's military became the focus of an ambitious and forward-looking parliament moved to re-build the land of the Magyars when the most of the world found itself drifting in a sea of debt. Hungarians reached to expand their borders to their former holdings to protect the region left vulnerable to aggressors. Hungarians were painfully aware of their former Empire having been whittled down by treaties and political compromises as Eastern Europe was whittled by punitive whims. Post-world wars, the United States demonstrated little understanding of historical ethnic lines drawn in blood for thousands of years. When the region faced the re-emergence of the new Russian Empire, once again threatening borders, it fueled a national fury. Hungarians did not ask permission to protect themselves.

The Hungarians made a decision to be self-reliant twenty years prior to the EMP disasters, prompted by an angry Russian bear that prowled former satellite countries of the Soviet Union. Russian leadership knew that neither the EU nor the USA was willing to stop world aggression.

The CEU recalled a history of false promises and betrayals in the name of freedom. It took little for the CEU to look toward Hungarian leadership in the geopolitical nightmares that had begun to unfold after the great eastern migrations into European and northern territories.

The regional traditions of husbandry were reborn with an explosion of agricultural yields that the CEU kept purposely within its closed borders. An international embargo quickly followed, meant to punish a region that had become increasingly self-reliant and upon which Europe depended for fresh produce. Food stores were carefully harvested and transported to the safety of the Wieliczka, Turda, and Aknaszlatina Salt Mines. These underground worlds provided an environment perfectly suited to emergency food storage. Unique microclimates were naturally endowed with air-conditioning, sanitation, and constant atmospheric pressure year round; in addition, the cavernous mazes of underground cities two hundred and fifty feet deep within the earth also secured the safety of medical supplies. It was one of hundreds of vast Hungarian and CEU underground facilities and military outposts that made for an extensive interconnected underground emergency network throughout Central and Eastern Europe.

Hungarians had always been ferocious fighters. It was a prowess born of necessity. In the crossroads of Europe, massive intrusions from the East chose to cross Hungarian territories for thousands of years. When it came to keeping predatory cultures at bay, the Hungarians knew no equal. It was at the diplomatic table where Hungarian losses had repeatedly occurred.

A unique culture by any measure, the Hungarians refused to give up their language. While linguists attempted to link the complex Magyar language to Finnish roots, it had no such relationship. If one asked the Hungarians, they would likely purport a linguistic relationship to ancient Sumerian text or themselves as beneficiaries of alien emissaries from Sirius, the brightest star in the Canis Major constellation.

"Why not?" a Hungarian might deadpan.

Most nationalities had been swallowed up by civil immigration, native currencies and languages long obscured by common device with an international agenda meant to homogenize the marginalized. Not the Hungarians. No strangers to trespassers, marginalized visitors who decided to become usurpers of cultural traditions were fought back tooth and nail. Hungarians were very compassionate people, although never accused of being politically correct.

The Meszaros family passed a sheepherder walking behind his black Puli. Dog and master urged the white corpus of fattened sheep to make their way along the steep grassy hills. It was a scene, thought Attila, unmarked by time. Thatched roofs fashioned to razor-sharp edges with rolling eyelets were positioned on immaculately coiffed yards, a small chapter of enormous Magyar pride. Summer evenings consisted of tables on cobblestone sidewalks with friends sharing food and wine lit by candlelight, embellished by ebullient storytelling. Cool breezes mingled with faint smells of fresh canning and melted wax that seeped through steamed windows. No one needed to be reminded of the significance of autumn preparations that heralded Hungary's rich natural resources.

Harsh political realities had been balanced with natural blessings. The largest and safest stretches of rich grasslands in Europe resided within Hungarian borders. Volcanic water from Heves was enjoyed for medicinal mineral baths. It was just one of innumerable natural springs throughout the country that filtered through ancient Turkish baths, making for underground networks that joined wine cellars and buried infrastructures. Hungary had amplified, modernized, and secured a second, fully operational subterranean nation. It was this immense assembly of multi-purpose tunnel networks that protected the Hungarians from the world's cascading decline into medieval status when the world darkened.

The Hungarians emerged from the Grid Wars and the EMP attacks prepared with purpose. There would be no further 'spoils of war' that did not benefit humanity; an altered mindset had changed traditional notions of national borders. Boundaries became a matter of a unified civilized world against savages. Everyone welcomed the Hungarian organization, remedial help, and military strength that kept the region safe.

"In every silver lining, there is a cloud" had once been the Hungarian take on optimism. Now, the adage had finally reversed with a more confident nation.

The Hungarian resurrection had been covertly enacted under the direction of official machinations over the course of decades. Concerned nationalists grew increasingly tired of getting the short end of the stick with every political alliance, with each leader willing to throw its citizens under the bus for larger or more selfish purposes. Scientists, mathematicians, artists, agricultural experts, and architects joined quietly to position Hungary in that which they predicted to be a major geo-political paradigm shift, given that the world had become dangerously short on resources and long on anxiety. Long accustomed to extrinsic political roadblocks and forever short of political clout that was connected to resources, Hungarian thinkers implemented novel policies that demanded cunning... a plentiful national resource.

"The issue is timing," began the newly-elected Prime Minister to his cabinet. "When we are strong and independent enough, others will follow our lead." A plan was hatched.

In the decades before the Darkness, the Hungarians offered their help to the Americans as their agent in Central Europe when the Russians and Islamist factions rattled the civilized world. Armed with American military strength as one of the most reliable EU representatives, the Hungarians had grown their arsenals for two decades, with the intention of becoming militarily autonomous. The seed was planted in 2008. Hungarians offered their country as the base for the Strategic Airlift Capability Partnership that included ten NATO nations, along with Sweden and Finland. Ostensibly, the Partnership would increase NATO's ability to transport large numbers of troops and supplies to remote places of interest around the Mideast. The base began with a supply of C-17s and gradually grew to be a holding port for aircraft and supplies either outdated or no longer supported by America's rapidly shrinking military budget. As the American military began to forgo ground and air capability in favor of drones, Hungary quietly grew her military strength.

Hungary's martial capabilities remained top-secret until the loose-lipped Major Molnar imbibed three bottles of homemade Pálinka gifted by his beautiful mistress. A grateful man, the major decided to show her 'his personal nuke' in his private quarters underneath the town of Papa. It was clear that the well-kept secrets of their true military strength were at risk; the Hungarian Intelligence suspected Molnar was either a Russian operative at the worst of it, or a weak link at best. Plan B went into effect.

The Hungarian Intelligence agent promptly sent evidence of 'Russian culpability' to the Americans. The Russians, said the top secret missive, had approached Hungary to house nuclear weaponry as part of their designs on greater Europe. To the Russians, the Hungarians sent another message that included bogus evidence of America's designs on Central Europe to thwart Russian geopolitical ambitions. They cited vast shipments of deadly chemical agents via the duplicitous Major Molnar.

It all went according to Hungarian plan. Taking a cue from the rest of the world, Hungarians casually dismissed the stories of hidden arsenals, new chemical compounds, or nuclear capability to the appropriate parties. Hungarians subsequently requested increased funding from the United States. With such funding, they promised to continue to operate their dangerous Strategic Partnership, the importance of which had grown proportionately to a Russian threat.

"Our relationship with the United States puts us at risk with Russia," the Hungarian Ambassador complained.

From Russia, the Hungarians leveraged monetary 'protection assistance' as compensation for acting as a holding tank for the deadly arsenals arriving from the West.

"If we refuse, it puts us at risk with our American friends," they justified to the Russians.

The Hungarians publicly and privately denied housing nuclear capability or defense weaponry, chemical stores or anything other than that which had been already sent or suggested for development by the USA—or, in other scenarios, Russia.

The Americans had no reason to doubt the Hungarians as vulnerable and, therefore, dedicated American partners. The American President dismissed the nuclear covert information as another Russian self-motivated ploy to re-invade Hungary and take over the Americans' valuable military base. The Russians, believing the Americans had developed the nuclear plan and supplemented it with chemical warfare agents, sent funds to Hungary to ensure full cooperation with mother Russia.

The Americans had long become friendless and feckless when it came to reliable international intelligence. Congress paid the asking price for the Hungarian base maintenance without fully inspecting Papa. In fact, it had been years since an American ambassador or official envoy had been directed to Budapest. Hungarian loyalty to the American partnership was taken for granted. Major Molnar had repeatedly assured Russia that the Hungarians trusted his advisements.

Taking a cue from the Russian way to solve a problem, the Hungarians managed to conveniently lose Major Molnar to suicide. The body, recovered months later from the turbulent Danube waters, made sense when it was revealed that the Major had been previously diagnosed with several psychotic disorders. It was discovered around the same time the major's grandparents' name was actually 'Petrov'. Everyone blamed the Russians for the murder of one of their own.

Molnar's Crimean mistress took refuge with a colleague in Budapest and disappeared shortly after the major's death. In addition to Russian assistance and trust, Hungary had been assured of a sixteen-billion-dollar annual defense stipend from the United States. The Hungarians negotiated access to two dedicated satellites launched beyond Earth's orbit able to off-set the Russians they believed had harbored plans to destroy CEU server farms. In the end, the United States offered two such satellites for sale.

Used for transmitting data and reconnaissance on behalf of anticipated asteroid mining, the deep space experimental satellites were equipped with a protective magnetic radiation shell made of hardened components that could immediately respond to an oncoming solar flare warning, able to shut down transmissions until the radiation danger had passed. When the American government decided to abandon asteroid mining projects and sell its hardware to private industry dedicated to such ventures, the Hungarians were permitted to assume part ownership of superfluous satellites as part of a broader military agreement. They shared costs with two private American companies that had a similar interest in energy and communication independence beyond erratic power grids. American law required a national entity as a partner. Pendergrass Enterprises and Hungary became the owners of two American made satellites.

The 'Crimean' mistress that had discovered and entrapped the Russian spy married her fellow Hungarian undercover agent, Attila Meszaros. They moved into tranquil Balaton before the worst part of the Grid Wars. Neither the Russians nor Americans uncovered the Hungarian duplicity. As the Central European Union, the region thrived during the Darkness as most of the civilized world tore at the seams.

By the time Ildiko was born, the Hungarian schemes came to light. Noemi and Attila had proven instrumental by positioning two major countries to support Hungary without either power suspecting the ruse. The couple became national heroes.

A grateful Hungary ensured ample compensation. A small farm and vineyard with a newly constructed shore-side Balaton home were wedding gifts. On the occasion of Ildiko's birth, the parents enjoyed a posh apartment and office near the Hungarian Parliament. It was not excessive. Both agents had operated at great risk since they entered the Military Academy. After the Russian-American affair, Attila found himself on the front lines for another ten years.

* * *

Attila was drafted as commander of the reinstated Hussar troops the moment the lights flickered on Hungarian borders. The military horsemen used in medieval Hungary were first created in the 15th century. Hussar militias were resurrected, enhanced, and made ready to patrol Hungarian boundaries on six fronts. Hussars assisted on other fronts on behalf of CEU friends. From Slovakia to the north, the former Ukraine and Romania to the east, Serbia and Croatia to the south, Slovenia to the southwest, and Austria to the west, Attila had positioned his troops armed with weapons hidden on each front in anticipation of another Muslim migration expected through Kosovo, Greece, Serbia, and Albania. The fighting was as brutal as it had been a thousand years prior but the Magyar forces had their energy feed back in order in record time via their operational outer orbiting satellites; Attila's troops were able to locate and engage ground missiles and stockpiles at every military base in the Carpathian basin.

Hungarian intelligence had taken seriously the threat of distressed countries that could no longer be subsidized by larger powers. No longer able to absorb migrants or political refugees, the European Union tried in vain to protect its borders as tens of millions from the Middle East, Africa, and South Asia reshaped the Western political and cultural landscape. More than one desperate nation had threatened nuclear war of EMP disasters in the hopes of leveraging funds from wealthier ones. Hungarians took note and prepared for a survival war. Along with access to satellites outside of Earth's orbit, the Hungarians had the foresight to establish hardened electro-magnetic defense systems as part of its infrastructure. That which was left was the task of defending Hungary and CEU neighbors from migrating forces on foot in the interim months of failed technology. Attila led a mounted charge across the exposed lands.

For the first five years, Central European territories were bloodied by the nomadic groups emigrating from Africa and Russia and those that funneled through Turkey and Bulgaria. Positioned with ample surveillance, the Hungarians once again stopped the favored route through their country into Western Europe. The wall they once built had been destroyed with the deluge of migrants from Syria, Afghanistan and Eritrea fleeing civil war, the Taliban rebels, and forced labor. Years later came the onset of the Semantic Wars. The Hungarians responded to territorial claims and humanitarian accusations with a rearmed citizenry that helped with the effort. Civilian Hungarian reserve units were trained and outfitted with guns and ammunition. While the world collapsed around them, Hungarians moved ambitiously forward with intact communications and concealed supply caches. The planning had enabled Hungary to coordinate and source military efforts on six of their fronts and on six others for as many years of battle.

The Hungarian Empire never fired a shot upon her neighbors. Cooperation was absolute. Resources and foresight that saved the CEU included important Norwegian trade agreements that yielded access to Norway's Svalbard Global Seed Vaults. Over 15,000 varieties of seeds resided packed and frozen on the Island of Spitsbergen in the remote Svalbard archipelago near the North Pole. Encased in 140 refrigeration units within bedrock at -18 degrees Centigrade, the precious gene bank's promise was fulfilled. At the crossroads of agricultural existence, the Hungarians planted their rich fields. After most of the world's farming came to a halt and fields went fallow, farmlands soon exploded throughout the regions formerly known as the CEU.

* * *

Ildiko yawned wide as the happy family made their way toward the village. Her parents worried that their daughter's spontaneous requirements for naps appeared to be narcolepsy. The doctors, however, attributed her sudden coma-like sleep patterns to a growing girl's hormones.

"I'm tired. Please stop, I'm so sleepy," Ildiko warned her parents of an onset of listlessness.

"Let's get some refreshment below. I know a great ice cream place," Attila suggested.

Ignoring a collection of injuries sustained from the strain of a battle-weary spine, Attila picked up his little girl and placed her upon his shoulders. Noemi walked beside them and kept a steadying hand on her thigh in case Ildiko suddenly passed out.

Once at the inn, the owners welcomed the famous family. Attila alerted Budapest that his holiday was concluded and requested transport back to the capital.

Noemi laughed, pointing toward a mop of tight curls spread upon the table.

"She passed out immediately," Noemi said quietly. "Let it pass."

Ildiko flew from her body effortlessly. Immersed in the sounds and smells of an unknown sea, she glided over the vast body of water under cloudless blue skies. Mountains were discernible from the periphery. The seagulls above her seemed aware of her presence and dropped to Ildiko's level, surfing the wind currents. A stronger, colder wind occasionally gusted; the salt air was peppered with flickers of light that reflected off the sun-kissed waters below. Ildiko was aware that ordinarily such light would cause her to shield her eyes, yet she stared through the water's mirrored blaze without difficulty. An enormous ship on the horizon, with its smaller service ships in its purlieu, drew her gaze.

It looks like a mother duck fishing on the Tisza surrounded by her babies, Ildiko thought.

A human baby cried and Ildiko puzzled over the misplaced sound amongst hustling men dressed in shiny yellow suits and green hip boots that bellowed commands to one another. She was unable to understand the strange language.

The field of vision released enough to encompass 360 degrees; from more than one hundred and fifty feet in the air, Ildiko could perceive details of the sailors' facial features, hear whispers, and the tinkling of eating utensils while absorbing the entire horizon. It was a cacophony of disjointed reverberations and sensations.

One of the men on the lowest deck looked skyward and pointed toward his co-worker operating blaring equipment that swelled to obliterate all other sounds. A singular mast with an enormous fiberglass sail enveloped the wind.

"He has the long, slanted eyes of the Asians," she noted. "I'm going to go see what's going on down there..."

Ildiko felt herself soaring toward the ship's railings that were twice as thick as the restraining rails at the Vaci Utca train station. Able to seamlessly travel through the steel hull, she enjoyed floating amongst the ship's interior corridors. Weaving in and out of stairwells and halls, mazes of dormitories with engraved brass plated doors came into focus inscribed with strange symbols. The little girl was awestruck by mysterious trappings.

Aromas from the kitchen, sounds of a man whistling in the shower, incense wafting from under a door, all replaced the ocean's salty smells. The wail of the baby she had overheard from miles beyond the ship reemerged, reached a crescendo, and then faded just as suddenly.

Without knowing how or where she had arrived, Ildiko hovered over a little boy asleep on a couch alongside a reclining man deep in slumber whom she intuited to be the boy's father.

As if touched by her thoughts, the boy opened his eyes and looked directly into hers. His furrowed brow and silent scream struck her as amusing and she giggled.

"I'm dreaming...my eyes are closed," the boy worried.

"Did I scare you? What are you doing in this place in the water?" Ildiko was sure that she was able to communicate and gave no mind as to how this might transpire.

"Go away!" the terrified boy screamed.

Ildiko became awkwardly self-aware that she was floating, disconnected to the earth, and therefore unanchored to the world.

I'm falling... was her last thought before she lifted her head from the ice cream parlor table; she requested pistachio ice cream of the waiter standing beside her chair for several seconds.

"One or two scoops?" the kindly waiter gently suggested.
"Two, please!"

Chapter VI

Woo Tsin-hang and Sonny

Patagonia Waters
Sunday, September 16, 2059

Woo Tsin-hang held the hand of his five-year-old son, Sonny, who was wrapped in a mountain of yellow rain gear, tethered to the railing of the fleet's largest cargo boat alongside the weather deck ladders. Father and son observed the turbulent waters quietly together as an antiquated Argentine vessel less than half their size drew within sight. Image processing radar revealed the lowermost decks overflowed with men. Gunners of the larger military vessel positioned themselves under the fiberglass kite-like sail that took an aerofoil shape with the wind that filled it. An alarm escalated to intermittent beeps then quieted. Flaps on the sail's trailing edge generated extra thrust that brought Tsin-hang's flag ship dangerously close to the oncoming vessel, whose baggywrinkled sails ripped in the vicious winds. The ill-equipped ship listed dangerously.

The Chinese captain called for the hydraulically controlled sail to be retracted by two men standing ready on the bridge. An anxious military crew anticipated the captain's signal to fire lasers upon the encroaching fishing ship. The captain, per his wisdom, waited for Tsin-hang's assessment of the situation.

"Wait and see. They see our size, know our capability," Tsin-hang recommended.

Tsin-hang was the formidable marine architect of the People's Liberation Naval Fleet that dominated international waters for over two decades that mercilessly depleted marine life.

Before the EMP catastrophe, militarized fishing boats had become a proxy for China's sovereign reach into international territorial waters. Desperate efforts were made by the Chinese to harvest nearly 200 million tons of seafood per year. It was not enough to meet or supplement the voracious appetite of the Chinese populace. In lieu of marine competition in deep waters, the sea life had begun to recover in their last five years at sea; billions of gaping mouths had closed abruptly and nature had recouped.

With a cargo filled to the brim with squid and fish, the ship's operators no longer had any intention of obeying their Beijing bosses who no longer exercised control of remote vessels. Countless crews had made a similar decision to escape China's survival horrors; most had smuggled loved ones on board on their final return. Thousands of vessels made a coordinated exit when it became too dangerous to dock. Ships encountered on the high seas were few and far between. Few dared to challenge Chinese naval domination prior to the E-bombs, and it remained that way post-recovery.

Within a few minutes, the polytarped-rigged mast signaled its retreat.

"It's fine. They can't do better in this wind. They're fighting for balance, as it is. Obviously, there's no auxiliary power on that ship and they're using deteriorating fabric sails and masts."

The captain, an ex-military attaché in China's fallen communist regime, could not deny the opportunity. "Shall we attack?"

Tsin-hang sighed, "No. We will not attack. Move on. They can't fish where we've fished and if they're coming this way, they've got nothing. They've no defense. What's the point?"

Sonny shivered with cold and tugged his father's hand. Tsin-hang unhooked the safety rope and led the boy below to their quarters, the most lavish accommodation on the immense fishing ship that represented the pinnacle achievement of the Chinese military fleet.

Not one ship meant to return to Mainland China after departing en masse with the 2500-member fleet years prior. Theirs had been one of a thousand such ships that independently made their way as maritime gypsies, roaming the seas gleaning life and transferring massive quantities of fish to huge refrigerator and processing boats that had once made their way back to the China Sea, passing a never-ending stream of replacements en route. South Atlantic fishing boats from China far outweighed British, American, Russian, Japanese and French naval strength in quality and strength. Chinese vessels that moved unchallenged blackened many horizons. An Admiral of the United Kingdom Royal Fleet protested the interminable assault as 'international food rape'.

Each Chinese renegade ship had remained within their former fishing waters with respect to sharing resources. Each vessel traded with chosen coastal cities for periodic provisions. The captains avoided conflicts with other Chinese ships.

Outfitted with nuclear power designed to sustain fleets for decades by processing spent fuel, everything from the aerodynamic sails to sanitation systems operated safely and flawlessly. No sailor or Chinese national intended ever again to harvest in the South China Sea, Yellow Sea, East China Sea and/or Sea of Japan. Even the Bay of Bengal and the Malacca Straits had been nearly stripped clean or purposely poisoned. What the fishing monstrosities could not capture, the poisoned waters finished off.

The sailors knew their job and it sickened them. They had not been emotionally immune as they witnessed the slow death of their homeland. Regardless of the tons of food provided, it was never enough. Septic soil could not be brought back to life. As hard as they worked to feed the first Darkness survivors, the Chinese navy knew the fate of their nation was seeded years prior to the EMP calamity. When the grid was destroyed, the exodus from the cities to the farmlands helped no one. Non-functioning hydroelectric pumping stations that had once redirected water to farms stood powerless. It was a testament to the country's fate. Within a year, most of China's interior population had died of starvation. Rumors were that millions had desperately resorted to cannibalism.

Those ultimately rescued by the sailors were family members able to transform the enormous ship and its six companion vessels into a comfortable nautical community. There was plenty of room and no need to ration supplies or food. Everyone gratefully and willingly contributed; families mutually assisted without reserve.

Cancer had claimed the famous marine architect's wife; Tsin-hang's precious Jia was gone within months of being diagnosed. Never considered members of the government elite, Tsin-hang's wife had limited medical options. Jia had no family history of cancer and chose the option of minor medical interventions such as organ cloning. Theirs was a calculated risk. According to the ship's medical team, the cancer was initially slow growing and incubated while Jia was still living inland. Cancer treatments were disallowed for advanced cases in any case.

Jia's cremation was just another harsh reminder of nomadic lives spent upon endless watery expanses. There was little promise of a territorial home other than the fortified ships that rarely docked.

Jia's portrait hung in Sonny's room. Below her beautiful face, father and son lit memorial candles. Tsin-hang touched her image each morning upon waking. On one such morning, a wife of one of Tsin-hang's attendants knocked at his door. Her question was whether there was a possibility of disembarking at the next trading port.

"I wish to examine the prospects of establishing an inland community for the first year of our baby's life. Perhaps we could keep one of the smaller ships moored for six months? I could deliver our baby and meet when you returned close to port?" she pleaded.

"Never," answered Tsin-hang, annoyed at the prospect. "You would be overwhelmed the moment you touched shore. You selfishly propose a ruinous scenario. The world is still unstable...it's in turmoil. No one docks semi-permanently."

Occasionally, a family or crewmember would opt to remain ashore to lay stakes in one community or another. No one objected and the settlers were given provisions. Besides the Western-educated leaders or those rescued from the Western world, no one had understanding of the foreign languages, as linguistics as an academic discipline ceased in 2023 in the Chinese school systems. There was little need with PM translators that equipped all personal and public spaces with live feeds. Without the monitor's satellite access, it was a challenge to learn a new language. He wondered how the Chinese pilgrims would fare in a world devoid of ready intelligence or the exotic virtual and augmented realities in which most of the population immersed themselves for too many years.

It wasn't the harsh acclimation to foreign environs that captured the architect's attention as much as his son's odd ability to understand the indigenous languages of each community port visited without a Personal Monitor. Sonny seemed to quickly grasp the language of the villagers in the hours that they unloaded their cargo. As the men and women brought their wares shore side in small boats, Sonny would listen intently as goods were exchanged and processed.

It was a few weeks prior when they sailed from Valparaiso, Chile that Sonny replied in perfect Spanish to one of the women carrying a large basket of cherries, wine, and Pisco bottles to the cargo elevator. He had also mimicked the Portuguese and Argentine dialects. According to the teachers on board, Sonny similarly grasped a wide range of the Chinese vernacular.

"It goes beyond the Mandarin, Wu, Yue, and Min varieties, as well as the five different subdivisions of the Min dialect in the province of Fujian," explained Sonny's kindergarten teacher. When Tsin-hang discovered that not one person on the ship spoke these nuanced sub-texts of Min, nor did anyone hail from the Fujian province, he summoned his son into his office to sit before a projection.

"Sonny, you can read. You have been able to read for a little while. It's apparent you've an amazing talent for linguistics. Who taught you this? Your mother began to teach you, but she has been gone for a long time. You even understand most of what I say...do you understand that this is not typical?"

"No," the small, frail boy answered. He adjusted his position to sit on folded knees on the Western-style chair so that he could look directly into his father's eyes.

"Well, it is, son," Tsin-hang smiled. He had no idea how to broach this subject other than to test his theory. At five years of age, it seemed impossible that a child could grasp meanings and syntax so rapidly. It was unlikely that a child could intuit meanings from hearing a language with such minimal exposure.

"I will read the transliteration text on the monitor. Tell me what you think about it," Tsin-hang instructed.

The Dutch language appeared from Tsin-hang's files onto the holograph.

"*Mijn naam is Sonny en ik hou van de Nederlandse taal.*

"I know my name is Sonny. What is 'Dutch'?"

"What did you hear it say, Sonny? Exactly, what did you understand word for word?"

"My name is Sonny and I love the Dutch language, it said. What is Dutch?" The boy liked games.

Tsin-hang ran a series of tests in much the same way. Sonny couldn't read the text. When the PM read aloud from the transliteration, he understood exactly that which was being said. Twenty languages later, from French to Haitian Creole, the boy translated flawlessly.

Tsin-hang did not know what to make of the phenomena. Sonny's ability did not fit into a savant category. *Perhaps he is telepathic*? He wondered.

Sonny had lost interest in the game. His focus was upon the salted and peppered fried squid delivered by the cook's assistant, who never failed to add plenty of precious rice.

Sonny, if you can hear my thoughts, tell me now. After several attempts, there was no reaction from the confused boy.

He's no mind reader, Tsin-hang concluded.

Sonny watched his father turn toward the tray of fresh urchin to retrieve the shears and protective cloth placed beside the large bowl upon the serving tray. With the precision of a brain surgeon, Tsin-hang carefully used the napkin to protect his hands from the irregular sharp black spikes, and an opening was cut to remove the outer top layer. Sonny cringed at the sight of the contents he found unappetizing. Tsin-hang offered a spoon filled with the orange roe sandwiched by bits of foam to his son each time the delicacy was available. Each time Sonny reacted with a gagging sound. His theatrics never failed to elicit his father's laughter.

"I agree it's an acquired taste and requires a little Pisco to make it better. No need to indulge in either at your age."

Tonight, Tsin-hang drank more than his customary glass of Pisco sour. Sonny cleared their serving trays, placed them on a small platform, and signaled the Monitor to have them removed. The wall opened up, retrieved the trays, and sent all to the ship's galley. By the time Sonny had completed the small duty, Tsin-hang had fallen asleep on the living room couch beside a half empty bottle of homemade Pisco.

Sonny climbed next to his exhausted father and huddled contentedly, his father's free arm brought up to place around his small shoulders like a favored blanket. Secure in the arms of the man he loved, Sonny promptly dozed off until 3:00 a.m.

The presence in the room was undeniable; Sonny opened his eyes with the prodding of the blue wide-eyed curiosity of an older girl peering down at him with strangely curled hair the color of the last vestiges of an autumn sunset. Her full, round face and the lack of facial definition struck him as odd; there were no sunken cheeks, no angularity. Her eyes, he noticed, were wide. The whites shined clear and moist as snow. Vaguely aware that the stranger was demanding something of him, Sonny was unable to divine her speech. Laughter pealed at his silence.

She seems to understand me, why is it that I cannot understand her? Sonny fretted.

He became aware of a racing heart and battled with words he could not recall. With her sudden disappearance, Sonny felt regretful that he had frightened the stranger way.

Tsin-hang awoke, alarmed. "Are you yelling, Sonny?"

"I saw a girl. She was looking down at me from the ceiling and was speaking but I didn't understand what she was trying to tell me. She kept looking and talking...laughing."

Tsin-hang thought the dream predictable given the testing earlier in the evening. He allowed the boy time to re-conjure the experience.

Sonny's nightclothes clung to a body now wet from panic. He struggled to grasp the moment of someone speaking a foreign tongue and it horrified him.

"Now I know what you mean, Father. I couldn't understand her words! I wanted to understand but I couldn't."

"A normal dream prompted by our games," soothed Tsin-hang. "Perhaps this dream arrived as a way for you to understand what it means for the rest of us to speak different languages, unable to communicate our emotions, ideas or strategies. Frustrating, isn't it?"

Sonny shrugged his shoulders, dissatisfied with his father's inability to fully explain something so dangerously alien. He vaguely recalled his father's story about the Tower of Babel from the Western Bible kept with other religious writings that lay by his bed. For the first time, he grasped the language challenges of the human race and found it frightening.

"It was Babel... she spoke Babel!" The biblical reference put Sonny at ease.

Father and son rose together and parted for their respective bedrooms and left their doors open. Tsin-hang turned on the monitor in Sonny's quarters as soon as he heard Sonny chanting strange cadences.

The following morning, the monitor transferred and analyzed the data pertaining to the strange song on Sonny's lips of the previous evening. From the earliest hymns of Rig-Veda, which originated with Indian Brahmin priests in 1500 BCE, its 'Vedic Period', Tsin-hang's son had inexplicably come to know some of the content of the Vedas. These were the sacred texts used for oral transmission of 'that which has been heard' rather than the information about human origin that was described as 'that which was remembered'. It was a small part of a great collection of liturgy, the exclusive responsibility of the Brahmin priests who methodically memorized their culture's story in a tradition lasting for thousands of years. Tsin-hang spent the remainder of the day studying linguistics and the chants purported to require a lifetime to master.

Chapter VII

CC's Gift

The Greenbrier Resort, West Virginia
Wednesday, October 9, 2060

C lifton Brown had lost the last of a thirty-man militia that had attended his needs for twenty-odd years. The last elected President of the United States made his way South, having escaped from his final hiding place. Brown emerged from government compounds in Butler County, Pennsylvania narrowly escaping the notice of a band of insurgents. It had been a long journey since the onset of the EMP crisis.

Air Force One and Air Force Two had successfully navigated their way to Nebraska, Arizona, Nevada, and Colorado, with a return trip to Butler County. Brown's final hiding place had been settled upon as a default.

At the first sighting of Air Force Two landing in Denver's airport, it was overrun by desperate citizens. Frenzied Coloradans unintentionally exploded the secret underground complex when their arrival was met with government firepower meant to guard the plane. Air Force Two exploded in the act of refueling when a rocket launcher answered angrily to the senseless slaughter of hundreds of innocent Americans seeking help. The president's duplicate plane rested above fuel reserves of 2.73 million gallons of jet fuel that could pump 1000 gallons of jet fuel per minute through a 28-mile network of pipes. Air Force One circled above as the presidential decoy tested the environment. Air Force I returned to Pennsylvania, narrowly missing the massive explosion that turned the region's skies pitch black.

Devoid of ample fuel, Air Force One landed short of Butler County. The entourage made the trip to a government strong-hold successfully on foot. It was there that Clifton Brown was nearly discovered within the cavernous limestone compound after decades of hiding. Storage units above ground had been searched a thousand times for food stores secured in some of the outbuildings, but the entrance to the hidden maze of apart-ments and deeper subterranean catacombs reserved for the government and corporate elite remained secret. Beyond those were the separate catacombs built for the president's personal security, assistants, and family members.

Brown's family had perished, his connection to the world was lost, and his mental stability tenuous. Without further safety options, Brown slipped unnoticed by the latest intruders in tattered clothes. He left what remained of his security men to contend with the small mob that had gathered not long after two guards on night watch were detected and killed be-side a fire. Their black gear emblazoned with the White Eagle logo flickered their identities to local hunters. The White Ea-gles, once admired and feared, were the worst examples of unregulated government power. In the name of law and order, the special forces of The Selective Service committed horrific crimes. A local hunter shot the two guards with a cross bow as their final breath was drawn from inside a shared whiskey bottle passed between them.

The two soldiers fell face forward into the fire meant to off-set a chilly fall night, not fifty feet from the underground entry.

"Let them burn," was the marksman's order. Their heads blistered and popped while the hunters removed weapons and boots.

Emerging a thousand feet deep into the surrounding woods, a trapped rat having made a clean break from a sinking ship, Brown was awash with optimism. He gazed hopefully into the clear night sky and took a deep breath of the cool, fresh air.

"The stars. Finally, the reality of stars," he announced to no one. An absence of artificial lights allowed President Clifton Brown to bask under heaven's luminescent blanket.

"I made it out alone," he reveled in the first moments of freedom. When the night guards failed to return, he knew it was only a matter of time before savages located and stormed his hidden apartments. As his last five-man security detail went upside to investigate the missing guards, they, too, never returned.

It was a mystery as to how the 75-year old man navigated alone to West Virginia without further incident. Clifton Brown could not believe his luck when West Virginia Confederation forces appeared before him. He raised his clasped hands in prayer and vigorously shook the hands of the Confederation security detail. Standing tall, Brown saluted the uniformed group even as they failed to return the courtesy.

"I'm President Brown, your Commander-in-Chief!" He stood awkwardly. Confederation military examined the man initially as a useless lone wolf expunged from nomadic pack of savages.

Brown's image and voice pattern was identified, marking the encounter as one of official interest. Morgan Pendergrass was contacted.

"We picked him up on the surveillance outside of the Greenbrier," began the colonel. "He was trying to force his way into the old underground bunkers. No one recognized him, sir. His voice pattern was identified quickly. When I called him 'Mr. President' he immediately responded. I think he thought we were there as his personal rescue party. He kept saluting, expecting us to salute back," the Colonel explained.

Morgan remained uncharacteristically silent.

"What would you like us to do? He's somehow made it past our northern border patrol...I apologize! Have no idea how it happened." The Colonel's frustration was evident.

Morgan laughed, "No apologies. He knows those government catacombs across the continent. Rats know how to hide. Probably other biometric entries remained responsive and he didn't know that we'd closed down the Greenbrier bunkers. It makes sense. He's most likely been underground for most of his travels and surfaced to gain entry through the resort since there was never any other portal. What's he saying?"

"He's aware of the Confederation, seems up to date, and expects us to take him directly to you. Claims that you'll welcome him with open arms, as he puts it. He insists that I contact you personally. Sorry to bother you with this sir, but Governor Hernandez says that he defers to your decision on the matter and adds that he and Minister Gant would prefer to have... I'm quoting here, sir... that 'ass-wipe' as far away from the D.C. area as possible."

"Well, well. If that idiot has been able to evade the public for two decades, I'm going to attempt the dubious courtesy of meeting him. He's alone, you say?"

"Looks that way, sir."

"Well, bring him on in. If you value your life or his, don't breathe a word of this. I don't want to be overrun with a lynch mob at my own home," Morgan concluded.

Morgan asked the Monitor to summon his wife.

"You pinged, Master?" Angela smiled as she entered the library.

"They got Clifton Brown trying to find his way into the Greenbrier bunkers through the hotel. We'd closed off the tunnel access. Imagine that?"

"Imagine what? We've experienced the unimaginable, thanks in part to that snake. What are you going to do?"

"That's what I'm going to ask you. You think you could stomach a snake for a short visit? Just us, mind you."

Angela hung her head as she struggled to regain her composure.

"Morgan, that man sent out the Selective Service and every American military unit he could muster to shoot down honest Americans in the streets for nothing more than trying to find their way out of a full-blown disaster. If you recall, the good young men and women of Annapolis, West Point, and the Air Force Academy were helping keep order, calming fears, transporting homeless children to college campuses, and the President ordered them to stand down.

"I've seen the Commons Archives. His directives were nothing less than a murderous campaign to retain Federal control without regard for frightened Americans. Those private troops of his raided the homes for weapons and took with them all food. Those cowards scurried underground and disappeared rather than deal with diminishing supplies, the injured, or the chaos. Everyone lost family and friends. We nearly lost our humanity thanks to President Brown."

"There might be things to learn, Angela..."

"I'll not allow that man to sit in my home. Nor will we serve him food our communities have personally sowed, nurtured, and harvested with bleeding, calloused hands. If he comes here, you'll meet him outdoors. Go to the barn. No, strike that. Don't dare take him to the barn. I can't imagine a place to send him other than straight to hell."

Morgan was all too familiar with the Commons reports of Federal government forces shooting at will to halt the frantic search of supplies. Rather than act as first responders, the Executive Office moved to protect the government's authority at all costs. For weeks, the first family and his military attaches were able to fuel and refuel at hardened military installations and fly the two Air Force jets that were similarly encased. National communications were knocked out yet the highest authority failed to return to the White House and its situation room. Those who sought refuge in the underground bunkers of the White House were left to handle overwhelming social chaos.

Within three months, there wasn't a Federal government representative to be found. A third of the population that qualified for Federal emergency life support had gone underground. Most of those had died slowly in their bunkers when life support systems miscarried. Unprotected citizens above ground starved or were slain in urban rampages. Additional numbers perished, overexposed to the elements, within six months. There were few survivors who had not cursed President Brown and his minions.

While thirty-four states prepared for emergency measures apart from the Federal government, few anticipated the scope of the EMP onslaught. No one was prepared to assist communities outside state boundaries. Morgan and Angela knew, all too well, the stories of those who operated without a modicum of compassion or duty.

"I know you're right," Morgan finally responded. "It's something I want you to consider, however. I've got questions," Morgan sighed.

A small knock at the door later, Caroline entered the room.

"Are you okay, Grandma?" CC looked puzzled at her grandparents' unnaturally slumped positions with heads bowed in silence.

"I'm fine, baby. What's wrong?" It was unusual for CC to find her way into the library mid-day; Angela was surprised.

"I have a picture for you. Mum told me to show you," Caroline smiled. Adele appeared behind her daughter in the doorway.

"Look at her drawing, Mother. We've a gifted artist on our hands!"

Angela took the large paper from CC's outstretched hand and covered her mouth. She handed it to her husband, who examined the clean pencil strokes, the finely defined features, and delicate array of colors highlighting the scene. Morgan flattened the drawing on his desk and secured its rolled sides with two books.

"How did you come to imagine this, Caroline?"

"That's the place I sawed and that's the place I drawed!"

"That's the place I *saw,* and that's the place I *drew*," corrected Adele.

"No, Mummy. I was making a poem. Poems rhyme."

Morgan pursued his questioning. "Where did you see this man, Caroline?"

"I don't know. Do you like it?"

"Your detail and technique is beyond excellent for five years of age. Remarkable. May I keep it?"

"Yes, Grandpa," Caroline said.

"Miss Langley contacted me to come see our little artist's work. She was amazed at Caroline's dexterity and suggested we run it over and surprise you. See you both at dinner," Adele explained and left abruptly with Caroline to return to school.

As soon as they closed the door, Angela let out a gasp. Together, Morgan and Angela examined the unmistakable image of a disheveled Clifton Brown, on the top left corner of the page, standing next to a tree. A likeness of the historical Greenbrier Hotel was situated at the page's center, the focus of the ex-president's attention.

Sunday, October 24, 2060

"Let's start to schedule CC's six month checkups on Sundays when her absences are less likely to disrupt her routine and others don't ask her whereabouts," Lex Collins submitted a schedule for Adele's approval.

"Sounds good," Adele approved. "She doesn't like to miss school and her teacher mentioned that her absences don't go unnoticed. She seems to have a calming effect on the class. She also mentioned that CC has wonderful leadership skills."

"Leadership skills? Like what?" Lex's face remained fixed on the Robicom's vids of the last week's monitoring of CC's activities that he religiously logged.

"Ms Langley was struck by something that happened about a month ago. She mentioned there were arguments on the playground regarding which toy should be shared by whom, what games the kids would play, who could and couldn't do what during recess. Anyway, these discussions would erupt into arguments, pushing and pulling, shouting...you know. When things got out of hand, Lola would bring CC's class back into the building and have them sit in a circle. They passed a stuffed bear. Whoever held the bear had the floor and could air grievances without interruption. You know, a drill in disciplined social behavior. So, this goes on for a few weeks and then, voilá, everything clears up."

Lex was puzzled. "So how's that reflective of CC's leadership skills? Just sounds like Lola's reasonable lesson," Lex offhandedly commented.

"That's what Lola thought. Lola said she was ecstatic that her strategy had worked, given that they'd gone over a month and a half without incident. Then she discovered that the perfectly peaceful playground was not her doing."

"Go on."

"One day Lola noticed CC sitting alone on the playground bench. Lola was concerned because CC wasn't one to isolate herself. She just watched as CC told her classmates that she wanted to think and leave her alone, ignoring pleas to join in this or that activity. When Lola approached CC and asked what was going on, it reflected something special."

Adele repeated the scenario as Lola had related it to her.

"Hamed," CC answered her teacher's concerns.

"What about Hamed, CC?" Lola asked

"He won't let me be the judge. He says that no one has to listen to me anymore."

"What kind of judge is that? CC, do you know what a judge is?"

"When everyone was fighting I said that we couldn't lose any more recess time. If there was a problem, I said that I could be the judge in my court and the people who were mad and yelling could go pass around the bear forever inside the classroom with you and miss playtime or I could hear the problem and make a judge."

"Judgment," Lola corrected. "Did they agree to your plan?"

"Yes. When somebody is mad we go behind the playhouse and anyone who wants to listen can listen or talk about what happened in my court. I make a judge about the problem and we go back to play. It's faster than just talking and talking for the whole recess. I hope that doesn't hurt your feelings but we always lose our time to play with that bear," Caroline explained to her teacher.

"I'm amazed that they trust you to be their judge, listen and abide by your decisions. It's a marvelous idea!" Lola said.

CC shook her head. "Not so much. Two days ago, Hamed starts shouting at me. It's usually Hamed and Kelly who start the fighting about the teams or who gets the bicycles first. He likes to be the boss of everybody and so does she. Hamed yells he's not going to go to court anymore and I wasn't going to be the judge. He screamed. He yelled, '*You are never on my side!*'"

Lola asked CC, "What did you say to him?"

CC said simply, "I told him there are no sides in a circle!"

CC slid off the bench, indicating that she was finished with the discussion.

Lola said she pursued CC. She asked where Caroline had heard that expression.

"I thought it," CC replied.

"Did Hamed understand what you meant? It's an amazing concept...very wise of you," marveled her teacher.

"I just thought it then said it."

"What happened then?" Lola asked.

"I said Hamed could be judge one week and then Kelly. Kelly said fine. They're happy."

"Any arguments since?" Lola asked.

"No. But now Hamed and Kelly always take the best stuff. It's still not right. They can't judge."

Lex sat dumbfounded. Adele raised her eyebrows knowingly.

"I'm telling you, she's an abstract thinker," Adele pronounced proudly. "I was watching the Robicom the other day. The robot points out to CC that she has left her doll on the stairs and the danger involved with her carelessness. So take a look at her response."

Adele indicated the monitor and Lex watched the cached sequences in which Caroline was summoned from her bedroom by one of the robotic maintenance units. CC entered the vicinity head held high, correctly suspecting a problem.

"Caroline, this doll was found on this step. It presents a dangerous obstacle to those walking up and down the stairs. This situation can cause accidents. Do you wish for me to remove it or do you prefer to remove the dangerous object?" the robot asked.

"Neither, Robot!" Caroline feigned indignation. "You should have called the hospital, not me. It looks like my doll tripped... her neck is broken. We needed a doctor! You should have saved her!"

"Wow," laughed Lex.

"Yeah. The robot just went blank then instructed that a live human was more valuable than an inanimate object."

Adele added, "I asked her the reason she would take an AI to task as to confuse the situation. She said that the robot had to learn that the first thing it should be concerned with was how to help others. I reminded her that the doll in question didn't have an AI component and it was Caroline that was meant to learn and fix the situation.

"What does she say? 'That's the excuse the robot used.'"

"What the hell does that mean?" Lex asked.

"I have no idea," Adele laughed.

Sunday, October 31, 2060

Adele arrived at CC's room in order to remind CC of her six-month checkup. CC was less interested in her medical assessment than Halloween. She wanted to dress in one of her costume designs printed the previous night.

"You want to wear a sequined dress with a tiara to see the doctors?" Adele asked her daughter.

"Grandpa calls me Princess. I'm going as a princess. He said a princess has a crown. I'm ready."

"I'm going to warn you that it's a little difficult to navigate those machines with glitter high heels and a crown," Adele warned. "Why not save your costume for Halloween tonight?"

Adele was grateful for uniforms and less grateful for the printers that lay vulnerable to her father's suggestions, CC's imagination, and a forefinger. Three of the medical printers were sequestered behind locked doors the day a queued mouse and a replicated nose found its way into Adele's bathroom sink, floating on a toy boat. They discovered worse when CC's class studied reproductive anatomy.

For three hours, the Collins brothers and Meredith Greene examined Caroline in the Research Hospital. Dr. Greene had been re-appointed 'Aunt Missy' per Morgan's suggestion. With that assignation, CC was in the hands of family. Angela and Morgan arrived to retrieve their granddaughter several hours later in order to leave Adele alone in conference to discuss results.

"Where the hell is your Princess outfit, Caroline?" Morgan asked his granddaughter. Adele's expression read disapproval.

"What did I say about giving CC free reign with the printers? It's expensive and it could prove dangerous."

"Nope. I've fixed the monitor. No more organs or people bits are queued. Lighten up, Babycake."

Connor and Meredith signaled Adele into their offices and waved goodbye to Caroline, who skipped toward her grandparents.

Adele took a seat and reviewed the monitor's images alongside the research team.

Connor took the lead.

"Let's go over general findings. CC hasn't had an earache, a virus, a cold, or a sick day in her five years. She's in the ninety-fifth percentile for our weight and growth indices; she has perfect vision and excellent responses. Physically, her coordination and strength are excellent...no medications, no allergies as of this time, no developmental delays. Occipitofrontal circumference is appropriate for her age, no skin blemishes or eruptions, and no dysmorphic features. CC's neurological examinations have been consistent. She's engaging, social and alert; exhibits a very good sense of humor, an advanced vocabulary, and a wide spectrum of information beyond her PM. Regarding the cranial nerves: her visual fields are full to confrontation. The fundi are benign with normal-appearing disks and retinae. Spontaneous venous pulsations are seen; extra ocular movements are normal. There is no abnormal nystagumus. Pupils are equal and reactive to light. There is normal upgaze and normal convergence. Symmetric optokinetic nystagumus is induced. Corneals are symmetric. Cranial nerves: the NLFs are symmetric. Orbicularis oculi are normal in strength bilaterally. Soft palate elevates symmetrically; SCM and trapezius are symmetric and normal in strength, the tongue is midline..."

Adele put her hands up in protest "Boys? Meredith? In English, please. Why am I here today?"

The three looked at each other.

"Because of the genetic cultivation and culling, we wanted you to know the ways in which we are examining CC's development. Look, you've mentioned many times that CC seems happy but you've worried that her even disposition may indicate a sort of peculiar complacency." Connor demonstrated his attention to his sister-in-law's concerns. Adele waited for more.

"I'm the last person to complain about her incredible disposition. But we recognize that something else is going on there. I just wanted to encourage you three to look at this matter of an unusual disposition more closely," Connor continued.

Adele had mentioned CC's consistently even disposition since birth. Had it taken nearly six years to sink in? It irritated Adele but she remained silent.

Connor pulled a graphic of a particular gene within the context of the entire genome. "We've long endeavored to understand how genes interact with environment to shape behaviors. It's the old nature or nurture debate. I'm prone to believe in hardwiring, with nurturing as critical tipping points. We find that sensitivity to the environment resides primarily in the nervous system and some people are more sensitive to outside influences than others. A gene like this DRD4 regulates a chemical in the brain called dopamine; it's a neurotransmitter that helps one experience pleasure, reward... even happiness, if you will. Despite our understanding of a supportive environment, we remain amazed at CC's enthusiastic disposition. Extreme extrinsic conditions, good or bad, aren't showing a blip on her radar."

Lex interrupted his brother.

"For example, when one of the hounds died, it bothered me that she just pulled up one eyelid on that old dog to check if the dog was really gone. She kissed him goodbye and watched me bury him. We said a prayer and all, but CC just remarked how happy he was going to be in heaven. Not a tear was shed. Not unusual, of course, but it was her certainty of it all as normal that struck me. No questions at all. I'm certain of her levels of compassion and empathy but there wasn't a trace of anxiety."

Connor continued with his report.

"We took a closer look at the gene and considered the evolutionary effect of increased dopamine and what it means that CC is developmentally malleable but so damn enthusiastic all the time. I'm taking this as a great sign that her genetic makeup is predisposed to a naturally calm state. I'm not going to cross-reference other extensive material here. It's now in your possession."

Displayed in the conference room were holographic images of Adele and Lex's bedroom. Lying between the couple was CC, who was prone to wake at night and make her way to their bed.

"So what's this, Lex?" Adele knew what she was looking at before the lights dimmed.

"We've become aware of an evolving phenomena and wanted to share it with you."

Lex asked for 'blue lights' footage.

"Various and randomly monitored nighttime scenes – pre-approved by yours truly – were played out in our bedroom and in CC's. You were aware of these recordings of our daughter's sleep patterns that were taken somewhat unsystematically. Seven sequences within the course of five years displayed brief moments of tiny blue lights that made an appearance in the vicinity of Caroline. They could be seen one or two at a time, and finally streaking away or vanishing in place. The scenes were mere seconds in duration."

Next to the video excerpts, Lex posted macroscopic images of the blue lights. Within the lights, there seemed to be an infinitesimal conglomerate of particles. Each particle was similarly enlarged. Each particle repeated the pattern of enumerable particles. The magnified pattern repeated itself fifty-two hundred times until the geometric pattern of a geometrical figure appeared with flower like patterns within the symmetrical structure of a hexagon.

Lex rendered the image three dimensionally and turned it slowly.

"This image is commonly referred to as the Flower, Fruit, or Seed of Life, depending upon the extent of geometric complexities. Its form represents a depiction of fundamental aspects of space and time," Adele observed aloud. She accessed her PM for a complete biblical, historical, and scientific account of the claims that the Metatron's Cube and the Platonic solids were derived from the geometric template.

"Here's the next image," Connor said, pointing to the geometric figure composed of 13 equal circles, with lines from the center of each circle extending out to the centers of the other twelve. "Here is the Metatron's Cube," Connor nodded to Adele.

"From this image, often called the Fruit of Life, we get the five Platonic Solids that include a star tetrahedron. Looking at it three dimensionally, we can see how all-platonic solids fit within the design of the Metatron's Cube. Please notice that these lights we have brought together here in the number of

22 times are those that we've macroscopically projected and are the same ones that surround Caroline. Each blue energy particle is a Metatron's Cube," Connor quantified.

"Blue lights. Yes, I've seen them," Adele stated. "This part is certainly interesting."

Lex was at once puzzled and relieved, "Seriously? What did you make of them, Adele?"

"Well, at first I wasn't sure of what I'd seen. I'm still not. I noticed the lights first in the maternity room. I see them mostly at night when I'm not distracted. CC is aware of them, as well.

"One night, CC woke me and pointed to you. She referenced the blue 'faeries' on top of your sleeping body. I was half asleep and went to the bathroom. When I returned, she was still standing beside the bed. She stopped me from climbing back in.

"'Do you see them, Mummy? Do you see them?' she whispered excitedly.

"I was groggy and crawled into bed despite her protests. CC climbed in over me to lie down between us. I pulled back the duvet cover to make room. CC shouted, 'See? See, Mummy? I don't want to sit on them.'

"She just sat on top of my head by the headboard as we jointly stared at six brilliant blue lights lying beside us. It was stunning. I guess that they may have been positioned there for quite a long time--might have followed CC to our room and settled on our bed, I suppose. My impression? They seemed organic, sentient. They sat quietly seemingly aware that we were examining them. Then, a gentle scurrying and they disappeared. Poof."

The men said nothing. Lex turned off the monitor. Noticing the move, Adele added, "Erase what I've said, Lex. You may never record me, our room or Caroline again without my express permission."

"Sorry, honey. Won't happen again," Lex quickly agreed.

Adele's annoyance surprised her brother-in-law. Both men waited to see if Adele would continue for a long minute. Adele rose from her seat and looked thoughtfully out the window upon the street below, her back to her small audience of three. Meredith Green stopped recording.

"Anyway, CC was thrilled that I was able to see the lights," Adele continued. "She'd never mentioned them before nor seemed to be concerned other than I verified them. CC fell asleep quickly. I didn't sleep well for days. It was, I don't know, somewhat mind altering. It seemed so hopeful, spiritual. I find it hard to explain."

"Why not mention it to me?" Lex seemed more curious as to the reason for his wife not sharing her observations rather than in the subject of observation. "And where was I when this happened?"

"Asleep." Adele ignored the first question and answered the second.

"What do you make of this, Connor?" Adele asked.

"It's inexplicable. That makes it fascinating and worth exploring," Connor enthusiastically replied.

"Has this anything to do with her DNA, genetic makeup, what?" Adele questioned her brother-in-law.

"Who knows? We're monitoring a sample of one. Who knows what happens to us, around each of us, when not caught on a research monitor of this caliber? Ours is advanced equipment; data is fed into our computers daily. We continue to be amazed at her continuity in health, even temperament, and intellectual curiosity. Her blood-work, her vitals...we've been involved in so many areas. The absence of negative genetic markers is tremendously encouraging. She seems so... forgive the word... synchronized. CC has yet to cry; we've never yet been able to gauge pitch variables, acoustic characteristics or been able to examine the complex of cranial nerves associated with the larynx and brain stem. Blue lights? Maybe a DRD4 gene in overdrive? Go figure. Her pineal gland is slightly enlarged and we're investigating that, too. Nothing to go on here, really, other than that the lights seem to be geometrically-configured energy pulses." Connor looked at Adele. "Ideas, Adele?"

"Well, we know the implications of the sacred geometry, as it's called. It permeates history as the God concept from which all life is derived. Were you able to gauge its frequency? What kind of energy is this?" Adele asked the men.

"That's the next step," Connor said. "We weren't prepared to do that without this conversation but we can. Don't think that she has the ability to summon or express the energy at will but you never know."

"It's energy, all right," Adele agreed. "It's part of a greater frequency. Everyone that has had exposure to CC seems to sense vitality. I'm prepared to allow this to unfold naturally. I'm not prepared to allow CC to become some kind of lab rat," Adele emphasized.

Sounding more like a neglected husband and less like a professional researcher, Lex moved next to his wife to question once more, "Why not share all this with me?"

Adele slowly turned toward Lex and held her exasperation in check. Her husband had never considered her observations as medically relevant and, therefore, had never engaged her to discuss outcomes before now. It was Connor who invited her involvement by personally contacting her to visit the facility.

"As you've reminded me, I have a few degrees but I'm not a medical doctor. I'm here today because Connor contacted me. Evidently, you'd overlooked the memo. Why did you not share these results with me, Lex? That's what's so peculiar."

Connor understood Adele's emotional gravitas. Over the years he had asked Lex repeatedly why Adele neglected to involve herself after frequent appeals. Now it was clear. Lex had not extended the invitations; he had not wanted his wife there.

"Please, Adele. You play a vital role. No one here has intentionally diminished your input," Connor assured his sister-in-law. "So if there's anything we've failed to report that you consider significant, please know that this has not been an intentional oversight.

"We've only been able to sequence a mere 1810 inheritable disorders and conditions amongst as many as 8,000 possibilities that can affect children. Our data expands daily. We are pioneers in a complex field that falls short of knowing the genetic spectrum of influences beyond disease. Then there's the decoding of sequenced bacteria samples of the entire DNA. Mutations of untreatable bacteria allowed us to decode dangerous pathogens that will help us stop viral outbreaks reported internationally that have been resistant to all antibiotics. It seems, for example, that CC is resistant to the entire range of mutated pathogens introduced in the last decades. We've done all of this without being intrusive to our beloved girl. We've amazing results and as many questions. We've discovered an amazing blue source of energy that represents that which has been termed the seed of life. Science has been so immersed in Artificial Intelligence, machine learning, and the Singularity theories, that we've forgotten to be impressed with our own organic sentience. To go from here, we need your help."

Adele smiled. Connor always had seemed more tuned to her than her husband. Lex, she thought, was dismissive and patronizing. Why had she not noticed it before?

"Thank you for that, Connor. There's something else I'll now share with you, if you're interested," Adele suggested.

The Collins brothers encouraged her contribution.

"CC knows things, absorbs information that hasn't been conveyed through the classroom, reading materials, holographic or virtual entertainment or normal means of exposure. At certain intervals, she sits quietly as if listening to transmissions but is able to carry on. It's not a trancelike state, just an altered expression I detect. I'm sure that CC's grasp of geometrics, abstract ideas, her level of humor and sense of the ironic, are well beyond her years. You three haven't paid attention to these elements."

Meredith sighed, "We've paid attention. We just don't know what to make of it."

Connor pulled from a long, flat folder a series of artworks divided by month and year that CC had either completed in school or on impulse. The last was the familiar pencil artwork of the Greenbrier Hotel and Resorts, a place his niece had never visited or seen.

"It's not about the Greenbrier or the skill, or the creative maturity it reflects; it's the fact that this picture is an accurate depiction of ex-president Brown right now, as an older man. We know his current appearance by way of the photos and interviews sent to Morgan after he was discovered trying to gain entry to the Greenbrier bunkers. CC's drawing happened the same day of his arrest in West Virginia a few weeks back. Interesting, huh?" Connor said excitedly.

"Yes, I was there," smiled Adele.

"All we're asking now is to refrain from prompting her... we know that you don't... and keep whatever you're doing going strong. Let us know if you notice any other remarkable traits that may or may not have a connection to her genome. You're a spectacular mother. Keep being spectacular," Conner smiled. "I'm sorry for the misunderstanding, Adele. We'll be careful to be less invasive and rely more on your input."

Connor replaced the drawings and filed them. Adele nodded appreciatively at Connor's kind words and said nothing to Lex, who seemed unusually silent.

Adele signaled her vehicle and spoke focused upon Connor and Dr. Green.

"Thank you for being there for CC. You two put her at ease, and she's crazy about her new aunt."

"Anytime, Adele. I'm going to meet with you regularly from this day forward. Your personal observations are vital. Sorry if you thought we didn't want you involved. That's going to change. You don't have to read it but the entire body of research has now been made available for your review. Call me if you have any questions," Meredith assured her on the way out of the office.

As much as Adele appreciated Connor's attention, she purposely ignored her brother-in-law's expectation to share the scope of her observations. Nor was she impressed with Dr. Green's offering reports while prompting participation. The phenomenon surrounding her daughter required careful stewardship and the responsibility for her daughter's welfare was ultimately hers.

Adele assessed her husband's exclusionary tactics. "Strange behavior," she concluded.

Climbing into the vehicle's back seat, Adele was greeted with an open monitor from her home.

"Mummy! Are you coming home now?" CC beamed.

"You bet I am! Who's that with you?" Adele asked.

"It's Lisa. She came over to play. You can play with us too, or just watch our new vid we made."

"Can't wait. Hello Lisa! Welcome!"

"Hello, Mrs. Collins," Lisa's magnified left eye filled half the screen. To her right was a room in the kind of disarray that indicated a wonderful afternoon.

"Be there soon," Adele smiled and closed the transmission.

Adele made a decision. "I'm sure as hell not telling them about the six other children that CC expects to arrive on our doorstep."

Adele adjusted her monitor's privacy settings and notified the research center of scheduled windows. She also left a personal message with the three doctors that was promptly returned by Meredith Green.

"Hello Adele! What can I do for you?"

"I'm going to manually set the monitor, Meredith. I want to have full control over investigative windows. Not Lex. Not Connor, or my parents, nor you, Meredith. Not anyone but me. I'm sure you understand my sense of things."

"Of course, Adele."

Adele blocked the car's monitor system at the Pendergrass gates and directed the car to the stables. As the car remained running, Adele moved inside her favorite horse's stall, reached into the barrel of sweet feed, and stepped on the newly distributed straw. Lorenzo munched from her splayed hand and nudged his mistress's shoulder with a nicker. Adele brushed away the dry straw under the automatic feeder and opened the hidden compartment under the floorboards she had discovered as a child. Normally, the space was used to store salt licks.

Having decided not to share her daughter's newest drawings, Adele retrieved the last three from her satchel and secured them within the hidden strongbox.

The estate monitor sought her whereabouts with a general announcement within the properties.

"Mrs. Collins, you are requested by Lisa Dawkins and Caroline Collins to inspect their costumes for tonight's festivities; may I ask where you are presently?"

"On my way. There in one minute..." Adele responded, carefully replacing the straw.

The side porch was decorated and included an impressive presentation of Halloween treats. Morgan busied himself by exposing shortcomings with his cane. He sampled delicacies with suggestions for improvement and corrected flow patterns. Caroline and her best friend, Lisa, appeared wearing versions of 'Tweedle Dee and Tweedle Dum'.

"What happened to the princess costume?" Morgan asked.

"It's stupid," Caroline said. "Lisa said so!"

"You have to be a stupid princess for it to be stupid," Morgan laughed. "You can wear whatever you want because you're smart!"

"Where did you get that makeup, baby?" Adele already knew the answer as she climbed the porch stairs.

"Your bathroom! You have lots of it. Like it?"

"What are you supposed to be? Creepy Clowns?" Morgan shouted from across the porch.

"Tweedle Dee and Tweedle Dum, Grandpa!" CC laughed.

"Let's tweak it a bit, shall we? Come on, girls...let's go back to the bathroom," Adele offered.

"What's the difference, Morgan?" Angela irritably asked as the three departed.

"Angela, I said clowns. I was thinkin' to say they looked just like ole President Brown and his sidekick, the Secretary of State... what's his name? That could be a great gig!"

"Just as well get Brown off your mind. I'll shoot him on sight," Angela pronounced.

"Get in line!" Morgan said. He spat over the porch, narrowly missing a platter of sandwiches.

Chapter VIII
Nicholas Bradley

Nicholas Bradley shivered from the biting cold along the New York streets and warehouse alleyways that bordered the former New York harbor. There were flickering lights from drumfires on the dilapidated dock; hundreds of men could be heard arguing, haggling, and begging for passage. These were the urban dwellers bereft of resources, the ones stranded for decades without access to private sailboats, vacation homes, or survival condominiums. Families of these weathered men and women stood along the pier closest to his position, huddled with children, each with a large knapsack or bag. Nicholas had no plan. He was left with nothing to barter. He only knew that he could not afford to miss another ship travelling south from Nova Scotia.

Nicholas crawled forward, trying to assess the ways he might navigate around and through the ship's guards. Splinters had made their way into his calloused hands but the pain was incidental to his objective. It was the only accessible port and the last Canadian ship for another month's time. The patterns he detected had been familiar to his father, who had spent years preparing for their departure.

Nicholas surveyed the heavyset men whose rifles suddenly dropped from their upright position and set upon two men arguing with the docked ship's captain who stood defiantly upon the pier. Wearing the familiar white hat from several days prior, Nicholas easily identified his father and sister's executioner. After an examination of the Bradleys' offerings of food and jewelry, the man with the white cap callously shot his father and sister with a pistol, kicking their tribute to the side to be sorted by subordinates. Within the briefest of moments, father and daughter glanced at one another lovingly in resignation of their fate; two point-blank bullet holes to their heads dropped them instantly.

Nicholas had stood beside the dead bodies of his father and sister, expectant and motionless. The men ignored the sixteen-year-old. His last living relations were tossed overboard to take their place among the floating carcasses of others, a mass of bodies that bumped rhythmically against the freighter's hull.

Nicholas ran for his life as the captain examined the meager Bradley possessions that had been summarily rejected as fare. If determined lacking, such offerings were confiscated and the owners killed. Nonchalantly, the foodstuffs, packaged seeds and ammunition were apportioned to the captain's sentries. Any items the captain fancied were tossed into a separate basket.

One of the guards mumbled to the captain about the loathsome chore of sorting canned food.

"Shit. Why can't anyone from the farms figure to bring some cured bacon?"

Porter Bradley, Nicholas's grandfather, had instructed his son in Karate-do. The teenager was no stranger to quick thinking. Therefore, the paralyzed state in which he found himself as a stunned non-participant in the murders caused Nicholas great shame. He rued fleeing the scene.

Crawling along the damp cold pier, Nicholas reflected about his life. No longer would his loved ones be able to prompt memories of the past, presently soothe his guilt, or offer future advice. He was alone and likely to stay that way if he could survive the next hours.

"Keep focused," he repeated to himself.

According to his grandfather's account, Nicholas was born in an upstate New York farmhouse attic. It was the grandfather who saw hope in his grandson's birth. Soon after his arrival, Nicholas lost his mother to post-partum suicide. His education had been adequate; his older sister and grandfather read and instructed him faithfully with the help of a township school seven miles south. When gangs overran the Bradley farm in the second year of the intermittent darkness, his sister was raped and left for dead in the fields. It was then Nicholas was determined to take responsibility for his family's safety. Daily Karate practice was inclusive of Kobudo skills. Rather than a samurai sword, Nicholas was gifted two of his grandfather's machetes, often used to clean brush in lieu of the farm's equipment that stood useless in the fields. Together, Porter and Nicholas Bradley cleaned and sharpened the 16-inch blade of the Bushcraft Machete and turned a new walnut handle. The Kukri machete was a solid 17 inches with a protrusion on the pommel that gave Nicholas a feeling of better control.

Using Kobudo footwork, Nicholas absorbed the requirements to wield the weapons against vital areas with strategies orchestrated by his seasoned grandfather.

Porter Bradley had inherited the family farm and had been its proud owner until the Grid Wars. An absence of energy had resulted in marauders ransacking food stores, slaughtering livestock, and cutting much of the forest for firewood. Nicholas's father, a government sanitation inspector, was ill-equipped to run a farm. The situation went from bad to worse during the winter of 2035. Given the previous year's raids on provisions, communities cooperated with coordinated lookouts that helped offset surprise attacks.

By 2045, communication had been reliably restored in the rural areas. When Nicholas was born, the family had joined a network of honest folk who resided on fertile land that enticed two sets of people: the peaceful farming communities and the pillaging groups migrating from urban landscapes that finally made their way into the more isolated areas. Many of the gangs included surviving orphans who had known no other life. Depraved from a lifetime of feral behaviors, the bands of scavengers knew no peace and allowed none.

After the farm's third raid, Nicholas stood guard alongside his 80-year-old grandfather on their front porch; a wood-burning stove helped to offset the blustering wind that blew unchallenged from the northwest. Nomads travelling in the area had long burned the farm's tall windbreakers that once kept the field's seedlings intact. With most of fields fallow and unprotected, Nicholas and his sister worked the acreage closest to the home. Farm animals were hidden from poachers. Such tactics had been successful until November of '59.

Like so many smaller groups migrating before them, five men had maneuvered around the town's defenses. It wasn't hard to do in the wee hours of the morning when sleep was most likely to overcome man and beast. Toothless and smiling, the elder of the five scavengers began to gain confidence as soon as the slumping figure of an old man came into focus, with a rifle that lay loosely in his lap. Their stealth approach through the Bradley gates broke into a full run; the harsh wind obliterated the trampling of dried leaves and twigs under eager feet. Without acknowledging Nicholas, they charged toward Porter Bradley and knocked him unconscious with a shovel that cracked bone and chair at once. The remaining four swept past Nicholas to break open the front door.

Nicholas made three moves. He rose from his chair, pulled his cold steel Kukri machete up toward his right ear and made a 45-degree slice into the neck of the closest man. Effortless as a cut of butter, the precision and power of Nicholas's response was derived from thousands of hours of practice. The blade's cut was as clean as those honed upon tightly-bound, thatched wet straw. As the group grappled with the double-bolted outer door, Nicholas manipulated the Bush machete mercilessly. Within seconds, the five men lay dying in pools of blood. Those who had not instantly died were rolled over on their backs, slit from throat to core like so much expertly quartered game.

Nicholas confiscated his grandfather's rifle from the grasp of his murderer. One by one, the bodies were dragged down the porch steps; their lifeless heads bumped and scraped against the cement as Nicholas made his way to a dirt patch near the barn. A telltale 'whoosh' of an ignited gasoline fire alerted Nicholas's father and sister from the barn to the scene of a crackling pile of corpses.

"Oh, God...not Papa!"

Nicholas watched his sister run past him toward the house to tend the man who had been their lifeline, teacher, and cherished grandfather. It was he who had taught the prayers, played the guitar, brought homilies to life, and kept the struggling family from starvation. Porter Bradley's son-in-law, by contrast, proved ineffectual.

Nicholas had believed his grandfather lifeless but he lay lightly breathing in the arms of his sister; the three managed to get him on a stretcher and summoned medical assistance from the nearest town.

"It doesn't look good. Head trauma like this? I'm sorry!" The doctor stayed for supper and prayed with the family.

After a week's time, the revered grandfather passed quietly in a coma with his frail hand held tightly in Nicholas's own. The family was inconsolable. When Nicholas went to the work shed to make his grandfather's coffin, he discovered the gravestone already prepared. It was simply inscribed without a name and date:

Here lies the grandfather of the two grandest grandchildren on God's green earth.

* * *

The remaining three Bradleys were resolved to finally make a move. It was unlikely they would survive another winter. After nearly two months of careful investigation, Nicholas estimated the timing of a transit ship that made its way to the south every four months from Canada. No other ship had come close to the Eastern seaboard shores until south of Delaware. Those were the Confederation or Canadian shipping and naval vessels that acted as border patrols.

There were rumors of how others had completed the near-impossible task of bribing and bartering for passage to Confederation safety.

"The more scarce the merchandise, the more likely they are to take you on," reported a farmer from the closest township. No, he hadn't heard any reports of successful journeys but passage on privately-owned ships was next to impossible.

"You'll never get close to anything but the pirates. These renegade ships don't come anywhere close to New York until they're sure that the Confederation patrols are nowhere near. No one we know has returned to tell us much. Most have gotten the hell scared out of them. And those pirates have no use for barter-bits. They want gold, gems or extraordinarily scarce food or drink. They're not even going to consider spare parts because they're not merchants," came the advice.

Following the route that had long been mapped as the safest path toward the city, the Bradleys had managed to avoid most of the dangers that entrapped less capable refugees. Nicholas's father went alone to scout the docks as they approached Pier 4; he directed his children to lay low until his return.

A few hours later, Gerald Bradley returned to their temporary camp in the lobby of a halfburned, razed hotel of black charred cement and exposed rebar. The exception was the refrigerator and freezer vaults of former kitchens. It was under and through the black carbonized ruble that the three had found a place to hide within the remains of vast storerooms.

"What did you find, Dad?" Nicholas asked.

"Dr. Jackson was right on the timing. That old freighter is waiting in port. She's been ironically named 'Hope' and renamed 'Hopeless'. The 'less' is crudely written in red. Its original purpose was to bring medical supplies distributed along the waterways of the East Coast. The Red Cross flag still hangs in tatters. I doubt the ploy works any longer because they've got gunners up top and roving guards with some impressive looking equipment. Got radios... an old monitor... a few generators on deck, some solar panels. I'm no sailor but the whole rig looks desperate at best," Gerald reported.

The family agreed to proceed and take the risk, 'or die try-ing.' The memory of his sister's adamant words made Nicholas gasp for breath, replaying the moment her eyes spoke fateful resignation. As the bullet pierced her forehead, Nicholas's sis-ter stood a split second over her father's fallen body with a lingering moment of sentience before crumpling.

Nicholas remained in the hotel's vicinity to steal food where he could find it, avoiding roving gangs and the rising bile with each lungful of a rotting city.

Desperately hungry, Nicholas realized that it was unlikely that he would ever make it back to the upstate farm without supplies and decided to make another attempt to board the Hopeless. Behind a pile of refuse, Nicholas observed the pat-terns of the men working the ship. From time to time, he caught glimpses of ordinary-looking passengers. There were women, there were young people, but he hadn't observed any men on board coming and going other than the guards, iden-tifiable by their guns and arrogance.

Filling a large canvas bag with live rats caught and collected beside mountains of street garbage, Nicholas marched toward the Hopeless and stood patiently in line. He was freezing and confused. The collection of rats made no sense.

I may have to sneak on board, Nicholas imagined. This was to be the last day the ship would be docked. If unable to board, Nicholas would avenge his family's murder sooner than later.

Nicholas did not believe he had any chance to get by the ship's men standing vigil. It was the evil man who had appor-tioned death to his defenseless sister and father that was on Nicholas's mind. The razor-sharp machetes were strapped to his waist, hanging inside loose-fitting pants.

Head bowed, Nicholas took his place in line with others, who alternately stood and then dropped out again. Scurrying from fear, the skittish watched the dangerous proceedings from behind a barrier of ten yellow sawhorses. Like mindless flies returning to the same trap, candidates scattered and gradually returned.

"Next!" called an unidentified voice. Nicholas was motioned forward at the head of the line. One of the returning families resumed their position they had forfeited hours prior in a panic, pushing past and around Nicholas. They rushed the 100 yards, arms flailing, and emptied the contents of their knapsacks on the dock for inspection. Approval shined on the captain's face. Pleased, he kicked that which he considered valuable to one side. Two men gathered a pile of packages and canned goods, wine and whiskey bottles. Outdated boxes of antibiotics and morphine quickly disappeared into a special container. Nicholas thought he might witness success. At the conclusion of the collective inspection and the captain's scrutiny, the husband was shot. The beautiful woman at his side was signaled to proceed on board.

She wailed, "My son? Please, my son, too?"

A little boy stood stunned beside his fallen father and bent to touch a listless hand.

"You best go ahead. We'll take care of the little tyke. You're granted passage so I wouldn't say much more," the captain sneered.

The woman refused to board and reached to grab her three-year-old son before the captain was able to scoop him up from the deck. He laughed as she stood wrestling against his advance.

"I won't let him die alone..." she screamed. "Oh God, please give him to me! Kill us both!"

Nicholas jumped the sawhorses and pulled his long machete, running furiously toward the captain. The blade was poised behind Nicholas's neck, his elbows elevated high above his head, and tucked together as one unit. Moments before the captain secured her son, his hands fell to the deck at his feet. Unable to grasp the quick turn of events, the captain's men stood riveted in an attempt to absorb the surreal scene. The captain screamed, staring wide-eyed at his detached body parts lying beside his shoes, palms up. The mother grabbed her son, hands kicked away from the boy, while the amputated man scrambled to secure two severed parts with hemorrhaging nubs.

Nicholas attacked the remaining men on the main deck and turned to look for others that were sure to come. Hopeful passengers that once stood in the line of death ran for their lives as each guard fell successively without firing a single shot.

Nicholas directed the frantic mother to grab the boy and move behind him onto the ship; Nicholas bolted for the stairwell after taking a final and fatal swipe at the captain's neck. The screaming head flew from its host. Finally silenced, it rolled across the deck with frozen, terrified eyes.

Discovering a service corridor, Nicholas slipped through a door designated as Laundry. He had lost the woman and child he believed had followed his lead. For minutes, Nicholas backtracked but was unable to find the pair. Screams of anger and confusion filled the ship as the monitor ordered 'clean up on main deck'. He gave up the search and retreated to the laundry room's safety.

Nicholas opened the portal in the stifling leeway; he was greeted by the familiar sounds of bodies being thrown overboard.

"Business as usual," Nicholas wept.

Within the hour, the Hopeless moved from its berth into the bay with the monitor's final call to 'get out of here' and 'where the hell did those rats come from'?

Panting and shaking from the ordeal, Nicholas prayed for his family who had sacrificed so much on his behalf, for the safety and welfare of a young mother and child he'd sloppily lost in the scramble, for the skill imparted by his grandfather, and finally for safe passage. The true meaning of his grandfather's admonishments about undue risks – 'don't jump from the frying pan into the fire' – dawned on the teenager.

"I just landed in the fire…," was Nicholas's last thought before exhaustion overtook him. On the hard tile floor, Nicholas slept as the cold bay air offset the boiler heat that adjoined the utility room.

Monday, December 20, 2060

The smell of food from the galley and the gentle rocking of the ship greeted Nicholas at 7:30 a.m.

"I've got to eat," he worried. With few thoughts of safety, Nicholas followed aromas to a table laden with foods he had never seen prepared in one setting. Gathering a plate from the neat stack upon the buffet, Nicholas piled eggs, bacon, pancakes and unidentified meat; he then selected a seat at one unnaturally quiet table.

Passengers ate in silence. An announcement blared about a crew meeting. No one spoke to Nicholas or remarked upon his unkempt condition; the blood on his coat or his sudden arrival did not seem to alarm anyone. He was left to eat his fill. Some passengers took time to say blessings over their food. Others protested the mention of God.

Nicholas returned to the buffet and filled his shirt with freshly-baked bread and jam. A young girl looked up from the other side of the table.

"Where did you come from?" she asked with raised eyebrows.

"Laundry room," Nicholas answered without looking up.

"I mean I didn't see you come in from Canada. Are you new?"

"Yes. Just boarded."

"Oh. I didn't see you. What's your name? There was a big mess last night. Lots of men died! Something killed that nasty captain, too. Did you hear the commotion?"

"No. I didn't." Nicholas stopped packing food and looked at the voice's owner.

Nicholas liked the girl's long, neat pigtails and the way she scrutinized him. He figured her to be ten or twelve years old.

"My name is Nicholas. Yours?"

"I'm Cynthia," she whispered. "Everyone is deadly, of course. Be careful. You're the only strong man I've ever seen allowed on the ship. They don't like strong men."

Nicholas liked being referred to as a man. He resumed wrapping extra food when the newly designated captain arrived. Sporting the coveted white hat, now splattered with blood at its crest, a burly man entered the mess hall bordered by a diminished group of armed guards. He politely asked everyone to cease all activity.

"We've decided to abort this trip at the next harbor. It's a mile to shore; we won't be able to navigate closer because they'll blow or board us. We'll get you as close as possible to something that looks approachable but we're not going to dock. Prepare yourselves."

"We'll die in the water within minutes," pleaded Cynthia who stood beside Nicholas. "You know we'll die."

"I didn't say you'd be swimming, kid. You'll be able to draw straws for two of the six lifeboats on board. Figure it out amongst you. The rest can return with us. Sorry about the change in plans. We figure assassins from the queue took out Captain Paxton and the other men. Can't figure how they slit everyone up. It's shit, but it is what it is. This isn't the only passage out; you'll be able to find another way." No one else dared a protest.

Nicholas followed the new captain out of the mess hall and tapped gently upon his shoulder.

"Excuse me, sir? Where will you be sailing on to?"

The self-appointed captain jumped. "What the... You scared the shit out of me. Where and when did you board?"

Nicholas wished he had remained quiet. With nothing to lose, he forged ahead.

"I got on in New York. I was let on... in... New York," Nicholas stammered.

"Bullshit. We don't let young bucks like you on board. What did you trade?"

"My machete. I traded my machete... for heads," Nicholas braved angrily.

A strange thing happened as adrenaline shot through Nicholas Bradley. His knees went weak and his throat felt scorched, ending any chance of answering further questions. Blood drained from his face and beads of sweat erupted from his forehead in the dead of winter. There was no machete at Nicholas's side; his weapons lay in the laundry room below. Without a thought of consequence, Nicholas stupidly believed himself capable of demonstrating bravado. His blood pressure indicated that Nicholas measured himself a dead man.

The captain also felt an overwhelming sensation of panic. His rising distress, however, far outweighed Nicholas's anxiety. It encompassed and squeezed the breath from his diaphragm;

an invisible vise rendered his lungs incapacitated, unable to fully inflate with another inhalation. In short order, Nicholas watched crippling pain double over the gasping captain. A long and eerie high-pitched wail emanated from the man's constricted throat.

Nicholas expected the guards to rush to their leader's aid but they, too, exhibited symptoms of extraordinary suffering. Nicholas remained uneasily in place as the men dropped, heedlessly smashing kneecaps into the ship's pitted steel flooring. Some held their heads and rolled in place. Two others grasped their right arms; all spasmodically rocked and howled. Another spewed bloodied vomit followed by an intense dry retching.

A young woman entered through the double doors and grabbed Nicholas's arm, "You poisoned them? Get out of here!"

"I didn't do anything. They just got sick," Nicholas replied to the woman he recognized as the mother of the child he had encountered the previous night.

"Please, come to my cabin... they'll kill you," she insisted.

Recognizing a rare gift of kindness, Nicholas calmed. And when he calmed, the men on the floor ceased to manifest searing pain. They began to breathe more evenly and their eyes opened wide, narrowing upon the teenager standing above them.

Cynthia followed the noises into the ship's corridor and surveyed the sight. Her older sister quickly followed into the overly-crowded space and panicked, having noticed the men lying on the floor had begun to regain composure. The sisters assumed an aftermath of a fight between Nicholas and the group.

"Cynthia, let's get the hell out of here now!" called the older sister.

"No. Look at them, Esther!" Cynthia insisted. "They're scared. They just can't move. Look at them look at Nicholas!" Cynthia grasped her sister's arm and the hand of the unknown mother rigidly standing beside her.

It was true, thought Nicholas. The men had been reduced to cowering mongrels too terrified to stand. Although somewhat physically recovered, they remained unmoving.

"What do you want?" one of them rasped toward the teenager he rightly figured was the source of their pain and grief.

Awareness washed over Nicholas and he understood three things. The first: sometimes he was visible and sometimes he was not. This condition depended upon his emotional state. Second, when panicked or faced with greater odds, he either was able to aptly focus and defend himself or cause emotional and physical pain in unknown ways to those who meant him harm. Sometimes, both events and reactions could take place. Third, he intuited, these abilities were commensurate with the levels of intended malice. He recognized these three elements of his strange abilities at once.

Nicholas turned toward the mother of the little boy whom he had saved the previous night and asked, "Do you know me? Have you seen me before?"

"No. I've never seen you before," she shook her head.

"What compelled you to try and save me just now? How did you know that I wasn't one of the captain's men?"

"I just heard screaming. You aren't one of that group, it's obvious...I knew you were in danger."

Cynthia's older sister tried to understand the situation. Men she knew to be vicious now cowered before one teenage boy.

"Whatever hurt them is going to wear off and they're going to kill us. It's that simple. We gotta go," Esther urged.

"There's nowhere to hide on a ship...where do you plan to go?" Nicholas questioned.

Nicholas was further puzzled by the lack of critical thinking he had experienced. First, he thought, there was the long, winding line of expectant passengers watching those that went before them having set a predictable pattern; they were randomly granted passage or murdered. In each case, their world's belongings vanished in the process. It didn't make sense. No family had been allowed aboard intact. Not one. It was a process of evidentiary value that been witnessed by potential victims standing in line for many hours. Small children were tossed overboard like so many useless ragdolls, as were the less comely females. Older males – skilled in some manner of need – were randomly quizzed and boarded only if determined non-threatening.

It doesn't make sense, Nicholas thought.

With these primitive behaviors were the juxtaposed civilized actions. Nicholas noticed the formally prepared meals, spotless quarters, and clean linens on a pirate ship. Where was the logic? He had never seen such behavioral incongruities. It was, he surmised, a microcosm of the planet that was erratically arranged in a semi-civilized limbo state. Little Cynthia appeared as some kind of Alice in Wonderland, able to see Nicholas at breakfast, whereas others had not seemed to notice him at all. *Just like the thugs that killed Grandpa. They never saw me at all.*

He had never known such maddeningly disconnected, vicious behaviors or the reason he reacted so mysteriously.

A new voice interrupted Nicholas's thoughts.

"They don't care what we do until they want one of us for something," interrupted the man who introduced himself as the chef. Pulling his beard, he added: "I haven't set foot on land for two years. Every route has a new crew. They don't know the ship any better than we do. They're just a series of smuggling pirates killing or replacing each other. There's always someone who can figure the routes, manage the monitor, the solar and energy cells. I'm the one who keeps the good food on the table and they won't let me leave. Most of the killing has to do with what needs to be put on the table. Every time I require an ingredient, I know someone has paid for it with their life," the cook shook his head sadly.

"Everyone wants to make their way toward civilization; all these guys do is eat and drink well while avoiding Confederation patrols near the former capital."

The cook surveyed the group that had managed to subdue the worst scavengers he had ever encountered. He examined the brutal men lying submissively on the deck and curiously regarded the young teenager.

The older sister, Nicholas reckoned, was around 18 years of age. Esther was frantic for an option and broke the silence.

"We have to take our chances with sea pirates or the land crazies? Isn't it possible to tie this bunch up and take back the ship? Could we make it to Confederation territory ourselves?"

The cook agreed and added, "Some of our group may get to shore with the lifeboats but we're going to still be long way from Confederation safety. We should try and take the ship," he decided.

"Confederation surveillance can pick up a lot, too. There's tales of migrating parties being rescued hundreds of miles north of Confederation borders by patrols. I think we can actually handle things and make our way somewhere until we're noticed. I don't mind killing this lot and personally tossing them overboard," the chef offered, turning a butcher's knife in hand.

It was not a decision that Nicholas wanted to make. Esther noted hesitation.

"Did you lose family, Nicholas?" she asked.

"Have you?" he returned the question.

"Who hasn't? I've looked after Cynthia since she was born. Where have you been? Not from the cities, that's for sure. You would know that there's little between us and a grave. These animals would kill us if they could. Cook is right. Finish them off!" Nicholas locked eyes with the cowering captain at his feet, who struggled with unbridled rage and pain.

In recognition of an opportune moment, the captain slowly moved to his feet. Nicholas's heart raced, and when it did, the captain's knees promptly buckled. Like a man pinned by the weight of the world, the captain pleaded for leniency.

"I won't do anything. I get it. Please, no more pain! Just listen! That worthless cook can't help you get anywhere. You need me. Only me," he begged Nicholas.

"Promises from murderers don't hold water...you stay where you are!"

Nicholas directed the cook, who had one foot inside the corridor and one inside toward the galley, to fetch his two machetes from the laundry room. He directed the sisters to secure the rifles. Nicholas didn't know the extent of his abilities but had witnessed their temporary nature.

"Let's move!" he cried to the sisters.

"No, Cynthia. Stay here...I'll gather the rifles from them," Esther instructed her sister.

Glaring at Nicholas, Esther gathered the weapons and weapon belts. Nicholas felt ashamed at having asked a little girl and apologized for his mistake.

"It's okay. You're just a little more than a kid, too. My name is Esther. What's yours? You alone?"

"Nicholas Bradley. My father and sister were killed and thrown overboard earlier in the week by this group. What's your last name?"

She paused as she gathered the weapons, not quite knowing how to frame the answer.

"Who knows? I can barely remember my mother's face," Esther answered bitterly.

Nicholas, who had not the luxury to shed tears since he'd lost his grandfather, felt an emotional aftershock. Welling tears spilled straight from eyes to deck.

The untied men began to wail from an emotional pain so intense that one began to hit his head full force upon the metal floor until it gashed and bled internally.

Nicholas continued his initial thought on the matter of his peculiar facility. In some manner, his emotions elicited analogous emotions from his predators. If the predators were guilty of aberrant acts, they would empathetically relive their victim's category of pain or injustice. The more victims involved and the more horrendous the acts, the more cumulative and intense the predator's pain. With that idea still taking form in his mind, two of the shrieking men, including the captain, died of embolisms. The remainder squirmed in agony for hours and stopped only after having undergone a rapid series of self-inflicted fatal wounds and repetitive concussing.

The passengers threw the dead men overboard and searched for others. Two men were found hanging in their quarters as suicide victims. Others had maimed themselves and died from ghastly self-inflicted injuries.

Calls went out on an open channel to the Confederation for help.

The cook made apple pies.

Chapter IX

Convergence

Thursday, December 23, 2060

*A*ngela and CC tackled the decoration of a twenty-two-foot Blue Spruce Christmas tree that stood halfway inside the crook of the home's grand spiraling staircase. The lopsided appearance of the ill-placed decorations spoke volumes of a grandmother's patience and love. Overloaded asymmetric ornamentation transformed the holiday ritual into something holy.

"Hey! All the stuff is mostly one side and overburdened at the bottom. What in tarnation? Like a bulbous leaning tower of Spruce," Morgan commented from the confines of his library.

"That's as far as I can reach, Grandpa. If you were here to help, we could put more on the top," CC suggested. She smiled knowingly at her grandmother, who had anticipated the criticism. Angela winked at her protégé and handed CC another string of popcorn.

"It's a testament," Angela sniffed her own brand of disapproval.

"Yup. I'll be right there," Morgan acknowledged with some resignation.

The three spent the last hours of the afternoon arranging the Pendergrass decorations from half-opened boxes. In the grand foyer, the disproportionate lopsided tree remained intact.

Robots busily vacuumed the remnants of freshly cut garlands and operated ladders. Freshly cut Hedera Helix was woven amongst the faux candlelight of chandeliers. The 'Gold

Child' of Ivy spun their green and gold serrated leaves intertwined with delicate holly swags.

Points of green cut crystal stars and red enameled berries spilled into climbing spirals along the staircase rails. Having presaged Christmas visitors, Caroline eagerly prepared for a night of entertainment.

A maintenance bot was interrogated. A not-so-sophisticated AI dutifully led Caroline to one of the missing printers that began to hum on command. Caroline allowed the printer to scan, select materials, and produce costumes. Twenty new outfits later, dolls were attached by twine to second-story light fixtures. Nooses were affixed to plastic necks and lowered toward the center of the home's main foyer.

"Finished!" she cried triumphantly.

Morgan emerged from a hallway and narrowed his focus upon the suspended menagerie.

"I'm just wondering if we're liable to get in trouble if someone comes in here thinking we're hanging these innocent characters till dead," Morgan said, hand over mouth.

"What's the matter, Grandpa?" Caroline looked toward the listless bodies and saw nothing but a great accomplishment.

"Shouldn't we be using this idea for Halloween?" Morgan suggested.

"It's a Christmas aerial performance! That means in the air. It's the Christmas JazzBazz Ensemble. Want to see the program?"

"Love to! Imagine, free entertainment!" Morgan found his granddaughter a never-failing source of enchantment.

"Not free. You have to donate barter-bits to the producer," Caroline corrected.

"You're the producer, Caroline?"

"Yes, sir. I'm going to help the children coming here. They need to buy things."

"Children? What children?"

"The visitors. They're coming here!" CC clapped her hands excitedly.

"What have you seen?" Morgan pursued.

"CC?" Adele interrupted the exchange with her hologram between Caroline and Morgan. "I need you now upstairs, please."

CC ran upstairs and down the hall scurrying toward her mother's room. Morgan, having picked up a clandestine scent, trailed. A door slam later, Morgan cursed his age when Adele's door bolted.

"I'm locked out?" Morgan tapped the door with his cane.

"We're having private time, Dad." Adele's flat tone aborted her father's protestations.

"Gotcha. Well, when you girls have time, I'd love to hear about the upcoming JazzBazz performance."

CC laughed but did not open the door.

"We can still see you in the hall, Grandpa. Don't bother to talk to the performers. They're not going to tell you anything!"

"I believe that, Caroline. Okay, then. Watch an elderly man sadly teeter away. My poor aching legs barely carry me from my precious family." Morgan peered into a hall camera.

"Bye, Dad!" Adele projected her image in the hall, motioning for him to return downstairs. "Love ya!"

Morgan knew what he heard. He also knew that Adele's overreaction meant something.

"I'm not getting enough information around here," he groused. "It's also boring with everyone getting ready for Christmas."

Morgan paused as Angela entered from the kitchen door's exterior. Two robots entered, laden with gift packages. Morgan watched silently as his wife followed to hide holiday presents in a hall closet. When the door closed, Morgan let out a two-finger whistle that drew Angela's attention skyward; her eyes fixed upon a life-sized Red Riding Hood whose red cape and green skirt swung wildly above her head. Angela's ensuing scream alerted Security. It took time for Morgan to convince security teams that everything was copacetic. Periphery alarms quieted sequentially. The chief of Morgan's security team made a personal visit.

"What happened, Dr. Pendergrass?" Isabella Moreno asked solemnly.

"Roving Bohemian artists startled my wife – all good now," Morgan explained through snorts of laughter. "Practicing for a Christmas pageant. My wife was a little startled," he laughed harder.

"I'm afraid that you'll have to find another pastime, Dr. Pendergrass. Our multi-biometric fusion of algorithms is a multi-sensorial combination of calibrated levels incorporating a wide spectrum of dissimilarly scaled scores into a common base for each member of your family and those that frequent the farm. Our system has merged hundreds of techniques, all of which require significant a priori database upon our input of normalization data, yielding a fixed, adaptive and/or robust score. Angela's levels of acoustic roughness engaged subcortical structures meant to ensure a person's warning system, a crisis recognition mechanism that ignites a biological behavioral advantage by a stimulated amygdala..." Moreno's justification for alarm was meant to impress.

"Stop! Moreno? What the hell are you trying to say?" Morgan agonized.

"It's the science behind our response, sir. You scared the wits out of your wife. Our monitors were off the chart. That's a fact. Cut this stuff out!" Moreno finalized and departed the room.

* * *

Adele and Caroline laughed at the monitor's scene playing out under the JazzBazz group. Adele turned thoughtful.

"Let's speak about your ability to see future events, CC."

"You don't like it when I draw the pictures?" Caroline asked simply.

"No, that's not it. I love your work." Adele patted a place next to her on her bedroom couch. "I worry that your work attracts so much interest. I've no idea what it means but I'm sure we should be a little more discreet. You know, like the surprise visitors you mentioned a few minutes ago. It alerted Grandpa, right? Draw all you want and whatever you wish. But if someone asks what it means, I'd like to be with you."

"I know that you hide the drawings. I think that people see my drawings and get a little scared. They're surprised because they can't see the way I do," CC said non-judgmentally.

The little girl began to pat her mother's head, she the comforter, her mother the little girl. Adele immediately relaxed.

"I shouldn't have said that kids are coming. It just came out of my big mouth," Caroline continued.

"You have nothing to apologize for. Sometimes we have to be careful about what we say, to whom we say it, and when we choose to say it. Not everyone hears the same thing in the same way. Communication can be difficult for everyone."

Caroline showed her mother a picture of pistachio ice cream she had recently drawn.

"The girl with curly hair likes this. We need to print this ice cream!"

"Arriving here?"

"Yes, but after some others. Then one more will come."

Chapter X
Heathrow Airport, London

Y"ou've got everything you need to make it across the pond. The Yanks better treat you right." Gordon Smith chuckled as he bade a final farewell to Amar Nishant's family on an abandoned runway, his private jet ready for takeoff.

"You can trust the crew; they won't be returning. They'll keep the jet and work for the Confederation.

"You already know your colleagues from the Crick research group, and their families. It's best to keep conversation about our work to yourselves until you formally introduce our findings. Betsy-x261 has done her best to analyze what's going on in our cells, beginning with the broad changes in the modulations of Schumann's Resonance, the ELF signals from the old HAARP space lasers to the electromagnetic pollution that has run counter to the human system. Our planet once communicated with us in a primal language of frequencies; we were once synchronized with planetary resonance. With the EM irregularities came RF destabilization. The result has been an asymmetric hemispheric function. Rage and fear will be permanent in most of our population until we are able to develop in vivo stimulation that might better protect cellular membranes that, in turn, protect us from the alternating electric currents that flow through cells and tissues. The latest onslaught has removed structurally important calcium ions from cell membranes. Our cellular membranes are literally leaking. Further cell membrane destruction has carried over to the bloodstream. Over the last forty years, prolonged exposure to erratic non-ionizing electromagnetic fields has resulted in electromagnetic hypersensitivity. Weakened DNA has caused cell membranes to permanently seep...there remains little to no barriers to toxins. Even the ATP is unable to amply help with the uptake of nutrients. The calcium levels in the cells also affect cortisol levels. Rather than the adrenal system going into 'fight or flight' mode, the stress hormone now induces 'fight or fight' mode. We can see how that's worked out.

"We're done with the cell phones and modulated ELF frequencies, radio waves for now. But we've inherited a great deal of damage. Our research is promising. We've seen that this can be reversed within glands, brain, blood...the works... by changing frequencies and building our cellular immunity. But we cannot save our species without fixing and retaining the natural resonances. We need to fix the damaged magnetic grid. We'd be shoveling snow in a snowstorm if that can't happen."

"We have prayed that the Confederation scientists can take it from here," Amar commented quietly. "We owe you our lives, Gordon. Why won't you come with us? I've never asked the things as I've intended...I respect your privacy... if I could just know more details?"

Gordon Smith ignored his friend and indicated to the rest of the crew to escort Mrs. Nishant and her son on board after the secured baggage and medical equipment. He lightly patted Aditiya on the head and bowed toward Indu.

"I wish you a wonderful new life within the American Confederation, Madame. It promises to be one of the best places on the planet. I hear that North Carolina is quite in keeping with your greatest expectations for Aditiya in every way," Smith guaranteed.

Indu removed the memory embedded in her family heirloom necklace and attempted to gift the emerald keepsake to their friend and benefactor.

"For you, from us, with fond memories and heartfelt gratitude," she bade Smith.

"Indu, I thank you but I can't use it where I'm going. My memories are intact and I can access our time together without effort. Give this wonderful memento to your future daughter-in-law." He clasped his hands over hers with the necklace inside her palms. "Now, you'd better board."

Gordon turned toward his friend.

"She's wonderful, Amar. He's a great child with exceptional talent. I wish I'd been so fortunate. Cherish them," Gordon advised. "They're expecting you at the Raleigh-Durham airport. It's a little over 4000 miles and you should arrive under four hours' travel time. There's no better equipment available out of London, Amar. The Confederation airspace will contact you...here's the call number that you alone possess. The pilots will ask for it when the time comes. It's an easy flight, plenty of fuel. It was once a part of the Royal Air Force's fleet for the Royal family."

Amar was expected to act as the official courier on behalf of Gordon Smith's research. The Confederation Research Triangle would be the Nishants' new home.

"You've my life's work. Don't blow it," Smith laughed. "Get the hell out of here. If you find that moment to speak of me, you are obligated to spin the most unlikely and exquisite tales," Smith concluded with an uncharacteristic hug and a final pat upon Amar Nishant's shoulder.

Gordon watched the jet roar down the runway through the vapors of his breath. A bright yellow sun rose. Crystallized dew sparkled on the overgrown green grass fields that resisted freezing temperatures. Gordon considered that which promised to be an unusually clear cold day and chose to interpret it as a good omen.

Gordon's chauffeur slowly drove an antique car toward his employer's position as the plane disappeared over the horizon. Gordon acknowledged it was time to depart.

"Ha! Let's do this right! Home, James!" Gordon feigned enthusiasm.

Once at 10 Downing Street, Gordon Smith contacted the UK royal offices in Sydney, Australia.

"Done and done," he reported simply.

King George thanked Gordon for his long years of service. "You will never be forgotten for your part in crafting a new world, Doctor. Humanity is in your debt."

"Thank you, Your Highness. God bless us all," Gordon bowed his head deferentially.

Gordon ate a robust breakfast and nodded toward his assistant. "The Japanese Samurai would sing a song or recite a poem before committing Seppuku. We English? We'd rather our kippers, a Bacon Butty, fried eggs, some stewed fruit on toast, perhaps sausage... and a proper cup of tea!"

"I will miss you, sir." Smith's aide of forty years bowed his head with great sadness and shook his employer's hand. "It's been an honor to serve you."

Within fifteen minutes, Gordon's body was removed from the bedroom and transported to the morgue.

Chapter XI
Rachel and Aaron's New Home

Friday, December 24, 2060

*T*he cargo ship, Wehr Elbe III, prepared for its return to its port of origin, the former US Military Ocean Terminal at Sunny Point, North Carolina. It had travelled from the Israeli port of Ashdod and then docked briefly in Astakos, Greece to load.

"It's Christmas Eve this evening, Aaron. Others on board are celebrating a very important moment in their religious liturgy," Rachel answered Aaron's puzzled expression. Christmas carols emanated jubilantly throughout the bustling ship preparing for its launch. Aaron beamed at the beautiful, strange songs.

"Do we fast?"

"It's a time to share celebratory foods. It's not kosher but I wouldn't worry about it," she urged.

Rachel had begun to feel relief after the exhaustion of a seventeen-month wait as Israeli scientists conducted Aaron's examinations. It had been her intention to help Aaron better understand his special abilities with the help of Israel's top scientists. The relationship had not evolved in the way she intended. Desperate to leave Tel Aviv, Rachel sought the influential.

"I'm going to need a heavier hammer to get out of here," she surmised.

Rachel accessed an international monitor through University friends; she searched Israel's joint research projects that included international cooperation, ranging from bio-fuels and static frequencies to genome research. Rachel scanned Aaron while he rendered objects weightless, encrypted the transmission, and sent it to Raleigh, North Carolina.

Believing it an official report, it was forwarded directly to Meredith Green and Connor Collins, who uttered the same spontaneous, if somewhat unscientific, one-word response. Green contacted Rachel to discuss her interests. Rachel wished to negotiate an international agreement between Israel and the Confederation.

"We'd like to immigrate to the Confederation at the earliest possible moment. Given Aaron's extraordinary ability to defend himself, I think it unwise to force the issue of keeping him confined here in a laboratory setting," she advised Dr. Green. "Israel can remotely cooperate if you'll accept such terms?"

"Your proposal might meet with some resistance, Ms. Ben-Tov; I believe that Aaron is regarded as a national treasure," Green explained diplomatically. "Press the matter from your end first. Let us know the outcome. We'll step in, if required."

As predicted, there was resistance; Rachel was obliged to listen to the appeals of Israeli notables.

"We're on the brink of something extraordinary. Surely you understand?" Israel's Prime Minister pleaded.

"I don't mind the research. I very much mind the disregard for Aaron's quality of life. You'll have all the research results from the Confederation of American States to consider," Rachel reasoned.

After many such audiences, Rabbi Herschel was summoned.

"You're a Jew!" Rabbi Herschel reminded Rachel. "This is a Jewish state. You are obligated as a Jewish citizen. God intends that I remind you of a duty... to abide by your role to nurture Aaron's Jewish loyalty..."

"So you have been brought here to represent the Jewish way of doing things?" Rachel responded. "Did you ever consider the matter of compassion over your interpretation of ritual, law, or commonsense guidelines? In this case, is scientific research a nurturing environment for Aaron? Is it his duty to be a human sacrifice, Rabbi? You have the nerve to speak of responsibility when you allowed an orphaned boy to watch his father's body transported by an orange cart, removed from his community, and buried without the benefit of clergy? Suddenly, Aaron is worthy of your consideration?" Rachel angrily chastised. "Why not personally conduct one more very important test upon Aaron? You may ask if Aaron would like to remain within these cold, white laboratories with sterile examiners. I'll do as Aaron says," Rachel promised.

* * *

Within the week, the Confederation ship arrived. The Israelis kept their word. The gifted child and his guardian left their shores.

The journey was nearly complete. The captain addressed the assembled passengers at their final breakfast.

"We've charted for Wilmington, North Carolina but will enter at Sunny Point, about 42 kilometers south. You'll go through a brief orientation at the Snows Point facility and have access to Pleasure Island and other first-rate accommodations. You've been issued monitors that are privatized with customized settings that include translators and accurate GPS maps...as opposed to the ones that are purposely altered for security reasons.

"You'll then be accompanied from there to Raleigh, North Carolina with Confederation representatives and escorts. I wish you Godspeed and His benedictions."

The captain, who'd never formally introduced himself to Rachel and Aaron, requested an aside to speak privately. He removed his hat and spoke softly to the pair.

"Son, you've something that might tell us a lot. You've been issued an angel straight from heaven; her name is Rachel. If this isn't what you want after all, I've entered my private contact on your Personal Monitors. Please set your biometrics as soon as possible. I'll take you anywhere on my route at anytime. I can do that... and I will do that without question. You're both a little young to know what you'll want in the future. Good luck to you both."

Rachel thanked the Captain for his courtesies and nodded to Aaron when he indicated a need to speak.

"I know you're worried about us. You don't have to worry. There's a reason we're here and it's a good reason. Your son loves you and wants you to know that you will be together again."

The captain gave Aaron his hat as a keepsake, and then retreated to his quarters, emotionally shaken. Aaron's words reminded the Captain of the loss of his son, who had been Aaron's age when influenza stole the tender life.

The passengers disembarked, with two exceptions. Meredith Green and the Collins brothers boarded the cargo ship to meet the Israeli pair.

Rachel and Aaron were asked to remain temporarily in their cabin to await personal escorts. As soon as Dr. Green knocked, Rachel placed a finger to her mouth to warn Aaron that he should not respond.

"Who's there?" Rachel asked.

"I'm sorry, we didn't realize you'd have your monitor off; it's Dr. Green and company," Dr. Green answered. "We've been appointed to greet you and Aaron. We're the team you initially contacted. We facilitated your transport from Israel. It's all been very mysterious but it's time we met."

Aaron unlocked and opened the door from across the room and grinned at the guardian he now regarded as his aunt.

Meredith Green was not normally a warm woman. However, she found herself impulsively greeting Rachel with a large bear hug.

"I know it's been hard. Welcome to the Confederation of American States, Rachel Ben-Tov and Aaron Shalit!"

Rachel felt Meredith's warmth and allowed herself to melt into her sympathetic embrace.

Meredith turned her attention toward Aaron and picked him up only to replace the boy suddenly. "Lord, I can't do that anymore. You're cute as a button but my back can't take it. Son, you're packed solid!"

"Pick me up again!" Aaron smiled at his Aunt Rachel. Rachel nodded.

Meredith braced herself for the 35-pound boost from a squatted position. Easily lifting the boy, she hugged him tight and kissed Aaron on the cheek. It occurred to the doctor as to the reason for an easier time of it.

"Marvelous! You're simply marvelous! Going forward, let's hug just like that."

"You can put me down now...it won't hurt," Aaron assured Green.

Rachel looked at Connor staring intently at her.

"You are?" she demanded.

"I'm Dr. Connor Collins," Connor said with an extended hand.

"You can stop examining me now, Dr. Connor Collins," Rachel responded.

Connor showed embarrassment and redirected his eyes.

She's much more than she reads on paper, Connor thought.

"I'm simply in admiration of the young woman who managed this long, difficult mission. Brava, Miss Ben-Tov," Connor compensated.

Rachel allowed a friendlier tone.

"I'll call you three Americans Lex, Meredith and Connor; please call me Rachel," she offered.

The helicopter silently turned its engines as soon as the pilot spotted the entourage. Rachel stopped short.

"Wait... we're supposed to be here for a while, right?" Rachel's panic at altered plans alarmed Aaron.

"You two were meant to accompany us immediately without processing," Meredith explained. "Those who accompanied you on the ship will go through a de-briefing. Theirs is a different mission."

"I see," Rachel said detachedly.

"It's a beautiful complex in Cary, N.C., where you'll live on a working farm with the Collins and the Pendergrass families. There's a girl there, too! She's Aaron's age. Lex is her father... her name is Caroline," Meredith Green said reassuringly. "If you aren't comfortable, we'll place you in your own home. Feeling at home within a loving environment is important, too."

Rachel shrugged one shoulder. "No one's thought about how we've felt before. We'll follow you, since that's the plan."

Aaron excitedly led the way toward the military transport that blew his aunt's hair into comical disarray. Their sparse belongings were brought aboard. Within forty minutes, the group peered from windows as the pilot circled Pendergrass Farm, signaling a landing on the front field. Six indistinguishable people stood outside of a home's entryway waving their enthusiasm; a smaller girl jumped wildly with two outstretched arms.

The group disembarked and made their way toward the Pendergrass' main home. Front and center, Morgan held high a handwritten sign on a thin long stick that read "Welcome Home!"

Adele whispered into CC's ear, "Is that him?"

"Yes ma'am. That's the ginger!"

"Let's welcome him as Aaron, shall we? He looks lovely."

Then to her father, Adele whispered, "How long have you known that this child and young woman were coming our way, Dad?"

"For a while. I couldn't be sure. When I heard CC mention visiting children I knew that this boy was likely to be one of them. Enough to make a person pause, wouldn't you say? By the way, how long have you two known?"

"For a while. I couldn't be sure either. I just had Caroline's expectations and a drawing to go on. I just now asked if this is the boy CC drew with the red hair and she confirmed it. We've got something special going on."

"We sure do!" Morgan yelled over the helicopter. "May I now see what you've recently locked away in the stable?" he added.

"Thanks for respecting my privacy. How did you know?" Adele asked.

"You've been hiding stuff in there since you've been four. Ever wonder the reasons there's no manure ever sitting on it? We always kept that buried box clean. Used to be where they kept the salt lick locked up till you found it. You can keep hiding stuff in there, if you want," Morgan laughed.

"Wait...you stole back your own chocolate?"

"Sure I did," Morgan laughed. "It was the chocolate wars."

"You share this with Lex and Connor?" Adele asked.

"The short answer is no. The long answer is hell no."

"Thanks, Dad!" Adele smiled.

As much as Angela tried to lead the new arrivals upstairs to their rooms, the group happily chattered in the foyer with no sign of wishing to do anything else.

Connor was particularly attentive toward Rachel. He explained the Christmas tree's origins, the ornaments and how 'fortuitous' it was to celebrate their Christmas Eve dinner together with special guests.

"Fortuitous?" Adele raised her eyebrows at Lex. "My, oh my. Is Elle going to come over here tonight?" she whispered.

"Turns out she's picking up Gloria Brackett around five," Lex answered. "Your father didn't want other guests around for this part."

"Good thing. I don't think Connor has any idea how far his tongue is hanging out."

Rachel and Aaron looked past the Christmas tree skyward and puzzled over the hanging dolls.

"I don't mean to be rude, but what Christmas ritual is this?" Rachel stifled amusement.

"They work for me," Caroline answered in a way that made sense. "They're the JazzBazz."

"Clever!" Rachel gave CC a thumbs-up.

"Do you like it here, Aaron?" CC asked suddenly.

"It's the best home I've ever seen. It smells good. It sparkles, too!"

CC took Aaron's hand and led him toward the kitchen to witness food preparations. Connor invited Rachel to follow his lead and Angela instructed the staff to take a tray of sandwiches and fruit to their guests' bedroom.

As a cultural exchange, CC took the opportunity to sample each type of Christmas cookie with Aaron.

"I'm a diplomat," Caroline explained to Aaron between bites. "Do you have sugar cookies in Israel, Aaron? How about ginger...cookies, I mean?"

"We have sugar but these are the best cookies I've ever had," Aaron muffled through the cookie samplings CC handed to him one by one.

"I think you can be a diplomat, too!" she noted.

CC grabbed another handful of cookies off the counter; her grandmother emptied them just as quickly.

"Let's wait until after dinner. That's enough for now," Angela warned.

"My grandmother is not a diplomat," CC remarked.

"What is she?" Aaron asked.

"*Security*," CC whispered.

* * *

With the household settled, Morgan messaged Meredith Green, Adele, Angela, and the Collins brothers to discuss the latest events in the privacy of the library.

"Where's Connor got to?" Morgan asked the gathered group.

"Otherwise engaged with Rachel Ben-Tov on a tour," Lex smiled.

Morgan clapped his hands. "Hey, this is a terrific turn of events. Should be a great Christmas dinner! While Connor is getting up to speed, let me do the same for you people." Morgan thought better of the idea and buzzed Connor to 'high-tail' it to the library and join the group's debriefing.

Connor arrived to see the assemblage gathered around Morgan's desk, where Caroline's pictures had been spread as the objects of consideration. The first was of her school friends. Best friend Lisa stood beside Caroline's own image as they peered out a window. To their left were two other close friends, a space, and then two additional unidentified children. Their teacher stood gravely behind the group, looking on.

The second picture depicted six children, ranging in height and age, of unknown origin save one: Aaron Shalit. His image was unmistakable, although the red hair was much longer.

The third picture was of a wedding. Connor's profile was also unmistakable. He was dressed in a tuxedo holding the hand of a woman whose face was obscured by a veil and long hair. Unlike Elle, the hair was chestnut brown rather than blonde. Signals fired rapidly clock-wise.

"We've already examined the picture of Clifton Browne and we know that story. We've got in hand another picture of someone in particular we know CC has never laid eyes on till today," Morgan pointed to Aaron Shalit's likeness.

"And here's one of Connor's upcoming nuptials to some Jane other than his faux fiancé; I'd venture to say that Miss Ben-Tov has that color hair. Wait. I'm right about that because I've been duly kicked under the table," Morgan grimaced and faced Connor.

"I'll just lay this out here right now because you're like a son to me. You may think Elle is the one. I know she's fine to look at. But you know genes, son. This is the kind of situation when y'all's children could have your looks and her brains. You're looking at the situation below your belt..."

Angela almost choked. "What in tarnation is coming out of your mouth, Morgan? This is not the subject of discussion!"

"I'm tryin' to say that Elle is nice enough – a looker, I guess – but she's an unlikely candidate for Connor. All I've been do-ing is praying. That lady's gene pool isn't something you want to dive into! I just can't see it."

"Sweet Jesus, Dad. Enough!" Adele pretended as if she hadn't shared those very thoughts. Elle, she believed, was someone to be tolerated until Connor came to his senses.

"Let's not go there; please stay on topic and spare us this," Angela begged.

Morgan was wired differently.

He continued, "For what it's worth, Connor, I'm the first to tell you when your fly's unzipped, too. Haven't we had this talk? You're still unzipped. You're still picking your nose!"

Meredith examined CC's strange picture that was, in con-trast to the wedding, a somber representation. A circle of nameless children stood somewhat sorrowfully, as if waiting in anticipation.

"What do you make of this one?" Meredith focused the dis-cussion back to CC's prescient talents. "I am not concerned about anyone's relationship, Morgan," she warned.

Morgan shook his head. "I'm afraid to speculate, Meredith. It looks like a serious group of young people, I'll give you that."

Adele interjected, "I'm not going to ask CC and neither is anyone else."

"You've seemed to have purposely omitted showing me these drawings. Why would that be, Adele? I'm her father!" Lex asked shrilly.

"Not the time, Lex," Adele cautioned.

"We can talk about these other crazy things and we can't talk about my daughter's activities now shown to everyone without the courtesy of soliciting my input?" Lex continued.

Morgan calculated that Lex had used two sentences too many.

"I'm the grandfather and I'm not nearly as partial to you as my daughter, whose common sense and brains happen to be first rate. I wouldn't go head to head with a mother who trumps a man's ego when it comes to parenting instincts. Best man up a little there, Lex Collins. I would trust Adele's instincts. I would never again doubt her direction, if I were you. I sure as hell don't. Got that?"

"I didn't mean it that way, Morgan," Lex's small protest and burning red ears gave away his indignation.

Meredith groaned, "Do we have to spend time on this? Let's recap, please."

Adele and Angela murmured the same and urged Morgan to stay on track.

"We've also a guest that has come our way by the raw chutzpah of one Rachel Ben-Tov from an Israeli Kibbutz; she made her way to an international monitor at Tel Aviv University. That lady traced the department's history and came up with our names and research. She spoke to Meredith and Connor and you know the rest. Aaron is able to move and maneuver inanimate objects at will. I'm wondering if he can move people, too." Morgan paused for a reaction that failed to display. "We'll have to test that out tonight when ten-ton Gloria Brackett rolls through the front door..."

"Stop it, Morgan," Angela reproached.

"Right. Anyway, we'll examine the ways in which Aaron Shalit is able to maneuver heavy objects. Historically, we might easily make assumptions about ruins that have inexplicably exceeded the technological grasp of the architects and whose massive stone structures are of proportions honed with precise seamless edges for which we also have no explanation. We've got the Israeli studies being entered now. That brings me to what else is forthcoming by way of London.

"Dr. Gordon Smith's work is due to arrive along with an Indian friend of his, Amar Nishant, a mathematics wizard. Smith, with the help of the British government, will be sending us a team that has worked on EMP and other frequency field effects on the populace such as Intermediary Frequency Fields, Radio Frequency Fields, Static Electrical Fields, Static Magnetic Fields and such. We've information as to the sources and distribution of exposure in the population prior to the EMP with the embedded chips. We'll coordinate our results with theirs regarding the aftereffects on such areas as carcinogenicity, genotoxicity, and developmental and neuro-behavioral effects. That which was speculation in my day has been well proven beyond case studies. The upshot is that we will have in hand proven long-range EMP genetic consequences that have heretofore been supposition.

"On top of this, I bring your attention to the little boy in my granddaughter's artwork... the six children referenced by Caroline as imminent visitors... this boy from India, named Aditiya Nishant, is Amar's son. Here he is...right here," Morgan tapped the Indian boy's image.

Morgan asked the Monitor to pull Aditiya's file.

"No one has mentioned a connection with any special abilities for the Nishant boy and I'm pretty damn sure Gordon would have mentioned something. We do know he's a math wiz like his dad but his genetic markers are nothing special for his class of genius.

"Within the next four hours, the Nishant family will land on a private airstrip near Raleigh-Durham airport. Our security team will house them within the Consortium Research Annex so that they can be close to work and we can easily set up the new equipment. But I wonder about the boy. Should we bring the family of three here?"

Meredith advised that an intact family would be able to acclimate anywhere but the boy might appreciate friends.

"I figure it's smart to keep the boy in the company of other children," Green summed up as she peered at the photograph of the small Indian boy who, by appearances, seemed inconsequential.

"If he had something going on like CC and Aaron, I would imagine that it would have been well documented by Nishant and/or Smith. I hate to say that mathematical genius isn't anything special in this context but that's what I'm saying," Morgan finalized.

Morgan turned it over to his wife, whose instincts he trusted on such subjects.

"I'm going to leave where they stay to you, Angela. You meet them and figure it, Cookie."

"Yes, dear. Thank you. I'll meet and greet. If need be, I'll have the guest cottage prepared."

"Finally, I've requested a search for these other children Caroline has drawn and described. The entire Confederation is on the lookout; we should have some feedback soon. For my part, I find these serendipitous connections exhilarating," Morgan reported.

"We've speculated for decades, wondering about the chances of evolution happening before our eyes; the rapid increases in certain traits, positive and negative. Autism growing to three-fourths of the population, the isolation of genes found in all elite athletes, others in gifted mathematicians, still more occurring in creative types. Our research has collated strange anomalies that we have been able to record and analyze.

"There's been probably hundreds of unknown species of man in our unrecorded or lost human history. I see a few more on the horizon, most likely a result of the EMP twenty years ago."

Meredith Green remarked to Morgan that it would be prudent to curb enthusiasm until they got back into the lab.

"Please don't go on a tangent that demands an urgent reaction, Morgan. We're out of immediate danger," she advised.

"Are you out of your mind, woman? I'm done with being prudent. You are unable to acknowledge what's happening beyond immediate threats from lunatics? Our world is rapidly adjusting with a genetic boost most likely to have been triggered by an overload of electromagnetic pulses. That we are witnessing a modification within our genetic codes—as we stand here blabbing--doesn't worry you? That there's been a rekindling of latent abilities and a destruction of normal ones doesn't give you pause, Missy? For better or worse, we've managed to change our environment and now it's changed us! We are in the lab, Green! We're the lab rats!

"I'm not just talking about the physical environment. We were culturally compromised before the Darkness, too. We fought for obsolete jobs like fools. We stood by as the Feds took on good religious folk and cultural norms in the name of progressive thinking. We also knew that certain research results were skewed. Scientific communities allowed for the politicizing of science for chump change. Like prostitutes standing on the corner of Government Grant and Personal Notoriety, we published at the expense of honest inquiry. The janitor at the University once brought to me the crushed bodies of roaches that relentlessly crawled in our labs and conference rooms. He told me that we had an infestation problem. Did we ever! They were all spy-bots.

"I'm not going to waste a minute being prudent, Meredith. Let's get on with it." Morgan pounded his cane on the coffee table for emphasis.

"You're right," Meredith sighed. "I once appealed to President Brown to fund a project on behalf of our department. We spoke initially about the University's inroads to reproduce organs and identify genetic deficiencies. It was difficult to bring the possibilities to light. Brown looked bored; Commission cronies representing obscure concerns flanked him.

"'What's new?' asked one. So I launched into the ways we could identify and modify the bioluminescent gene from a deep-sea jellyfish and make mammals glow. Sort of a dog and pony show to bring genetic research home. I brought out the holographs. Under certain wavelengths of light, puppies and kittens lit up like Christmas trees. By using the bioluminescent gene from coral, for example, the test animals were yellow, red, and other colors of the rainbow, depending on the source. Our nation's leader envisioned the possibility of encoding convicted felons with fluorescent markers. Law enforcement, he says to me, could more easily identify glow in the dark color-coded criminals. He had a color code for every crime under the rainbow of possibilities.

"'We could expose criminals publicly... we'd be able to use special equipment to see offenders glow in the dark or identify the criminal element in other ways,' Brown exclaimed. Police, you see, would have special lights, Brown envisioned; they'd use these lights to distinguish convicted criminals from everyone else in a crowd. Tax evaders, he suggested, could glow green. I tried to explain that this process took place in the *embryonic* stage."

"'What are you saying?' the president pressed.

'We have no way to know who is going to be a criminal, Mr. President. It can't be done de facto', I said.

"He lost interest. I altered my approach. I moved to the financial savings our genetic inroads would bring our country, the market share on such research advances, the kind of thing that would once more make the United States an information leader. He didn't want to hear of it. He comes back with 'how are we going to support all those people living healthy for an additional 30 or 50 years?'

"That idea never actually occurred to me. All I managed to do was to scare the President of the United States. Healthy Americans that lived a healthier, longer life was not on the table. Brown saw most Americans as financial liabilities.

"I agree that we've got long reasons to be concerned. But yours is an undetermined agenda, Morgan. You're jumpy. Too many new outliers exceed the purview of our current research. It's too broad a brush stroke to properly examine that which you term a new evolutionary stage. We're going to get the bottom of it, but we're going to have to pull this in. We have international cooperation but I don't want to look crazy without defining our methodology."

"You're wrong, Missy!" Morgan noticed for the first time that Dr. Green felt overwhelmed. "You've got to have faith that something has landed in our laps in a way that is crazily beyond coincidental and we are geneticists! Get that tail out from between your legs, Meredith. Put on your big girl pants and think big."

"You don't go pushing around heavy objects just because of frequency influences on genes," Greene protested.

"Who says?" Morgan gritted his teeth with impatience. "Where the hell do you think this is going? I say it is because of radical environmental changes. Think about it...

"What makes a healthy genetic outcome as opposed to the kid who kills the neighborhood pets, Meredith? We've got basic societal evidence but it's time to examine the reasons that we have nature suddenly popping out kids with super powers and others that have remained amoral, non-thinking predators for generations. All of a sudden we've got altered or latent genes that are diametrically at odds. It puts our entire species at risk."

"You have a plan? These kids show up and you have a plan, Morgan, to treat them like guinea pigs until you can figure a specific path of inquiry?" Meredith asked.

"My own Adele had intensive work. I hardly regard our child or these special cases as test animals. Angela and I were thinking of our age difference and wanted a child. We did whatever was possible to help ensure Adele's future. We felt that way about genetic screening and we felt that way about good nutrition and intelligent, compassionate treatment."

"Wait a minute, Morgan. Angela, you knew that Adele's genes were tampered with?" Meredith asked.

It was Angela who was now annoyed.

"Of course I knew. I thank God we had the opportunity to screen and remedy in the embryonic stage as much as we have with attention to her cultural influences."

"See why I had to marry her, Missy?" Morgan crowed.

"And thank God they 'tampered' away," Adele added. "There were diseased, life-threatening genes discovered while I was in the womb." Adele took her mother's hand in support.

"It's not the time to gather support, to get permission, to come to a safe consensus. It's time to be brave and move forward," Adele emphasized.

"I know how people can be frightened. I'm not going to soon forget when bricks were thrown through our lab windows," Meredith frowned.

Angela did not hide her disappointment.

"This isn't the Meredith Green I remember. Better get your mojo back." Angela excused herself and departed the room with a final advisement. "Get yourself together, Meredith. Take the questions one by one. But we're not publishing university papers here. We're trying to save the human race."

Upstairs, Aaron and Rachel enjoyed their quarters. Rachel scrambled the house monitor with her own in the event it might pick up or record their conversations.

"How do you like CC? She's so cute, right?" Rachel smiled.

Aaron thought about his new friend and said, "She's the one with the lights I told you about. CC knows about me, too."

"How did that happen?" Rachel asked.

"Somebody visits us," Aaron attempted to explain. "I can see what the older girl sees. I saw CC and CC saw me through the girl."

"What does she look like, Aaron?"

"Really curly hair. And yellow!"

"Has she shown you anyone else?"

"A boy on a bigger boat than the one we came on. Huge. I would never be able to move it. I could see him through the girl's eyes."

A knock at the door interrupted them.

"Rachel, sorry to disturb you two but our monitor was unable to send you a schedule. I've taken the liberty to write it out. If you're too tired to join us this evening, please don't feel pressured," Angela said and slipped the week's meal plan under their door. "Please let us know if you have special dietary requirements or concerns," she added.

Rachel opened the door with apologies.

"Please don't be offended. I've been safeguarding Aaron for a long time and I get nervous about surveillance."

"Of course, dear. If anyone understands these precautions, it's our family. I'd do the same," Angela reassured.

"We're looking forward to celebrating this evening with your family," Rachel said eagerly.

"If we're lucky, we'll have three extra at our table. A family is meant to arrive from India. The boy is around the same age as Aaron and CC."

"Forgive me, please come in," Rachel invited as she moved from the door.

Angela took a seat beside Aaron, now sleeping soundly.

"What a lovely child," Angela commented, much as an admiring grandmother might.

"I'm prone to wonder about yet another child the same age showing up here. What about you?" Rachel asked.

"Well, we were expecting you and the Nishant family, although it's peculiar that everyone's schedule had an arrival time of today."

Rachel shook her head. "You know what I mean. Do CC and this boy have special abilities like Aaron?"

"You're just like those old attorneys," Angela laughed. "They never asked a question they didn't know the answer to. My guess is that you've got reason to believe that?"

"You first."

"I'm not exactly in the loop but I hear bits and pieces about everything, and the rest I research. When I take action, I like to have a firm position with Morgan. You know that old line regarding the matter of convincing the father that he may be the head of the family but I'm the neck?"

"When women didn't or couldn't have much say?" Rachel asked.

"Well, when women tended to more clever as to how they were saying it, anyway," Angela lightly chuckled.

Rachel relaxed and confided her thoughts.

"The way I figure it, these children communicate on another level. Previous generations got sucked into a swirling vortex of data and noise that destroyed our ability to self-reflect or hear naturally occurring external cues. It was a time of proxy realities that drowned, rather than amplified; information normally meant to enlighten us was unable to process. There was so much distraction and entertainment that humanity got played out of their minds. A flood of data...all that noise... and no room for solutions. I've thought about it as I was following the Israeli research. They correlated half a century or more of hyper-arousal to a sort of auditory exclusion. We couldn't hear ourselves think. We sure couldn't hear others think either. Now, it appears as if that might be changing."

"I assume Aaron knew about CC?" Angela asked simply.

"Yes. He insists that she knew about him, too. I know at some point we'll sit with them and discover how it works."

Angela rose and kissed Rachel on the forehead. "You'll discover you're in good company, Rachel. We love these children."

"Aaron is special in ways you can't imagine," Rachel claimed.

"Funny you say that. I've always thought all children were special in ways that escape us."

Chapter XII
The Nishants' Arrival

Friday, December 24, 2060

*T*he Nishant family disembarked along with research teams and their families. Pendergrass security identified the Nishants and convoyed them. The three exhausted travelers nodded off on the ride to Cary.

In anticipation of the arrival of new friends, CC rehearsed the JazzBazz troupe from the main floor, a flailing baton punctuated commands.

Aaron leaned over the top railing to examine the activities that had CC yelling encouragement. He puzzled at the lack of response from inanimate, non-motorized dolls. CC exited and reentered the room, sporting a feathered hat that had no immediate effect upon the performers.

"Welcome to JazzBazz!" CC announced to the empty seats. "All PMs must be turned off and you can't eat. Please leave barter-bits at the door on the way out because we need them. Lights out please, Monitor!" On cue, the lights faded and a 21st century techno version of *Entry of the Gladiators* swelled. CC bellowed directions that went unheeded.

"Do you need some help?" Aaron yelled from above. "I don't have theatre experience but I think I can make things move. I mean, I can probably swing them around if you tell me what they're supposed to be doing." Without waiting for a response, Aaron manipulated the dolls.

"Oh, Aaron! You have magic! Can you make them bow together at once?"

As much as he wanted to please his hostess, Aaron was unable to puppeteer to such nuances. They agreed to have the dolls respond with awkward jerking when CC called their names.

"If they want an encore, just plaster them all to the ceiling and I'll turn the lights out. We'll just drop down Sugar for the encore. Can you do that?"

"I think I can..."

"...everyone will just laugh their crazy heads off. You have skills, Aaron! We're going to be great friends."

"Thanks, CC. May I have another cookie?"

CC had never been asked for permission from anyone to do anything. Considering the sign, CC assumed the heady role of taking a new friend in hand as the savvy one of the pair. Should she allow a cookie or not?

"No, I'm so sorry... you may not have a cookie," came the decision. "We're going to be eating dinner and there is a table just for desserts. There is a mountain of them. I'll get killed if I try and sneak back into the kitchen now, with everyone losing their minds and running around and yelling at each other and then yelling their heads off at me as soon as I stick my head in the door. Stay away from that place till the robots take over. If we eat one dessert, my grandmother gets crazy. Unless you can float them out, you're going to get hung by your toes!" came the reasoning.

"Killed? Hung by my toes?" Aaron looked alarmed.

"Monitor, explain terms," CC directed her PM.

Morgan, Adele, Lex and Angela entered the foyer and eyed the two children suspiciously.

"What's the fuss?" Morgan laughed.

"I hired Aaron," CC replied absentmindedly. Her mind focused upon Aaron's aunt upstairs. "Rachel needs help. Can you help her, Grandma?" Caroline suggested. "Rachel doesn't know what to wear to dinner."

Adele volunteered, "I'll go up this time, Mother. Lex, please wait here with Mother for Elle and Gloria Brackett and keep a lookout for the Nishants. Don't leave Dad alone to greet them, please. They may run for their lives!"

Morgan cringed at his daughter's warning. "Give me some credit."

"I did," Adele said as she forwarded a selection of proto-types from her closet to Rachel's room.

Aaron and Caroline left the adults to inspect the tree. Angela returned to oversee dinner preparations. The three men stood to wait in the foyer with Meredith Green, who gritted her teeth the moment Morgan lit a cigar.

"I detest smoke, Morgan!" Meredith waved away the first puffs that sought her out.

"Hold your breath!" Morgan said testily. "God, woman. This is my home!" Morgan sauntered toward the library and motioned for the group to follow.

"All right boys – and the poor excuse for a woman – shall we pregame?"

Meredith took offense at once. "You talking to me, big guy?"

"No. I was talking about our unofficial daughter, Lex. Don't be so sensitive, Missy."

"I think we'd better be on our best behavior when the Nishants arrive," Connor suggested to offset Morgan's insult. "They're five minutes away. I'm pretty sure we've been warned to make them feel at home and we'll need our wits about us."

"What are you saying, boy?" Morgan groaned. "We're trying to be witless; that's the point."

"They don't drink," Connor tried.

"Okay. They don't have to drink," Morgan argued the point.

In this instance, Lex was of similar mind. Lex longed for relief. A Pendergrass gathering, anticipated Lex, promised a desultory exercise. His lackluster repartee sparked uneasy pauses that prompted Morgan to snort and chortle. Expected to be a good sport, Lex came up short as others spoke over and around him while he sought untimely retorts. Lex hated Pendergrass holidays.

Lex had once preferred alcohol to a tablet of Calm. In the last four years, Lex had begun to take equal doses of each as a holiday remedy.

"You want a tablet of Calm?" Lex held out one small white pill toward his brother while tossing another down his throat.

"Why would I want Calm? I've never taken that junk," Connor said.

"Your fiancée is about to arrive and you haven't taken your eyes off Miss Israel. I'm prescribing either Calm or sunglasses," Lex laughed hard and pushed a tumbler toward Connor. "Name your poison."

"Rachel Ben-Tov," Connor announced. Morgan's eyes grew wide at Connor's uncharacteristic candor.

"Well, you better be clear-headed. I don't want annual Christmas stories about the time your almost fiancée got jealous, started blasting insults at Miss Ben-Tov and then got blown out a window or something worse by her boy protector."

Meredith Green cringed at the careless reference to Aaron Shalit's ability.

"Morgan, not only should you not say those things, you shouldn't be thinking such things until we know more about how these children communicate."

Only one thing irked Morgan more than being reprimanded by Meredith, and that was Meredith's lack of humor.

"If there's anything we shouldn't be thinking, it's opinions about everything that can go wrong. Tip-toeing around stuff? Not going to do it. We're good people. If these kids know anything, I'd put barter-bits on them getting that picture. After all, it's called evolution. Need I remind you that not one of these youngsters has nanobots in their bloodstreams? No neural amps? Yet, they seem to have superb health and pretty edgy capabilities and insight. They've likely been endowed with a sense of humor, Meredith. This isn't an episode of the *Twilight Zone* and you're not Judge Judy," Morgan said apoplectically.

Meredith poured a tumbler of scotch into a glass and sighed.

"What in Sam Hill are you talking about, Morgan? I'm not going to waste a moment reckoning obscure references from your glory days!" she said, sipping the scotch. "Let's just forgive and forget...it's Christmas Eve!" she concluded.

Morgan scoffed, "Missy, I'm not Lord Jesus and I don't have Alzheimer's, but I'll toast a noble capitulation!"

A buzzer signaled the arrival of the Nishants. Morgan and Lex had forgotten Adele's instructions.

"We're coming," Morgan yelled into the PM.

"Do you like chicken?" Morgan suddenly turned toward Meredith.

"Sure?"

"Here," he said, offering his elbow, "take a wing."

Morgan escorted Meredith out of the room, followed by the Collins brothers. The robot waited instructions to open the door.

"Let's welcome the Nishants!" Morgan's cigar spewed enthusiasm, his chin jutted upward, and he adjusted a red and green bowtie for emphasis.

"Stop!" Angela rushed into the room past the group to the front door. "You're letting the Bot open the door, Morgan? I recall Adele asking that Lex personally meet and greet!"

Angela opened the door and crossed the threshold. Her face morphed from furious to festive before Morgan processed the scolding.

"I'm so, so happy you've made it here on Christmas. We're so pleased to have you as our guests! Welcome!" Angela gushed.

Morgan muttered under his breath and Meredith whispered in his ear.

"Be thankful for the woman still in your life who makes you appear decent."

"Get a breath mint," Morgan whispered back. "Be thankful they still make them."

Indu, Amar, and Aditiya Nishant walked slowly amongst the welcoming party, who were careful to avoid speaking over one another in the event simultaneous remarks could not be effectively deciphered. To this end, Angela signaled the household to gather into an organized reception line.

Two of the family hounds by the fireplace raised their heads with interest and barked. Neither moved to investigate. Facing the prospect of meeting strangers in a strange land, Aditiya grabbed his mother's sari like a lifeline.

CC introduced herself as 'Caroline Collins, the producer of JazzBazz' and turned to introduce her new friend. "This is Aaron Shalit from Israel!" CC reached around Indu Nishant to offer her hand to Aditiya, who reluctantly released his mother's skirt.

"Come on! We've a lot of Moravian sugar cookies!" CC shared that which she considered to be the Pendergrass kitchen's best-kept secret.

Aditiya envisioned the cookies in CC's mind and followed her lead. Angela pointed toward her running granddaughter and Aaron, who broke from the reception ranks for the pantry.

"That was my granddaughter leading your son to trouble," Angela apologized to Amar and Indu. "The other young boy is Aaron Shalit, and this lovely woman is Rachel Ben-Tov, Aaron's guardian from Israel," Angela introduced pleasantly.

Morgan thought the introductions irritatingly time-consuming and thrust his hand toward the Nishants.

"I'm Morgan Pendergrass and it's my pleasure to have you in our home. You can ask anyone here for help or answers. But I'm going to be the one you'll eventually mean to search out. Best to start with the Big Cheese."

"The Big Cheese?" Indu repeated.

"The biggest!" assured Morgan.

"Certainly the cheesiest," Meredith added.

Unable to explain all things cheese, Angela maneuvered the Nishants toward all things Collins.

Blue moved into the room with Caroline and Aaron. Never having seen a dog, Aditiya bowed low to investigate. Blue licked the length of the boy's face.

CC felt that she should let Aditiya know that he needn't lick the dog in return. "It's a kiss. You can just pet him back," she advised by way of demonstration.

"I don't lick animals," Aditiya indignantly declared.

Introductions were interrupted by a new set of arrivals.

"These would be our friends Gloria Brackett and Elle Smythe," Angela announced.

Gloria entered the home with six homemade pies on a bot.

"The pecan pie has your name on it," Gloria called to Morgan. "And by the way, I never once spilled cranberry sauce in your home, you storyteller."

"Wait...I told Meredith that she was the cranberry slob, not you, Gloria!" Morgan objected.

Meredith laughed, "That's the only way I was going to get Gloria to bake six glorious pies; I told her that you said she couldn't cook worth a damn and spilled cranberry sauce. She got mad as a wet hen."

"Well done, Missy," Morgan admired; he slapped Meredith Green on the back as she emptied her drink and began to choke.

Gloria regarded Meredith and Morgan. "Merry Christmas, you two troublemakers."

Morgan eyed the pie-laden bot cart and said, "You are as resplendent in pies as your ample bosom, Gloria. It's that same bosom that keeps the cranberry and gravy from ruining heirloom tablecloths. So, no worries there either."

Shortchanged for a rational explanation, Angela gave none to the struggling Nishants, who tried to reconcile breast and pie references.

Elle's arrival startled everyone when she ran in from the kitchen entrance. Squealing with delight, Connor's girlfriend twirled in the foyer like a drunken dervish.

"I love the tree...lights...the flowers...!" she twirled and commented, arms stretched upward and wide.

"Thank you," Angela smiled, a stock version of the gesture. "May I introduce our guests who've traveled from London?"

Elle Smythe's mind made a forced landing.

As everyone suffered the introductory redundancies, Rachel's eyes followed Connor as he slid silently away from the reception line. He turned and signaled Rachel to follow suit.

Coats were removed and presents placed under the tree. Refreshments were passed amongst guests. Morgan supplied eggnog separated as the genuine variety from the less authentic teetotaler version. Rachel slipped away unnoticed to join Connor in the dining room.

Elle had not sought Connor, nor did she ask about his whereabouts. It was Adele that Elle cornered.

"What do you think of my new dress?" Elle asked as the twirling began once more.

"You'll have to stand still so we can take a good look," Adele suggested.

Elle ceased to call attention to herself one way and launched another that focused on a dress. Given the depth of the topic, everyone struggled mightily to feign interest.

"I'm not the person to ask about fashion," Adele excused herself. "I just care if it's comfortable or not. How do you feel in that dress?"

Elle frowned and asked, "What's that mean? You don't think I look good?"

"It's Christmas eve, Elle. We have guests. Let's get to know them. They can't relate to fashion choices or the elaborate wedding you have in mind. They've escaped a very restricted life down to being chipped and monitored. Let's make them feel the power of our celebration of family and God."

"You're saying I'm tacky, right?" Elle's hands rested petulantly upon her hips. "You always kinda look at me like I'm not up to Pendergrass standards. I know y'all make fun of my name. You made fun before I changed my name and after I changed my name. Y'all are just plain mean Polecats."

Adele apologized earnestly. "May I please explain that episode?" Adele meant to correct a misunderstanding between them.

"Elle might be pronounced like the letter but it's not spelled as the capital 'L'. We thought at first that you were light-hearted; it didn't occur to us you didn't know the French spelling. I wrote out the proper name. Then there was the matter of your new middle name that you changed to 'Channel'. With two 'ns', it was no longer the former fashion house but a synonym for a waterway or bandwidth. You misunderstood the spellings of your preferred names and when we tried to help, you threw a tantrum, insisting that it was a matter of creative interpretation. Which is fine. But if it weren't for Connor, you'd be walking around with the name L Channel Smythe. In that case, your first two names would have shared the frequency that broadcasts North Carolina's Commons daily fishing reports from Bass Lake," Adele explained.

"You have to always correct me. I get tired of everyone trying to fix everything I do or say," Elle sulked. "This happens all the time. Why don't you like me?"

Adele considered the timing. Should she come clean or once again sweep Elle issues under the rug?

"It takes but a moment to ask the monitor the proper spelling of Elle and Chanel by simply pronouncing or spelling. It's the lack of curiosity, the surety of knowing things you've yet to investigate, and then the resentment of constructive criticism that bothers me. If you want to have my opinion on matters, I think you should have informed opinions on those matters, too. Reach out a little bit, Elle. Let's move beyond what you want or what you're wearing and observe the world around us," Adele finished and prepared for the backlash.

"Whatever. You can't tell me what is correct and not," Elle said furiously.

"I rest my case, Elle. I'm not pretending to talk fashion ever again. Please don't ask my opinion. Ultimately, it's your opinion that matters. I want out of decisions that are never made and reoccurring questions that endlessly loop. You love the process. You like to hear yourself talk. Talk to a mirror!" Adele challenged Elle.

Elle glared at Adele and said nothing.

"For the record," Adele added, "that transparent pea-green laced-up dress hugging your hips so tight your two girls are popping out inches from your chin is literally over the top!"

"You do like it!" Elle squealed happiness to Adele's astonishment.

CC tugged on Elle's dress and said, "Merry Christmas! I think you look very pretty in that dress."

Elle smiled down at an admiring fan.

"Well, Merry Christmas to you little Miss CC. I love your dress, too!"

"I have cookies. Would you care for one?" CC offered one of many retrieved from her pocket.

Elle smoothed her hands over her hips for emphasis. "If you've got a dress like this, you can't go eating sugar cookies, sweetie! Gotta watch it or you'll end up looking like Gloria Brackett over there," advised Elle without malice.

Caroline took Elle's hand in hers and held it. Adele thought CC's approach curiously out of character.

Elle relaxed while Caroline stroked her hand for several minutes. Neither spoke.

CC gave a final squeeze and departed to join Aaron and Aditiya, who had discovered the joys of sliding down stair railings. The pair landed in an overstuffed clothes hamper filled with Blue's bedding.

Elle remained transfixed and motionless for several more minutes while Adele lingered. As if infused with an inner understanding, Elle looked apologetically into Adele's eyes, contrite tears quietly brimming.

"I'm not very smart. I'm jealous green of y'all and I don't know why. Y'all have been nothing but kind to me. I just never know what to say. I'm sorry, Adele." Elle hung her head.

"I wish that you would pay more attention to what you could do to help yourself or lend a hand to those around you, Elle. That's what I meant to get across to you. Perhaps if you'd donate some time at the school or help out on the farm? When you get to know how we spend our time you may understand a great deal more about Connor," Adele suggested kindly.

"I'm stupid, Adele. I didn't get the education. You know that. But I'll try," she said with a faraway look. Elle walked away and sat alone by the fireplace.

Good God, thought Adele, *I think she's having a moment of reflection.*

Aditiya and Aaron became fast friends.

"Can you tell me why dolls hang in American homes?" Aditiya ate a handful of chocolate almonds CC had given him.

Aaron laughed, "That's CC's theatrical group. We have a show later. You can help us if you want."

Aditiya wanted nothing to do with playing with dolls and said so.

Caroline entered and announced, "We have new friends that will come here."

"How do you know?" Aaron asked simply.

"I don't know how I know. Everybody keeps asking me why I said something or drew something or where I saw something or how I thought about something. I keep saying I don't know because I don't know. I knew you two were going to be here but I didn't know you were coming at Christmas. I would have gotten you some presents or something."

"You saw the blond girl with curls?" Aditiya asked excitedly. "She laughs a lot. She arrives in dreams."

"She likes some kind of ice cream called pistachio," Caroline confirmed.

"I thought she was just a dream. Then I didn't."

"I can see people in the day, or just walking around. I saw you two..." CC stopped short. She recalled her mother's warning to avoid certain topics.

Aditiya poked CC lightly. "What's wrong?"

"I was thinking that I should be quiet and wait," she finally said. "My mum asked me to be careful when someone asks questions about seeing people when they aren't here. I think that means y'all, too."

Aaron laughed. "Same here! Aunt Rachel doesn't like questions. I think she means adults."

"Can you just answer something for me?" Aditiya's eyes popped. "One thing?"

Aditiya, thought CC, wiggled and fidgeted unnaturally.

"I said no questions about things until parents are with us," CC finalized in a way that mimicked her grandfather's style of handling a usurper. Seeing the effect on her guest, CC was regretful.

"Ok, one question." CC held up her forefinger for emphasis.

"When you look around at things do you see tiny little dots on everything? And sometimes can you see your hand kind of melt into the dots? And at night...it's easier at night... you might see through the walls and ceilings when the lights are off?" Aditiya carefully asked.

Aaron remained adamantly silent. He thought CC wise to suggest restraint and foolish to retract the suggestion. CC thought Aditiya's question no more than a harmless observation.

"Everyone sees that, Aditiya." CC tried to process the reason for Aditiya's confusion.

"No one sees dots. Just ask. My parents don't know what I'm talking about!" Aditiya insisted.

"Rachel can't see circled hazes or blue lights either," Aaron corroborated Aditiya's predicament. "I can even see through my closed eyes!" he added.

Aaron recounted an instance in the research center as he settled down for a nap. Rachel rose from her seat to open a window. Aaron noticed a guard making a gesture to another that stood behind her back. The meaning of the gesture escaped him, but Aaron was compelled to tell the guards to stop what they were doing.

"What's so weird about that?" CC asked.

"My eyes were closed. I could see through closed eyes. Sometimes when I'm sleeping or tired and it's dark, I'm not sure if my eyes are open or shut. My Aunt Rachel replayed what the guards did on the monitor. It was something bad because she kicked one of them between his legs. He yelled and the alarms went off. The other guard reached for Rachel and I floated him..." Aaron paused recalling the expression on the second guard suspended briefly inches under the ceiling. "We never saw them again," Aaron finished.

"You see the dots though?" Aditiya asked specifically.

"Yes."

"Do you notice that sometimes the dots are in motion around here?" Aaron's mind went to several times he had noticed waves of pulsating streams on the Pendergrass horizon.

"No. Just dots that don't move," Aditiya clarified.

There was silence among the three children that connected them in a new way.

"Let's get out of here. Want to see Blue again? We have a lot of animals but Blue and Traveller are the only ones that can be indoors. Blue is put away in his room by the kitchen," Caroline suggested.

"He's already sniffed me and put his tongue in my nose. I'm fine," Aditiya flatly refused.

Morgan watched with interest the exchanges between the children. When the Nishants were escorted upstairs, he made his leave.

"Excuse me. Take your time freshening up. I'm going to have a word with the children."

Indu and Amar Nishant passed the three joyful children who chattered like excited birds, the young innocent sounds of discovery. A long-forgotten memory of her family prompted a smile. Glancing skyward, she caught sight of suspended dolls in altered states. Indu erupted with delight. The foreign sound of her own laughter troubled her.

"We'll be singing some Christmas songs instead of JazzBazz and going to the Church for midnight service," Morgan called to Indu from across the room. "We won't be having the doll show. My wife says it's inappriate and you'll be too tired…"

"May we go with you to the church service?" Indu quickly responded. "We wouldn't want to miss a real Christmas cele-bration in an actual church!"

Morgan yelled with thumbs up, "You betcha!"

Morgan took an awkward seat beside Caroline and her new friends; a motorized leg quietly calibrated and whirred into position on a lower stair.

Aditiya tapped Morgan's leg and offered his approval. "It's hard! What happened?"

"I wore out this leg running track in college. I couldn't give it up. So I had more operations and finally I've got this thing that can kick a football twice the length of a stadium."

The children smiled politely. No one recognized the term 'football' and the translator was set to verbatim.

Morgan took his granddaughter's hand and whispered his reservations. "Look Caroline, I appreciate your efforts but we're going to forget JazzBazz. We have guests here that may not be ready for Aaron's kind of talent. I'm thinking we want to be as normal as possible for at least 24 hours," Morgan explained.

"Ok with you, Aaron?" CC whispered, following her grandfather's lead. Aaron nodded his agreement. "I know how people act when I move things in the air..."

"Wait. You move things...how?" Aditiya exclaimed.

Morgan smiled. "He doesn't know exactly how he does it, I suspect. I'd suggest that we remain a little quiet until we understand more about your wonderful abilities. We'll have to take a rain check for tonight's performance."

"What's a rain check?" Caroline asked.

"We'll do it another time. Postpone the show for another time when everyone is properly prepared. When something gets rained out in open theaters, they used to give a ticket to let the audience come back on a clear day. Trust me on this."

"Okay, Grandpa. I'm just saying this is inside and it's not raining."

Aditiya tugged on Aaron's jacket. "How do you move things, Aaron? Can you show me?" he pleaded.

"Not now, okay?"

Aditiya frowned.

Morgan rose and CC handed him the cane her grandmother had removed after Morgan flipped Blue mid-air when the dog jumped for the couch. The dog landed on his back. For thirty long seconds, everyone thought the dog dead.

"Can I show them Blue and the stables?" CC became an eager tour guide.

"Give your guests some breathing room," Morgan suggested and left.

"We're leaving," Caroline directed the boys. "Grandpa says you need breathing room. We're going to the stables."

Adele carried a tray of tea servings up to the Nishants' rooms. She served refreshments and took the opportunity to open closets that accommodated clothes as well as concealed a control panel.

"The monitor is yours to use as you please, doctors. You know how this one operates, I presume?" Adele ventured.

Indu and Amar touched the controls and examined the options. "With the exception of our time in London, we've been at the other end of Monitor controls for the previous nine years, I'm afraid. We've never owned a central Monitor. Thank you. We feel as if in a sweet dream, Mrs. Collins."

"Please call me Adele. If there's anything you need only refer to the bot numbers. Everything can be manually or voice controlled, with or without security, with or without hologram projections. We've secured the home and farm as well as possible.

"The reason?" Indu asked.

"We conduct research on site; there's a children's school on the property and then there's Morgan's position within the Confederation," Angela explained.

* * *

Downstairs in the Pendergrass kitchen, the action had culminated with spectators and too many cooks. Elle joined Angela, Gloria and Meredith in the kitchen standing in a semi-circle, intently focused upon simmering poached pears.

"Looks like y'all are birthing a baby cat," Elle announced. Everyone squirmed at the reference.

Elle selected a position amongst the women and surveyed the process. Gloria finished brushing the glaze on peeled, half-baked red Anjou Pears. Indescribable aromas emanated from food platters that fought for space.

Elle grew up without the benefit of field-grown crops that had been planted, harvested, and prepared. She was accustomed to government-issued Nutrition Cubes until the Darkness stopped production and distribution. As did hundreds of millions, Elle and her father ran out of cubes. By the time they made it to their Nutrition Distribution Center, the warehouse had been emptied.

Fate had intervened when Connor and she met. It was not long afterwards that a wide-eyed Elle encountered 3-D printers that magically produced whole food from capsulated ingredients.

Most food items in the Pendergrass kitchen were, therefore, indistinguishable to Elle. She struggled to pronounce, categorize, and refine her knowledge of a modern kitchen. Rows of colored spices with alien names and histories filled her ear as she touched each item with her PM. Elle marveled at the women whose pride in cooking skills became evident as each shared small secret tricks of the trade amongst the group. Elle had once considered the act of cooking insignificant and tedious. For the first time in her life, Elle was able to absorb the complexities of what was going on around her.

"I want to learn how to cook. I've never learned," Elle announced. In startled unison, the women looked up with the unusual pronouncement. Only Gloria regarded Elle's as an important moment.

"Cook what, dear?" Gloria asked.

Elle thought about it then answered, "As soon as I learn how to make pies, people will smile when they see me coming."

Even though the Pendergrass kitchen was fully bot-equipped, Gloria agreed to engage an eager student on the spot.

"Come watch me. I'll prepare and brush the glaze. We'll return the pears to the compartment and reduce the heat. By the time we're ready for desert, you and I will run back in here and crank the temperature up for three minutes. It'll be perfect. Then we're gonna spruce it up to look fancy with a mint leaf and a little whipped cream!"

"Can't a bot do that temperature thing?" Elle asked.

"The point is we can do it, too. We'll take pride in the work we invest with attention to detail. Our messed up blouses and wayward splattered spots will bear witness to the love we share. We'll cherish the smiles our friends will dispense with each bite. It's like that, Elle. Cooking teaches us science, math, and it's art, too! It's most of all a tribute to nature's gifts while an intimately shared experience. Still want to be my student?"

"Absolutely!" she cried.

* * *

Connor and Rachel stood in the corner of the grand dining room, bathed in the flickering light of a listing Christmas tree. Candles placed throughout the rooms made the crystal sparkle.

She's exquisite, thought Connor as Rachel's wide, moist green eyes caught the candlelight.

"Why did you signal me?" Rachel asked.

"Why did you follow?" Connor smiled.

"You'll have to adjust that passive-aggressive translator," Rachel retorted.

"That didn't come out right. I just meant that I'm happy as hell you're here," Connor frantically corrected.

"You're staring again, Connor. If I'm not mistaken, don't you have a fiancé running around here in a long green and white lace dress?"

"That's Elle, all right," Connor agreed. "I've yet to give her a ring. Everyone assumes...I assumed...until tonight," he awkwardly spurted an explanation that made Rachel flinch.

"Are you serious?"

"I'm dead serious," Connor continued. "It's important that you understand my situation."

"Get hold of yourself. Shame on you," Rachel said without disguising her disgust. "You have no idea who I am. You've embarrassed us both. How dare you not take me seriously?"

Connor laughed, "I know who you are, and I'm the last person who would underestimate your standards. We've a lot of data sent per the Tel Aviv research. I know the risks you took, your compassion, your interrogations that bordered on an inquisition, the insistence to be part of each part of the study conducted on Aaron, and your suggestion that you undergo the same scrutiny in order to be beside Aaron, so as not to traumatize him. It was a grueling experience. I know all of that. I also appreciate that your parents and loved ones were brutally killed. I'm aware of your friendship with Shoshanna and the pains you took to befriend the Shalit family after her death. You took care of the Shalit household for nearly five years. I know your IQ and the way you searched each day, many hours a day, about our genome projects at the Research Triangle. It was part of my job to understand the nurturing stages of Aaron as much anything else that came across my monitor. You learned about the Confederation, our history, and our laws. You investigated the Research Triangle and the Pendergrass stories as well as Cary's school system. What I didn't know – what no amount of data could possible tell me – is how wonderful you are in person. The pretty part is right and that's just fine, too," Connor said, very much aware that he was staring.

"Interesting," Rachel commented. She could not resist peering back into Connor's intense blue eyes but said nothing more.

"Look, all I'm saying is let's get to know each other..." Connor asked.

Rachel scrutinized Connor's face for half a minute, until Connor's uneasiness confirmed his intentions.

"You're old," Rachel shrugged and took another sip of the spiked eggnog.

"I'm older than you. That doesn't make me old. You're just a little younger..."

"I'm just playing. But no way am I going to get to 'know you' with a woman around who talks about a wedding. It sounds weird. I'm not going to be played like you're clearly playing that poor girl."

"You know that's not true. You know it, and I know you know it. She's never been for me and she even knows it. She's living a fantasy."

"You are now embarrassing her one way or the other," Rachel insisted.

"That's not true. I've said it a million ways and times. I'm not equipped to hurt her by shunning her completely. I'm not equipped to marry her either," Connor admitted sadly.

"I don't know your history so you have me at a disadvantage. You can be sure I'll have all I need to know by tomorrow!" Rachel sneered.

"You admit that you're a little interested?" Connor asked hopefully.

"I don't deny it," Rachel allowed as her right cheek's dimple took shape.

Lex and Adele entered the dining room, failing to notice the whispering couple in the far corner. Adele checked place cards.

"I could have sworn I put Connor here and Elle across from him," Adele puzzled aloud to Lex.

Before Adele changed the altered seating arrangements once more, Connor spoke up.

"I took the liberty of rearranging some of our guests!"

"You scared the hell out of us, Connor," Adele accused.

Adele's attention moved toward Rachel, who stared awkwardly into an empty glass of eggnog.

"Of course. Whatever you think," Adele finished. Lex and Adele requested the chandelier light to fade as they departed. Candlelight swiftly warmed the room once more.

"Dinner in thirty, Connor...heads up! That is, if it isn't already," Lex laughed.

"What grade are you in again, Lex?" Rachel objected.

"Just a bad joke," Lex quickly offered.

"Yes, you are," Rachel finished.

"Wow," Connor gasped, "the chutzpah!"

"I'm the one with chutzpah? Your brother is the one with the gall." Rachel eyes narrowed upon Connor's.

"I meant my brother, Rachel. I'm sorry for his outrageous remark," Connor said with seriousness. "I would appreciate some quarter here. My brother isn't a mean guy. He is socially awkward at best."

Connor had observed Rachel for over a year. He had reviewed daily transcripts of everyone's interaction with Aaron Shalit. He had been witness to Rachel's reaction to two guards who had unwisely ignored protocols. When the young woman decided to remove Aaron from Israeli scrutiny, she mindfully and passionately presented her case before the country's best minds. Connor had concluded that the woman's energy and purpose was without equal. As Connor thought all of this, he impulsively drew her delicate hand to his cheek and held it there.

"May I kiss your hand?" he smiled.

"Yes," she said simply.

Chapter XIII
One Door Closes

Budapest, Hungary
Friday, December 24, 2060

*F*amily and friends of the Meszaros family walked slowly behind the horse-drawn coffin moving in light snow flurries that softly sprinkled and blew like crystallized dust across the Kerepesi Temeto. A funeral would forever blemish their Christmas holiday. Attila Meszaros held the hand of daughter Ildiko with one hand, the other resting to the side of his wife's coffin upon the carriage. To the front was the priest who led the cortège of mourners. From a small chapel, bells rhythmically chimed their solemn message.

The 19th century, 55-hectare graveyard had once lain in disrepair, the resting place of iconic Hungarian cultural and political luminaries. Hungary had rebuilt its infrastructure and restored historical landmarks that included the famous cemetery. Statues and graves that were ravaged by time and the 20th century Soviet Union Communists were finally restored. Mausoleums were returned to original marble luster, the grounds cultivated into gardens, and each small gravestone lovingly resurrected. The remains purposely left untreated were those that hosted leaders of the Communist regime who had once conjured excuses to exhume political leaders accused posthumously of capitalistic crimes. It was a cemetery that had always accepted those who either committed suicide or were executed as casualties of Hungarian nationalism.

It was in this restored historical graveyard that Attila would lay to rest his loving wife, Noemi, whose life was prematurely terminated by a covert Russian agent's spouse. Orchestrated to appear as a suicide, Attila knew better. The Hungarians discovered the long-forgotten wife of Major Molnar within hours of discovering Noemi's broken body. Attila's wife had been thrown from the fifth story over a balcony railing onto the cold cement of their apartment building's enclosed court-yard. The murderer mistakenly believed she had discovered her husband's assassin.

Attila sat in an insignificant meeting across the Szabad Ter quad, a two-minute walk from their home, the moment his wife had answered the door to be bludgeoned with a metal pipe. Ildiko collected favored drawings, poems and photo-graphs and spent two days crafting a keepsake. Noemi's only child gently placed the memorial beside her mother's resting body inside the coffin before the lid's final closure.

Prayers were recited and the priest spoke while the elev-en-year old stoically stood beside her father. Ildiko kissed the back of her father's hand, patted it softly, and whispered child-like reassurances as the coffin was lowered. Without warning, Ildiko fainted into a small heap at her father's feet, miscon-strued as the result of exhaustion and grief.

Ildiko floated effortlessly far above the gravesite, detached yet able to observe her earthly surroundings. Attila bent to recover his daughter's limp body from the frozen ground. Sit-uated in the warm cabin of a waiting car, someone's coat en-veloped the girl's body. The priest consoled the sobbing father.

"I've never seen him cry," Ildiko marveled above the scene.

"He's cried, precious," her mother's voice was unmistakable.

"I'd like you to come back with me, Mother. Please come back to us." Ildiko turned and faced her mother. It was the same illuminated beautiful face that had softly sung her to sleep, kissed troubles away, and uttered an endless stream of encouraging words, smiling once more at her.

"I can't live without my mother," Ildiko's eyes and soul pleaded a desperate case.

Noemi had a message that filled Ildiko's mind.

You have abilities that will grow. Your obligation is to remain moral and trust in the path you will take. You have a purpose...

"I cannot live without you..." Ildiko repeated.

We are forever connected...always near one another. Please listen, my love. Her mother's soft image became clearer. *You will move to a place called the Confederation of American States. It will be your new home. Tell your father this.*

A mother's love enveloped Ildiko and pierced deep within the daughter's soul with a love so strong that it supplanted searing pain with faith. Ildiko felt her mother's peace and assuredness.

Tell your father to train the horses, follow the blue light, and love well, her mother advised before fading.

"I love you," Ildiko reached for a fading light.

I love you more, Noemi's essence whispered throughout her daughter's soul as Ildiko returned to her body.

Without a word between them, father and daughter attended midnight mass in Ybl's St. Steven's Basilica near their home on Perczel Mor Utca. Friends and neighbors surrounded them during a time when most were happily celebrating Christmas Eve with families. The priest who presided over Noemi's burial walked over to offer communion to those grieving. Attila stared ahead with swollen eyes and waved the priest away.

Saturday, December 25, 2060

Attila refused the prescribed tranquilizers and rose at 4:30 a.m. He meant to finish the decorating interrupted by a knock at the door three days prior. Hidden presents were retrieved from the attic and placed neatly under the tall fir beside Linzer cookies that had been pre-packaged in tight-lidded tins.

At 7:00 a.m. Ildiko was awakened by the traditional ringing of St. Nicholas' bell and to aromas of freshly made palacsinta rolled in dark chocolate and crushed walnuts. Baked cinnamon apples sat as an aside for unfilled pancakes. As her father sprinkled the last of the powdered sugar atop the Hungarian crepes, Ildiko walked into the kitchen.

"Merry Christmas, Papa," Ildiko quietly greeted. She didn't know what to make of a traditional Christmas breakfast that followed her mother's death.

"Was it a dream?" Ildiko asked in tears. "I woke up and I remembered...my mother is dead. Is it a bad dream, Papa?" Attila spread his arms, summoning his daughter into them.

"We're not going to let this tragedy overwhelm us, my darling daughter. We have each other and we will honor your mother with a good life," he said confidently.

Ildiko nodded in agreement. "I think that's what she meant when she told me that we should love well."

"When was that, Édes?" Attila served the baked apples and made espresso for himself.

"At the funeral. She spoke to me when I fell asleep and told me to tell you that we should go live at the Confederation."

Attila took a seat. He knew that his daughter would have no idea of the word "Confederation" and their country's decades-long cooperation with the entrepreneurial American, Dr. Pendergrass. How could she know of the relationship between Hungary and Pendergrass Enterprises? He had a reason to trust his daughter's post-mortem experience. He, too, felt his wife's presence.

Attila struggled to remain composed. "What else did she say?"

"That you would understand about going to the Confederation...that she loves me and we are always connected...for us to love well...something about training the horses and to follow the blue light. She was there!"

Their sadness could not be eradicated and the day passed slowly. The monitor was set to mute, although there were countless condolence notes and food containers sent to the home. The exterior monitor explained the privacy settings and kind neighbors collected the food and flowers in the interim. It was the aftermath of a funeral. Attila had attended too many with his wife. He was lost without her.

Father Hajtos visited late in the afternoon and sat with father and daughter for hours in the darkened room amongst an array of candles meant to offset the growing shadows. Attila drank three shots of Unicom within as many minutes. With a raised eyebrow, Attila signaled Ildiko that he was ready to speak.

"Let's share our experiences that we had with Mother, shall we?" Attila broke the uncomfortable silence.

Father Hajtos was encouraged. "I agree! It's good therapy to speak about your life together..." he sympathized.

"No. I'm talking about our experience after Noemi passed," Attila corrected the priest's impression.

Ildiko shared with the priest her mother's image appearing at the burial site, the messages she intuited, and the loving words and feelings that had been exchanged.

Attila expressed a similar experience that he felt initially as a dream but realized there was a physical sensation of his departed wife being beside him. "I also was urged to move to North America."

Father Hajtos listened. He thoughtfully ate another cookie, dipped it methodically into his espresso and said nothing.

Ildiko spoke once more when the old priest finished the last bite of his fifth cookie.

"Do you think it's true?"

"Of course, Ildiko. Why wouldn't I?" The priest placed his empty coffee cup and plate back on the dining room table and stood to leave. His wrinkled, calloused hands clasped those of a man rarely seen in his church but whose financial contributions had helped it thrive.

"I might not see either of you again. Are you prepared to actually move to North America?"

"Hell no. But we're going," Attila smiled at his daughter with the decision that had just been made.

Ildiko watched as the elderly priest rose and struggled with his heavy black coat.

"Have faith...know that God loves and protects you," the priest advised, brushing away the cookie crumbs from his pants. Attila broke the afternoon's civility and the priest's words of comfort with a tidal wave of frustration.

"Believe in what?" Attila angrily interrupted. "I believe that life's undeserved horrors are evidence of random chaos, Father.

That's not to say that I don't believe in what you do or can't admire your community service. God? I'm not going to believe in fairy tales!"

"You speak that way now, when your daughter is most in need of reassurance?" the priest asked.

"I've no reassuring thoughts about how to fill this emotional void with anything but the rawest pain. Why does the Church always seem to fall short of spiritual nourishment? Here, take the travel kit. You'll get what you want in the afterlife. We can't seem to get a full meal, a real explanation in the here and now. Frankly, I'm starving here. People operate best with stringent dogma and rules with cause and effect. I get it. Do this, do that...go to heaven!? Guys in robes do our thinking. Isn't that so, Father? You eat cookies and tell me to be brave and keep the faith? You have nerve to tell me to reassure my daughter with the same pap you are peddling to me?

"Rather than extrapolate a common theme amongst all the religious tributaries, we ignorant sheep are instructed that there is one route to God on top of all the other rubbish. You represent all of the bureaucratic religious middlemen acting as gatekeepers to God Almighty!

"We actually pay you to translate for us, guide our decisions, and even allow the idea of excommunication if we deviate from official dictates. Good or Godly men who are so sure that they know what's best for us that they intimidate without reserve while telling us how much we're loved. How can you sell benevolence and hell at the same time? You don't find that a bit confusing? Oh yes. For that kind of answer, we need to keep coming to Church.

"It seems to me that we get whittled down to cowards, so afraid of life and death but for the intermittent bubbles of hope, happiness and a sense of duty that sustains us. Hoping in God, supporting religion, is like carefully nurturing rose bushes in anticipation of their ever-so-brief beautiful blooms. Yet the wandering deer managed to nip off each of those budding roses, leaving us with only the systemic plant in desperate need of more care, robbing us of the payoff every time. I'm sorry if I suspect those pontificating high above the crowds on organizational pulpits that nip off the tender rose buds of our souls."

The priest watched as Attila began to pace. Ildiko stood motionless.

"These religious institutions are also political institutions, creating needs, vying for allegiances--the exact behaviors of nation-states. We are inculcated to believe that it's our filial duty to protect our way of life against others, we've been told, who mean to destroy us. Us against Them.

"Humankind has had the option to coordinate the best of history's cultural messages, reconciling the best ideas that promise to make us whole. Whose fault is it that this doesn't happen? I say it may be little men with little minds wearing oversized hats and robes that carry emotional weapons – the big God promise – for heaven and redemption. No, Father. We're a long way from spiritual stone soup. Keep the faith? It means that I should righteously refute my spiritual intuition and follow religious and political leaders who manage to financially drain us then point toward the next enemy of the moral state. You don't think I know when there aren't answers? The Church kicks the answer down the road...wait until heaven? We can't have faith in our own feelings about what's good and what's not without big parades, charades, and basilicas?"

"I understand you are upset. The church is here to help you cope with your grief, Attila," Hajtos offered softly.

"How exactly has the church helped me cope with all of the senseless deaths I've experienced? How do you explain millions of deaths that have culminated in the one that has injured me beyond all healing? How many people have to die to make the point that this world is nothing but random chaos by those who would define our goals? How did we become scared, angry little creatures in a sea of hope and wonder? Religious leaders have removed or altered whole sections of biblical history in the interest of the best spin so we won't be confused. Exactly what are we supposed to have faith in? I'd like to make my own decisions about what is and isn't relevant to my life.

I want all of the information. Don't clarify it for me. Don't chew it for me.

"We have become half-brained, overly stressed animals doomed to spiritual crumbs. And those crumbs are most likely what's left of a worthwhile meal. Who did that? Who robs us of our inheritance? I think it's a good portion of self-appointed heads of state that sit their fat asses down first at the table, that's who! It's all about control. When honest, fair-minded, good people show the way, must they be so rare that the Church moves to canonize them?

"I'm in pain. You can't help. Eating cookies with us? Some coping mechanism! That beautiful Basilica blocks from here can't help. Where is this big God right about now when I could use a little relief?" Attila angrily demanded.

"Why go to such efforts to support my work in the Church?" the priest asked simply.

"You're an earnest man. Simple, good-sense plans to be-have correctly with a moral code are critically important. I'm just asking that you understand that I object to the very idea that the Church has answers and rules that morph politically. I resent the manufactured polarity.

"I don't need you to tell me about God without acknowledg-ing a learning curve in science or believing in our divine gift to know right from wrong. Tell me you don't recognize what I'm saying."

The priest answered deliberately.

"I don't believe we've ever had such a discussion as this. I would be lying to say that I'm without doubts, too. I agree that we cannot fully grasp what God means. I do say that God is easily felt and accessible. All I ask is that you keep your mind open to that part of you convinced of something more yet to be pursued and shared. Be willing to be inspired. Be ready to accept that God represents the known and that which is un-known, the very miracle of life. Don't let the loss of your wife make you bitter. Some challenges are meant to create spiritual muscle, Attila. Pain is required to bear more spiritual weight. Emotional scar tissue can turn into spiritual muscle; you will be able to bear more challenges, go farther, in the interest of the heavenly father.

"I'm in agreement about the robes," Hajtos laughed. "We always figured the pomp and circumstance represented trappings of authority. To most, poverty signifies piety. Both impressions are unreliable."

With a final pat on Ildiko's head, the priest moved into the exterior corridor of the apartment house, ignoring the low iron railings over which Noemi Meszaros was thrown.

"I will pray for you. You're a good man and a practical one. God has a plan for such a man and his daughter."

"Sajnálom," Attila apologized. He closed the front door and turned on the kitchen light. Attila dictated a missive to the Confederation of American States.

> *Madame Secretary,*
>
> *I am unsure whether you've heard of our recent tragedy. My wife was murdered by way of vengeance, a result of our involvement in undercover activities designed to tip the scales in favor of Hungary's autonomy so many years ago. While we never discussed our plans openly, our ongoing cooperation has proven invaluable. As is, I have decided to make a new life outside of Hungary. I count on you to welcome us as my daughter and I prepare to leave for the Confederation at the earliest possible opportunity. It is my intention that we continue our relationship in North Carolina, where I will continue to work as a liaison between our governments. While we have been invited many times throughout the years, the reason for my past objections is no longer a factor.*
>
> *Most Sincerely Yours,*
> *Attila Meszaros*

Chapter XIV

Good Vibrations

Saturday, December 25, 2060

S onny chanted hypnotic melodies. The innumerable nuances resonated vibrations that put his father at ease despite his growing concerns. The monitor recorded each session of the Vedic recitations, an oral tradition that had been traced to the early Iron Age. Each night, Tsin-hang poured over the versions by replaying the ancient Hindu mantras. These mantras had historically been relegated to Pathins, the scholars charged with mastering the word-by-word recitations. Yet Sonny had hurdled to the advanced stages of chanting with words that rapidly evolved in complexity. Rather than a linear level of chanting words with Vedic pitch-perfect accents, Sonny's acumen had grown without the aid of mnemonic device or access to an experienced Brahmin priest. He had never practiced the thousands of hours usually required to perfect the intonations. According to the monitors' research, the soothing effects of Tsin-hang's son's chants were not accidental. Such vocalization was the spiritual tool by which divine sound was conveyed, the first step in liberation meant to build the bridge by which humans were able to cross from their primal levels of existence toward spiritual enlightenment. By the data's reckoning, Sonny was in the class of Supreme Brahman.

Tsin-hang approached his son with a simple question.

"Why do you chant?"

Sonny smiled as if he had been waiting for the question.

"So that others can hear the vibration when they are ready for it. I want to help keep the vibration spectrum alive so that anyone can connect to it when they are receptive."

Tsin-hang noticed for the first time that this translation was not via the monitor's earbot; Sonny spoke without the aid of a translator that helped to extrapolate meanings.

"Father, you wonder how I understand so many languages? I think that I have an ability to touch the vibrations that ride on so many fields...magnetic fields, radio waves, low and high invisible frequencies... like the monitor does," Sonny answered his own question.

"How do you speak with such elevated understanding?"

"Is it elevated understanding, Father? It's just the knowing..."

Sonny retrieved his earbot translator, unable to explain his intuition on the subject of accessing and channeling information at will.

"The consequential, the conscious, the meaningful...." he repeated translations in different Chinese dialects until Tsin-hang put up his hand and laughed.

"There is probably no satisfactory explanation or translation," Tsin-hang clarified. "Yes, like the human vocal chords that formed the vibrations millions of years ago and the disappearance of the air sac 600,000 years ago that once interfered with language. It took another half million years to learn the vibrational range just to speak. We learned from the animals, especially the birds. Then we made language for speaking amongst ourselves. Now it's possible that we should be able to make another level of vibrations, hear the Knowing, as you say, and become one consciousness," Tsin-hang theorized.

"Father, I've been listening. Sometimes you say it's quiet when I hear many different things. The chanting just helps me to focus on something when other noise becomes too loud."

"I follow that. Please tell me more."

Sonny was pleased with his father's altered tone. It had a tenor of interest rather than one of nervous apprehension. Sonny became animated, free to spill ideas that had built in his mind.

"The vibrations help us understand. They can even change the way we clean the litter left behind by lower vibrations. We knew these higher sonic and wave vibrations at one time. We moved stones as easily as ideas – without technology—but we forgot how. The world became too noisy and people interpreted the higher vibrations for us; at least they said they could. Then some people said that they could hear the Knowing but they couldn't. We soon forgot it was there and it was sad...we went deaf.

"A few who knew Sanskrit kept the sounds alive until today. I can hear the sounds and they bring me happiness here on the great water. It's the water that makes it easier to hear the different frequencies."

"What else do you hear?"

"I'm trying to ignore the other noise, Father. I know it's there, but I want to hear and make the sounds from the Knowing before they go away. I don't know what they mean but I know how it feels. It's a good thing. The other sounds are manmade and they cover these vibrations if I let them. Does that make sense to you, Father?"

"It happens to make absolute sense, Sonny. The question is what one does with such ability. We'll cross that bridge when we come to it. In the meantime, I'll keep records and do what I can to categorize your utterances and impressions."

They ate their dinner in silence. Tsin-hang tried to listen in the void. He heard nothing but the occasional monitor announcements on the ship, the low hums of Bots moving through the corridors, and the eager chewing and swallowing of urchin and rice from a little boy engrossed in the act of enjoying a favored meal.

"You're my best friend, Father," Sonny remarked between mouthfuls.

Tears rolled down Tsin-hang's face even as he maintained a stoic countenance.

Chapter XV
Christmas Crazy

W e absolutely cannot go to Gloria's this year," Angela voiced adamant objections about the annual Tons of Fun Holiday Festival hosted by Gloria Brackett. "We have guests, Morgan. They'll not understand what it means to see grown men and women in military fatigues drive old Sherman and Chieftain tanks blasting at painted drone targets!"

A collector of WWII tanks, Gloria Brackett hosted the annual Tons of Fun Festival on behalf of charity. The Christmas Day event meant an afternoon of buffet dining, gifts for underprivileged children, skeet shooting, and knife throwing contests. It was also a food fare that featured pulled pork, creamy slaw and twenty enormous barbecued apple-mouthed pigs from spit to table. Bonfires were scattered around the farmhouses; her team of Clydesdales and Friesians were harnessed to large twentieth century carriages for the children's joy rides around the property, while spiked hot toddies were liberally distributed to adults. The culmination of the activities was Gloria's moment to simulate war games that featured twelve refurbished military tanks outfitted with live shells. Covered in Tons of Fun plaid blankets, hundreds of spectators watched from portable bleachers. A crowd cheered their pleasure as teams maneuvered the fields, churning and spitting mud, blasting targets that had been arranged on an obstacle course. The winning team took home an enormous trophy and 20,000 in barter-bits to donate to their favorite charity.

Morgan disagreed with his wife's idea to forego the event.

"I'm not going to miss it," Morgan insisted. "The kids are going to love it! Gloria is expecting us and that's that. Just tell the Nishants not to drink the hot toddies if they ever intend to walk again. I may back out of the spitting contest but the rest is on, Cookie. We don't want to go cultivating humorless friends, do we? And there's fireworks!" Morgan pouted mightily and pleaded like a ten-year-old boy for mercy. "Let's just name your alternative Done with Fun!" Morgan groused.

"What about Rachel?" Angela continued.

"What about Rachel? Most romantic setting I can imagine. You know damn well that Connor and Miss Ben-Tov won't notice a thing. Those two are smitten; Connor is going to be as busy as a one-legged man in a butt kicking contest."

"I was thinking about the pork and kosher laws," Angela worried.

"Nah, she's not kosher and the Nishants don't even ask."

"The boys... won't they be terrified?"

"If those boys aren't crazy happy out of their minds to see things blow up all over the place, then they don't have the right to penises! Now's the time to know that kind of thing, don't you think? Let's go back into the dining room and finish that incredible breakfast. First rate!"

Twenty-two people ate at two tables in the dining room, with one smaller table set up in an adjoining alcove by the foyer. Maintenance bots removed remnants of strewn Christmas gift-wrappings while others removed and stored coats, hats and scarves. The sun filtered through windows, catching scattered dust particles in streaming beams of light. Chattering overwhelmed the piped music. Holographs intermittently appeared that amplified festivities with cheerful greetings and well wishes from friends and neighbors.

CC filled Blue's new dog dish with leftover sausage gleaned from plates removed to the kitchen. Aaron hoarded fruit and described memories of Israeli blood oranges. Champagne cocktails were served with bitters and the Nishants insisted on sampling it all. Indu drank the champagne too fast and smiled too much.

"You've a serious set of white choppers," remarked Morgan admiringly. He offered Indu wine as a chaser.

Angela diplomatically described the afternoon's plans as an eccentric charitable event. Everyone nodded agreeably without paying attention to details. There was great happiness in the Pendergrass home and Morgan felt his heart swell. He remained uncharacteristically circumspect until his PM buzzed an urgent message that demanded privacy.

"Excuse me..." he announced to no one and departed the party for the library. "Go ahead..." Morgan signaled the voice at the other end.

"Sir, we've picked up a message from a pirate freighter off Boston Harbor, picked up by our drones. They're requesting a rescue operation from the Confederation. It's a familiar vessel we've noticed that travels from Nova Scotia. It's one of the hundreds running hopeful immigrants toward our borders. We don't know for certain but we figure no one makes it to anywhere on this particular ship, having never docked on shores far south of New York. The pattern, we assume, is to dump its passengers midway to nowhere. This is the first time we've been messaged."

"What's the message?" Morgan asked impatiently.

"*We've taken the ship and need Confederation rescue,* regularly for ten hours."

"I hate to get near those ships. It compromises everyone...a lot to lose including our hardware if it's a trap. Any ships in the vicinity? Talk to DC?" Morgan asked.

"They're inclined to send a ship because they've scanned it and don't consider it a threat...not from the ship itself. Don't know what to expect from the pirates, though. Can't really trust the message, of course. We've observed some women and youngsters walking the decks. We could get closer and instruct them directly to lower the life boats and motor our way."

"No bargaining. You know these crazy pirates. If you're satisfied, get them off the ship and bring them in. Copy plans to the capital and Hernandez. After they're safe, be careful when you revisit to examine the ship. Scan it before boarding," Morgan advised.

"If they're actually passengers, where do you want them?"

"Wilmington, maybe. I know DC is overwhelmed with refugees. Clear it with Raleigh. They'll make arrangements," Morgan concluded.

A circumspect Morgan returned to the family living room and surveyed his home's growing community. Aaron played with Blue. Indu and Angela were engrossed in conversation. CC trailed Aaron; Aaron tried to figure the workings of more modern bots. Friends that rarely visited caught up with familiar stories that began with 'remember when'; groups exchanged familiar bursts of laughter at familiar cues. Morgan viewed the montage of happiness, relieved that there were recurring moments that remained the same.

Meredith Green and Adele sat on the floor, engrossed in a genome puzzle the geneticist designed and printed as a gift. Adele tried to grasp a scientist's attraction to DNA puzzles over Christmas scenery. Despite overwhelming boredom, his daughter graciously worked the puzzle pieces while Dr. Green spoke about their latest genome inroads.

Aditiya strummed a guitar perfectly even though it was the first instrument he had ever touched. Hyped on ginger cookies, CC jumped from couch to couch and added chairs to her obstacle course, demanding that the safety Bot manically shadowing to 'watch out'.

Neighbors eventually made their leave. Gloria bade everyone goodbye hours earlier to prepare for the afternoon's festivities on her farm. Morgan surveyed the frenetic scenes for hours and wondered if there was a missing party.

Lex settled on the couch beside his father-in-law.

"What's up, Morgan?"

"Seems someone's missing from this group but I can't figure it."

"There's twenty-two with the guests, neighbors, and the security teams. One regular is missing. Elle was a no-show. She ended her unofficial engagement with Connor last night. No drama. Said she just didn't feel right about being his wife but wanted to remain friends with the family."

"You're lying'," Morgan exclaimed incredulously.

"Truth, Morgan. Seems she's not as insensitive as we figured. Acted like a lady about it and they wished each other well. I guess it's hard to miss what's going on between green eyes and my brother...even for Elle."

They looked toward the fireplace across the room at Rachel and Connor speaking, knee-to-knee, convening in a private world. Morgan liked that Connor was smiling and laughing with another green-eyed woman.

"Hey! That little uptight fart is even showing some teeth!" Morgan slapped his knee.

Lex laughed, "Adele thinks it's crazy how quickly Connor came to attention. Anyway, it's good. Rachel is keen on the Tons of Fun activities this afternoon. She wants to enter the shooting competition. Not a good sign for our Cary boys."

"I'm going to miss crazy Ellie. She never failed to remind me the value of genetic research. So pretty... like a flower... able to draw all the bees. Just dumb as mud," Morgan sighed. He recalled untold millions just like Ellie that had been unconcerned and uninvolved. *They slowly tortured our country by self-interested inches,* he thought

"Not to change the subject," Morgan said to Lex, "but I want to bring Clifton Brown here for a conversation. Least, I think it'll be no more than a day or so. Trouble is my wife might have objections if she finds he intends to set foot around here. Not that I blame my beautiful bride. I'd like to figure how to keep him out of sight with your help."

"Sure," Lex agreed. "What do you hope to learn?" Lex asked confused. "We know how he acted from the archives. He's nothing but a liability at this point. We'll have to spend resources legally addressing perfidious crimes if anyone in Cary figures he's around. Then what? Lock him up? We have to have our first murder conviction? A lose-lose situation," Lex posed.

"Just a conversation, that's all. I've got questions. I'd be remiss if I didn't learn information kept secret that may relate to our research. What do you say we have extra security around him and he stays in the old tobacco shed? It's decent. You and Connor stayed there in the old days and no one goes near there anymore. Elle is gone, too. There's no monitor but I can arrange surveillance. I'll have the entire farm under lock and keys and then we'll have a New Year's party that'll take everyone's eye off the ball."

Lex suddenly disagreed with the sophomoric plan intended to counterpoise Angela and Adele.

"One of the most dangerous things you could possibly dream up is to go around Pendergrass women. Just tell Angela, Morgan. You're the one who says he refuses to play games; you're the one who demands and extols the bitter truth."

"I meant anyone I didn't have to sleep with, you fool," Morgan growled.

"Morgan, it's simple. I'll speak to Angela and tell her that we don't want to leave any loose ends. When we've concluded an interrogation, we send Brown away," Lex explained. "On second thought, where would we send that monster, Morgan?"

"Trouble is, he's an evil political animal that needs to be isolated. I'm pretty sure that he knows of resources out of our scope... couldn't have kept himself alive this long if he hadn't. I sure as hell don't want him around the Confederation," Morgan pondered a second dilemma.

"I'm not as morally equipped as you, Morgan. I've seen the vids of families his security forces mowed down, the last vestiges of civility that vanished due to Presidential directives. That includes my family left to burn in the Chicago mayhem. He should have died decades ago in his mole holes. I'll help with Angela. I've no solution after that," Lex offered.

"All right. I'll count on you to speak to Angela when the time comes. We'll show him around a little... the animals, the labs. He won't believe the strides we've made, the health benefits, the trade agreement. I'm just that small and angry and I'm expecting him to act out his ego by spilling information..."

Lex shook his head. "Morgan, do you honestly think that Brown would be impressed with the Confederation? That he'd be envious? You think he knows something we don't? All you're expecting is spontaneous combustion from envy?"

"That's exactly the plan, son," Morgan acknowledged.

Angela appeared in the center of the room to remind everyone to depart for the Tons of Fun afternoon festivities.

"What are you two scheming up, Lex?" she focused to Morgan's side.

"Well, when this all dies down, we'll sit down and talk. In the meantime, what's your call on Rachel and Connor?"

Angela followed Lex's eyes that indicated the fireplace. The living room had emptied and quieted. Rachel and Connor remained oblivious.

"Same as yours. I'm putting my money on CC's drawing," Angela chuckled.

Angela handed Morgan his personal monitor to tape on his wrist. "It's been beeping furiously. Thought you'd better check in."

Morgan read the message from the Hungarian Prime Minister with an attached missive from the Confederation Secretary with Attila Meszaros's travel itinerary.

"Better put more water in the soup, Cookie. We've got visitors soon arriving from Hungary."

"How long, Morgan?"

"Permanently. We'll find them a place but we'll have to fix something up around here. Mr. Meszaros from Budapest has worked with us for the better part of 15 years. He has a little girl around eleven years old. She'll feel better amongst the kids, right?"

Angela sighed, "What happened?"

"The mother was brutally murdered by an enemy of the state. They buried her Christmas Eve."

"Oh, Lord. Leave it to me. We'll take care of them," Angela promised.

The Brackett Farm

Two Pendergrass Farm transports emptied an assortment of jubilant passengers at the front of Gloria Brackett's restored antebellum plantation home. The home, thought Indu, looked curiously familiar. The main home was an approximated replication of the two-story white wooden structure, Tara, from the 1936 *Gone with the Wind* movie set. It was an image the Indian doctor recognized of the former American South featured in one of her favorite films. "How strange and wonderful!" Indu exclaimed, as a figure appeared aggressively trotting their way.

Rather than a soft-spoken Southern belle, Gloria Beckett had been nurtured of hard-core Texas stock that thought, walked, bought, and fought big. Outfitted with cowboy boots and jeans, Gloria excitedly hailed the Pendergrass visitors.

"Howdy, y'all! Come on now...you're makin' an entrance like prissy debutantes," Gloria peered at Morgan.

"I'm fashionably late..." Morgan retorted.

"Without the fashion..." Gloria completed.

Open-air transports ferried groups of six toward the fields of activity, where hundreds of visitors milled amongst festively covered tents. A strange combination of Christmas decorations, guns, and whistling targets, the Brackett's annual festival drew the most eccentric and fun-loving participants because it was decidedly outrageous. No one minded the use of expensive outdoor heaters, roving decorated animals, or the liberal distribution of spirits; the only fast and hard rule was to cheer one's favorite members of the Tons of Fun teams that marked the festival's climax. Targets would be jettisoned high and others dropped sporadically onto the fields by flying drones. The tank with the most successful hits would win.

The Pendergrass group was greeted by the war cries of old fashioned Glocks, antique 12-gauge Smith and Wesson shotguns, and AK47s fired on one side of a field. Opposite the targets on the other side of the expanse stood twelve older men and women. The latter group of marksmen was outfitted with precision-guided firearms with the ability to calculate every environmental variable including wind speed and the handler's heart rate. Bull's eye destinations, whether standing or moving 1000 feet in the distance, were a trigger pull away as the gun's computer calibrated temperature, barometric pressure, and the magnetic pull and spin of the earth, ensuring that every bullet pinged its target. So the shooters and audience could appreciate the moment, impact was amplified by holographic visual loops on PMs.

"What's the use of using smart weapons against those that exhibit real marksmanship skills?" asked Rachel as the group walked amongst the crowd.

Connor laughed, "The smart weapons are for our more nefarious, slightly inebriated gang of community elders. If you notice, they're sectioned off with professional security personnel watching their every move. The real marksmen are trying to prove themselves the old fashioned way with no computational weaponry...over there to your right. Fact is, the older guys on the left side are the ones that underwrite the event with Gloria Brackett; it's just a way to look good, have fun, and donate to charity. Folks in these parts don't mind ending their Christmas with a bang. That part over there is for the guys that can't quite make it up into those tanks anymore. Guess which group Morgan is in?"

Rachel laughed as she watched Morgan Pendergrass scurry across the field toward his friends, hooting and hollering with a security escort; the Confederation security teams retrieved the weapons from the shooters after each round and pulled back the bolts to reload. As soon as Morgan arrived, he was handed his smart weapon, the one equipped with a Pendergrass biometric trigger.

Pulled pork sandwiches and coleslaw hardly fit Rachel's ex-pectation of Christmas fare but she was delighted. Aaron, Adi-tiya, and Caroline left Connor and Rachel's side to walk with Adele and Lex toward the children's archery and shooting range with other attendant parents. Angela and Meredith Green played host to the Nishants, who found the event ever more palatable with each sip of hot spiced wine. Amar and Indu smiled at those who arrived on horseback until one horse was spooked at the first tank shell shot during practice drills. Its flailing hoofs almost caught Indu's arm as it reared.

Gloria and a safety bot instantly appeared on the scene. Gloria's ability to monitor minutiae amongst countless activi-ties, noted Indu, was a sixth sense.

"Sorry if that animal scared you, ma'am. But sometimes a horse has a sense about things we don't give it credit for. It's pretty crazy right now around here but all my horse cares about is a novice rider in its mouth. You came mighty close to being hurt. My apologies!"

"We are enjoying every minute of it! And I'm sure that's the reason they call good instincts good horse sense," Indu said calmly.

As Connor and Rachel explored the grounds, Elle appeared on the horizon. She waved a broad greeting to the couple and kept a respectful distance. It was odd, thought Rachel, for a woman to be so accommodating and understanding of a bro-ken engagement "even if it was Elle that ostensibly made the decision," Rachel concluded as the couple returned an awkward acknowledgment.

"How'd you meet Elle, Connor? You two don't seem a likely pair."

"She was eating my dog," Connor replied matter-of-factly.

"Hot dog?"

"No. My hunting dog, Senior."

"Stop!"

"Elle and her father were camping in the woods. I'd gone hunting the day before with the hounds and Senior Blue some-how got distracted. He'd find his way home ordinarily but still hadn't shown up by the morning. I went to track him in the woods with Pup-Dog and Traveler, my best trackers. We tracked some smoke and marched right up to a ratchety tent by a smoldering fire. Ellie had cooked up Senior. She and her father were just finishing the dog off, picking their teeth. His collar was just sitting there by the chopping block."

"Sick."

"It was survival. Times were bad, Rachel. I was pissed as hell, though. There was plenty of stupid in that move; they could have used the dog for hunting. Instead, they capture Senior with a live squirrel and butcher him for food. That hound never met a squirrel he didn't like," Connor said sadly.

"And how was that experience a turn-on?"

"It wasn't like that. Ellie was skin and bones. She and her father were ill. What could I do? They didn't deny capturing or eating Senior. They said they were sorry. The sad fact was that they had been living outdoors trying to trap squirrels and such for about a year. Father and daughter had lost the rest of their family and it was just the two of them struggling to get by. By the time Senior came along, he looked like top sirloin.

"You fell in love...?" Rachel prompted.

"I took the pair of them back to the farm with their belongings. They received medical attention and decent food. Neither Mr. Smythe nor Ellie was too resourceful, however. We just couldn't find much in the way they could do. I continued to check on her regularly to see how she was doing because her father died while they were still on the farm. She was always grateful and excited to see me. I guess I was sort of just like her. By the time Ellie...Elle...showed up and filled out, she looked like top sirloin to me, too," Connor shrugged with a sigh.

"I see."

"I never had time to socialize, Rachel. My group was pushing twenty-hour days to get things back in order as fast as we could. I worked with the same twenty or thirty people every day, each night. I'm forty. Yeah. She looked great when she cleaned up, and she didn't ask for a lot of attention then. I thought that I could fall in love. We began to talk about what it meant to have a family. Least, that's how Ellie saw it, and I believed her."

Rachel changed the subject.

"Did you get a new dog?"

"I cloned Senior."

"How's that working?"

"Interesting. I'm the best one to distinguish the differences. They're negligible, except the dog doesn't remember me, of course. He used to be by my side all the time and knew all of my signals, facial expressions, and such. He's now under the influence of ginger cookies but he's still a great hound, hunts the exact same way... just has a different personality because he hangs with CC most the time. I find it disconcerting. CC prefers to call him just 'Blue'. That's the dog story," Connor finished with a touch of sadness.

"Christmas heralds harmony and peace, right?" Rachel again changed the direction of their conversation.

Connor chuckled as they watched army tanks grinding over the hill in formation. Bugles blared, unnecessarily magnified by monitors. A rousing cheer erupted from the stands.

"Don't even try to make sense of a Christmas connection with those monsters. See that WWII Chaffee tank and the M4A1E8 Sherman in the middle? That belongs to a Raleigh outfit. See that 1966 British Chieftain? That's the only women's team, with our own honorary General Brackett at the helm. She used to bring the tanks in from Texas and started a club to exhibit on Veterans Day. Her grandparents were wealthy landowners in Dallas and left a fortune to their only grandchild. She wasn't from the 'all hat, no cattle' bunch. The Brackett family was the real thing."

"Only an heiress could afford to maintain those dinosaurs," Rachel underlined.

"Those tanks were about 300,000 barter-bits a pop ,excluding the restoration and maintenance. They're money holes. Take up a lot of room, too. Playing around with them can wreck a place when these guys go knocking down trees and churning up dirt. But they came in handy. When we needed to secure our borders, it was these antiques and crazy owners that kept the meanest groups out. They had ammunition, too! Gloria's friends were armed to the teeth. Called themselves the 'Tar

Heel Terror' unit. It was weirdly awesome the way they scared off the gangs from the North. We honor those years of vigilance by letting these guys go senseless at Christmas. They saved our hides while we got organized."

"There's a lot of danger having a tank without eyes. How did they know friend from foe?" Rachel wondered.

"The Confederation owned operable satellites. We could easily make out the bad guys by the path of destruction before they hit our borders. It wasn't hard to pick up the heat markers of those savages. Nothing seemed to interest that bunch more than burning the landscape. They targeted defenseless homes first and plundered food stores, then burned what they left behind.

"Our Tar Heel Terrorists were camouflaged. They waited on coordinated points selected by our militia units in Raleigh as the crazies drove antique cars on the freeways. The EMP didn't hamper some of those really old cars. The less crazy of them had figured out how to get fuel from stores probably used for emergency generators when the pumps stopped. They were smart enough... re-rigged some of the electrical systems or forced the smarter communities to help them.

"When intermittent power came back on line they tapped into Confederation resources and were able to start the newer hardened transports closer to our borders. Anyway, those tanks you see were really useful."

"That's it?" Rachel remarked sadly.

"So far, the only damage these days has been when Jackson Galloway filled up his tank at the local farm depot gas station and flattened the car in front of him, situated under his scope. Luckily, no one was in the vehicle but Galloway was prohibited from using artillery or ever filling up at Jones' station again."

Rachel considered the easy-speaking, laughing Carolinians that surrounded her as drones whizzed overhead projecting and dropping targets. Each tank took turns shooting. Hit or miss, the artillery blew the bordering pine trees apart; bots quickly sprayed fire-extinguishing chemicals. The firepower drew hysterical screams of approval.

"Clearly, this somehow makes sense," Rachel's eyes softened.

"Like us, right?" Connor put his hand on the back of her head and pulled her gently toward him. He had never kissed someone he loved. Connor knew that the moment their lips touched.

Monday, December 27, 2060

Morgan answered his PM; the frequency indicated the highest priority.

"Sir? We've picked up a party of 16 off a limping freighter called the Hopeless. It was the ship's chef that contacted us. Evidently, a long string of desperate passengers over the years were promised passage within the vicinity of the Confederation. According to the chef, he's been held captive by a series of teams of pirates that collect goods and trade with other pirates. He's tight-lipped about what happened to passengers. No children of the Confederation's description on board…"

"So, why in the hell contact me with an urgent signal?" Morgan yelled.

"Long-standing search orders indicated 'special tendencies'. I had ears for that, too. According to monitor reports, two sisters – one preteen and the other around 18 – were advising this Nicholas Bradley to keep quiet about what transpired on the ship. The more we picked up tags, the more I paid attention. The passengers had been able to finish off armed pirates with an unarmed group of mostly women. The young man in question mentioned to his newfound friends that he suspects an undefined prowess… specifically invisibility…that most likely allowed him to board the ship unnoticed. There was other talk about two captains dying within 24 hours of each other. We're going in now to inspect. The teenager seems to be at the center of the coup."

Morgan recalled CC's picture on his PM and the row of children with a noticeable gap. A blank spot between two of the kids meant something.

"Bring him in. I've got a feeling you're right. Please include the two sisters if they are now a trusted group; I don't want to cause any anxiety. All you have to do is drop the 13 survivors into Raleigh. Bring the three others to the Farm after they've rested. Good work. Forward the transcripts."

"Will do, sir. I'll ping you our findings on board. We'll remove anything of value or danger; we'll have it tugged into the Wilmington port."

"Sounds like a plan."

"And sir? Shall we also arrange transport for Brown at this time?"

"No, I haven't figured what to do with him. I'll get to that once we're done here."

Tuesday, December 28, 2060

Morgan called his transport and let his research team know that he would be arriving within the hour. He contacted the Nishants, Adele, and Rachel with the request to accompany him to the Research Triangle Research hub.

"Dr. Pendergrass, would you mind sharing today's plans?" Rachel asked.

"For a day of fun at our Research Facility in Raleigh," he answered and closed his eyes for the remainder of the trip.

Dr. Green met and escorted the group into one of the vast buildings. It was only Green's shoes that echoed in the enormous hallways. Low hums and clicks of the ventilation system could be heard within the massive building that smelled as sterile and antiseptic as the appearance of the interior looked.

Morgan's retina was scanned at the door; the party felt the gravity of a meeting yet to be defined as they entered a large conference room. An assistant assured the synchronicity of everyone's Personal Monitors. Names of participants appeared on individual monitors that graphically depicted and stewarded the seating arrangement.

"I'm not going to dismiss anything as out of the scope of possibilities," Dr. Green began as seating was identified. "I'm going to try and bring everyone up to speed today. Consider yourselves part of a think tank that's only a quarter full."

Morgan took charge of the proceedings. Unidentified men and women took their places around the long table. Morgan ignored the unidentified white coats and left his guests without introduction.

"If you have questions, it's all on your PM. So let's get started," Morgan began.

"I'll start with my granddaughter. Caroline Collins has a talent for drawing prophetic images. Dr. Green and I were aware, for example, that Aaron Shalit and Aditiya Nishant would be our guests but CC was not told of this. Yet she knew and drew their images.

"By way of background, Adele – my daughter – and her daughter, Caroline, have both been screened for genetic frailties. Adele has been devoid of illness, has keen insight, and an even disposition. There has been no indication of unusual aptitudes except one. My Adele is able to love her crotchety father 95% of the time. I'd call that a unique ability.

"Caroline is another matter. Beyond the images of children she expected to meet in our home, she also knew of another visitor whose image was identified to her before I was officially notified. It's the ex-president of the United States, Clifton Brown.

"Hearing what's happening in real time is one thing... that which might be categorized as telepathic frequencies... but foreshadowing specific events is quite another. The monitors are secure and encrypted; my granddaughter would not have access to transmissions in our home. In any case, Caroline drew the picture of an accurate person and scene prior to any transmission to the Confederation.

"That being said, one of her drawings includes five children inclusive of a blank spot. I just thought it odd...didn't ask Caroline about that because her mother would have hanged me by these fat thumbs. Adele watches CC like a hawk but she trusts our direction even if she draws privacy lines. I say that because we carefully navigate those boundaries with all of the children. Keep that in mind."

Morgan paused to gauge Rachel's reaction aware of her overprotective tendencies. Her face remained expressionless.

"Well, today I hear of a teenager who is one of a small group being rescued from a pirate-run freighter supposedly transporting tribute-bearing passengers...people that believed the Confederation would be their destination. During this escapade, meant to rob and discard hopeless refugees, a teenager on board managed to overcome a team of armed cutthroats. It's what we've heard but haven't substantiated. We'll get the details of that soon.

"I'd requested Confederation militia to comb for clues as to the whereabouts for unidentified children my granddaughter had drawn; these were children that she was sure were bound for Pendergrass Farms. In addition, we asked Confederation surveillance to have ears for unusual abilities or occurrences. Our people picked up a particular distress signal and listened in. There is indication from conversations that a teenager named Nicholas Bradley has abilities that were discussed the last few days amongst his newfound acquaintances; they're all passengers on said pirate freighter.

"Of note was the boy's ability to escape notice and overcome fully armed men. The idea of overcoming great odds and having an ability to escape notice has puzzled him as much as two young sisters who've advised him to keep mum. It appears that Nicholas expanded upon his theory that he is able to become invisible specifically when alerted to danger.

"I refer to the blank gap within a circle of young children on this particular drawing."

Morgan indicated the drawing projected on the room monitor that clearly showed the likenesses of Aditiya and Aaron amongst others. Rachel's eyebrows rose; Indu Nishant drew a breath and held it.

"Aditiya...exactly my son," Indu finally commented.

"Interesting," Rachel agreed.

"That's it? Interesting?" Morgan incredulously asked Rachel.

"I already knew that Aaron and CC knew of each other. Where are we going from here? I get that there is a group of kids who communicate and have exceptional abilities. That's it?"

Morgan considered Rachel's statement rude.

"Am I working for you, Missy? Nah. I'm working for us all! I promise to move as quickly as possible to evaluate and examine these youngsters further in the most noninvasive scientific way possible. I remind you that you contacted us for help! Snarky isn't going to take us anywhere."

"Understood. My apologies, Dr. Pendergrass. Just wanted the bottom line first. I'm not a patient person either," Rachel responded with all the contrition she could muster.

Amar had another concern. He had yet to find an opportunity to privately address his host or the Confederation research team. He was under the impression that Gordon felt the utmost urgency when he brought Amar into London and then facilitated the transfer of his family to North Carolina. Amar failed to grasp the priorities of his host. He put his hand up in the air to take advantage of the moment.

"We've yet to share findings, Dr. Pendergrass. As soon as my team is relocated in town, I would like to bring everyone up to speed with regard to the mass effects of the EMP on the population. It's the reason I was more than a year in the UK and sent here with earnestness. Respectfully, I'm sure that our findings are integral to your genetic findings," Amar stated with some urgency.

"Yes, I'm aware. We're moving on that. Within the week, we'll have your EMP research reconciled with our own trials. You'll see that you've brought the most important confirmation of this genetic puzzle. Gordon has been sharing findings for many years and we've cooperated for decades. There is much to discuss; this meeting is just an introduction to the latest topics. I'd like your formal input later, if you don't mind, after Dr. Goodwin presents his theories about Nicholas Bradley. Dr. Goodwin has taken great interest in this idea of invisibility within marine biology," Morgan finished by way of introducing one of the speakers.

Dr. Green stood upon Morgan's cue and invited one of the attending specialists to take the floor.

"Dr. Goodwin?"

The biologist weighed every bit of three hundred and fifty pounds; his voice boomed baritone and he frequently patted a perspiring head with a handkerchief tightly wadded in one hand. Goodwin began his address leaning heavily upon the table with the other.

"Good morning. I'm Dr. Harry Goodwin, biologist and bio-chemist. I've been asked to give today's briefing with regard to anomalies that have biological footprints. Today's subject is invisibility. Invisibility is the latest topic that focuses upon Nicholas Bradley.

"We've numerous examples of species that have evolved be-yond normal camouflage capabilities. One of our planet's most invasive species is the Comb Jelly, Mnemiopsis Leidyi. Its hunt-ing prowess is amazing given that it is slow, blind, and brainless. It's so brainless we've nicknamed it the Sea Walnut. It combs the coast of North and South America, capable of eating ten times its bodyweight per day. I might add that the Comb Jelly almost devastated the fishing industry in the Black Sea almost eighty years ago. The anchovy-rich Black Sea was almost no more. No one could figure it. Turns out that these Sea Walnuts are voracious consumers of everything at the bottom of the food chain. Anyway, one of the Comb Jelly's favorite meals is the Copepod... a miniscule crustacean but vital to the ocean's food chain. The Copepod is also one of the swiftest animals in nature able to travel 800 body lengths in a second.

"We wondered how it was that this agile fast creature 100 times bigger than its prey was unable to avoid being consumed by the brainless, sluggish Mnemiopsis. Well the Comb Jellies – scientists discovered – were somehow made invisible to their prey. The mindless Sea Walnut evolved to be imperceptible to its prey's antennae that are sensitive to the surrounding water current. The way in which the jelly slurps up the water stream is so wide and slow that the process by which it is able to scoop up its prey is an ability to be hydrodynamically invisible. The jelly has evolved to offset the sensitive vibrations of its prey that are normally well-tuned to the water's pulses for danger signals. The Sea Walnut can consume its prey without notice. In the most practical sense, it is invisible."

Morgan couldn't ignore the opening.

"This is the way you've managed to sneak up and suck down buffet tables, Dr. Goodwin?"

Meredith groaned. "Please continue, Harry..."

"There are many natural concealments that act as properties of invisibility. We've rethought our approach and have added numerous studies that challenge traditional concepts of invisibility. We included the critical roles played by the visual and cognitive systems of the observer. We'll come back to that idea later.

"Now, let's jump a little here about our ideas about evolution. They don't pan out. That's clear. Too many missing links... too any quantum jumps in too short a period of time. Among other mysteries, humans are simply not heretofore considered symbiotic. Has our species evolved without a predator? Most radical changes in nature take a long time to adjust... or risk elimination. While this young man's claims or theories about being invisible to his prey may sound strange, nature has developed such abilities at lower levels. Perhaps our organism once had abilities that have gone dormant.

"That which geneticists have considered junk DNA is something we're looking at now more closely. We once considered the unidentified, un-connected DNA material hanging around as so much rubbish. Junk DNA represented our inability to account for genes no longer functional. We had little understanding of this broken-up grouping whatsoever. It was certainly convenient to call it 'junk' coding.

"Scientists reckoned unused portions of a genome sequence were no longer an adaptive advantage for an obsolete coding set. Under the file of non-coding DNA, scientists theorized our species had outgrown its usefulness. Yes and no.

"We took another look at this superfluous genetic junk decades back. It's that research focus that got shut down by the Federal government in Dr. Pendergrass's day. It made us all suspicious. What did they fear? We're still unsure.

"We had long been operating on the premise that rather than this grouping of DNA being useless to our evolutionary needs it might remain relevant to our survival – but in what way? These segments did not have an obvious biochemical function. Protein coding DNA was seemingly a minuscule part of the puzzle. It's big, of course but it's only 20% of the enigma. There is another 80% of DNA that includes switches that signal instruction for proteins. It's the non-coding sequence that

displays complex long-range power law correlations while coding sequences do not. We are still decoding higher functions.
Duons have parallel codes and meanings. One is how proteins
are made; the other concerns how genes are controlled. And
now we know that our entire DNA switching mecanism with the
Dark Matter reacts to frequency!" Goodwin pulled his massive
body erect to emphasize this point.

"That brings me around to this invisibility question with the
young man on his way here. Under what circumstances would
humans need to be invisible? Second, if this Nicholas Bradley
is able to become invisible... whether at will or not... what are
the survival conditions that spark that ability from our past,
present, or future conditions? Third, we often assume that we
humans have been programmed from the get-go with full functionality. Perhaps this is not the case if not sparked by need.
Genetic factors are significantly ingrained... sixty million years
or more worth. Without amplification of certain genes under
specific conditions, we might have inadvertently rendered
some of our programming and its integrated wiring dormant.

"Maybe we're wired to capacity but for whatever reason
have been thus far unable to authorize it. There've got to be
other reasons for vast amounts of DNA... and ways to use it to
enhance our genome. Our programming may be incomplete.
Perhaps we've yet to factor environmental influences properly.
Again, we'll revisit that idea."

Harry Goodwin dabbed sweat, drank water, and looked for
questions. There were none.

"All right, so we've got some indication that one of the
anomalies that has come to our attention is the ability to evade
detection... to be invisible. What's that mean? We tend to think
of camouflaging as undetectable to one's eye, as in chameleon
color changes. We think of invisibility as anything from cloaking or light refracting devices to vanishing in thin air. Like the
Sea Walnut, it might include evading vibrational capabilities.
It may mean that conceptually we cannot adjust to an unidentified image if that image is not on our frequency or escapes
our cognitive abilities. Slight changes in color arrangements

can mislead our perception, as we know. Anything that escapes our experiences often qualifies as cognitively invisible.

"It is feasible that humans had once developed highly sensitized intuitive capabilities that kept our species from harm's way. From what kind of harm would you imagine beyond the earliest animal predators? Perhaps harm or the threat of harm springing from our own species or another? Disease is a threat and we have responded. Natural disasters are threatening and we got busy predicting and offsetting those dangers, too. As of late, our greatest threat has taken shape as irrational or malicious behaviors at the hands of our own species. Moral cannibals, as it were. It's conceivable that certain survival mechanisms lay dormant because of an overlooked empirical change.

"Civilization has long depended upon institutional security, religious codes of moral conduct, and civil codes of punishment that may have relieved us of personal survival instincts or defenses. It's the reason that cunning human predators are literally able to get away with murder; they are able to evade our instinctive radar. These predators wear the invisibility cloak of civility. We have been led and lulled to ignore much of what is left of such vibrational waves. Our natural instincts that evolved to give humans valuable lifesaving cues have diminished with technological advances that mimic instinct. Stop. Go. Wait. Warning signs, security alarms, our Personal Monitors telling us when we are sick and when others have a virus or temperature. What else happened? Social engineering happened, for one. We were inculcated to never think negatively about others, to ignore our wariness of strangers even if we felt otherwise. We were rightly and wrongly convinced that many among us were bigots, pre-judging others unfairly, and were made embarrassed or pressured out of our insightful assessments. Anxiety about others was considered paranoid in the event some rationale could not substantiate a need to separate. Given this tact, there may be a lot more of unidentified Dark Matter in humanity's future. That is, if we survive. Having relegated our safety to institutions with prescribed social conventions, we may have lost the greater part of our survival instincts that signal a threat to our operational integrity.

"A seemingly passive, brainless, irresponsible, less capable predator can get close to us without setting off alarms. Sophisticated or pathological criminals murder without remorse, avoiding our internal radar. Sound familiar? Like the brainless and deadly Sea Walnut that interrupts the fragile food chain, able to maneuver under evolved preservation radars, creeping upon on its prey, able to operate on an entirely different vibrational level, we just cannot see the danger coming. In this case, sense it.

"Another aspect of invisibility relies upon one's cognitive perception. If we've never experienced a certain predatory behavior, we may not recognize it as a danger even if we've heard or observed it second-hand. Certain behaviors might first woo us into complacency, seduce us into comfort and security, then slowly extract our resources, consuming us slowly with outcomes as deadly as a direct attack..."

"Like Elle Smythe! She almost sucked the life out of me with those awful stories. Just about married Connor! His mind went invisible..." Morgan stopped when Green kicked his leg under the table.

"What's wrong with you? Please allow Dr. Goodwin to finish!"

"What's wrong with your foot? You just kicked the hell outta my mechanical leg," Morgan knowingly smiled.

Goodwin resumed with Dr. Green's signal to ignore the interruption.

"It's only the most obtuse and overtly aggressive predator that makes our adrenaline race, for example. We've gradually misdirected our 'fight or flight' mechanism in favor of a societal consensus.

"My point: until we examine someone who is said to be 'invisible', we cannot dismiss the possibility. Accounts are on record of people going about their daily business and noticing that no one noticed them. Not ignored them, mind you, but absolutely didn't see them. There's a difference. That extensive data is in your files," Goodwin finished.

Rachel had spoken with the Israelis at length. She understood where this was going. "Are you making a correlation to Aaron's talents? Others, too?"

"I don't think it should have taken us this long to untangle our DNA challenges", Goodwin speculated. "It was the sudden apparence of this genetic anomalies that made us reconsider recent events and their effects upon the genome. There have been a lot of political challenges, coupled with the solar flares and the EMP blasts most recently from off-shore in the Atlantic Ocean, just to name a few of man's trials. For what inherent need is there this impulse to obliterate ourselves, along with the rest of the civilized world? What is it about our species that conceives of such a thing? Cooperation means more to our quality of life than wholesale destruction of resources. Ants cooperate better. What we do know is that some humans fear losing power and seek control even if it means self-destruction. This behavior seeps into our environment; then it becomes molecular.

"I'd like to add my own unproven observation. When daily survival does not depend upon brainpower, cooperation, individuality, or innovation, we may lose our evolutionary track. Unable to pursue our curiosity, use the full measure of our human competencies and imagination, humans may possibly render our species genetically neutered at untold levels."

Harry believed that there were trigger mechanisms for the unidentified codes. That there was 80% of dark material unaccounted for said something about the human timeline being delayed or sidetracked on its way toward maturation. Civilization had been a matter of quantum steps forward, only to be destroyed by our species' inexplicable failure to identify, protect, and nurture our best selves. That included scientific inquiry.

"We have in our midst a grouping of genetically altered young people having appeared in a nanosecond of time. Historically, this may not be unusual. This group of children drawn to our area may be a sampling of a greater population," Goodwin tried to summarize for Rachel.

Goodwin opened the room for discussion. "These are seemingly random theories brought forward by concrete science. Thoughts?"

Amar had been involved with the EMP research; he had no idea of its applications to genetics as it pertained to examples of unusual behaviors on the other side of the spectrum. He was aware of the negative effects and had not considered the positive.

"You are saying, Dr. Pendergrass and Dr. Goodwin, that you've identified someone who can make themselves invisible?" Amar clarified. "And could someone also explain to me the reference to Aaron Shalit?"

"It's clear that Aaron has unusual abilities. I'm simply not prepared to risk a haphazard discussion in front of strangers as a matter of general speculation," Rachel answered.

Morgan became agitated. He took the trouble to stand to emphasize his objections. "I could agree with you, Miss Ben-Tov, but we'd both be wrong!"

Rachel wanted to explain her reservations; Morgan raised his palm forward. "Stop, don't talk. Give your ears a chance," Morgan growled. "In American parlance, I don't give a rat's ass. So listen up. You're late to the game.

"I sensed impending disaster many decades ago. I processed the craziness going on in the world and I prepared for it, Miss Ben-Tov. It's the reason you're able to sit in this air-conditioned room or eat a wide variety of foods or communicate with us from across the world. I will remind you that unless I'd subsidized our state's hardened transformers, bought satellites, prepared for auxiliary power, cached valuable data, and had working relationships with like-minded communities, we'd be dead in the water. That took a hell of a lot of mutual respect and trust. It also took relying on my personal instinct. Take a lesson. Take a seat. We've no hidden agendas here."

"Maybe you can give Miss Ben-Tov insight as to how coordinated is this effort. Dr. Nishant? If you don't mind?" Connor invited.

Morgan regained his seat with a grunt as Amar awkwardly stood. "First of all, I apologize to Miss Ben-Tov if she felt as if my question disrespectful." Amar bowed his head and nervously cleared his throat.

"As the solar flare threats loomed, we tried in England so many years ago to not only to pinpoint the timing but to investigate the possible environmental effects. One such study came under the European Scientific Commission's interest in electromagnetic fields and the effects on humans. This came as a result of smaller influences like cell phones, Monitor frequencies, Radio Frequency Fields, Personal Monitors and True-View glasses, Static fields, Intermediate Frequency Fields, and so forth…on and on. Those studies returned alarming information at the 'lower' levels of exposure. It included everything from the balance of epidemiological evidence of RF fields in vivo from our vitro research to acoustic neuromas and increasing neurovegetative symptoms as a result of the cumulative effects of generations of exposure to electro-magnetic pulses and frequency fields.

"No one anticipated that there would be overwhelming simultaneous EMP impacts on top of the cumulative exposures we faced up to that time. We had been focused on the requirements to safeguard our military, communication and transportation… with one area reserved for a cursory look at what consequences electromagnetic pulses and wide range of frequencies would have on organisms… specifically on the human organism.

"I worked on the data shared within the UK office for some years prior to my return to India. The information was supplemented when an old friend rescued my family. The evidence for DNA alterations, enhancement of known carcinogens and cellular damage, was found to be rampant before the EMP's concentrated forces hit our planet.

"It began with simple studies that provided evidence suggesting that strong electromagnetic pulses may have substantive and long range effects on the cognitive processes of the brain's left hemisphere. Studies hoisted a red flag early on. One such study began with a few words that researchers transposed while the subject read a prepared text. We simply asked the test subjects to read lines from a book or poem. These test subjects were all university students. Prior to the application of a low-grade EMP to their brain, the text was read perfectly by our study group. After? The words were jumbled. The research suggested that the EMP application temporarily short-circuited the logical circuitry of the left hemisphere. 100 percent of our test subjects muffled the readings at some minor level.

"Then the study expanded. They identified a region of the brain just above and behind the right ear that we theorized controlled morality. After using magnetic pulses to block cell activity in that region, a strange thing happened. It impaired the study group's notion of right and wrong. Morality, as we know it, was skewed immediately.

"Moral behavior, we'd been led to believe, is an ingrained organization derived from cultivated behaviors. Yet when a magnetic field was applied to this specific brain region of bright healthy university students, moral judgments were not only quantifiable, they were negatively altered.

"The key area, according to the study, is a collection of nerve cells known as the right temporo-parietal junction, or RTP. In one study, the question was put forward whether one would allow a loved one to board a plane that had a history of serious mechanical problems. After receiving a 500-millisecond magnetic pulse to the scalp, the verdicts were based upon outcome rather than moral principle. In other words, if the plane didn't crash, a positive judgment to board the faulty plane was acceptable. Intentions didn't factor; value of the subject and consequences didn't matter... morality was altered in case study after case study. 'Sure... I'd send my girlfriend, boyfriend, mother, father, child on an airplane with a faulty engine', they said. That particular study concluded that if the subject was killed, the decision maker assumed marginal culpability.

"Then we added another element. This region of the RTP is highly engaged when people consider the intentions or consequences of actions of others. A transcranial magnetic stimulation, or TMS, created weak electric currents that stopped brain cells from operating normally. The volunteers were exposed to TMS for 25 minutes before reading stories about morally questionable characters and scenarios. We then subjected them days later to a much shorter millisecond of TMS while being asked to make another moral judgment. The moral judgment deteriorated further; they no long considered whether or not there was a harmful outcome and had no discernible concern..."

Morgan interrupted, "How long did it take to return to normal moral behavior and interpretation?"

"All except one returned to normal functionality within the week," Nishant explained.

"Well, shit. Nice experiment, Dr. Nishant. You send that kid to another school or what?"

Nishant stammered, "They're volunteers...I..I..did not select the sampling."

"Ahh. And you didn't administer the low level shocks either? Interesting study when the scientists aren't that concerned over the greater outcome. Please continue."

Amar hesitated, clearly embarrassed at the irony. Dr. Green encouraged him to finish his presentation.

"Dr. Pendergrass always speaks what's left of his mind. I remind you that he was born this way, although we wish we could blame it on an experiment gone haywire. Please continue. We're very eager to hear."

"Yes. Up to that point, we thought that moral development was late to come about. It doesn't solidify until the mid-twenties, we thought. The overwhelming question here is what effects does an EMP, the likes of what our planet endured, have on children? What effects did it have on our DNA? It seems as if some children who might have been dosed heavily with the EMP energies might never develop a moral sense, while others do...or have...developed traditional or alternative ways to compensate for moral decay caused by the consistent low frequencies.

"I think I should stop here, Dr. Pendergrass. It's the second part of that study now in your group's hands that we are here to investigate. It deals with reproductive effects that have a direct correlation with a wide spectrum of spontaneous brain and nerve abnormalities. We suffered the environmental inability to cleanse the planet of the cumulative effect of low frequency lifestyles suffered by the time we were hit by the EMP disasters. Most of the world's populations were already operating with a carcinogenic overload. The EMP disaster put a large population segment over the edge..."

Meredith Green took charge as soon as she noticed Morgan nervously tapping his cane on the floor, a lingering personal protest to that which he considered an overload of redundancies.

Meredith kicked Morgan's cane from under the table and stood to continue Amar's train of thought.

"Solar flares, coupled with the e-bombs, affected human behaviors. We now suspect there are other long environmental influences. We know that these EMPs have disrupted the earth's natural resonance of 7.89 Hz and/or the resonance of life ELF frequencies as well. I'll skip a reference to vibrational forces at work in the Sea Walnut and what it means to innate survival; I will bottom line our collective studies: these anomalies that have come to our attention are the result of a convergence of interrelated events, the upshot being the triggering of heretofore unrealized talents and survival mechanisms in our genetic code, and something more sinister at the other end."

The room fell silent.

"To what other end?" Rachel asked softly.

"We have morally, physically, and emotionally polarized the planet. By this time, shouldn't there be a return to civilized behavior in regions previously civilized or cultivated? Where's the effort after two decades to return to a better way of life? There is evidence that there's a strange mix of logical and illogical behaviors in regions where the EMP effects should have faded. It might mean that those who are ordinarily charged with inculcating moral patterns were unable to act morally or sustain moral behaviors, much less instill moral tenets to the younger generations. Yet, there are countless examples of unaffected people in nearby areas who have restored working communities. We could well attribute this irregularity to the irregular patterns of the magnetic field in the first place. It could also be a result of certain cultivated traits that have been maintained in community-based conclaves. Dare I submit that cumulative electromagnetic damage that caused extreme molecular damage was sustained and amplified by not living a culturally balanced life?

"The magnetic pulses may have also triggered dormant switching mechanisms meant to offset behaviors for historical or cosmic cycles of events. Maybe these onslaughts of environmental attacks have happened before and we are wired for a survival response, while other responses represent those victims of long-term brain impairment. As we unravel DNA wiring that directs highly sophisticated DNA strands, we can see how quickly evolution may come about in the interest of dealing with crisis management."

"Let's take a lunch break. I'm starved," Morgan announced. "My brain hurts."

"If you have to excuse yourself, Morgan, please do so." Meredith eyed him suspiciously.

"My prostrate was regenerated years ago, Missy. I'm hungry and I think we need a break. Too many big thoughts, ya' know. Let's digest them over some sustenance."

As they stood and began to talk amongst each other excitedly, Rachel moved to Morgan's side.

"Please accept my apologies, Dr. Pendergrass. I have difficulty trusting anyone."

Morgan rolled his eyes and smiled.

"You're too smart and pretty for me to hold a grudge, young lady. Now, by way of excuses: I'm too old to have to convince other people around me to move in the right direction. And I've never harmed anyone in my life. Spare us the suspicions. This involves my own flesh and blood, my home, and humanity's future. Get a grip."

Connor approached Rachel and took her aside. "You're amazing...did I tell you that?" he murmured.

"That's hormones talking, Connor. One kiss and a few days later, I'm just amazing?"

"Damn right."

Chapter XVI
The White House

Washington, D.C.
Wednesday, December 29, 2060

*I*n a windowless, white-bricked room, Clifton Brown played with a former twenty-dollar note examining the picture of the seventh U.S. president on one side and the White House featured on the other. It had long been removed from circulation with the advent of new faces that replaced those of the Founding Fathers. Brown rued that the entire currency was defunct before his own image was placed upon the 100-dollar bill.

"Used to be called the Double Sawbuck because it was twice the value of a ten-dollar bill. Twice the value of nothing is always going to be nothing," he laughed to himself. "Better to have the double eagle. Gold means something. At least Jackson had his picture on some kind of currency. That means something, too. All I got was the wrath of Americans when the world decided on the Yuan even as it declined. In the end, all the banks held in trust were useless paper promises when the smart ones moved on to barter-bit currency", he thought.

Brown returned the mint condition bill that was among a collection of transparent museum strongboxes stored in an old utility closet. He rummaged amongst other boxes and letters that provided distraction.

Since transported from West Virginia, Brown had come in contact with three people. When he asked questions of the examining doctor in those first days, they went unanswered.

When she returned for a second examination, Brown called her a disrespectful 'bitch'. A no-nonsense Confederation colonel, the tall lean woman quietly placed her equipment to one side and slapped Brown hard across the face. Since that episode, he'd received no music, sparse food, and vitamin drinks in place of dessert. There was no monitor, news, writing or reading material. The matter of Brown's surveillance was made clear by the hum of an old turn–of-the-century oversized camera meant to remind him of his predicament.

The room was clean and agreeable; he thought it was one of the secure rooms for mid-management staff under the West Wing but could not be sure. It was clear, however, that there had yet to be an official decision as to his fate.

"They don't know what the hell to do with me," he smirked. "Means they're a virtuous, careful group. Pendergrass will see me. He's going to want answers," Brown reassured himself.

The room went black. Without a clock, the sporadic stretches of light and dark were meant to confuse the ex-president's sense of time. He was accustomed to alternate rhythm cycles having lived underground for twenty years. Brown could not have cared less.

This isn't Pendergrass' style; someone's pissed, Brown thought. As if reading his mind, the monitor came to life with an unidentified male voice.

"If we had our way, Mr. Brown, we would have replayed many thousands of hours of images for you. We would have begun with the children dying of starvation and families being randomly slaughtered as your Secret Service invaded homes. We would follow with your hightailing it out of the Situation Room and into your two planes with your family and staff. Then we'd have included that heartwarming expression of the Brown brand of leadership... ordering four people killed on Air Force One for 'insurrection and treason' when they advised you as to an emergency plan for the greater populace. As it is, we've left you in the company of your conscience. As a man without one, we assume that yours has been a very satisfactory stay. We'll transport you to another location within a half hour's time. Please prepare yourself."

"What's the dress code?" Brown remained prone on his bed, hands behind his head. His sarcasm was meant to aggravate the unseen tormentor. "Are we going anywhere special?"

There was no answer and the lights returned.

In the Oval office, Confederation Minister Robert Gant gritted his teeth as he terminated the communication with Brown.

"I've got so much I want to say. It's all I can do to remain calm," he complained to Governor Mario Hernandez's hologram.

"I'm wondering what Morgan has in mind. If it were up to me, I'd have him just take a stroll downtown in any North Carolina town around lunchtime. I sure as hell can't imagine how he's survived the last twenty years undetected! No illness, acting smart as a baboon's ass," Hernandez grumbled.

"Think that's what Morgan is wondering, too," Gant agreed. "The guy was not someone to go it alone. He as an evil leech with no backbone so what and where were his resources?"

Governor Hernandez figured that if anyone could figure Brown riddles, it was Pendergrass.

"He'll know what to do with the scum. Hate the idea Brown will be in my state. Parasites are known to spread viruses. His special brand of discontent and hatred spread like wildfire.

"We'll expect your transport tomorrow at noon in Raleigh. Take care, Robert," Hernandez said resignedly to his friend.

"Thank you, Mario. Want anything from here?" Gant asked.

"What have you in the way of happiness from that extraordinary wine cellar?" he pleaded.

"Gotcha. On its way!"

Minister Robert Gant was typical of the men and women who assumed responsibility for Confederation administration. Theirs was a sense of responsibility rather than a power grab. Morgan Pendergrass had handpicked each official before he handed over the reins and re-instituted the vote. There were term limits this time around for the Congress, and civics classes were once again a part of the national curriculum. 'We trust in God' was returned to the gold-based currencies and the barter-bit allowed to continue and fluctuate independently with market demand. In the interest of transparency, the Commons news reports ran live 24/7. Gant had been Morgan's right hand man.

Security measures included the return of private ownership of weaponry. The latest weapons used biometric triggers. Everyone realized the dangers of traditional guns that landed in the hands of the 'crazies'; the ammunition, however, had a shelf life. To date, there was no evidence of the capability for severely brain-damaged survivors to manufacture new ammunition or override complicated codes for smart guns.

The first rounds of leaders responded to challenges without praise or remuneration. Confederation currency was goodwill.

Colonel Komor knocked on Gant's door and was buzzed in.

"Want to slap him goodbye, Krisztina?" Gant laughed hard.

"I've never done that before," the doctor sighed.

"You've never slapped a man?"

"I've never had to hold my temper like that," she said in a way that suggested exhaustion. "What I wanted to do was administer a quick hypo to his carotid artery in that nasty chicken neck. The man is a creep. I reviewed the chronicles and can't imagine how prior generations sent a Brown our way. What happened? Were people completely out of their minds? Even a child could read his duplicity."

Robert Gant, and millions of others, shared similar opinions. And not everyone was privy to the documentaries. Gant recalled the president's confusion at the onset of the solar flares that further complicated an overburdened electronic grid section-by-section, coast-to-coast. The bombs put the president's sanity on the line as wholesale panic ensued.

"First thing he wanted to do was retaliate," Gant recalled the situation as a lowly advisor. "He yelled to respond with nukes to the offending nation. No one could explain it well enough; the e-bombs came from the middle of the Atlantic... no way to track its origins or launch a response. Besides that, he couldn't grasp the science that predicted the solar flares for twenty years. Brown sat and twiddled his thumbs while publicly blaming the flares on climate change. If he'd moved, we'd been able to get most of the population to safe areas or have given them assistance.

"He ran...literally trotted out... from the Situation Room to the duplicate Air Force One planes. Then he ordered four of the top brass to be killed...on the spot...on the plane. That's not what bothers me. It bothers me that his orders were immediately followed. The embedded chips with cyanide were activated without a singular protest," Gant ranted. "No one wanted to be next."

Krisztina sighed, "Pendergrass has been an amazing counterpoint. But he's too highbrow to mete the appropriate measure. Brown will live out his days confined within civilized surroundings. Sickening. Did I thank you yet for making me accompany him to Raleigh?"

"About that. We're required to have medical personnel on board. You're the right person to handle him. Thank you... I owe you a dinner. Sorry?" Gant smiled apologetically.

Komor sighed as she pulled back her brunette hair into a tight bun. "It's fine. I'll be in touch from the Consortium. I'm supposed to profile Brown. Like you need a doctor to do that?"

"I'll miss you around here," Gant added.

Chapter XVII
The Hopeless Rescue

December 29, 2060

Nicholas, Esther, and her younger sister, Cynthia, boarded one of the six lifeboats with four other passengers. Each lifeboat teetered as untested riggings alternately lurched and slowed throughout their descent into the rough waters. Heliports roved the scene, intensifying the sprayed waves that angrily crossed bows. A loudspeaker instructed the passengers to motor to a barge with a platform secured for their rescue.

"Disembark carefully with personnel. Please leave personal belongings on the ship..." came the bullhorn directive.

As their lifeboat approached the floating platform, Nicholas spoke quietly to his two friends.

"They'll ask what happened. How much do you think the others know?"

Esther tried to calm Nicholas as the helicopters hovered above them and removed passengers.

"Look, it doesn't matter. You don't even know what happened. The question is why it happened and you seem to know that much. These are the good guys. We're away from the bad guys. They're dead. Don't over-think it."

"That doesn't make me feel better because nothing is the way it appears. I don't think we can count on 'good' guys' and 'bad guys'. Why does everyone act so bizarre?" Nicholas posed. "The captain of the ship says we can draw straws to go ashore and the others return? What the hell? I mean those were the same guys who just casually pumped bullets into innocent people. Why not just kill us and dump us overboard? At one level, stuff seems reasonable and then it turns nuts."

Esther had another idea about Nicholas' sudden angst.

"You're just nervous because you've never flown before. You're fretting like a little girl. The thing I'm worried about is flying with you. Don't make the pilot throw up or beat his head on the ground...if you don't mind."

Nicholas agreed that he was a little nervous about flying but insisted that the source of his uneasiness was random behaviors.

"Why is it that things don't follow a pattern? Don't you notice how some people are afraid, some are oblivious? Most of those passengers didn't seem to figure that they were standing in line to die even after watching the sequences of murder for hours!"

"Sure. It's even worse in some places. I think it has to do with the chipping from a long time ago. All those welfare recipients and federal employees had implanted chips to help track their records for medical assistance and all. You know, make sure that people didn't buy things with welfare money they shouldn't. Who knows what else went into those chips? Some old Canadian told us all about how the solar flares probably finally rocked their brains. My mom said that tracking chips were attached to the nervous system..." Esther chattered eagerly.

"Was anyone in your family embedded with a chip?" Nicholas wondered.

"Hell no," Esther said. "We weren't on government assistance, even though we could have used it. We believed in being nice, compassionate, and independent. Our parents died for it, too. There wasn't enough compassion to satisfy starving thieves. Nice couldn't stop bullets. Fair couldn't get us admitted into a hospital either. They died for all the right reasons except for being around for their kids. We were abandoned."

"How did you guys get on the ship?" Nicholas asked.

"*Shut up!* Don't ever ask us that," Esther said abruptly.

Nicholas, Esther, and Cynthia watched as groups were lifted away by the heliports. The three of them remained waiting.

"They could have taken us on the last one," noted Esther.

Nicholas had no sense of urgency.

"I don't feel threatened, if that's what you're asking," he answered.

A large uniformed man approached them.

"Please follow us. We've been instructed to take you three to North Carolina."

He signaled the last helicopter to land rather than hoist the three. He spoke to someone at the other end of the platform then turned to the three waiting patiently in the ripping wind.

"We've identified the passengers and we know you as Nicholas Bradley, and you two ladies as Cynthia and Esther, correct?"

The girls nodded in the affirmative.

"We'll be relocating everyone else to places that can accommodate refugees. You three have been personally invited by ex-governor, Dr. Pendergrass... we'll leave in the morning after you're able to rest this evening."

"That's a good thing?" Nicholas looked hard at the officer.

The man immediately removed his sunglasses and extended his hand.

"I'm Sergeant French. It's a good thing, Nicholas."

Nicholas shook his hand and felt at ease for the first time in more years than he could remember.

As the three were seated in the enormous Confederation heliport, all welcomed the rare sensation of relief. Nicholas felt the light squeeze of Esther's hand in his as the engines quietly lifted them into the clouds. Cynthia fell asleep on her sister's lap. Esther's head rested on Nicholas's shoulder.

Thursday, December 30, 2060

Scott Reid stood at the entry gates to the Pendergrass Farms and stared at the stone pineapples sitting on either side of the iron gates that seemed more suited to Charleston, South Carolina shores than Cary, North Carolina.

"May I help you?"

Before Reid could answer the gate monitor, the security system had identified the man whose last two visits raised alarms in the Pendergrass household.

"I wonder if I might have the opportunity to speak to Dr. Pendergrass? He'll only recognize me from a security breach and a Halloween party about five years back," Reid explained.

"We have you, Mr. Reid. Please wait while we check Dr. Pendergrass's availability."

The next voice was Morgan's.

"What the hell you doin' here, Reid?"

A well-rehearsed speech rushed forth from Scott Reid.

"Sir, something happened five years back when I brought my boy here for your Halloween party. He used to be emotionally upset until a chance encounter with your granddaughter when she was an infant. I'm bringing it to your attention now because I had no idea the meaning of that transformation until a visit to the doctor last week."

The minuscule lens on the monitor rotated. A bird drone dropped, too.

"A visit to the doctor? You telling me what, son?"

"That my little boy touched your daughter's hand and he was... I really don't know how to say this, sir..."

"Give it a try."

"Would it be too much for us to just meet for five minutes? I feel a little weird out here."

"Keep goin'. I feel a little weird in here, too."

"He was healed. From the moment your granddaughter touched his hand he was calm. There's more. He's highly intelligent."

"My granddaughter healed your son? He's good? Great. I won't bill you."

"It's not a joke, sir. He has half a brain, and I mean that literally. I think your granddaughter somehow put him right. I remember the complete change in him that Halloween night. My wife and I didn't know the reason for his emotional temper tantrums...we didn't have evidence of the cortex being 95% gone... it had lesions and was disabled. Somehow, the right hemisphere took over, the doctor says. Your daughter rewired him."

"How come you just now goin' to the doctor, Reid?"

"I've been in survival mode. My wife left me right before that night I was caught wandering around your farm. I've been busy feeling sorry for myself and my boy hasn't needed a doctor. Not once. I'm sure it has something to do with your granddaughter."

The gates slowly opened and a security bot picked up Scott Reid. Morgan answered the door.

"Come in. Sit down. Listen good."

Reid did as he was told and watched as Morgan paced in front of him, twirling his cane.

"This is the way it works. Your doctor would have told you, if you'd bothered to ask, that the brain has the capacity to rewire itself. There will always be some gaps, some special needs, but the brain has a way of compensating for injuries, illnesses, strokes...get the picture?"

"He did say that, sir. But my son doesn't have the usual functional flaws that go hand in hand with this condition. His basic language abilities are fine... everything is fine. The main issue in this situation was that some of the deeper structures that control movement were missing and there was an issue with emotional tantrums.

"He couldn't be calmed. He screamed, and squirmed con-stantly. My wife was a wreck. She couldn't take the pressure and left. The moment your granddaughter touched him he soothed. I remember the moment his face changed. It's re-mained that way ever since."

Morgan decided he didn't need this problem and weighed the possible outcomes.

"Let's go into my library...I'll order up some sandwiches for us. I'm hungry."

Reid recalled the library, the floor to ceiling books, and the fireplace surrounded by leather furniture. In one corner sat the wheelchair that his host had used on that odd Halloween night. Pendergrass abruptly shut the door and remained silent until Reid had a long look around.

"Look, I don't think that my granddaughter rewired your son's brain, nor do I think he's highly intelligent or healthy because of her. What I do think--and this is the first time I'm saying this outside of my head--that my granddaughter might have fixed his temperament. She has a gift to calm people. I've noticed this happens with her direct contact as well as being in proximity. What do you say to that?"

"That's what I'm saying, I guess. Something magical happened that made my boy peaceful. I just wanted to bring it to your attention. Most of all, I wanted to thank you."

"You're welcome. Now, this is what I want from you. I need to protect my granddaughter. So you're not going to bring any attention to any so-called talents by way of this jibber jabber. I've acknowledged what I know. You're going to honor my request, son. Is that an agreement? You're not going to use the words 'magic' or 'strange' in the context of my granddaughter."

It occurred to Scott Reid that Morgan Pendergrass had been more than honest; the Confederation's most notable citizen had positioned his granddaughter as vulnerable to public scrutiny.

"I'll never say anything. The fact is, I was drawn here. I couldn't explain it then and I'm not sure about the reason now."

Morgan frowned and snapped, "Ok, that kinda statement gives me the willies. What you sayin'?"

"That your granddaughter has a God-given gift; I think I was led here for a reason."

"You have a job, Reid?"

"Yes sir. I've been working with Failsafe Enterprises."

"How'd you get that job? They're a pretty tight group."

"You recommended me, sir. I thank you for that gift, too. Thanks to the good pay, I've been able to spend time on school...getting another certificate soon."

Morgan's heart sank.

"Look, Scott. I didn't recommend you for any job. They offered it to you or you applied? Did you make any statements about your son or my granddaughter at the time?"

The men looked at each other. Scott Reid didn't need the ruse spelled out.

"They asked me about the reasons for my being on the property at the time they picked me up like they were supposed to. I'd have to get the transcripts to see if I said anything about my son or your granddaughter, but I'm 99% sure nothing of the kind was ever mentioned. I don't think it has anything to do with that, but somebody made a connection or maybe an assumption when you told Failsafe to let me go free. They told me that I'd come highly recommended by you about three weeks after the incident. They said I had the job because Governor Pendergrass recommended me."

"It's okay. I'm going to make a quick call."

Within five minutes, the Pendergrass Farms security had discovered the bug on Scott Reid, embedded within the FS shirt logo. Isabella Moreno, head of security, frowned with concern.

"Failsafe knew you were coming here?"

"They sent me on a periphery check of the properties. They probably thought I might check in. I don't know how. I drop by here every week. This is the first time I thought about actually ringing."

Morgan recalled his son-in-law's suspicions about the Confederation's lack of vigilant security.

"It's our first indication that the Confederation is no longer secure and/or has an armed security force breaking the law. I hope its limited to Failsafe. You're invited to now work for me, Reid. It will require an undercover investigation of the Failsafe group. You in?"

"Yes, sir. Have I been jacked around for five years like a carrier pigeon?"

"Not sure about that. My guess is that any security group has the potential to be a private man's army... a mercenary group for hire, anyway. Most probably there isn't a person on the Failsafe force not tracked and bugged. We made that illegal so I'm going to make this investigation a priority. In the meantime, we're going to reverse engineer that bug and see if we can figure what – if anything – was transmitted."

Isabella was head of Pendergrass security. She was also Morgan's personal bodyguard, doubling as a personal assistant.

"We're on it, Dr. Pendergrass... just handed it off to my people. There's more than a conventional bug, sir."

"What did you find?" Morgan worried.

Moreno glanced at Scott Reid.

"Did someone require you have a RNM implant in your brain?"

"What the hell is that?" Reid stammered.

"Yes or no?" Moreno asked

"Not that I know of," Reid answered.

"The good news is that the Remote Neural Monitor was always flawed and detectable. The NSA started research at the turn of the century to map an individual's bioelectric field. It was meant for intense National Surveillance. With special EMF equipment, the former National Security Agency could remotely detect and monitor possible terrorists. For electronic surveillance purposes, the NSA tracked electrical activity in the speech center of the brain with the hopes that it could be translated into the subject's verbal thoughts or intentions. A RNM was also able to send encoded signals to the brain's auditory cortex. After a RNM implant, the government would let a captured terrorist leave prisons and then track – and hopefully control – an unwitting spy as a spotter and plotter. There are bioelectric resonance frequencies in the brain...the Motor control, auditory, visual, somatosensory, and thought cortexes. It is possible to disrupt a person's images and personality by transmitting incompatible frequencies for any of these regions. In this case, your RNM is meant to test as a lie detector for employees. Your impulses have been mapped; deviations from your standard indicate something is wrong."

"What happens now?" Morgan asked.

"We've determined Reid's standard profile. His implant is now neutralized from any remote control. It is set permanently to his bioelectric profile and will not fluctuate. It's essentially non-functional. When anyone tries to read his patterns on a brain-to-computer link, Reid's pulses will read even," Moreno explained in simple terms. "He will always be telling the truth... by those indicators," Moreno assured.

"You've already done all of this?" Morgan asked.

"Done and done," Moreno said. "Regarding Failsafe, shall we authorize the use of planting some spybots within their facility? Shall I put in a call to the Governor?" Moreno asked.

"Oh, yeah. Authorize the hell out of that idea, Isabella. Bring him up to speed on the current use of the old implants."

Governor Hernandez approved the investigation and asked to speak with Pendergrass.

"Morgan, this is serious. I hope it's just a case of being overambitious and nothing more. I remember Cain... a pain in the ass. Got any ideas?" Hernandez asked.

"Let's hold on to our shorts. I'm just going to request that the Confederation put a stop on sanctioning any more private security firms," Morgan directed and signed off the moment Isabella Moreno called in with her report.

"The bug and the RNM implant were operable until Mr. Reid got close to the call box monitor at the entry gates. Our technology is way beyond this piece of junk. It's useless around here," Moreno assured.

Morgan spoke to Reid and Moreno.

"This is how this is going to work. Isabella will activate your exterior bug by turning off our equipment. Our departure chit-chat will indicate that I think you're a little nuts and not to be taken seriously. You're going to say that you were given a job at Failsafe and just wanted to check in. Got that, Isabella? Bring the bug back over and put it back inside the logo. Give me a high sign before you allow it to activate. I'll walk Reid outside the gate."

Isabella disabled the Pendergrass security to revive the Failsafe feed with an enhanced bug.

"It's got a visual, too. Are you ready for this? Better be a good actor," Moreno smiled. "Are you ready?"

"Yes, ma'am. But, how do I control it? What if I have to get in touch?"

"You'll be able to turn it off and on at will...but be careful about Failsafe's visual surveillance when you move to trigger. Trigger it by your arm monitor and don't touch the logo or the shirt if you can help it. A simple touch is fine if your PM is ever removed. Any time it's activated, we'll be listening and watching but you won't have two-way communication."

Isabella wished him well and left by an underground entrance that led back to her offices.

* * *

Morgan Pendergrass considered that there were not many accidents in life. A man had initially appeared as a lurking suspect five years prior. The same man reappeared as the window to corruption that had operated under his nose. *Tip of the iceberg,* Morgan thought.

Scott Reid and Morgan walked toward the library door.

"Ok, showtime, Scott. I'm going to cover our asses in the event that Failsafe had surveillance that picked up our initial conversation at the gate. I'm also going to underline that I think highly of Failsafe. You play along. We'll end on a friendly note. Got it? I'll begin by opening and shutting this door. They'll figure a time lapse was spent in a protected space. Ready?"

They moved into the foyer and Isabella activated the Failsafe bug. She signaled Morgan on his PC and he began as they made their way down the long driveway toward the gates.

"Well, I'm mighty glad you're enjoying your work at Failsafe. They used to work here inside the compound for the Confederation but they went private. You're in good hands, son. You've come a long way since that crazy Halloween night five years ago. But remember... it's a scientific fact that the brain rewires itself. Got nothing to do with anything but God's plan to help the body heal itself. Your doctor will explain how your son recovered," Morgan said on script.

"I guess the doctor did try to explain it. I really didn't understand all that was said. You're the only doctor I know. Thank you, sir, for helping," Reid played his part.

Morgan handed over a small bag to Reid.

"Well, look what the kitchen sent us! Leftover sandwiches. How about you take these?"

Scott Reid looked into the bag that contained three sand-wiches and twenty miniature bugbots programmed to find their way inside the infrastructure of the Failsafe Security complex. They would automatically seek various temperature settings and were controlled by Moreno's team.

Reid rode back to Failsafe's parking station. He selected one sandwich and dropped the bag's contents in the transport sta-tion's trash repositories that connected to the office building. As he entered the building, the lobby-bot's floor receptionist announced Reid's name.

"Scott Reid...check in upstairs, please."

Scott Reid had made mistakes in his life but he decided that this wasn't going to be one of them.

The office door buzzed open as he approached a mid-man-agement office. Inside were eight men, including the COO of Failsafe Enterprises, Richard Cain.

"I'm sorry... got a message to come up here to check in. I didn't know there was a meeting." Reid tossed a half-eaten sandwich in the waste disposal by the door.

"You're in the right place, Scott," Richard Cain's voice as-sured as he examined his employee's startled expression. "Sorry if we alarmed you. I've got a special interest in making sure that our biggest client is a happy man. I understand you paid Dr. Pendergrass a personal visit today? Mind sharing what made you do such a thing?"

"Yes, sir. I had an unfortunate encounter with the Pender-grass Farms years ago. It's on record. I sort of stumbled my way onto the Pendergrass property without permission. Fail-safe security took me in for trespassing when I tripped the perimeter line."

"Go on..." Cain said.

"I took my son to a Halloween party a few months later. Dr. Pendergrass recognized me on his porch. He invited me into the home with my boy. We came to terms and he's forgiven me. I always felt pretty bad about that episode. Anyway, I looked around the Kuykendall perimeter today and it all looked good. I took the opportunity to buzz in just to express my gratitude."

"That part we know. I see that you were invited inside the old man's house," Cain leaned in.

Scott Reid detected a tone of disrespect for the man whom everyone credited with saving half of the former United States. Reid spoke calmly.

"Yes, sir. Nice guy. I apologized again for having trespassed years before and just let him know that his security was on my beat today. I guess I should have cleared that?"

Cain ignored the question by asking one.

"What else did he ask?"

"He talked about his leg. Twirled a cane around a lot. Pointed at things in his living room and his library. I told him about my son who...well, it's kind of crazy talk...I just imagined that a meeting he had with his infant granddaughter cured him of a brain injury. Dr. Pendergrass explained that this is a very normal function and his granddaughter had nothing to do with it. The brain has a way of repairing itself. I felt like an idiot because it's exactly what the doctor told me," Reid finished.

"That's it?" Cain pushed.

"He was nice about it and ordered something for us to eat and drink. I think he's lonely. He asked about my boy, said he was sorry about my emotional stresses, suggested some rest, and that was about it."

"What was in the white bag that you brought through the door this afternoon?"

"Leftover ham sandwiches. Did I do something wrong?"

Richard Cain was considered the best at surveillance in North Carolina. He had been troubled having to share his flagship account with a private staff that Pendergrass preferred for his family's personal security. Cain's ambition showed when he pressed too hard to become the Confederation's Security Council chair. Confederation officials thought his suggestion that other contenders were 'incompetent' reflected poorly. Cain regretted his subsequent temper tantrums at Board meetings. Cain had a bad habit of expecting more; he was told that his outbursts suggested instability.

In the end, Pendergrass dismissed Failsafe from the Pendergrass interior compound but kept the company on for a few of his local businesses. When Governor Hernandez formed the Confederation Security Force for the state, it dug deep into Richard Cain's revenues. Cain figured that he needed to keep on the good side of his largest account or suffer a larger hit to his reputation. He arranged for Scott Reid's position, figuring him a harmless, brainless agent likely to represent Failsafe as nonthreatening to Pendergrass's private security personnel.

"I'm good with you having a relationship with old man P. The account is important to us, and I'm going to make you head of the Pendergrass perimeter patrol. If you see or hear of anything unusual, dispatch it. Sound good, Scott?" Cain stated the plan as a given.

"Thank you, Mr. Cain."

"Do a good job and it's going to mean bonuses, too. I'll check in with you regularly to see how things are going. Just be sure you know who you're working for, Reid," Cain emphasized.

"Of course, sir. I'm perfectly clear on that point," Reid confirmed.

Reid departed the room and Cain reviewed Reid's brain EMF results on his monitor.

"No trace of duplicity. The kid is squeaky clean," he smiled.

At the end of the day, Scott's transport drove him by his son's school and returned to their modest one-level brick home with its small, neat garden. Christmas lights flickered on the home's eaves. Scott Reid saddened as he recalled a time when the decorations were strung and arranged to loving perfection.

Jordon sprinted in front of his father, slamming the screen door mindlessly behind. Reid removed his company shirt indoors and retrieved the encrypted glasses given to him by Isabella Moreno. Morgan Pendergrass's welfare was on his mind and he made a call. Moreno connected Reid with her boss.

"Sir, you're right to be suspicious. Nothing specific. It's just Cain's tone and the number of men in on our conversation. I've been assigned the Pendergrass Farms operations bordering

Kuykendall Road; I've been given a raise with promises of bonuses and will be reporting directly to Richard Cain."

"Not sure what this all means. What you say is understandable from a business point of view. However, I do know that he's not supposed to be bugging employees without their knowledge or using remote tracking frequency chips, and that he's got a bad temper. He was pretty ticked off when I refused to use his group officially or fit him into a Confederation position. Fact was, I'm glad he had that nasty rage or he might have made it to an official position. Guess you're an official double agent for our investigation. Mind yourself, Reid. This isn't a nice business. What did he say in particular that put you on edge, son?" Morgan added.

"You're revered in these parts, Dr. Pendergrass. He blew you off as an 'old man'. I don't trust his intentions. I sure didn't like his sneer."

Morgan laughed, "Fact is, I'm an old man and that sneer is the guy's natural resting face. Be objective and be thorough."

Friday, December 31, 2060

Lex was eager to ingratiate himself with his father-in-law, who rarely asked a favor. He considered every approach possible that might convince his mother-in-law to be open minded with regard to Morgan's idea of Clifton Brown's arrival.

Lex was quietly situated at the kitchen table when Angela walked into the room. Angela held a vase in her hand that she aimed at Lex.

"Angela...it's me!" Lex warned.

"You scared the bejesus outta me. Why are you just sitting there?"

"Just wanted a minute of your time. I ...need...to..." Lex stammered.

"You're an emissary for my husband. You're supposed to persuade me to be receptive when Clifton Brown comes to town, stay around here, for the sake of God and country?" Angela presupposed.

"That's about it..." Lex tried.

"You just trot off back to Morgan and say what you want to say but promise me now that you'll be watching the security around here."

"Yes! Of course I will. Thank you!" Lex was overjoyed at success.

"Make sure Isabella puts bots all over the place...insects... everything we've got."

"Drugs? Shock collar?" Lex asked.

"Exactly."

"Joking, Angela."

"I'm not. Something is terribly dark. Brown shows up alone without a single member of his family? Everyone dead? Better take note."

* * *

It was arranged. Clifton Brown was to fly from Washington with CAS security guards. Dr. Komor was directed to accompany Brown as the attending medical officer and senior representative. Brown attempted a discussion by way of an apology as the entourage prepared to land in Raleigh, N.C.

"Hey! Trying to apologize here, Miss Doctor. I've been under stress for twenty years. You've got to understand what it means to be the President of the United States...to ensure the safety and welfare of those who operated the country. It was..."

Without turning, Krisztina raised a middle finger high above her head.

"One more word and I'll have to give you a special time-out. Not another peep until Dr. Pendergrass says so," Komor warned.

"You're telling me to be quiet? You'll answer for your behavior, you piece of nothing. Morgan and I are..."

Krisztina locked and loaded her medgun, stood up, turned, aimed and injected Brown in the side of his neck from ten feet away. Brown's head slumped to one shoulder.

"Wow, Colonel!" the Confederation guards on board hooted approval.

"Yeah, well, sorry you'll have to carry him to the transport. I'll explain it," Komor apologized.

From the cockpit, the pilot spoke.

"No need! Dr. Pendergrass has a live feed and is laughing pretty hard. He wants to talk to you on your personal monitor, Colonel."

Komor adjusted her settings for privacy. The last chuckling of Pendergrass filled her head.

"My apologies...the man is beyond annoying, sir," Komor explained.

"No one knows that jackass better than I. Good job. There's no known tonic I know of other than the one you delivered. Komor, I'd like you to record whatever's going on with Brown during your stay. You're going to have to curb that temper," Morgan warned.

"Yes, sir!"

Brown awoke bleary-eyed in a converted tobacco shed. It was a step down from his last confines.

"Another windowless room?" Brown scowled.

A security guard observed the ex-president warily from across the room without response.

"Giving me the silent treatment, soldier?" Brown struggled to steady himself. "How about a little help? You had to cuff an old man's hands together? I'm so frightening?"

The guard stoically regarded Brown. He tried to reconcile heinous crimes with the person before him. Brown, the young guard decided, was the type of man who would never evoke pity, regardless of age or condition.

Brown chattered mercilessly. The guard contacted Pendergrass to let him know that his guest had awakened 'full throttle'.

The Pendergrass New Year's party was scheduled to begin at 9:30 p.m.; Morgan glanced at his wrist PM and wondered if he wanted to speak to Brown at all. He decided to let the man rest and sent instructions for Dr. Komor to oversee security.

Another call interrupted Morgan; the three young people rescued from the freighter had arrived. In another 24 hours, they would be on the farm.

"Make the young people as comfortable as possible, Captain. Take them out to see the fireworks."

Morgan summoned Indu and Amar, Rachel, Angela, Adele, Lex, and Connor in his library to bring them up to speed on Brown's residency.

"I've got a dodgy guest nearby. He's a prisoner so I don't want anyone to be alarmed, just aware of the situation. The ex-president of the United States is here."

Indu's distress transformed her usual calm.

"The man who encouraged India to implant half the population with RF tracking chips? In the end, we couldn't move for the dead bodies. He is here?"

"I've got a mother lode of questions and that's one of them," Morgan nodded sadly. "We also have three teenagers on their way. One of them is Nicholas Bradley, per our conversation. The other two are unknowns but they're sisters. I'd appreciate it if your children are told to expect visitors and to welcome them. Before they arrive, we'll do some screening but there's no reason to believe that they're on the wrong side of things."

Indu relaxed. "I'm sure that they will be as warmly received as we were. We'll help in every way possible," she smiled assuredly.

Chapter XVIII
Cosmic Clicks

Friday, December 31, 2060

*I*n the Pendergrass upstairs recreation room, CC played with Aaron and attempted to do the same with Aditiya. Aditiya preferred to immerse himself with the super-computer at his disposal to design and collect geometric forms that floated unconnected around the room. He had worked for days identifying and assembling patterns. Multicolored three-dimensional images finally came to organized life the moment Aditiya asked the computer to synchronize the geometric patterns to known scientific forms.

The three children stared at the rotating spheres take shape, creating a symphony of designs.

"They're beautiful, Aditiya. What are these?" CC stared at the enumerable superimposed geometric shapes defined within natural images.

"They're being labeled now," Aditiya said absently transfixed upon the patterns. Aditiya directed the monitor to narrate the action and answer spontaneous questions.

"*These are longitudinal and latitudinal lines that signify energy lines...*" the monitor spoke as the patterns interconnected.

"*...Magnetic circles, symmetrical clusters of fifteen great circles, creating one hundred and twenty identical triangles. The Sioux tribes referred to these as the fifteen hoops that signify Earth's life force...*"

The monitor highlighted a series of celestial globes that symbolized Plato's belief that the basic structure of the Earth was an evolution from simple geometric forms to those of greater complexity.

"*In the order of complexity are the five patterns that form the blocks of the crystalline matrix are: tetrahedron, hexahedron, octahedron, dodecahedron and the icosahedron...*" The computer asked if more information was required.

"Yes," Aditiya answered immediately.

"No," corrected CC.

"Yes," overrode Aditiya. "This is my stuff, CC."

"I don't understand it!" CC protested.

"I want to hear. Just adjust the level of your translator!"

"My translator says you're rude," CC countered.

Aaron directed, "Just let the monitor illustrate, CC... we'll figure it out later. Monitor: continue!"

"*These are the five Platonic solids. To achieve perfect symmetry between the vertices, each face of a regular polyhedron must be a regular polygon and all the faces must be identical... Plato explicitly addressed the role of 'necessity' in the design of the universe as exemplified by the five and only five Platonic solids. Do you wish a direct quote?*" the monitor asked.

"Please," Aditiya confirmed.

"Noooo," CC pleaded, "I love to see these things!"

"CC, the images will stay. Now, be quiet. I want to hear the quote," Aditiya insisted.

"*Shall I continue?*" the monitor asked.

"Please continue until I say to stop," Aditiya glared in CC's direction.

"*Plato wrote: Although God did make use of the relevant auxiliary causes; it was He himself who gave their fair design to all that comes to be. That is why we must distinguish two forms of cause – the divine and the necessary. First, the divine, for which we must search in all things if we are to gain a life of happiness to the extent that our nature allows, and second, the necessary, for which we must search for the sake of the divine. Our reason is that without the necessary, those other objects, about which we are serious, cannot on their own be discerned, and hence cannot be comprehended or partaken of in any other way.*

"*In Plato's Cosmology, The Timeaus: 360 BC: the polygons include the triangle thought by Plato to be the building block of the universe. This idea and others make up the four elements and heaven...*" As the Monitor continued, CC jumped, excitedly circling one of the spheres glowing in its transparent geometric complexities.

"I have no idea what it's talking about...what is this one?" Caroline called out at the top of her lungs. "I love it!"

The monitor paused for Aditiya to confirm.

"CC? Stop!" Aditiya yelled. Examining the unusual image, he reconsidered CC's question. "Ok, what's that one?"

"*This correlates with your renderings of the geometric hexagons. Leonardo de Vinci named it Fleur de Vie, the Flower of Life. It is a figure used in countless motifs throughout ancient history as ancient symbols significant to spiritual beliefs depicting fundamental aspects of space and time. The Fleur de Vie figure consists of seven or more overlapping circles; the center of each circle is on the circumference of up to six surrounding circles of the same diameter. It is referenced as figures of sacred geometry and the Platonic solids within as being a template from which all life is generated...*"

CC interrupted, "Aaron, what do you think of Aditiya's art? Mathematical art, right, Aditiya?"

Aaron walked around the images and smiled his pleasure at the geometric patterns. "I love them. Like the Tree of Life...I see resemblances. These are spiritual. Very holy, I think."

The monitor beeped an incoming summons from Rachel, Indu, and Adele who had requested the three to come downstairs to dinner.

"Save!" directed Aditiya to the Monitor.

Caroline mimicked her friend's exhilaration.

"Yes...save, save, save! I love the block images. They're like the genome pictures at Dr. Green's office. Those are cells that split into patterns sort of like these pieces that are pieced together deep in the earth that Mr. Plato thought about."

Adele's voice filled the room.

"CC? You three need to show up downstairs in the kitchen tout de suite. A little dinner before the party has been prepared. Grandma and Grandpa will meet you three in the kitchen."

"My mother gets too excited, don't you think, Aaron?" CC wondered.

"She's a great mother, CC. She loves everyone around her except the new visitor," he said as the three moved rapidly toward the kitchen.

"What visitor?" CC poked Aaron as they raced downstairs.

"Someone in her mind. An old man with a big nose and long ears."

"My grandpa?" CC speculated.

"No. An angry man," Aaron said, "Don't know him."

"I don't like people coming here and surprising us and making my mum nervous. Aditiya is nervous enough for everybody," CC concluded.

As children are prone, Aaron announced a challenge to a race to the bottom. CC, house veteran, used her home court advantage by straddling the banister and sliding furiously down the well-oiled handrail. Aditiya, unused to spontaneous fun, preferred to take the steps one by one. Aaron skipped two at a time.

CC hooted victory and Aditiya lost his footing and fell.

"Who's the winner? Yes...it's Caroline Collins!" A victory dance was had.

The three burst into another spurt as soon as Aditiya caught up. This time, Aditiya kept pace but ran face-first into Morgan coming around a corner; the impact into his mechanical leg knocked the boy to the floor.

"Ouch!" Morgan regarded the Nishant boy's plight by rubbing his own forehead.

"That's what they mean when they say not to run head-first into things. You ok?" Morgan advised straddling Aditiya.

"Why do you say ouch and rub your head when I'm the one who hit my face?" Aditiya tearfully asked.

"How should I know? Must be that empathy bone acting up. Here, let me give you a hand up before I get in trouble for hurting poor, helpless small people."

Angela entered the room and surveyed a yellow racing stripe on the front of CC's white dress and Aditiya's imprinted forehead.

"I'm not going to say a thing," she commented.

"You just said something, grandma!" Caroline laughed.

"Yes, true." Angela hustled the children into the kitchen. "It's a good idea to get something in your stomachs now so you don't rob kitchen platters."

"We're staying up tonight?" CC peered up at the JazzBazz dolls still hanging from the second story.

"Baby, sorry. We aren't going to have time for JazzBazz. People are coming over and we just won't get anything done if we have to explain Aaron manipulating the dolls. You okay with that?"

"Got cookies?" Caroline countered.

"Nothing wrong with a good negotiator!" Morgan winked at Caroline.

The children ate a small dinner in the kitchen while Angela spoke discreetly with Morgan at the far side of the room.

"He'll get nothing from my table. Sorry, Morgan!"

"I'm not asking for Brown to attend the festivities. Just taking him a home made dinner plate is all I'm asking," Morgan urged.

"Don't ask me to share food with a man who took so much from so many. I'm not so virtuous," Angela insisted.

"Do you think the man that is here is the Trickster?" Aaron suddenly interrupted.

Morgan and Angela's conversation abruptly ceased. They crossed the kitchen toward the children and sat at the table.

"Please explain, Aaron," Angela said calmly. The other two children came fully to attention.

"Rachel wants to be here when we speak about... things," Aaron tentatively suggested.

Rachel was summoned and took a seat at the Pendergrass table, too. "What's bothering you, Aaron?" urged Rachel.

"A soft voice has been speaking to a man's mind; the man is near us and lying on a bed. The Trickster speaks in whispers. I heard it a few hours ago."

"Please tell us what this Trickster says, where he's from... whatever you know," Rachel advocated Aaron's full participation.

Aaron's pupils appeared slightly dilated; his monotone delivery and motionless body affected channeling. It was evident that Rachel was familiar with Aaron's ability to stream information in an altered state.

"I advise everyone to adjust your translators. To the highest setting, please. Go ahead," Rachel advised.

"The Trickster is of no time, inside of time, behind the curtain and sometimes in plain sight acting on stage. He is Edshu the ancient Nigerian. He is Loki of the Norse. Sometimes, he is a she. He is called the spider Anansi, the horse of Odin, the devil dogs called coyotes. He is Olifat, son of a human woman and a sky God from the Micronesian Islands. He is Gwydion and Aengus. He is the teller of half-truths, a shape shifter, the one that feigns to be the messenger of the Gods, the one often called 'defender' or 'helper' by and for the common people. He uses flattery, wealth, weakness and ego; people follow his advice, terminally foolish in their quest for power. He begins with the good path that has significant yields in order to garner the victim's faith and to build one's courage. A façade of instant friendship and benevolence is part of the Trickster's mask, meant to gain greater influence. His cunning countenance and valuable knowledge is prematurely shared with innocents, who look upon unfamiliar gifts with inexperienced eyes.

"He speaks quietly to victims as a divine muse and leads disciples to a moral sinkhole that sucks down overeager lemmings. The Trickster's appetite for damage, debauchery, and irony is insatiable, his laughter commensurate with well-executed treachery. God is not on the side of humans, he says. God fears human progression, says the Trickster. The Trickster pledges to be the human advocate. Yet it hates humans.

"He is the Monkey King stealing the Peaches of Immortality. He is the Tragedy of Man and the Mysterious Stranger, the maker of mischief, the perpetrator of folly. All is confusion and confusion is his purpose. He is jealous of man, of God, of truth, of wisdom, and, most of all, the canons of values and morals that help safeguard humankind. He locates the holes in wisdom, questions God's path, and muddies our faith. He is sub-human, and superhuman, a bestial and divine being of duplicity, contradiction and paradox. He crosses all boundaries and shows us the ways that boundaries are meant for fools. Discipline and patience foil his favored tool of temptation.

"The Trickster's breath is drawn from turmoil, his delight pinched from false miracles. He praises mediocrity, takes joy in the overlooked detail, throws fuel on the fires of discontent, and relentlessly points to the unmerciful nature of the noble path. He is the agent of evil, able to convince man to focus upon imagined threats. The Trickster represents God, it says. This is the most spiteful trick of all.

"As much as it tries to destroy the human race, man proves resilient. The ultimate trick is to coerce man to kill man. Humanity, says the Trickster, is unworthy of God's attention and the Trickster tries to prove this. The trickster whispers here," Aaron concluded.

Everyone sat silently in an effort to absorb Aaron's stream of consciousness. The young boy's eyes relaxed and he looked at Rachel sadly.

"I think the Rabbi heard the Trickster. Rabbi thought himself God's messenger. He enjoyed ritual and authority more than God's gifts of forgiveness and love. A Rabbi should have known when the Trickster told him to obey God's law and not to bury and bless my father. The man who is here near us listens to the Trickster, too."

Rachel hugged Aaron, who appeared drained from the experience. "Thank you, Aaron. Don't worry," she wanly assured.

"Fear is just Trickster food. I don't worry," Aaron warned.

"Well, that scared the holy shit outta me!" Morgan announced. "I'm not used to small people talking like that. It's rattling. I'm going with my bride's advice!"

Morgan pinged Moreno's office. "Do whatever you have to do to contain and isolate Brown. I've got it on good authority that he cannot be trusted at any level."

Angela had moved on to another idea. "I'm going to suggest that we just get Brown out of here now."

"There's no need," Aaron protested. "The Trickster cannot be held to boundaries. It can go anywhere. It can appear as anyone, anything. This is the way of the Trickster. We only have to keep to our path, our side. It moves through time and space. But the Trickster can only entice you to cross your moral line. If you know who you are, its words mean nothing and have no power. The Trickster needs man to doubt his best instincts. With God's help, man will remain the gatekeeper of his soul. All it can do is suggest how we can harm others and ourselves. It can threaten us with pain and fear but is unable to offer redemption.

"Why is it here?" Angela asked.

"The Trickster is listening and speaking because there is a powerful influencer here that threatens it...or helps it...I don't know which," Aaron tried.

"I don't know why everyone thinks that a trickster is scary," CC protested. "They just want candy. That's all!"

Angela corrected her granddaughter's impressions.

"Not someone who goes trick or treating on Halloween, Sweetheart. We are speaking of something that embodies a bad influence, a keeper of secrets, the gossip on the street corner that says something to you to put something negative in your mind, planting a needless anxiety that wasn't there before. Tricksters come in lots of everyday disguises and deceive people year round. The tricks work for a while for people's benefit then cause great harm. At first, no one realizes that the trick is harmful. It's the trademark of evil work."

CC looked blankly as she strugled to understand the concept of evil.

"Well, that can't be good. Why is the Trickster here again?"

Angela struggled to form an appropriate explanation. Morgan took over.

"The President of our once-great country is here in the converted smoke shed," Morgan answered matter-of-factly. "He misled people who trusted him. He used the Trickster's advice..."

Aaron disagreed with Dr. Pendergrass's assessment.

"Dr. Pendergrass, the Trickster uses the man. Man cannot use the Trickster. Man doesn't always believe the Trickster exists. He calls these ideas primitive thinking," Aaron paused. Morgan urged the boy to continue.

"The man called President thinks he has done his best and he listens thinking that it is God or his divine connection that speaks. God made him rich. God made the President a great man. God told him how to win, how to survive. That's what he believes. Only people who are willing to hear half-truths can heed a Trickster. Then they begin to think like the Trickster. They think everyone will cheat, be weak, be a liar, and a thief. Man's laws, they believe, are good for control but are not meant for leaders. The Trickster needs man to do his bidding. It is important that the Trickster convinces followers that they have been chosen to lead toward the right path toward their rightful place in the world and the hereafter."

Morgan was thoughtful. The expectant faces of the children around him meant something. Would they know how easy it was to swell up with one's self-worth when rewarded with minor successes? Did these little children have the moral discipline that would stop them from thinking themselves more entitled than the less gifted?

Will these kids understand moral myopia? How does that happen when you've got evil staring at you on the precipice? We need a no-nonsense approach to this situation, he concluded. Morgan decided to deliver his lesson right then and there.

"I don't know how to talk kid talk," he blurted. "I hope your translator explains it fine and you get the guts of this thing. I'd say Aaron is onto something that history bears out. It's like this: The Trickster politely knocks on your door for breakfast. He's just passing by and needs a little bite of food. He's a friendly fellow and before you know it, it's time for lunch. You like the traveler because he tells you ways to get around and make friends. You invite him for dinner and offer a bed for the night. He decides to hang around and stays for dinner. The Trickster is in your home and will stay until you kick the bugger out. You're friends now, anyway. You let the devil stay because he's so damn indispensable. The guy has shortcuts and hacks you've never considered.

"He's clued you in on stuff you never thought about. Your friends and family aren't quite what you've imagined. Of course, he just hates like hell to tell you the awful things said behind your back. But he does so because he's your honest friend. You realize those that criticize have never fully appreciated you. The deadbeats criticize you, hold you back...they're jealous! They're just not on the same level!

"This character is depicted everywhere. That damn Trickster goes against the Greek gods when he thinks that man could use a good hot fire and deserves it right away, even when warned to stay out of man's lives. He just hands fire right over and he's a big hero, too. Zeus, the CEO of the Greek gods at the time, sits down in a board meeting on Mt. Olympus and gets mad 'cause he had his own ideas about when humanity should learn about fire. This idea wasn't even on the agenda, objects Zeus. On the face of the thing, it looks pretty damn generous to give fire to the ordinary people running around on earth shivering their butts off. I mean, people needed fire to cook food, warm them up, and protect them from animals trying for an easy snack. Give 'em fire! Let there be s'mores! It looks bad for Zeus; he looks like a selfish jackass keeping good people in the dark and cold. These myths warn that certain gifts are game changers and time sensitive. At first, fire looks like a great thing. The Trickster is a damn hero lighting twigs and showing off. Maybe nuclear power was a great thing, too. Given our latest delivery package, we clearly were lacking some common sense. In my day, there were idiots who let firecrackers go off in their hands. Not much has changed. We're still blowing ourselves to pieces.

"People's minds can be changed with a neat little lie, a sneaky nuance selected out of context. A leader may begin with noble intentions but decides to bend rules for the greater good. It's a slippery moral slope. In hindsight, the clues aren't so subtle. You think your wife is great, then one day you get a notion – that little whispered thought – and you are now convinced that she is cheating on you...because you're thinking of cheating on her! Guys can be dogs...."

"*Morgan?!*" Angela yelled her objection at tangential unsuitable subject matter. The children looked blankly at Morgan.

"Tough crowd," Morgan shrugged. "I'm just saying it doesn't have to be fire or ginger cookies. That devil can get into everything, convince everyone that there's reason to be suspicious. That Trickster stirs the shit!"

"Morgan!" warned Angela of language usage.

"Stirs the soup!" Morgan corrected. "We tell ourselves that we are small, just pawns on the planet. Then we swing the other way...arrogant, without a trace of humility. No one misses a chance to pontificate, be righteous, and hate the other guy. It's tough to be true and constructive. It takes nothing to hate and destroy.

"We've received some greatly inspired codes and information that have served as civilization's building blocks. Where did our amazing insights, technological advances, arts and architecture come from? God? The Trickster? How do we stay on course when the devil we've created is always popping up with an easy way out? We do it with wisdom, the harder choices, a cultivated meaningful journey."

Rachel continued, "Somehow a promising leader inspires and excites us with promises of greater strength, clarity of thought, or absolute fairness. This leader seems able to touch us, articulate our apprehensions, and offer solutions. Most are good men and women. But there's another insidious variety of leadership that encourages us to redirect our energies toward restricting or fighting others who threaten the quality of our lives. We rarely discover the extent of hate or restrictions until it comes full circle. You know, like if Caroline baked an overabundance of cookies but she didn't think of sharing with others. Rather, she froze them to eat later. Angrily, I move to forbid cookies if they aren't available to everyone...

especially to me. I'm going to teach her a lesson. Even though I love cookies I might deny myself rather than make my own cookie."

"Whhaaat?" Caroline gasped.

"She's just saying it could happen," Morgan winked. "It's been done before. I mean, without certain regulatiions or considerations for others we should just figure ourselves as lawless, unmitigated trash-talking monkeys. We bicker about what's right, who does and doesn't deserve this or that, how we should raise consciousness and all that crap but it's just manmade laws trying to imitate the big plan. We are all on our paths to a higher consciousness. Then man decides to try on God's britches, telling everyone what's fair. Absolute power corrupts absolutely!

"Birds sing, newborn babies enter the world; the seasons change and there are beautiful sunrises and sunsets. Why do those miracles fail to inspire us? Cultivation starts to feel like too much work. Art, the signature of civilization, becomes illegible or smudged and we still dare to call our smallest versions inspired. Our tears are born of frustration rather than gratitude. We've been tricked out of our humanity, our moral birthright slowly dripping away like water from an ill-begotten leaky spigot."

The room fell silent. Morgan took his wife's hand.

CC spoke first.

"I understood Grandpa's meaning. I don't have a baby translator. It's the same level as yours," she smiled triumphantly at the adults. "I know what you mean because I feel it when somebody is confused or scared. I can't make them feel better when they are angry. So much is coming out of them I can't get in. When they are wondering what to do, I can touch them and then they seem to know. They feel better. I think it's the Trickster whose big mouth keeps whispering over everything that is soothing and sweet. Blah, blah, blah... he makes too much noise."

It was the first time that Caroline spoke openly about an ability to rectify angst.

"Can you try to make me feel better?" Aditiya pleaded. "I'm always worried. Now, I'm really worried about the Trickster."

"Not now. Maybe later when no one is just staring their big eyes out of their heads at us," Caroline replied.

"Well, can you make Blue stop peeing on me?" Aditiya pointed to a wet stain on his pant leg. Blue lay innocently beside his master.

CC sensed a lesson was in the offing.

"I can't fix that. You'll have to act like you're not going to put up with that mess or he's going to pee on you all day long. He doesn't pee on anybody else, Aditiya."

"What am I supposed to do?"

The talk about dog piss annoyed Morgan but he recognized the call for a man's lesson.

"Pee on him first, before he gets to you, young man. Do it!" Morgan insisted.

Aditiya unzipped his pants and took as much aim as could be expected of a child. Part of the wet message reached Blue's head.

"Morgan? I'm going to..." Angela's frustration with her husband's methods turned her ears bright red.

"Okay, enough of this right now," Morgan clapped his hands gleefully. "Kids, finish up. We've got a party coming up and we're going to bring in 2061 with love and happiness. Wash your hands, pants, and shoes, Aditiya," he added. A kitchen bot cleaned the floor and dog.

CC separated chicken skin for Blue and treated the humiliated dog under the table. Aditiya's own table scraps matched CC's contribution. Toward the end of the meal, Blue rested his contented head upon the foot of a new friend.

Rachel ate ice cream and thought, *God, but that man can rant. How depressing can you get?*

Aaron burst out laughing.

Chapter XIX
Hopeless to Hopeful

Nicholas, Cynthia and Esther surveyed their surroundings. The converted resort retained luxurious appointments. The group's attention turned toward a glass enclosure.

"It's heated. Look at the steam. Imagine! In the middle of winter!" Esther stood beside Nicholas, taking in the fountain and spa that adjoined the swimming area.

"Let's eat. Then we can go swimming," Cynthia announced.

"You can't swim," Esther said matter-of-factly. She and Nicholas stood together taking in a scene known to them through fairy tales and stories related by older family members.

"It's so calm and clean," Esther smiled. "It's just here for people to enjoy!"

Cynthia scampered toward exotic aromas. Within minutes, she returned with a tray of bread, hot pizza, raspberry jam and something recommended to her as peanut butter.

The three sat poolside and passed the treats amongst themselves.

"I'm taking off my shoes," Cynthia announced.

Nicholas and her older sister followed suit and the three sat with their feet dangling in the water.

Firework displays for the New Year began hours before midnight. Camp regulations required residents and visitors to return to their quarters before 10:00 p.m. The three young visitors had never celebrated New Year's Eve and the sight of exploding colored lights mesmerized them all. Cynthia fell asleep in a lounge chair with a towel wrapped around her slender body. Despite the cracks and whistles that exploded skyward, Cynthia lay in a semi-coma.

Esther's eyes welled with tears.

"What's wrong?" Nicholas moved to comfort the eighteen-year-old whose thoughts wandered to a life of struggle, a lost family, and the fleeting adolescence with an unknown future.

"I'm fine. I'm just a little tired of running and wondering if we're going to be okay now."

"I like that we're protected from the scavengers. I figure I've got a new family... if that's alright with you and Cynthia?" Nicholas said, searching for appropriate words of comfort.

Esther smiled gratefully at Nicholas. His black hair and blue eyes outshone the exploding pinwheels beyond the glass enclosure. She wondered if Nicholas knew how attractive he was.

"Of course. I'd like that, Nicholas. Just remember I'm the senior member here."

"Oh, right." Nicholas was aware that the men assigned to their safety watched them rather than the fireworks.

"Let's wake Cynthia and go to bed. These guys must be pretty tired of babysitting."

Esther gathered their robes and belongings, wrapped the leftover food, and helped Nicholas wake Cynthia.

As they said goodnight, Nicholas could only manage a "Happy New Year". He wished he knew how to kiss the young woman standing inches from him. She stirred and comforted him at the same time. Nicholas felt the humbling signs of a new sensation. He'd felt weak-kneed before but never in the context in which he now found himself.

Esther took his hand and pulled Nicholas toward her. She kissed his cheek and moved her lips that whispered warm breath in his ear. "I'm pretty sure this is going to be the happiest year of my life. I think it's going to be yours, too." Esther turned and went into her room.

Neither Nicholas nor Esther was able to sleep that night.

Cynthia slept for twelve hours straight, until breakfast call. It promised to be a new year heralding a new life. They would arrive sometime soon at the Pendergrass Farm.

"Are we just a bunch of refugees?" Cynthia asked her sister. She knew the word since the age of three.

"If there's a refugee tier, I'd say we might be at top right now. It has something to do with Nicholas. Don't know exactly the reason they'd separate the three of us from the rest of the passengers but we'll find out soon. We're going to stick close to Nicholas."

Chapter XX

New Year Surprises

Saturday, January 1, 2061

*A*t the stroke of midnight, the Pendergrass party toasted the New Year amongst streamers and confetti. The children showed no signs of slowing down. Angela, Indu, Adele and Lex shored up the youngsters and stewarded the reluctant group upstairs to prepare for bed. Morgan and Meredith finished off the decanter of Bourbon; Morgan bemoaned the lost football seasons and grand parades of decades past. Meredith sat in a semi-stupor pretending to agree with him.

Rachel and Connor lingered outdoors in the cool night and enjoyed the crystal clear skies.

"Romantic enough for you?" Connor pulled Rachel into his jacket.

"Pretty nice," Rachel agreed as she nuzzled and kissed him. "It's not what we Jews usually call our New Year and it's not what we usually do but it's much more fun! Happy New Year, handsome!"

"Handsome? You think I'm handsome?" Connor prompted.

"Obviously."

Connor held her thoughtfully. "I wonder what this year will bring? So much has happened."

"So many inexplicable things are about to happen," Rachel said with conviction.

Connor turned Rachel around to look into her eyes. "What makes you say that?"

"We're riding some force, some kind of wave that's taking us quickly somewhere entirely new. We've evolved to some kind of crossroads after almost falling into an abyss. It all seems chaotic and planned at once. You don't feel that?"

"I'm just glad you're here for the ride. I like you so much. I'm falling for you, Rachel."

"Like me so much? Falling?" Rachel said indignantly.

"Fallen," Connor corrected himself. "As a matter of fact, I've fallen in love with you. I'm a believer in CC's drawing."

"What are you talking about?"

"I'll show you tomorrow. It's a picture she drew of me with someone in a wedding dress. I was with Ellie at the time my niece drew it. It's a drawing of you, Rachel. It's written. That's all I can say."

Ignoring the cold, the pair kissed until Morgan and Meredith began to shoot pistols in the night air, hooting bourbon-induced salutations to 2061. Swirling rockets sent skyward by the Nishants barely missed Morgan on the second story balcony. Angela and Adele summoned a bot to help them extinguish a pile of pyrotechnics that Amar had ignited at the stroke of 12:00.

"You don't wish to light the whole pyre?" Amar lamented.

"Not to worry," Adele laughed.

Lex appeared next to his startled father-in-law on the balcony standing in the midst of flying pinwheels that shot overhead.

"I've called Meredith's car. You two should return inside. Your PM has sounded an alarm; someone is going to get hurt. Angela's orders: *put the pistols away*!"

Lex was unable to convince his father-in-law to relinquish the firearms to him.

Morgan snapped at his son-in-law.

"You'll blow your own toes, man. I'm fine. Help Meredith. The good doctor is three sheets to the wind!"

As Connor held Rachel in his arms, a sense of foreboding overtook him. He called to Morgan and Lex on the balcony, "Anybody check in about Brown in the last hours? The ten o'clock guard never reported."

Morgan stopped wrestling with Lex and instructed him to contact security. "See what's going on; we should have had an hourly report."

Seconds later, Failsafe Enterprises contacted Morgan. It was the owner himself, Richard Cain, on the other end.

Rather than answer, Morgan contacted his security officer, Isabella Moreno. When she arrived, he texted his thoughts via an encrypted channel; she did the same.

"You contact Failsafe?"

"No, sir. We removed our automatic signal system when Reid first visited remember? Failsafe here?"

"Not yet. Got Cain on the other line. He doesn't know that we cut him out of our emergency loop. Connor mentioned security issues, then I get this call. Be careful what you say. Go straight to the Brown shed."

"Just left there, sir. Everything is fine. Guards checked in with me right on time. I didn't want to interfere with the festivities. That doesn't answer how Connor's remarks were intercepted. Say nothing. Give me time to find out how Failsafe was notified, sir."

"We're on the same line of thinking. I'll speak to Cain now."

Morgan affected slurred speech. "Cain? That you?"

"Dr. Pendergrass? We're on our way. What's happening?"

"Hellooooo, Richard. We're just shooting our way into the New Year. Stay put... everything is fine!"

"Happy New Year to you, Sir. Mind if we send someone out just to check? We've got Reid in the vicinity."

"Sure. I'll give him a bottle to take home," Morgan laughed.

"Will do, Governor. He's been notified as we speak. Goodnight."

Morgan put his forefinger to his lips. Connor and Rachel were riveted by the exchange of information they could hear from below.

By the time Moreno appeared with a scanner, Morgan figured that a bug had been implanted within his mechanical leg. The scan indicated the same. Not a word was exchanged until Meredith vomited over the balcony onto the lawn below. She yelled 'heads up' after the fact.

"That's the party. Come on, Missy. You're going to stay here the night," Morgan said as Angela maneuvered her away.

Reid showed up within minutes, spoke with Moreno, and asked to speak with Morgan. Moreno was curt. "He's busy."

Moreno did not trust Reid.

As if he heard her thoughts, Scott Reid shook his head vigorously. Moreno realized he was correct to protest. Whoever planted the bug had to have had done so at the time of the operation years ago.

"See what you can find out," Moreno wrote the text and flashed concern. She meant to omit the part about the implanted bug.

"I'll find out. You can bet on it. How is it possible? I thought there was no interior surveillance anymore by Failsafe since they were fired?"

Moreno keyed her concerns. "Find out what excuse they'll say caused them to call in. My guess is that they'll say that they picked up the sounds of the firearms going off street-side. You better be trustworthy, Reid. I'm going to de-digitize you if you cross the governor. I'm talking about fingers and toes here."

Moreno felt certain that the Failsafe Enterprises had infiltrated the property with spy equipment when their services were terminated. Now, a bug showed up in Morgan's leg. Cain was the kind of man that would do that. She would have to scrutinize everyone on the Pendergrass estate more closely.

Moreno nodded toward her boss as he wrote a message with the two of them in the library.

"Get the doctors to the research center tomorrow. Let's get this bug out. Find out who was in attendance for that operation. Do a complete sweep of all personnel and double the surveillance on Brown," Morgan instructed.

Morgan then encrypted a simple message to Confederation governors: "Code shit."

"How long has this bug been activated?" Morgan's throat dried as he considered the amount of personal and vital information that could have been leaked in the span of six years.

"We have a scanner in place 24/7. Nothing showed until now. Don't think the worst... my guess is it was properly rendered dormant each time you passed our security. Outdoors on your porch, it somehow reactivated. You must have been beyond the hotspot. We'll correct that immediately. I have no reason to believe that this was anything but a fluke of an overlooked location on the balcony."

*　*　*

Sunday, January 2, 2061

Nicholas felt protective of the sisters. He found himself attracted to Esther and wondered if she felt the same. Safe, well-fed, and in the company of Confederation military, the three breathed evenly in one of the government's signature black transports. Esther took Nicholas's hand in hers, squeezed it, and then rested her hand upon his thigh. "We're safe. We're together," she whispered in his ear.

As the Pendergrass Farm gates came into view, Nicholas's heart accelerated even more.

"It's been the Pendergrass family farm for over 100 years; it's now occupied by Morgan Pendergrass's extended family and assorted guests that come and go," the driver said, noticing Nicholas's expression.

"Do these guests come and go as they please?" Esther asked.

Their Confederation guard escort smiled and assuaged the teenager's anxiety.

"You're with friends. You'll be able to ask anything that comes to mind. You'll get a straight answer, too. You three are lucky people," the guard assured.

Morgan wasn't on site but his wife, family and guests stood on the front porch waiting to greet the three visitors. CC and Blue ran to the car, kicking up gravel.

Esther and Cynthia grinned broadly. The warmth of the greeting party overwhelmed the cold air.

"I'm CC. My grandfather can't be here so he made me the head welcomer. So, welcome, welcome, welcome. This is Blue. Don't mention the c-l-o-n-e word," Caroline warned in one disconnected, breathless sentence.

The three moved onto the porch and Angela embraced the sisters while Lex and Connor each shook Nicholas' hand, accompanied by reassuring pats on his back. Two hours later, Rachel and Adele had settled the arrivals into private rooms with personal monitors. The group had never worn personal monitoring equipment but learned quickly how to affix the transparent thin tape and disposable audio dots that responded to verbal commands.

At 5:00 that afternoon, Morgan returned home without the bot-tap. It wasn't difficult to find or remove. Neither was it difficult to determine the research lab assistant who had connections to Failsafe Enterprises. As soon as the woman was taken into custody for questioning, she spoke without having been prompted.

"They gave me a chip and I slipped it inside the casing. I'm a tech assistant. It was no danger to the patient and it meant a lot of money. Richard Cain asked me to do it. We'd been intimately involved. I thought he loved me. Eventually, I figured otherwise," she offered immediately.

"In what way did he direct you?" Isabella Moreno asked.

"Cain told me that the implant was to help ensure the governor's safety but I can't pretend that I believed that. Sure, he worked for Pendergrass and I knew that as security chief there were things he couldn't share with me. But you don't usually implant illegal spy-bots for any reason. Richard went to a lot of trouble to let me know that Pendergrass could never find out, told me where to place the tracking chip, and how to activate it. Look, I didn't want to think about what I did."

Moreno and Pendergrass sat silently as the woman tearfully spoke of Cain's security operation and the ways in which he kept tabs on people. She hadn't had a conversation with him since being dismissed from his bed but feared repercussions.

Clifton Brown's name unexpectedly surfaced.

"How do Richard Cain and Clifton Brown know each other?" Morgan interrupted with a not-so-wild guess.

"I'm not sure. Richard said once that it's only a matter of time until he gets the information he needs from Brown. I asked if Clifton Brown was still alive...where he was...what information he had, if he'd ever actually seen him. Well, Richard began to brag that he'd been tracking and directing Brown... that no one knew he was alive. Just as quickly, he regretted having said it and slapped me. I thought he meant to kill me. When Richard left the room, I was told never to open my mouth again and that I had a RFID chip implanted inside of me. He injected it personally one evening when I was sleeping. It was insurance, he said. It had poison in it, too."

"Why are you speaking now to us?" Morgan glanced toward Moreno, who had indicated the woman had been screened and was clean of any implant.

"I don't care anymore. It was wrong and I've felt guilty for most of my adult life. How could I have been such an idiot?"

Moreno answered, "No chip. No poison. He just left you with an ample dose of paranoia. That works, too."

"Can you forgive me?" she wept her relief and guilt.

Morgan, never known to deal with a weeping woman, did what he could.

"Just stop crying. You don't see me crying," Morgan tried. "Moreno isn't crying, either. Now y'all move along...you'll be debriefed. You'll show up tomorrow in the hospital as if nothing happened. Let's assume that there might be others on Cain's payroll. We'll take care of him."

Pendergrass left the building clean of Cain's bug. As he approached the waiting car, a call came in from Scott Reid.

"Sir, the last transmission from one of our bots came in; you have a bug in your leg. Cain's people heard your exchange with your son-in-law regarding security and reacted prematurely rather than wait for a call. They know they made a mistake and there wasn't a physical breach. The guy on Cain's special assignment monitoring your property in the office called it in and then... disappeared. I mean disappeared. Anyway, Cain looks worried. He called me in to talk. He wants me to go over to your place today and say that I was on patrol and heard the gunshots and called in. Just letting you know."

"I figured as much. The bug only worked in one location anyway. What time you supposed to be at my home?"

"I'm here now. Just ready to buzz you."

"Give me an hour. I'm not there."

"Sir? They also reported that someone referenced Clifton Brown, the ex-president?"

"You were able to locate and send that transmission to Moreno?"

"She's got it all, Sir."

"Good man, Reid. Thank you."

"Is the ex-president really with you?"

"Feel free to share the fat but stay lean on the questions, son."

From the car, Morgan contacted Moreno, wondering what she had discovered about Cain.

"Nothing brilliant. Just looks as if our man Cain is fishing like crazy to find some opening to get back into your good graces or debt. I've alerted the Confederation to conduct an intensive security sweep. Cain made the mistake of prematurely moving in on a bogus alert when he was listening. Maybe he was eager to remind you that he's around," Moreno puzzled.

"Cain wants to be the FBI/CIA and NSA rolled into one. How the hell does he figure to overcome the fact that we knew he wasn't allowed to survey the property's security interior? He's an idiot," Morgan groused.

"Sir, it's the reason the governors wanted him out in the first place. He wanted to make the position of Confederation Security Minister something much more ominous than it was. He envisioned building and activating a separate military force. Remember what Hernandez said? 'You mean to have your own army, Cain? That's not happening.' Cain blew up. We all remember that day. Hernandez pushed his big chest into Cain's face. A week later Hernandez discovered Failsafe bugs all over his building."

"Thanks. I'm home now, Isabella. Keep me posted," Morgan signed off as Angela hurried from the front door to greet him. Morgan smiled at his wife, who beamed enthusiasm. *I miss that part of Angela,* he thought. *She's had a lot on her for too long.*

"These people that are arriving here from all over the world, Morgan! It's wonderful. As soon as I think it can't get crazier, in walks a new bunch," Angela effused.

"What do you make of the latest three?" Morgan asked.

"Nicholas is entirely visible and polite, too. CC, Aditiya, Aaron, and Blue won't leave the poor young man alone but he seems to have taken to them like a big brother. Esther and Cynthia just folded into our arms. They immediately trusted us. I heard that the Hungarians are going to arrive any day now. I enjoy this role enormously. It's wonderful for CC, too." Morgan changed the subject with something more serious on his mind.

"I'm going to visit Brown soon. You're right. We have to deal with him as soon as possible and then get him away from these good people. I'll have a conversation with the governors as soon as I finish with him."

"Don't dare go without Lex and Connor with you. And take some security guards. It's a feeling, Morgan. Trust me on this," Angela pleaded.

"Oh, I do, Cookie."

The buzzer rang and the monitor displayed Scott Reid at the front door.

"You again, Reid? Always dropping by to pick my kitchen clean?"

Scott Reid laughed and delivered his lines.

"Just came by to check things out and let you know that I was the one that contacted Failsafe on New Year's Eve. I realized as soon as I called in an alarm that you people were just blowing off some steam. Those guns sounded pretty bad. I followed up and found everything otherwise in order."

"I just leave the security to the security people. Don't keep up with who does what. Tell your people we appreciate the good work and I'll try to keep our enthusiasm to a minimum next year," Morgan gave the scripted response previously discussed.

Reid thought he was supposed to go inside but realized that Failsafe might think it out of character for Morgan to be that familiar. "Well, thank you, sir. Happy New Year to you and your family," he finalized.

"Ditto," Morgan replied.

As he drove away, Reid realized that Pendergrass was as clever and good a man as could be imagined.

Chapter XXI

A Dark Conversation

Monday, January 3, 2061

The seven-person cluster that strode purposefully toward the converted tobacco shed alerted Blue, who joined the entourage from inside the horse stable. The dog kept low to the ground, expecting Morgan's wrath for his mischievous habits that disturbed the animals. Blue liked to wriggle his way under freshly distributed straw or amongst the bales of hay, camouflaged by his brindle coat. Startling the horses was the dog's favorite pastime.

Morgan snapped, "Damn...you at it again? You're that dog in the manger...can't eat hay but gotta keep the other animals from feeding?" Blue slunk to the ground, guilty as charged.

Connor patted his pant leg but Blue took refuge behind the Collins brothers.

"Good idea," Morgan huffed.

As soon as their monitors beeped an alert, the security guards came to attention.

"Dr. Pendergrass is on his way with two Confederation replacement guards, Doctors Lex and Connor Collins, Isabella Moreno – Pendergrass security – and a Confederation medical officer, Dr. Komor," read the PM messages. One of the guards prepared Brown.

"I'm in for a visit?" Brown indicated a glass of water that was handed to him. Having drunk half the glass, Brown dropped the glass to the floor.

"Oops. Sorry about that."

The guard cautiously kicked the glass to the side before retrieving it.

Brown sneered, "You don't really think that an old chained-up man is a threat? Ha! Who's coming this way?"

The guard ignored Brown.

A knock at the door later, two security agents entered with Krisztina Komor to inspect the cabin. Komor arranged the seating and directed two guards to stand outside. Lex, Connor, Isabella, and Morgan entered the room and each selected a seat around the ex-president of the United States of America. Komor stood alert bedside.

Brown spoke before Morgan could get settled.

"It's good to see you after all these years, Pendergrass. Who are these fine fellows with you? Didn't know you had sons."

Morgan studied the man lying prone before him in the blue pajamas that extended beyond a white bathrobe. He noted calloused feet and manicured, smooth hands. Blue settled beside Morgan's feet; like his Alpha, Blue did not take his eyes off Clifton Brown.

"You in there, Morgan?" Brown's sarcasm voided the cordial greeting. "Who are these people?"

Morgan kept his poker face half a minute before responding.

"Just because you asked me somethin' doesn't mean I have to answer, Cliff."

"What happened to the respectful good citizen I used to know? You can't bring yourself to call me Mr. President? So much for Southern manners."

Morgan bent low to stroke his dog. He noted Blue's bristled back, steady stare, and rigid tail. Lex and Connor said nothing. All present deferred to Morgan's instincts on the matter of dealing with Clifton Brown.

"Well, you've met the smart and accurate Colonel Komor. Believe she shot you in the neck with a sedative. Hope that gives you some kind of idea how we deal with bullshit." Morgan straightened and settled back comfortably in his chair. "Let's begin with some questions, shall we? Hopefully, you'll answer them. If not, all the same to me."

"Shoot."

"Be careful what you ask for, Clifton."

The monitor's camera lens could be heard widening. As Clifton Brown spoke, his personal monitor indicated whether or not the truth was being spoken.

Brown objected, "Am I on trial?"

"What's it feel like?" Morgan looked him in the eye.

"Feels like I'm on trial," Brown retorted angrily.

"I can't help that. Why are you here, anyway?"

"You brought me here."

"Ha, fair enough. Why have you been lost to us for so long?"

"I've been hiding. Didn't know what I'd find. Lost my way. Lost my mind. Lost my family. You want a recap of 20 years of hell?" Brown rolled to his side and regarded Morgan, propped up on rearranged pillows. "You want the minute-by-minute version?"

"Not really. We've got our own versions. Let's get to specifics. Where are the NSA and NASA archives? I'd hate to think that the American government destroyed or lost precious information like that. Haven't really started to search your crypts, though."

"What are you looking for in particular, Morgan? Maybe I could help you? Maybe you can help me?"

"I'm pretty sure that we could use some of that scientific data to help us along. Course, now... we're building things and not destroying them, so we may not be on the same beam."

"A little bitter, Morgan? Are you seriously blaming me for the ills of the world?"

"I'd say you're a big, ugly part of the nasty times profile. You were mighty busy two decades before the Darkness making trouble for honest Americans rather than searching for solutions. By any measure, you failed humanity in our darkest moments. We recovered records of the first months in the EMP aftermath. Your reaction to the disaster was nothing short of subhuman behavior. You were screaming and whining like a long-tailed cat in a room full of rockers. You had one thought in mind: saving your own sorry backside," Morgan indicated the monitor's docu-vids.

"I was there. Where were you?" Brown protested.

Morgan was clear that the man lying before him was sans a sense of guilt. For whatever reason, Brown felt justified in ignoring the pleas of half a billion Americans suddenly without resources to weather 48 hours.

"You feel as if yours was a decent stewardship of our country? You feel justified about implanting radio-frequency identification chips that, unbeknownst to government employees, had cyanide in them that could be remotely triggered? You also knew that the chips amplified electromagnetic impulses and could seriously burn cells from the inside, not to mention compromise the entire neural system. As we discovered after the EMP bomb, that was certainly information you had in hand, right? You feel good about using our taxpayer's resources to build underground survival bunkers earmarked for government personnel while families fought upside for survival? Thought it was a solid move for our crumbling infrastructure to be in disrepair, unhardened, and unprotected? Let me bring it home for you. I figure something is wrong when you order the death of your own family. They must have been a hell of a threat to national security, Cliff," Morgan rhetorically asked. "Let's start with what it takes to murder your loved ones."

"Where in the hell did you get that sick idea? My men didn't exactly want to pamper women who couldn't keep up. The Eagles were moaning and groaning about their own families. I knew that it was a matter of time until my wife and girls were left behind in some critical situation. I showed my men that we were on the same page. Showed them I could be hard-ass in hard-ass times. My family knew I was doing the right thing for our country and no one questioned my leadership after that."

"You're all heroes. Did they suffer, Brown?"

"Of course not. What kind of monster do you think I am? I signaled their chips in the night in their sleep. No one felt a thing. It was what my wife begged me to do. That was the kind of heartbreaking decision that is required to put your country back on track. I needed to demonstrate that kind of sacrifice.

"You have no idea the chaos that ensued within three days of the bombs. You sat in your little Southern town in your

big Southern mansion with your generators, hardened transformers and satellites, and then Monday morning quarter-
backed a civil war? Streets were burning; people were burning.
I was the only point of leadership in an endless heap of
desperation."

"You get a lot done after that?" Morgan asked sarcastically.

"As a matter of fact, we did. We inspected the entire underground network and rebuilt many of the connections. We were
able to finally connect to a satellite in this region and tap in.
It was rightfully the American government's equipment in the
first place, Morgan. We were working the whole time, assessing what it would take to recover, rebuild, and reorganize the
country. Most American cities were burning. There was rampant disease without so much as an antibiotic. It's still going
on. I couldn't risk too much until we rebuilt our strength. In
the meantime, people like you step in and separate our entire
country? Nice work. Leave the better part of America to just
burn and die out? When do you plan to check the remains?
You never once moved to help urban areas up North or on the
West Coast. Not once. You've been sitting here in North Carolina spitting tobacco and sipping bourbon? Who the hell do
you think you're talking to?"

Komor stared through Clifton Brown. She struggled to isolate and identify a certain sickness rising deep from within her.
Similarly, Lex sat incredulous, gaped mouthed.

Connor recounted the conversation Rachel and he had regarding Aaron's references to the 'Trickster'. He replayed the
boy's reference of a subliminal subversion of logic and recognized it in play. Connor stood and walked toward his mentor
and quietly whispered 'sidebar' in Morgan's ear.

"Excuse me, Clifton. My friend here wants a word," Morgan
explained.

The two men and a dog left the building. Moreno followed
with her scanner to ensure privacy. After giving a nod their
way, she returned inside.

"Look, it occurs to me that the man in there is more than a
sick puppy. He's insanely delusional but his ability to pinpoint
your weaknesses is uncanny. We know you felt guilt at not

having tried to sort the Northern mess, eradicate the illnesses, but until recently, we didn't even have enough medical supplies to take care of the Confederation. This guy reached into your head and successfully discovered your remorse and plucked it out. He's playing you like a maestro.

"I've referenced the conversation with Aaron about the 'Trickster'. I say we bring that kid here to have a listen. Aaron knew Brown was here. He invoked the name of something or someone occupying or influencing Clifton Brown with all kinds of references to a malevolent force. Let's bring Aaron here... see what happens," Connor implored.

"Are you out of your cotton-pickin' mind? Bring a child around this monster? I'll have none of it. Just because they saw him coming, know he's here and called his MO doesn't mean that Cliff can't do them harm. What's wrong with you?"

"He'll never give you the information you seek, Morgan. He's sure as hell not going to give you any other kind of satisfaction either. The guy figures himself blameless. Question is, what are you looking for and what will it take for him to spit it up? Why the hell did you bring him here, Morgan?'

"I'll consider Nicholas Bradley, who can handle himself. It's Nicholas who has an unusual coping mechanism," Morgan reconsidered thoughtfully. "You're right, though. I feel like crap about our inability to assist good people outside our borders. We are few. They are many. Compassion sounds good until the bear eats your arm when you run out of Cracker Jacks," Morgan said with defeat in his voice.

"Cracker Jacks?" Connor was used to obscure references.

"Never mind. Just remember Gordon Smith's report via Nishant. Civilized boundaries are now holding back great numbers of survivors whose minds may have been permanently altered. Not all, and not all completely, but enough predators are out there to compromise the human race. I'm not kidding around, Connor. We've got to figure our options, take a good look at secret research that meant something and went nowhere. We have to do what we can to correct the human condition. I know the government hid the Tesla schematics that could have saved us trillions of dollars. They shut down important genetic inroads. Why hide or kill so many great innovations?" Morgan sighed his frustration.

"Maybe there's no good reason at all, Morgan. I tend to believe Aaron's assessment of darker forces at play. Some things can't be explained. Forget that part. I just want to point out to you that Brown has demonstrated an ability to take you off course," Conner re-emphasized. "The monitor didn't beep once that he was insincere. The man is a pathological liar. He believes what he's saying and you're taking it in! That's not you," Connor said with the kind of conviction meant to shake Morgan back to task.

Somberly, the men reentered the tobacco shed. Clifton Brown broke the silence with laughter.

"Looks like I've got a hand, right? Don't know how to call it? Ha-ha. You're going to have to deal if you want any information. I know plenty. I know the reason that your research was stopped cold. I know that our plans were worldwide strategies to control the public, secure resources, and the information that had to remain in government hands. We've got intelligence you'd never dream of. I saw it all. I was never alone on this, Morgan, and you know it. There were plenty of scientists who threw you and your meddlesome kind under the bus.

"You righteous idealists make me sick. You just went your merry way with trainloads of criticisms and no solutions. Our planet was drowning because we were expected to feed and nurture everyone, protect every plant, save every dying species, help every downtrodden, needy newcomer. You wanted to let these people lead their own lives, lead ours, when all they wanted was the monitor, some drugs, enough food, a decent education. We could do that. We did that. So what if the rest were promises on the table? We paid people a minimum wage to keep them on the government payroll. It worked. They ate, they could study, and they could breed at will.

"The Grid Wars were a planned distraction after we controlled all the water and land. It was just one of the things that we did to monitor our precious resources. Energy problems were something only governments could fix. Every time we stepped in and came to the rescue people remained grateful and marginalized the pigs that might have designs on what rightfully belonged to everyone. It was like a deck of cards... we could pick from terrorists, capitalists, communists, Jews, Christians, racists, Muslims, corporate interests, any group that threatened American assets. We kept everyone dancing fast and hard. The Romans had circuses; we gave Americans Grid Wars. We ran a well-organized shell game. Keep your eye on the boogey man; beware the modified crops, your freaking genetic research, and climate change. It was the climate change that gave us the real power worldwide! There wasn't a government in operation that didn't want to use that one. In the end, you couldn't build a campfire without government sanction or tax. Name it, we used it! Why would we want energy independence or cheap energy when the government owned it all? It was our bread and butter. It bought us time to get the masses under a system, keep the riots under control... feed the unemployed. It would have been chaos otherwise.

"No one dreamed the solar flares could possibly couple with an EMP disaster from a renegade country or two. With a little more time, we could have culled the planet of dissidents, criminals, and deadbeats with those RFID implants. No one would have been the wiser. Things would have been squared away and under control. What was RFID to the lives it could save? No more kidnapping; we would have all medical records on file...able to track down those Alzheimer's patients and end reoccurring felonies. It was only the US that resisted RFID implants and the onus was on me to lead the free world. I had to convince the Western countries to get in line. The Americans? Oh, it was hellish to get around that religious bunch talking about the Beast and crazy shit.

"India and Mexico were the first to buy in. Hell, we didn't have any intention of adding the poison until Mexico figured out how to finish off the drug lords. The cartels vanished. The chips became a permanent solution to the police and government employees who weren't loyal to national directives or worked the black markets. It just wasn't coordinated well. It got away from us. Too many idiots and self-serving workers at play. We had most of the country processed with welfare recipient implants that tracked drug addictions and junk food. Then the game was up. We just flat ran out of funds. So we focused on what was left of the private sector. No employee chips? No government contracts! Easy peasy.

"You played it out to your advantage just fine, Morgan. Game, set, match, you hypocrite. People, institutions, and states like yours moved to be self-sufficient while screwing the rest of the country. Where was your team spirit? Teamwork is what made our country great. It's what the civil war was about. United we stand...an indivisible nation...with liberty and justice for all..." Brown emphasized.

"What happened to the part about under God? You dared to remove it from the Pledge of Allegiance and then got rid of it entirely. Team spirit?" Morgan sniffed his ire. "Team spirit? You mean an autocratic socialistic state?"

"It's called leadership meant for the collective welfare. Where's your brain? Environmentally and financially, we had mismanaged the planet and we needed smart people to lead the less inclined. God references were always a monkey wrench thrown our way and you know it," Brown rationalized. "Let everyone pray away in private. Prayer should be a discreet and intimate moment; it has no place in public policy or law."

"Like sex?" Morgan laughed, "The Feds sure legislated the hell out of sex, Cliff. How does government align its duties with determining the morality of sexual conduct?"

"You know what I mean. Icons of God... like the Ten Commandments outside of courthouses? Government represents all religions. You wouldn't want the Koran sticking on public housing, would you?"

"You're right. Graffiti was fine," Morgan smirked, "Who needs to be reminded of the basic tenets of moral conduct?"

"With few exceptions, American holidays were white Christian ones or white Christian wars, or white male leaders... until we understood the impact of such apathetic emotional triggers."

"You had a Christmas tree in the White House, Cliff," Morgan rolled his eyes.

"A holiday tree, Morgan. You didn't see one cross, star, or other unseemly ornament hanging from it. It was beautiful," Brown proudly recalled.

Morgan wondered to himself, if Brown and other leaders wanted to remove 'dissidents and dead-beats', who was left when one half of the United States citizens were welfare recipients and the other half was unhappy about it? If God was the culprit, who was the prophet?

"I'm listening." Morgan pulled out a pipe and packed it thoughtfully. "Tell me about how things really worked in Washington."

"Quid pro quo," demanded Brown. "You've got an insatiable thirst for details. What do I get? Your business should be to make me comfortable and allow for my long, sweet life."

"Whatcha got?" Morgan puffed.

"I can connect the dots, Morgan. You're wondering about the reasons your genetic research was stopped. You thought me stupid or shortsighted? No. It happens that we had in hand the perfect prototype for cyber-sapiens. While each field was fiddling with synthetic biology, bio-computing, nanotechnology, and neuroprosthetics to develop diagnostics for improved quality of life, you ignored the possibility that man had already developed the best version of himself for purposes of survival. Any more development and we'd be challenged to control the masses. You had to be stopped. You and your groups had to be portrayed as demons. It was perfect. It was more within the grasp than what was happening with Artificial Intelligence. AI had already displaced 78% of the work force. The rest? That 78% was on government subsidy. All would be chipped and in line. No riots. No fuss. Better IQs? Better health? Who needed that?

"But God was everywhere. It was most annoying. If we were to bring singularity to fruition, we had to reconcile God to the notion of transhumans. We could evolve into our best selves. But how to control the worst of ourselves? As it happened, Mother Nature stepped in and did it for us. The EMP was the modern flood that wiped out the driftwood. You have no idea what the future holds for us, Morgan. It's going to be a new age. We can do this together."

Morgan thoughtfully puffed on his pipe for several minutes, tapped the dottle from the bowl with his heel, and rose from his chair. Brown's grin fixed itself into a self-congratulatory smirk.

Morgan reached for his cane that balanced upon the armrest.

"Well, if that's it, I'll be moving on. I'm declining the chance to offer any compensation...the comfortable, sweet kind of life, anyway."

Komor and Blue were the last to leave the room. On her way out the door, Komor leaned down and wrinkled her nose at Brown like a mischievous rabbit. Brown snarled at the Colonel, "He'll be back. You're not so smart. I know how this works."

Komor shrugged. "He won't be back. You're not so smart. I know how this works. If you miss me, I'll be right outside this door."

Brown touched Komor's arm. "What do you think they've got in mind? For me, I mean?"

"Who cares?" she scoffed.

Komor closed the door just as the ex-president lost composure. A string of expletives made their way through the thick wooden walls.

A circumspect group had walked minutes together back toward the main house when Morgan broke the silence.

"Isabella, bring Nicholas Bradley and Aaron to me as soon as possible. Bring their transcripts, too. I want a copy of that Trickster stuff. Invite Rachel to accompany them if she's nervous about Aaron."

"Yes, sir."

Connor patted Morgan's back reassuringly. "These kids are here for a reason. This is no accident, Morgan. I think they can help."

"How am I supposed to suggest such things to children?" Morgan countered.

Connor disagreed, "They're gifted children. They've got unusual senses and abilities. If they've reservations, we'll listen. We can only ask their sense of the situation. I mean, Aaron offered his take on Brown without ever meeting the man.

Didn't sit in judgment of him; that *little* boy just warned us to remain morally vigilant. No one told the boy Brown was here. CC saw Brown, too. A six-year-old with astonishing artistic technique rendered his exact image. Who knows the extent of their emotional maturity? We're the ones late to the table. We're the ones with a lump in our throats, the sick stomachs. They've got survival mechanisms and talents that have risen from an evolutionary crisis. It's like those kids stuck their fingers in a cosmic socket, Morgan.

"We're dealing with an animal in blue pajamas who eats his own. As much as we would like to ascribe current widespread amoral behaviors to the electromagnetic pulses on the human brain, you've got to consider that Brown's brand of evil preceded the disasters. I find it curious that we had research since the turn of the century that unequivocally demonstrated that those RFID implants would further impair judgment. He knew that. The first thing he did was implant illegals and welfare recipients as a condition of pending sanctions and welfare. No resistance from anyone. People like Brown wanted more lab rats to study and people lined up for the cheese!"

Morgan was thoughtful. He grasped at straws.

"I'm focusing on natural genetic predispositions and trying to quantify a wide array of such immoral behaviors. Is this our natural state? Aren't moral challenges the irritant that provides the grist by which pearls are made?" Morgan tried.

Connor put his arm around the shoulders of Morgan, whose gait had slowed, his back stooped from an invisible burden.

"One thing at a time. We have wonderful human anomalies right here that defy the rules. Let's see if our visitors can offer a way out of this mess. We're not going to be able to alter the world's genetic makeup, establish some kind of Utopian society, Morgan. It's a process that's currently beyond us. One thing at a time."

"They're flipping kids, Connor!"

"Infinite intelligence and special talents thus far displayed seemed to have escaped known categories. We'd better start listening a bit more," Connor insisted.

Midway, Blue sprinted from Morgan toward his mistress, now approaching the group at a fast clip. CC pumped short breaths in the cold air like a small locomotive.

"Grandpa, the gold-haired girl is here!" CC exclaimed.

"What's that?" Morgan stooped to pick up his granddaughter.

"The curly-haired girl is here, Grandpa."

"Where?" Morgan asked.

"I don't know. Can't you find her?"

"What made you think she's here?"

"I don't know. Just I know."

Isabella Moreno answered her monitor first. "Thank you, we'll get back to you as soon as we get indoors."

Moreno grinned, "CC, you're spot-on. The Meszaros group is situated in the Hungarian Embassy in Raleigh. Landed a few hours ago. They'll be staying in the Hungarian ambassador's guest house."

"Where were you when we had a stock market, Babycake?"

Morgan kissed his granddaughter's flushed cheeks and followed her into the home's warm foyer. Nicholas Bradley and Aaron Shalit stood together with Adele and Rachel to meet them. Behind them stood the Nishant family and the sisters, Cynthia and Esther.

"Who sounded the alarm?" Morgan surveyed the expectant faces of his household guests before him.

"I told them that Goldilocks was coming here, Grandpa. Right?"

"They're here all right," Morgan nodded.

"And we were told that you might need Aaron and Nicholas?" Rachel stated.

"Yup..." Morgan indicated a trip to his library.

Morgan sighed at the sight of the expectant faces now scattered about the room.

"I don't have the slightest idea where to start. I'm advised by my better self not to bring children into this discussion. I'm going to throw this out there. Feel free to speak up. It's about engaging the children to help ferret out some things that have eluded us. I think they can do that. I think they're supposed to," Morgan introduced awkwardly. "Each of them has certain insights that may help me grasp things I can't figure."

Rachel spoke before Morgan could continue.

"We know finding our way here is no coincidence. I think I speak for all of us that we now realize that this is uncharted territory, requiring risks."

The women nodded their heads in agreement. Meredith Green knocked on the door and was invited to join the group.

"Well, where's CC?" Morgan looked toward Lex. CC appeared from behind her mother's body. Reluctant to speak to everyone, Adele conveyed CC's message, spoken directly into her ear monitor; Adele nodded her head.

"CC tells me that she senses everyone is nervous and their minds aren't calm. She says that she wants us to hold hands in a circle before we speak together and make plans," Adele explained.

Morgan raised his eyebrows toward his granddaughter.

"Sure, why the hell not? What are we doin', CC? Praying for cookies?"

"I'm going to calm everyone. Everyone is thinking everything very loud and fast. Everyone is scared and worried," she uncharacteristically whispered.

The group awkwardly formed an erratic circle in the library that wound around chairs and tables. Rather than join the circle, CC moved toward its center.

"Everybody hold hands," CC directed.

The group tentatively did so.

Nicholas gasped as small blue lights darted around CC's head. Blue points of light swept and zipped about the room. A few returned toward the circle's heart, where CC stood with arms languidly resting with open palms. The blue lights glowed brighter until blended into an aura of blue haze that enveloped the room's assembly. A few deep breaths later, the bright blue light expanded throughout the room. Small spheroids within the sprawling halo became more defined, yet connected within a haze. Just as quickly, the blue orbs separated and darted back toward the circle's center, where CC seemed to re-absorb them. The blue force inside the hazy cloud like atmosphere disappeared in a flash.

"Everyone feel better?" CC clapped her hands joyfully in the midst of stunned silence.

The Pendergrass library filled with an indisputable sense of peace. Morgan grasped many things at once. The first was the enormous relief and healing his granddaughter must have afforded Scott Reid's ailing infant son. It also occurred to him that CC was an emotional tuning fork, having transformed Cary's citizenry into an unusually harmonious place. It was the reason that people were drawn to her and felt an urge to touch her.

He thought about the way in which the Pendergrass household had operated, with disagreements that never manifested into enduring bad feelings. People were calmer, more receptive, and forgiving.

Morgan also considered a specific transformation. He never understood before this moment how it was that Ellie graciously accepted the realities of a failed engagement. It was as unlikely an act as anything he had ever witnessed in the name of civility. Moreover, Ellie had been changed into a curious, productive citizen. He understood that his granddaughter had a part in that, too.

Other than Meredith Green's one too many champagne cocktails on New Year's Eve, people had restricted alcohol intake. Lex's bottle of Calm remained half full since Christmas dinner. Morgan felt lighter, too. He was without the heaviness that had grown so steadily inside him. With each passing year, a new item of concern had been added to his emotional baggage, ever so gradually wearing him down. Suddenly, his granddaughter had appeared to him, much as a spiritual porter, whisking away the accumulated burden. Morgan likened the blue lights having left the residual gift of spiritual relief.

Nicholas Bradley spoke first. He touched his chest and tapped it.

"I've been carrying something sad and I was used to it. It's gone now. It's different than happiness. I feel, I don't know, smooth?"

"Like a clock that doesn't skip a beat," added Indu. "You're confident of its rhythm. Have I been holding my breath my entire life? I feel as if I can breathe easier," she said, awe-stricken.

Aaron recalled his mother, father and homeland with fondness rather than melancholy.

One at a time, excitedly speaking over one other, those in the room expressed a similar sense of congruence. Meredith Green described the harmonic sensation as one of personal 'synchronization'.

"What gave you this idea, CC?" Meredith smiled toward the little girl she had scrutinized in the womb. "Why hold hands?"

"Goldilocks. She visited me and said that I should try it out because I need practice to make the blue light bigger and bigger. She said that I needed to help bring the boy in the water here as soon as possible, too. But, I don't know what she's talking about."

"What else did she say?" Adele asked her daughter.

"If we had some kind of ice cream," CC answered.

"I'm betting you'll be able to introduce Ildiko Meszaros and her father to all kinds of new things, too," Adele smiled and kissed her daughter.

"I'm shelving any further discussion or plans until we can get the Meszaros father and daughter here. Let's arrange that, Isabella," Morgan demanded. "They'll be exhausted but it seems the little Hungarian girl has communicated an urgency to get here to my Caroline."

Morgan instructed Moreno to make the arrangements.

"Bring the Meszaros family here at once."

He slipped outside the room as the gathering bathed in the aftermath of a viscerally exceptional sensation. Morgan tried to grasp and sort the ideas filling his mind.

Morgan speculated that adverse behaviors might be offset by energy conducted from a gifted agent. He had no idea what happened inside his library or what it meant. He did know with certainty that what had transpired was in direct contradiction to the state of mind of the man on the other side of the estate. Was it possible that someone like Brown could be positively affected by CC's experiment, too? Was there a chance that this energy permeated the tobacco shed?

Morgan peeked back into the library. "Look, forget my little speech with everyone. I'm going to pay Brown a visit now. I want to try the new me out on that jackass." His announcement, however, was drowned in the sea of excitement. Morgan slipped out of the house with Blue at his heels.

Morgan walked briskly across the hardened ground toward the shed. Blue trotted behind in the smooth trail created by Morgan's heavy boots that crunched and flattened the mud's frozen stalagmites.

Colonel Komor responded to Morgan's knock and pulled a chair toward Brown's bed. Morgan ignored the gesture meant for his comfort and stood tall, preferring to peer down upon Brown.

"How you feeling now?" Morgan examined him with a hopeful squint.

"What do you mean, good Governor? You have an itch you want me to scratch, Morgan?"

"I used to. Now, I find myself just wondering if you've had time to reflect on things. Don't you think that would be a natural response to your life's work? I mean, do you feel relieved or remorseful?"

"Are you asking if I would have done things differently? You think I liked what happened? You think I enjoyed seeing our country being buried and burned alive?" he offered with accustomed self-importance. "We were treading water. My job was to identify and save those who could help us rebuild. That wasn't a bad objective, Morgan. It's called being in the real world. Noah had nothing on me, Morgan."

"What about before the EMP disasters?" Morgan asked. "You knew that you were misleading citizens with false information. What good did it do? I struggle with a lot of your decisions. For example, what were the reasons you rejected nanotechnology rather than pesticides and fertilizers? We had the ability to secure food and its viability, for African dairy farmers to preserve milk for the day it took to reach a cooler; we had plastic storage bags lined with nanoparticles capable of reacting with oxygen and preventing cassava from rotting. We could monitor plant growth and detect diseases, create additives that would be easily absorbed by the body and deliver nutrients and omega fatty acids to cells without causing any changes to taste or color of food. We could grow plants faster, healthier, and without the issues of past GMOs. Why stop all that? We could have fed the planet!" Morgan asked earnestly.

"Nano capsules added to food products? You meant to deliver nutrients and nanoparticles added to our food to increase the nutrient absorption? Why would I go down that road when it was meant to feed the world? Why would I grow Africa or Persia, Morgan? It would have fallen to our government to fortify others and then defend our country against those same ingrates?

"Hell no. To what end? Our money was on designing micro-chips in the bio-med field. We could connect motor nerves, sure. But we noticed that the frequency of the chip could not only track but had an effect upon behavior. So we pursued behavior modification. Unless we could identify people and their needs we couldn't very well help them. We needed to first embed chips in all those billions of people you were trying to save, Morgan. You have to categorize people's habits and needs before you do anything else.

"It was a boon to the largest retailers and made American products more competitive. American RFID technology forced every supplier to adapt and ramp up or be dropped. The re-tailers discovered they could function without half their work-force. Then they'd eventually operate without their entire workforce. We knew what every customer did while shopping, where they took the merchandise, everything automatically deducted from bank accounts. There wasn't a major business not on board. Those that protested government sharing were soon dropped as suppliers."

Brown paused to take in Morgan's shock. "The only problem we could point to was fraudulent scanning of credit cards. Every credit purchase would eventually require an implanted chip in the cardholder rather than the card. What's the big leap? You talk about feeding the planet? What about identify-ing and distributing to the masses?"

"What made you stop from implanting everyone?" Morgan asked.

"We didn't stop. The frequencies made people go a bit crazy. We needed more fieldwork so we implanted the Indians and the Mexicans to figure out how to smooth it out for Americans."

"Why shut off our work?" Morgan asked about his own research. "You lied about our efforts to eradicate disease while you conducted unethical research on unwitting citizens in the name of safety. You implemented a medical framework that required a national ID chip embedded into a singular card, then moved rapidly into requiring government RFID chips...you knew that it was all about ending all individual options," Morgan seethed.

Brown chuckled at Morgan's naiveté.

"People supported me because I understood how to make them feel secure. Who wanted to bother with the details? No one. That was my job and I did what I could to keep people who couldn't compete clothed, fed and educated. To hell with those greedy bastards who had 80% of the wealth! Americans were starving to death. Children were dying for lack of clean water. We could not respond with jobs. There were no jobs. We were spent out keeping people in nonsensical menial government work at 20 dollars an hour just so they wouldn't riot and burn.

"You rich hyenas kept talking about merit, fairness but wouldn't own up to carrying the less capable, the less educated, the less inclined. Who owns the earth's wealth? You capitalists sucked up America's goodwill, along with our resources, complaining all the way to the bank about having to pull the nation's cart, paddle with one oar, and all that bullshit. All that elitist talk about our constitutional rights. We were debating a charter wholly unsuited to the needs of the 21st century! No one could even understand the Constitution.

"We plumbed the Constitution rather than to waste time with political infighting or legislation. People were suffering. Enough was enough. Here we stand...a remnant of the wishful thinkers taking me to task for moving mountains to save the country?"

Morgan calmly assessed Brown's face as he absorbed the skewed tenets adopted in place of more difficult ones. Brown's was a perverse version of leadership.

"Humans should be the beneficiaries of the resources of the planet and I was one of the ones called upon to oversee those resources," continued Brown. "There are always causalities, bad feelings, and collateral damage. I stepped up to the plate with a plan. You? You're just another entitled elitist talking about your work ethic but at the same time taking advantage of the failing system so that you could secure your little fief-dom. Then you talked most of the other productive states into doing the same, calling for the Constitutional Convention. Sure, cause a national schism...that's all you managed to do. Form your little state sovereignties when urban America was suffering. Who feels like shit? Not me, Lord Morgan. You've always felt superior and entitled, right down to your genetic research. You researchers who feel as if you've a calling to eradicate human failings through better science and at the same time pretend you aren't playing God? What's going on inside of you, Morgan? Your academic buddies dared to play around with genetic advantages? You would let billions of humans eat themselves alive? Fight for dwindling resources until we'd burned the planet bare? Where was the balance?"

Have I been an elitist? Morgan considered to himself. *The idea that citizens were too limited to steward their resources is an elitist idea in itself!* Morgan shook his head at the ruse.

"The Trickster. The mischief-maker who sprinkles evil with just enough truth in order to make the lie palatable or conduct the righteous execution. Of course!"

Brown looked quizzically toward Pendergrass, as did Colonel Komor.

"Are you aware that you said that nonsense *out loud*? What the hell you talking about? Your synapses aren't firing, Pendergrass," Brown said.

Morgan ignored Brown's comment and continued, "I'm inclined to believe that you believe that crap yourself. This explains your lack of regret or self-reflection. You're too big for guilt. You harbor those really important big ideas! Yours is a grand plan to provide for the welfare of the little people. Keep them in check...keep them in line... throw them crumbs, until they're grateful for the chance of being alive, forgetting that it's their right to the opportunity to live fully and well. How big of you, Brown! The only opportunity presented to them was contrived as the magnanimous government subsidy route. It was a dead end and you knew it. Government schools, government teachers, government medicine, government food, government jobs, government votes...the lack of nutritive value cut them at the knees.

"Your track record speaks volumes. I couldn't conceive of killing my family for the good of the nation. Any nation that would require such an unnatural act is unworthy," Morgan's voice was as clear as his conclusions. "If you'd sacrifice your family, what chance did ordinary Americans have?

"You hid like a rat. Did whatever possible to save your skin. Conspired to create manufactured suffering by segregating the populace, polarizing the country, with every hateful notion having been neatly plated and served with pride. Produced nothing. Helped no one. Endorsed false privilege to the level of class envy. Your White House was sullied by vileness and confusion. You figured yourself as a benevolent despot who cared for the welfare of the nation but used every resource at your disposal to ensure your tactics went unchallenged, lest someone knew the facts. Since the majority of voters no longer cared about our government charter, it's no wonder you were successfully confused with the knight on a white horse. Saving Americans from the enemies you defined and redefined at will must have been a full time job. Most charismatic leaders relied on enemy nation states to rally against. Nationalism always worked. Protect the motherland! You had a sicker stratagem. You pitted Americans against Americans. It was the rich against the poor. God-fearing people were portrayed as disingenuous hate mongers. God became laughable fodder for politicians and comedians hell-bent on being progressive thinkers. The joke was that you denied good science, too. Never mind using our minds. Hate and division was the game.

"The rich? Who the hell was rich thirty years ago, Clifton? Few institutions were alive, much less thriving. We were a country of hand to mouth. Those with money paid 85% of the taxes until you nationalized, leveraged, or blackmailed them all. Then the government ran out of money. Flat-ass broke.

"Most of all, projecting your own character flaws upon others is telltale. You hate any notion that threatens absolute power. I don't think like that. You think like that. And since when is elitist thinking wrong? You're an idiot. You're damn right I wanted elite levels of everything. You mix a lot of bad cement, Brown. You sank good ideas with bad ones and even that cement couldn't hold water. Elite doesn't mean exclusive. It means a slice above... better education, better health, better government, and better business, better opportunities that don't happen at the expense of the freedom of others. America was the best place of opportunity for personal freedoms, imagination, and vision. You and others like you skewed founding principles, then screwed good Americans in the bargain.

"American exceptionalism was a dream and we dared to imagine it! From our dreams came reality, and good men and women died to defend them. It meant our collective abilities would be able to raise the highest common denominator rather than accommodate the lowest. It meant doing our best as a community, helping our fellow man, and doing that as our duty to God and a country....in that reasonable order. I don't care what your notion is about a damn thing because it will never work without a moral compass. To me, humans are endowed with a nature to explore something bigger, broader, and mindful with a curiosity that compels us to spiritually reach, intelligently armed with faith and humility.

"Our country represented a right to worship freely and the opportunity to dream big without fearing ridicule and censorship. America was supposed to be a democratic beacon for the world. Why not elevate parity? Why did people begin to think that it was acceptable to attack those that worked their ass off? We don't have it; you do, so give it over? Where were you going with that? Americans were always the most giving, charitable people on earth! I don't mean just giving help... I mean we think *highly* of others.

"You can't pull that crap speech on me, Brown. I think better of people. You had a responsibility to work harder toward noble ends. You didn't have a dream, you ass wipe, you had and made nightmares the moment you expected and encouraged people's worse nature. Your type killed excellence by propagating envy," Morgan railed passionately.

"Please," Brown laughed, "you're nothing but a dinosaur."

"There's not one person in this room who doesn't know how to plow a field, tote water, dress a wound, or bury loved ones," Morgan clarified, his eyes unwavering upon Clifton Brown. "You know how to kill your family and arrive at a rationale for doing so. That much is clear."

Brown's cynicism oozed.

"All you have to do is rid American society of the dissidents and the deadbeats? Then everyone will be harmonious, God-fearing, and hardworking as hell? The Confederation is so different? The names have just changed. Yeah, you're such a big damn deal. So honest it's frightening. We're cut from the same cloth, Morgan. You're no different from me. You're delusional. Some beacon of truth. What a pile of lies. You're a self-absorbed moral revisionist, Morgan. You use God as a cornerstone for all kinds of excuses..."

Morgan texted Isabella: "*Please bring Nicholas to Brown's shed. Trust me.*"

"You know what, Clifton?" Morgan squatted by the bed so that he was at eye level. "I think I am very, very different. I think everyone in this room is very, very different. You're the one full of horseshit. I'm betting on it. I'm going to prove it."

Nicholas and Isabella were inside the cabin within minutes. Nicholas surveyed the scene and sized up his mission.

"I know the reason I'm here, Dr. Pendergrass. I heard Aaron, I heard CC, I heard you, and I feel the very strong vibrations here."

Morgan took the boy in hand and left the room to go outdoors. Nicholas preempted Morgan's explanation.

"I know you know what happened on the Hopeless. I can't say what will happen here but I mean no harm to anyone. The thing that I cause is a reaction of some kind. I'm nothing more than an echo, Dr. Pendergrass. I didn't feel guilty because when I was cornered, I didn't imagine or expect it. Whatever happened was a result of someone else's purposes. Actively threatening my life either made me invisible to my predator and/or allowed me to fight on a different level. I know now that I was protected from evil one way or another.

"The man inside that little cabin is not a good man. You know that, I know that, and it doesn't take any special powers to sort that out. You think I can offer proof or something. You think that you are on the right path and the man inside has low vibrations of destruction. I have no control over what happens. I do know that once he thinks of threatening me, he gets back what he's dished out in life."

"Well, crap if I care. Let's go, son!" Morgan directed.

Morgan re-entered behind Nicholas, who returned courageously into the cabin to test the ex-president. Komor had never been briefed on Nicholas nor knew the extent of his abilities. The Confederation guards were trained specialists; not the least of their skills was complete discretion. They had been briefed on Nicholas and the sisters before they were allowed to escort them to Cary. They stood observing Brown's every move, ready to intercede if Nicholas was in any way in danger.

"I don't mind if you all stay. I have no idea what to expect, however," Nicholas stood erect, with the poise and confidence of a seasoned soldier.

Nicholas examined the man in blue pajamas, who seemed unusually calm. Brown stared expectantly back at Nicholas.

Nothing happened. Nicholas thought about it. He knew instinctively that the man was as evil as the men on the Hopeless. Yet there was no reaction. It occurred to Nicholas that unless Brown meant to attack him personally or threatened others directly, he was unable to elicit or conduct a reaction. Was it conceivable that the man's energies were entirely devoted to sequestering compromising thoughts? Was it possible that the ex-president knew he was being tested? Or was it, Nicholas wondered, that he believed himself justified and had no guilt?

Yes. That's exactly it, believed Nicholas. The man on the bed remained contained, affecting boredom. Nicholas was unable to aggressively or proactively test out the man lying confidently still, shielding certain memories, pathologically confident of his guiltlessness.

Nicholas turned toward Morgan and Morgan understood the challenge at once. Brown's hidden thoughts and associations would make him susceptible to guilt that had long been pathologically firewalled. Morgan intuited Nicholas's conclusions and moved to prompt dark memories that had been carefully crafted to neurotic acceptance by the man who harbored them.

"Allow me to introduce a fine young man, Cliff. He's a great kid, this lad," began Morgan. "He was born and raised in the aftermath of the EMP disasters in upstate New York. Marauders raped his sister as she tended the fields, his mother committed suicide and his father was clinically depressed. Nicholas Bradley's grandfather – murdered on their farm by five thugs – inculcated a most excellent education that included community activities and religious study. Their loose-knit community was one of the islands of sanity in a world of raw insanity. Many such provinces, like the one in which Nicholas matured, kept irrationality at bay with moral behaviors and cultivated habits. These were hard-working folk from all walks of life. Their collective faith, cooperation, and discipline worked miracles on the brain and soul. It wasn't enough to keep them from being isolated from civilization. Nicholas, his sister and father decided to make their way to the safety of the Confederation.

"This remarkable young man made his way toward us through some of the worst territory on the continent and sneaked onto a ship of pirates in the business of ferrying desperate people to safety near the Confederation borders. I'd say he has a guardian angel or two." Morgan paused and watched as he stated, "Unfortunately, the rest of his family was murdered by pirates. It's admirable that he survived."

"What's this about? Get that kid out of here. You call your-self civil?" Brown exploded with loathing. "I'm an old man tied to a bed in a windowless old shack. You're boring me to death. Who's in a world of evil? You look like you fit right in, Pender-grass. Give me some dignity. Take these shackles off, give me some clothes and allow me to speak as a free man," Brown demanded.

Morgan signaled Komor to remove Brown's restraints.

"Finally. Now give me my clothes," Brown growled.

Komor handed Brown his clothes and shoes. Nicholas stared at Brown blankly as the immodest man stripped and discarded his clothing. He replaced them with a Confederation prisoner's orange jumpsuit. Stained pajamas were tossed toward Komor's head. Without batting an eye, Komor whipped the flying clothes from the air and threw them back at the ex-president. Brown's face turned red; his bottled wrath spewed forth upon Nicholas.

"What exactly do you have to say for yourself, migrating miracle boy that failed to do miracles? What in the hell are you here for? You think you're looking at a freak show? Want to learn some history? I know exactly what went on, what goes on, in the North. Plenty of people escaped that hell-hole. Your family should have gone north into Canada, not south. You're not bright or brave. You sound like a lucky fool. Probably ditched that sloppy family of yours and went on your own!"

Nicholas recoiled in his seat as a montage of images formed in his mind. First came screaming children separated from their homes. Displaced families roamed the streets in freezing temperatures to gather clothes from the dead. Government agents appeared in robotic exoskeletons and forced their way through burning buildings to retrieve ammunition in large steel boxes; charred bodies lay in their wake as goods were loaded onto armored vehicles, carried on backs, pulled by handcarts. Through smoke-filled streets, civilians were forced to act as the military's mules.

Gunfire rang in the blackness, interrupted with streams of lights from affixed cameras on roaming helmets. Laser beams cut the night, followed by screams. The scenes in Nicholas's and Brown's minds rapidly transformed.

A White Eagle Security team hustled a much younger President Brown to massive airplanes that sat side-by-side, prepared to exit on a vast runway. Helicopters were lined up on another. White House personnel carried the luggage of the President's family. That staff dropped listlessly to the ground as the remainder of the President's entourage callously made their way around the fallen bodies. Two Air Force pilots moved rapidly toward the President's entourage to explain the dysfunction of the plane's automatic and remote systems. They were allowed on board after much arguing. The co-pilot, said one White Eagle, was 'redundant'. The young man's body slumped and was thrown back down the long ramp and dragged from the runway.

Brown's mind played these interwoven scenes, straining with simultaneous effort to self-edit the flood of memories. His face appeared momentarily terrified and contorted, and then reverted alternately to the composed face of the former commander-in-chief in self-appreciation.

Nicholas heart rate shot up. Komor became alarmed at the sudden spike. The monitor beeped its protest with rapid reads of a heuristic medical report. His medical avatar pleaded attention with ECG metrics and warned the omission of implanted medical nanobots that could reveal a complete picture:

"*Warning! No profile on subject; DNA data base non-existent... acknowledge ambulance requirement... signaling medical emergency assistance now...*"

"Are you all right?" Komor manually felt the boy's vitals." I'm going to ask you to come with me," Komor advised.

Morgan motioned Komor to refrain from interference. Komor reluctantly removed the boy's wrist monitor that was without access to internal personal data. She remained by his side.

Nicholas continued to observe images, looking through, and around, the man before him. Nicholas was privy to a story now unfolding in Clifton Brown's subconscious. With thinned speech, Nicholas recounted his interpretation of the images and the emotions they elicited. Without moving his eyes from fixed space, Nicholas spoke distantly to Clifton Brown.

"Can you recall the moment your wife asked you to spare your daughters? She begged you to let them live..to just kill her and free the girls. She cried on her knees and the two girls began to weep, too. The younger one wore an oversized leather flight jacket. She ran into her mother's arms. They held each other and wept their distress on a cold cement floor. Your wife began to recite the Lord's Prayer and your youngest daughter joined her. She was rocked and hugged by your wife; the name 'Marcella' is softly repeated again and again as your wife buries your daughter's head into her chest. Your oldest daughter stands upright. She screams at you. She hates you. She spits at your face and calls you an animal..."

Nicholas played the thoughts he was dealt. He grasped that mention of his sister's rape ignited the briefest recall of Brown's oldest daughter when she was dragged to the side of the room by three of his security guards. Brown had allowed his wife and youngest daughter to cower for over a half hour on a bunker floor. Then, he watched his security men—one after the other—ravage his 22-year-old screaming daughter without protest.

Nicholas felt the ex-president's stoic regard for the anarchy around him; Brown's singular concern was one of personal survival. One of the rapists held a chip activator. When they finished with the eldest daughter, Brown held out his hand for the small instrument and pressed the handheld weapon three times to release the poisoned chips embedded inside each of his family members. Nicholas relayed the quick, painful deaths and the subsequent removal of the bodies, piled on a cart and deposited into a crematorium.

Nicholas continued to relate events even as Colonel Komor's own monitor beeped her internal protest; Nicholas rapidly recounted incidents of horrific proportions that included a locked room of kidnapped women in what looked like a cement bunker.

"Shut up!" Unrestrained, Brown lurched for the teenager but collapsed the moment his feet touched the first floorboard. With the slightest trace of moral conscience ignited, Clifton Brown's body began to furiously burn out of control from the tinder ignited by the minutest tinge of culpability.

Slowly and painfully, a guilt-ridden life of meting pain, death, and destruction began to hemorrhage. No matter where Brown attempted to compartmentalize memories, his mainframe was hacked by the single word 'rape'. Brown beat his hands upon his head.

Nicholas objectively noted the difference between his prior experiences and the one transpiring before him. He did not feel physically threatened. Although Nicholas' heart rate climbed to an alarming rate, it stabilized just as quickly. CC's light had calibrated him, he believed. Nicholas stoically regarded Brown thrashing on the floor in another soiled jumpsuit and moved out of range.

"I've no control over this, Dr. Pendergrass," Nicholas walked toward Morgan for advice.

"It's time for you to leave, son. This has nothing to do with you. You've been no more than a catalyst. The poison in that man is erupting like molten lava, burning his insides as it spews and spills over. Go back to the house. Thank you for proving something I needed demonstrated. He put doubt in me. I needed to know," Morgan added gratefully.

Nicholas left with one of the guards and looked up toward the sky, allowing the drizzling rain to wash the last of Clifton Brown from him. The guard urged Nicholas to move quickly away, hoping that distance would help heal them both.

Morgan's disgust was held in check. Brown demanded an explanation in gasped breaths.

"What the hell is happening?" Brown choked in vile green matter.

"The way I figure it, you've come up against an earthly karmic warrior...a mirror of your intent and actions, perhaps? The pain you are experiencing seems connected to the pain you inflicted upon others. If you survive, it might convince you that empathy exists...in your case, after the fact."

Komor and the guards, immune to Nicholas's effects, knew that the young man was the facilitator of Brown's current condition. Komor suggested that Brown be again restrained so as not to self-inflict injury. It took four of them to manage the crazed man.

Komor taped the transparent, thin medical monitor on his wrist but it showed nothing of interest except high blood pressure, a slight temperature, and dehydration. Komor considered a sedative and then thought better of it. She might be a good person, but 'not that good', she decided.

A guard asked what Dr. Komor professionally made of the fact that Brown was foaming at the mouth with undiagnosed causes.

Dr. Krisztina Komor coldly regarded the man lying now prone in tight restraints on the bed, drowning in uncharted, spontaneous agony.

"My bet? There's a God."

* * *

Angela and Adele were of the same mind once they heard of what transpired in the tobacco shed. Neither thought anything positive would come of having the ex-president on the farm.

Rachel and the Nishants concerned themselves only with justice served and reviewed the monitor's rerun of events.

Lex became pale and silent as he observed the confrontation he avoided.

Connor assured young Nicholas that he was on the right side of the equation; Nicholas concurred that there was no malice involved. Nicholas excused himself to join the sisters, who were engrossed with Aditiya's holographic images floating within the recreation room upstairs, oblivious to all things Clifton Brown.

Angela felt a new urgency to remove Brown from North Carolina.

"Stop the hysteria right about now, Cookie. Who's his audience? The man is in cuffs, under guard, fighting for his life, if not his sanity."

"How long will he writhe in pain?" she asked. The monitor transferred the muted images and Angela closed her eyes, repulsed by Brown's self-loathing rising to untold levels.

"Not long enough," Amar Nishant said without emotion. "This seems to explain a term I learned long ago. I used to think I knew it."

"Of what term are you speaking, Amar?" Indu's attention was riveted upon the scene of a man sinking painfully in a personalized pool of depravities.

"Purgatory. He is, perhaps, expunging. Do you think there is an end to such purging of the soul? Is it possible that this process allows him to physically or spiritually recover?"

Adele tilted her head toward the image of the man who allowed his own daughter to be brutalized.

"Ordinarily, I would be unable to conceive of such an act. Since my exposure to Caroline's lights, I recognize this evil without becoming vulnerable to it. If it's purgatory of some kind, it's extraordinary. I think the religious notion of purgatory happens post-mortem. Save this torment, I believe that Mr. Brown had not a clue about the pain he caused others."

Indu concurred, "Your daughter's evolutionary gift has given us the composure required to deal objectively with amoral predators I would have otherwise been unable to look at."

Morgan and Connor looked at each other knowingly. Indu had said that which was on everyone's mind. CC had an undefined ability to adjust the emotional condition of others to an optimal state. That included the calibration of Nicholas' abilities. She had been able to better affect the unwieldy powers that Nicholas unintentionally caused. When Clifton Brown's mind brushed against a memory in Nicholas's presence, the pain was sparked, and then continued, whether or not Nicholas felt threatened. Justice was served as soon as Clifton Brown connected to his culpability.

Connor watched the monitor as Brown continued to scream protests, pulling at his restraints.

"CC's influence on Nicholas was the fairest solution," Connor began. "We're, in fact, watching what happens when the man awoke to an imposed conscience ...all in one sitting.

"I suspect that we'll discover other survival mechanisms at the molecular levels that protect us against evil. Our systems of justice have been morally based. In the end, we've had to define criminal behaviors and bring up the rear with consensual, de facto justice. Our collective compassion and psychological profiles try to excuse sick behaviors but our good will has never eradicated crime. We've had to incarcerate or execute the worst criminals. Still, no permanent moral justice was ever served. Humanity rose to the challenge to demonstrate the compassion they felt was denied victims of circumstance...and then what? Not much. Evil grew.

"With the EMP overload it became worse. There was no counterbalance. Post-EMP, extreme behaviors begot extreme responses in the name of survival. This inherent defense system we see in Nicholas is just enough to render the predator inoperable with commensurate pain for the crimes committed."

Connor thought in terms of genetics and evolution.

"I noted when Dr. Goodwin mentioned there is no obvious symbiotic relationship between man and his habitat. We wouldn't be missed; the world would move on. Dr. Goodwin was right. Our natural predators are those of us who lack moral conscience. Is our evolution connected to this conflict?

"I also ask myself what has made some large groups and individuals able to withstand a constant bombardment of chaos and thrive with moral productivity after the EMP overdose while others were unequivocally drawn toward the negative? How could man be so divided, so at odds, in their programming? I've got to figure it's not all about hard programming. Our cultural habits, the way we think, the things we expose ourselves to, seeking to situate challenging ideas, a developed sense of harmony and beauty--all of this and more affects our DNA. Some people were already in a weakened state. Others survived erratic frequencies because their internal connection to sophisticated cultivated rituals and positive thoughts was greater. Perhaps cultural habits-or the lack thereof- have the ability to enhance or diminish our brains, our neurological pathways, and even our cellular structure?

"Nicholas tells us a lot, too. I say that evolution has finally provided us a means by which to recognize evil, ferret it out, render its image, find its hiding place, feel its vibration and weigh it against that which is wholesome. On the other side of the coin, our more resilient predators represent a vibrational virus able to infiltrate society like the Sea Walnut...a predator from another vibrational field that slowly destroys an entire tier of the crustacean sea life as an invisible agent that, on the face of it, lacks the power or resources to threaten empowered, superiorly-enhanced sea life. It seeps into our infrastructure unseen. Evolved life can be diminished or destroyed before it knows what's happening.

"Human predators traditionally look like us, act like us and even agree with us. They find common ground...usually a common dissatisfaction... so that they can engage and become closer to us. This kind of predator often mistakes compassion, trust, love, and ethical conduct for weakness. That kind of predator is always surprised when good people have the wherewithal to hit back and hit back hard. We eventually do.

"Like the Sea Walnut, human predators share the same waters, live like us, and seem to have the same goals. Yet they remain among us to sabotage our existence, unwilling or unable to forge an independent life. This kind of predator is mostly imperceptible to a higher vibrational frequency. We find ourselves opening our homes, our coffers, and our hearts to those in need. The predator that preys upon human kindness is the cleverest and most insidious. We've been taught to give others the benefit of the doubt or risk self-doubt. Are we paranoid, biased, hateful, or even irrational when they manipulate with platitudes of friendship, mutual satisfaction or goals? We feel something, of course. Something is off, you know? But do we act on it? We risk being accused of paranoia, bias, hatefulness, and irrational behaviors. We lament our lack of good heartedness, wishing to do the right thing. That radar system beeped alarms and we ignored it. Whether it was depleting our system of resources or causing anxiety, we were reluctant to act on our behalf. We were somehow, I don't know, unworthy of such selfishness.

"Nicholas's ability doesn't require quiet self-reflection for a higher moral authority to kick in. This is genetic coding able to stop an organism's predatory intent. Nicholas had DNA equipped with the kind of radar that doesn't need a conscious trigger," Connor concluded.

Rachel took Connor's hand to lead him from the Monitor screen to sit beside her.

"I was in charge of the supplemental vegetable garden for a few years on the Kibbutz," Rachel began. "You'd think that insects would be the main things to look out for. But it was actually something more insidious. I became aware of a member of the plant kingdom's Dodder Family, the Cuscufaceae. It looks like a bit of nothing of a plant. The Dodder, I can tell you, is the sneakiest parasite imaginable. It attacks other plants mercilessly. Left unchecked, it kills every living plant in sight.

"That plant hasn't enough water, minerals and carbohydrates to live on its own. The flowers are sweet looking and numerous. It's not something that appears threatening. No big thorns, no foul odor, no poisonous berries, nothing alarming. Each plant produces 16,000 seeds and each seed's viability ranges from 20 to 60 years; a seed can lie dormant for five years. It lies in wait for a permanent host plant... sucks life from it and kills it.

"The young Dodder seedling gropes in the air, sniffing nearby plants; its stem moves midair, along irrigation ditches in water, travels embedded in livestock manure. Cows eat infested alfalfa or eat crop seeds that can be infiltrated by even a few Dodder seeds. The Dodder plant will spawn and then moves fast to make contact with a host. It coils around the stem of its victim and the basal part of the Dodder plant will disintegrate so that no soil connection exists.

"It doesn't normally wait around for a suitable host to show up. The vine creeps and crawls, shoving competing plants out of the way, expanding its territory as it stretches toward countless types of ornamentals and food crops. As it turns out, it loves tomatoes. It slithers, virtually undetectable; its tiny, thorny bramble whips from side to side frenetically, on the hunt for a tomato plant like a five-star restaurant. Our monitors caught it on time lapse. Its jungle vines entwine with the tomatoes', stretching up toward the sunlight and snuffing out the tomatoes' lifeline. It sinks tiny nozzles into the tomato plant to suck out its vital juices.

"There's extensive collateral damage beyond killing plants one by one; the Dodder also carries and spreads plant diseases, causing dramatic declines in produce. Phytoplasma is the cause of more than 200 diseases once thought spread by some kind of virus. It's the Dodder's work. The parasite's wide range of suitable hosts, coupled with the long life of its dominant seedlings, makes the Dodder almost invincible to eradication.

"The Sea Walnut would have been best buddies with the Dodder. Neither has a natural predator. So I get what you're saying. What do we do when nature produces such parasitic killers? There is nothing in nature that eradicates the Dodder or the Sea Walnut but the higher authority of human interference... or the complete destruction of hosts."

"How does it detect a tomato plant?" Aaron looked curiously at his adopted aunt.

"It can smell them. It's developed the ability to sort chemicals emitted by each plant variety. The vine sniffs out its hosts and grows toward telltale scents released by neighbors. It's selective, too. Sick plants are bypassed. All this was discovered by one of our Israeli botanists," Rachel explained. Finding the room listening to her conversation, she shared her conclusions.

"The Dodder has no way or reason to derive its nutrients from the environment. Other than to feed on another plant, it can't be satiated. It drains the host dry, multiplies, and carries diseases to other vegetation in the process. All the while, it appears with flowers and small fruit beneficial to no other living organism. There are many parasites that are facsimiles and mimics but few are as devastating as this plant. The Dodder can even absorb chemicals from its host plants so it can also prove toxic if eaten by animals. Beyond the plant devastation, it has the ability to kill grazing wildlife," Rachel observed and waited for input.

Meredith Green looked at the children and considered the lifelong alignments with genetic determinism versus naturalistic terms. It seemed to her that the appearance of the children with extraordinary abilities was nature's answer to irrevocable corrupted coding caused in part by the electromagnetic forces.

"We know that variations of a gene predicated antisocial behaviors in mistreated children. We know that monoamine oxidase at low levels is linked to aggression. We know that children who were neglected had a variation of the gene that produced low levels of MAOA were likely to develop antisocial personality disorders with violent dispositions. And we know that others able to produce more of the enzyme didn't have such problems. We've known that the psychopaths, the kind which now roam our planet in unprecedented numbers, have a diminished ability to recycle serotonin in the brain. All of these and more have been set in DNA stone? Such inherited traits that are irreversible mean either we come up with a solution and cure behaviors by tweaking genes or it's a war of the species," Meredith ventured.

"I'm telling you," noted Adele. "I never thought that an air-sniffing, water-slithering, tomato-sucking, spore-producing, disease-transporting plant could make me associate behaviors with the likes of Clifton Brown."

Morgan terminated the monitor.

Indu joined the discussion.

"I'm afraid Westerners struggle with the fairness of hierarchy. Indians have long lived with polarized souls at the center of debate. There was no lack of pain as we've tried to come to terms with classified systems.

"You know the caste system in South Asia that separates people into high, middle and lower classes? When I was a student at University, we were able to identify this development from genetic analysis. Over five thousand years ago, there was a departure from a long-practiced endogamy. Evidence showed that there was a brief period of intermarriage between genetic populations. About two thousand years ago, the mingling abruptly ceased and strict caste divisions crystallized. We Hindus have been born into one of four major castes—with subdivisions, of course. To move from caste to caste by intermarriage was strictly forbidden. We're not sure what happened that made intermarriage suddenly become taboo. But we were able to test the DNA and connect historical developments with texts like the holy Manusmruti that explicitly forbade caste intermarriage. With a simple blood test, we were able to list the caste as a category with exact proportions of genetic 'purity', if you will.

"Gradually, we University researchers canonized those groups from the Near East and Caucasus region, as well as another South Indian group more closely genetically connected to those of the Andaman Island. While the DNA was mixed, we could determine exactly the proportion of ancestry. It wasn't anything but scientific inquiry. But this cursory study played into political hands.

"The next thing we know, the USA is testing a strategy to implant chips into welfare recipients, supposedly to offset fraud, drug use, and other errant behaviors. The way the Indians viewed this was from different eyes. We have a unique historical perspective that embraced separation of classes. Chips that tracked activities for the 'sub-humans' appealed to the Hindu ideas of karma and caste. Frequency tracking looked to some as a practical way to get around our constitution that forbad job discrimination based on class, too. Indians in power weren't worried about jobs; they were worried about an inferior group of people that were multiplying in a way they thought put our country at economic and social risk.

"Everyone seemed eager to believe that the Dalits, the untouchables, were the troublemakers...the rapists, the thieves, the muck of society. Those of us who protested this unfounded theoretical implantation were dismissed from the research program. Soon, we realized that there was more than simple cooperation from the US. The Americans were everywhere on campus, and so was your military.

"The Americans convinced our government there was a way to manage illiterates so that they could be 'protected' with appropriate medical attention and education. This was an obvious fraud to Indian academics. We knew that these poor beings rarely ever made it into a proper hospital.

"Within a short time, millions of Dalits were implanted with frequency chips. It was that man on your monitor lying there screaming with pain that gave our country the idea of controlling behaviors in the streets rather than bother with justice.

President Brown visited India personally. The program was swiftly implemented as a testing ground for leaders like Brown. They used our research in the worst ways.

"Before long, the undesirables disappeared. If a Dalit was accused of a heinous crime, he or she never made it to court. Slowly, more and more dead Dalits were discovered. Curiously, the medical schools had more and more organs to transplant and plenty of samples with which to experiment with regenerative techniques. We didn't miss the connection. Our friend Gordon Smith divulged the conspiracy. It was a concerted effort by a group of so-called democratic countries to get a handle on the least productive classes that outweighed dwindling government funds while enlisting them at necessary levels of support: the vote, the worst jobs, a counterbalance to the influence of 'elite' numbers. Self-styled progressive causes and groups turned out to be led by the most insidious racists.

"Gordon quoted your President Brown. Brown said he had the way to get rid of 'dissidents and deadbeats'. We had gotten used to untouchables for thousands of years, so it was not too difficult to convince a large percentage of Indians. Dissidents, however, were another matter. They were classified as disloyal government-funded companies, employees, or individual citizens unwilling to follow government social directives. That was put in American terms. Brown repeated it everywhere.

"We were somewhat ashamed but not guilty. We did our best within our means to protest the scheme within academia. Then, the Darkness came. Within a week, I couldn't move ten steps without stepping over a dead body of every caste," Indu said as she bowed her head and clasped her hands together tightly.

"Here is what I wish to say. I do not ever want such an evil to rise again. Whatever it takes to do that, we must do that. Maybe that means something drastic.

"Amar has scientific evidence that human capacities for evil and good tendencies have solidified one way or the other in extreme ways in our DNA. This has accelerated due to the EMP impacts. If we can't correct the genetic defects, we need to identify this new caste of killers while the Confederation is strong. Our children here are the beneficiaries of genetic game-changers. A new generation of gifted children will likely be the first targets for extermination from the worst of these primal, amoral predators. That is, if these hysterical humans are not exterminated before we are overrun," Indu explored without hesitation as to the proposed solution.

Morgan narrowed his eyes on Indu. "If I played it back, you would realize that your suggestions carry overtones of Brown's initial strategies. Subspecies: two distinct genetic codes? One evolutionary and one retroactive...less intelligent, predatory, unusable. I know you don't mean to represent that which Brown prompted. But you're speaking of identifying genetic markers and eliminating carriers.

"Smith's collective studies indicate that half the planet preys on the other half and, therefore, we're the better half? My first instinct is to recall our innumerable mistakes in allocating such justice.

"If someone attacks my life, livelihood, or highest princi- ples I am compelled to action. Yet it's a slippery slope to anticipate such a thing and proactively intercede, Indu. It's not what we do."

Indu was disturbed by the doctor's hesitancy. It was not the time to wax philosophical.

"What are you trying to say? That hasn't already happened? You of all people should know what it means to be proactive. This element isn't just dead weight. We're speaking of an ele- ment that is programmed to kill. We're at a genetic crossroads calling for an intelligent human decision to preserve the best of our species. I wouldn't wait for some cosmic green light. Our sense of urgency, these enhanced DNA codes, are all the evi- dence we need to understand the ultimate fight is here."

The room fell silent when they realized that CC was present behind a couch. She stood to ask a question, revealing herself. Morgan acknowledged her with a nervous smile.

"The Dodder is a plant, right?" she asked.

"Right you are."

"The tomato is a plant, too?"

"Yes."

"Why doesn't the tomato plant protect itself somehow? Why does the Dodder always win?"

"What do you think?" Morgan asked.

"I think because the tomato plant is needed by people who like to eat BLT's and tomato soup and spaghetti sauce. People are supposed to protect the tomatoes like Rachel did. People are the higher power that can protect the cultivated plant over the angry one."

"You are trying to correlate an idea, Caroline?"

"Who looks after us? Who protects the good people? Who is the higher power?"

"What do you think?" Morgan tested.

"I think we are always being protected but maybe we can't understand what protects us, or how it protects us, just like a tomato plant probably doesn't understand how Rachel watches out for them. We can't understand God, but God understands us. God protects us in ways we don't know.

"If Nicholas can stop the bad people we will all be able to protect ourselves from the bad people in the same way. We will all have a little of Nicholas in us. We will learn Aaron's ways and others, too.

"Maybe a tomato plant will one day learn how to protect itself and the Dodder will learn to make its own food or die. Rachel might even figure out how to give the tomatoes a smell that the Dodder doesn't like..."

Caroline stopped speaking abruptly, her face showing deep concern. "What's the matter, Caroline?" Morgan asked.

"Rachel isn't at the Israeli farm. Those tomato plants will die if someone doesn't do something. Maybe no one comes because they're doing something else. Maybe a tomato plant has a Nicholas tomato in its group. A Nicholas tomato plant can make the Dodder sick and die when it means to suck his friends up."

"Ok."

"When Rachel is gone, the tomatoes have to do something to help themselves. Just like us. We have to do something to help ourselves now. Aaron can make things move; we all will be able to move heavy things of stone and metal."

"Go on."

"And the blonde girl can go anywhere in her mind. She can find people like us. And she can see the wrong kinds, too, and warn us."

"And?"

"And I can make people be a little happier and not so mean so they feel the right way."

"I see that."

"I think the parasites die out when there are no more hosts. Or a new kind of host is born and stops the feeding and the Dodder has to stay connected to the ground."

Aaron pinged his translator.

"They adapt. They learn to feed another way?" Aaron asked, as he stood up next to Caroline.

"Maybe," CC shrugged.

"You may be on to something there," Morgan smiled at the children. "I like the thought of the final stage of human adaptation as the motivated self-sufficient kind."

Adele kissed her daughter on the cheek. "You're trying to grasp the philosophical. I'm proud."

"I feel sorry for the tomatoes but I still feel like eating a tomato sandwich..." Caroline scratched her head.

Indu laughed at life's ironies. "One way or the other, the tomato gets eaten."

"Let's get a move on and pick up the Hungarians." Adele glanced at her PM and her daughter, who now waited impatiently by the door.

* * *

Confederation officials were instructed to prepare Attila Meszaros and his daughter for a transfer to the Pendergrass home within the hour.

"It's what the little Hungarian girl had been insisting on all along," the Hungarian Ambassador's attaché commented with surprise as he spoke via monitor with Morgan and Governor Hernandez. "From the time we met them at Raleigh-Durham, the daughter instructed us to drive directly to your farm, Dr. Pendergrass. Her father couldn't have disagreed more but she was persistent enough to have spoken to Governor Hernandez earlier from the airport. She badgered me all the way to the Hungarian Embassy. I mean, Governor Hernandez knew exactly of whom she spoke but had no inkling how that information would be in the little girl's mind. He asked Ildiko Meszaros how she knew of this plan."

"What did she say?" Morgan asked.

"She just said that she saw the home, the children she knew. She explained clearly that she had a way by which she could envision, in real time, scenes and people she had yet to meet personally," the attaché summarized.

"Can you replay the conversation?" Morgan asked.

"Yes, sir." The attaché forwarded the girl's security vid taken in the transport.

"*I used to fall asleep and move around and just watch. There was no way I could figure where I was going, how long I could stay there, or who I would meet. Sometimes, I just listened to the birds or flew toward the stars. Recently, I feel a need to look around and I am able to revisit the same places, watch the same people. I've seen the iron gates and the bright lights, the big home, and the horses. There are smells there, too, that I like. A funny dog with many other dogs, children older and younger...*"

"Are you able to describe the home? The children?" Governor Hernandez had asked.

"*There are tall black metal gates with fruit or something on top of the sides. You can see the brick home from the long driveway but not before arriving there. There are thick rows of green trees that border the road like tall thin soldiers. But from above, you can see all the little homes, the barns, three lakes, and the animals that graze on the small hills. It smells like animals around the barns and a little short-haired dog sometimes eats the horseshit. It's disgusting.*

'*I've seen a beautiful, tall woman who kisses another man in the house and whenever they walk around. They're outdoors a lot. There's a little brown boy who is nervous and loves the numbers and shapes that float around his room. A very handsome boy is there, too. He has black hair and blue eyes, and he always looks at a girl that has a sister. I know that there is a kind-looking woman... she looks after the old man with a cane. The old man is worried all the time and the woman makes him happy. They love each other very much.*

"*There's a red-headed boy who carries around a little black cap in his pocket and cries lightly at night in his bed. He can make the gravel in the driveway swirl in tight circles one way and then do it the other just as fast. It's beautiful. I told him that. He always seems happy to see me but has never told anyone.*

"*And my favorite is the little girl who is able to see me all the time. She draws and her mother hides the images in a long tube. The tube is under the ground in the horse stable.*"

Hernandez interrupted, "What do you make of that, Morgan?"

"She's got that right. We've brought in guests with the children," Morgan substantiated.

"Shall I continue?" the attaché asked.

"Yes, let's hear the rest," Morgan instructed.

"*...I also saw the crazy red-eyed man in the little building. He's there, too. He thought that I was a ghost in a dream. He's held down and watched like a rabid animal. Around him is a black thing...a very large, black, gooey kind of thing...that churns around him and smells strange. It doesn't scare me. When I come near, it shrinks.*"

The attaché waited until Dr. Pendergrass finished the monitor replay and remarked, "They're both waiting in the Embassy. No one unpacked. Ildiko Meszaros was adamant that they were going to your home tonight."

"My daughter and granddaughter are on their way. It was my daughter who felt the urge to retrieve them," Morgan explained.

When CC and Adele walked in, Ildiko and her father were waiting in the Embassy lobby. Attila was slumped in an overstuffed chair snoring. Ildiko poked her father.

"They're here!"

They thanked the confused ambassador and Governor Hernandez by PM and left with Caroline and Adele Collins. Upon meeting, CC and Ildiko hugged like long-lost sisters.

In the transport, CC ran her hands through Ildiko's unruly hair, scrunched the tight blond curls, and then laughed when they bounced back into place.

"I'm so glad you're here!" Caroline exclaimed.

Adele marveled at the immediate bond between the girls, even though they were six years apart.

"Tell me about the boy in the water, Ildiko," Caroline asked.

"Have you gotten to him?" Ildiko smiled with excitement.

"Heck no," Caroline said. "Where is he exactly?"

"He lives on a floating city. It's enormous. He doesn't like seeing me. Once I tried to speak directly to him. I can't communicate with him when he's upset because there's noise that's always around him."

"Is he special?"

"The people I see now are different than most I know. I never travel to the places of pain. Never. I am usually taken to places of sweetness. That's the reason I don't understand the red-eyed man that's in a little house near your home. He sits in bed all day and yells," Ildiko added seriously. "I don't like that thing that hangs around him."

The transport delivered the newcomers to the Pendergrass estate and drove to the main home. The gravel predictably pinged the car's undercarriage; rather than an onslaught of disturbing memories, Adele was charged with enthusiasm.

The Pendergrass household excitedly appeared outdoors to meet the Hungarians. Aaron had been occupied with the driveway gravel every day for weeks. Beautiful swirling funnels of stone columns took shape on either side of the driveway that met at a peak and formed a welcome arch upon the transport's approach. The eddying stone arcs separated and fanned out over either side of the adjoining fields, returned as a single large spiraling sphere, stretched long over the driveway and dropped pebbles and gravel neatly back into place behind the car. The Nishants cheered their approval, Rachel beamed with pride, and Angela greeted the new arrivals with open arms.

"We're going to love it here, Papa. I can't wait!" Ildiko hugged her father.

"Did you get my message about pistachio ice cream?" Ildiko suddenly asked Caroline.

CC ignored her question with one of her own. "Have you heard of ginger crisps?"

"No"

"Ginger crisps are good, too."

"I'm going to be pretty impressed if there is a bigger show than flying stones," Attila remarked to Adele. "You've got *dancing cookies*?"

CC laughed, "Everybody knows cookies can't dance. You eat them."

Adele took Ildiko by the hand and introduced her to a growing household. Attila looked on as the children, parents, and newfound friends crowded around his daughter.

"They all know my daughter?" Attila puzzled.

Adele smiled knowingly. "They seem to. I know Caroline has expected a laughing girl with curly gold hair. According to your daughter, they've got work to do. The first order of business is to gather a young Chinese boy in some faraway ocean. From the description, we gather he resides on a large fishing vessel accompanied by a flotilla of processing plants. It's also militarily equipped."

"My little girl told yours all of that? Strangers apparently know more about her than I," Attila said with a tinge of embarrassment.

"Her mother just passed," Adele softly reminded. "She knows you're grieving and understands the issues associated with changes. How about thinking Ildiko wise rather than remiss?"

Attila appreciated Adele's sensitivity and wisdom.

"You're not unlike my deceased wife. She had that kind of inner understanding, too. It's true. I'm mourning and wouldn't have been exactly receptive to telepathy, swirling stones, and such. I still don't understand."

Adele and Attila turned their attention toward the group outside the home that had formed an impromptu circle with CC once again at its hub, affecting a wheel's spoke. Blue orbs appeared suddenly, moving and streaking about them. Gathering together around and above CC, a blue bubble of shining light stretched a hundred feet in diameter, encompassing all that stood as a working part of the phenomenon. As it happened once inside the library, the aura expanded out and retreated toward the epicenter and dissipated. A few remaining orbs lingered around Ildiko and disappeared.

"Along with dancing rocks, there are Pendergrass light shows?" Attila spoke with renewed energy.

"We've been part of this before, yes. How do you feel?" Adele asked.

"I admit that I feel less stressed, more rested. No, that's just talk. I feel like I've just taken excellent drugs of some kind with a few shots of Pálinka. I feel pretty damn good," Attila announced, almost cracking a smile.

"This is my second round. I feel even better than the first time. Crazy, right?" Adele and Attila laughed together at the rush of vitality.

"They've all such facilities?" Attila wondered, observing the instant friendships being forged.

Adele explained, "We don't know. Some of our guests accompanied others who were here for other reasons; yet they've begun to show signs of absorbing abilities through some kind of osmosis." Adele indicated Aditiya Nishant and Cynthia, who had recently taken to referencing ideas and conversations through 'visits' with each other.

"They communicate on an evolved level, it's certain. They associate telepathically or intuitively. It appears as if they don't bother to answer each other but I'm sure the question or idea has been expressed. I, too, am becoming much more attuned to sensations I'd never felt prior to these blue light experiences. I first noticed the blue orbs at my daughter's birth. My guess is that the phenomenon is coming of age with her."

"Well, Mrs. Collins, I wholeheartedly buy everything you're selling today," Attila said simply. "This is a remarkable phenomenon."

"Please, call me Adele. Why are you convinced?"

"Because I never said what I was just thinking aloud, Adele. You just answered a specific thought of mine."

"What can I say? I haven't done that before," Adele said nervously. "Let's get out of the cold and move into the house."

Lex approached the pair in the entryway and offered Attila hot chocolate.

"Welcome to Cary, North Carolina! I hear you're a military man? You actually led a brigade of horsemen that defended Hungary's borders?" Lex asked excitedly in the doorway.

"I did," Attila granted while squeezing Lex to the side and allowing Adele to pass them both toward the interior.

"I can't imagine riding a horse, much less fighting on the back of one. You Hungarians knew to procure satellites. Imagine! Horses and that kind of technology was incredibly prescient! Just leave me in a lab. That's where I do combat..." Lex rambled as he followed Attila. "Can you tell us what that was like?"

Attila silently sipped his drink and was not prompted by the protracted silence but by Adele's rapt attention.

"I've been fighting my whole life. There's a lot of blood on my hands," he began. "Hungary had a chance to save herself from a global war between super powers, an untenable position for our small country. It was treacherous but we did it. I spent years mowing down infiltrators from the East from the back of a horse. We took our territory back while helping our European neighbors recover. We have the same concerns as the Confederation. You, too, are surrounded by new generations of displaced tribes who've grown in numbers and strength. The older ones are dying out and along with them go the teachers, the cultural legacy, and the memories of civilizations. I have to say it appears impossible in our lifetimes to put things right," Attila put down the hot chocolate, wishing for something stronger. He thought his story would stop Lex's overreaching interest but it had the opposite effect.

"We've never met anyone from Hungary except the Ambassador," Lex remarked. "We viewed what happened, of course, but would like to hear whether you're presently gaining an upper hand?"

"Plundering has become the predominant way of life to the East. It's no good to feel properly situated while that's going on. What are we going to do? We never willingly opened the gates to the barbarians from the East in Hungarian history. We sure as hell aren't going to do it now. The wave of brutality and aggression has only grown in terms and numbers. Maybe we'll stem the tide with answers in your laboratories?"

Lex had not expected such a serious man with such a serious response. "Well, that's a thought. Excuse me while I refresh your drink."

Attila examined Lex's pale complexion and asked, "Are you sick?"

Feeling nauseous, Lex Collins scurried away toward the bottle of Calm he kept in the upstairs bathroom. Adele was left to host Attila.

She chose to change the subject.

"This blue energy you just witnessed is no parlor trick. It's a combination of frequencies from a spectrum we've yet to categorize or understand fully. It emanates from the children and returns to the children. It's a healing agent of some kind."

Attila said nothing and blocked his thoughts on the matter. He smiled at her and she smiled back.

"Who's that?" Attila indicated Rachel, standing alone, overseeing the children's activities.

"That's my brother-in-law's new girlfriend, Rachel Ben-Tov. She adopted Aaron Shalit as an orphan in their native Israel. He's the one who can move metal and stone. As far as we know, he can manipulate all materials, both non-organic matter and biological, at some level," Adele paused for a reaction that did not come.

"Aaron is a quiet, polite boy who daily practices his skill," she continued, indicating the boy. "We've noticed that cars seem to be parked and re-parked in the most irregular manner outside of the garage. Farm equipment has been covered in mud having been temporarily stuck in ditches. I found a bicycle on top of the horse barn last week. He's getting the hang of it."

"Horse barn? Mind if I take a tour tomorrow? Wouldn't mind taking a look around by horseback... when your time permits?" Attila asked eagerly.

"Of course. Our plans have begun to take shape by way of regular morning meetings after breakfast in my father's library. We do the same each evening. The children are now tutored together by a local teacher."

"Those two aren't kids," Attila noted Nicholas and Esther nearby.

"Nicholas' abilities are the most directed and defined. We imagine that with age, the abilities grow in quality, strength, and scope. Perhaps as a grouping, they may assume each other's new strengths. So we keep them in proximity," Adele said. "The other teenager has yet to display any special properties."

"You're saying that they adopt each other's abilities by association? Interesting. It appears as if everyone is affected in some way," Attila theorized with Lex in mind. "Maybe it's not all positive for everyone," he added.

Attila took note of two men positioned next to a portable bar. Dr. Pendergrass spoke with Connor; Attila focused on the amber liquid drunk from crystal glasses.

"Is it possible to get something stronger?" Attila suggested.

"Of course!" Adele led the tall rugged Hungarian toward her brother-in-law and father. The men introduced themselves and enthusiastically embraced a new drinking partner.

Chapter XXII

The Bane of Cain

Friday, February 4, 2061

Richard Cain regarded Scott Reid from behind his massive excuse of a desk, his back arched, arms folded high behind his head, until he reached into a drawer and dropped minuscule spy-bots upon its surface.

"Any idea where these came from, Reid?"

"None, sir. Where'd you find them?"

"I've been collecting them ever so gradually. We weren't able to find the little buggers with our sensors. That means that there is one – and only one – person that could manage this. Right, Reid? This comes from the Pendergrass group over in Raleigh; that's what I figure. What do you think?"

"Don't know, Mr. Cain. Dr. Pendergrass sure doesn't seem like the type to spy and he sure wouldn't spy on his own people. Don't think it's the Governor."

"Everybody still calling that old guy a governor? I guess I don't get how that works. Nobody called me minister after I'd been fired," Cain complained bitterly.

"I've been wondering how these bots could have infiltrated in these numbers around Failsafe offices. Hell, found a little one in the bathroom drain in the shower room. Had to eyeball them really hard. They're translucent with reflective coating that makes them practically invisible. We've got nothing that picks them up. Crazy, huh?"

Cain's agitation meant trouble. The question was rhetorical at best. Reid thought about his son and his throat went dry. The conversation might end with his only child left an orphan.

Reid was alarmed the moment his PM was removed by security when asked to visit the office floors. He managed to manually press his shirt logo, activating a live feed to Isabella Moreno. It might mean seconds, minutes, or longer until he was discovered with a listening device. However long it proved, Scott knew that Moreno would recognize any contact as an emergency situation. For as long as he was able, Scott Reid would have to keep a conversation going until Moreno's group arrived.

Cain was the deathly Shahyar to Reid's Scheherazade. A self-righteous king, Cain postured as an entitled, misunderstood man that had been wronged by the fates. Scott Reid was armed only with his imagination against the tight-fisted, mean-spirited man that stood expectantly before him.

"Sir, why would someone want to sabotage Failsafe?" Reid began with feigned curiosity.

"You tell me. I figure you're the only connection between Failsafe and the guy able to develop and fund this kind of technology. Whoever developed this knew it was beyond our tracking and that means Morgan Pendergrass. His heart always betrays him. Thought he'd give you a chance, did he? Felt bad for the lost soul? Typical Pendergrass. I'm guessing that the Moreno woman has been filtering your bug? You working for them now?"

"Bug sir? I have a bug on me?"

Cain considered that Reid might be innocent.

"Tell me what you know about what's going on in that old shed...the one the Collins boys used to live in years back."

"Don't know a thing about a shed," Reid said. "I'm not permitted anywhere on the property."

"Well, you're going to have to know about it and do something about it because there's someone held captive in that building that I'd like right here in my office. You're going to get him out. You're going to take a personal interest in the safety of that farm and walk right up to that shed and neutralize whoever might be guarding the prisoner held there. We'll pick you up with a helicopter. I'll be responsible for recovering him. Got any questions?"

"I'll never get close to that shed, sir. As accessible as the place appears, it's heavily guarded 24/7. That's the reason they'll never let me go past the gates. If I do manage to get past the gates again, it'll have to be something a lot more compelling than a possible security breach. Failsafe is restricted to the perimeters."

"Seems to me you think more than I thought you could. I don't give a damn how you manage it. Pendergrass isn't ready for a direct retrieval and that's what we're going to do."

"Why?"

"Because I'm going to prove that there's only one person who should be in control of Confederation safety. Second, the man they're holding has information I want. That information belongs to me, not Morgan."

"Why not ask to speak to him directly? What's good for Failsafe has got to be good for the Confederation." It was a statement Scott Reid figured would endorse his naiveté.

It seemed to work. Cain laughed hard, pointing his finger accusingly at Reid's chest, "You think the Confederation gives a damn about the rest of the continent? The world? It's only a matter of time before the insane overwhelm this little Shangri-La. I'm not waiting around for that day. I'm going to make my move. We need to secure this foothold and move aggressively. The only way to do that is to obtain top-secret technology. Brown knows where that information is hidden, not to mention the gold reserves and countless other valuable assets.

"I'm going to need an equipped army before I'm through. You're going to help me regain my rightful position." Cain put his two hands heavily upon Scott Reid's shoulders.

"What exactly is the plan, sir?" Reid's eyes met Cain's.

"You're willing to stake your life on this, Reid? 'Cause if you want a piece of the pie that's what it's going to take. Let's face it; you're expendable. You're not the brightest kid on the block but you've been able to worm your way onto and into the

Pendergrass place twice now. Let's see if you can do it a third time. If we're successful, I'll make you a happy, wealthy man."

"Mr. Cain, sir? You're going to be immediately targeted by the greater Confederation forces. I'm not sure you'll make it out of the state."

"That's insightful of you, Reid. That's the reason you've got to do a good job of not being discovered."

If there was a weakness in Richard Cain it was his manic ego. He began to strut his vision around an overly bedecked office.

"I'm way ahead of the game. I've got my own supporters within the Confederation. They'll move when I move. Pendergrass and his cronies have taken their eyes off the game. His time has come and gone. We'll grow this country the way Hungary did. We're going to move when most of the world is still stuck in the mud killing each other and fighting over clean water, roaming like starving rats. We'll all be wearing suits and ties again and talking English. We're going to take it all. We're going to be the United Countries of Planet Earth." He laughed hard and waited for Reid to join.

Scott Reid tried to grasp the maniacal absurdity that had grown in a man once trusted by the Confederation. Reid did not believe that there was any cooperation or a possible coup. Given Cain's wild eyes, Reid believed the man utterly mad. A plan for removing a guarded prisoner – if one existed – from the Pendergrass stronghold was strong evidence of irrationality. Storm the place? Did Cain not know that satellite images could pinpoint and identify movement, heat, and frequency down to the size of a roach-bot?

I'm just a decoy, a pigeon to see exactly what the Pendergrass compound can do. He can't be serious about wanting to remove Brown in high security circumstances, Reid tried to process.

"Wow. I never thought of it that way. Count me in, sir!" Reid tried buying time.

"I'm mighty suspicious of these spybots all over the place. Not sure I trust you. As soon as you help retrieve our target, you can have your son back."

"You've kidnapped my son?"

"As we speak, partner."

"That's how you treat a trusted partner?" Reid yelled angrily.

"I don't trust anyone," Cain derided.

"I can't allow you to threaten my son...you're not going to hurt my son!" Reid lost composure.

"Gosh. I was getting used to you calling me 'sir'. Not many people do that anymore. I'm not sure I like the new you, Reid. When I can't figure you in, I figure you out. It's time I just finished off the Reid family."

"What do you mean, 'finish off?'"

"Remember that pretty wife of yours? Mmm, I remember! Thanks for sharing." Cain licked his lips.

The sickening revelation overwhelmed Reid. Richard Cain knew his wife? She was with him? He killed her?

Cain drew a smart gun from his desk drawer and played with it in the vicinity of the man whose face went pale with fear.

"Sit down and stay there. Tell me about the bots, choir boy." Cain enjoyed watching his prey squirm. "Tell me the real story."

"You tell me about my wife," demanded Reid.

"Saw her, liked her, found her, had her, offed her, dumped her. I literally dumped the body in the city landfill. Anything else?"

Cain spoke to his monitor.

"Send up the clowns. Check this idiot for bugs and check his vehicle, too. Encrypt all feeds. When his kid arrives, keep him in storage."

Scott Reid had never been outfitted with, or trained in, weaponry. He had never had a martial arts lesson or been in a fistfight. The closet to physical confrontation had been the occasion when a coyote was discovered in a chicken coop. He swung a shovel across the animal's backside as it scurried off with a squawking chicken. Reid now contemplated his inability to save a chicken.

Tears of frustration welled. Reid dropped to the floor and commenced to beg for leniency. Cain was enthralled by the dramatic appeal.

Scott Reid crawled across the floor toward Cain; his arms stretched flat, pulling one after another, head bent low in primitive submission. Cain had yet to witness such abject supplication and found himself worthy.

Reid appealed to Cain's vanity in every way possible.

"Spare my son, sir. You don't have to take my life. Let me offer it to you in exchange for my son's."

Cain lowered his gun toward the head of the man now at his feet wailing as a child, forehead flat to the floor. Reid desperately implored, his clasped hands held high above his head.

"Keep talking dirty." Cain kicked Reid in the ribs. "What've you got to offer besides flattery, boy?"

"My wife was always too beautiful and smart for me. If you took her life, you spared me pain as part of the bargain. When she disappeared, I already had a hundred reasons she didn't want to be with me."

Cain tired of Scott Reid but didn't want to make a mess of it.

If I shoot him this close I'm going to shoot through those hands which might just spray all over, Cain supposed. He considered having the guards take him elsewhere. Cain lowered his gun and began to laugh.

"You're just crazy enough to use, Reid. Oh yeah. I've done that already," Cain released the biometric lock.

"And one more thing. What makes you think that the kid is really yours?"

Reid had crouched while pulling one knee underneath his chest; with his hands grasped above his head fervently in prayer, he sprang double-fisted and caught Cain under the chin, knocking the gloating head backwards. Reid catapulted his body up and over onto Cain, forcing the man's torso onto the desk, and secured Cain's position with his own. Cain was stunned but kept a tight grip on the gun within his pinned, outstretched arm. Reid dug his fingers into Cain's throat and head-butted the man beneath him but did more damage to himself than Cain. Cain's outstretched legs hanging from the desk offered Reid an opportunity to knee him in the groin, but freeing his leg would have released weight. Reid struggled with no strategy, fueled with rage. Able to keep Cain's right arm immobilized, Reid couldn't manage to free his own to extricate the gun.

Cain touched the gun's trigger. The bullet's trajectory fired toward the opposite wall and just as quickly turned to search for human heat with a different biometric signal than the owner's; Reid jerked left and was able to pull Cain partially on top of him as a shield. The bullet that entered Cain's temple bored through the opposite side of his head and continued through Reid's shoulder, finally embedding within the desk.

Rather than Cain's security, it was Moreno's team that forced the door. Throughout the building, the monitor sounded the nervous chatter of employees as they were rounded up and sequestered by the Confederation security forces. The building was locked down.

"My boy?" Reid appealed to his liberator.

"He's fine," Moreno assured him. Moreno looked on approvingly as the office monitor replayed the last minutes that transpired in Cain's office. Cain's eyes remained open, fixed upon the ceiling cam that had captured and replayed that which was officialy determined to be a suicide. The legal irony of 'biometric safety' features did not escape Moreno. "Cain pulled the trigger and Cain is dead. End of story," Moreno called in.

"Well played," she smiled. "We got to your boy before those thugs ever showed. You couldn't have been more effective, Scott. Let's get you medical help."

Isabella strapped a personal monitor to Scott Reid's arm. It analyzed the shoulder wound, detailed immediate care, and pronounced an excellent prognosis. It then communicated with the building's system and summoned an ambulance.

Reid remained anxious and asked Moreno, "Did you get that Cain said that he had help within the Confederation?"

"We got everything since you triggered your bug. We're on it, Scott. We retrieved your son. We've got the Failsafe people quarantined now for questioning. We've have all PMs and we're analyzing Cain's files."

"Thanks."

"For what?"

"For making my son your priority. Calling me by my first name is pretty good, too."

Ambulance personnel arrived and escorted Scott Reid toward the Failsafe lobby. Confederation and Pendergrass security men and women lined the halls; they clapped rhythmically and saluted an unlikely hero.

"Mind if I go back to get my coat and retrieve that gun?" he asked Moreno.

"It's yours. We have the evidence we need."

It took only minutes to run back to Cain's office to gather his coat, the spybots, and Cain's gun. It was then that his knees buckled.

Moreno waited patiently in the hall until Reid reappeared.

Isabella smiled broadly as Jordon Reid ran forward to embrace his father.

Morgan Pendergrass's dispatch pinged Reid as the ambulance sped away.

"Couldn't have done better myself. Get patched and get to the Farm for a conversation. Give that boy of yours the hug of your life every time you revisit this day." Then Morgan added gravely, "If you want to test out Cain's last words, we can do that."

"Absolutely not," Reid replied. "One way or the other, Jordon is my son."

Chapter XXIII
The Circle

*W*ith the combined talents of Ildiko Meszaros and Caroline Collins, an enormous Chinese fishing fleet was located along the 2,600 mile Chilean coast- line. The Chilean fishing industry had been overwhelmed by the Chinese military naval strength for nearly half a century. The only other pinpoints on the horizon were family-owned fishing boats of the simplest construction, free to once more fish their Chilean coastline at will. No one paid mind to the insignificant villagers.

One flagship fishing vessel now dominated the Patagonia and it was the ship that was home to the boy called Sonny.

It took two days for Ildiko to describe the surrounding topography to Caroline. From these descriptions, Caroline crafted a crude map. Finally, the girls decided to try a differ- ent approach.

"You can come with me!" Ildiko suggested.

Caroline confirmed Ildiko's suspicions; she was able to jointly examine the strange ship and its coastline. The result of their paired venture of remote viewing yielded a paradig- matic geographical chart.

With Morgan's prompting, the White House made contact. It took another week to convince Woo Tsin-hang that they were being summoned to a place in North Carolina because of a remote viewing as described by a twelve-year-old Hungarian girl and a map graphed by her sidekick. Tsin-hang also needed time to accept that Morgan was making a serious attempt to locate children with special abilities.

Dr. Pendergrass spoke with Sonny, who comprehended every word. Moreover, the boy recognized the truth of the matter. Woo Tsin-hang was won over by an overwhelming sense of relief. When he heard that there were other children in Cary, North Carolina who had similarly arrived in the world with supernatural gifts, he looked forward to a support group. He remained wary, however, of the Confederation's political intentions.

"There will be no more than a week spent at your place. You will not be allowed to test or question my son without my presence and you will return us to this ship. The orders are for the ship to militarily retrieve us if this does not happen," Tsin-hang bluffed.

There would, however, be no military rescue in Confederation waters. The captain had been clear about that from the start. In fact, the Chinese captain hesitated the moment Tsin-hang was not forthcoming for the reasons of Confederation intervention.

"Why do they want you? This is a political cooperation?"

"Yes," said Tsin-hang. "It's a new government eager for a new cooperation. I can't see the harm."

"I'm not convinced. We don't need trade. How do they know you?"

"Perhaps their intelligence is far superior?" Tsin-hang flippantly posed. "It's a time for collaboration and this is the perfect opportunity to pursue options. We've got to think of the future. We are three years away from having to refurbish the ship's reactor. We're going to need help with that."

"When do you return?"

"I'll insist upon a few weeks. You can be assured I'm not going to compromise our people. You've always trusted me and you should continue to do so."

The captain was satisfied and dismissed his initial idea to keep Sonny on board. He needed the technical expertise and goodwill of Tsin-hang to maintain the ship's reliability.

"Keep me informed," the captain finally agreed.

"Will you move to help if we need it?" Tsin-hang asked hopefully.

"No. You know that's not the question to ask. Your safety does not balance with our community's welfare. Say what you will and I won't deny it. Know in the end we will not help. I'm agreeing to let you go, take you both back whether a week or more, and not destroy aircraft coming near the ship."

The Confederation helicopters and drones alarmed the ship's community as they circled. Sonny suggested that he and his father travel alone to Concepción via small motor transport toward the rocky shore for a transfer to the CAS airship. In that way, they would not compromise the flotilla. That's precisely what Tsin-hang suggested to the captain and that was the plan followed.

The small passenger boat stayed tied to a Concepcion pier and the pair walked toward level ground next to a former vacation resort that had been transformed into a local community fishing facility. There was no way to tell what kind of people Tsin-hang and his son had arranged to meet. Confederation forces swarmed the area; father and son were quickly escorted toward the transport helicopter. It was a long ride back to Confederation territory. It was also a silent one.

Nor did Sonny utter a word within the Pendergrass household for two days. The children approached the Chinese boy with care. Only Ildiko, as a familiar face, could approach Sonny. Once again, she proved intolerant of his behavior.

"Why are you scared? Does it look scary here? You're a chicken gizzard," Ildiko repeated her favorite taunt. Chicken gizzard references confused Sonny. He ignored Ildiko. Sonny fully grasped everything that was transmitted without a translator but idioms and colloquialisms eluded him. He watched his father carefully and only ate what his father ate, went only where his father moved. As Tsin-hang became more comfortable, so did Sonny.

It took seven days for the pair to settle in, despite the reassurances of the other guests. Ildiko and the rest of the group decided the newcomers were not much fun.

Sonny watched as the children played amongst themselves. He attended tutorial sessions set up on the farm's schoolhouse but rarely participated.

Caroline approached Sonny on the estate where Blue had tracked him. She introduced her dog. "This is Blue. You can pet him if you like."

Sonny smiled. He awkwardly petted the dog. Blue promptly rolled on his back for more of the treatment on his stomach.

"Scratch him. His foot goes stupid," instructed CC. Sonny scratched Blue's stomach and the dog's hind leg pumped. Sonny laughed at the reflex.

"You can understand without a translator, right?" CC watched Sonny and wondered how long Blue could pump his back leg without stopping.

"I understand everything I hear. I know a lot about every spoken language."

CC was pleased with their first conversation and asked, "What else do you know?"

"That's a lot to know, don't you think?"

"I guess. What can you do with that?"

"I understand what everyone is saying, and what do you mean what can I do with that?" He stopped scratching and the dog whined neglect.

"Can you talk Dog?"

"No!"

"Well, we have translators so we all know all the languages. But if you could understand what Blue was saying, that would be unusual. What else can you do?"

Sonny answered irritably, "I don't know; what can you do? My father says that the children here are like me and have some special talents. I don't see that."

"Well, almost everyone does something. Like Nicholas can make people go crazy!" CC exclaimed.

"That's nothing special. What else?" Sonny readdressed Blue's stomach.

"Aaron can make things move without touching anything."

"Machines do that, too. Just like translators can do what I do. What else?" Sonny challenged.

"Aditiya understands a lot of mathematics. I mean a lot."

"So do computers. What else?"

"I can make you feel better when you can't make yourself feel better," CC added softly.

Sonny felt the sincerity of CC's remark. "Do you think I'm sad?" he asked apologetically.

"You don't laugh or smile. Your eyebrows are down. I think you're sad."

"The chanting makes me feel better. I think that's really the time I'm not lonely. I can clean the ship of bad feelings. I get rid of the crying and the dreams of past sadness, the deaths, and the burial burnings for everyone else. Sometimes it's hard because it makes me tired and I don't know how to do that for myself," he admitted for the first time to anyone.

CC recognized an opening and yelped, "I can help you! The others will help, too. It'll make you feel better, Sonny. Your father can do it with you. I don't sing, though. Don't be asking me to sing or hum."

It was agreed that the group would help Sonny feel more comfortable by forming a circle when they finished the school day.

On the walk home from school, Nicholas and Ildiko chuckled at the younger kids chatting with Sonny. Cynthia and Esther paid special attention to the part of the discussion regarding special abilities. Esther was grim.

"We don't have any special skills. It's weird for us," Esther remarked to their group but looked directly at Nicholas. "You make us feel like outsiders."

Nicholas disagreed quickly. "So what constitutes a special talent? Aditiya is a brilliant mathematician. I have little understanding of what that kid is talking about when he spins those numbers and images. Some people are better musically. I can't carry a tune and have no idea how to draw. CC can see the future and draw it like a master, but she can't carry a tune. Ildiko can travel with her mind. We grew up on a quiet planet. Maybe people have always had these abilities but now we can concentrate on them because there's no interference. Maybe there are tons of talents we no longer think are special."

Esther turned to Nicholas and asked, "So, what special talents have I? What about my sister?"

"That's easy. Cynthia has guts. I mean, she can face off with anyone anywhere. I was frozen with fear when my father and sister were killed next to me. She could see me on the ship when no one else could. She came right up to me and asked who I was and how I got there. She stood up to the captain and protested being put off the ship when she thought it meant being thrown in the ocean. That girl is brave as hell."

"What about me?"

"That's easy, too. To me, you are magic in every way. When you listen to me and smile when we speak, I feel amazing. Touch my hand and you turn me into butter," he smiled with twinkling eyes.

The secondary group slowed to eavesdrop on the banter that had become intimate. Cynthia groaned and Ildiko snickered. CC observed Nicholas and Esther gazing tenderly into one another's eyes.

"I think they're going to kiss!" CC whispered to the group. Then loudly she yelled, "Bet you wish you could make us disappear, Nicholas!"

Sonny stopped and turned toward the pair as they took each other's hands. He recognized at once one of the special frequencies used throughout the centuries by the Sanskrit chants and Georgian monks as part of the healing frequencies.

"You hear that?" Aditiya tapped Sonny's shoulder.

"You hear it?" Sonny returned the question.

"I see the numbers and shapes taking form from a background of dots. When it comes to focus of a special frequency that's electromagnetic, there are correlating geometric shapes and numbers that appear," Aditiya explained. "This melody is very clear!"

"All nature has vibrational code," Sonny agreed. "It's nice that you see it manifest in shapes and numbers. The Hindus have a saying, 'Nada Brahma', that means that all creation is sound. When we are able to hear the primordial sound of Aum or Om, we are attuned to the creative spirit.

"In the Judeo-Christian culture they might understand that concept by saying, 'In the beginning was the Word and the Word was with God, or the word was God'...the tying together of nature and vibrational frequencies with Creation. Other cultures speak of that which the Creator has thought, then spoke the word of that thought and how creation was then manifested from the intent of that thought," Sonny relayed some of his studies on the matter.

Aditiya considered the frequencies that yielded specific numbers and the correlation of those numerical values to geometric shapes common in nature.

"I figure that these sounds come from a numerological manipulation of decimal representations of frequencies in cycles per seconds... hertz representations of the sounds you hear naturally, Sonny. The numbers I see in nature are different from those that are represented by the music we play from the monitor..."

"I know. I can't listen to it," Sonny stated with surprise. "It's not the same vibration. It has the wrong kind of power except for certain pieces. Most of that music has been altered; it carries something that is slightly atonal and does not help the human condition, as music should. This is the reason that I can hear so clearly this frequency right now...it's so harmonically strong!"

Aditiya glanced at the numbers he visualized accompanying the melodic frequency and announced, "It's at 528 Hz."

Sonny interpreted the sound in terms of Western music. "I hear what you might call the middle C note in a symphony of others. Nicholas and Esther are surrounded by the most beautiful sounds. It is love making a connection. And while it is very beautiful, it is unfortunately very rare," Sonny quietly said as tears formed.

"It's a pattern of six repeating codes around a series of sacred numbers, 3,6 and 9," Aditiya observed. "I've been playing with those numbers and shapes since I had CawCaw but this is one of the few times that I've seen them actually dance! It's beautiful to me, too." Aditiya smiled in recognition of another dimension connected in the way he saw the world geometrically interact. "It's all music!" he concluded. Aditiya did not empathize with Sonny's sudden sadness and patted him on the back. "I think it's fine. You don't need to cry about it."

Sonny and Aditiya watched the numbers, shapes, and frequency that connected Nicholas to Esther. They also noticed a strange energy link that formed from Nicholas to another person in the group.

"You know what that is?" Aditiya asked Sonny, pointing to the blue light and an appendage stretching elsewhere.

"No idea." Sonny stared at the clean lines taking form, a new glimpse into Aditiya's world.

"You going to say something about it?" Aditiya asked Sonny; he continued to marvel at his precious shapes and numbers singing a cosmic song of love.

"No way," Sonny smiled.

"Same," Aditiya agreed.

Chapter XXIV

Comeuppance and Betrayal

Thursday, March 17, 2061

Woo Tsin-hang was pleased that Sonny had spent the day with the other children who had also planned a group activity after dinner. He was satisfied that his son had begun to experiment with new foods and exercise. He had returned from school with color in his cheeks.

"What's this circle thing about?" Tsin-hang had questioned Amar at dinner; Amar deferred to the head of the table.

"Well, Dr. Pendergrass?" Tsin-hang asked his host.

"Can't say we know. As far as we can tell, it's spiritual medicine of some kind conjured by my granddaughter in ways we can't figure. The effect is immediate and the aftereffects seem to linger. I'd say if you don't want to feel more peaceful, don't take part. As it is, I'd call it some kind of synergistic phenomena that puts us emotionally, physically, and spiritually on line. You feel things, hear things, and sense things with a clarity and understanding that interconnects and grows. I'm of the mind that it's something that's inborn. Until triggered correctly, it remains inert. That tell you anything?"

Tsin-hang nodded his head knowingly. "I'm unable to explain my son. He knows things from places and in ways for which I have no awareness. I admit to being puzzled by his chanting..."

"Chanting? Like the Brahmin?" Indu and Amar asked in unison.

"I know how strange that sounds. I have it on my monitor." He handed a chip to Connor Collins as one of the researchers. "Hopefully, you'll be able to enlighten me as to how my son was born with this familiarity?"

"We'll do our best and run it along with the information collected from the other children," Connor assured him. "We're almost ready to present our findings thus far; I'll add Sonny's linguistic abilities along with this data. That is, with your permission?"

"You understand our reluctance to meet and come here under these odd circumstances? Let me sleep on this, as you say. I hope you understand."

Having taken social cues from Morgan, Rachel sniffed her disapproval. "You see and feel that we're trying to quantify phenomena and map everyone's genetic profile. What's your problem? Haven't you had enough real horrors in your life as a point comparison? These are good people trying to do good things."

Indu gently interceded. "Rachel has traveled far with Aaron. She's taken great risks on faith. We've all done the same. Nicholas Bradley, for example, has just turned 17 years old. He made his way after his family was murdered. Let's work together, shall we? None of us are strangers to risk or horror."

Tsin-hang objected to Rachel and Indu's contentions.

"I'm a military man. Our ship survived a holocaust because of my clear thinking. Forgive me if I don't take any chances with the person I love the most in the world. My wife is gone. My life is Sonny. I'm going to deliberate as long as it takes to ensure that Sonny's interests are being served."

Morgan tired of the talk.

"Look, Tsin-hang. I'm getter older by the minute here and I don't have that kind of time to waste. According to our Hungarian cutie, your son is beyond just another piece of a DNA puzzle. I'll have you know that my granddaughter drew his picture months ago. She and Ildiko figured out where you were located amongst a thousand similar ships dotting the planet picked up by our surveillance. It would have taken a long time to pick up conversations in each of those ships. The kids located your son – not the Confederation. By the way, Ildiko already has had conversations with your son somewhere in space and time. You're not curious as to how these kids know each other? What the hell it means?"

Tsin-hang conceded an argument before it swelled.

"I like you, Dr. Pendergrass. I think I'm ready for that bourbon you mentioned."

"About time!" Morgan slapped Tsin-hang on the back.

After dinner, the adults entered the library and were surprised to find the children next to a mountain of empty dishes that once contained ice cream.

"Ice cream, Ildiko?" Attila Meszaros asked.

"It was vanilla with a ginger crisp on top. I loved it!" Ildiko had yet to lick the white traces from one side of her mouth.

Sonny's bloated stomach told a similar gluttonous tale. He lay on the floor with one arm across Blue in a similar condition.

CC closed the door behind the group and asked that everyone join hands. She need not have urged them. At once, they came to life and scurried toward a circle configuration, a school of open-mouthed fish abruptly changing directions. As the newcomers to the technique, CC repeated instructions for Tsin-hang and Sonny.

"Join hands, I go to the middle. A blue light comes. It goes away and everyone feels happier. Got it?"

The group joined hands. Sonny gazed up at his father, whose bourbon-induced smile sprang more broadly than usual. Everyone felt excited, newcomers and veterans alike.

CC concentrated on the circle, with special attention upon Sonny. She raised and wiggled her eyebrows then playfully winked the way her grandfather did to her when he prepared to trip someone with his cane.

Blue orbs gathered around CC, grew into an aura, and expanded throughout the room. Rather than recede, the light silently exploded once more onto the Pendergrass estate and throughout most of North Carolina before receding thirty seconds later. Alarms sounded everywhere.

"You're right. Pretty impressive!" Tsin-hang and Sonny began to laugh hysterically. The group joined in.

"That's new. Wow!" Connor and Rachel couldn't stop chuckling.

Attila and Ildiko Meszaros spoke excitedly to each other. For the first time in a long while, father and daughter hugged tightly.

Morgan yelled, "Better call security and let them know it was a new warning system the Confederation was trying out or some damn concoction. Isabella Moreno is going to have a fit explaining something I can't begin to." Morgan was more amused than concerned. Calls came in by the thousands reporting UFOs, strange lights on the horizon, and the large flash that preceded its disappearance.

"Some things never change," sighed Morgan.

"Don't believe in life beyond this planet?" Tsin-hang asked.

"Just trying to figure life forms like you first!" Morgan teased.

The group seated themselves about the room to savor the experience.

"I'd say that you'd understated the nature of this circle sensation," remarked Tsin-hang. "You're quite right. The effect is positive and immediate," Tsin-hang turned toward his son to gauge Sonny's reaction.

"I know the reason we're here," announced Sonny as he walked toward CC, still situated in the room's center.

"You're the key to everything. We're going to help you reach everyone, everywhere. It will be the beginning of a great change. Each of us has a part but we are meant to help you, CC."

Caroline smiled at the boy who would now be their friend.

"What else do you think you know?" Caroline asked.

"The light will help a lot of people into a place of higher vibrations. For others, they will not be able to be helped at all. Some will be happier; others will move away."

Sonny turned toward the group and carefully examined the pale streams of blue light that lingered between participants.

"It's like the merging of magnetic fields," Aditiya validated.

"Everyone see that?" Nicholas asked.

"I see it," Aaron confirmed. "Pretty nice!"

"Great, I don't see any magnetic fields..." Rachel puzzled.

Esther agreed sadly, "Neither do I."

Cynthia was quietly amazed that she could indeed see the light connect to others.

An idea suddenly occurred to Connor regarding Clifton Brown. He wondered about the effect of the light on others in proximity.

"Let's check on Brown again, shall we?" Connor suggested.

Morgan nodded in agreement. "You thinking there's a half-life for evil jackasses?"

Angela grimaced. "No, Morgan. Please? Remember Sonny and Aditiya said that the effects of these lights go one direction or the other. If it reached Brown, he is most likely in the negative category, not a better man."

"Can we go with you to see him, Dr. Pendergrass?" Nicholas asked earnestly.

"Me, too?" Aaron and Aditiya each repeated. CC joined by pointing two fingers toward her head.

A singular word meant that CC was too young. "*Nope!*" Adele said, folding her arms across her chest.

Rachel demanded that Aaron stay behind, too. In the end, only Aditiya and Nicholas would accompany the adults. The remaining children briefly complained about having been left out of a group adventure until Caroline's offer of more ice cream diminished the impact.

Connor and Morgan looked inquiringly at Lex, who sat with a blank expression. Lex gave no indication of an interest in anything more to do with Clifton Brown.

"Headache," Lex answered the unasked question. Lex had no stomach for the tobacco shed. If he had any curiosity, Lex typically stopped short of ordinary confrontation; his reluctance to seek it out surprised no one.

Colonel Komor and Isabella frantically pinged Morgan regarding the matter of the blue light seen outside of Brown's confines and speculated as to the source. The truth of the matter eluded both women. Neither Morgan nor Connor offered answers as they walked toward their position in the shed. They had an experiment in mind.

"A group of us are on the way to you now," Morgan told Komor and Moreno. "Ignore the calls for right now. Assure NC that nothing we know has indicated a threat. We're looking into it."

Nicholas and Aditiya outpaced the adults while Nicholas spoke with Aditiya.

"I've an ability to thwart an attack from such a person as Brown. That's the only reason I'm going. What's yours?" he asked Aditiya.

"I see something around that shed," Aditiya answered. "I see geometric shapes. After the blue light I could see the magnetic field above us and toward the horizon because the blue light tracked its lines and shapes...even though it was night!"

"What's that got to do with this evil guy?" Nicholas pressed the issue.

"I usually see the world in dots. Now, those dots have been making waves around the shed. Can you see it? Everything is pulsating..." Aditiya asked hopefully.

"I don't see any waves or anything," Nicholas answered.

"Do you see that thick blackness without colors?" Aditiya asked as the shed came into view.

"Nope."

"Well, I do. It's not normal. I've been watching it. I want to see what's in there!"

The boys entered the shed, ignoring the protests of lagging adults. Moreno and Komor, standing outside to greet them, re-entered and took their places beside two attentive guards. The security team circled the final resting place of ex-president Clifton Brown.

"He's dead," Komor announced as the adults entered. The medical monitor told the same story. "He arrested minutes ago without a sound until the PM announced it. No warning whatsoever," Komor puzzled.

"Yeah, he probably wishes he was dead. He's just stuck between places," Aditiya noted.

Nicholas and Aditiya gawked at the wall behind the bed at something no one else in the room could distinguish.

"See the black thing?" Aditiya nervously asked Nicholas. "Now, do you see that thick slippery thing?"

"Oh, yeah," Nicholas' eyes stared.

"Somebody tell me more," Morgan demanded.

"I think that the dots I usually see are just a kind of screen that blocks us from other places," Aditiya stammered. "The screen that usually keeps us from hearing and seeing into another dimension is supposed to make room for this man. But he can't pass into the other place. The black stuff is fighting against the millions of dots that are squeezing to regain their space. It's like there should be a door, a portal, or an open space that he can melt into but the man is... *unwanted* there," Aditiya struggled. "He's unfit. He's being pushed away; he can't move through the planes. The dots don't want to separate for him. The black mass has been waiting like a kind of fly-trap or something," Aditiya strained to describe that which was transpiring before his eyes.

"Fly-trap? A dimensional fly-trap?" Morgan pressed for more.

"The dots I see are usually with color and the spaces are constant. I put my hand up and I see a seamless area of the same kind of dots without variance. It's like I could melt into everything if I had to. It's like everyone could melt into it if they had to! But here, there is a place around the man that has no color but it does have a kind of working mass you can see as a matter of contrast. Everything just closed around him, squeezing him, pushing him, pulsating, to regain its original position. But the man couldn't be..." Aditiya tried to come up with the right words for the scene.

Nicholas intervened with the word. "Digested!"

"Yes! He's stuck," agreed Aditiya. "He sees and hears but Mr. Brown no longer lives in our world and he isn't going anywhere else either. The black blob that surrounds looks like a floating amoebic oozing sludge meaning to take him away. It reminds me of the river banks in India after the monsoons."

That's about as close to hell as I can imagine, thought Connor.

"Hey!" Aditiya yelled. "The dots are closing... becoming closer again. The man is being forced into a kind of hole... the regular dots are waiting to go back into place."

Aditiya understood the reason others could not share his ability to see another dimension.

"I think people can't see the space between our plane and others. Their eyes stop somewhere else before the veil of dots."

Nicholas and Aditiya put their hands to their heads, covering their ears for a few moments, and then regained their poise.

Nicholas squinted, "He's gone. He's sucked away. The veil is back where he was and it looks like the black thing is alive... looking for something. It's anxious about what to do or it wants more to do! Hope it can't move out here. That thing is an ugly sucker," Nicholas watched and called with disgust.

"Where did the man go?" Connor couldn't help but wonder if the kids knew. Aditiya answered with some authority.

"There's a nether land in between the dimensions. Each dimension is within a greater hierarchy," Aditiya observed with uncharacteristic calm. "He's now anti-matter. I think the black thing processes people like him.

"It absorbs in lieu of transformation, transition, or an ability to return," Nicholas suggested. "It's like there was some kind of argument between forces going on. And while it was going on, President Brown's soul was screaming."

Komor asked incredulously, "*Who are you people*?"

"I'm Aditiya Nishant. My parents are Doctors Indu and Amar Nishant." The boy turned and extended his hand toward Dr. Komor. "Nice to meet you!" They shook hands and Aditiya turned his attention upon a lingering trail of evil.

"The man leaves filth. Dr. Pendergrass? Could you ask Sonny to come and clean this house and get rid of that black thing, too? He can do that!"

"Meaning the chanting Sonny does, son?" Morgan asked.

"Yes, the chanting. He should come now and make the place clean again. The black thing has to go away. It can't stay. It makes me nervous."

"Same!" agreed Nicholas.

"Ditto here!" echoed Komor.

"Count me in," Connor raised his hand.

While they waited for Sonny and his father, Komor asked the boys the reason they suddenly covered their ears.

"The shrieking!" they answered at once.

Sonny entered the tobacco shed with his father. "It stinks!" He recoiled with the statement. No one else smelled an odor.

"Can you clean up?" Aditiya asked matter-of-factly.

"I'll try," Sonny agreed.

The monitor recorded Sonny's chanting mantra for healing from the Rig-Veda dating from 1500 B.C. The little boy intoned the oldest unbroken form of an oral tradition that melodically began and continued syllable by enunciated syllable for two uninterrupted hours. The tradition of cleansing the environment—a daily ritual for any Brahmin Temple--now made sense in the former tobacco shed, chanted precisely at 110 Hz.

No one moved for the duration of the acoustic phenomenon except for Morgan whose neck jerked spasmodically when he fought, and lost to, sleep. Snoring ensued within twenty minutes of the ritual.

Tsin-hang finally smiled approvingly toward his son. "Done?"

"Yes, father. That was a foul soul. It was as foul as the rancid, rotting fish the seagulls won't eat," Sonny said, pleased with his accomplishment.

Krisztina Komor coughed loudly and Morgan came to attention. "Let's go!" Morgan boomed. "Komor and Isabella... you might as well stay the night in the main house. We can get an early start tomorrow morning."

"What about the body?" Moreno asked.

Connor did not hesitate. "Burn it."

"No last rites?" Komor wondered.

"Seriously?" Connor objected. "This is where the incinerator behind the warehouse makes perfect sense. That's about as decent a removal system as I can imagine for that carcass."

Morgan shook his head disapprovingly. "Can't do it. Wish I could. We'll clean and prepare him for burial and put him on ice overnight. If we can't bury him or give him a service of some kind, we'll send Brown's body to the hospital crematorium."

As the groups made their way back to the main house, Dr. Komor quizzed the elder Nishants, who now were on site to meet their son.

"I'm getting the picture that we've a group of little experts in different fields of... what? Exactly what are these children capable of?" Komor directed toward Aditiya's mother.

Indu threw up her hands with a nervous laugh. "I'm sure Dr. Pendergrass can explain better than we."

Komor and Moreno sprinted back toward Pendergrass and Collins. Moreno tried first.

"An explanation, sir? We have inquiries coming in from Raleigh about an explosive blue light from here to South Carolina."

"Can we debrief in the morning? I'm about to collapse."

"Looking forward to it, sir," Moreno quipped.

"You looking forward to the morning debriefing or my collapse?"

"Now that you mention options..." They laughed together.

Komor pursued an official concern.

"Do we answer questions about Brown? I'm sure it's a matter of time until DC wants an update. He was the ex-president...

"Send the calls to me," Morgan cut her off. Moreno pushed her agenda angrily as a security chief without answers.

"Let me put it this way...I know you may think this is none of my business but I want to know what the hell is going on around here! Little smart kids running around here are more knowledgeable than your security team. You trust visitors and strangers without giving us much of a clue," Moreno accused while she blocked Morgan's path.

"I second that," reinforced Komor, joining the blockade. "These children are aware on a level never before categorized!"

Dr. Pendergrass wished he had an answer. One was forming in his mind, of course.

"Want to hear it? Outside in the cold?" Morgan leaned on his cane.

"Absolutely," Komor insisted. "I don't get it. How are they so insightful? I get the translator's capacity to extrapolate language and ideas but it's translating complex *concepts*!"

"I see it like this. There's going to be variations here and there, but it's likely that much of the DNA dark matter, that we've come to expect having control over genetic behaviors, is waking up to a new dawn," Morgan attempted. "I suspect these unusual kids have triggered abilities long dormant until the electromagnetic overload. Or worse, we never noticed what was going on before the world went quiet. Perhaps we are now forced to take notice.

"We're not strangers to these abilities, ladies. Historians have long regarded sages and prophets as having access to a particular wavelength to the Divine. These men and women meditated and seemed able to receive information beyond what others regarded on a spiritual realm...or worse, of course. Our greatest thinkers have all shared a deep curiosity about what it meant to be a part of the universe; they cued connectivity much as we searched the Internet on behalf of our particular interests. The more one searches, the more the right questions follow, the greater the investigative impulse. But a guy has got to ask the questions first. A person has got to show some interest and actually persistently explore. Origins of the word religion were to seek, to bind to, piety. I guess you could call a vested search for answers a prayer. From such a focus, springs frequencies of relevancy.

"Is it surprising that this group of children who've come into this world without an overload of electrical pulses and distractions connect to their universe in a way that might be termed natural and organic? Remote viewing is just another wavelength available to someone who doesn't have alternate means or unnatural interruptions that ground our otherwise forceful electrical balance. Not new stuff. If you're willing to listen, relax, and open your mind a bit, sometimes you might receive signals others miss because they are less inclined. Hell, if you listen at all without your own self-importance screaming for attention, you witness a lot. You ever fly in your dreams?" Morgan suddenly asked.

"No, sir," Moreno answered. Komor said nothing.

"I have. Just takes a few such adventures to alter your mind about such possibilities. Couldn't tell you if it was a dream or I actually went scouting around. I can tell you this: I could smell the night air and lift effortlessly. I had a new understanding of freedom. No guilt, no worries. I realized we're likely anchored to the earth by the weight of our negative thoughts, self-doubt, and other self-imposed restrictions. These kids? They're different. One of the gals is able to astral project her image as well as view others from great distances. Goes through material! Walks through steel. Sees the terrain around her, distinguishes smells...she feels it all! There're reams of scientific studies about remote viewing. Military intelligence communities usually underwrote those studies. What was proved? That consciousness is projected to another place? Nah. It just proves that we are all pieces of something larger; we're all connected. Connecting to another point just seems physically remote. In the quantum world, it's just another part of you.

"We had to get away from the noise. Prior to the EMP disasters, I couldn't even see the stars anymore, much less hear myself think. Imagine what we couldn't receive or transmit!" Morgan added thoughtfully, looking up to the night sky.

Isabella wanted specifics rather than a chapter out of the Morgan Expedient meanderings.

"Sir, I overheard from one of the security guards that the Bradley boy went briefly invisible. They had his voice recorded but no image. What's up with that?" Moreno's tone meant that her role had been overlooked.

Morgan ceased to examine the cloudless heavens. He spoke to Komor and Moreno, realizing that he had been negligent. Those most responsible for his security had been ignored.

"I apologize," Morgan said. "I'll tell you about this matter of invisibility and self-preservation that the Nicholas boy exhibits. He's recounted having been undetected by predators who killed his grandfather. They overlooked Nicholas during the act. He observed the murder and killed them while unnoticed. He has told of events on a ship that triggered a state of invisibility at similar life-threatening moments. In graduating stages that began with invisibility and ended with a karmic chain reaction, Nicholas involuntarily separated evil from innocence. In this way, the teenager defends himself. Don't we have references to this? We talk about intent and outcome all the time. Countless stories surround those with 'guardian angels' whisking people to safety, avoiding certain death, empowering the weak with unimaginable powers, the Goliath to David ratio. Could these not represent extraordinary acts of self-preservation, too?

"Consider such undefined gifts as God given. I don't know how to get my head around the science so I'm going to use the word God because it means intelligent design and ultimate balance. The kid, for example, can't use his powers aggressively. It's purely a self-defense mechanism against overpowering odds. I'd say that's intelligent design.

"Then, there's Aditiya. He's the one we refer to as mathematically gifted. He references the idea of seeing the world geometrically. We're not shocked when savants pop up with extraordinary talents, even though these are singularly focused at the expense of other functions. Savants should be able to operate at a superlative level but can't seem to coordinate all the neural levers. Aditiya appears able to visualize mathematical concepts like a holographic quantum computer... and with full control over all his levers, is simultaneously able to socially relate well to others.

"We appear to have some programming that has yet to be enacted, triggered, and configured. Historically, we only have the tiniest glimpses of such brilliance. The Mozarts and the Einsteins arrived fully functional. They were appropriately synchronized. It's not their talent or insight that just helped jump-start civilization, it's the very idea that high functioning humans brought attention to that which might represent an extraordinary human birthright. What's the surprise here? We as a human race have yet to come of age..."

"Who else? Are there others?" Komor interrupted Morgan's drifting thoughts.

"There is the Israeli kid, Aaron Shalit, who can move things. He retrieved twenty-five pound underwater stone-carvings as souvenirs twenty-five feet below the water's surface. We should also figure that these talents are prepubescent skills! Perhaps Aaron embodies a sonic connection to basic elements yet to be harnessed by our technology?

"I hardly discount other universal life forms. They're there. I'm just saying let's not underestimate our own species. We're erratically evolving. One step forward, two steps back. Perhaps we've been taking four steps back too many times. Maybe our technology was meant to mimic innate talents we've yet to realize as a primer for our imagination..." Morgan finished. "I'm boring myself. That enough?"

"That's certainly more than I wanted to hear. I'm back at square one." Komor peered up toward the stars. "I hate to admit I truly appreciate Brown's punishment," Komor added wistfully. "It was fitting. A portal opening up and trapping bad energy so that it doesn't escape, crushing the life out of something that has no business being kicked down the road..."

"I'm freezing! I don't mind the cold when I'm preaching but can't stand it when I've gotta listen," Morgan moved quickly on down the frozen path to the house.

"*Where are you*?" Angela messaged Moreno impatiently. "Morgan with y'all?"

"On our way," Isabella acknowledged.

"Everyone is here and tucked away but your group. You've some anxious parents and friends waiting," Angela explained.

Morgan, Komor and Isabella stepped onto the entry portico, only to be met by the stricken face of Adele Collins.

"Dad? Could you follow me, please?" she half whispered.

Angela directed the rest to follow her inside and hurriedly took coats. "Time for bed, people!" she prompted and the group reluctantly made their way upstairs.

Komor looked toward Morgan to remind him of his invitation to stay on site for the night.

"Oh, yeah. Two flights up. Turn right. You can use the room at the end. Bathroom is in the hall on the way there. Have a good night. See you in the morning for our de-briefing."

Moreno sensed a problem in the household and said, "I'm going to sleep in my office, if you need me."

Morgan followed Adele into his upstairs sitting room. Angela joined and sat in a chair beside Scott Reid, who stood at attention.

"Reid? You sure show up at the weirdest times. You got some weird information, too?" Morgan noted with surprise.

"He does, Dad," Adele said. She turned off the monitor and signaled security to insulate all quarters and to signal any movement within the estate quietly only to her PM.

"That sounds ominous," Morgan remarked. "You got me worried, girls."

"This is about Lex, Dad."

"Where's Lex?" Morgan grimaced.

"Allow me a presentation," Scott Reid interrupted. "I'd like to bring your father up to speed."

Reid indicated a recent surveillance feed on the room's monitor display. "This is about an investigation," he introduced as Morgan watched with interest.

The scene focused upon Lex Collins in footage captured by security cams that surveyed the cryogenic vaults at the Hospital Research Center. Adele's husband came into focus. Lex carefully removed a steel canister from the vault's interior and closed the heavy metal door behind him.

"This next sequence tracks Dr. Lex Collins behind the facility unlocking the doors to the incinerator intended for lab animals and body parts. Lex is now emptying the vials from the canister, throws them into one of the door slots, and presses the green button. Whatever was entered was vaporized by intense thermal energy within seconds," Reid narrated.

"When was this?" Morgan tossed his cane on the floor and leaned forward to freeze and magnify the canister label and numbers.

"This afternoon, sir."

"What time?"

"A few hours before dinner. During work hours."

"Why not ask the man what he was doing? Lex does research. It's a research facility. What's the problem?" Morgan asked angrily.

Reid explained the matter as he related it to Mrs. Collins and Mrs. Pendergrass.

"When Richard Cain showed me the spy-bots on his desk about three weeks ago, I noticed that they weren't the bots given to me by Moreno. He thought that they were ours and assumed that the state-of-the-art technology was patent Pendergrass funded research. But they weren't the bots I planted. I asked to return to the office to retrieve my coat and took the bots Cain had thrown on the desk. Clearly, they didn't belong to Failsafe. I wondered about their origin. So I put them in my jacket. Moreno never noticed them on Cain's desk when she came to rescue me – they're transparent – or maybe she just ignored them in the rush. I kept this to myself. For all I knew at the time, Ms. Moreno may have been at cross-purposes.

"I took a trip over to the labs at the Research Triangle after all of this went down. I had clearance there. I pulled out the plastic transparent bots and the guys in our Confederation Military Research group were amazed. They weren't amazed at the technology. They were surprised that someone had poached their project before its release. They asked me where I'd gotten hold of so many prototypes and went to inspect their storage. Every one of the originals was missing except for the larger models. We tried to figure who had access to locked storage units. We compiled a comprehensive list of scientists. Moreno didn't have any idea of the latest spybots being developed, nor did she have clearance. No one had spoken to her. She didn't show up on the monitor archives either. I figured she knew nothing about missing bots.

"The cold storages, the medical research cryogenic units, are back-to-back to the military research facilities. Lex Collins was the only biometric entry registered on the doors other than military scientists. He'd been there before yesterday, too. We traced Dr. Collins entering the medical vaults in December of 2054. Our records show that he opened the cryogenic vaults before yesterday, and the military vault's main door, only once.

We have no other records--or monitors, for that matter--inside each door of the storage vaults. The temperatures are too frigid for most surveillance cameras for purposes of ample resolution."

Morgan looked toward his wife and daughter and asked, "Mind telling me what you've made of this information?"

"When Scott gave me this evidence, he took a chance that I'd bite his head off," Adele began. "He assumed I could put the pieces together, and he was right. Lex and Connor used to have identical schedules. Things have changed. They rarely know what the other is doing these days. I wondered if it was Connor's fault. Was it Connor's new girlfriend, new distractions, different research directions, or what? I began to take note of Lex.

"Lex has become nervous and agitated. It was gradual, then lately he's barely able to contain himself," Adele displayed three empty bottles of Calm. "He hasn't touched that quantity in years," she emphasized. It's like he changed overnight," Adele quietly said as she looked toward her mother.

"Go ahead," Angela prompted.

"He avoids touching me and rarely shows CC affection. She, by the way, was the first to notice a change in Lex's temperament. He wouldn't let her touch him either. She tried to hug him one day and he backed away! Caroline didn't pursue it but we were both shocked. It was if Lex feared his own daughter. When we returned from her last check-up, CC whispered to me as we re-did makeup; she confided that her father was worried about lab tests. She said that his mind was 'full' and indicated that her father was confused. I asked Scott to be on the lookout for Lex's activities. He found something."

Reid once more indicated the monitor.

"I combed the Failsafe files and Cain's computer. On the later, was a dossier on the Pendergrass family. While in college, Cain had befriended Lex Collins. Cain was already teaching law when Lex was a freshman but they certainly knew of each other socially. They had friends in common, although all were older than Lex.

"The Dark years came and went. Cain moved toward security when the opportunity presented itself. He couldn't very well eat off a law profession. Anyway, there's a file of communications between Lex and him that have continued on and off until as recently as last month.

"It was curious that Lex mentioned Elle as topic matter. He evidently disapproved of Elle's association with his brother in a way that didn't make sense. He seemed obsessed with the idea that Connor would marry at all. I bring that up for a reason.

"Lex, I've learned, contacted Cain and asked him to dig up dirt on Elle. There was none to be found. She was just a simple country girl and Cain said as much in his report. I went back to the beginning. I recalled Cain's congratulatory letter to Lex when Caroline was born. It was a cryptic message. Cain wrote that he was 'available' if ever Lex found himself 'compromised'. It's not a typical goodwill message on behalf of a newborn. Cain knew something about Lex. It seemed to have something to do with Caroline's birth, too.

"Cain guessed about Lex's deception or else found evidence in his planted surveillance that explained Lex's strange concern about Elle. Cain connected the dots that I didn't figure out until today. Today, the records show Lex's visit to destroy vials from the cryogenic lab at an extraordinary time."

Morgan rubbed his head. "I saw the name Collins. What are you saying?"

"As you are well aware, sir, genetic samples of all kinds are kept there... stem cells, vials of eggs and sperm, all kinds of tissue samples for regenerative purposes. Registered to that vault are your daughter's eggs and your granddaughter's stem cells. It also contains Connor's genetic samples. It's all kept there in the event that Connor...or anyone...would undergo genetic screening when it came time for him and a future wife to have children.

"Then Elle came along. Connor's sperm samples remained untouched. Rachel replaced Elle. The samples were still untouched. It was unlikely that Connor's samples would be touched without a plan to proceed with testing and fertilization. To date, there have been no concrete plans for Connor to marry or have children. So naturally I wondered if Lex's visit had to do with his own plans for more children? Why else would he be entering the genetic freezers?"

"I suppose," Morgan huffed.

"Why all of a sudden remove all of the vials with 'Collins' on them? I theorized that Lex might have acted on Connor's behalf. His brother may have shared his plans to get married to Rachel. But the sample Lex retrieved didn't actually belong to Connor Collins... it had been switched years ago.

"If Rachel and Connor decided to have kids--or even if it had been with Elle--the sample with the name Connor Collins might show sterility, if my theory is right. Connor's girlfriend or future wife may decide to get pregnant naturally but he's a scientist. The sample was there in the first place because he would take a look at his sperm's integrity as soon as Connor wanted to start a family. Lex couldn't allow that to happen.

"We might have figured that Lex has one child and was finished. Having made genetic alterations, Lex may have confused or conflicted feelings about his daughter's special abilities. Or Lex had decided to replace the sample with a new batch, even though he didn't bring a replacement vial with him. There could be several explanations for Lex being in that vault. But nothing explains his actions of *sneaking* into the facility. He was obviously trying to avoid detection when he decided to destroy both his and his brother's vials. Lex wanted to get rid of all the evidence. Lex's metrics of behavioral functions by the security cam and his PM leave no doubt that he was nervous to the point of devious behaviors.

"I brought the information to Mrs. Collins. Only she would have insight to confirm my suspicions. Mrs. Collins knew me. She was aware I had made a connection between Caroline and my son's recovery years back and that I'd been discreet. I told her what I suspected and showed her the images.

"Your daughter confided to me that she and Lex had trouble conceiving. Lex assured her that nothing was wrong with either of them but proceeded with an in vivo fertilization after mapping rather than 'take chances'. They were successful the first trial."

"Stop!" Morgan demanded and looked at Adele for confirmation. Adele nodded in the affirmative

Morgan blamed the messenger and exploded with rage. "You had no right to march in here and confront my daughter with this information. You should have approached me first!"

Reid would have none of Morgan's rage on the matter.

"Sir, I tried to contact you many times; it wasn't something to convey by other means. You were otherwise engaged with critical matters, according to your security office. I suspected Lex Collins and Cain of serious wrongs and I didn't waste a minute to move on it with the person most involved. We have no idea where this is going or the reason this seemed to be an urgent move after five years' time."

Adele crossed the room and held her father's arm. She tried to calm the wrath that had yet to fully break its emotional dam.

"Dad, calm down. Let me cut to the chase. Lex was sterile and used Connor's sample. Lex was shooting blanks the whole time. Who would have dreamed Lex would do such a thing? Lex thought it was important that he sire the Pendergrass legacy. He probably figured that was needed to be accepted. He switched his sterile vial for his brother's, then had to destroy all of the vials in light of Connor's new romance."

"The timing of the first monitored entry was correct?" Morgan sat with clenched fists.

"Right to the day, Dad. December 10, 2054," Adele confirmed the evidence.

Morgan eyed Reid and Angela. Reid explained further.

"Cain was head of surveillance in December of '54. Cain figured what was going on. He later connected Lex's dislike of Elle, then Rachel. He also watched Lex raid the vaults by cams and entry codes never replaced. Cain saw an opportunity; he recently played his card when he demanded of Lex the latest covert technology. He instructed Lex to smuggle Confederation spybots to him. Lex took the first Confederation bots he laid eyes on and stole military prototypes still in development. Cain's threats to reveal Caroline's true paternity had Lex over a barrel.

"No one knew about the bots Moreno gave me to plant in Failsafe. When Cain found the evidence of bots around the building, he didn't know what was what. He obviously hadn't spoken to Lex about the bots. Lex took it upon himself to deliver something, anything, to keep Cain's mouth shut about his sterility. It was the only technology he could put his hands on. So he grabbed them but hadn't delivered them.

"Those prototype bots were mixed with Moreno's. But they had never been activated to transmit. So, I'm guessing that Lex discovered the issue, lost his nerve, and just let them go on site before he reached Cain's office. They weren't programmed to broadcast anywhere. He was in panic mode. Crazy. So he just let the critters out somewhere and they just ran around Cain's building transmitting nothing till Cain found them. A few were mine, the rest were stolen from the Confederation labs.

"Cain had likely been spying in the Pendergrass labs since the Collins boys worked on the farm. He knew just about everything there was to know until Isabella Moreno did the sweeps that finally shut him out. Cain's records include thousands of hours of conversations between Lex and Connor.

"The vials weighed on Dr. Lex Collins as evidence of his sterility, duplicity, and betrayal. Cain was in a position to demand anything he wanted of Lex."

Morgan disagreed. He thought Reid was out of his depth, his logic flawed by a personal bias against Cain.

"Don't be stupid. We could find out anything we wanted. We would discover whether Lex was Caroline's father or not. Caroline's data is extensive; Lex *is the father*."

"Says the data," Adele protested. "Who the hell controls that data? Garbage in, garbage out. What would make you dream of checking that out? Only Cain had evidence of Lex's predicament. My husband has lived a lie, made a mockery of us, morally reprehensible acts of betrayal so that he could secure some kind of manly image. Cain figured that out fast."

Morgan felt sick and roared, "My God, it's genetic rape!"

"He was weak. Always been weak, Dad. My guess is that he's never loved me. He certified his manhood by proxy...stolen at that! I suspect five years of confusion and guilt was amplified by exposure to CC's blue light," Adele elaborated.

"Everyone else was receptive to the light except for Lex. He immediately became withdrawn, a cowed animal. The man isn't a murderer like Brown but every time those kids got together he became uncomfortable, a little more distant. Lex has been definitely negatively affected.

"He manages to avoid all of the kids now. He's involved at all levels of the RT genetic research but his focus has switched to covering his tracks. It's the reason that Connor has been complaining about the research not getting enough traction lately with these new children. There were a lot of complaints leveled at Lex for the last months, wondering why a lot of data wasn't up and running. Lex has spun quite the web of deceit by altering algorithms.

"How much did he share with Cain? I've no idea. Maybe he couldn't stand it anymore so he destroyed the evidence. Next? He's going to screw up all the data in the research project at the Annex. Perhaps blow the building. Who knows? How does a person come clean with what he's done?" Adele warned her father.

Angela interjected a plan.

"We've got bigger fish to fry here. First, we'll test out our theories. My guess is that Richard Cain and Lex have been long associated in more ways than one.

"Second, I'd venture that Cain was in touch with Brown for years. It answers a whole lot of smug that was going on. Lex is an idiot for opening us up like this. He's never made a move to protect this home. He didn't care that Cain might undermine the Confederation."

"You going to tell me where that SOB is right now?" Morgan yelled.

Adele assured her father that Lex was clueless, sick, and should not be alerted as to their information.

"Sleeping like a lamb. He's been taking heavy doses of Calm. He kept asking when Nicholas was returning. 'Where is Nicholas?' over and over. Then I got the call from Scott on my PC. We met in the barn. By the time I returned, Lex had passed out. I got CC to lie down in her room and told Mother the story. Here we are."

"How are you, Babycake? How are you handling this terrible betrayal?" Morgan asked heavily.

"I have the most wonderful child in the world. I have a weight off my shoulders you can't imagine. When we have time, I'll explain what I mean by that. Let me tell you, I'm focused."

"What about Caroline?" Morgan's throat began to constrict. It touched Adele to realize her father's pain.

Scott Reid paused the conversation, calling attention to Caroline standing in the doorway. She walked toward her grandfather and sat beside him.

Blue lights circled the room and hovered over Scott Reid as a newcomer. They moved from Morgan to Angela to Adele and back to CC. With the exception of Morgan's heavy breathing, there was not a sound. The lights disappeared together at once in place.

Why are you awake, Caroline?" Her grandfather did not know what to make of her sudden appearance.

"Everybody is sad. I came upstairs to see what's going on," she said, examining those around her.

"Well, nothing much is going on in here!" Morgan laughed. "Just a bunch of tired old people."

Caroline Collins, however, had something to say.

"This is about Daddy. Daddy is the only one that doesn't have a light that connects to anyone else. All the kids that can see the lines of lights know that Daddy had no blue line to anyone else. The rest of us are all connected. All of the adults had blue lights to each other except for Daddy.

"Daddy is not the only one who doesn't like the blue light. There will be more. I'm sorry. It just can't stay with him. He's getting sicker. Daddy made and kept secrets. It doesn't matter if people don't know the secrets. He shouldn't have made them because they hurt him."

"I knew that stealing the ginger cookies and pretending that most of them were for Blue was wrong before I got caught. I know the difference about these things and so did Daddy," Caroline answered what had, at one time or another, streamed through their minds.

Scott Reid terminated the monitor images and watched as the delicate six-year-old girl comforted her mother and grand-parents.

"I'd just like to ask if anyone saw blue lights darting around here?" Reid tested in the quiet room. "Blue lights? Anyone?"

"I'll talk to you later about that," Morgan nodded. "Your job now is to touch base with Isabella and start a serious investi-gation into Cain's former activities at every level. Hopefully, this is about Lex and Lex only. You breathe a word of this particular issue and you'll be a sorry man!"

CC lightly slapped her grandfather's knee. "Mr. Reid is our friend. I think you have to say 'sorry'. Anyway, everyone knows that Daddy is not well. It isn't a secret."

"Sorry, Reid!" Morgan shook the man's hand that was intro-duced to him as a confused intruder when CC was three months old. "I'm upset."

"Understandable, sir." Reid nodded to those in the room and departed.

"What about Lex? What do we do?" Angela asked her husband.

It was Caroline that answered, "Let Daddy be Daddy. We will be us. I don't think we can help if we make him sicker and sicker."

"You mean Nicholas will make Daddy sick?" asked Adele.

"No, all of us. We can't help it. Now everyone is beginning to have what everyone else has. Daddy will begin to feel a little ill everywhere, not just around Nicholas and not just af-ter the lights. We all have some of Nicholas in us now. Ildiko can move some little things. I understand math better, see dots, and can understand without the translator. Nicholas un-derstands some of the chants and can hear the adults like the younger ones do. For grownups, it's the same. Everyone trusts each other more. Mr. and Mrs. Nishant understand Aditiya; they realize what he's been able to see and they're happy that he isn't always nervous and biting his nails. Ildiko's father thinks about his wife and misses Hungary but believes he's doing the right thing. He knows that the Confederation needs him and he's making plans to help. Rachel loves Uncle Connor and he loves her, too. They feel that they were meant for each other and so does Aaron. Granddaddy and Grandma...I know you love everyone here. It happened fast because we're connected. Everyone understands how we have to work together. Everyone hears and sees the same things... but *not daddy*.

"Tonight, Dad walked out of the library without the light and I knew he may hate us one day soon. He's changing as fast as we are changing. The blue light should have helped. I don't know why it didn't. It makes everyone else so happy. I never would hurt my daddy or anyone," Caroline soberly justified.

Morgan eyed Caroline closely.

"Of course you wouldn't hurt your father. Are you angry with your father?" Morgan worried.

"I've never felt angry, Grandpa. I'm surprised that my father doesn't understand that lies and love don't mix. It's like Daddy mixed sand in the ginger cookie dough. You don't want to eat a ginger snap, no matter how much you love cookies, with even a little bit of sand in it. I don't know why he doesn't like the lights. Just like you said: you can lead a horse into water but the horse has to swim out by himself."

Morgan laughed and corrected her, "You can lead a horse to water but you can't make it drink."

"Same thing, isn't it?" CC kissed him on the cheek, happy to see his mood change.

"We'll go back to our rooms now," Adele yawned.

"The hell you will, Babycake. You've got a confused animal in yours and I'll just feel better if you both stay here for now," Morgan insisted. "Lex's room is being monitored. He won't be unmonitored from this moment. Weakness is the fodder for evil. My son-in-law is without spine or scruples. He's not going to take a piss without observation. Confederation friends have been notified. We've got this," Morgan assured his family.

"I do find it curious that it was Lex who mentioned that we had to be more vigilant, not to be so lax about Confederation security when Caroline was born. He knew then and there Cain was up to something. He never had the onions to say it like a man. Just threw it out there in a moment of guilt. What a piece of...pie!" Morgan regained decorum for the sake of his granddaughter. "Well, Cain and Brown are history. I'd say we've been doing things right for batting blind," Morgan shook his head sadly.

Chapter XXV

A Reckoning

Friday, March 18, 2061

L ex Collins woke up with a fever; his PM advised as to his condition and the appropriate response.

"Yeah, yeah, I know," he groaned. Lex reached for the bottle of Calm and swallowed four capsules. The cold sweats ceased.

Moreno and Komor awoke early. They received the memo regarding Lex Collins having compromised Confederation security and his conflict of interest as a Confederation researcher. The women remotely monitored Lex, reported his illness, and made note of an overuse of Calm by 8:00 a.m.

Morgan, Scott Reid, Adele and Angela had no more secrets between them on the subject of Lex Collins. By 9:00 a.m., Colonel Komor was appointed as North Carolina's Confederation Security Chief. She agreed to serve for a year. Moreno couldn't have been more pleased with the decision. Matters had changed and the scrutiny with it.

At 9:30 a.m., Morgan spoke with Governor Mario Hernandez and Confederation Minister Robert Gant about the recent spikes in violent activity just beyond their borders.

"It was a matter of time," Gant commented on the topic of improved vigilance. "It's not even tribal warfare from where I'm sitting. Violence has increased without a discernable pattern. The way you see it, these are lines drawn by unseen forces that may have been with us, since the beginning of time. I just see a shit-load of trouble! I'm not sure how those children you've got there can help, but we sure could use a secret weapon right about now," he added.

Hernandez decided to weigh in.

"Now, you want to know what I think about Cain's confederation conspiracy? He was a mixture of snake oil and crap. Lex Collins? Hasn't the gumption to follow through on anything he might have gotten mixed up in. He'll fold and run as soon as he knows he's been compromised. Don't get paranoid, Morgan. You've got a tight and committed group," Hernandez assured Morgan.

Gant reiterated Hernandez's conclusion and proposed a plan.

"We'll monitor the former American territories and see if there are any specific migrations that indicate saner groupings. We'll segregate them from those that erratically move. Right now, the crazies move like hornets, erratic and angry. Hungarians gave no quarter to that kind of encroaching enemies; their lasers were able to target from 300 kilometers along with those son of a gun horse battalions. We need that kind of permutation. You've got an expert right there in your house, Morgan. I'd listen to what Attila Meszaros has to say. He worked both the satellite images and military brigades in the fields by horseback. They've managed to reclaim their former empire and are now supporting the new territories with organized communities established on borders every day. Former countries are clamoring to come under the Hungarian flag. Hungarian research recognized immediately that the electromagnetic overload skewed the magnetite in the brain..."

"What?" Hernandez interrupted. "Magnetite?"

"Magnetite is the most magnetic substance known to man," Morgan explained. "It exists in the cerebral cortex and is in the lining surrounding the brain and the spinal cord. Magnetite crystals turn bacteria into swimming needles that react to the earth's magnetic fields. Our magnetite crystals actually sway back and forth in the brain, conveying the magnetic sense by which we are able to judge direction. When we studied animals' ability to sense earthquakes prior to major disasters, it was the subtle changes in the geomagnetic field that we suspected acted upon the brain tissues of animals. We've known that magnetite helps migratory species to migrate successfully by allowing them to follow the earth's magnetic fields. When it came to humans, we made the association between the ethmoid bone and the magnetic field."

"Ethmoid bone?" Hernandez questioned.

"It's located between your eyes just behind the nose. When they say 'follow your nose', it's almost the fact of the matter," Morgan laughed. "So that's the navigation issue. But what we're referencing here is that our brains have an entire magnetic system built into them. We're a mass of electrical activity with all of its frequencies, pulses, bursts...all sharing within one common medium: Earth's magnetic field. Imagine what happens with the electromagnetic bursts? It caused disruptions in segments of the population with compromised cellular magnetic functionality. Sure, magnetite. Without its proper functionality, people can go navigationally crazy at the least of it. Magnetite is located roughly at the center of one's head, filled with crystals. The glandular structure is connected as a discrete quantity of electromagnetic energy. We're connected, for better or for worse," Morgan underlined the topic.

Gant continued, "From our reports and observations, we pick up tribes now unafraid to set up camp alongside protected farming communities. Thousands of boating communities have sprung up with shoreline outposts. They are constantly under siege from crazed individuals that may or may not want supplies. Many times, they ravage without taking anything. Given this blue light thing, I made an association with your son-in-law's erratic impulses and those that have escalated their attacks," Gant stated without judgment. "Any ideas, Morgan?"

"Connor and Meredith Green are looking into ways it might be possible to transmit this special energy on a broader scale. I'm not even sure that's a good idea other than it may separate those that need our immediate attention as opposed to the feral ones in need of remedies we've yet to discover. Let me know when we should all meet. Sooner than later, right, Robert?" Morgan asked.

"I'm good with sooner," Robert Gant agreed. "And one more thing, Morgan. Can't tell you for the life of me how Cain knew

Brown was even alive. My guess? Brown located Cain and not the other way around. Makes sense since Brown finally made a beeline toward North Carolina after 20 years of hiding."

Morgan agreed, "Never thought of that. You're right. Thought he had something in Cain. But how did he know Cain? To hell with it," Morgan sniffed. "They're both dead."

"Allow me to mention an overriding concern here." Robert cleared his throat for emphasis.

Morgan grunted, "What's that, Robert? You won't live long enough to finish off that wine cellar?"

"Krisztina is leaving D.C. You're a no-'count thief, Morgan. Pure and simple," he accused.

"You got a love interest going, Bobbie? Ha. You had plenty of time to move on that one. I recognize talent. Not above stealing it either!"

"I'm crazy about her. Just never got around to popping the question. Thought it was too cool around here for her to want to serve elsewhere. Take care of her, Morgan. Put in a good word for me and don't keep her too long," Robert Gant asked in the moment he decided to marry Krisztina Komor.

"You're an idiot. Someone else is going to pick up your option. It's my job to poach every good soldier. I'm especially fond of Komor, too. She ignores my bad behaviors and she's got a wicked temper. Watching that woman explode is a grand thing to behold. Watching her walk isn't too bad either. Got that long neck, dark auburn hair and legs for days that can kick asses and doors," Morgan whistled in a fashion meant to further irritate his colleague.

"Finders keepers?" Gant appealed. "I'm slow but she's the one for me. I'm begging you to not let the guys too close."

"Not my job. You need to man up and let her know how you feel. I'm not cooperating with a non-plan," Morgan warned.

"Take care of that family," Gant said before they disconnected.

It was left to Morgan and Adele as to how they would tell Connor the sordid tale as to how he, and not Lex, was Caroline's father. Morgan wished he were a younger man. *I'd tear him into pieces, bait my hook, and go fishing,* he thought.

* * *

Adele met her father downstairs at the breakfast table and stared at a spittle-flecked monitor in his hand as she bent to kiss him.

"Still spitting nails?" Adele observed.

"This guy has been busy betraying everyone: you, our family, our research, and even Caroline. I could spit...."

"You've done that, Dad. Let's figure what we're going to do," Adele took a prepared meal from the kitchen bot.

"Who knows how Connor will take it? It's likely to be a scene like no other between Lex and him," Morgan opined.

"I'm sure he'll be civilized about it," Adele said as if saying it would make it so.

"I'm sure he wishes that. A man doesn't usually take this kind of news lightly!" Morgan pushed the monitor from him, no longer able to count the times and ways Lex had purposely covered his tracks with false data entries. "When Caroline is older and finds out what a scoundrel he's been..."

"The rate Caroline and you are going, everyone is going to know this degenerate's secret in two seconds flat when she hears us even thinking about it," Adele clarified. "I'm just wondering the right time to tell Connor. The tragic thing about betrayal is that loved ones deliver the worst kind..." Adele fought back tears. "I can't even look at him."

"He's milk gone wrong. No way to bring rancid back, Baby-cake," Morgan agreed that Lex was a lost cause.

Blue barked and scurried from the room to the back door, exiting with an unknown party.

"There goes my loyal dog," Morgan sighed. "Damn clones!"

* * *

Blue made himself comfortable outdoors within the horse arena; he turned four times in a tight circle and settled upon a discarded coat lying on the ground since summer. The dog watched Connor Collins and Attila Meszaros lunge two horses and sneezed at the wisps of dust kicked up and blown his way.

A whip gently urged the German Warm Blood one way, then another. Attila's hand was steady and he spoke encouragingly to the gelding. Compliant and eager, the horse responded to Attila's easy confidence.

Conversely, Connor had difficulty convincing a skittish Tennessee Walker unaccustomed to sharing attention or space.

"I've got a princess here. Exactly what are we looking for, Attila?" Connor called as he struggled with the gelding.

"Footing, stability, intelligence, and a calm disposition!" Attila drew his pistol and shot it into the ground. Connor's horse skidded short, reared on its hindquarters, and bolted into a full gallop, furiously bucking disgruntlement along the inside perimeter of the arena.

"What the hell was that for?" Connor scrambled for the flying lunge line.

"Most of all, a horse that doesn't spook," Attila frowned. "We're going to need steadier stock."

Connor managed to halt the panicked horse and pulled the line until he had hold of the halter. White manic eyes peered down a long stretched neck through snorting vapor.

"These horses may look like fluff but they've pulled plows and can hunt anything. Just caught off guard," Connor justified.

Attila laughed, "Exactly my point. A military horse maneuvers obstacles in the heat of battle with no thought of anything but the rider's objectives!"

"What's going on here, Attila? I thought you just wanted to go riding." Connor believed himself a drafted tour guide for their guest.

"I do. I want to get an idea of the local terrain and these horses. I've got a lot of work ahead of me. Going to help? What else you have?"

"A really nice Arabian, two quarter horses, a Thoroughbred, two Morgans, and some others. What kind of work?" Connor asked.

"The Confederation is going to need a Hussar type regiment at some point. You're going to have to go into uncharted fields of battle. You'll run into people who seem compliant because of fear but are still mentally unstable. And then there are those beyond compliance or fear; they are too far gone. Crazed wild survivors will come at you without any regard for life, their own, the lives of women, or children. They'll do anything to cut you down. They'll sever the legs of your mounts. They'll burn the forests to prevent refuge, including their own. In the cities, the horses will have to contend with steel rubble, broken cement steps, a wide variety of crumbling surfaces. They'll need to take to water without hesitation, swim and ferry you by their tails so you don't rise above the water line, and do these types of maneuvers with confidence. Without these mounted troops, we could never have secured our borders throughout Central and Eastern Europe."

"It's not the same situation..." Connor stammered a protest.

"It's the same, Connor. You will not maintain civilization with this ever-growing madness that escalates each generation. It's just a matter of time. The only difference between Hungary and here are the numbers and spaces. We faced hundreds of millions from the east that cut down every living thing in its path," Attila said without emotion. "They were venomous swarms of unending locusts."

Attila returned to the horses to further survey the situation.

"We can't use Arabians. They're basically sand poodles. They're good for distance but too finicky and fragile. The Tennessee Walker is smooth enough for Sunday afternoon outings but I'm not sure of the breed's footing on rough ground. I like the looks of the one you call 'Chocolate Lady'."

Connor laughed. "That's the one Caroline renamed. It's Adele's horse and my sister-in-law can ride to hell and back with that one. What's a Hussar?"

"Let's go riding. We'll talk about it," Attila said emphatically. "Contact Adele and Lex and see if they want to go with us. I'd like to see how they work. I'm going to need help with training."

"Training? Oh sure. I'm going to throw that one out there so I have to spend an hour convincing Lex. Lex won't go. He'll never ride. He doesn't like horses and I'm pretty sure the feeling is mutual. Not really the outdoor type. He's that guy with an apple in his hand that drops the offering as soon as he's approached. Lex picks his way around a barn trying to avoid manure. On top of all that, he's got allergies."

"Forget I asked," Attila laughed.

Connor pinged Adele: "Saddling Chocolate Lady for you. We'll be showing Attila the Hun around these parts. Hurry up."

"Lex is sick. I should stay," Adele regretfully suggested.

"All the more reason. Take a break and get some fresh air. It's perfect riding weather. Bring some water, would you?" Connor urged.

"I'd like that. I'll have to be back by the time CC gets out of school. Could we swing around to that side of the property on the way back?"

"Sure. Get ready for some heavy work, though. This guy means business. He means to build a Confederation Cavalry by the way he's talking."

"Be there in twenty," Adele enthused with an altered mood. She imagined sun and wind on her face. It would also provide a way to avoid confronting Lex for a few more hours.

Attila and Connor mounted and met Adele making her way to the stable. She pitched water bottles their way and swung herself on the back of her beloved horse. Lady's ears signaled readiness and they walked toward familiar trails to warm up. Ten minutes later, Attila urged his horse into an easy canter. He approved of the animals' stamina and training. They had been riding wordlessly for nearly forty-five minutes when Attila put his hand up in the air, signaling an abrupt halt.

"Follow me," he ordered. The three riders moved toward the edge of the woods that hosted thickets of oaks and cedars with an underbrush of blackberry brambles that obscured large timber stumps. Attila urged his horse toward an old oak tree with thickened branches dripping with wayward ivy. Standing on the saddle, the Hungarian launched himself toward the lowest branch and pulled himself upward five more within a few heartbeats. By the first brittle crack of the first tree limb, Attila had moved to the next three.

The Hungarian's eyes zoomed and magnified the terrain, interfacing with a memory chip wired in his brain's hippocampus. The hundred billion tiny nerve cells that made up Attila Meszaros' brain fired a series of neural implants, recording and assessing everything he could see, hear, and smell. It took 15 seconds to cache hundreds of thousands of images and corresponding notes. He directed his attention to a spring-fed lake where he imagined future water drills.

"A lot of cotton-mouthed moccasins in that lake a few miles north of here?" he called down to his companions.

"A breeding ground if you must know!" Adele yelled her objections. "Not going there, Attila."

"We've got remedies for that. We'll outfit the horses for indigenous wildlife for regions we investigate," he explained.

He jumped twenty-five feet to the ground; his effortless cushioned landing had been seamlessly calibrated.

"You're amped!" Connor appreciated the science that the Hungarians had developed and honed for the last decade. "Never saw so much going on at once. Impressive!"

"It helps in the kind of fieldwork we encounter. Laser sharp hearing and vision, memory and access to information, either banked or streamed from the brain-net, has helped immeasurably. The Australians and my country have been cooperating on animal amplification, too. Hungarian Hussars have been successful greatly due to our technological advantage in hand-to-hand confrontation."

Connor puzzled, "Hussars? A little more on that, please?"

"In lieu of your own cerebral implant, allow me to read this off," Attila said as he mounted his horse from the ground without touching the stirrups. The horse felt little or no impact as he landed.

"The Huszár dates back to 1432 in southern Hungary. During the Ottoman wars in Europe, King Mathias Corvinus introduced the idea of conscription of mounted soldiers to run the Hungarian borders. 'Husz' means twenty. For every twenty serfs, the nobles had to equip one mounted soldier to guard Hungarian territory. Bands of mounted Turks that fought the Hungarians inspired King Corvinus to organize large trained formations in the Hungarian Black Army. It was these horse regiments that pushed back the Turkish Spahis, the Bohemians, and Poles. Our ancestors' successes were copied all over Europe and into Russia. No one could quite do what the Hungarians did," Attila added with national pride.

"Why was that?" Adele asked.

"No one had the skills to train the horses like the Hungarians. No one could ride like us either. Our equestrian gifts were considered so superlative that special orders were given by Frederick II in the 1740s to never offend or try to direct the Hussars as long as they were part of the Prussian army. Successes were so impressive that Hungarians were not subject to disciplinary measures. My predecessors could be unruly. Some might call us brave and independent types but we were mostly considered hard-nosed. We were handsome and charming fellows all the same. As you can see, I'm here to carry on that legacy in the 21st century across the ocean," Attila said with cheek. He sat erectly, poised for examination.

"We see, we see," Adele laughed. "So what's the plan? You're planning the same kind of thing for the Confederation?"

"Morgan and I have been discussing lately what it means to drive a large rescue mission. He hadn't counted on stories like ours. Horses have to be equipped to move through rough terrain, urban areas, amongst rubble, and contend with attack dogs. It's what we did every day of the week, all year, all ten years. We never had the luxury of rescuing anyone. We didn't believe that there were significant numbers of survivors worth saving. Even if we could figure the sane ones, that fine line was quickly crossed when our people were falling into pits and burned to death fighting to keep our borders intact. We're not as mawkish as Americans.

"In all of our patrols, we only lost 1% in battle. It was due to careful strategizing and amping our men and women who faced a ruthless onslaught. We didn't have half the technology we do today, so you may be more successful with Morgan's idea of retrieving the sane survivors."

"How much have you listened to? I mean, have you overheard our private conversations in the Pendergrass household?" Adele asked suddenly.

Attila looked at her knowingly. He was able to hear every frequency of surveillance and noted the increased activity since last night. Angela and Morgan spoke of Lex's activities in the den as Attila had headed out to the barn. He didn't miss much of the discussion. It was what he was trained to do.

"Nothing, Adele. That would be eavesdropping and I would never do that," he assured her. It was code for 'I heard it all but it's none of my business.'

Adele felt as if the wind was knocked out of her. She was broadsided by the realization that never again would there be secrets. In her father's day, the government intruded mercilessly with the Internet, had tracked each American's communications with a handle on every location of every vehicle and phone. Then came the tracking devices and chips. Visual aids were never one way; direct observations by unseen sources were a given. Now there was a paradigm shift with the arrival of a strange blue light that linked people in a way that thoughts and feelings could transform everyone into empaths. Today she had been made aware of implanted neurotransmitters that boosted hearing and sight ranges with brain-net connections. Attila had the additional luxury of receiving information via his neural transmitters that could interact with diagnostic nano-bots in his bloodstream. He could also cache, cull, analyze, and send information at will to the brain-net.

Adele hoped for simple, civilized understanding. "If Attila's response is an indication of things to come, it wouldn't be so terrible," she factored an appreciation for his thoughtful discretion.

Attila acknowledged her grateful smile with a nod and changed the subject.

"We're going to change how we communicate with the horses. It makes our work almost effortless. Our mounts have to know what to avoid, quietly position, and recall strategic maneuvers within days and minutes instead of years of high level repetition. Once conditioned, they move seamlessly. When we break up mobs, our riding line is knee to knee and sends a vibrational signal that upsets the opposition. The thing

I've noticed is that those horses get smart. I mean really smart."

Adele and Connor looked doubtful about such a project.

"I know you think this idea is premature, but the signs are all there," Attila said. "We've already been through this cycle throughout my continent. If you're not proactive about the movement toward the Confederation, it becomes problematic to sustain one's population while regulating war zones. You can't imagine what it means to have your people taken hostage; children ransomed one hand at a time until food stores and ammunition stockpiles are emptied.

"I suspect this round in North America might be worse. I saw what happened with that light. I may feel these effects more acutely because I'm hyped electronically but it certainly fits the theory that it amplifies one's nervous system at the very least. We'll be better at who we are and it will be clearer as to who is our enemy. Our enemy has no reason, no mercy, and no scruples. That force is nothing but an overwhelming urge to destroy the energy that makes them sick. That's us, folks. We're going to destroy the energy that makes us sick, too."

Connor knew at once that Attila had been briefed on their research.

"You've read the Nishant report, too?" Connor asked.

"It makes perfect sense. We've also got the Israeli reports on the magnetic field's flux since the EMP disasters. There are soft spots in the atmosphere portals in the magnetic fields. It figures that our cellular levels have been affected. Humans have been transformed negatively and positively. Consider the polygenetic issues for schizophrenia that we once thought to be mutations rather than problems with dopamine, glutamate, and other brain chemicals shared by the autoimmune system to keep balance. We ignored the genetic abnormalities that should have been fixed prior to the Darkness. We might have avoided the irreversible damage we now face. Billions of people stood teetering on a mental precipice. Never mind frequency overloads since the turn of the century.

Now we're talking about a war for the species. I see no prisoners, no half measures."

The intermittent sound of the harmonic cadence of the three
horses walking across the field underlined the gravity of Attila's
theory. Adele laughed nervously, "Here I thought this day in
the country was going to be a little stress relief. I'm suddenly
scared out of my wits."

Attila and Connor smiled, too.

"We'll just do what we have to do," Attila stated. "We're
doing it for our kids. I'm not a man who prays to God, believes
in churches and people dressed up as religious potentates. But
I have to agree with a certain religious view there's something
inherently wrong. I've never dismissed the notion of sin or evil
because you've got to ask yourself how people can wake up
one morning, drink a cup of coffee, and trot off to work to slit
throats, slicing heads, and rounding up innocent people for
more of the same? How does that happen? Don't like the wife?
Hell, chop her nagging head off! Disrespectful teenage girl
problems? A little acid should fix that. That's what went on
decades before the EMP disasters! Where was everyone on the
subject of psychotic terrorists? As if random chaos had some
reason attached? That alone should have signaled wholesale
moral detachment. Just like those studies in the UK I looked
at recently. Hey, if it didn't come out bad for me, what's the
problem?

"Look, the Confederation means something. Hungary's ambition to fulfill a national vision meant something, too. Now,
our entire region is working together. Australia was actually
the first to forge its borders and interior, long before anyone
talked about an EMP. As an island with great naval strength
and committed leaders, Australia had a relatively easier time
of it. Boldly, and without apology, their Navy met and turned
back the masses moving in on them illegally. Like the Hungarians, they were prepared for self-sufficiency and public con-
demnation. Not so the UK. Under siege from its interior, the
English folded from within. The interior sieges exploded with
social fires. Hate breeds faster than you can imagine. I intend
to help prepare to defend what's good and decent in this part

of the world the way we succeeded in the CEU. I had no idea of these gifted kids. Clearly, their presence tells a story of possibilities. We have to face the fact that hostile forces will sense their existence and actively target them."

Connor believed Attila. It was clear that he had to make his stake known.

"I'm going to get in touch with every equine group. We can practice on the farm or any one of twenty farms around these parts," Connor announced committedly. "Then I'm going to propose to Rachel," he added.

Adele and Attila laughed at the non sequitur.

"You have our permission to do both," Adele smiled.

"What about your research? This is going to take significant time away from the lab, Connor," Attila reminded.

"Lex and Meredith don't need me. It'll be fine. I am going to ask that our doctors talk to Hungary and amplify our troops. Morgan has to have some additional medical work, too. He's going to need to go another country mile if we're headed to this kind of military campaign. Deal?"

"No question. Let's ride on it!" Attila hooted.

"I'm in!" Adele announced. "Not that you guys asked," she mumbled to herself as Lady bolted forward.

The cool winter breeze brought welcome relief from the unrelenting emotional turmoil that churned within Adele Pendergrass Collins. Moving across the gentle Carolina hills on the strong, sure back of her horse, Adele blew past the lurking shadows that had appeared the previous night. A familiar cool, sweet wind filled her hair and washed Adele's senses anew. Moving in unison, the moist earth was pulled and tossed by the galloping unit that tore across turned soybean fields. Laughter erupted as the three riders gave free rein to their passions.

Attila loosely tied off his reins and began a series of vaulting maneuvers while in a slow gallop. Connor and Adele were captivated by the equine voltage display Attila was able to execute upon a clueless Pendergrass mount. From side to side, ground to saddle, Attila demonstrated exquisite control with forward and back chest rolls that ended with a double tucked vault to the back of his horse. An attempted handstand brought Attila's mount to an abrupt halt; Attila's trajectory sent him up and above the startled horse's head. Attila landed softly on his feet.

"Need you make us look any more pathetic?" Connor laughed as hard as he had in years.

Adele joined the hilarity. It was Attila's mud-splattered face that made the Hungarian look a little less polished, a bit more human.

"Let's walk," Attila announced when he remounted.

As the horses slowed to a walk for the final leg home, Adele pointed toward the schoolhouse.

"Ildiko enjoy school here?" she asked Attila.

"Entirely enthusiastic," he said. "She misses her mother. These new friends have helped."

Connor noticed a man in the distance that stumbled and faltered across the hill toward the school.

"Attila, can you make that out?" Connor worried. "The guy looks drunk."

"It's your brother," Attila identified. "He doesn't look well."

Adele squeezed her thighs hard and moved her seat into full gallop toward the man she suddenly recognized. Lady's chest heaved with the acceleration needed to meet her master's urgent purpose.

Lex Collins ceased walking when he spotted a horse galloping his way. Attila and Connor, startled by Adele's reaction, followed her sense of the moment and tracked closely behind. Neither man believed Adele could possibly be so eager to see Lex.

Adele painfully observed Lex in slow motion pull a long black launcher from his side and raise it toward the schoolhouse. Blood curdling primal screams of terror seemed to arise from somewhere else other than her.

Attila released the reins and pulled his manual weapon from its holster. His was not a smart gun; he relied on his amplifications to make adjustments with lightning speed as he took aim. The rate at which Lex's rocket launcher flew from his left hand and spiraled into the air astounded the three riders. As they raced toward Lex, Connor and Adele realized that Attila had never gotten off his shot.

Attila bolted from his horse and jumped Lex. It took little effort to subdue the man who, at his best, was too fragile to resist.

"What happened to the launcher?" asked Attila, baffled as to the whereabouts of the weapon, throwing Lex to the ground.

Connor pointed upward toward the schoolhouse roof. Aaron stood quietly at the window regarding CC's father, who intended to end their lives in a hailstorm of fire. CC appeared beside Aaron as they witnessed her father held face-down into the hardened mud beside a swing set.

The teachers quickly pulled the children from the windows and the bots sounded alarms.

Lex had full clearance; security had ignored his presence. Only Aaron had a feeling that something was not quite right. He was compelled to move from his classroom seat toward the window. The launcher was easily manipulated away from Lex Collins' grasp through the glass.

Adele rushed inside the building and pulled her daughter close. For the first time in her life, slow, quiet tears rolled down Caroline's face.

"He wanted to hurt us?" Caroline asked her mother, who stood frozen in disbelief.

"Yes, he wanted to hurt us," Caroline answered her own question.

Connor had never been a violent man but never had he shied from a fight. He stood with his boot between his brother's shoulder blades.

"What were you doing, Lex? You aimed a launcher against a schoolhouse of children, one of whom is your own child? What are you?" Connor grasped for reason.

Attila swept Connor aside and pulled Lex Collins from the dirt by his hair and flipped him over on his back. Lex lay face-up and motionless, a physically transfigured man whose red veined eyes stared back, devoid of white. Lex's breath blew hot, foul vapors into the cold air.

"Why shouldn't I break your neck right now?" Attila snarled at an all-too-familiar sight.

Nicholas Bradley walked deliberately toward the man who had as recently as the previous night offered him a dish of ice cream. Lex was the man who had spoken encouragingly to Nicholas about studying genetics. This person, thought Nicholas, had become another creature within a span of twenty-four hours.

Lex spoke feverishly. His shaky finger leveled toward Nicholas.

"He's making me sick. They're all making me sick. They're trying to kill me. Exterminators! Altered Humans, demons! Adele? Help me, Adele! They're evil," Lex alternately accused the children and appealed to his wife.

Aaron retrieved Lex's launcher from the roof and held its long neck, examining its lethal potential. Undaunted, Ildiko took a position next to her father, who now controlled Lex with a foot leveraged against the man's throat.

Aditiya, Cynthia, and Esther quietly regarded the scene and couldn't imagine the circumstances. At the same time, they had intuited Aaron's thoughts of extreme danger and the man's wild hallucinations.

Sonny began to chant an ancient Vedic prayer. Lex pulled himself into a tight fetal position and Attila released him. CC moved quickly from her mother's arms to stand by her helpless father, now whimpering like a wounded animal resolved to its fate. The children joined Sonny's invocation. A few minutes later, their vibration dissipated the man's pain and anguish. Lex Collins ceased to live.

The children drew close to CC and held her. They touched her arms and hugged, while some softly chanted. Attila and Connor similarly moved alongside Adele, who stood listlessly next to the lifeless body of a man she had once loved. Her husband's contorted face was now a frozen mask of terror. Connor gently closed his brother's eyes, a mirror of vacant humanity.

With a light breeze came tossed dried leaves that crumbled in the wind. Chocolate Lady sauntered behind Adele and nuzzled her distraught mistress. Adele's gaze remained temporarily transfixed upon Lex's expression and then she moved quickly away, without touching the body. Chocolate Lady reared high and came crashing down, pawing furiously, stomping and tearing the man's remains to pieces. The other horses neighed frantically then quieted as Attila pulled Chocolate Lady away.

Connor bowed his head and prayed silently beside Lex's mutilated corpse. The children joined in the ritual of contrition, forming an impromptu semi-circle around the grief-stricken brother.

Despite his small stature and age, Aditiya stepped forward with insight meant for the moment. He spoke softly to reassure Connor that his brother had passed safely through the vibrational veil into another place.

"He has no pain. He is in a better place to be healed," Aditiya shared.

"If I hadn't heard my mother's warning, I wouldn't have known," a circumspect Aaron remarked to Attila.

"Your mother? You mean Rachel?" Attila asked.

"No, my birth mother. She touched my back and called my name. I knew something was wrong," he answered.

"I was split second off from getting within range. I would have been too late," Attila acknowledged. "You saved everyone, Aaron."

Pendergrass security forces and the coroner met at the school. An entourage quietly walked back toward the Pendergrass home with horses in tow. There were no more tears. Death and violence were not strangers.

Nicholas and Cynthia walked on either side of Esther, who seemed the most unsettled. It was apparent that she felt estranged.

How did everyone else know how to chant in that language? How did that happen? Esther thought to herself.

It similarly occurred to Attila that Adele had first anticipated a crisis.

"How did you know, Adele?" he asked tentatively as they walked.

"I just knew," she answered. "I could feel Lex's craziness, his intentions. He's never visited that schoolhouse once. He's never shown interest. I don't even know what made me want to go there since this morning. Oh God," she said softly, "I think I've known something was wrong for a long time."

Morgan Pendergrass received the news, held his wife's hand, and gently gave her the upshot of the day's events.

"Lex turned quickly. Genetically compromised people will do the same. This is what we can expect in the next wave, Angela. It's beginning to look like a viral infection reacting to a powerful antibiotic. Our grandchild and her friends are the antibiotics. Each successive dose of blue lights has a cumulative effect; you can see the horrific results," Morgan spoke with gravitas. "There are worldwide reports of migrations moving toward civilized points. What happened to Lex is spreading like wildfire all over the world.

"That's the bad news. The good news is that Green and I have an idea. I take that back. That midget mathematician Amar Nishant figured it and we've found his theories on track," Morgan's tone turned optimistic.

"What is it?" Angela tested.

"There may be a way to channel this phenomenon via the damaged geomagnetic grid. It's the field that acts as a bio-magnetic connection to our cells. I'm betting on an idea that involves the Allegheny mountain range that has a high density of crystallite that can act as a powerful medium for this energy that requires a wider distribution. We might expedite this process...perhaps change marginal survivors the right way and quickly identify those that are lost to us. But I'm wondering how it works with a billion people on the planet?"

"Billions," Angela corrected. "We have to sort billions of people."

"No dear. Most of the planet's population is gone," Morgan said gently as he stroked his wife's trembling hand.

"I'm going to arrange for Lex's burial tomorrow," Angela changed directions. "Let's not try to explain anything just yet," she suggested. "Let Connor, Caroline, and Adele mourn."

"Mourn what?" Morgan said with undisguised contempt for Lex Collins. Then he spat.

Connor Collins, in fact, wasted no time mourning the monster he once knew as his brother. He did wonder how it came about that the children's forces sickened a good man. Could it be possible that they had actually caused his transformation and death? Were his brother's final death threats justified? He'd never hurt anyone, supposed Connor.

"No," stated Meredith Green when Connor asked her opinion at work the following day. "He wasn't as innocent as you thought."

It had not taken Dr. Green long to investigate Lex's life and work when prompted by Morgan. Lex Collins' research involved data analytics. The trail of his concern always led back to Caroline's blood work entered periodically. Every six months, Lex had re-entered skewed blood work to falsely reflect his paternity.

"It meant your brother was hiding plenty," Meredith clarified with a clinical air. "It doesn't distort all of our work. On the positive side, it demonstrates a psychological weakness that CC escaped. Caroline might not be the gifted child she is if it hadn't been for Lex's substituting his sperm with yours. As your offspring, she was spared, Connor."

Connor excused himself and threw up in the bathroom. When he returned, he tried to make sense of things.

"You were saying, Meredith?" Connor asked in as calm a manner as possible.

"The children's powers may be able to pinpoint duplicity that had exponentially exploded into a physical illness so dire as to make a person go mad with guilt. Without a blip from the nanobots in his bloodstream, criminal intent or past crimes were identified. Lex's anxiety grew with this contact within the group. It finally sparked an unidentified illness. Lex may have died sick with guilt," Meredith proposed.

"Who else knows I'm the father?" Connor suddenly asked.

"I'm not sure. I know Morgan knows; he told me. I'd bet Angela and Adele know, of course. Whoever you've shared it with, I suppose."

"Lex always seemed more interested in CC as a specimen than a child. It makes sense now," Connor said quietly. "It's probably the reason Adele cut Lex off from information. Intuitively, she didn't trust him. I know that she was unhappy with Lex's preoccupation with tracking CC's stats. My question is how he could have moved into the category of murderer?"

"He exhibited a base survival mechanism to attack that which was threatening his reputation," Meredith replied. "For a long while, he kept his most basic impulses under control. The children's effect somehow exacerbated a frail psyche gradually, and then acutely. The last dosage was too much for his body to handle. He grew physically drained and mentally insane."

"Are you kidding? Lex's lapses were hardly akin to someone like Clifton Brown's. Where is this moral line? Lex never killed or hurt anyone," Connor argued.

"Lex suffered guilt that exponentially turned on him. It's a combination of events. Why do you think we call it dis-ease? The levels of guilt grew with years of compound interest. Everyone has a tipping point. Without intervention, he imploded. Most probably its effects were heightened by proximity," Meredith attempted to make sense from a case study of one.

"There are redemptive options?" Connor theorized.

"I'd say so. Absolutely. The people in these parts and throughout the Confederation are less likely to carry guilt. They've been working to survive and thrive for nearly two decades and practice discipline within a spiritual-centered community. They have constructive outlets for their anxiety. You can't go through hell and come out the other end without some humility and a personal strategy. A collective sense of what lies just across Confederation boundaries reminds them of what they might have forfeited if not for their values and good fortune.

"Weakness knows no nationality. Yet, certain cultural rituals may offset damage. Your brother's duplicity and psychological illness was somewhat insulated by an edifying environmental influence. The Pendergrass household is faith-based; the family practices an elevated work ethic, and a community of the same mindset surrounds and buffers them. Faith, discipline and moral aptitude could ultimately not offset Lex's betrayal. I'd say he never felt deserving of trust or love since December of 2054. Day after day, Lex destroyed himself with guilt until the blue lights broke all vestiges of false design."

"What should I say to Adele about being CC's father? Help me out here, Meredith. How do I approach Caroline?"

"You haven't spoken about it?" Meredith asked with surprise.

"Just found out, Meredith. Didn't have a clue until you told me a few minutes ago."

"Well, shit!"

"Adele and I have to figure this out. I've got Rachel to think about, too. The most important person is Caroline. I do love her so much," Connor stated his intentions. "If any of us expect to have a future, I'm going to have to take an active part in being on the front lines of this thing. When I saw that launcher aimed at the school, it changed me. There was nothing theoretical about the way I was too dazed to act. That moment required no lab work. The response needed to save others completely escaped my skill sets. I hated that. If I need to learn how to shoot bastards that kill children, I'm going to learn. Attila is right. We have to move," he said angrily.

Connor left the lab without saying goodbye to anyone.

* * *

"I know, I know. We found out about Lex last night," Morgan answered Connor matter–of–factly. "Adele knew about Lex's actions from an internal investigation she authorized."

Connor sat down and considered his second shock of the day.

"Aren't we going to need an explanation for my brother's intention to blow up everyone's children...at school?"

"They're all bright. They're scientists and military people. They've all seen worse," Morgan narrowed his eyes. "The kids? They already intuit the situation. The Nishants and Tsin-hang came directly to us and offered their condolences. We all get it. We're living in a world of a whole lot of crazy but we also have a whole lot of tolerance, too."

"I just don't want them to be offended," Connor tried to explain. Morgan spat out his drink with gurgled profanity.

"Offended? Where'd you dig up that old saw? Must have found it wrapped up in your first girlfriend's sorority shirt. Attila and Tsin-hang aren't offended, princess. These guys were witness to the horrors of the EMP consequences on their families, their friends, and the greater populace. Tsin-hang anguished horribly that they couldn't feed people fast or well enough. He witnessed seas of corpses feeding seagulls in the water and his countrymen chomping on each other in port. The entire Chinese naval shipping corps finally shipped out and never returned. Tsin-hang's perspective doesn't lend itself to your tender sensibilities.

"Attila fought bitter battles on five fronts. He describes it as desperate as anything he'd ever studied in warfare. Children were forced to the front of enemy lines. Some were buried to their necks across the plains so that the military couldn't move in equipment. Half of them were already dead. By the time the children were dug out, the enemy had moved beyond reach. They saved the children only to have most survivors institutionalized for life.

"Women were nothing but bait. When the Hungarians moved in to free women tied to trees, and remove some hanging dead from tree limbs, the men in hiding shot the good Samaritans where they stood. Like cunning starved jackals, semi-humans slaughtered without leniency. Those that survived with their equilibrium intact were saved only after the most ruthless military objectives intervened with long hard campaigns. You don't have to worry your little head about offending anyone. You better think how we're going to go into the interior and fix things. By comparison, Lex was a pussycat."

"You think everyone is willing to march into hopelessness?" Connor imagined the horrors.

Morgan walked slowly and opened a leaded pane window to allow fresh, cold air to fill the room. He noted several cracks in two of the window's panels.

"Of course. It's called duty. It'll take us some years to do this correctly, however. We have to build an experienced military. Attila is invaluable to that end. Our people are tough and they'll recognize their responsibility to restore law and order. The only question I have is to whom do I trust this leadership? I'm hoping I hear your 'yes', Connor Collins."

Connor couldn't imagine himself in Morgan Pendergrass' shoes. He measured himself an unlikely candidate in every way. He did, however, recognize a rhetorical question when he heard one.

"I came in here to tell you that Caroline is my daughter. That my brother...."

"Yes or no?" Morgan ignored Connor's sidetrack.

"Yes," Connor replied.

Morgan closed the window and pulled the worn, sun-bleached curtains away to invite the full spectrum of the sunset's crimson hues to filter inside.

"You'll take over this project as of today," Morgan clapped his hands.

"No."

"That was fast."

"I'm here and I'll take over when the time comes. You're not going to get to kick back one minute. In fact, we've got you scheduled for surgery next week. You're going to be kicking ass until you're 130, Morgan. That is, if you don't get murdered first for your insults."

"Lord, Connor. I'm already renewed, restored, and re-fitted up my ass and back again. This is as good as she gets."

"We're going to amplify everything. Eyes, motor skills, neurological pathways, memory, your manners..." Connor encouraged.

"Those procedures aren't safe yet. And there's not enough needles or chemicals in the world to make me want to be any more polite," Morgan said dismissively.

"The Hungarians and Australians are way ahead of us. Attila is going to get his back fixed with a whole new system. See you in the Annex next week. I'm getting work done, too." Connor paused at the door. "You knew about the lab switch this entire time?" Connor asked.

"Nope. Found out from Reid last night. I told you. He had a hunch that panned out."

"Adele? She knows!" he repeated strangely.

"Are you okay, Connor? Yes. She knows. Reid reported to her first. Get a hold of yourself, son. You've a wonderful daughter. We're all grownups here."

"Thank you, Morgan. It's just a shock. I suppose for you, too?"

"I've always thought of you as my son. You and Adele figure the rest. You've been close friends for many years. I know she's going to be fine. Your Rachel will, too. Time to move forward."

"Caroline? What will she think?"

"Caroline knows it all. Haven't you noticed that we're playing catch up to a six-year-old?"

Part II

Chapter XXVI

Confrontations

Thursday, May 15, 2070

*I*n ten years, the expected progress for the international consortium of scientists to harness the powers that lay within the 'circle' of empowered teenagers had yet to meet expectations. There had, however, been significant changes on the Confederation's outskirts, a microcosm of the human predicament.

Formerly diffused and diverse populations had collectively focused attention upon the lights, crops, and hums of civilization that lay in the Confederation's interior. Frenetic offspring of former Americans had become more aggressive and disoriented with each generation of social neglect that grew with incessant exposure to leaking environmental magnetic fields. It was irrefutable that DNA single and double strand breaks in human brain cells had become commonplace. Brain cells, unable to divide, repair, or replace themselves, were part of the endless cycle of cellular damage that resulted in a plethora of neurodegenerative diseases. Among a host of cellular threats were moto neurons damaged by the myelinated nerve fibers that were particularly vulnerable to magnetic fields. There was long-lasting DNA damage, chromosomal conformational changes, and cancers initiated by damage to a cell's genome. The aftereffects of erratic electromagnetic fields on DNA lingered painfully with no forthcoming solutions in sight. No one could explain the reasons that DNA integrity remained stable in the bloodlines of those that had emerged from the EMP disasters relatively intact.

The former Northern, Central, and Eastern European territories had made a dramatic decision concerning the unabated threats of wild gangs, disease, and ignorance that had bred and spread too fast for containment. Their struggles against migrations swelled with each new generation of altered humans. It ended with the cruel decision to massacre any human collective within one hundred miles of civilized borders. Women and children, the human shields of crudely equipped males, were the first victims. Wave after wave of primitive frenzied factions moved senselessly, overwhelming border settlements squeezed between chaos and civilization. The Hungarians withdrew their armies; the Scandinavians and the UK withdrew their naval deployments. There was no dissenting discussion about the innocent dying with those that meant to destroy the last bastions of civilization.

Hungarian artillery rained for 24 hours on a cold December morning until a hundred-mile swath of blistered ground marked the demarcation between cultivated territories and the 'crazies' throughout the continent.

Spybots were dropped on all borders, airborne drones reported heat traces; within moments of targeting, ground troops and drones blasted entire urban areas. Sane humans who were trapped stayed trapped. Reasonable survivors, concluded the civilized world, would have found a way to indicate peaceful intentions, plan an escape or flag help. After many years of search and rescue, it was agreed that the governments had done their best. No one was willing to risk more.

On and off for five years, the migrating hordes were visually reminded of Hungarian and European scorch techniques. It didn't take more than basic animal instinct to avoid charred parched areas that had zero yields with poisoned watering holes developed to deceive intruders.

Tens of thousands had been rescued by sea and air. Tens of thousands had also been stranded and cut off from communication. Hundreds of thousands had died at the hands of merciless gangs. Billions had disappeared from the planet. Most died each successive year from disease, the elements, and starvation. Heat signals indicated that since the EMP, the planet was reduced to approximately somewhere under a billion people, with higher concentrations in Oceania and North America, the tip of south America, Antarctica, and Scandinavia.

Child mortality rates were astronomical. Generations of amoral neurologically and hormonally unbalanced parents had abandoned their offspring to natural forces.

Morgan cautioned Connor Collins not to lose his humanity while trying to protect it. Everyone studied and discussed alternatives to genocide.

The Confederation citizens often referred to their 'Circle of Hope', with faith that Providence had provided a tacit endorsement of right action with the gifted children. Now grown into young adulthood, Confederation citizens remained hopefully expectant as the Circle members had come of age.

In addition, the young adults acquired the advantage of technologically enhanced abilities to cache information with superlative augmented physical properties.

Each Circle member worked diligently within the Research Triangle to develop personal projects, many of which proved insightful. Their IQs proved off the charts. Their health was far outside excellent. Hormonal levels were never anything but even and predictable. Moreover, they showed signs of self-healing.

Aditiya and Sonny eventually developed the theories by which their concerted powers could be funneled and connected to the earth's magnetic network. The circle felt strongly that this was the answer to safeguarding survivors from the magnetic pulses that, no matter how slight, kept generations from functioning properly. Ildiko was able to pinpoint erratic or weakened atmospheric portals; Sonny, Aditiya and Aaron worked together to trace patterns of portal irregularities. With the help of cosmic markers determined by Aditiya, located by Ildiko, and vibrational timing sensed by Sonny, the circle focused its blue light energy on each magnetic anomaly and portal within friendly territories. They were able to plug or patch most of the holes but knew that there were other factors that prevented wholesale genetic recovery.

"We're just using Band-Aids," lamented Aditiya. "We need major surgery to fix the earth's grid."

Caroline thought that if they were allowed to personally move from place to place as a group they could patch the protective field regionally, section by section, leaving a permanent fix in the hostile territories that might connect, reconnect, and heal naturally over time.

Morgan was reluctant to risk the group. Therefore, the best part of field experiments had already been conducted.

Attempts had been made to connect the satellites and drones that passed over the interior as conduits. No matter how funneled the energy on specific targets, the blue-hued energy patterns dissipated. Within twenty-four hours, soft portals opened and shut as the earth breathed its exhaust and once again allowed the solar magnetism to seep back into the atmosphere. Yet, even those few hours of the circle's influence proved to have a positive and lasting effect on the populace. Conversely, those lacking cellular magnetic equilibrium quickly became ill and died within days or weeks, much as Lex Collins had done a decade earlier.

Adele and Attila felt strongly that in the ten-year interim, the unbalanced population had grown exponentially faster and would likely overtake the civilized world.

Morgan insisted that there would be a natural solution that allowed nature to 'take its course'. That stance had worn thin with everyone.

"We ARE nature taking its course, Morgan," protested Meredith Green. "Since when did you get so off course? What happened to the Morgan Expedient? You've lost your mojo. We have feral animals impersonating humans. You're allowing them to survive naturally, feeding on the weakest, stalking sane survivors, burning stockpiles, and raiding farms without the impulse to cultivate themselves or crops. There are going to be natural causalities until we can figure how to reach the remaining good people we cannot ferret out."

"Tell me how you really feel, Meredith," Morgan deadpanned.

"Not a damn joke, Morgan," Meredith flicked a chip across the table.

"Those who could think straight have already gotten out, Morgan. The rest are most likely down in those luxurious survival bunkers, hidden communities, and remote regions offshore hiding from the crazies and the magnetic storms they rightly fear are ongoing. We don't even get a signal from them. We won't. Those bunkers and upscale survival condominiums are hardened and self-sufficient. According to our research, they're geared for a century. The others? How do we know that there are any thriving communities beyond the ones already rescued?

"Meanwhile, our safety buffers are shrinking. You're so frightened of compromising that Circle of young adults that we don't have a chance to see what they can do naturally."

Caroline insisted that Dr. Green was correct.

"We know that without certain stimuli we can't properly understand our capabilities. That comes with direct contact and you know it, Grandpa. You're keeping us in a box. We can't do what we're supposed to do with so much distance between the threat and us. It's time to get our hands dirty."

Adele agreed with Caroline's assessment. She outlined for her father the way it would go.

"Connor, Attila, and a host of experienced men and women will accompany the Circle. Attila has made sure that everyone can handle themselves.

"Texas is in a vulnerable position right now. As much as the Mexicans have been trying to help, the former Californian region has bred a relentless breed. Tribal hierarchies have begun; any kind of organizational framework is a bad sign. Washington State is now protected by Canada. Oregon is lost. Look at the map, Dad!"

Attila weighed in as the argument closed around a very reticent Morgan.

"An important part will be the horses that have nano-transmitters and amped reflexes. We've doubled our strength with these incredible animals. The tech troops should go to Texas and move toward California. Mexican troops have been losing ground without the opportunity to blast. Somebody has got to make a decision. You aren't making one. The governors still defer to you, Morgan."

Morgan said nothing.

Adele's impatience moved into decision making mode.

"Connor and I will pinpoint lasers along the California line from the Pacific. Let the Mexican authorities plant field traps and bots. We also need new prisoners to examine..."

While Morgan worried about the crisis, he did nothing. Adele, Connor, and Attila took the reins the moment Pendergrass waxed sentimental. He had begun to term the predators 'fellow Americans' in need of medical assistance.

Woo Tsin-hang had helped the Confederation effort, having convinced the Chinese military fishing vessels to post in the NC harbors within a year of his arrival. Within another three years, two hundred former Chinese military vessels joined the Confederation Navy. North Carolina became their permanent home after the Chinese captains vied for Confederation citizenship. "The best place from which to help humanity," Tsin-hang represented.

New generations of men and women trained at the Citadel in Charleston, South Carolina, and the Naval Academy in Annapolis. Confederation technology upgraded ship weaponry as soon as Robert Gant felt confident of the timing and technology.

"I propose taking ten ships toward the Virginia coast, the most logistically compromised area. We'll be able to monitor by sea and air. The horses will have a short distance to travel inland toward the Allegheny Mountains. The Piedmont gives us an advantage. We have no evidence of traces of fossil fuels, batteries, or machinery in use in the areas that we'll target first."

Attila agreed. Morgan, he felt, had become a reluctant man. Keeping his granddaughter safe overwhelmed all other considerations. Moreover, Morgan wanted assurances that innocent people would not be hurt. Such a solution looked unlikely. The Morgan Expedient had all but petered out.

"You've grown a hemorrhaging heart!" Gloria Brackett accused one day. "Get your damn act together. I want those crazies out of my family's future!"

"I can't be responsible for innocent victims," he stammered.

"You've grown sponge balls, Morgan. Give it over to those young adults. And stop calling them kids. Let them get to work." Gloria kicked Morgan hard in the shin. She knew which one to kick.

Attila had trained four thousand troops within eight years. Spring exploded with azaleas, and summer was close behind. "Enough training!" Attila exclaimed one Sunday afternoon. He pushed himself away from the lunch table set on the back porch and anxiously paced. Wooden planks creaked their protest under his heavy stride.

"I want everyone to get it in their heads that I am no tomato plant. No one is going to sniff me out and stick little suckers into me, draining me dry, while I happily congratulate myself of peaceful intentions. To hell with that!"

Connor, Adele, Indu, Amar, Rachel, Tsin-hang, and Angela nodded their heads in agreement.

"Let's move," Adele demanded. She turned her back on her parents as she looked across the farm's lush fields, "I expect you and Connor to have plans on that desk of yours, Dad."

It was agreed that the Confederation would move to eradicate the threat that had stood at their door for too many years.

* * *

It was with sadness that Connor realized that the sweet pieces of life, so carefully fitted since the Darkness, were about to be disrupted. They had existed in an interim bubble of peace and love. He thought of friends that had become so familiar. They would all face danger once more.

Rachel and Connor's child, Edward, had proved as gifted as any of the original Circle. Their little boy's initial power was closest to that of Nicholas Bradley, with a slight twist. Edward would disappear from sight from time to time. Connor laughed to himself; it was most often when the five-year-old was doing something expressly forbidden. Like CC, Edward had a penchant for cookie pinching. Unlike Nicholas, his own guilt often made him invisible. Aaron, who had assumed the role of an older brother, could best sense Edward's whereabouts. Connor imagined the times that Aaron suspended a cookie jar out of Edward's reach; with a confession of wrongdoing, Edward would reappear.

Aaron had matured into a young man of wisdom and compassion. The sounds of his family laughing at mundane happenings gave Connor the greatest of pleasures.

And then there's my other unofficial protege, Nicholas, Connor smiled to himself thoughtfully. *There's a man with extraordinary equestrian and martial arts skills. Ildiko is as brave a fighter as her father. I'm not sure if she's a brilliant strategist or she actually sees what's coming. Caroline? So calm, so willing, and so detailed. She's the emotional glue...saying little until it needs to be said. Aditiya and Sonny are wildcards. You think you know their range until they surprise us with more. All of their lives will be changed forever.* Connor surveyed the fields, contemplating the upcoming challenges.

* * *

There were sixteen stables of twenty stalls per stable situated on fifty acres on the far side of the farm. The troops jumped, ran endurance steeplechases and conducted ambitious dressage drills, cooperating with drones and transmuting solocopters from miles above. With their powerful infrared cameras, the drones could pinpoint targets by tracking heat traces in lieu of direct visuals. If required, they connected to Confederation surveillance orbiting. Lifelike bots were meant to challenge the horses and rustic settings. Solocopters were individually manned and could transition from airborne to ground, mechanically folding and repositioning the hardware. Able to float to the ground without need of a runway, their quiet maneuvers further tested the troops' ability to avoid ambushes. Attila did not presume the impossibility of a sophisticated enemy.

Drones identified Confederation Hussar signatures via implanted neural sensors that pinged markers to discern friend from foe. Without a six-inch gap from an opponent, Confederation drones ran the risk of collateral damage. Hand to hand combat was, therefore, an integral part of the training program. It was Attila that passed along his weaponry skills to countless young men and women; the same group became proficient in vaulting while operating smart crossbows. For the challenge, Aaron and Nicholas had teamed their unusual talents. Aaron would suspend and propel Nicholas as high as thirty feet to attack from airborne positions. Sonny added an ability to disrupt the harmonic fields of enemies. Practicing frequency skills, however, had mistakenly caused a few days of vomiting and arguing amongst the Confederation trainees until Sonny got the hang of it.

Within five years, the cadres were able to clean out opposing mock forces on field, within forests, through treacherous waters, and in urban settings with a 96% success rate. Four distinct seasons gave Confederation trainees time to experiment with natural conditions inclusive of mudslides, snow, ice-covered rock, and blistering heat.

It was decided to develop and test a lightweight protective covering for riders and mounts that could render them invisible and emit indigenous frequencies that offset auditory signals. Aditiya pointed out that such protection would be required for the more extreme electrical magnetic pulses in the Northern states. "If we make it that far, we can also expect intensified resistance."

"It's unreasonable to think that we won't run into military challenges," Connor began. "Our primary mission, however, is to see what we can do to permanently correct the erratic magnetic force field that protects earth. We'll initially focus on areas that are relatively close to safety. If moderately successful, scientists will explore the ways to reverse the cellular damage. Our priority is to do what we have to do to ensure the field's restoration."

The time had come for Confederation troops to merge on the Pendergrass farms in the late spring of 2070. They would move in a months' time. An early spring thaw was predicted for the Allegheny Mountains. Final practice drills were scheduled across North and South Carolina.

Gloria Brackett and her Tons of Fun ran their maneuvers on the Pendergrass estate with refurbished antique tanks that had been maintained with loving care. The club members happily compared their functionality to the later multi-million-dollar tanks made with silicon carbide chips instead of silicon ones. The 21st century equipment moved after the EMP but failed to consistently or accurately discharge the lasers. Brackett liked artillery. "Technology that depends on outside support is not for me! Aim and fire! That's what we know and that's what we'll do!" she declared.

Gloria's field strategy was simple. "When all else fails, blow some shells," she would yell the club's mantra.

Attila ignored the old timers. Gloria Brackett noticed. Tanks often sat idle on the field watching the perfectly synchronized teams of soldiers. Gloria pined for more action, having imagined Tons of Fun leading the charge.

"She's been gnawing at the bit for her whole life," Morgan explained to Attila, charged with Gloria's management.

Gloria stuck her head out the top of her tank a week into final drills.

"When are we going to get some action, Attila?" she yelled over the drones that whizzed by, shooting blanks toward the mounts. Gloria had no use for alternative transmissions. She loved the sound of her voice.

Attila ignored her.

"Morgan has turned into a little girl," she continued to bellow. "Time to poop or get off the pot, commander Attila Meszaros! We're goin' to war or just playing around for another year? Let my Tons of Fun into a few of these maneuvers!" she demanded with a fist that waved an angry protest in the air.

Attila said nothing. Gloria Brackett was not a person to let a little silence stop her.

"We should be running in front!" Brackett repeated.

"A... little... patience... please?" Attila turned slowly, with punctuated exasperation.

"I got everything but duct tape keeping this body together. I'm clean out of patience. I've got to get some kind of action. It's hot as Hades in here," Gloria screamed to the heavens.

Attila moved his horse next to Brackett's tank.

"We haven't set up the theaters for your group," Attila reminded her. "We'll need the tanks to blast through in the event of fort-like metal or cement structures. In Turkey, there were embankments of automobiles. We were attacked from atop buildings and from bunkers made of rubble. Tanks would have been perfect to clean out a path for the horses so I appreciate this great addition of your equipment. It's just not timely to run your drills today," Attila placated.

Gloria's eye's narrowed suspiciously.

"What...are...you...saying?" Gloria mimicked Attila's warning.

"I asked you to wait, Madame. You're not scheduled until next week. I asked your patience and you said that your group wanted to observe. Here we are. Not ready for the tanks. Never were," Attila finished testily.

Gloria turned and slid back inside her enhanced FV4202 55-ton Centurion with a reclined driver position and mantle-less gun mounting. Computer sensors situated in the turret's casing offset the necessity for a gunner but could run manually, too. With its own infrared system, the turret had a large searchlight inside an armored box with a range of 2.5 kilometers. As Attila surveyed the field maneuvers approvingly, he heard the rapid turn of the tank's gun whir into action.

"NO, Gloria!" Attila warned.

...which came too late. It took another two seconds for the decimated drone to finish its descent thirty yards in front of the tank and separate in as many pieces.

"What the hell are you shooting our drones for? Are you crazy? I can't even hear right now..." Attila screamed after a string of Hungarian profanities.

The engine turned off with a heavy metallic belch. Gloria popped out the top once more and snarled, "Nobody gave you permission to target my tank. You keep those damn drones away from my team or I'll shoot 'em all."

"It's a drill!" Attila pleaded on behalf of reason.

"Drill somewhere else. Don't even pretend to practice within range of my babies."

"You're acting crazy," Attila accused.

"Go tattle to Morgan. Tell him to put it on my tab. My sensors will shoot anything that locks in on me."

"You shot manually. Nothing locked," Attila seethed.

"Could be. I'm just sayin' that these tanks are juiced. Impressed?"

"Madame Brackett, next time you might consider just letting me know how clever you are without blowing expensive equipment along with my eardrums."

"You'd best learn the element of surprise, sonny boy. Trot off now with your prancing ponies, sabers, and little bows and arrows. We'll be back at my farm shooting stuff to smithereens! Tons of Fun...rolling out!" Gloria Brackett yelled directly toward Attila. Eight of the Tons of Fun corps turned sequentially and backed off of the mock battlefield without regard for the mechanical target bots caught, trampled, and spat by the tanks' massive treads.

Nicholas and Caroline were so amused at the exchange between the Texan and the Hungarian that the Circle, scattered throughout the fields, began to laugh in unison. Tuned in to each other, the friends were mutually affected by sensations, reactions, and spirits. Private jokes no longer existed.

"Somebody kindly retrieve Ms. Brackett personally and tell her it's their turn to work maneuvers," telepathed Attila. "We don't want to lose her goodwill."

"I'll do it," Nicholas understood and spurred his massive Hungarian Warm Blood.

There were many occasions when words failed to reach the lips of those residing on the Pendergrass Estate. During the mock battle, seamless communications occurred between most of those on site. When Adele practiced, she, too, was able to intuit everyone's thoughts. With the exception of Esther and the Tons of Fun group, telepathy had become the preferred mode of communication.

What Esther lacked in telepathic skills, she made up for as a talented strategist who unofficially tested the limits of tolerance. Esther regarded translators with disdain. For those less inclined, neural implants were used. Esther refused the implants that similarly offered brain-net connectivity. Field assignments began to reflect her limitations and she bitterly complained despite the available options.

"Of course you're frustrated because you can't communicate!" Attila defended without hiding his growing frustration. "What the hell do you think we're doing? You refuse to act as part of this team meant to fight hostiles. Get amped!"

"You people are all assholes," she screamed back. "I'm sick of having to ask all the time what's going on."

In the unenviable capacity of placatory boyfriend, Nicholas tried to address Esther's concerns.

"No one knows exactly when they're not speaking aloud, Esther. It just turns out that it's easier to telepath during the heat of the action. We're not trying to be secretive. It's much more effective – an automatic response," Nicholas once again tried to calm a woman who refused to cooperate.

Esther was not interested in that which might prove easier for the group. She was unable to intuit or receive the signals that others took for granted. Her unreasonable ire had grown into bitterness. She believed she had been robbed of talents and, therefore, opportunities.

"The only way I know you all are communicating at all is because you special people forget to use hand signals. There are thousands of others around who may not hear your thoughts. Ever think of that? How do you expect to lead without some damn signal or Attila's ridiculous whistling directives for the horses? If I hadn't memorized those toots and hoots, I'd be caught constantly out of formation.

"Please, Esther. We've been running the same maneuvers for years. You still need a PM audio or text? They were always crude emergency measures. You refused neural transmitters. Most everyone picks up our thoughts with those receptors, intuitively or telepathically. What are we supposed to do?" Nicholas appealed once more.

Esther found herself frustrated for more reasons than field signals. She felt excluded, lonely, and a minor player in life's theatre. Cynthia, noted her sister, no longer followed her lead. Having had the good fortune to be exposed to the Circle's influences at a much younger age, Cynthia had assimilated talents more easily than most. Esther felt as if she was the only one with a dearth of talent.

Complaints about Esther's temper tantrums piled high. It was left to Connor to sort. Attila's solution was to remove her completely from Confederation duties of any sort.

"You're fully capable of being an asset to our efforts even if you haven't the same capabilities as your sister. You can be sure of that," Connor spoke optimistically to Esther over lunch at the Research Triangle.

"That's not true," she corrected. "I'm not sure of anything. I'm not even sure what my boyfriend thinks. I do know what he's not thinking. He certainly isn't thinking about marriage. He won't even talk about it. I'm almost 30. He's a few years younger but that's not the issue. He's lost interest in me, just like everyone else."

Connor felt ill-equipped to speak to a grown woman about a personal relationship that had run its course. He tried to draft Rachel to have a word with Esther about appropriate behaviors.

"You're around the same age. Doesn't seem like it, but Esther can relate better to you," Connor suggested carefully to his wife.

"Not doing it. She hates me," Rachel said evenly.

"Esther is part our family."

"The nasty part," Rachel corrected. "She's always creating a problem, discussing something that's been a problem, or gritting her teeth because we haven't recognized a problem. The worst approach is trying to help solve these vague, manufactured problems. It leaves her without anything to be problematic about!" Rachel ranted in one breath.

Connor suggested a solution. "Maybe she needs to get into town and get involved with other people? Perhaps get her mind off of herself and a failing relationship?"

"I'm ahead of you. I introduced her to Elle and Lisa's aunt. They invited Esther to lunch and insisted that I go, too. It wasn't a minor disaster. Esther found ways to insult everyone. Elle called her out on her bad conduct and Esther lost all traces of decorum that begun with a long nonsensical rant. The security bot on site responded with a directive to amend her tone and volume. Esther excused herself to go to the bathroom by way of kicking the bot and swiping Elle's head with her elbow. Elle was still seated with a fork of food in her mouth. Elle is no slouch; she decked Esther so hard we all felt it. Esther began to rise off the floor and Elle kicked her right back down. Elle tells Esther to apologize to everyone for making a scene and we all received a citation from the security bot."

"Wow," Connor sighed disbelief.

"I'm not going another round with that woman. Doesn't that knife between her teeth tell you anything?"

Connor tried to convince his wife to give it another try. "We can't have a loose cannon like Esther on this mission. I'll give you an example of our problem that came to a head recently.

"As you know, we will need to feed ourselves on the move. Supplies could easily be cut off from the coast. Hunting wasn't a problem for Esther; she did a great job. But when it came to preparing the game she sat on the ground and whistled our horse signals to upset the tethered mounts. Attila was furious."

"Let me guess. She's too good to skin and cook?" Rachel suggested the problem.

"It was the way she took out her protest on the animals that stunned us. Hers was a butcher job and I don't mean any half-sane butcher. She let the rabbit scream while she hacked. We corrected her. No one, however, believed her cruelty was a mistake."

"You want me to have chitchat with the animal torturer?" Rachel asked incredulously.

"Can you just give it a try tonight after dinner? We've got to come to a decision about who'll be traveling. That first group has got to have the entire Circle in it. If we can't count on Esther, she can't go. If she isn't needed...that's one thing. Being a destructive element or a distraction is another. Before I have to tell her that she'll be staying behind, it would be the right thing if we've done our best to bring her around."

"Only for you, handsome," Rachel smiled. "I'll catch her tonight after dinner. Make sure everyone leaves us alone."

"You're amazing. I'm so in love with you."

They kissed and wordlessly held each other for a few minutes.

"You're worried? What's wrong?" Rachel felt her husband's unease. He had held her too tightly.

"We've got plans to leave North Carolina in two weeks. You're coming with us. I wasn't going to allow it because we need a good group to remain here. There's Edward to think about but Angela convinced me that he's in good hands."

"What changed your mind?"

"According to Caroline, you're critical to the mission."

"You don't say. I like that. Did CC draw the outcome?"

"I figure that she'll offer her impressions if they're relevant. If things weren't on course, she'd certainly speak up. It was Caroline that insisted that you be part of the mission. Sonny says he wants to teach you some new chants. As always, my wife is in demand."

"I just can't go. Edward needs me. What if something happened to us both? Caroline has to be more specific to convince me of leaving our son without parents."

"I agree. There's nothing that needs you that can't happen within hours of our delivering you on site. She'll understand. But I'll miss you by my side."

Toward the meal's conclusion, Rachel pinged Esther, who maintained a tight grip on Nicholas's hand under the table. He looked relieved when Esther spoke to her PM.

"*Sure. Where?*" Esther answered Rachel's invitation to meet.

"*Conservatory. Ten minutes.*"

The women met in the music room's corner by the piano. Esther played a few notes lightly and then ran her thumb roughly across the length of the keyboard.

"No one ever took the time to teach me an instrument. Wish I could play."

"With neuro-transmitters, you'd learn in no time," Rachel encouraged.

"I'm not going to let those freaks stick needles in my head," she snapped. "Look what happened to everyone with those frequency chips. No way."

"Mind if we talk?" Rachel smiled as an elder sister might and advanced as smoothly as possible.

Esther sneered knowingly and bristled like a cornered cat. "Why? Can't you hear what I'm feeling or something like that?"

"I don't need special powers to hear or feel what's going on. Not even the lizards outside can miss that vibe. You're annoyed. Let's see if we can sort whatever issues are troubling you the old fashioned way?"

"What's that mean? You're going to share your wisdom?" Esther mocked. "Wise, wise Rachel. How does it feel to be so mature?"

"You know what, Esther? I know I have a long way to go, because I sure feel guilty about how awful I react to you sometimes."

"What do you mean?"

"I'm ashamed at the way I see you right now. It seems you're angry and frustrated all the time. I had the best intentions to see if we could talk about what's upsetting you. Now, I can't help but want to get out of here. You're eternally spinning yourself a victim sweater, holding a pity party, or creating the nasty topic du jour.

"Each week, I find myself listening to your gossip. You force me to process words and ideas that I reject in ordinary circumstances. All those fabrications you conjure force me to clarify intentions conveyed by your skewed interpretations of meaningless exchanges. You go your way and I'm left to clean up emotional puke. Imagined slights turn into collections of injustices.

"In the beginning, I'd just say to others, 'she didn't mean it that way' or 'I'm sure you misunderstood' or 'she's stressed right now'. I've now been asked to speak with you! Is it possible to make things better around here by a civil discussion?

No, I figure it's easier to call your game. Just like the bot...just like poor Elle. You prefer an attack!"

"Don't hold back. What game are you going to call?" Esther smirked.

"We can do without the drama and temper tantrums. What makes you unable to respond in kind to those who care about your welfare? You seem to purposefully disrupt any assemblage, distrust everyone's representations, and manage to concoct contentious topics out of thin air. As Attila puts it, you manage to 'spit in everyone's soup.' I'm sorry. Please forgive me for being so frank. All I want to say is that you might consider that there are alternatives to being a petulant, pea-brained jerk."

"Anything else?"

"Glad you asked. I think Nicholas deserves better than being the Patron Saint of Awkward Behaviors!" Rachel said with disgust.

Esther was overcome with rage. She had watched for ten years the ways in which the beautiful Rachel Collins had wrapped the Pendergrass household around her little finger. When Rachel spoke, everyone listened. Rachel was a great athlete. Rachel had a new research project. Aditiya thought Rachel's designs were brilliant. Rachel could out-swim and out-maneuver most on horseback. Connor adored his wife and managed to say so in public. The Israeli could bake a perfect Southern pecan pie and presented Ildiko with Hungarian retes for her last birthday. Caroline trusted Rachel as a second mother and Nicholas revered Rachel as a smart, sympathetic friend. Sonny worked with Rachel on the cleansing chants and entrusted her to new amalgamations. It was, to Esther's mind, a nonstop Rachel B. Collins fan club.

These thoughts gained momentum until Esther's hand flew impulsively toward Rachel's face to slap the mouth still speaking its owner's mind. The offending hand, however, froze and remained motionless mid-course. Rachel stared unbelievingly at the aborted assault inches from her face.

Subsequently, Esther's body was catapulted upward toward the ceiling, her hand still frozen in position. Screaming protests set off alarms.

"Conservatory, security red alert," warned the security monitor. Esther's wail sounded throughout the home.

A human starfish, Esther was discovered by the household pinned flat against the ceiling with arms and legs stretched wide. A panicked face peered down upon Aaron's own; he examined the situation from the doorway.

"You? Again?" Esther screamed at Aaron.

Nicholas entered the room, pulling Aaron with him. "Get Esther off the ceiling, Aaron!"

Aaron gently allowed Esther to return to the floor feet first.

"What the hell did you do that for?" Esther demanded of Aaron.

"I'd like to know, too," Nicholas joined.

Aaron yelled his objections as Esther moved menacingly toward him. "You're not a person to be trusted, Esther. For the record, I said that out loud. If you don't understand what I mean, I'll translate: You're dangerous!"

Cynthia arrived on the scene and worked her way around the horrified group that had gathered. Just as Esther faced off with Aaron, Cynthia intervened.

"What have you done now?" Cynthia's long-simmering embarrassment was clear.

"Oh, right. Excuse me, exalted ones, great Circle of love and light. Aaron, the altar boy, attacked me," Esther spat back. "Clearly, it's impossible for Aaron to have glued me to the ceiling without reason. Don't bother to ask me what happened, sister."

"What happened, Esther?" It was Morgan and Angela who now stood by her. "We want to get to the bottom of this," Morgan assured her.

"Rachel and her condescension are at the bottom of this. She insulted me. She's the one who asked me to confide in her, work things out. She lures me in here just to insult me." Esther felt the room close in about her. "I'm excluded. Period. No one wants me on the research projects. No one tells me what the hell is going on during the war games. I asked for the big Frisian and I get some low-grade Pinto because Attila says the Frisian doesn't want me. What does that even mean? I should be on the front line with Nicholas. Attila tells me to help the newcomers without asking my preferences. When Angela asks what I want to do on my birthday, I say 'absolutely nothing' and that's exactly what I got. No one even bothered to figure what kind of cake I prefer. I hate chocolate!

"I've got no super-duper uber powers. That makes me the only one without a skill. Why not just say it? Tell me to get out, to leave. Go ahead..."

Hers was a rave with little connective tissue. Morgan was provoked at the flying profanities and insults meant to describe his home and family that had welcomed and nurtured Esther for more than a decade.

"Finished, Missy?" Morgan demanded. "Your long-winded tirade seems pretty simple by half. It's a message of extreme disgruntlement and entitlement, at the base of which may be some boyfriend trouble. This, too, will pass. Like a kidney stone... but it'll pass," Morgan attempted his brand of guidance.

"Screw you!" she screamed.

"Don't flatter him, dear," Angela tried her best to diffuse the situation. It had the opposite effect.

"I'm sick of all of you," Esther stood tearfully with her head turning toward a window; she looked longingly past her audience as if trying to draw breath beyond the closed glass windows.

Nicholas took Esther's hand in his and guided her through the parting crowd, from the crude scene playing out as high theatre. His hand rested assuredly on her trembling shoulder as they moved into a sunroom through an attached green-house. Gardenias were in bloom; Nicholas selected one for Esther and placed it upon the small table between them. They sat for a few minutes until Nicholas broke the silence.

"Speak to me. This isn't who you are," Nicholas implored.

He waited patiently for the girl he met so many years ago on a pirate's freighter to reappear. He examined the face that had altered with a declining disposition. Once attractive and bright, a furrowed line between her brows deepened with its owner's discontent. A once glowing, clear complexion had become sallow. Once thick and shiny, her hair had thinned by an incessant habit of pulling and twisting its strands.

Esther fondled and smelled the gardenia selected from a group of plants that was grown, per her request, many years ago as a teenager. Angela encouraged each visitor to select his or her favorite ornamental plant to propagate. Everyone agreed that Esther's gardenias were extraordinary and the pride of the lot.

"I couldn't hold it back anymore. I blew it," she admitted. "If there's one power I possess, it's the intuition to read your reluctance to marry an inferior specimen. You're just too nice to say it. Nicholas, you're making me suffer more than any of your prey ever agonized."

She hoped that Nicholas would prove her suspicions wrong. Esther stared into her love's large blue eyes until they moistened with regret. He took his time before answering.

"I loved that part of you that was eager, optimistic, brave and kind. Those wonderful attributes have deteriorated. It's difficult for me to tune into where you are. I've thought about it. You're someone else. You think it's the opposite. It's not. I can't find the girl I used to know...the thoughtful, kind one. Your bitterness is now part of you in every way. Today's Esther taunts horses, ignores the screams of helpless animals, and forces those who would otherwise care about you to contend with your erratic disposition. If you hadn't wanted to use unnecessary physical force against Rachel, Aaron would never have sensed danger. I felt it, too. I just couldn't believe it," Nicholas sorrowfully explained.

Esther crushed the flower in her hand and let it fall to the brick floor. "It's simple to say. Let me say it for you. You don't love me. You don't find me interesting. Maybe you're not so interesting either! Maybe my interests aren't fighting imaginary devil people. I get tired of galloping horses and Pendergrass breakfasts, lunches, and dinners. I'm tired of getting excited about every ritual occasion and laughing at jokes that no one bothers to share. I don't even like the music you play. I'm sick of blue light cults in town groveling around you 'gifted' types all the time. What the hell have the Cary Circle clowns ever actually done that's so amazing? You think plastering a helpless woman on the ceiling is noble? It's pathetic."

For years, Nicholas ignored the impenetrable slippery walls of mire that had built within Esther's mind. Cynthia was the first to distance when Esther bitterly accused her sister of disloyalty.

Nicholas hung his head. He had dreaded this moment. It took time for him to appropriate words for a mind irrevocably blocked to decent intentions.

"Who is she?" Esther finally demanded of Nicholas.

Nicholas remained silent.

"Who is she?" Esther repeated. Veins along her neck burst into blue long streaks, her enraged state firmly escalating. Nicholas was as direct as possible.

"I don't love you enough to marry you; please forgive me if you thought we were committed partners. I've done nothing to lead you on, even if I never looked for another. I promised you nothing. Many times you suggested our future together; each time I said nothing. If your anger has something to do with me, I want to clear it up here and now. We are now in the position to be friends. Nothing more. Nothing less."

"You're wrong there. We're much, much less."

"Esther, our characters can be determined by the way we leave a relationship, not by the way in which we enter it. Loyalty can only be determined when one doesn't stand to benefit from prior expectations or those derived of the relationship. Let's remain loyal friends and not part bitterly."

Nicholas stared at the greenhouse floor covered with shattered door glass left scattered by Esther's furious exit. Before the bot appeared, Nicholas swept the glass along the tiled floor. A large piece glimmered its hiding place and he reached to pick it up. Blood sprang from his fingers. The cut was long and deep.

A fitting departure gift, Esther, he thought.

Wrapped tightly with the bottom of his shirt, Nicholas held his wound and made his way to the kitchen.

"How did that happen?" Angela asked as soon as the PM sent the extent of his injury.

Angela returned with a small tube and examined two sliced fingers. Sonny and Caroline looked on with interest.

"It's healed. It closed. I didn't have time to apply the bond. I'd say I'm confused," she said while replaying the injury report.

Angela's PM related an update as it read Nicholas's status. "*Healed; without bacteria. Prognosis: accelerated rate of healing, no scar tissue.*"

"Ha! I knew it," Sonny smiled. "I've been working on healing mantras. Excellent!"

Nicholas groaned, "You could have worked on the ex-girlfriend mantras and saved me the real wound."

The fingers pulsated with some discomfort, but the skin had smoothly joined without a trace.

"Those healing chants, Sonny? Thanks!" Nicholas added.

The PM updated its report once more. "*Wound: completely healed.*"

"Not all wounds," corrected Nicholas.

Chapter XXVII
Mission Strategies

Tuesday, May 20, 2070

*A*ttila announced that the Confederation troops would travel to Virginia on the Haijian-100, an 8,000-ton, 25-year-old Chinese ship ostensibly constructed as a Marine Surveillance Vessel. It was originally created to ensure the safety of fleets of 1000 to 4000 ton vessels in the South and East China Seas. Refitted to accommodate livestock, medical supplies, and airborne military equipment, the Haijian sat elegantly in the still Wilmington waters. Angela privately referred to it as Morgan's Ark.

No one could be sure of what Attila's scouting militia would find or how long of a campaign could be expected. It was hoped that the Confederation Hussars would be able to situate the Circle in advantageous positions. Theoretically, this could be done by transmitting the energy atop the parts of the crystalline Appalachian Mountain chain and Piedmont regions. Tests justified such locations as having enough crystallite to magnify the force's properties.

Per tradition, key players and planners met in Morgan's sanctuary. Junior Blue had passed, having been fatally bitten and clawed by a wild cougar. CC insisted on saving the canine's line. By Morgan's feet, lay two cloned replacements separated by five years, Bluer and Bluest. Bluest was the more ambitious of the two and stood erect, eyeing the assemblage. Bluer preferred to rest on his side dangerously close to Morgan's chair. Bluer's tail was perpetually bandaged as result of a reluctance to move out of the way of slamming doors, a rolling chair, or an advancing Morgan.

"Who's on first?" Morgan commenced.

"We have the equipment to calculate error margins and adjust any miscalculations on site," began Aditiya. "We have the military reconnaissance to offset surprise attacks if we attract that kind of attention. All I can see is a series of scientific tests by which we can fully assess the powers of the Circle, ascertain how much of an amalgam the Circle has become and whether this melding of power increases with exposure to unknown stimuli. Not insignificantly, we have to develop a plan to assist those who have been generations in hiding," summarized Aditiya. "It's a hell of a field trip... what can I say?"

Sonny had worked with the Nishants for some years investigating vibrational fields. Various experiments indicated that healing chants of choice could be transmitted to what Sonny referred to as the 'cosmic vibrational generator'. When Morgan heard the name, he choked on his drink, barely able to disguise his amusement.

"You want to explain that a little more, son?"

"Our chanting vibrations will use CC's planetary generator – that means Caroline – to offset the extremely low frequencies that have been corresponding to brain waves; these low frequencies have negatively affected behavioral patterns," clarified Sonny. "Man is a bio-cosmic transducer with transmitter and receiver. We are able to train our brain waves to lock on and modulate along the Earth's Universal Magnetic field in a healthy way: our cellular magnetite is just one way this has been done. Since the EMP caused fissures, humans have been affected by extremely low, erratic, and, therefore, disturbing frequencies. Those that seem unaltered were those pockets of communities and individuals who maintained their higher frequencies with a general integrity of thought, word, and deed. They simply have a higher sense of things that ends up protecting them."

"How you figure that?" Morgan asked.

"I speak of prayer, community involvement, productivity, contact with nature, music, and ambitious education as the kinds of practices that helped people from becoming too introverted or narcissistic. With that kind of high-frequency protection, people have been able to offset disease, depression, and other adverse psychoses. In other terms, they made a practice of stretching mentally, physically, and spiritually.

"Post-disaster, some people got to work. They were resilient and made efforts to join forces with like-minded communities. Such joint efforts created positive frequency fields. People were able to read from the same page that took into account a greater purpose. Others went on rampages and eschewed law and order. Both groups propagated their particular frequencies of choice. One was parasitic. The other remained optimistically productive. The first faction devolved into what we might term a natural malevolence. The second grouping tended toward compassion and altruism. One has a low erratic frequency; the other a harmonically complex one," Sonny recapped.

"Okay, okay. One faction is God-centered and the other end is full-blown evil? That's the guts of it, right?" Morgan quipped. "You've got the God notion or you've got the Devil?"

Sonny was thoughtful.

"Most people feel a harmonic visceral urge we sense is possible. For whatever reason, cooperative efforts require a careful balance of disciplines. Beyond physical elements, shouldn't we expect a certain evolutionary spirituality that matures us emotionally? Doesn't that maturity help prepare us for proper use of our full capacities? We're always evolving.

"Do things go wrong during that evolution? When people realized there is no such thing as perfect design in the way they imagined, some lost faith. It's hard to conceive of a perfect designer producing an imperfect code. We try to philosophize our way out of it all. This perfect designer, this great programmer, caused the Darkness and included all the pain that went with it? No perfect world, the reasoning goes, no perfect God.

"Who says our world is imperfect? We recognize evil but we can't seem to reconcile the reasons for its existence. Our primitive concept of balance, therefore, precludes the concept of ultimate design. That idea, in itself, demonstrates a serious lack of insight.

"Ask yourself: Is our desire to improve upon technology or bio-chemistry more relevant than our drive to explore our Godliness? We love to borrow technological ideas and applications. Why not delve into the different paths of human spirituality? It's low-hanging spiritual truths...or falsehoods...that we would do well to investigate along with scientific inquiry. They work together.

"Take my own gift, for example. It's hardly new. For over five thousand years, there's been a science dedicated to vibrations and frequencies kept to letter and tone in order to assist our emotional balance. Vedic texts, sacred utterances, or mantras were practical tools. Beyond healing mantras, there were incantations used thousands of years ago to defeat enemies on military fields. A good mantra will be able to override the smaller vibrations by absorbing lower frequencies. The upshot is to bring the environment into harmonic levels that vibrate just under 7 Hz. Today, this resonance is entirely measurable.

"Man's ability to reset vibrational energy levels has existed for a long time. Holy men kept alive many kinds of chants addressing challenges of all descriptions. Somehow, I am able to tap naturally into these chants, so I think it's possibly just another unrealized natural inheritance. My ability to attune instantly to linguistic complexities and transmit frequencies is hard evidence. Our DNA has intricacies heretofore not fully grasped. I just want to bring this home: we are enabled to develop in ways that unlock sequential doors to full consciousness. We just have to find the keys that unlock the doors between that which is, and that which ought to be..." Sonny stood proudly and smiled at his audience.

"Sonny, that's nice. Let's get to the point of the mission, shall we? Give me something as to the reason we're going to send you toward Pennsylvania rather than Mt. Mitchell, the highest point in the Appalachian Mountains?" Morgan asked. "You've lost me, son. Did we just go to Pluto?"

"Sir, I understand your impatience. I need to expand upon this issue of frequency to explain that, too. It's for everyone's benefit. Permit me?"

"Go ahead," Morgan said as he urged Bluer's tail away from the wheels of his desk chair.

"The most beneficial frequency on earth is around 6.8 hertz, right? It was first discovered around and through the Giza Pyramid before it was destroyed. No one understood the origin of this energy or the reason it permeated the ancient pyramid. That doesn't matter except that Circle's frequency happens to be exactly 6.8 hertz. We act as a sort of Multiple Wave Oscillator...we present a magnetic field of multiple waves of inherently beneficial frequencies that do everything from healing the body to re-connecting to an appropriate frequency. I think that the Circle acts as a filter. We can transmit the beneficial and subdue the negative occurrences that threaten or drain us."

Morgan peered at the source that had drained his reserves. "Wind it up, Sonny!"

"When Aaron spoke of the Trickster, it reminded me of a design that has forced compromises in it. Have we ever pointed to manmade innovative design that we disliked or didn't think could be improved? We do it all the time. We may not know its function or be able to replicate it but we decide that its unfamiliarity is offensive, irrational, or useless. Similarly, we may not know a creator's purposes but it's pretty arrogant to dispute all aspects of a design when we are ignorant of the totality of its mechanisms or purposes. Worse still, is for a critic to espouse improved variations without first being able to replicate the program or design. Where is the human version of a wholly improved DNA? Who are we to take advanced design to task by saying it's not benevolent enough?

"Intelligent design may be completely benevolent by incorporating opposing forces that prompt development. It's the resurgence of the Trickster factor – a range of challenging variables – intentionally and cleverly introduced to occlude, analyze, or experiment as to the design's integrity.

"Our purpose, the Circle's purpose, is a genetic way to offset our present challenges. Throughout the universe, negative frequencies perpetually threaten spiritual – not only technological – singularity. We are each meant to do our part as cells of a greater whole. We should be able to bring our unique experiences to the human field of information that, in turn, connects to others. If we ignore a wayward cell within our midst, it will mean only one thing. That cell will replicate by way of imitating healthy ones until it sucks the life from its host, taking the system with it. At the least, it inculcates destructive elements that likely confuse our optimal state of consciousness.

"At this point in time – as we understand time – EMP disasters hit the planet at once. We assume it was a tragedy. It also may have done humanity a favor. It was these manmade and natural occurrences that rid some regions of overwhelming frequency interference at the lowest, most damaging vibrational levels. It was this discrepancy that allowed some of us to realize a supplementary natural state while others slid to its lowest. With high frequency partially restored, we may be able to save people by resurrecting a natural resonance."

"How do you see evil now?" Morgan asked.

"Anything that threatens functionality or evolution without constructive value?" Sonny answered with a question.

"Give me a prospectus based upon your sense of what is happening now," Morgan clarified.

"Every program has viral threats that prompt better programming. We have a chance to do a re-set. No matter how empowered our genetics, no matter how advanced our technology or trained our troops, ours is an unforeseen but very familiar battle. It's forced upon us...that is clear. Fight or die. Grow or whither. I can't see how destructive dark elements disappear without intervention."

"Do you see yourself as cosmic martyrs or what?" Morgan asked.

"I'm not sure what that means," Sonny puzzled. "I think we're compelled to maintain healthy design because we sense its supremacy. Aditiya understands numbers in terms of texture, shape and color ...sees his environment with shapes geometrically linked... it's his reality whereby he can actually visualize the mathematical elements within a balanced state. You know the way Ildiko worked with Caroline to methodically discover my exact location? They were able to go beyond my location. They replicated the exact numbers of windows on our ship and a coastline with 100% accuracy. Clearly, it means that we can combine our talents if we hold a common purpose. How was it that I could listen to any dialect and learn to speak them all? I was receptive to an electromagnetic spectrum of living data that, for whatever reason, I wanted to connect to.

"Circumstances actually invigorated my generation. We believed that anything was possible; no one feared anomalies. We were living an anomaly.

"Information that reaches the brain field is bound together with all the other signals in the brain. It's this field that binds what we might consider consciousness. It's not just a dumping ground for gathered information we've considered relevant to be retrieved when we think about it. Our developing consciousness also proactively influences our actions. Some neurons are fired and others aren't, depending upon how we conduct our lives. Our environmental exposures... those learning experiences that we seek out...determine whether or not the brain will determine a need for firing or latency. If we insist upon certain paths, the brain tips those neurons into firing. It's up to our free will to expose our EM fields to those ideas and experiences that will make up our consciousness. If we keep pushing in a particular direction, the brain keeps firing that way. If we want to be simple-minded receptors for whatever comes our way, we'll absorb ideas and images that are meant to distract or direct us. If we think we should be unable to remotely view happenings across the world, we will not remotely view anything without the net. If we cannot imagine what it takes to subconsciously bind experiences and unconsciously stop predatory behaviors, we won't. If we consider that we have an obligation to ensure moral action and involve our brain until we have a solution, we will succeed.

"You ask how we see ourselves. From that which has pre-ceded us, we've transformed. Our transcranial magnetic stim-ulation did not just switch off the frontal temporal lobe; it rather turned on exceptional mathematical, artistic, and bio-logical abilities. Caroline's blue light somehow triggered an amplified capacity. Or it locks the door to those unsuited, un-willing, too long exposed to limited destructive experiences.

"We've also developed a sort of synesthesia. We can cross reference senses that allow for a deeper understanding of our part in the world. There's no doubt in our minds that we feel connected. We're not martyrs, Dr. Pendergrass. We're survi-vors," Sonny emphasized.

"Connor?" Morgan turned to his surrogate for his report.

"We know that we sail June 10," Connor announced as he sent the reconnaissance information to everyone. "We're going to see what's out there and see what can be done. The ship carries military support. We'll move into the northern interior and face off with any challenges to securing our borders, rec-onciling the ill to sanity, and ensuring that our once-great country is re-established."

"That's a pretty tall order. But I like to think big," Morgan said in terms that endorsed the mission to commence.

Morgan spoke gravely to Attila, "Guard everyone with your life."

"I've prepared with my experiences and my family in mind," Attila reminded Morgan.

The terrifying high-pitched yelp that appropriated relief from the room's gravitas emanated from the latest cloned Plott Hound. Morgan's chair now sat upon Bluer's bandaged tail. "No more dang clones," Morgan warned Caroline and Angela.

Chapter XXVIII
Emerging Leader

Sunday, May 25, 2070

*T*he Appalachian Data Repository, once the mother ship of government and private industry's data protection, was built deep within the limestone mountains of Butler County, Pennsylvania. Miles of underground tunnels held vaults containing invaluable original paper copies, precious artwork, and everything from the microfiches and crystal chips of Fortune 2000 companies to the former government's Social Security and IRS records. Connected to the vast temperature-controlled vaults were mazes of many more subterranean miles of upscale survival bunkers intended to house top industry leaders and key government administrators in the event of a national emergency. The extensive living and operational accommodations were upgraded annually to meet disaster scenarios and contingencies. Much had been invested into the security that would ensure protection and sustenance for an elite community for an undetermined amount of time.

In addition to the small army that assumed observation posts on the interior and exteriors of the massive facilities hidden 250 feet beneath green turf, were biometric security systems able to identify each resident. Retina scans were coupled with reads of implanted frequency tracking chips able to locate and classify each owner that resided in luxury behind ten feet of hardened concrete walls.

Within these quarters, were extensive storage rooms, medical supplies, food stores, and aesthetics via a sensory menu that affected seasonal environments replete with auditory and haptic sensations. Beyond the individual storage banks, meant to serve a century of needs, were the interior and surface farms fed by underground water sources with filtering systems. That which began as a preparation for radioactive poisoning or deadly viral outbreaks ultimately served as the White House's safe house following the EMP disasters. With the sole exception of passengers on Air force 1 and 2, not one resident intended for the bunkers had access to hardened transportation by which to reach their alternative dwellings.

The current resident of the conclave's most opulent suites was a man known as Grayle. The young man was pleased by the discovery of his master bedroom equipped with extraordinary enhancements. Grayle discovered there an astronomer's dream of perpetually clear nights upon which dynamic constellations were projected onto his bedroom ceiling. For its previous occupant, the room provided an aesthetic cocoon of never-ending diversion and privacy. The former president of the United States did not find his pleasure in astronomy.

It took the young man a year to break into the ex-president's quarters from the hidden entrance discovered along with security guards drinking whiskey by a fire above ground. It took another year to safely open the vaults throughout the mazes of the ADR. Grayle was able to decipher the ADR Operational Manuals within the entry's offices.

Grayle found his way as he travelled from one of the rare civilized outposts that thrived cooperatively with similar communities in rural Pennsylvania. Like so many others of his generation, he found his family as a migrating survivor. A kindly elderly couple adopted Grayle. But like so many others, he had also been made weary of manual labor and isolation. Unlike others, Grayle's restlessness and ambition overcame fear of the unknown.

A decision to explore came one afternoon as Grayle contemplated the future prospects of living a life without ever having seen offerings beyond the thick fifteen-foot walls of his hometown. Dismissing the failures of others, Grayle intended to make his way to Confederation borders, with a promise to return with help. Although heartbreaking to his family and friends, Grayle was resolute. He was a dutiful son but had eyes and heart fixed upon a young woman. If it was freedom and security he wanted for his future family, Grayle knew it was time to make a move.

With supplies piled high on his back, Grayle set out unaccompanied toward the Southern territories. Compasses were worthless and no one from his town had marked such a long trail for others to follow. Natural navigational instincts belied everything he read in the sky. For weeks, Grayle wandered lost in the woods until coming upon five men, much like himself, foraging for food. Grayle panicked and shot their night watch before realizing that they were friendly sorts. Repentant for the rash act, Grayle offered his hunting services in exchange for exoneration.

Within a few days, Grayle's uncanny survival skills ingratiated him with the others. Loaded with deer, rabbit and fowl, the small band agreed to find their way South with the talented young man able to provide food. With one exception, the group had no understanding of mangled metallic directional highway markings. The eldest, however, had no intention of trying to venture far from the familiar rolling hills.

I'm too old to fight, the eldest man thought. He decided not to assist beyond the foothills and kept silent on the matter when the confused group groped to make sense of former navigational markings. As much as they hunted and marked their trails, no one could count upon directional instincts mere miles from previously chartered routes.

On a still, clear night, smoke drifts attracted Grayle's group to the location that later proved a secret entry to underground hidden bunkers. The men crawled on the forest floor until they could see the flickering light.

Having suffered memories of earlier times, the eldest of the group was made fearful by the sight of the men warming themselves by the fire. Grey Man squinted at the faces and forms of those identified as security guards. Disheveled remnants of the former regime, the two men were clearly drunk on their watch.

"They're still wearing those lightweight bulletproof shirts and weapon-concealing shin boots," Grey Man observed. There was more fear than awe in his voice. His frail voice rasped the story:

"The infamous White Eagles represented thousands of personal body guards appointed to the President. Extraordinary physical specimens were the elite of our military forces. They were a minimum of 6'4" and wore infrared glasses that could scope 360 degrees. Pumped up monsters is what they were... pushing crowds to the side, staring down anyone who dared to gawk their way, dragging anyone suspected as a threat to the state or the welfare of its leader into FBI transports. Once in their custody, few returned. Without business or government ID cards, anyone wandering on the streets was easily lost in the system." Grey Man wiped away the sweat that appeared on his forehead. "White Eagles made those old Nazi Brown Shirts seem tame by comparison. Mean as they come," Grey Man trembled."They had the drones do the dirtiest work. If a tagged criminal got beyond their reach, those drones could cut the perpetrator to pieces. Any crime that threatened the operation of the Federal offices gave the Eagles legal authority to eliminate. I saw an elderly woman decapitated on the street. Crime? She canvassed for tax relief by promoting tax evasion. She held her sign high in the street, despite warnings. The crowd grew by the hundreds urging her on. Then a laser sliced through the air."

"What is tax evasion?" Grayle asked.

"Money collected by the governments, local and federal, to keep the country in good shape. Good roads, schools, living conditions, safety...that sort of thing. We paid a national government that promised to support and protect citizens from enemies outside of our borders," Grey Man explained. "They also protected us from criminals that didn't obey laws or wanted to take away our personal freedoms, or threatened our homes or businesses...they kept us fed, too." Grey Man laughed suddenly at the irony of his explanation.

"Didn't you just say government agents killed citizens?" Grayle asked.

"Sometimes it was necessary. There was so much chaos toward the end," Grey Man sighed.

"These are not biblical laws," Grayle pursued. "And it's not in keeping with the old American constitutional ideas. Where is the personal freedom of living your life without paying protection money to a group of people that had the authority to kill you on the spot?"

Grey Man wept. "I always dreaded such a question from the new generations."

Grayle rose up in the woods just thirty feet from his intended targets and took aim. The wind howled and so did the drunkards. A struggling fire made sloppily of pinecones and dank wood crackled its protest in fits and starts. Two crossbow arrows flew in rapid succession, passing through the back of the men's necks toward the flickering light. Two White Eagles were sent choking, face down into the fire before Grey Man began a new sentence. Grayle wordlessly retrieved his arrows and discovered the path by which the dead men had made their way above ground. Grayle silently explored the underground and the group followed.

Beginning with this group of five, Grayle was able to identify and collect hundreds of migrants within the Appalachian foothills and valleys. Most were wayward and confused but eagerly followed a man with a plan. Some were so consumed with vitriol that Grayle personally executed those that tested out as insane when they threatened his authority or attacked members of an emergent community. Every week, there would be hundreds of new candidates.

"Can we use this one?" one of his men would ask about borderline aspirants. "He's healthy, pretty strong. Doesn't look threatening but won't or can't communicate. What do you think, Grayle?"

Grayle would individually examine each candidate to determine suitability for New America. One by one, day in, and day out, Grayle acted as the community's gatekeeper. A personal cache of smart guns determined martial superiority within untold miles of survival bunkers able to accommodate and sustain untold thousands. Thousands arrived and Grayle devised a system to ferret out troublemakers.

It was Grayle's habit to ask one simple question of those who exhibited dubious behaviors:

"Do you believe in God?"

Those that answered in the affirmative would be allowed a follow-up question.

"Have you tried to obey God's commandments?" he would ask again.

Grayle wanted those who were earnest in building a civilized community and were willing to follow his organized path to that end. He had no interest in watching his back.

Per usual, one afternoon Grayle entered yet another roomful of new arrivals. From the Community Hall's stage podium, Grayle addressed the newcomers.

"We mean to see if you are suitable within a month's time. I expect you to abide by our codes of conduct and adhere to God's laws. Your citizenship will be my decision," he bellowed to the crowd.

"Or what? What are you going to do about it?" came one surprising response. Grayle feigned bewilderment and weighed the upstart standing defiantly in line below his position.

"I'm open to suggestions. Our goal is to welcome those willing to learn the merits of morality. If you can't manage that, you won't thrive here. With too many of your kind, our existence is threatened," explained Grayle.

The strapping young man approximated Grayle's age; he clearly disapproved of the process by which one was expected to gain entry.

"You're sitting up high. I'm down here on the floor. You're already looking down on me. I want to sit where you're sitting," the man challenged.

Grayle regarded the newcomer who had tracked his way to the Boyer site.

"Please, stand here. I'll take your place," Grayle invited. The role reversal pleased the visitor enormously and the stranger's mood changed accordingly.

"Would you like to have my position of ensuring that every-one has food, is treated equally and well? Are you able to embody the spirit of giving and grace?" Grayle tested.

"Oh, sure. I could do that," the man quickly agreed.

"There are terms to your position," Grayle clarified.

Grayle was a leader. He knew to teach reasonableness by example. Taking cues from biblical scenarios, Grayle grasped opportunities that promised lasting impressions.

"You are now in my position. You will take charge of one of my duties. You'll have my room, too." Grayle stated terms. "I don't eat or drink until the citizens of New America have been fed, and that's what you'll do as well. Each citizen has at least one good meal daily, provided by the hunters, farmers and preparers. You will be responsible for that one duty and that's to make sure that everyone has had ample nourishment. If one person goes to bed hungry or thirsty, you will too."

Duke, a rough man with four serrated knives strapped to a belt, was typical of castoffs who had no memory of family. He had lived his life hunting in the wild, following the ways of others, living on scraps while observing survival skills of those he served. He eventually provided for the older hunters; when strong enough, he left the pack.

According to his account, Duke ingratiated himself with various groups by periodically exchanging wild game for shelter. After the winter months had safely passed, Duke would slit the throats of his hosts and abduct a woman or two to serve his wishes. With one such female, out of her mind with fear and grief, Duke appeared at the compound. Grayle calculated that the girl was about fourteen years of age. With regard to apology or further explanation, there was none.

Finding himself in Grayle's quarters, Duke was ecstatic when the perquisites of his new position revealed themselves. He was given clean clothes and escorted to the bathroom, where there was a deep drawn bath. Duke slipped his scarred, calloused body into the hot water with a sigh. When the wrapped soap products proved inedible, he threw them against the mirrors.

Steaming soup and vegetables were prepared and delivered by the kitchen. Duke asked for more, and more food arrived.

He laughed hysterically and stretched out on the clean, comfortable bed, kicking sheets and throwing pillows about the room.

Later in the day, Grayle visited the commune's newly-appointed leader, still slumbering in his quarters.

"I hope you're well, Duke. Remember that this is the last free meal. The rest will rely upon your fulfilling obligations."

Duke sneered, "You like words of old people. I don't care. I know what I need to know. You and your puppies can go now. Bring me my woman."

Grayle refused. "That may happen when she is able to walk and speak correctly. She's eating now. She is very, very sick, as you must know. How do you explain the girl's injuries?"

Duke hurled a soup bowl at Grayle and jumped a table that separated them. Before Grayle's men could react, Duke had his knife at Grayle's throat.

Grayle smiled calmly as he clasped the man's neck in return, his fingers inching around the circumference of Duke's trachea, then digging for a firmer hold.

"Duke, do you know how to leave here? You were blindfolded on the way down. You will never find your way out for a lack of direction and any other number of reasons. I want to also say that if you so much as flinch, I'll rip your throat out."

Duke choked. "Ha! I like you," he said as the knife was returned to its sheath. "I'm joking. But tomorrow may be different."

Grayle left and never returned. For two days, Duke lounged in luxurious quarters waiting for food. He had no idea how to read or figure the words upon which organized life operated. He waited until hunger overcame him on the third day.

Duke screamed for help and none arrived. Upon exiting the room, the door locked behind him. For half the day, Duke wandered the mazes of corridors, unable to discern an exit. Finally, he discovered an open stairwell and climbed the winding steel stairs until arriving at a floor with a door leading to muffled noises of life. He slammed the butt of his knife upon the steel mass; the rhythmic clanking drew attention and the massive door that separated Duke from civilization slowly opened.

Duke identified himself while pushing past a young boy.

"I'm Duke. Bring me food and water," he demanded, taking in the sight of a large community hall populated by groups engaged at orderly workstations.

The young boy guided Duke into an explosion of noise and activity. It was a place teaming with community-focused industry for which Duke had no use or understanding. He had never bothered to ask Grayle's name but recognized the leader directing activities across the enormous hall.

"You!" Duke pointed an accusatory finger at Grayle.

"You!" Grayle roared back.

Grayle's visceral reply filled the room, which fell into a sudden stillness. He was a man who did not react well to aggressive salutations.

"Did you fulfill your duties? Did you make sure that everyone was fed properly?" Grayle demanded with obvious displeasure.

"How could I? I couldn't find my way anywhere. You kept me prisoner. I'm dying of hunger, haven't eaten. Get me something," Duke indignantly countered with demands.

"As you can see, we're busy." Grayle spread his arms to indicate the proof of the matter. "I've allocated myself other duties. When you didn't show up, I substituted and others had to help me cover other commitments. We counted on your help and you let us all down. Let me see if your friend is now able to help you out," Grayle finalized by motioning Duke's captive to come forward.

The young girl Duke had abducted stood quietly beside a table piled high with harvested dried seeds neatly dried, counted, and prepared for packaging. She responded eagerly to Grayle's summons. Matted hair had been cleaned and secured back from the young girl's face. Open, angry eyes peered out from bandaged wounds. Discolored bruises, now healing, peeked beyond ointment, bond, and adhesive that melted into what was once a delicate face and décolletage.

"Your friend asks for food and water; will you do that for him? We've covered his duties for three days...we can't waste more time," Grayle gently put to the girl.

"No," rejoined the girl through cracked, blistered lips.

Duke yelled his objection. "You idiot. All you have to do is go to the place they serve the food and bring it here."

"We've eaten," the girl replied curtly.

"Then a piece of meat. I'm dying," Duke demanded.

"No," came the response once more.

Grayle addressed Duke by way of interpretation to those now paying witness.

"Everyone would suffer here without thinking of others. You could have found your way out three days ago, before retiring for the night. You might have asked how we managed to feed thousands of people in the bunkers or above ground. It's a complicated system but I could have met you and walked you through the ways we operate. There would have been assistants to help you, and they put aside the time to do just that. They, too, waited for three days. You had no intention of helping. You had no questions. You had no concerns. There was no effort. No one held you prisoner. You didn't care about the welfare of anyone but yourself. We can see how that worked out. You've claimed one friend," Grayle pointed toward the frail teenager. "Broken bones and teeth offer testament to the merits of that friendship. Do you wonder the reason that she isn't eager to help the man who saved her? I think not. She needs time to recover, that's clear. You'll have to find food and water for yourself from now on," Grayle declared.

"Show me where it is," Duke bellowed.

"Not here. You have your knives and you're free to go find what you will outside the way you want...away from here. If you don't want to leave because you feel this is the place you'd prefer, you can ask someone else to volunteer to fetch food right now. It's up to you."

"Who will help me?" Duke shouted in the hall.

An overwhelming resurgence of activity emphasized Duke's predicament.

Grayle made his way halfway across the room. As quietly as he spoke, no one missed the exchange between their leader and the man who wanted to be one.

"They don't know you. They've never worked with you or seen you work or contribute to this community. Your only acquaintance has been beaten and starved, a slave to your desires and sick imagination. She has rejected you to embrace the goodwill of others. Even as an ailing, recovering victim, she's eager. Within a week or two, she'll join us as a full-fledged contributor and a welcome member of our community.

"On the other hand, you are a man who was given the responsibility of leadership who sees only the power he might wield. Yours is an animal's thirst. You've exhibited no human curiosity, humility, or compassion," Grayle leveled at Duke.

"What do you do exactly?" Duke felt for his knife.

"I never eat before our helpless farm stock is fed. The last plate served of the day or night is mine. If we've run out of food, or feed, I'll know. I manage the many operations that run our fast-growing city. It falls to me to ensure moral principles of governorship. And I deal with people like you that expect something for nothing. But I give them a chance, too.

"You were given food and a bed as hospitable gestures. You were trusted. You crawled out of bed only to eat and drink... three days late. You enter here with a demand on your lips to be attended." Grayle stood and waited mid-way in the hall.

Duke narrowed his eyes upon Grayle.

"I don't know these words. You left me alone. You tricked me," Duke squeaked confusion.

Grayle stood rigidly and silently. Duke tried a different approach.

"I'm a lost hunter. You said you would help me," he pleaded desperately. "I expected help. You just gave me a job to do. That's not what I need," Duke whined unreasonably.

"I'm unconcerned with your needs at this time. Now follow this escort outside and never return," Grayle added with a pointed finger.

"My woman!" Duke insisted.

"It's her decision," Grayle answered.

Duke looked toward the nameless girl. "Come here," he demanded. "We're leaving!"

"No," she said.

Duke's rage was immediate; he pulled a knife, flipped it and grabbed the blade midair, then lobbed it toward the girl's heart.

Grayle was able to reach and push the stunned girl aside, and turned, in one fluid motion, toward Duke.

Duke was fast to close distance, brandishing two more hunting knives that sliced the air. Weaponless, Grayle signaled the onlookers to move back as he met his challenger.

A seasoned hunter, Duke had no doubt that he would prevail in the sea of startled sheep that surrounded their sweet-tongued shepherd.

Duke's right hand rose high across his left shoulder, the blade prepared to slice forty-five degrees downward into Grayle's carotid artery. In his left hand, a second knife was positioned to simultaneously puncture Grayle's lung on the same side. At the moment of closure, Duke's knee pulled upward to offset Grayle's counterattack but his prey elected to maneuver around and behind him. Grayle grabbed Duke from behind; his massive hands gripped and jerked his attacker's neck by the shirt collar, pulling him off balance.

Duke's knees buckled when Grayle's boot buried deep and sharp into his thighs. His boot searched its way down into Duke's knee joint. With Grayle's leverage and weight, the knee buckled violently and landed Duke kneeling with his back to Grayle. With one hand positioned around Duke's throat, Grayle's free hand splayed wide and slid from the man's chin until it touched the familiar indentation of eye sockets. Grayle's fingers found their marks then buried an inch down, skewering the eyeballs until one popped.

Duke released the knives. Flailing arms failed to ease Grayle's grip that hooked deep and high within his skull. The man squirmed wildly but the slightest movement of his head exacerbated the pain. Duke's predicament was no less than the thousands of trapped animals he had left for days to slowly perish with severed limbs.

"Let. Me. Go!" screamed Duke.

Grayle released Duke by pushing the blinded man violently to his side. Leg cocked high into his chest, Grayle's boot met Duke's larynx and crushed it flat into the cement. A stomp to the man's temple followed and blood gushed from the ears that heard nothing but its own dark opinions.

Duke, Grayle had concluded, proved an unsuitable candidate for rehabilitation.

Followers, shocked over their leader's close brush with death, quickly joined Grayle to fuss over his welfare.

Grayle's hands reached upward with an earnest providential appeal to forgive the man who had no inner understanding and for forgiveness having to needlessly end the man's life.

"We ask your continued protection as we build our community toward a New America. Help us understand the need for vigilance against evil and an ability to temper this vigilance with compassion...."

Several minutes of prayer passed and the body was hustled away to the crematorium. Duke's former human possession scrubbed her tormentor's blood from the floor with bleach and grateful tears.

Chapter XXIX
Beyond the Borders

Saturday, June 14, 2070

Morgan's Ark!" Ildiko laughed with her father. "We've got horses all over the place, all kinds of equipment, tons of provisions. We're supposed to be gone no longer than the summer, Papa?"

"We hope that's the case. Our plan is to direct Confederation help to a meeting point and transport survivors to the main ship and transports off New Jersey or Maine. Some might rather relocate to another Confederation state west of the seaboard. We'll contact air transports, if that's the case. Part of our mission is to begin to administer reconstruction of cities and towns," Attila smiled at his daughter. "I'm actually trying to be an optimist. That alone is an enormous undertaking."

"I've been training most my life for some serious action. But I don't see danger. No one does." Disappointment rather than relief resonated in Ildiko's voice.

"That right, Édes? I'm no psychic but I certainly don't underestimate this situation. Don't let your guard down. Never wish for action that will likely scar you for life," Attila frowned.

"I'm not looking for trouble. I've remotely searched the area for over a year now. I've mentally flown over this territory and all I see are occasional hunters, some smoke here and there, and farms surrounded by fences. We've marked those. I can't see any dangers. I just can't. We might be able to reunite the United States successfully and quickly," Ildiko assured her pensive father.

"I hope you're right."

Father and daughter stood thoughtfully on deck as the cool water washed away the blazing heat of the Carolina sun. Attila recalled his wife and sighed deeply to offset emotions of such moments. He thought that so many years and so many tasks would have staved off painful memories of his happiest moments in Hungary. When tired or stressed, he nevertheless imagined Noemi's beautiful, kind face in every natural beautiful setting in which she belonged. As much as he tried, he could not erase the image of his soul mate's crumpled, lifeless body lying in an apartment courtyard.

Ildiko felt her mother's presence. The feeling was undeniable. "I love you," Ildiko said simply to her father.

He turned and pulled his tall, strong daughter into one of his arms. "I couldn't be prouder. I love you, too."

Behind them, Adele pressed the heavy door and moved onto the uppermost deck, allowing the wind to fill her nostrils with the scent of salt spray. When Attila and Ildiko met her eyes, Adele asked softly, "May I join you two?"

"Sure!" Ildiko eagerly beckoned.

As Adele made her way to where they stood, Ildiko was startled by the sound of her mother's voice. It whispered, "*This is the one.*"

Hearing a long-lost familiar voice and the message it bore made Ildiko erupt with happiness. Adele paused midway on deck.

"No... I'm not laughing at you!" Ildiko corrected the impression. "It's the excitement of going on this adventure!"

"I would never think you meant ill to anyone, Ildiko. I thought that I might have interrupted a rare and private moment between father and daughter. I can come back later," she offered.

"No, please stay. I'm going to meet Nicholas and CC below before the meeting," she answered. "Apa? See you later!" She quickly kissed her father and winked.

"She winked at me. That was weird," Attila wondered aloud.

"I've got to admit, I'm pretty enthusiastic, too," Adele remarked, drawing close to Attila's position against the railing.

"This is going to be extraordinary. We'll travel on this magnificent ship in the company of four other ships packed to the gills with soldiers and mounts that know no equal in the world. It's surreal. It's a meaningful mission, trying to reunite our country after so much horror. Great stuff!" Adele enthused.

Attila was not so optimistic, "Onak négy a lába, mégis megbotlik...The horse has four legs and still stumbles," he translated. "No matter our measure, neither Hungary nor the Confederation has assurances. We've united a greater Hungary but still find pockets of the murderously insane for which there is no remedy.

"You know the reason Hungary grew her territories so rapidly? Our nation became the primary safe haven; we were the last ones with resources and the compassion to help others get back on their feet. Together, it was the collective civilized fighting that stopped overwhelming numbers.

"I'm afraid of what we're going to find here. Things don't make sense. I know they're out there. But where?"

Adele stared toward the setting sun and pulled her coat tighter around her. "It's cold on the water," she said to fill an awkward silence.

"Yes, always cooler on the water," Attila agreed, peering into the horizon. "I'm not used to large bodies of water. My country was landlocked, until recently. We had great sailing on the Balaton but not on open waters. Now, the Hungarian Navy sails the Adriatic and Tyrrhenian Seas. I have to see that before I die. A proper Hungarian Navy would be like horses flying," he mused.

"I wouldn't mind going to old Europe and seeing Hungary. Sadly, I've never been beyond Confederation borders."

"It's sadder that the Europe you read about no longer exists. Borders are arbitrary. Man tends to respect borders when we've exhausted all other options, or we're too weak to resist... or decide to invade. The migrants have redefined the meaning of nation-states. We're busy maintaining civilization's boundaries on behalf of humanity. We're called Hungary and we've expanded but our purpose is to ensure cultural traditions, to progress without hindrance. All nationalities work to keep the insanity at bay."

"How do you go about it?"

"People have been encouraged to return to cultural roots, spiritual pursuits, and family life to shore up optimism. Hungarians are a proud culture, but we take pains to recognize and respect those cultures we've welcomed under our governance. It's simple, really. It's brutal to escort families out of Hungarian borders. Yet, we must make those decisions when irreversible mental illness is evident or in the cases of superimposing another culture at our expense. It sure as hell isn't tough to spot either tendency. I need no written research to figure what constitutes a crazed, predatory animal. I didn't hesitate to take out every one of those monsters that mistook compassion for weakness."

"You helped rescue most of Europe from being overrun. I'm guessing that there's room for one more statue in Budapest's Heroes Square. You'd look right at home sitting atop the Millennium Monument riding on Kincsem. Wasn't that a famous horse?" Adele flattered.

"A thoroughbred. Not the kind you'd choose to take to war with rough terrain. You know about Hősök tere?" Attila turned to look at Adele, his side to the railing.

The cenotaph is dedicated to the memory of heroes in the name of freedom of the Hungarian people and national independence. It's all here," she tapped her head, indicating the implanted neural amplification rods that were able to cache all that she had researched on the topic of Hungary.

Attila approved. "I'm complimented anyone would think of me in that context. I realize that the most important statue is of the Archangel Gabriel holding in his right hand the Holy Crown of St. Stephen, our first king. In the left, Gabriel holds a double apostolic cross, a gift from the Pope in recognition of Hungary's conversion to Christianity and for fighting the Islamic invasions that meant to take over northern Europe. Hungarians recognize that the archangels are always poised to kick satanic ass. It's not so alien to the world's current situation."

Adele listened to the history lesson. She preferred the less serious Attila whenever and wherever that side of him surfaced. He brooded a lot and preferred to read and walk alone. If there was a celebration, Attila was the first exit without notice.

Yet, Adele considered, the man was dynamic and straight-forward, emitting pure male magnetism. His brand of humor ranged from dry to sardonic, preferring to withhold jokes to ensure a worthy audience. Adele noticed he was more amused by actions than words. Lately, her heart began to jump when he caught her eyes from across a room.

He's nothing like the man I married. Adele's mind compared the stark contrasts. Lex was the only man she ever knew. Time had taught her how an impressionable young girl could be convinced of anything. Still, she had no regrets. Adele concluded that their unlikely union was nothing less than a miracle. Caroline was proof of that serendipitous truth.

Attila turned to rest upon one arm to examine Adele. He reluctantly allowed a smile to grow slowly across his well-defined face, roughened by years of exposure to the elements. It was out of Adele's character to have sought his company; he knew to be flattered.

"Does your face hurt?" Attila tilted his head and examined her.

"No..." Adele blushed. "Why?"

"Because it's killing me," he grinned. "You're a beautiful woman. There, I've said it." Attila's intensity emanated from dark eyes that remained fixed on hers.

"Thank you," Adele smiled. "I mean it. It's been a long time since I've heard that kind of compliment. You begin to wonder..."

"Nervous?" Attila drew closer and took her hand in his. Adele's heart beat rapidly. His thumb gently rubbed the back of her hand with an unexpected tenderness. It stopped her breath.

"Why would I be nervous?" she coolly asked.

"Well, it's this mission of ours. Dangerous, right?" He held her gaze and released her hand to lean his on the rail in front of him.

"Red sky at night, sailor's delight. Red sky in the morning, sailors take warning. Isn't that the English saying?"

"Not sure but the view is definitely delightful." Adele wished he had not let go of her hand. She wished she had responded in a warmer way.

Attila turned from the sun that spread its orange, yellow, and red hues across the horizon and examined the woman before him with renewed interest. Sea spray caught prisms of light and flickered across Adele's face; her sea blue eyes offset the warm hues that enveloped the ship.

"You're more enchanting than any sunset. The sun and heaven's sky will never hold a candle to what I'm seeing at this moment."

Attila turned Adele fully to face him. The fading sun created a brilliant halo of color around Attila's head. With the blocking of the sun, Adele fully opened her eyes and held her breath when the tall Hungarian squared off to make a point.

"I've admired you for years. So you've a right to be nervous. I've no will to resist you any longer. You should know that."

He kissed her lightly on the lips and lingered there until she responded more passionately.

"That settles that," Adele laughed when they parted minutes later.

"Regrettably, it took this pathetic excuse for a Hungarian male around ten years to get this close. My compatriots would string me from my toes in Heroes Square if they knew my true cowardice." He tilted Adele's head up with a finger to her chin and began to kiss her lightly on the lips, face, and neck. As he pulled away, Attila kept his hand on the nape of Adele's head and ran his other hand through her thick ash brown hair, taking care to capture and smooth flying strands from her face.

"Expect happiness, Adele," he murmured in her ear.

"You made me come to you," Adele stated with a certain resignation. "Why not the other way around?"

"It took me a decade to convince you that I was worthwhile?" he smiled down at her. "From the moment I saw you with Lex, I knew two things. He was no man for you. In fact, he was no man. In the second case, I knew you would come to me when the time was right. You are a strong woman, very used to saying no. I am a strong man and not used to hearing no. There could be no mistakes. But why do you approach me now?"

"If we lose everything, I cannot afford to lose a love I might never have allowed to take its first breath. When I boarded the ship, I thought that it's entirely possible that I could die without ever having kissed you."

"Now that I've kissed you, it's impossible for me to live my life without you. So all of this is easily remedied," he sighed softly and kissed Adele so tenderly that she lost herself in the moment, melting into his arms. His large hand now fully cradled a head that had gone limp.

"You have patience, I give you that," Adele murmured.

"Patience is expected for a woman like you, Adele. You have been worth every moment."

The ship's monitor blared the call to the Conference room.

Adele and Attila held each other as the last rays of the sun faded, immune to the sudden temperature drop.

"Am I supposed to walk now?" Adele asked as he took her hand. "The knees...my knees are seriously shaking..." she shook her head at a condition no longer held in the abstract.

"It won't be the last time," Attila assured.

Sunday, June 15, 2070

By morning, a brief storm had sobered the passengers' mood and slightly agitated the horses.

"Thanks for helping move the containers," Connor said gratefully to Aaron. "Your maneuverability is incredible."

"I'm just waiting for the pyramids to come back in fashion. Otherwise, I'll be looking for work," Aaron half-joked. "I'm not sure how amazing it is to control objects."

"I'm counting on your help, Aaron," Connor said. "We may need you to help blast through the barricades and assist with transporting refugees and goods over difficult terrain. I can think of a hundred ways you're invaluable," Connor patted Aaron's back.

Sonny greeted everyone in the galley with uncombed hair and a Confederation-issued shirt worn inside out. Tsin-hang peered up at his disheveled son from the breakfast table.

"It's an incredible ship. I know every inch of it," Sonny announced with pride. "It brings back a lot of memories. It's crazy to see it in these waters with my father helping out again. They wouldn't give us our former cabin, though."

"Your father deserves some privacy. You're bunking with friends your own age," Cynthia suggested dryly. "You're not a kid!"

"I concur, Sonny." Tsin-hang signaled his displeasure at Sonny's disheveled appearance. *All that linguistic and frequency talent and not one clue as to how others feel about a military man showing up like an undisciplined child?* Tsin-hang messaged his son. *Go change!*

Attila and Connor combed the hourly reports of the terrain they would travel. The computer analyzed the predictability of the weather and the time required to cover the five hundred miles toward the Appalachian Trail into Pennsylvania, with estimates as to numbers and condition of inhabitants.

"I'm not sure we'll get as far as Lake Erie but our first team will try to move toward what was once wilderness parks. The horses can handle most anything but I'd like to keep this expedition as conservative as possible," explained Connor.

"What happened to the Tons of Fun group?" Adele wondered aloud.

"They're posted on North Carolina's northernmost border, ready to roll when summoned," Connor answered.

"Are you joking?" Adele chuckled at the image.

"Nope. You never know. And there's no way I'm going to tell General Brackett that there's no place for her in this mission. Her duty is to protect the Research Triangle area."

"Good God," Adele exclaimed. "She's going to roll that battalion around the state until you get back. Does the Governor know what's going on?"

"He will!" Connor laughed. "I expect he'll be amused."

Cynthia had yet to recover from losing her sister to an unseen influence and imagined what might have been if Esther had not been so susceptible to molecular changes. It was her hope to save others from a similar fate. Ildiko and CC felt her melancholy.

"Esther isn't lost, Cyn. It's possible that Esther, and those like her, can regain their equilibrium," Ildiko consoled her friend.

"I'm hoping that's the case. It's as if she sat teetering on a fence, blown slightly this way and that. But she'd always recover her balance. Then a wind came and blustered past her resistance. We prayed together, we lived together, we dreamed and studied together with the best group of people imaginable. What makes you think she'll recover?" Cynthia probed.

"I don't know. It surprised us all. We're supposed to have a special sensitivity about these things. I picked up nothing," Ildiko supposed. "Aditiya and Dr. Green say that normalcy and one's optimal state is always the most delicate of balancing acts. We'll try and figure if we can reverse engineer this horrific frequency that keeps so many people unsteady," Ildiko reassured Cynthia, now fidgeting with her fingers.

From her bunk, Caroline asked, "Where's Esther now, Cynthia?"

"She's been helping out at the Research Triangle and says that she really likes it. Some guy has taken an interest in her and they communicate daily. Best thing for her was to have someone to show her attention."

"Who is he?" Caroline asked.

"An out-of-state researcher processing international data. They're working on frequency variations, including the ones we generate. She doesn't want to discuss any of that. It's all about how 'hot' this guy is. He plans on visiting her soon so it's made her happy for the moment." Cynthia was secretly pleased that her sister seemed contained, if not happy.

"Maybe Nicholas was too much to handle, girlfriend," teased Ildiko. She pursed her lips, considering her own lackluster love life. "I've ever had anyone to go crazy over me or vice versa. I'm pathetic. I do love pizza, though. Now, there's something hot that loves me back."

Cynthia and Caroline sympathetically nodded in agreement.

"Looks pretty bleak from where we're all sitting," Cynthia smiled. "Hard to meet guys with family and bots watching your every move. It's going to take somebody crazy in love or just plain crazy to make his way through the Pendergrass gauntlet."

Caroline groaned. "I'm pretty sure I won't be able to drive somebody whacky enough to handle my grandfather."

"Forget your grandfather. Who in their right mind is going to want to come up against Nicholas, Aditiya, Sonny or Aaron?" laughed Ildiko. "Imagine it. Nicholas asks where we're going and my guy has something else on his mind. He pukes or something before we get out the door. Aaron has the same tendencies. Who wants to be flipped across the farm because of a goodnight kiss? Sonny will transmit chants of civil behaviors that will ensure we're never kissed. And Aditiya will remind every poor soul of their actual chances of success. We've got brothers from hell."

In cabins two decks below, Nicholas, Aaron, Aditiya and Sonny similarly commiserated.

"I'd like to find a nice Chinese girl. Where am I going to find a Chinese girl?" Sonny complained to his cabin mates.

"You speak a million languages and dialects and you've got to have a Chinese girl? Where did that come from? You can communicate with anyone you want without a translator. I wouldn't mind that ability," countered Aditiya. "If I were you, I'd start practicing up first on some manly chants."

"Or begin with a few grooming techniques," added Nicholas.

"I'd like someone like my mother," Sonny continued. "I love the Chinese culture."

"That's fine. But even a nice Chinese girl isn't going to want to hear she's supposed to be like your mother, Sonny," Aditiya warned.

"Nothing against your mother, Sonny, but you've just defined yourself as searching for a mate that you recall as a three-year-old," Nicholas said dismally. "Think about those hopes and dreams. Give yourself a little wiggle room. I ended up with the first girl that smiled my way. We see how that worked out," Nicholas complained lightheartedly.

Aaron ignored his friends with his own challenges. "Rachel thinks I'm ten years old. After this mission, we've got to get our own place. Not kidding."

"Who's laughing?" Nicholas exclaimed.

The young men laughed together with hopes for an independent future.

"We've got a larger objective: get our place, find some women, have fun, settle down, and live happily ever after," yelled Sonny.

"Not sure what to do with you, Sonny. We may have to identify and splice a certain fashion and fun gene that's eluded your map," Nicholas joked.

"Like you'd need that for survival," Sonny scoffed.

"Like, it might be a problem in your case," Aaron shrugged. "You need to get some game."

"By the way, Nick. You don't have to find your woman," Sonny taunted. "I'm pretty sure your love match is right here on board."

"Anyone in particular?" Nicholas asked, truly puzzled.

Aditiya shot a disapproving glance across the room. "Shut up, Sonny.

"I'm not saying who it is," Sonny antagonized. "But I can tell you that I knew from the beginning that Esther wasn't going to work."

"That would make you a jackass. You could have saved me a decade of Esther hurt," Nicholas said angrily.

"These things aren't supposed to be told. Ask Caroline. She knows things she never talks about," Sonny insisted.

"I'm not talking to Caroline about love matches. I'm pretty much finished with talking to you on the subject of women, too." Nicholas threw a pillow across the room. When Sonny ducked, a shoe quickly followed, hitting Sonny as he triumphantly regained his position.

"Let me tell your future right now," Aaron warned. "You'd better warn me of any troubled women headed my way or I'm going to empty whatever I can find on your idiot shaved head... after flying you around upside down."

Nicholas yawned, "Have any special love chants?"

"Why?" Sonny asked, rubbing his head unnecessarily.

"Practice... we all need to learn those tunes." Nicholas pulled his covers over his head.

The young men fell asleep early and woke to the captain's announcement to prepare for shore transport. The monitors displayed the transports already ferrying horses toward shore. Media drones projected two thousand troops being transported to port onto other smaller transports.

"It looks like an invasion rather than a rescue mission," observed Aaron.

In the cabin above, Adele complained to her mirror's reflection. The skintight camouflaged suit left little to the imagination. Regardless of its chameleon-like ability to automatically modify to shifting environments, color changes could not hide her curvaceous body.

Adele examined a 3-D image rotating in her mind. "No way," she decided. When she asked for a projected image of what she might look like riding a horse, she exclaimed aloud, "Oh hell, no!"

The officers and the Pendergrass group met in the ship's largest Conference room. It would be their last meeting before joining the Confederation Minister and readying for departure. Adele scurried into the room late and was greeted with a burst of laughter.

Adele's upper half moved inside the room, the lower part of her body obscured by the uniform's refracting feature. Half invisible, Adele had solved a body image problem.

At the conclusion of the meeting, Attila challenged Adele.

"It's not what the invisibility feature is meant for. Save the juice for when we need it. Fact is, I like that part of your body. Please don't deny me the pleasure of seeing you. You are absolutely beautiful."

Adele meant to educate Attila. "I'm following in the footsteps of a great American leader. You know what Adlai Stevenson II said?"

"What did he say?" Attila raised his eyebrows, feigning playful interest.

"'*It's hard to lead a cavalry charge if you think you look funny on a horse'*... that's verbatim what Adlai Stevenson II said. I'm going with Adlai," she countered.

The horses loaded on the flat transports equipped with tacky pitted flooring that allowed for traction; the animals boarded boldly. Gleaming trimmed hooves were one of the many the Research Triangles' inroads in animal husbandry. Nutrition and advanced water resistant sealants made hoof wall problems, chipping, and incessant trimming a thing of the past. The horses were optimized in every way, head to hoof. While novice mounts would have once presented a problem, the Confederation horses were quick students and bred to the job.

Kabardin genetic lines brought sure footedness; the robustness of the Mongolian breed had ensured the best of centuries of bloodlines of Persian, Karrbahk, and Turkmene crossbreeding. The horses could also be used for all-purpose driving. Hungarian Warm Bloods were altered to Attila's specifications to ensure a workhorse equipped naturally with exceptional intelligence, disposition, and muscularity without excess weight. Seventeen hands high, the new broad-backed breed proved animated, disciplined, and agile. Known as The Pendergrass, the unique horses were bred into the thousands. The colors ranged broadly, but the regimentation of the military horses proved an irrefutable tribute to genetic engineering.

Two thousand of the magnificent steeds would ride into the nation's capital and split into different directions within 24 hours. A parade was scheduled, then abruptly canceled.

"Are you out of your mind?" Attila yelled incredulously at the Minister of Defense's attaché. "This is supposed to be a discreet military mission. Why a parade?"

"I guess that's a no?" the attaché asked thinly.

"What's your name?" Attila asked.

"Lovejoy Hopewell, sir."

"You're joking."

"I had optimistic parents, sir. It's a joke... but not on you."

"You coming with us?" Attila shouted at the Hopewell's image.

"Hadn't planned on it," Hopewell answered, a confused man.

"Then save the parade for when you fight or sludge hundreds of miles through unexplored dangerous terrain. No parades. Why tell the world about our plans? Do you have a speech prepared about our strategies, too?"

"I don't have a clue as to your plans. You and Dr. Collins have yet to share anything specific with our office, sir."

"On point! Doesn't that tell a military attaché something?" Attila testily pointed out.

Viewing the desperate expression of the clueless attaché, Attila decided to rein in his Hungarian temper.

"Sorry, Hopewell. I'm in charge of keeping these troops alive and well. If we need help, our other troops, and all the air power the Confederation can muster, will come to bear. We have our ships off shore. Does this seem as if we're taking any chances? It's one of the reasons our preparation has taken so long. We've bred special horses, used new technology and trained to enter isolated territories expecting the worst. We don't know what we'll find. Why advertise?"

"We haven't had any conflicts, no signs of any significant trouble or advanced tech. There's absolutely nothing of interest transmitted from satellites except small groups living in hiding that regularly reappear to farm and tend livestock. What's the harm in a little parade in the capital?" Hopewell protested his position.

"What good does it do?" Attila's voice rose once more when Connor entered the room.

"It helps lift the spirits of the citizens?" the attaché suggested meekly.

"What are you, a party planner or a military attaché? I hope meeting my knuckles won't dampen your spirits, you twit!"

 Connor motioned for Attila to step away from the images.

"Mr. Meszaros has picked up too many of my father-in-law's temperamental traits, I'm afraid," Connor attempted to mitigate the feelings of a stricken young attendant used to peacetime duties.

"I know that Dr. Pendergrass and Governor Hernandez have been in touch throughout this week. Please understand that Raleigh is the source of your data. Clearly, we have the same information. Rather than nothing evident, you might consider that something seems purposely hidden from our view. There have been few signs of mass movement or dangerous conclaves of any kind in our target regions. Given worldwide trends, this translates as unrealistic, Hopewell.

"We will move through our once-great country laid to waste. With few exceptions, most of us were never privy to its original glory except through historical records. The point comparisons of what could have been and what remains will challenge us all. It's going to be a long road to restoration that's not short of complications. Do you understand the mindset?"

"Yes. My apologies," Hopewell replied in a small voice.

"Good. Please make sure that the mounts and the militias are well fed and assisted with the morning's preparations. We'll meet this evening at 18 hours," instructed Connor.

"I can't wait to see how all this animal amplification works," Hopewell exclaimed in an over-enthusiastic rebound.

"We're not going to have some dog and pony show, Hopewell. If you have questions or want information, you'll have to speak directly to Dr. Pendergrass, Governor Hernandez, or Minister Gant," Connor's tone and message translated as distinctly irate.

"You know that's going to be a flat negative, right?"

"Right," Connor answered. "Dismissed, Hopewell. I'm preparing to disembark."

The monitor abruptly was terminated. Attila and Connor looked warily at each other.

"Lovejoy? That's a real name?" Attila asked.

"Very much so. It's the combination that's killer," Connor chuckled.

Connor poured a shot of Hungarian Pálinka for himself and offered another to Attila. The men downed the first drink together and savored the heat that passed quickly through their bodies. Attila was pleased with one of his homeland's specialties. "How did you manage?"

"Your Prime Minister sent a case to Morgan when you arrived ten years ago. Morgan sends the 'white lightning' with his best regards. Says he's not prepared to be that drunk ever again in this lifetime." Connor read the note attached to the neck of a very long, thin bottle.

They toasted and downed a second shot of the potent clear fruit brandy. Attila threw his emptied glass over his shoulder appreciating fully that the shattered crystal rang its fatality against a cabin wall.

"What the hell?" Connor feigned horror.

"I'm a Hun," countered Attila. "We like to punctuate."

"Good thing Morgan just spits," Connor observed.

The men surveyed the coast as the silvery mist burned off with the morning sun. The remaining transport rocked on the water, idling nearby, awaiting orders to move in for the last passengers.

The Circle members joined their leaders on deck and Adele moved in behind her daughter.

"This is a bit wild in the scheme of things. A mother-daughter venture of extreme proportions," Adele whispered and squeezed Caroline's shoulders as they viewed the activity on the water.

Caroline turned and smiled down at her mother, who was now four inches shorter than she. "I wouldn't trade this for the world. I love you."

A familiar face waved toward Connor. Connor returned the salutation, unsure as to the transport passenger's identity. His amplified eyes and brain-net quickly accessed face recognition and history of Robert Gant. Connor shared the information with Attila.

"Who's the woman with him?" Connor cued his brain's message center.

"*Gant is joined by his wife, the former Krisztina Komor. Your latest message on the topic indicates that Dr. Komor intends to accompany the contingent on its mission,*" it revealed textually and via audio.

Attila groaned, "What do people think this is? A party?"

"I heard that," signaled Gant.

"As did I!" Komor added as they embarked.

Attila and Connor were surprised at the last-minute addition. Dr. Komor pinpointed Attila's remark that dismissed her qualifications.

"I've been in surveillance my entire life. I'm also a medical doctor and can technically assist with your amplifications if something goes wrong. I'm also the person who accompanied Brown onto the Pendergrass property years ago and got a lesson in things that fade with black slime into oblivion. I think it prepares me to accompany your group, Attila Meszaros," Komor snapped a staccato retort.

"Apologies, Mrs. Gant. Can you ride worth a forint?"

"You know I'm half Hungarian?" she smiled.

"Half will do," Attila smiled back.

"What do you expect to find, Attila?" Komor asked.

"Extremes," Attila answered soberly.

"What do you hope to achieve?"

"Reconciliation, with God's help," Attila said hopefully.

"God?" Komor said with some surprise.

"Yes, God."

* * *

Tuesday, June 24, 2070

The Confederation troops moved together from Newport News into the nation's capital via Chesapeake Bay. Their path would take them toward what was once known as Morgantown, Pennsylvania. From that point, the plan was to separate and define safe perimeters from Philadelphia up the coast through the northernmost states of the former United States. The ships would correspond by tracking their route up the shoreline until the two groups met either in New Jersey or, if things went smoothly, in the Gulf of Maine. One half would trek toward Lake Erie and follow the water until Buffalo, then cross back through New York. If met with challenges, the expedition could be easily assisted and the convergent points reassigned. Along the way, the mission expected to identify communities of sane survivors, help reestablish safety borders, airlift medical supplies and/or accompany groups toward the port for transfer. Everyone acknowledged the necessity for flexibility.

When it came time to part ways, the expedition had performed flawlessly. Smaller drones sent signals to the leads and flanks about obstacles, weather changes, dangerous animals, and tributaries. Satellite images did the same. Morgan kept an open feed to follow the two expeditions in real time.

Ten troops were left with each community until Confederation boundaries were expanded and secured. With the exception of starving children wandering the countryside and remnants of burnt-out rural and urban areas, there was no sign of large hostile groups. The stories of the community citizens told another story. Survivors had lived decades in dread.

"The crazies have hit us since the darkness. We could never tell when gangs would assault. Maybe as many as fifteen or twenty at a time, but we could never take the chance of leaving our fortresses," explained an elder to Connor.

"But you've got a few thousand in each community here and some are within twenty to fifty miles of each other. Why not join forces?" Attila puzzled.

"It wasn't that simple. Some communities have wild cards. We're not all the same. They might be civilized enough to have a solid grouping but they're just not interested in farming or progress of any kind, for example. You can feel the tensions of those kinds of groups. They tend to be aggressive and unpredictable. They may or may not want our kind of help or be able to understand our set of rules. No one was willing to take the chance on taking in wandering people without children or join forces with communities without farms, crops, or schools. Some were simply stagnant and not so dangerous but no one was willing to bet on unpredictable behaviors. Others? They mean to steal our resources, if given the slightest opportunity.

"We've had our own people go mad with few warning signs. We've got no idea the reasons. We'd gone back to the old ways; it seemed to keep everyone on course. Until the moment that someone goes sideways," the old man shook his head sadly, "they appear fine in every way until they turn."

"What do you do when a crime is committed? What happens to people who suddenly lose their equilibrium? What grouping tends to be affected?" Adele asked.

"It's odd. We don't seem to have issues with kids. It's just those in early adulthood or the more fragile older adults that turn one way or the other; it happens usually in the early twenties or under the stresses of old age. When someone changes they have an urge to up and leave. They pack up and exit the compound. No goodbyes, no regrets, no fears of what's out there. We just let 'em go into the wilderness and wish them well if we know about it. We've never reached the punishment stage."

"They leave without weapons?" Attila asked.

"Nothin' but maybe a hunting knife and enough dried food to keep them for a week or so. Telling you, it's like a call of the wild or something. They go peacefully and never return."

"How do you know they're 'off', as you say?" Sonny asked.

"Sometimes it's gradual but it all happens over a month or so and then hits a crisis point within a few days' time. Usually, the person first withdraws from activities. They become abrasive and sometimes have verbal outbursts, accusing people of not liking or including them. Once in a while, they just go quiet. Not a peep. I could swear that they even seem to have facial alterations. I'm not lying; they'll actually begin to look distorted. When you get down to it, the nastiness often begins with the so-called victim who just pulls a really nasty stunt for no apparent reason.

"I had to personally intervene once. I watched one young woman stalking one of our older members busy harvesting apples. Gracie was picking way up on a ladder. For no reason, this young 19-year-old goes and steals a few pieces of fruit from her basket at the base of the tree. Okay, I think. Naughty move. But then, the girl doesn't eat the apples; she drops them at the base of the ladder. Gracie climbs down to protest the theft. It's certain that the old lady is headed for a fall. I caught her just in time as she reached the last rung. The young lady laughs. Really laughs. It was pure evil. Next day, the mischief-maker is gone. It's the way it happens. We never hear from them again."

With the wondrous eyes of a young child, the white-haired elder moved to touch one of the horses and trace his hand along its long, warm, sleek body. Bending over to pull up long blades of grass, he sighed with delight when the gentle, soft muzzle of a grateful horse nuzzled and slipped the sweet offering from its upper lip into its mouth. It was a familiar, reassuring sound that brought back childhood memories.

Attila and Connor watched the man examine the rows of resting horses; he also took measure of those that stealthily arrived, able to take an entire town by surprise. Tears formed in the eyes of the weathered man who had come face to face with the world that had moved on without them.

"We should have fought," he anguished. "We should have gone together South or tried to make our way to the shores. We sent out groups that never returned and it frightened us. I guess we just prayed and wished ourselves into a stupor. We weren't weak but we weren't brave either. I blame myself. Where was my faith? People looked to me to lead. All I did was play it safe."

His sadness resonated with the troops that silently observed the physical state of those who had lived decades in seclusion. A crude cemetery within the compound was testament to the high mortality rate. Children were shadows of their potential selves, even though there was laughter and curiosity that belied their stunted, fragile bodies.

Those townships along the way with medical resources could reproduce simple antibiotics or generate natural remedies; others that were not the beneficiaries of a scientific legacy of medical information or rudimentary engineering skills were doomed to nineteenth century tools and results. Yet in each of these civilized populations, poems and stories had been written, music composed and sung, dances choreographed, and paintings drawn.

In such communities, troops were left to maintain order or provide simple oversight. Often townships needed the Confederation intervention to remove a small group of savage leaders that had overpowered and then threatened an otherwise moral community into submission. Confederation presence meant establishing a democratic society, administering medical attention, and laying out rules of simple hygiene and food preparation. Sometimes, it meant listening to their survival tales and congratulating the populations for their fortitude.

"We're not prepared for this," complained one soldier, regarding tasks that seemed insurmountable.

Connor admonished the man, "We don't have the luxury to consider an alternative."

There were times Confederation troops were met with extreme hostility. Confederation contingents would be attacked no matter how nominal their approach. Nicholas would lead when drone images or scouts suggested brutal primitive behaviors. Hallmark warning signs included women relegated to menial jobs, public beatings, vacant homes, or buildings in vast disrepair.

In such cases, Nicholas became invisible when faced with ruling thugs. With a singular confrontational thought, Nicholas's karmic effect proved immediate and transformative. In agony, the leader would inevitably respond humbly to physical pain. After many fits and starts, it became evident that something significant was attached to the idea of hurting others. If that failed, Aaron was quick to move boulders to hover over someone's head, threatening to knock sense into the situation.

"Wish we had a Nicholas and Aaron at every one of these wackier communities," groaned one officer.

"This evil momentum can be turned around. Think of it as something important, your duty," Connor advised.

A mitzvah, thought Aaron, *a demonstration of one's understanding of our commandments that offers us a closer relationship to God...*

"Mitzvah?" Nicholas repeated.

"There're commandments within the Mishnah Torah. Jews are reminded that their relationship with God greatly depends upon adherence to these commandments but also our ability to exemplify the idea. We may not, for example, 'rebuke a sinner' as it says in Leviticus 19:17. We should try to 'imitate His good and upright way'... that's said in Deuteronomy 28:9. We just do what we can to help others to carry their burdens, love the stranger and assist the needy. Other laws go to taxes, agriculture, criminal law, property rights..."

"Listening now. Thanks, Aaron," Nicholas answered.

"Where does a hovering half-ton boulder come in?" Ildiko laughed. "Seems like a pretty hard-hitting commandment to me."

"It's not covered in the commandments but I can extrapolate that we don't want to have any unnecessary deaths. It's just the kind of language some of these people understand," Aaron looked toward Ildiko, gauging her approval. She smiled at him and held his gaze longer than usual.

Caroline routinely summoned the Circle to privately convene in the vicinity of each community site. The group would join hands and the blue light would funnel upward to the sky and stream over the countryside as far as the eye could see. Satellite images conveyed exponential swelling of the light's influence. Each time the light grew in intensity, the communities with which they had come in contact responded, flushed with intuition, health, and motivation. For the less inclined, an inexplicable irritability manifested and people departed without a word, just as the Elder had once explained to Connor.

As anticipated, crystal geodes and quartzite within the mineral-rich foothills of the Allegheny Mountains magnified the effect. Bodies of water, Confederation scientists discovered, offered an intensified outcome, too. The light began to show signs of healing the magnetic fields.

On site of Morgantown, the blue light shot upward toward the evening skies as if reaching desperately to attach itself. Fractured in different directions, the blue blazes left crisp traces of brief attachment to geometric patterns that marked a concave horizon. Each time this was done, the intersecting geometric patterns grew wider and brighter until Aditiya excitedly pointed to the clear intersections of the electromagnetic field.

"There it is!" Aditiya sent the others his mental image of the magnetic field that covered the earth's outermost orbit. "It's beautiful. Each time the light attaches, it stretches a little more."

"What is it? What are these traces of light that connect for moments from the earth to sky?" Connor asked Aditiya.

"It's a split second of a divine connection manifesting on many levels. We are beginning to make visible a sort of consciousness unit. It's octave based... follows the mathematical principles in the physical universe at every parallel. Some call it sacred geometry. It's the fabric of our electromagnetic field but it's more, too.

"There are connections between harmonic ratios, for example, and everything we know and see in nature. A seashell depicts the phi spiral; an atom's structure has a process by which each electron is released sequentially through different isotopic stages. The atom morphs into the next element within the Periodic Table. There's always an energetic evolution that emerges from its epicenter. One cell becomes two cells and the division continues until there is an exact copy. That same cell represents the first note of the octave that also represents how all consciousness operates, whether it's on a submicroscopic, cellular, planetary or cosmic level. These patterns and Platonic forms are within everything from minerals to the cell organizational framework of a developing zygote. It's in the grids of planets, too. The same frequency numbers are also in the sunspot cycles. The grids that mirror land mass are the same types of energy patterns that form a precise analog of the nuclear membrane of the cell's continuing expansion, division, and repeating of the process. It's as if everything in the universe is all geometrically decreed as wondrously precise connective tissue," Aditiya recalled his mind's eye of connecting geometric forms since childhood. He quickly sent examples of sacred geometry to those that now tuned in.

"We are witnessing an incredible balancing act that sustains – or threatens – the balance of man's harmonic nature. These numbers and patterns are everywhere, permeating everything we can see or imagine. From pure white light, from its vibrational beginning, our world has been distilled to a spectrum of frequencies, each of which represents our 'wholeness', our optimal state, emanating from the time of creation. Evidence of these connections can be found everywhere when you think about it. We should be able to discern that there is a universal code and symbols of that code at every level of our existence, no matter our interests, focus, or passions.

"Renaissance scientists were able to make clear connections between harmonic ratios and the human body's proportions. The same for those that passed down Vedic or Georgian chants note by note. What we are doing here, I think, is reconnecting; rebuilding the harmonic consciousness that has been disrupted on our planet or connections we have forgotten. A much greater harmonic integrity may be connected beyond what we are now witnessing," Aditiya waxed ethereal.

"You are theorizing a connection to other life forms, dimensions, cosmic life?" Connor asked.

"Of course. We're like the two-dimensional forms in the 1884 novella by Edwin Abbott, *Flatland: A Romance of Many Dimensions.* Flatlanders were those geometric life forms of a two-dimensional world unwilling and, therefore, unable to grasp multidimensional concepts. We cannot allow ourselves – we as humans – to be the reluctant errant cell rejecting possibilities because we lack an abstract facility. Each cellular structure within our own biosphere has the responsibility to remain as healthy and open-minded as possible. That doesn't just mean doing our best by preventing physical illness. We're also expected to harbor healthy mindsets with a willingness to deposit the coin of the realm in the spiritual bank," Aditiya tried to explain. "We should know to give without quid pro quo – give to others, our planet, without remunerative expectations. Give because we know in the deepest part of us that we are assisting ourselves as a connective part.

"Those of us who survived this cataclysm are like so many ancient survivors before us. We're likely residues of many civilizations, many lifetimes, and innumerable collective experiences. We've been serendipitously pulled from the spiritual abyss so that we might try again. Civilizations have failed many times. I suspect we've been redeemed in as many.

"There couldn't be more messages compelling us to build with joy, to love life. I mean, it's Sonny's main gig. He senses the low frequencies and begins to chant as if cutting away bramble that's obscured the sunlight. Every culture has a way to access rays that feed, light, and warm us. It reminds me of the yellow faces of Attila's Hungarian sunflowers that reverently follow the sun's path from dawn to dusk. We, too, need to respond to our source. We're meant to follow the light," Aditiya surmised.

"Proverbs 6:22-23 ...for the commandment is a lamp, and the law is a light..." Aaron added thoughtfully.

"There are countless such directives," agreed Aditiya. "Consider written mathematical codes, great structures built around the world, brilliant concepts of our classical roots, and reams of binary code etched in rock from civilizations dating eight thousand years ago. Some scientists suspect ancient civilizations over 100,000 years ago. Evolved, enlightened messages, over and over again repeated throughout the ages come to us in every way possible. The cues are undeniable yet we've chosen to fight over who has the most reliable providential clue. Religions weren't meant to compete. We were supposed to compare notes, connect the dots, and work together.

"Each disaster and hardship tests the mettle of man's commitment. The EMP disaster, the rampant evil that starved and tested our planet, is just one more catalyst, just another working day, in the business of spiritually cultivating the human race," Aditiya explained his perspective.

"Look at us," Aaron agreed. "Our small sampling converges from all over the planet, awakened in a period of time we can barely gauge. We are gifted a biological talent to manage some kind of crisis. We get yet another cosmic boost to fix ourselves after fully screwing things up.

"Can't you hear it? Let's see if humanity can get it right *this* time! Adversity has a way of changing one's perspective and this time around it's no different. Right now, earth's protective field is gasping for breath, skipping beats, has a dangerous frailty with sputtering pulses unable to maintain a natural seamless energy flow, corrupting literal and moral navigational abilities inside the brain, altering our DNA... think we have a habit of ignoring signals? *Word* – in the harshest, loudest possible way," Aaron concluded.

"So let me get this straight. You people are human jumper cables?" Morgan Pendergrass's voice abruptly interrupted Aditiya from his Cary office. "That's what you're saying? You've arrived to jump the planet?"

Everyone laughed at the image.

"Earth's battery is faltering... like the old cars. Humanity is endowed with abilities to recharge it," Aditiya confirmed.

"Try to avoid metaphorically using the word 'old'. 'Classic,' you can use," Morgan corrected and signed out.

* * *

Caroline sat thoughtfully the evening prior to the Morgantown departure and smiled within the blue light's afterglow. It was stronger than any previous exercise. "Instant healing," Caroline observed as she sat with her mother.

"Instant healing," Adele agreed. "Another day, another miracle," Adele approved happily.

It proved a calm evening for the Confederation troops that celebrated their final evening with the town's residents. Townspeople viewed with special pleasure the horse rides given to children. Their squeals of laughter pealed up and down the town's center road. Relief was palpable among the adults.

With technical direction from Confederation experts, the failing energy supply had been repaired. Expert hands refashioned, restored, and replaced faulty equipment. Dr. Komor and her staff examined hundreds of Morgantown citizens in the church and distributed medicine and counsel. There were six minor surgeries, "and a lot of tooth extractions," according to Komor.

In the warm moonlit evening, the good Morgantown people stared at the thousands of tents they knew were constructed but disappeared by some kind of magic once erected.

"So we aren't easily detected," explained a soldier.

"By the crazies," one young boy finished. "I wish we had that magic. Will we know these things?"

"You will, son. I promise that the worst is over for you, your friends, and family," smiled Jordan Reid, who recalled his own transformational miracle.

Attila and Adele relaxed on a hill upon a blanket as the moon rose, overlooking the campfires within a town too excited to retire. Faces of Confederation soldiers flickered with the intermittent yellow flames prompted by long sticks and fresh logs. Long shadows stretched across a meadow, strangely altering directions among invisible tents. Worries seemed to disappear along with the frail sparks that took flight and dissipated in the cool wind far above the quiet valley. Families gathered to listen to the soldiers' stories of a life without fear. Spontaneous bursts of merriment echoed beyond the lush green basin below.

Attila held Adele tight to him when she wordlessly rested upon his shoulder. At the mound's crest, moonbeams sought out Adele's hair, causing it to glisten and beckon Attila's admiration.

"You're as beautiful and mysterious as the moon," Attila said, stroking Adele's hair.

"Mysterious?" Adele asked.

"Like the moon, part of you is always hidden," Attila smiled.

"As it is with everyone, I suspect. Your intentions are certainly partially hidden from plain sight," Adele said as she leaned away and onto the crook of her elbow.

"I demonstrate my feelings; I rarely speak of them. Do you want to hear my intentions?" Attila mirrored Adele's position and stared at Adele from the opposite side.

"Why do you ask permission?"

"It was merely a warning," he smiled.

"Could you be any more unromantic?" Adele scowled.

"You could accuse me of restraint only. My feelings for you require every sinew of my body and mind to calm itself; if let loose, I would fear losing you in an explosion of expression with the slightest spark of hope. Therefore, I mean to convince you of marriage."

"That's a terrible proposal. You'll have to do better."

"I'm sorry. It's the translator," he stammered.

"No, Attila. It's not the translator. You should put yourself out there without caveats," she corrected. "That's the way it works. A marriage proposal usually requires a demonstration of humility and risk. It must make your heart beat with anticipation, your throat constricts...that's the way I've imagined it. I need you to see my value and be told as much. We're too experienced to hope for something less. So go for it or say nothing. This requires an over the top approach," Adele advised.

"You're training me?"

"I'm training you. No whistles or special shock amps, but I'm doing my best here."

If two hearts could beat as one, it occurred that night on the Morgantown Hills. Smells and sights became sweet and crystalline. Adele suddenly realized a long-lost sensation of contentment. It was a feeling that had eluded her until Attila made his feelings known in no uncertain terms. A symphony of cicadas lulled the pair as they shared dreams of a life together.

Cool, moist grass beckoned Adele to remove her boots so that her toes could move freely throughout the tufts meant to amuse then obligingly fold softly like a cushion. Impulsively, Attila did the same and they strolled barefooted together along the hill.

"I thought I was amped until you kissed me on the ship. That, my dear Attila, was my real moment of amplification," Adele recalled their first intimate exchange.

Dropping to one knee, Attila took Adele's hands in his and cleared his throat.

"Share this moment and every moment possible with me, Adele. I will do everything in my power to love and protect you. Whether yes or no, you have my heart, loyalty, and respect from this day forward until I die. Please say you'll allow me to be your husband."

He placed a circle of diamonds on her left ring finger and explained, "This is for you, to remind you of my promise. Please say yes..."

"Yes," she replied. "That was *so* much better!" Adele complimented. Examining the ring, Adele knew that her fiancé had indeed waited a long time until the right moment. "I love you," she said as they kissed.

Arm in arm, the couple made their way back to their blanket and picnic basket on the hill's crest. Attila's infrared eyes zoomed into the city and commented, "I think everything written about a full moon is not without reason."

Far below their position sat diminutive figures of a man and a woman similarly enchanted with one another; they embraced sitting on the schoolhouse steps. Attila patted Adele's hand and sent visual coordinates. Adele zoomed and recognized her daughter with Nicholas. Nicholas's chin rested upon Caroline's head.

"They're just friends," Adele stated.

"Very good friends," Attila teased.

"Should we listen?" Adele whispered conspiratorially.

"You should never listen to young love, any more than they should listen to us. It's meant to be their experience, a touch of pure joy, and discovery. The same for us...an ecstatic rush shared only by us," he kissed her cheek.

"I'm just so surprised!" Adele said, embarrassed by her impulse.

"I'm surprised that you couldn't see that coming. I've been watching Nicholas watch your daughter for years. It's a good thing that Esther never figured it."

"Caroline was in danger?" Adele said, suddenly alarmed.

"Some of these things are out of our hands," Attila said. "That being said, I kept an eye on all of them."

"I notice that you believe in fate all of a sudden."

"I don't intend to qualify or quantify that which is beyond my understanding. There's no denying the wonder of it all," Attila answered.

"You've killed and are prepared to kill again. How do you reconcile preemptive murder with God's purposes?"

Attila laughed, "You sure know how to sweet talk a man."

"I'm no good at this," Adele apologized.

"Why try to reconcile anything? I can't. Some things are beyond man's purview. Love is the easy part. We feel its satisfaction and it's good. You're in my arms and I'm home. We have an inner drive to get home to our best selves and to those who help us feel protected and happy there. We similarly feel a terrible ache of an analogous homesickness for peace, beauty, and tranquility. That's when we get to the hard place. Who are these mud people without conscience or reverence, able to sabotage our precious dream of humanity's homecoming? I feel you next to me and know a part of God's greater dream for us is played out in our small bubble. I try to reconcile that bubble of happiness with my hellish memories and find it impossible.

"I'll never forget the crazies that come at you screaming, jumping from trees to slice your throat, that linger in shadows outside the tents, quietly setting a blaze that burns a ring around their victims. It's all in another day's work. They'll stand stoically as blistering flesh turns the air putrid. Suddenly, someone will react. Hey! They've forgotten to do the same to the children! They round up the children who've been hidden away and throw them screaming into the fires, too. I've had to helplessly watch as precious few of us were forced to lie in the fields with our horses hugging the ground.

"I've seen children protecting their homes barely strong or tall enough to wield a weapon. Hundreds of thousands of amputated limbs and bodies dumped into tributaries floated from other countries that nearly choked the Danube. I witnessed yoked women pulling carts of conquering tribes, only to be strapped to trees nude when they could no longer serve. You see that and you're crystal clear that this thing you are fighting is pure evil making its way to its home, too. Something terribly altered is always looking at you – for you – until you come eye to eye with that something that looks like you. Even so, each of you believes the other is the monster. You are forced to engage with the evil derived from someone else's worst self-image. I would not believe it. I would not be part of it, I told myself. Yet, as I killed, I could never imagine enjoying the snuffing out of life. Never. The Crazies? They loved it. They were home.

"We had to temper our disgust with compassion so we didn't lose our humanity. That was pretty much what your father said, too. I went home to my wife and child, following a tenuous thread back to my humanity. I never prayed. I never did that. I just knew that I was trying to fight myself back to a place for which I've had occasional glimpses of happiness. Once you have loved, Adele, the feeling never leaves you unless you let it go.

"How did you feel when you lost your wife?"

"It didn't diminish my morals but I didn't see the world as anything but a random environment that can be temporarily domesticated by hard work... only to lose the last vestiges of cultivation with brief neglect. Sweet gardens could be overrun in a month by weeds after a thousand years of painful attention. Poof. Nothing seemed to hold without constant vigilance. As I heard your father say once, we're all shoveling snow in a snowstorm; that was my general feeling. My wife changed all that. I loved her so. We were partners during our life together. However, it was posthumously that I felt something more. It was my wife's parting gift.

"You heard her?"

"I heard her, saw her, and felt her on Christmas Eve. Ildiko had a similar experience. I eventually lost my anger to Noemi's everlasting love that connected to me from somewhere in some way. She got through to me when I was utterly in despair. Every day I was exposed to the darkest corners of the human mind. Noemi's posthumous experience was an epiphanic one. She let me know that I had the love of Ildiko to keep me in check. I will never let the darkness overcome me. It's our appreciation of the miracle of life that makes a person willing to protect that precious miracle at all costs. Love can be discovered on a beautiful fall day on the back of my horse galloping freely on solid ground, the burst of blooms after the hard winter, the first coos of your newborn that connects us to those echoed by newborns everywhere. I will do anything to take proper account of providential prompts. I'll kill to keep those ideas intact."

"Who's the sweet talker now?" Adele touched his cheek.

"It's my way of saying that I've been blessed twice. I have been blessed because I didn't give up. Need I say that I love you the long way again?"

"You've said what I needed to hear," Adele smiled.

"I love you, Adele."

"For the first time in my life, I believe I deserve such love," Adele said gently. "Caroline and my family were enough, I told myself. My good fortune, I believed, was enough. Yet my soul was starving. I love you, Attila. Please share your great love with me."

Attila held Adele until they fell asleep in each other's arms. They woke at 4:45 a.m. when birds chirped their morning activities.

By 8:30 a.m., the troops were packed and ready to move. Half the cavalry would migrate toward Philadelphia and the other would move in the direction of Lake Erie. Troops would remain within each community until help arrived to ensure their continued welfare. Confederation airlifts regularly flew in and out of the mainland to rescue the infirm and relocate isolated parties.

A headcount revealed there were twenty fewer members who had disappeared in the night from the sixteen-foot high walls of Morgantown. It was assumed that the energy emanating from the Circle negatively affected that set. It had become a pattern.

"What about these people that suddenly left Morgantown? Are they now more dangerous?" Sonny asked with growing concern.

"Those that departed are not only more dangerous, they've become shrewder. While we bring our type of resolve and strength forward with the light, that same force seems to bring acuity to evil," Caroline answered.

Chapter XXX

A Whisper

Monday, June 30, 2070

ordan Reid helplessly watched as the first hundred of his cavalry disappeared up to their necks in mud that smoothly sucked the soldiers to a suffocating finish. It took thirty seconds from the time the line touched the camouflaged bog. He struggled to grasp the complexity of the ruse.

Single-purpose systems of sewage joined 3,000 miles of watershed managed infrastructure, hybrid detention ponds, and holding tanks. All had been purposely released into the city's vast infiltration basins and funneled to fields on the city's perimeter. Rather than miles of unobtrusive fields of green expanse, the land had been overwhelmed with billions of gallons of water overflow that seeped deep from within the city.

Reid's troops had worked hard over difficult terrain. Able to move naturally for the first time since circumnavigating former highways and burnt cities, that which appeared to be a clean, hard stretch of long green grass fields was hard to ignore. Reid felt an overwhelming urge to allow the troops to move freely and signaled a five-minute joy ride. The lines excitedly moved abreast of each other. Fifteen long rows of horses galloped hard and happily in the summer breezes. Meant as a brief respite, it was a carefree coupling of riders and horses until it wasn't.

The first rows fell rapidly upon each other mid-stride; others that followed closely behind balked abruptly to avoid the same fate. Forced to helplessly witness their friends struggle mightily against impending asphyxia, anguished cries joined the whirring blades of rescue drones that swooped in. Retractable metallic ropes were expertly targeted seconds later than arms could be freed. In the frantic struggle to keep their noses and front legs high, the horses expedited their descent into depths that reached more than twenty feet.

The water trap of green silage and loose mud was thin enough to rapidly pull horse and rider down and thick enough to prevent recovery. It had proven a well-planned and insidious execution.

"Fall back but not into the woods. Circle up. Prepare," came the instructions as stricken soldiers drowned.

The cavalry had been reduced to less than three hundred. With no other imminent threat, some of the closest horses and riders were located within the muck and removed with the arrival of more powerful drones. The lost soldiers ran into something that required a combination of engineering skills and stratagems that was without known precedent in the Confederation's recent history. Moreover, the manmade ambush was specifically suited to their use of horses.

The sights and sounds of the senseless loss to an unseen enemy for unknown motives made the mission dreadfully authentic. Reid ordered the burial of all retrieved corpses, man and horse. An intelligent, ferocious, well-situated enemy remained undetected.

Reid attempted to signal the ships of their situation in hostile territory. Accompanying drones automatically did the same. Clearly, Reid realized, they were in a dead zone.

Hundreds of miles away, Ildiko screamed and signaled her alarm. Her remote viewing was within seconds of the tragedy. Minutes later, Connor directed the location and circumstances of the troops on Philadelphia's periphery to the ships.

Before dusk, heliports and soloports dropped reinforcements and equipment.

* * *

For five days and nights, the urban fighting was non-stop. Cloaked jamming devices situated upon the highest buildings were discovered as the reason for undetected activity. The Confederation caught no one by surprise. Even though horse and rider were veiled, there were casualties within the tight confines of buildings and lairs. Close quarters and the dysfunctional drone transmitters meant the use of offshore laser cannons presented a high risk. The satellite images and orbiting infrared visuals were of marginal use in the case of close combat.

Wild dogs in the city quickly caught the scent of the horses. Although the horses kicked and killed the hounds, the animal struggles made horse and rider simpler to target. Molotov cocktails, grenades, and explosives were thrown in the vicinity of the yelping and gnashing animals; twenty horses and riders died together, their corpses reappearing amongst slaughtered dogs as Confederation reflective shields disintegrated. Riders were retrieved for burial in the morning hours but the horses had to be left where they fell. Chemical alterations of rigor mortis left the gruesome sight of the beloved mighty steeds on their backs and sides, legs stiffened in undignified positions. Confederation troops fought fiercely, mindful of fallen friends.

Overwhelmed by that which promised to be a Pyrrhic victory of search and rescue, Jordan Reid remained unwilling to fire into masses of people sacrificially thrust into the streets, nor did he explode buildings that might house innocent survivors. Even as the lasers from the ships had eventually locked in, it was impossible to separate the innocent women and children used as shields.

As rocks, bullets, and missiles pelted them, there was no regard for collateral damage from opposition forces. The crazies killed their own as mercilessly as Confederation forces; their lifeless bodies were left without regard. Confederation troops acknowledged that complete insanity ruled. Rather than visceral battle cries, ecstatic screams of unbridled lunacy echoed amongst building corridors in the night.

On the fifth day, the sight of childrens' decapitated heads greeted Jordan Reid's troops. From ruins of buildings and the remnants of rusted green metal signage, the frozen expressions of terror on human gargoyles were meant to ward off the Confederation. A singular word was written in large black lettering on a hanging placard from each child's severed head and neck: LEAVE.

Connor sent Reid orders to immediately withdraw into the wilderness area and continue northwest.

"Don't try to make it through to the coast. It's no longer a search and rescue. Even with coverage, it's a bad idea to take the risk with so many civilians," Connor explained. "There's too much threat to innocent people, too much sophistication. We'll return better prepared now that you've identified the blocking source."

Reid agreed, "It's a nest of traps from here on out. We'd have to retreat in any case. Even if we'd hadn't been ambushed, I'm sure that this is more than guerrilla warfare; we have to come in eventually by air but I've no idea how to tell who is who. My guess is that the inner city fighting and fortifications have been developed to keep people in as much as it is to keep people out."

An idea occurred to Attila. "No!" he shouted. "I want you to stop signaling the horses. Stop trying to re-direct them around those who are thrown in front. Let the horses figure out the enemy. I'm sure of this. They've got great instincts...they'll know the innocent from the crazy predator and they've got the amps to do the job. They smell it! They can maneuver on their own, fight their own battle. Riders can act from the saddle without parsing innocents," he demanded of Jordan. "Don't think about it... act!"

It worked. The horses were left to their own strategies when Reid led the final inner city charge. Their instincts coupled with highly engineered senses and were able to forge a greater telepathic connection, easily targeting feral threats and foregoing the innocent. Riders became reactionary elements. Adroitly avoiding some and sensing the strong predatory behaviors of others, the horses kicked, bit, threw and trampled an enemy they identified with animal instinct. The final conflict ended suddenly with the enemy's hasty retreat into the night. Left standing were grateful hostages.

The CAS air force hovered over the mounted soldiers until they met the overgrown Appalachian Trail. A third returned to

Philadelphia's outskirts while others were ordered to return to the ships.

Drones pinpointed the buildings with advanced installations that had successfully blocked satellite signals. With laser accuracy, the technology was destroyed from hundreds of miles away by the ship's laser cannons. Reid's troops moved rapidly to join Attila's regiments moving toward Ohio. Confederation reinforcements moved into the center of Philadelphia en masse.

That night, Ildiko and Sonny engaged the Circle to try to direct the blue light to a specific area with Vedic frequencies meant to help ensure Confederation success within a war-torn city. Satellite images reported an enormous blue light of gigantic proportions enveloping Philadelphia. Two days later, there were reports of the American Liberty Bell floating on a barge on the Delaware River.

"A replica?" asked Meredith Green in Raleigh, examining an established feed.

"No. We've discerned the interior crack and the extra copper patches. It's the original. I don't know how they got that two-thousand-pound bell on a barge, but there it is floating down the Delaware. People are lined up on both shores cheering. I don't know what to make of it," Dr. Nishant announced from the Research Triangle's military building.

"They're celebrating their freedom. Where did the hostiles go?" Indu wondered.

"That's the big mystery," Green answered. "Our drones and troops have not found one hostile. They landed full force... there's no trace of the enemy!"

"Very odd," Indu commented worriedly.

Chapter XXXI
Two Sides of Mona

Wednesday, July 2, 2070

G rayle woke with a start in the middle of the night. He moved from his bed and wandered into corridor 22 toward the vault that accessed the international satellite feeds that once diverted communications and decided to activate it.

"How do I do this?" he wondered when nothing responded. He'd forgotten the requirement to activate the controls upside and followed the hidden escape route outdoors into the hardened concrete communications building. There was no longer a reason to fear EM pulses but Grayle rejected the compulsion to observe a dying world more than necessary. Communication access was his secret. He already had enough evidence that the Confederation was moving closer to his community.

"Horses? Military?" he considered while reviewing reports. As much as he tried to trace the path of ingress or regress of Confederation troops, their trajectory was unclear. It was an opportune time, however, to prepare. Grayle figured that the confederation troops would underestimate the challenges in his part of the world. A superimposed 3-D map clearly marked the site of a terrible battle as 'Pennsylvania'.

I'll need to keep close watch. These poor souls might find their journey more than they bargained for. They're going to need our help, he thought.

Grayle attempted to organize rudimentary dressage drills on the unseeded fields surrounding the cultivated farms. There were a few dozen horses used for packing but no one knew how to ride like the images captured of the Confederation's mounted militia. "We have no such abilities," he sighed his disappointment. "They'll never learn such skills in such a short time."

Among the thousands of residents underground, and in the ever-expanding town now named 'Grayleton', were able-bodied men and women who knew plenty about how to survive and fight in the wild on foot. For the most part, Grayleton was seeded with those who had managed to survive violent situations. Grayle welcomed those who trekked into the vicinity or crossed paths on hunting trips. Word spread and the trickle had turned into an unsystematic migration toward the safety and comforts of Grayleton.

Grayle was aware of the need to protect Grayleton. He had at his disposal almost every strategic device known in history. Access to thousands of original books in the Military Vaults had its advantages. Prototype weaponry and manuals offered means by which to create ammunition. More importantly, Grayle felt as if he was a conduit of knowledge from a source able to process through him extemporaneously. This he attributed to a guardian angel that carefully guided his actions.

"Civilization is coming!" announced Grayle in the community hall. "We're finally going to meet the Confederation, for better or for worse. We'll remain cautious," he advised the assemblage. "We aren't interested in helping, supporting or joining those that would lead us down a path of war only to re-institute sins that destroyed our once-great country. Am I wrong?" he yelled to the crowd.

"No!" came the resounding cry.

Grayle spoke gravely, referencing the Philadelphia tragedy. "I've witnessed Godless savages slaughter without mercy. I've also seen those who mean to rid us of this intrusive evil.

"If Confederation soldiers come this way, we'll prepare to meet and shelter the survivors. Let's pray that these men and women are believers and have God's protection."

Dutifully, those present bowed their heads in silent prayer. Grayle entreated privately for something more. It was with disappointment Grayle realized the world's complexities eluded his audience's interest or intellectual capacities. All direction, he realized, lay with him. Grayle's loneliness was offset by an intense desire to establish a specific brand of society.

Grayle's passion for life, his voracious thirst for knowledge, and his will to restore a God-centered community, drove the town to confidently follow the charismatic leader. Nevertheless, Grayle missed having informed or motivated friends with whom to exchange ideas. His was an intellectual isolation that represented more desert than oasis.

Grayleton citizens were satisfied to work at specific tasks. They were receptive to stringent laws and regulations. Automatic pilot tended to be the preferred mode of operation. No one argued in the town bearing the founder's name. Few demonstrated curiosity about the vaults or the ways others functioned at respective jobs. Their faith in Grayle was absolute.

Grayle came into the world with a passionate message on his lips, a gift of oratory known to transform lesser men into sweet-tongued demagogues. Such leaders, Grayle considered, were no different than the illusionary green field that lured Confederation men and women to their untimely deaths. In a moment of simple folly, trained soldiers rode toward a slice of heaven and slipped carelessly from life.

"Safe ground and grassy plains will not lower my guard. Our survival requires consistent vigilance," he concluded.

As much as Grayle thought about past love, Grayle knew that the freckle-faced girl of his younger days was not his equal even then. Even so, he imagined a safe haven, a family, and a working society. Reminiscent elders conveyed images of former times that he was unable to get out of his mind.

With every tome and chip, Grayle's soul grew keener for the information held deep within the Boyer earth. For many days on end, Grayle slept in the art and music vaults; he watched the vids and original films threaded on antique equipment and digitized ones. Millions of data bits at his disposal consumed the leader and fed an insatiable craving for former and future times.

Among the historical artifacts were coded stone fragments dated 11000 BCE. Government records of advanced technologies, underground pyramids in Alaska, Giza fragments, samples of rock and soil that had been solidified by a nuclear blast in a time that predated modern civilization, were scattered and left unexplored for want of time. The stored collections of anomalies, rarities, and the priceless seemed endless.

Inventions of every description were catalogued and kept in temperature-controlled rooms. One vault was dedicated to wines that dated back 7000 BCE; Chinese was scrolled on the massive mechanical drawer that hydraulically rolled from floor level to thirty feet. Jewels from antiquity and Renaissance artwork that had never seen a museum lined hundreds of thousands of feet within the underground mazes of precious items, selected by anonymous authorities.

As much as Grayle wanted to immerse himself in the signatures of civilization, it was the data centers dedicated to securing massive statistics that most interested him. Stored within ambient temperatures of 55-63 degrees, the vast facility operated on an efficient geothermal system deep within the mountain. Meant as a disaster recovery option for major industry and government, Grayle also recovered top state secrets within the US President's quarters amongst passageways of additional covert tunnels and treasuries.

For whatever reason, the ex-president of the United States kept certain less important information close to him in smaller temperature-controlled biometric vaults. Original Bibles, religious texts and scientific studies with margins of notes had been read and re-read. Grayle studied the manuscripts, artwork, and communiqués discovered lying outside of the bedroom safes.

He lay upon his bed and stared at the lesser known Isleworth Mona Lisa painted by Leonard da Vinci a decade before his subsequent version. According to Clifton Brown's journal, it was painted between 1503 and 1506 in the artist's native Florence. The former resident had hung the original painting at eye level, so as to be comfortably viewed from a prone position. It was from this identical perspective that Grayle stared at da Vinci's first rendering of the more famous Mona Lisa that followed the Isleworth version.

Grayle decided that the model for the original version, Lisa Gheradini del Giocondo, might have been a simple, innocent woman as evidenced by her easy upturned smile. The second try, thought Grayle, was conversely a glimpse into da Vinci's mind. The succeeding, more provocative Mona Lisa, was worldlier.

"She was a woman of secrets," Grayle determined. Grayle discovered Clifton Brown's carefully written remarks within a bedside journal that agreed with his assessment.

"*The second Mona Lisa is supposed to be something of a mystery. She's made cryptic, defined as much by the viewer's perspective as the painter's own. With the smallest alterations from the original, I realize I have no idea of the mind or temperament of this woman. The first Mona, by contrast, looks transparent, not at all profound*," wrote Brown in one entry. It was followed a year later by an additional notation.

"*I see this woman and I am not threatened or confused but confident that she is what she is. Not so the second Mona. She gives me pause. What does it mean?*"

Grayle was more baffled about Brown's obsession with this particular version than the painting.

From under Brown's former bed, Grayle discovered another da Vinci treasure that was still labeled from a vault formerly held by an industry leader. The Vitruvian Man illustration of arms and legs extended aimed to represent divine symmetry. A young man with wild hair illustrated architectural principles. Vitruvius, the architect upon whose theories da Vinci's Vitruvian Man was based, appealed to da Vinci. Vitruvius theorized that the exact proportions and measurements of the human body were divinely created, perfect, and correct. A house of God, therefore, theorized Vitruvius, should reflect and relate to the part of the human body noting that the human body could entirely be encompassed and symmetrically depicted, within both a circle and a square.

"*If man is made in the image of God,*" began a passage from the ex-president's notes, "*the human's perfect proportions*

503

embody a divine and cosmic order. Each circle represents this divine perfection and is always at the center. The five Platonic solids are the building blocks of the cosmos...." It was too much for Grayle to grasp entirely but the massive illustrations upon which the encased illustration lay correlated the theory with graphic church designs broken down in a perfectly illustrated series of connecting squares and circles. It helped him grasp clues of intelligent design; he liked the reassurances that stood solidly on paper and were carved in stone. It drove him to search for similar scientific clues in the underground tunnels that alluded to spiritual connections. His mind, each night, returned to the journal and the paintings hanging over the foot of his bed.

I must be like the first Mona Lisa. My people should feel as if I'm transparent and safe – one of them, was his last thought before drifting off to sleep.

Chapter XXXII

Esther and Stanley

Thursday, July 3, 2070

*E*sther now longed for her sister and former friends who once comforted her. Her erratic temperament had considerably calmed; she believed the cure had been concurrent with the onset of true love.

Meredith Green was charged with Esther's oversight. Esther was grateful for the tedious office job, given the alternative of working manual labor on the Pendergrass farm.

After hours, Esther spoke happily with the man who worked remotely on similar projects. They exchanged jokes, noticing that they tended to cross reference similar files. Both acknowledged themselves as 'lowly' employees that didn't mind work of little consequence.

"Hey, there. I see we're always in the same space. You as bored as I am?" he messaged first.

"No oversight, no reports, no thinking. It's perfect, right?" Esther replied.

From that point, they spoke about the world, their families, ambitions, and pets.

"You don't have a pet?" he once asked.

"No. I spent a lot of years with way too many dogs, most of which were named variations of the favorite sire. The indoor dogs were fine but the hunting hounds all looked the same, too. I called them all 'Stupid' because I couldn't tell one from another."

"I've got some kind of mix. She's part somethin' and part somethin'. I've got no idea," the young man joked. "Maybe a cat would be easier to care for," he suggested.

They met holographically and the chemistry was immediate. Finally, they spoke on a regular basis for hours at a time through the TrueView that had haptic features.

"My boyfriend's name is Raga... half white, half Indian. Raga means 'melody of beauty' in Indian Classical music. He can play the sitar!" Esther excitedly blurted one morning to Meredith Green who had merely mumbled a 'how's it going?' on her way through the lobby.

"That's nice. How'd you meet?" Dr. Green continued politely with Esther trotting beside her.

"Online. Work. He's in data filing, too. He wondered who it was that was working within the same work space."

"Works for us?"

"Yes, in a university part time job. He's so handsome with enormous green eyes and beautiful black hair. His voice is so pleasant – soothing and calming."

Dr. Green mumbled 'that's nice' once more and hurried from the hall, having zero interest in personal relationships. Her job was to keep an eye on Esther and that was that. Esther was working and logging long hours and surpassing her quota. The idea was to engage and distract Esther. "She's certainly engaged and distracted", Green thought with satisfaction.

Esther and Stanley interacted regularly. They planned to meet in the flesh but Esther was not yet off probation.

"Why is it that you're on probation?" he worried.

"This old guy that calls the shots – pretty much my boss – thinks he owns the world and it just so happens he almost does. He thinks I was unstable after a long relationship that didn't work out. I lost my temper pretty bad and lost my place at the family table while I was at it. Even my sister doesn't talk to me."

"Where's your sister?" Stanley asked.

"Don't know. She's off gallivanting around the country with a bunch of Confederation yahoos who think that they're rounding up wayward cattle. She's supposed to come home by the first of August but they've got flexible plans."

"You think I could come and visit?" he asked.

"I've got a small apartment near here. I don't see why not."

They made plans to spend time together the last two weeks of August in Raleigh.

One day there was a pause in the conversation while they stared at each other's images via the TrueView.

"I'm sure you're the one for me, Esther," Stan broke the silence. He touched her face with the TrueView's haptic application; it identified a mutual predilection for intimacy. Stan's proposal for an intimate relationship was made viscerally clear. Never had Esther felt so prized.

Angela Pendergrass made note of Esther's elevated mood when they crossed paths in downtown Cary.

"I think she may be ready to return home, Morgan," Angela reported to Morgan later that afternoon. "You won't believe the difference. She's genuinely happy with this fellow."

"Well, there's never been a cloud so dark that the sun can't shine through," Morgan said sarcastically. "Anything's possible, I guess. If this miracle lasts more than three days, we can invite the young man over here for lunch or something but don't hold your breath, Cookie," he concluded in a puff of smoke.

Chapter XXXIII

Random Pieces

Friday, July 4, 2070

"We will call ourselves New America, hopefully a temporary name," began Grayle. He surveyed the township that stood in rapt attention. "This town of Grayleton might be an epicenter from which we may rebuild our great country once more. The United States of America once celebrated this date that commemorated the adoption of the Declaration of Independence, composed by Thomas Jefferson and signed in 1776 by what was called a Continental Congress in a great city called Philadelphia. With their signatures, brave men declared that thirteen defenseless colonies regarded themselves independent from the dictatorial rule of Great Britain. Rather than primitive outposts, these founders considered themselves civilized and their colonies much more than Britain's subservient outliers. They had gone through countless hardships for many years. There came a time when they wanted to govern themselves rather than be indentured servants of a kingdom an ocean away. Today we will celebrate Grayleton's ability to govern ourselves against all odds. We also recognize the spirit of our once great national heritage that lives on in us!" decreed Grayle at the onset of the day's festivities. "We will celebrate July Fourth in honor of the God Almighty, and our right to freedom with bonfires, parades, and sharing food!"

Grayle had routinely followed the Confederation troops moving toward their hidden township on his monitor feed. He knew that they would pass through some of the most treacherous territory in the state as they journeyed northwest.

"They're going toward the Lakes," he surmised.

Grayle apprised the Grayleton citizens it was likely that they would have visitors from the Southern parts of the country that survived the darkness intact. He could not hide his enthusiasm.

"We'll give these people a great welcome!" he announced daily in preparation for Confederation interaction. "Let's celebrate in anticipation of a promising future..." Grayle surveyed the sea of blank faces.

"Any questions?"

There were none, ever.

An American flag was hoisted on a field that day and families gathered to see the strange symbol rise above them. Grayle explained the meaning of the flag and what it took to erect a nation per the vision of the Founding Fathers.

By nightfall, the food had been finished and remnants of the day's activities began to disappear. Blankets and tents sprang up along fields and small bonfires lit irregular paths. Those that had learned how to play the old instruments played upon them, albeit deprived of any harmonic faculty.

"Horrible," Grayle lamented. He made a note to himself to arrange for the children to listen to music recordings the way he did. "Even the singing is off key," he cringed.

A strapping young man, the strongest and most eager of his personal guards, made his way brutishly through the dispersing crowds toward Grayle. Although just 6' tall, the young man towered over most of those whose growth had been arrested by malnutrition. A few years after his arrival, Grayle discovered possible potential in the teenager named Anton. The eager boy was more wide-eyed and focused than the typically inept newcomer. As a young man, Anton announced a name change that would demonstrate his admiration.

"My name is now Grayleson," he declared in front of Grayle one afternoon. "Like I'm your son," he added.

"You should honor the name given to you by a loving father," Grayle insisted otherwise.

"What makes you think my father loved me?" Anton challenged.

"What makes you think he didn't?" Grayle returned.

"I was beaten. He beat my mother. My mother died and he threw her body into the woods. The same for the babies that came from other women. What do you think now?"

"I think he was an ignorant, vile man. I'm still not your father and your name is still Anton," Grayle reiterated.

Anton, recalled Grayle, tended to express opinions. Grayle liked feedback in measured doses but recognized in Anton a basic lack of respect that typically accompanied arrogance. Given an opportunity to usurp Grayle's authority, he would do so. Grayle knew that he could never be so foolish, nor Anton so empowered, as to be politically leveraged.

On several occasions Grayle had eyed Anton manhandling people when they failed to respond promptly to his demands. Grayle noticed bullying tactics that gradually moved into physical abuse. Bruise marks appeared on women ranging from young to old, from extremities to face.

"Do you see me acting this way, Anton?" Grayle asked Anton, caught in the act of hitting a young woman who resisted his advances.

"No, Father. Forgive me, please. I'm learning."

"Stop calling me father," Grayle ordered in the first instance. "You must never use your strength against citizens again. If you've a problem, you'll take steps 1-2-3 before taking any physical action. 1: come to me. 2: come to me. 3: come to me. Understand? You do nothing."

"Yes, I come to you and tell you of any problem. I do nothing." Anton bowed his head deferentially.

Another incident followed this warning, however. Rather than a woman, Anton repeatedly struck a man from behind who accidentally brushed by him in the dining hall. Grayle appeared behind Anton, bumped his shoulder and demanded, "Now hit me, Anton."

Anton refused to strike Grayle.

"You will hit me the way you hit others. Do it now while I'm watching, able to defend myself. That would be fair."

Anton still refused. "I cannot hit my father!"

Grayle warned Anton in a way that sent shivers down his spine and turned him white. No one heard the warning whispered in his ear but Anton's terror was unmistakable. He stood shaking as Grayle walked away and then fainted. Anton never again touched a Grayleton citizen.

"I'm going out with the scouts tonight," Anton reminded Grayle as the last of the campfires died and doors closed on the street fronts. "We'll meet the Confederation people if they stay on their path."

"If you run into them, make sure they read this message the moment you deliver it."

"Yes, Grayle," Anton said as he ran his hand around the envelope and tucked it away. He had no idea of the word 'deliver'.

Grayle worried about his unpredictable, overzealous lead scout. Yet, he had factored Anton as a necessary player.

"Be careful. Remember, you're not permitted to speak for me or answer questions. You stick to the script. If they're unfriendly, we need to keep our location a secret."

"Yes, Father!" Anton feebly rolled the words 'permitted, script and location' over in his mind.

"Stop the father business, Anton!" Grayle growled his disapproval.

Anton departed with a large group. They anticipated crossing paths with the Confederation troops that had joined and proceeded together trekking toward Lake Erie. Anton knew the territory by markings and he knew how one mile could be friendly and the next stretches might become a snare. There were no great numbers anywhere but the foothill people were familiar with opportunities for surprise attacks. He figured the Southerners were going to welcome their assistance by the time they met.

At 3:00 a.m., Anton's fully equipped group slipped out of the town unnoticed. Their frequent scouting trips were planned so as to avoid undue attention of citizens. Grayle wanted it that way, even though no one seemed to care.

Sunday, July 6, 2070

Jordan Reid conveyed his post mortem account to Confederation leaders in the outskirts of what was once Harrisburg. There was silence until Attila could no longer contain his fury.

"You decided to go for a little joy ride? Where did you get that idea?"

"I don't know what I was thinking," he painfully admitted. "I let my guard down. To that point, there were so many little villages of varying degrees of development, but we never came close to anything formidable enough to have figured such an entrapment. The idea came to me from nowhere... impulse... I can't believe it myself," Jordon anguished.

"And the reason you didn't finish off those in the streets in plain sight? You took five days?" Attila furiously pursued.

"The children. I couldn't see blasting innocent children. They were different than the ones we found en route. They seemed alert, well-fed, cognizant of everything going on," he whispered. "I could hear their parents screaming for us to stop...they weren't all crazies. And the crazies killed them just to get us to enter the city streets." Jordan searched for a way around his failures.

Attila was well acquainted that such levels of histrionic insanity that escalated decades before the Darkness. The world stood by, ignoring the sacrificed innocents – including their own children – to the call of hatred. They committed suicide, strapped bombs to their chests, and walked into crowded buildings and streets demanding attention toward never-ending passions they termed causes. Extremists overwhelmed most of the civilized world until the ever-contentious Islamist fundamentalist leaders turned against one another once more for absolute authority. The resulting internal tribal conflicts stemmed the tide of worldwide massacres but never fully ceased to drive millions away from their homelands, like so many lemmings, drowning and dying in their attempts to escape certain death.

"What about our dead? You get them and the equipment out of there, Reid?" Attila's tone leveled.

"We did, sir."

Attila and Connor dismissed Reid and turned toward the group that sat together gravely at the campsite headquarters.

"We'll move together from this point," announced Attila.

"We should have always been together," Caroline announced with her eyes resting upon Attila Meszaros. "I'm afraid that you underestimated the resistance. That wasn't Reid's fault."

"I would have sent Nicholas but we felt we needed the Circle as a unit," Attila acknowledged.

"Reid is a good man. He pulled a dumb stunt. We're lucky that they didn't lose more," Caroline reminded him.

"It doesn't make sense that those guys could be that advanced. Blocking our satellite surveillance? How about the knowledge required to flood the city and create that bog?" Cynthia posed.

"Most of all, how the hell did they expect the CAS? They didn't hear a twig break," Connor added.

"They may not have expected the Confederation," Sonny suggested. "They just expected something. That blue light has been lighting up the heavens for a while now," Sonny emphasized. "Scouts look around for threats. That's what they're supposed to do. The light, and the energy it conveyed, was such a threat."

"That Liberty Bell was floated down the river," Cynthia marveled. "Crowds of people were there cheering according to reports. They're the good guys. Just where did the bad guys originate? Where did they go? All of a sudden they rule the city, throw people's children into the line of fire, and then capitulate? Run away?" Cynthia asked. "How did they sneak in there in the first place? Or were they always there keeping the good people captive?"

Ildiko raised her hand, suddenly a schoolgirl in an over-talkative classroom. "I'm not picking up any movement other than small bands of people here and there. I've never had an inkling of organized rebels."

Nicholas insisted that it was important to move the Confederation troops forward only after a better equipped scouting party preceded in 25-mile increments.

"Enough people should be involved in our scouting group in the event we find similar technology or numbers beyond our expectations. I'll lead and Aaron should flank us. It'll take longer but it's safer. I'll go without a suit; the rest will all be invisible so our numbers can't be quantified. If we're about to be attacked, I'll disappear. It's what I do, right?" Nicholas proposed.

They agreed on Nicholas's plan and contacted Raleigh.

Dr. Komor spoke privately with Attila and Connor. "I agree with Caroline and Cynthia's concerns. They fought as a unit with plans and strategies. This is not something we've ever come up against in the last twenty years."

Attila nodded. "They factored our compassion and civility, too. No other group but Reid's would have hesitated to run over children in the midst of fighting for our lives."

"What do you mean other than Reid's regiment?" Adele asked.

"I can tell you right now that I would have done anything to preserve our people. If the Hungarian Hussars hesitated to defend our borders, there would be no Hungary. It wasn't pleasant. It was dark business. Our message was clear; if an invader or crazy faced a Hungarian they knew that we were going to ask questions from the dead. It didn't take long for our dimwitted enemies to get the picture. I didn't hesitate to replace every slaughtered woman and child nailed to posts with one of his or her own. That's the purview of war. Don't fight if you don't fight to win."

Adele shared his disgust at half measures. For too long, crazies counted on Confederation compassion. Many innocents died but many more were saved as a result of the stoic approach.

Caroline changed the subject and asked if everyone was prepared to 'spread the light' within the hour.

Sonny smiled his approval. "It's making a difference. Each time, there are less and less low frequency areas."

Caroline hesitated thoughtfully. "You know, I grieve for the horses. Our good friends...they fought so valiantly."

After the meeting had concluded and Sonny chanted prayers for the dead, Connor contacted Cynthia.

"You've got a call from your sister. Do you wish to receive?" Connor asked.

"No, thank you," Cynthia refused.

"She's been given the chance to contact you because Green considered Esther has an improved mental state," Connor added as a suggestion.

"Still no," Cynthia finalized.

It was 9:00 p.m. when Esther's call to her sister was refused. At 9:30 p.m. she pinged Stanley.

"Hello beautiful," he greeted before noticing the tears. "What's wrong?"

"My sister won't speak with me. My former friends won't accept my calls either," Esther sobbed with disappointment.

"Why is that?"

"I've had a bad time of it. I treated the people that loved me the most in the worst possible ways. I'm not sure what happened to me. Their energy was different. I couldn't get along."

"Energy?" Stanley asked.

"There are things I'm not supposed to talk about if I work here. If that happens, I'll be sent to the moon or something."

"I don't like to see you sad," Stanley commiserated.

"I remember the way I acted. When my sister returns, I'm going to make it up to her. I'm going to make it up to everyone," Esther resolutely planned.

Stan spoke about future plans he had in mind.

"I wouldn't mind seeing Hungary, Esther. They say it's the most intact and beautiful of old Europe and the best of the new world," he mentioned excitedly.

"Hungary? It's so odd you mention Hungary."

"What's so odd about it? It's huge now, has everything the Confederation has and is much more organized. Want to go with me? I know that I could find work in the Carpathian basin," Stan encouraged.

"I've a friend from there who speaks about Hungary all the time," Esther smiled. She felt the moment was serendipitous.

"I'd like to go anywhere with you, Stanley Raga."

Stanley couldn't believe his luck. Esther was beautiful, smart, had a great sense of fun. They both knew that keeping their Research channel open for private conversations was against the rules but she was willing to risk her job for him. He loved the way she listened intently to his every word and was so eager to please.

With a woman like Esther by my side, I could take over the world, he mused happily.

Tuesday, July 8, 2070

With alternating scouting parties ensuring safe passage many miles to the anterior, the Confederation Hussars moved confidently through the countryside until they made their way into what which was once mapped as the Gallitzin State Forest. The mountainous terrain was made more difficult by the gnarled tree roots and windfalls that had compromised formerly groomed hiking trails and footpaths. It was now an unspoiled territory teeming with wildlife. The tall, dark forests from which the troops emerged were filled with dried treetops and enormous rotting stumps. Without fires or human management, the second growth had failed to materialize. At the western edge of the Allegheny Plateau, the lower reaches of the alpine climate filled with birch, alder and balsam trees. Krisztina Komor assessed, recorded, and catalogued more than five hundred species of plants within the first thousand acres of their travels through the former state park.

"Wild ginger!" she marveled.

By the time they reached Glendale Lake, the Confederation regiments had begun to enjoy the sounds of wildlife. Given the Confederation's collective alien scent, their invisibility meant little to the animal population. Besides a few broken steel traps and discarded fishing poles scattered around the lake's edge, the only other civilized evidence was deteriorating cabins with moss-laden roofs.

Woodchucks scurried everywhere, spiking their heads from crater-like homes and retreating just as quickly as the horses pounded their way amongst their coverings, able to nimbly avoid each hole. Centuries-old wooden traditional windmills, once used to harness energy to pump water and grind grain, joined 21st century turbines, most of which had ground to a rusted halt. Working windmills served only to capture and channel gusts of wind that had gained momentum up and over the hills for no one's final use. Herons and geese glided and honked their way toward the wetlands that bordered the 26 miles of the sprawling lake, suddenly made aware of the unseen presence below them.

Paradise, thought Komor as she ambled beside her horse, Temper, categorizing images for later analysis. As dusk began to show, the tents were erected but the curious doctor had yet to arrive camp-side. Komor had lagged for miles, riveted by the bustling life that had matured in the absence of technology's intrusions. It was clear that the animals were periodically hunted because humans sent alarms throughout the animal populations many miles before they'd arrived. It was an emerging pair of polar bears that stalked her, with a baby elephant in tow, that caught Komor by surprise. A spider money sat contentedly on the head of the baby elephant.

The strange menagerie appeared to Komor as an illustration borrowed from a Russian fairy tale. Rather than run for her life, Komor stifled her laughter. Temper remained motionless.

Dragging one of his hind legs, the first emerging bear was clearly worse for wear. Another smaller bear, thought Komor, was probably only three or four years of age. Komor's information told her that there had once been several zoos in the area, making logic of the odd alliance. She decided to lead Temper from their migrating path toward one of the rivers that would take them closer to the lake. She signaled Attila to expect some strange company that might be headed their way to fish and graze.

The animals passed the invisible rider and horse then abruptly scattered into a gaited run. Komor mounted Temper and followed closely behind. Breaking off path, the bears trampled small trees as they cut a new swath of trail toward the wetlands. Komor galloped toward the Lake. She questioned the reason no one had responded to her unusual message.

Entering camp, it was clear that there was a problem. The newly staked tents were being retracted. It required a singular snap of a button for the tents to self-erect and repackage themselves, but the hundreds of snapping sounds at once were disconcerting. Once visible, the troops re-activated their refracting field.

"What's happening, Attila?" Komor signaled.

"Where've you been?" Attila snapped. "Go inspect the injured."

The scouting party had returned with four wounded. Nicholas drank water while his arm rapidly healed. Sonny and Caroline worked to expedite the group's healing properties and their wounds began to close rapidly, too. It had come to pass that the entire contingent had been able to maintain exceptional health and heal just as quickly. It was clear that the blue light and chants had permanently shared effects.

"Here's the point," Nicholas continued as Komor took a seat beside Adele. "I was unable to stop anyone. Although my life was threatened and I turned invisible without any gear, there was no reaction as I've experienced in the past. Maybe around five older men fell to the ground in agony but the rest of them were unaffected. I knew immediately that they had no conscience. None at all. Given that they intended to attack us, I realize my power is limited to those who have an understanding of their treachery. Those that reacted to me were aware that they had wrongly killed and otherwise caused pain. These guys? Nothing. They're immune."

Nicholas looked as surprised as everyone else when he said, "They were there to ambush us. They were waiting out of sight but our drones picked up movement. These guys were crawling on their bellies in the wood per images in four second time-lapse counts; 46 men moved amongst the brush toward our position. We stopped and waited for about an hour. Another series of images came in of the same men that suddenly turned away from our position. I tried to contact base and we'd been jammed. Jammed! We could reach our drones but nothing else. The red light was clear...no one was receiving. I tried to message telepathically. Zero! The only thing I wanted to do at that point was to go in hard and finish them off.

"We moved forward and came upon some lean men with their toothless swag standing with their knives and assorted weapons hanging from waist holsters. One of them threw a knife toward my horse mid-chest and it began. From the trees, from under the ground, from all around us, we were attacked by crossbows, guns, flamethrowers and lasers. The lasers were ineffective because of the outdated technology but managed to cut some of our screens by bits and pieces. Then they began to target the horses' legs. They were unable to cut through their protective gear, too."

The horses and Aaron saved us from a protracted fight. Aaron felled every tree and stone he could levitate from the back end. The horses didn't let anything stop their momentum. They cut through the swelling groups like butter moving in tandem, hooves slicing through those that came near. We shot and defended from our mounts and left a lot of decisions to the animals as to which attacking groups were priorities. They separated in groups of four. If they decided to charge through, we aimed high. If they reared, we hung to their sides and shot lasers and arrows.

"It was brilliant. Even as we felt victorious, the horses checked the dead bodies for movement. One of the horses took off running after someone hiding that escaped far into the wood. We'd already dismounted. That mare finished what we started.

"Aaron buried those that came from behind at us; they're now underneath half a hillside of embedded boulders he summoned to the surface," Nicholas finished.

"Boys and girls? There are more coming now our way," Ildiko interrupted to alarm the troops. "I see them!"

"She's right!" Cynthia yelled. "I've the same report coming in now from the drones. Raleigh confirms that they never received our former distress signal. They're coming in with reinforcements from the ship," she added.

Attila set defenses based upon drone coordinates and Ildiko's moment by moment tracking.

"We're being attacked from a heavily armed group, a thousand yards of here northwest 35 degrees," Ildiko coordinated with others. "From the other side of the Lake, the positions of some of the advancing predators have appeared," she warned.

Attila stared unbelievingly at the scene in real time.

"This doesn't look smart. Too obvious; those guys are sitting ducks. Send the third regiment to go east wide around the far end of the lake... they've got to have another group closing in from behind you," Attila instructed. "Aaron, you go with that group around the lake and block any ground attack that might come our way. Send drones to pick them off."

Nicholas and Attila scanned the area along with the entire contingent; reports rapidly detailed images of the tall wooden and cement outposts once used as fire watches. Each structure indicated human movement from their bases all the way up to the top. Zooming in on the images, Attila spotted and marked each man and woman prepping their guns and crossbows secured vertically up the multiple 200 ft. edifices. They were preparing for the retreat they had expected to happen below them.

"But from whom?" wondered Attila. "Who was supposed to come or go that way? Us?"

Within thirty seconds, the heron-like drones circled and blew the outposts from the face of the earth. Screams emanated from the towers, now transformed into fiery torches.

Those that stood across the lake facing the Confederation camp moved aggressively into the water closing on the opposite bank.

"This is insane. Why would they move into the lake and come straight at us?" shouted Attila. "They must know their comrades meant to sandwich us are now toast. Keep a look out...this isn't right."

On closer inspection, Attila and Connor realized the choice of their assailants to rush into the lake was not aggressive nor an option. Behind those now struggling across the cold water came the war cries of a second rapidly advancing group. From across the lake, arrows picked off the desperate swimmers one by one until the west bank of the lake floated red with dead bodies.

"What the hell?" Aaron yelled. His attention turned toward the hill that separated them from the forest. As predicted, from the rear came those that had separated from their main group, now floating dead on the lake. Like the thunderous rolling of an earthquake, huge multi-ton boulders were lugged from the depths of the mountainous plateau up into the air only to rain down again to pound the screaming men and women on the attack.

The ground shook its protests until all that could be heard was unconditional silence, broken by faltering broken timbers and branches in the aftermath.

The ambushing groups had finally been laid to rest in the crudest of burials. Like so many earthly icebergs, huge boulders peeked from the earth in hardened, smoothed mounds; smaller boulders that had cracked in hundreds of shards lay as sharp reminders of the eerie deluge. Dust clouds rose from the surrounding forest and blanketed the moist green floor of ferns, moss, and shrub. The ambushers that flanked Confederation troops, on all sides but one, had been at once bludgeoned and buried. An unidentified group stood on the opposite bank facing the Confederation troops.

Aaron returned to the front lines on the lake's banks in time to see the strange group across the water represented by a frenetic man hoisting a white rag upon an arrow. Behind the flag bearer were those that forced their attackers to flee into the lake. The lack of movement seemed to indicate that the man with the white makeshift flag awaited a response.

"We're friends!" The man finally bellowed.

Attila continued to stare wordlessly.

"I'm coming over alone. Don't fire!" The spokesman rolled over a downturned canoe from the gravel bank and began to paddle. Attila, Adele, Connor, Aaron, Nicholas, Caroline, and Cynthia stood with arms folded as the canoe skidded on the sand bank at their feet.

Nicholas placed himself between the stranger and his friends. The representative offered an old fashioned envelope.

"My leader sends this message," Anton spoke breathlessly.

Nicholas handed it to Connor without altering his eyes or position. "You knew we were here?" Nicholas asked simply.

"We know people come to hunt and fish. We know the crazy ones hunt them and steal their food. We always help. We kill the crazies. Sometimes we come and everyone is dead. Sometimes it's a fight like this one, with the biggest groups coming together from different sides. They take what they want and kill. You are the first from the South."

"How do you know we're from the South?" Connor asked.

"Where else would you come from? We know the North," Anton reasoned. "You have the clean. You have the smell," he laughed.

Attila observed the exchange with interest.

"We are sent to protect the wood! They'll be on the path toward the big lakes, too. Looks like you and us killed a big group together. We're lucky, right?

"Your name?" Attila finally spoke.

"Anton is my name. You can call me Grayleson."

"I'm sure that doesn't make sense," Caroline piped up as she approached. "Thanks for the help. We were caught between two well-prepared divisions," she added more graciously.

Attila motioned for the man identified by one name with the strange preference for another, to follow him. Aaron and Nicholas stood vigil on the water's edge.

"We also sent out scouts. A group meant to attack us; we thought we killed them all," began Attila, speaking measuredly to Anton. "I suppose that they had several groups, one situated deeper in the woods. They had us surrounded; somehow our communication went inoperable. That means technological sophistication. We're also surprised by your behaviors," Attila challenged with a hostile barrage.

Anton appeared confused and offended, but mostly confused.

"We help. That's what we do. We watch out for the weak ones. You ride animals. You have magic but you don't hunt. Why are you here? You're making surprises, too."

Attila said nothing, preferring to stare at Anton.

"We have technology that reflects science, not magic, Anton," Connor interjected. "We're from the Southern regions, a small representation of the Confederation of American States. We, too, hope to be able to offer the kind of assistance that could protect the vulnerable. It appears as if we are compatriots on that score," he smiled and extended his hand.

Connor's language or the meaning of a handshake escaped Anton.

Connor withdrew an unmet hand.

"The note says that we are welcome to follow you back to your camp. Where is camp, Anton?" Connor continued.

"Three days walk from here. You would make it faster. You can follow us. Our camp is big. We call it Grayleton. It's safe."

"More ambushes?" asked Ildiko.

"Ambushes?" Anton repeated the foreign word.

"Surprise attacks from groups like these?" Ildiko tried to clarify.

"Always and everywhere. Human animals don't care how much they lose or who they lose. The people who don't like killing go to big Philadelphia or Grayleton."

Jordon was puzzled as to the reference to the city that was able to ambush and kill some of their troops.

"Philadelphia was overrun with human animals, as you call them," Jordan said. "They managed to trap us within the streets for a while. We didn't have an easy time of it. A lot of civilians died in the effort to annihilate us. What kind of safe haven is that place?"

"Crazies don't live there. They are on the trails. They see you go that way. They tracked you, got around you... I don't know," he said. "It's the safest and largest place but the people can't leave. If you were attacked, it's from the crazies that live around big Philadelphia. Not the Philadelphia people."

"So these nomadic groups just move from place to place and prey on solid communities? I still don't know how you handled them when our technology was ineffective. Any explanations?" Attila asked. "Where do they have access or the know-how to block our frequencies?" he barked before Anton could respond.

Anton looked blankly and replied, "I don't know the words."

"Well, we've been invited to visit a man named Grayle," Connor said aloud, examining the note in his hand. "The place we've been invited to is named after him, I gather?"

"I give the letter. I say no more," Anton replied, jutting his chin upward.

Attila smiled at the young man's inability to keep his mouth shut. Within seconds, Anton predictably turned toward Connor with a question. "Do you believe in God?"

"I think you're asking whether we are also compatriots in this fight against insanity. We hope that we'll be able to protect the welfare of others, including your community," answered Connor. "I think we'll save the God discussion for another time. God may mean one thing to me, to you another."

"Grayle will know the words you say," Anton said. He was frustrated that Connor did not give a simple answer of yes or no. He felt Attila's wariness and suspicion. He felt comfortable with Connor's authority. Connor, he analyzed, was too weak to defend himself.

Caroline moved closer to examine Anton and squinted her eyes. "Your place is underground?"

Anton was startled. "How do you know?"

"I can see and hear it," Caroline explained to the others. "It's huge. You've got thousands of people living there. This is no camp."

Ildiko confirmed Caroline's impressions. "Technology, industry, farms... heat pumps, rudimentary and advanced weaponry..."

Sonny approached from behind with a concerned look on his face but said nothing.

Anton turned ashen and stammered, "You...you are witches and demons?"

Caroline moved to take Anton's hand in hers but he would not have any of it. "You stay away from me, witches," he hissed.

"I mean to calm you," Caroline explained.

"You?" Anton examined Caroline up and down and decided she lacked the qualities he sought in a female.

"If you don't want me to touch you, it's no problem. You're free to go, of course."

Anton panicked. He had ignored Grayle's instructions to say nothing, represent no opinions, to deliver a letter and return home. If they wanted to follow, they would. If they didn't, they would not. He had done something very wrong, for which he had no understanding or remedy.

"How about some food for you and your men?" Connor invited.

"I'm hungry," Anton agreed.

The meal served was spat out in disgust. "This is not food. In Grayleton, we know what is food!" the Grayleton emissary shouted his suspicions.

Connor appealed once more to Anton, "We're here to help in this region. Everyone has different needs. Some need medical assistance, some are in need of evacuation and some need military protection. How can we help Grayleton, Anton?"

"Help us? We don't need your help," Anton answered indignantly. "We help you. We have...." He began a thought, then thought better of it.

Nicholas nodded in response to Attila's telepathic instructions and moved toward the water's edge to make an appearance in full view of the other side. He peered across the lake at the men and women standing expectantly. One by one, they slumped to the ground. Some began to rub their heads. Others held their stomachs, while others vomited violently. The ones left standing turned and disappeared into the thick woods.

Anton doubled over with stomach cramps, unaware of what had transpired. "I feel sick," he complained. "You did poison me!"

"What were your instructions? What did your leader tell you to do here?" Nicholas asked.

"Just what I said," he whined.

"He's simple, there's nothing more in his head other than the expectation that we will follow him to their compound," Caroline messaged the others. "His reaction may be due to other duplicities, not necessarily malice toward us. I'm still wondering the reason that the group suddenly has a reaction to Nicholas?"

Sonny shared his own concerns.

"He and the others are all operating on an identical frequency. It's a low level hum with no alterations. They've been conditioned to think and react at a minimum. It's not that they're evil. But they've reacted to Nicholas knowing that they have done something similar before that might have ended badly," explained Sonny. "My impression is that sometimes they bring people back to their home and they assimilate fine. Those that don't fit in are killed or exiled."

"There's a leader. He is orderly. He's fair. He's calculating," added Caroline.

"He's highly intelligent. He holds prayer meetings," Aaron added.

"He sees the grid and has vid streams of the blue lights. He examines the frequencies and he speaks in a monitor that is in a darkened room," Ildiko continued.

Ildiko examined the lake as she spoke; her eyes stared without blinking while her mind travelled to Grayleton. "I see groups of people working hard at jobs that indicate an advanced society. I see no other monitors here. I see little technology above ground. I cannot see very well underground and I don't know the reason," she said as her mind travelled throughout the town.

"It's hardened," Sonny interjected. "It's built to interrupt most of our frequency fields. It's an enormous bunker. You can tell by where the frequencies begin and end. It's miles long, buried deep within the mountain."

Connor received the same information from Raleigh. Morgan and Meredith weighed in from their TrueView.

"It's most likely the same bunkers that housed Clifton Brown's group in the limestone mountains south of what was once near Butler County," Meredith Green transmitted. "They've at least two thousand upside and we've no idea of what lies underground," she said. "I'm unsure how they've escaped our notice."

"You going to do exactly what with that ailing scouting party from Grayleton lying by the water's edge?" Morgan yelled from his Cary home.

"Caroline tried to calm their leader by coming in contact," Nicholas accounted. "He recoiled like a rattlesnake. His reaction caused that chain reaction. They're connected in a weird way. All I did was examine them from across the lake," Nicholas explained. "There was no initial reaction the first time I looked their way."

"Enough of these hiccups," Attila insisted. "We've got to investigate Grayleton. I'm going in with troops with Confederation backup in the vicinity. There is no indication of air power or drones but there's plenty of evidence of technology. That means we've been set up."

"Explain," Morgan demanded.

"I don't think Anton's search and rescue crew were sent to save anyone. I don't think it was just another scouting party to guard their territory," Attila emphasized.

"What's that mean?" Morgan asked.

"It means the various Confederation troops and contingents have been tracked the whole way since landing in Newport News. It means that someone knew exactly where we were going from Philadelphia to here and our intention to move northwest," Attila continued. "It may mean that this Grayle knew what we've planned from the beginning."

"Impossible," Morgan barked.

"Very possible," Connor said. "These people are pretty primitive that we have here. I'm not so sure that's the case regarding the person directing them, Morgan."

"How's that possible?" Adele wondered.

"We'll find out," Attila said. "For now, I'll call for back up forces for here and for our target area. At the least of it, we'll need transports to get Anton's guys out of here. These people don't realize they need rescuing."

"What makes you think they're ready?" Cynthia asked. "Sonny indicated a very low frequency of thought. It means they're neurologically damaged and won't be altered until we're able to patch the magnetic grid around them. It just endangers everyone."

"They're operating at a low common denominator now," Adele noted.

Caroline suggested that they should collectively move the blue energy. "They've been in these parts. Why aren't they one way or the other? They're sort of in a limbo state. If this is a sampling of Grayleton with thousands of citizens, let's figure out right now how they will, or will not, react."

"Do it, honey," Morgan directed.

Caroline and the rest connected their thoughts and energies without touching one another. The power had significantly grown between them, leaving each more empowered with analogous abilities and enhanced communication. There was no longer a reason to physically connect. All they had to do was wish it.

The blue light began to stream and connect, first with the Circle members, and then moved amongst those with evolved frequency levels. When the connections completed, the light focused to a center point high into the atmosphere until it attached to the geomagnetic field that connected and protected the earth. Where there were gaps, the blue light stretched to emerging geometric lines that outlined renewed connections. For a few moments, the sky became a perfect series of interlocking geometric patterns pulsating at intersections of twinkling star like points. Caroline felt the sensation of magnetic bipolar adjustments edging to an angle of 20 degrees, the righting of an angle at the center of the earth, her skin tingling at the streams of overly charged particles from the sun suddenly rejected. Her feet warmed as if intuiting the geodynamics of molten iron alloys adjusting in the earth's outer core as convection currents eased its escape by gentle waves.

Anton looked toward the heavens in wonder as his pains subsided. On the far end of the lake, most of the Grayleton people stood carefully, now erect without sickness. A small sampling of the recovered chose to escape into the forest. Another sampling remained prone to the ground in amplified agony. For the second group, their pitched torment echoed across the lake then ceased abruptly.

For the most part, the effect was uniformly positive. The horses neighed their pleasure and troops smiled with satisfaction. Whatever the blue light's purposes, it reliably left the

Confederation representatives with an indescribable sense of peace.

As the light receded, the group looked at one other.

"It's beginning to work the way we planned. These marginal people reacted quickly and well. I think we're making big headway at this point," Caroline smiled. "The process is faster, broader, and more effective each round."

"What happened?" Anton asked meekly. The group ignored him.

"We'll try to find the way you're being monitored," Morgan promised. "I don't want us surprised again. Easy does it...and don't depend too much upon our technology. There's too much evidence of being successfully blocked or foiled. Everyone should close down some of their amps and rely more on intuition and remote viewing," advised Morgan.

Anton grew anxious. Events far escaped his understanding; he decided to flee. Along the water's edge, he seized his canoe unnoticed and slid it into the water.

Attila issued orders to prepare to move toward Butler County. Jordan Reid was instructed to keep the Grayleton scouting party in their newly established base camp, where they would remain until further instructions. Attila didn't need Anton to find the camp and instructed Jordan to make sure that Grayle's emissary remained with the Confederation in the interim.

"Where the hell did he go?" Jordon frantically searched the vicinity for Anton.

Aaron spotted Anton paddling his way toward the opposite side of the Lake. With little effort, the boat was picked from the water and suspended slightly. Canoe and Anton were skimmed across the water's surface and came to rest once more on the Confederation shore.

"I'm a prisoner?" Anton wailed.

"We've never taken prisoners, Anton. Do you?" Connor asked.

"We send them out from Grayleton if they're too crazy," he spoke between pants.

"Who decides if they're 'too crazy'? Your leader, Grayle?"

"Father knows," Anton clung to the sides of the canoe frozen in place.

"Father?" Caroline repeated.

"Grayle is our father. He knows everything. He gave us everything! Before Father, there was nothing but darkness, cold, and lightning that burned us..."

"Do you pray to father?" Aaron asked simply.

"Why would we pray to Father?" Anton asked confusedly.

"Not yet they're praying to him," Aaron telepathed the circle.

"He's just impressed with civilized behavior and a little know-how," Caroline shared with the group. "Let's go and see what we find."

Adele telepathically asked how they intended to get the Grayleton party to their side of the lake peacefully. "We should convince them to come over here from the other side."

Nicholas signaled for the terrified group. Without hesitation, they moved quickly toward the canoes that once served a resort area and paddled. Others swam next to the boats.

Anton moved from amazement into indignation. "You can't tell us what to do! Only Grayle tells us what to do."

"Your people...do they have freedom to do as they please?" Connor asked.

Anton stood and waved his hands for the encroaching group to turn around. "Go back! Run!"

Anton seemed invisible, inaudible. An enraged, displaced leader turned his attention toward the leaders of the Confederation troops.

"We'll never take you to our camp. You'll never enter. Father will know what to do with demons and he will cast you out," he warned. "Go back to your home. Leave us alone."

If there was one thing that the Confederation citizens and troops knew well, it was the myriad of ways erratic behaviors manifested. Tales of primitive tribal communities were rarely the same. It didn't surprise anyone that his or her presence was overwhelming. It was no surprise that there was little logic. It did surprise the troops that they were construed as demonic forces from those that professed God and touted a protective mission...

"He's confused, Mother," Caroline answered her mother's doubts telepathically. "Our skills denote demonic powers..."

"He's brainwashed, Caroline, Dangerously brainwashed. Almost everyone else is altered in a determinant positive or negative way by the blue light, except this group? Strange, don't you think? These people act like empty shells reacting to whatever force is in proximity."

"It's this man called Grayle. He's perceived as omniscient," messaged Sonny.

"Maybe. But something else is happening there," Ildiko interjected. "It's that enormous stronghold that operates without our ever having picked up a clue that they existed. How is that? What do the drones pick up? What have the satellite feeds told us?" Ildiko rhetorically asked. "Nothing."

"You're right," Aditiya thought back. "We've nothing that indicates even the farm work going on there. We don't pick up any of the frequencies or spectrums whatsoever. It's so low it escaped Sonny's attention until recently. I've asked for every kind of surveillance. We'll get those reports as we close in."

"Anyone recall the Sea Walnut referenced from those old research transcripts?" Attila asked. "The frequency so low-slung that it operated under vibrational radars? With any kind of similar cloaking or blocking tech, I can see how we completely missed Grayleton."

Anton shouted, "Why are you all quiet? Why are you staring? Somebody answer me!"

Caroline smiled kindly at Anton. "We're sorry. We've just decided that we need to think about things a little more. We'll travel to Grayleton; you can stay with your friends. You've nothing to fear."

She walked away and the others followed.

Ten troops escorted the very wet Grayleton scouting party to makeshift shelters and tents; they appeared compliant and grateful. Anton, however, refused to move.

"We have other things to do than watch you pout," Aaron implored. "Please move toward your quarters."

"Only Father tells me what to do," Anton snarled.

"Fine. You can hang around. Let us know when you want to go to a tent or eat some dinner or relieve yourself. Or not."

Aaron suspended Anton twenty feet mid-air over the water and walked away.

Someone brought Anton's belongings across the lake and handed them to the nearest soldier. Unfolding the large parcel, the soldier gasped then took the contents to Attila.

"This belongs to the man called Anton. I think you'll find this second parcel interesting, sir."

Attila unfolded the large white fur pelt. "What the hell? What kind of fur is this?"

Tapping his Cortana cache, it identified the pelt as bear; it expanded upon the possibilities that the pelts were of former zoo animals once in the area that might have escaped and bred in the wild. But rather than a polar bear, the sample bore out as an albino black bear.

Attila and Komor simultaneously recognized the significance of the pelt.

"Anton had time to kill and skin bears? I thought his group arrived in the nick of time late today to save our own skins?" Komor analyzed, "Anton's group knew we were coming. They knew we'd be ambushed. They knew they would appear as if they were saving our backsides. My guess? They sacrificed their own first group so Anton's could look like the good guys," she continued.

"That's what I've been saying," nodded Attila. "A greater group of Grayleton fighters was sent in to attack with orders to kill. They had divided into four initiatives. One group would go deep into the woods flanking us. A second would climb the watchtowers and pick us off as we were squeezed by the third group that appeared poised to attack from across the Lake. It would have taken at least a day to set that up. Anton's fourth group ostensibly saved us. Nothing but staged. I don't have to remind you that every single one of those in the water was murdered. Not one survivor. What does it take to self-sacrifice or kill one's comrades for Grayle's purposes? We're looking at amoral and well-ordered performances.

"This Grayle somehow knew that we were too formidable to take on but we could be fooled if we considered him our confederate. Then we might be foolish enough to walk into another trap as friends of a burgeoning civilized world. We'd trot behind Anton, Grayle's minion, into his little town. I wager that it was Grayle who also strategized the attack on Jordan's regiment in Philadelphia, knowing that he'd double back to join our forces," Attila concluded. He put his head in his hands like a man who had been hoodwinked. His thoughts quickly circulated.

Nicholas added his assessment, "And that's the reason for the odd reaction from their troops to my presence. They were following orders but were conflicted about killing their own. Only Anton fully understood the plan of sacrificing their men for a ruse."

Ildiko immediately channeled Anton's thoughts as he viewed his large pelt being unrolled high above the water from his unfortunate vantage point.

"Anton is thinking that the fur is a gift for this Grayle person. He's had it for a few days. It's from another sloth of bears; not the one I ran into. They're not three or four days from their compound! They're one day and a half.

"He's thinking about how pleased Grayle would have been with the gift..." Her mind dispersed images now shared by everyone. "...the meat was cooked but only eaten by four of the people in their camp. Anton was served first and he threw the remainder to three women..." Cynthia recounted. "He recalls that episode from many days ago."

Everyone looked toward Anton, still suspended mid-air.

"Where did your girlfriends run off to?" Aditiya yelled. "Where are the other three?"

"Don't waste your time," Adele reprimanded. "We need to move out; let them go. The point is that Grayle and this guy want us to go there. He's gone to a lot of trouble to maneuver us his way. Let's get our hands on this Grayle first and talk later," she advised.

Komor retrieved her medical kit and loaded a med pistol. Taking aim at Anton, she shot him in the neck with a sedative strong enough to keep him immobile for 24 hours.

"Why?" asked Aaron "He can't move a muscle, Doctor. There's no pain."

"He was able to think and observe, Aaron. I'm going to assume that someone else can read this moron's thoughts just like us. Now the lights are out. Story over."

Attila and Adele finished packing their gear and prepared their mounts. Attila asked Adele for a moment alone with their tethered horses.

"I'm worried. We'll likely face something new. I want you and Caroline to stay to the rear and not move into camp until I give you an all clear."

"We're soldiers, Attila. We go in together."

"There's bizarre activity going on. It's getting to me," Attila sighed.

He pulled her toward him and wrapped her slight body into his. They kissed and he stroked her hair. Neither uttered a word and the world stood still.

"It was good until you patted my butt," Adele laughed.

"An admiring gesture from an old Hungarian soldier," he smiled. "It's time to go before we're heard."

"What's to hide? Everyone knows we're a couple," Adele smiled.

"If that's the case, listen to my heart rather than my words," he replied. "Please say we'll marry as soon as we return to Cary."

"As soon as possible," she agreed.

They walked toward the camp's clearing and found the waiting militia mounted. Uniformly, the troops applauded their approval.

"Congratulations, Mum!" thought Caroline. "It's perfect!"

"Congratulations, Papa!" echoed Ildiko.

"Let's move out," ordered Connor. He sent the good news to Cary via Rachel.

"Tell Morgan and Angela to test out their Hungarian goulash. We're welcoming Attila into the family," Connor announced the engagement with a great deal of joy.

* * *

The Pendergrass Estate

"You hear, Cookie?" Morgan yelled his pleasure.

Angela smiled at her husband. "I'm already on it. Wonderful news. Adele seems as happy as she's ever been in her life. I can't wait for this to happen. Happiness in the midst of all of this!"

"I'm going to feel better when we get this nasty stuff taken care of," Morgan worried.

"Nasty? You don't think it's under control?"

"It's all speculation. How the hell does this outfit around the outskirts of Bumblefork, Pennsylvania know how to track or stop our forces without our having a fig of a clue? Not normal. I'm thinkin' it's a leak on our side. I'm also thinkin' that those Grayleton sorts are housed in those government bunkers chock full of munitions and intelligence. Moreno is pulling records as we speak. She and Scott Reid have been confounded over the same issues. Meredith Green and the Confederation military brass combed records but we've no indication of transmissions."

Hernandez and Gant located and sent historical records and images of the vast bunkers that included a map of vaults that snaked underground. The largest holdings for government records was the one in which they suspected Grayle had established a settlement.

"We should have known to examine those catacombs. The assumption that they'd wait till we got there was insanely shortsighted," Gant complained from the capital.

"Too much on our plate," Green sighed. "Always, too much to be done, fixed, filled, addressed. We'll get it done now."

"We've omitted certain environmental sounds and have picked up human voices and mechanical activity," noted one technician. "Farming mostly. We looked for refraction cloaking this round and discovered twenty outbuildings that cloak temperature readings. We read the soil and discovered artificial turf and rock disguising the compound's entrances and exits. There's plenty of doo-dads," he reported.

"I'm not surprised at the level developed decades ago," Scott Reid surmised. "I'm surprised that EMP victims have been able to figure it operationally."

"Damn right," Meredith Green chimed in. "There was no evidence of brain damaged survivors, even close to that aptitude, or anywhere near those numbers. How is it that they act uniformly vacant but have proven this effective?'

"Let's assume this leader is immune to the EMP and intellectually gifted to boot. That's what our analysis says, given the reports we're now sorting. All of the recorded conversations and images support this supposition," reported one researcher. "I point to the algorithm's result of the data."

"Where is the analysis of moral certitude?" queried Green. "It makes a difference. It's what we're after at the moment."

"We've run it both ways. Nothing conclusive, I'm afraid. See for yourself, doctor."

Meredith Green reviewed the models that played multiple scenarios. Nothing was conclusive regarding the moral intentions of the man referred to as Grayle. There was an even fifty-fifty chance of either good or malevolent intentions, depending upon extrapolated and direct reports of below par specimens. Few such survivors had the ability for critical thought one way or the other.

"This Grayle is running the show," Scott Reid blurted. "What are they going to find there?"

Chapter XXXIV

Sorting

Wednesday, July 9, 2070

C ynthia daydreamed as the troops made their way toward the limestone mountains in Pennsylvania. She disregarded and cached the messages pending from Sonny's father, Tsin-hang, from offshore. Hundreds more lingered from the Research Triangle. Detailed accounts about transports, the Philadelphian remedial assistance, and a hundred other similar reports were disregarded. Somewhere in her mind, Cynthia registered that the Confederation was successfully locating and helping cities and towns identified as Confederation receptive. Studies showed that the magnetic grid was in the process of healing, not only in local regions visited, but worldwide. Large and small, facts faded into her net storage. It was Cynthia's preference to replay a series of dreams that had haunted her.

"I saw the fight coming. Why didn't I say something?" she asked herself. She remembered Anton's image but not his face and heard his pompous, broken language addressing those under his command. "I recalled so many details as they took place," she fretted.

"I've seen the Grayleton place, too. It was both primitive and progressive," she reflected while reviewing the images. "Freshly-clothed children were trying to figure what it meant to take a bath, eat from a plate, and take an adult's hand. Others were studying and reading. There were flowers that

537

bloomed without any blemish. The fruit was uniformly shaped."
Cynthia struggled to find a common thread.

She now realized that parts of her dream had passed, some
images resided in the present, while others might represent
images of things to come. It was not quite a dream state nor
was it remote viewing as described by Ildiko.

Curious, she thought.

What disturbed Cynthia more than the horrors of feral brutes
burning on the watchtowers, were the feelings that rushed over
and through her that emanated from a tall, muscular man. Hers
was a magnetic attraction for a stranger who washed his face
but never peered into the mirror. His raw sexuality frightened
her but there was no impulse to look away.

"How incredibly handsome," Cynthia held her breath as he
splashed water on his face and towel-dried his neck. In her
mind's eye, she recalled the way he smelled of the sweet outdoors, the smooth, deep, visceral tone of his voice, and a slight
even smile that hinted at pleasure. As he strolled the streets,
children waved his way. There were occasions when he chose
to touch the shoulders of elderly citizens, then summoned
assistants to attend their overlooked needs. Farm animals
seemed to sense the man's presence and relax. Goats and
sheep were examined with a gentle touch; he felt his way
around their bodies with an appreciation for the delicate equilibrium required of gaining an animal's trust.

He followed the narrow steel-barred channels that funneled
the animals to the nearby slaughterhouse. Whether fowl or
beast, the animals did not protest their fate. An entire area
dedicated to death was absent of bleating, mooing, and
squawking. Cynthia observed as he pushed the heavy door of
the slaughterhouse; her heart rose in her chest at the sight of
blood-splattered workers pushing and pulling carcasses, wash-
ing the floors of bits of bone, flesh, and feather. The scene
quickly changed.

She felt the cool corridors floating beside him, hovering over
and around the man, as she happily followed along nooks and
crannies of an underground world. Stone and cement walls were
carved and rounded seamlessly into high-pitched cathedral like

walkways; signage was engraved rather than posted, markers purposely created that conveyed solemnity, lest anyone overlook the importance of intents or purposes.

A strange darkness overcame Cynthia's dream carrying an unmistakable fear of the unknown. Although Cynthia felt his presence and heard his feet walking, she could not easily see the man. When the darkness gave way to light, she saw her own image standing in front of a hall of doors situated on one side of the corridor, the ceilings much lower, with an appearance of having been handcrafted rather than machine fashioned. Nothing was to the right of this corridor but a smooth, uninterrupted cement wall. Then her image disappeared and, once more, she focused upon the man. Grayle was his name. The name came to her clearly as soon as he peered down the hall and tentatively moved forward. Each door that lined the hall to the left, thought her host, had been opened. Cynthia could feel his sense of wonder and determination, touching each door and then moving to the next. At the end of the long corridor his gait slowed. Grayle approached the last door on the long row and simply stood to regard it. The entry was modern, an obvious design departure. It was the last vault that had yet to be explored. The door lacked an engraved number. He backed away before making his way back toward the entry. The lights closed sequentially behind while igniting an advancing path.

Cynthia intuited an ongoing dilemma.

"He's surrounded by people but so very lonely," she sensed. "He has things to do and is growing impatient to finish his mission, fulfill a vision for the future," she recalled the impression.

Then Cynthia assumed the man's point of view and lost the sense of an observer. She felt as he when people crowded his space, demanded attention, and spoke platitudes of admiration, their body language suggestive of a familiar subjugation.

"This is not real admiration," he had thought. "This is only ignorant fear or need for affection," he felt. It pleased him that they followed his direction but it felt empty of substance, like the animals that walked into the steel gates toward their deaths, willing to die for the community welfare, for him, for the collective's future. "I've got to keep moving forward; I need to finish this..." he told himself.

"This is Grayle. He seems to be a good man," Cynthia concluded as she once again drifted amongst rapidly morphing scenes and moods that Grayle sensed with each encounter. A recently opened vault was being re-investigated. Piles of files had been removed and stood taller than the man that had rummaged. She felt his frustration and then perceived his plan to circumvent the sorting challenge.

"I can't waste time figuring it all out. I've just got to learn to operate what's necessary," Grayle decided. He pushed away heaps of artifacts and antique strongboxes formerly dragged from their neatly labeled categories. Cynthia sensed Grayle was searching for something in particular but was now pressed for time.

Something indescribable blurred Cynthia's intuition. It was these scenes that she struggled to understand. As much as she replayed them, she was left only with a sense of their import without specific evidences. She was not alone. Grayle seemed frustrated by an inability to collate the clues that signified something out of reach.

The clearest image had been Grayle moving outdoors toward an outbuilding. He swept his palm quickly in the vicinity of a biometric unit and moved into a dark, dank room smelling of neglect. He slid into a chair situated midway inside a tight semi-circle of computers that remained in the shadows with other unidentified equipment. A singular light shone from the central monitor that activated upon Grayle's entrance. Grayle's eyes sparkled in the monitor's glow, his even white teeth gleaming with overt joy. Engrossed in streaming images, Grayle did not bother to illuminate the rest of the room.

"He's catching up," concluded Cynthia. "He's been isolated most of his life. He's discovering a world he wishes to become reacquainted with; he's knows it's now his turn to make things right...."

Music filled her mind. There was classical music, then the sitar, followed by a wide range of cultural influences. He rapidly played samples of instruments that jumped to holographic life.

The images and music samplings flashed at extreme speeds but Cynthia sensed his ability to grasp the smallest nuances, imprint mental notes, and prioritize their significance at the pace of their appearance.

"They must learn all of this," he said aloud, departing the building. "We've a clean slate and cannot waste precious time!"

Cynthia felt the breadth of the constellations above when he peered into the night's sky. She basked in the night's warm breezes and shared a quiet appreciation for a thriving town built around one man's idea.

There were men and women she understood as experienced combatants meant to guard the city, languishing dogs that roamed dirt paths, and finally a soft tune lifted from Grayle as the bunkers came into his field of vision. He paused and laughed suddenly, as if sensing Cynthia's intrusion. For a split second, he peered into her eyes. She gasped. Over and over, Cynthia replayed her dream as recorded. Grayle never looked her way but that once.

Annoyed by her obvious absentmindedness, Cynthia's horse changed cadence.

As the horses picked their way along the trail, Caroline and Ildiko rode together. They imagined what it would mean to be sisters in the likely event that Adele and Attila were to marry. Ildiko spoke of her father's eccentricities and Caroline spoke of her mother's ability to hold her own in the face of a very confused childhood.

"Excuse me? What the heck is a normal childhood?" Ildiko asked pointedly.

"Excuse me! Who isn't eccentric?" Caroline laughed.

Nicholas caught up to the two friends, hoping to spend some time with Caroline.

"Hello mind-reading, future-painting, remote-viewing, female types," he smiled.

"Hello vomit-inducing, guilt-amplifying, emotional boomerang," Ildiko laughed. "I'm guessing you lovebirds want to be left to plod romantically alone together?"

"Sure, super powers," Nicholas replied. "If you could spare the blue light goddess?"

"Done. I'm going to find Aaron," Ildiko called as she cantered away.

Nicholas and Caroline rode quietly together. Theirs was a connection that surpassed that which might have been called a 'love' relationship. In every way, they sensed each other's delicate sensations and reactions to the world. As each new positive sensation was discovered, they were careful to retune or refine that which was meaningful to the other's happiness.

Caroline was able to sense the pain Nicholas carried as a young teenager separated from his family. She had shared intermittent images and felt his heart racing while witnessing the brutal murders of his sister, father, and grandfather. She was even able to grasp his first longings of lost comfort after Mrs. Bradley's suicide.

As an empath, Caroline also felt how Nicholas had been able to absorb emotional discomfort while immune to the horrors of those who presaged or endorsed evil. Aware of the depths of his love for her, Caroline understood that Nicholas considered her as his true connection to the universe.

Caroline did not feel emotional needs in the way that ebbed and flowed with human contact, or imagination, or were modulated by hormonal and chemical exposures. Caroline was wired differently. She understood the waves of emotion as she tuned in and calmed others, yet analogous emotions did not originate from within her. Caroline's capabilities allowed her to emotionally commiserate with others beyond sensing a familiar experience. When their hands first touched, Caroline felt the rush that flooded through Nicholas. The first time they kissed, she made the mistake of laughing out loud when she realized it was the onset of emotions coursing through his body rather than her own.

"What's so funny?" Nicholas had asked. He had been hurt. It had taken him the better part of six years to gather the nerve to reveal his feelings to Caroline and she laughed at his first approach.

"The feeling! It's amazing!" Caroline sang her joy.

"But is it your feeling or mine? An empathetic connection only, or yours?" Nicholas was puzzled as to how to handle the situation.

"I'm not sure. I feel your joy, your excitement, and the flood of happiness coming from inside you. Isn't that feeling now somehow mine, too?"

Nicholas never fully understood how Caroline experienced the world but he trusted that Caroline was the one for him. For her part, Caroline seemed content by his side.

"You've never been off center, CC," came the newest observation.

"Nicholas, you've never been sick either," Caroline looked into his mind and laughed.

"I'm lovesick for damn sure. I can't wait to get back to Cary," he announced excitedly. "Your grandfather offered me a position. I thought I was going to spend the rest of my life fighting for truth, justice, and the American way, sending blue healing light out to the heavens," he smiled.

She did not reply nor did she think his statement merited one.

"I love you," he finally announced aloud. "I'm asking you to marry me," he shouted.

"I love you, too." Caroline smiled. "Let's not speak about marriage right now. We've a lot to do. I'm still getting used to my mother's situation!"

Her sense of the moment was quickly interrupted by a sudden anxiety that had nothing to do with Nicholas Bradley or anyone's marriage.

"Move!" she warned the twenty or thirty that were in closest proximity. The horses pulled hard into a full gallop, maneuvering faultlessly around and over the overgrown roots and brush that obscured what was once a secondary route leading to Appalachian Trail's main artery. The news travelled instantaneously and the entire regiment was aware of undefined distress.

"What's happening?" came the messaging en masse.

"Don't know yet," answered Caroline. "No image. Just the sensation to move out as quickly as possible."

"Same here," thought Nicholas. "A bad feeling and I think I've gone naturally invisible." It was his reaction to impending harm, a most reliable and foreboding signal that no one ignored.

Sonny looked toward Nicholas and confirmed, "Yeah, he's gone! We're facing something unusual."

"Good for everyone to enact their shields. We'll meet at the coordinates I'm now sending. We'll update as we go," messaged Connor.

Drones answered the questions with images of mechanical discs whisking erratically fifty feet above them through the air. A sonic frequency undulated and subsided causing disorientation in the horses.

"Shut down the hearing amps on the horses," Attila directed.

"By what measure is this frequency carried?" wondered Sonny.

Aditiya answered, "It's simply a reaction to the ground's impact to ward off unusual biological threats. A few hundred horses pounding the ground can do that. We've alarmed sensors that send discs to randomly emit high frequency deterrents. Don't ask me how they were set. Who would have that kind of capability today? We can't be sure if those maniacal discs are equipped with lasers...until they fire."

The militia was ordered to slow to a walk as Confederation drones quickly identified, targeted, and destroyed the screaming discs.

Cynthia answered the most important of Aditiya's lingering questions, as the troops meandered forward.

"The Grayleton compound has enormous vaults housing all kinds of strange armaments and technology," Cynthia offered.

Aditiya messaged a singular thought. "And how exactly do you know this?"

Ildiko answered for Cynthia.

"Cynthia and I have remotely seen the bunkers and vaults. Cynthia described specific images of armaments and is transmitting them now."

Attila and Adele conferred quietly offline.

"We're definitely walking into a trap," analyzed Adele.

"I believe that's so," Attila concurred sarcastically. He signaled a cessation of movement and called the leaders forward for a meeting. Before they finished congregating, Caroline intervened.

"We all know that it's likely that this Grayle personality is aware of who we are at the least of it. Also, it seems he has had a pattern of locating and corralling loose bands of wanderers for over five hundred miles. Over the many years, voila! Grayleton!"

"To what end?" asked her mother.

"Personal security at first. Then, it probably evolved as a compassionate gesture as the stronghold grew. Now, I'd guess he has assumed responsibility for these thousands of wayward survivors. Those that left communities, attempting to make their way south, could easily been murdered by the time they made it to this region. Grayle's hunting parties discovered pilgrims but didn't threaten them. He took them in. For whatever reason, that's how the leader saw it and that's how it was done."

"We'll assume we're expected," Adele concluded. "We'll assume the highest technology at their disposal. For my part, I'm going to presume entrapment. Let's apprise everyone accordingly."

Tsin-hang opined that Grayle was more strategic than compassionate. He advised the Confederation to assume the worst.

"Sonny can figure the frequencies from where you are. Let him investigate the environment. It can tell you a lot," he suggested.

"I like the idea," Connor said.

Morgan weighed in, too. He recommended taking a few days to camp short of their destination, allowing the Circle to intuit or presage the situation and to use the time to interrogate the Grayleton scouts left at their base camp.

"I'm sending the ship's larger drones to circulate and rest within fifty miles of the compound we've now triangulated."

At the lakeside camp, Anton's thoughts had been mined and distributed as he shared both disposed and disinclined impressions of Grayleton life with an interrogator who sat prettily across from her subject. It was a process that required no special skills. Much as one might kick a loose layer of dirt from a bit of shiny glass revealed in the deep woods by the sun's rays, Anton came to life. The beautiful interrogator remained in rapt attention as he spilled his guts.

Sonny isolated himself and identified Grayleton's frequency levels by its marked contrasts to the surrounding environment. Ildiko concentrated upon remotely viewing per the compound's map of hidden outbuildings and farms. Caroline reverted to her childhood technique of drawing spontaneous images of future events.

Aditiya and Sonny conferred their findings and were the first to explain conclusions when the group re-convened.

"This city's organizational heart operates underground, meant to inhibit certain frequencies. It does this successfully. However, there are other frequencies that permeate our universe," Sonny stated. "Some of these frequencies leave vibrational traces in the environment and, if significant, I can identify these vibrational levels that sometimes tells the story of that data..." began Sonny.

"How is that done?" Connor asked.

"This isn't new. Pythagoras attempted to explain musical harmonics to the Western World by describing stone as in a state of 'frozen music' in 6 BC. He intuited the mathematics of frequency in all that surrounds us. The planetary rotations, seasonal changes, the atomic composition of elemental matter, all reveal rhythmic variations. From these variations, my mind identifies frequency differentials that respond to the immediate and persistent stimuli in the environment in which it resides. Perhaps an object has adapted to its environment and sometimes it hasn't."

"You may wonder as to the harmonic standard from which our own DNA is harmonically ordered," added Aditiya. "To that end, I have tuned into Caroline's exceptionally consistent frequencies to set that standard for our purposes. Her vibrational sound has a self-organizing power that emulates – if not reflects – universal harmonics. She is absolutely in tune with the sounds of our universe. If you've ever wondered the reason for Caroline's even temperament, that's likely part of it.

"I think that the reason Caroline responds to people in distress is that their frequencies are unreasonably discordant to her. As a kind of tuning fork, she's able to re-set the frequencies to harmonic levels. At first, it was her presence that could affect those in her area. Then, by physical touch, Caroline was able to alter molecular functioning. Finally, as a group, we are able to amplify this ability of hers, focusing our collective energy on a much broader scale.

"Survivors have been sorely damaged on the cellular/molecular levels by an unnatural exposure to EM infiltration. That kind of existence tends to resist the process of a programmed evolutionary track. I'm not just referring to physical evolution. There's another kind. We also have to spiritually evolve. Many of us might, therefore, spiritually die on the cosmic vine. Others are able to correct and transform into an evolved state. Those that are able to receive the blue light, or hear Caroline's 'tuning fork' as it were, are motivated immediately. Others are repelled... they will revert to the lowest frequencies, where they find their own level of comfort. They prefer to exist in a place that requires little effort to function. This is the state where one is unmoved to replenish or grow personal resources. Spiritual evolution is as important as the physical plane. Otherwise, lower frequencies test the mettle of those seeking higher frequencies. Perhaps that's the plan. The upshot is that those creating obstacles may end in self-destruction but it also helps others become better spiritual specimens.

"It's the 'birds of a feather' phenomena. Groups tend to collect on similar frequency levels. We may love music but we should also love and crave the frequencies of soothing sounds able to connect to our own DNA naturally embedded with cosmic symphonies. Discordant, disconnected or disengaged, anxious people may prefer to seek familiar levels of discordant frequencies. The more predominant these low frequency groups, the more corrosive our planet's vibrations.

"For over sixty years, the cacophony of external lower frequencies grew and disrupted our intrinsic tendencies. Who cared? Who knew? Everyone believes his or her frequency of choice is harmonic. Yet, we know that it requires effort to move into higher vibrational strings...at least, until it becomes a natural state. Effort distinguishes such levels.

"When the hour of our so-called darkness came upon us, we noticed the heavens suddenly light up. We could hear a stream's gentle current gliding over stones in the night; we were lulled to sleep by a symphonic oscillating wave of stridulating crickets and awakened by chirping, warbling birds heralding dawn. Some of us of a new generation were altered to the point of communicating with each other unencumbered by time and space. We've touched that optimal moment when we are able to 'hear' the DNA state of the world...a connection to our inner universe."

Adele asked how vibrational standards could explain Grayleton.

Sonny carefully measured his interpretations.

"I can only theorize according to the chants I transmit. Some things become clear to me that depend upon whether chants are received or not, absorbed or repelled. It's not a matter of a person being resistant to a message; it's a matter of their mind being too full to receive a drop of information, hear another note, or having the appropriate psychological receptors. In the case of Grayleton, the vibrational level of those living and working there is on a communal level. It's harmonically consistent. They're filled with the music of their collective lives, listening to a uniform sound, driving a uniform rhythm, with uniform goals. This sounds ideal. It's not. A uniform rhythm is no more a natural state than a symphony is made up of one instrument, a consistent singular beat, deprived of contrast.

"Our universe is dynamic, with varying rhythms. We have expansion and contraction. Lightning will streak violent, erratic patterns against a blackened sky followed by rays of sunshine bouncing off rain drops, – a rainbow appears that even a child will notice! Nuanced trickling waters conjure our sweetest thoughts and lull us into a dream, while savage tsunamis draw life from the ocean depths, requiring us to run for our lives. Life is hardly monotonous.

"We learn new tones, new rhythms as events mirror irregular and complex natural phenomena. Volcanoes and shooting meteors might be considered symphonic crescendos. Order, as in a monotonous drum thumping, should not operate at the expense of the wide spectrum of stimuli that permeate our psyche, our cellular structure, and our electrical signals that are meant to connect and resonate with new meanings. So I find it odd that the vibrational frequencies I receive from Grayleton are at one hormonal level, one auric field, at very low energy levels. There's a higher auric and hormonal field that helps to express creativity, just as there are variations in music, architecture, dance, and scientific inquiry that range from the simple to the complex. In Grayleton's environment there is plenty of contentment but no curiosity. No crescendos. No surprises. No contrast. Flat-lined. It's just like our fifth grade teacher Miss Polskiniski's endless drone. We couldn't keep our heads off the desk," Sonny inferred his impressions of the silent city.

"This hum may be Grayleton's optimal level for damaged survivors. They are functioning without animus. Is this not an optimistic analysis?" Aditiya posed.

"Not being dangerous isn't exactly optimistic," Attila interjected. "I need for you to expand on their weaknesses."

Sonny complied. "Regarding the harmonic fabric of DNA, we are all inferior to Caroline's bandwidth. With regard to Grayleton's environmental information, I don't recognize our own electromagnetic patterns. I'm not calling that exactly a weakness but it's plenty weird."

"I'm bottom-lining 'weird'," Connor recorded. He turned toward Nicholas and asked for Jordan Reid's report regarding Anton.

"Jordan spoke to other Grayleton camp residents before speaking with Anton," Nicholas explained as he forwarded Anton's transcripts. "Anton was very chatty after hanging over the lake for six hours, wetting his pants, and sitting across from Marge Hathaway.

"According to Reid and Komor, our Grayleton guests are naïve and innocent participants without much moral or analytical insight. Our Grayleton samples acted upon that which they've been taught as ethical or moral prescriptions. That interpretation is directly associated with their leader's own.

Grayle determines what is moral. If Grayle asks for cooperation in a task, there's no over-thinking it. No questions asked.
Which brings us to the Grayle messages carried on the tip of
their tongues.

"These messages are all morally based, taking into account
the Judeo-Christian Bibles as a moral compass. Passages have
been memorized, rituals observed, community contribution
required, compassion and patience encouraged at every turn.
The Ten Commandments act as the foundation.

"There are stories, lots of them, regarding Grayle's equita-
ble handling of errant or dangerous outsiders. By these accounts, Grayle has standards, trial periods of observation in
which wayward candidates have time to adjust. Grayle separates those whom he deems receptive from those considered
incorrigibly wicked. He exiles rather than eliminate or imprison.
We've perceived no tales of sexual deviance, undisciplined, or
erratic behaviors. These people idolize Grayle and believe him
a medium of God's message. He's Solomon incarnate."

"Did anyone ask if they disagreed – at any level – with
Grayle?" Cynthia asked.

"Komor put those sorts of questions forward. She asked if
they liked the directives, working their tasks – that sort of
thing. Not one person questioned their level of satisfaction,"
Nicholas reported. "It's as if they'd never entertained the idea
of an opinion.

"Anton idolizes Grayle. He has some ideas that differ from
the others we interviewed. Anton is transparently envious of
Grayle's access to vaults and places that are off limits. Anton
harbors images of standing outside of locked doors and buildings. He has never been invited into Grayle's personal living
quarters, for example, and his disgruntlement is clear. Anton's
finest ambition is to gain access to Grayle's world as a way to
become closer to Grayle. That world is much too complex for
Anton's state of mind. He's aware of his limbo status and harbors inner longings to end-run Grayle. If this is a slice of conscience, it explains his illness as a reaction to my presence.

"Grayle, we've come to understand, is privy to advanced
information enclosed in the largest government bunker in the

world. The man understands the value of these holdings and has somehow managed to put the entire complex in working order. And we've encountered something that Anton certainly knows about: the sonic discs. Anton reported that he helped position them with Grayle but had no idea of their function. When you read our report, pay close attention to the crude pictures of equipment and animals that Anton drew for us."

"Speaking of drawings," Caroline interrupted, "I've come up with some samples. I tried to draw impressions. For whatever reason, my sense of the future stopped abruptly when we got around these mountains.

"I was watching my horse and admiring her when something finally came to me. I drew it." Caroline transmitted her drawings, typically more analogous to photographs than art.

"I drew the horses and livestock to scale. As you can see, the horses are upward of 20 hands. The chickens are enormous...as large as any turkey I've encountered. If you examine the environment, you might notice there aren't constraints of any kind. No stalls, no pens, no cages. The animals are just standing around without any kind of activity. All of the stock seems beyond domesticated or secure; they seem mindless. Contented, sound in every way, but compliant without an instinct to seek food outside of that which is duly served."

"It seems as if this leader, Grayle, has successfully organized wayward wanderers that might have transformed into full blown crazies," Cynthia offered. "He might teach us something about an interim state that is receptive to remedial help."

Grayleton Secrets

When Anton and his scouting party failed to return, Grayle worried whether to send help or wait. It was only a matter of time, he figured, until Anton would go off track. The man could follow orders five times and neglect the next five.

"He probably decided to do something else or is now leading Confederation troops toward us days late."

No one in Grayleton asked about the missing group and that troubled Grayle. He decided to wait and see how long it took for someone to show concern.

"Typical," Grayle despaired.

"We're missing one of our scouting parties," he announced in the community hall. "Let's offer a silent prayer for their safe return."

A few minutes passed and Grayle said 'Amen'. Those present did the same. Still, no one speculated as to the missing friends and neighbors.

"Anne? Are you worried about Franklin?" Grayle asked the young woman whose husband volunteered to accompany Anton.

"Worried?" his wife responded blankly.

"Thinking about Franklin and when he might return? They were supposed to be back yesterday at the latest," Grayle urged.

"I'm thinking about him now. Is that what you mean?"

"Are you worried about his safety?"

"Are you worried that he is safe?" she repeated with a blank expression.

"I'm wondering where he is...where everyone is...right now, this moment. How about you?"

"Yes. I'm thinking that now, too," she acquiesced with little conviction.

Grayle looked over his flock of mindless, malleable sheep. They helped repair the remnants of civilization. They imitated the signs of society. They could espouse a memorized script. However, they were not the architects. The question was, could they ever be?

He would know the answer when their youngest children showed signs of critical thinking. To date, there were few dissenting voices or examples of spontaneous action within Grayleton.

Grayle sought refuge in unexplored vaults that afternoon and, as was characteristic, asked not to be disturbed. He locked all access. Grayle often elected to disappear for a few days at a time. Townspeople knew that they could contact their leader in case of emergencies by pressing a red button in the community hall. Such emergencies typically occurred no less than forty times within 48 hours. Grayle ignored them all. When able to enter the vaults, Grayle cared for nothing more. When able to explore the secreted treasures of civilizations, Grayle knew that he was preparing himself for something greater.

It was curious the items removed from public scrutiny, he thought. Why was it, Grayle wondered, would people not find it remarkable that there was a mechanism by which one could move tons of boulders hundreds of feet at a time with formulaic acoustic levitation? Or that there were thousands of square feet dedicated to freezers filled with samples of Telomeric Activation vaccines that could offset aging by half a century by essentially turning off the molecular switch of deterioration? Vaccines labeled in subcategories, under the singular heading of 'Cancer', were dated back to 1978. Why allow for the proliferation of cancer when it could have been eradicated so much earlier?

There were warehouses that reverse engineered equipment that lay intact and inert. Foreign looking script accompanied binary code accompanied by hundreds of translations. There were unlabeled massive lockers and freezers erected beyond Grayle's reach or ability to purpose. He was not compelled to blast his way into anything unlabeled after having read the warning signs that indicated deadly viral diseases.

"Ancient Codes" was a favorite area of interest. Without full contextual knowledge, it was difficult to figure the nature of the vault's contents. Grayle, information starved, could not imagine a period in which so much information had so little time for analysis, application, or implementation. It occurred to him how greedy and possessive man had become to have sequestered so much in the interest of absolute authority. In the end, priceless information was left unexpressed in obscure environmentally-controlled hardened cement vaults 250 feet below the earth's surface. Strange rooms reflected an historical shift of humanity's priorities.

"It doesn't require technology to control man's simple mind. It's getting man to account for the purposes of his or her mind that's the challenge. Where is the non-thinking antidote around here?" Grayle smiled to himself. "It's surely the most secret and protected potion in all the world!"

Grayle happened upon a vault labeled Strategic Plans. The strategies listed included disaster plans for the American government's personnel. Scenarios ranged from economic collapse to nuclear war and alien invasions. It was clear that every governmental body worldwide had similar ideas, given the stratagems were internationally cooperative. Self-preservation meant that these collaborating nations would continually update their priority lists for those with relevant skills. Grayle termed political leaders as the Keepers of Secrets.

"The Keepers professed a desire for the good of the people," Grayle theorized. "They all seemed to figure that the key to man's happiness was minimal information for the masses while pertinent information remained with leaders.

"It takes nothing for the mind to resist all evidence, to kill for a manufactured reason, to see another as an enemy because they simply exist. The best lessons about humanity are learned over great stretches of time with extreme sacrifices. And then they are lost in an egotistical heartbeat," Grayle concluded with some satisfaction.

"Human arrogance – so predictable. We need to eradicate this pattern of returning to the same problems every other decade, growing and killing off thriving civilizations every other millennium. I'm the one to do this," he pleaded to the heavens. "Rectification needs to happen once and for all!"

Grayle figured that one of the first vaults he discovered held information that required closer scrutiny. It held frozen stem cells of human specimens considered genetically gifted. Of all the themes, it was the one that read Abnormal Genetic Codes that captured Grayle's attention. Recalling the `Rainmaker` near his home, Grayle knew that heaven's liquid gold was recompensed in wild game for the boy's part in helping ensure a good crop. The child that could produce rain died of a viral infection when he was not yet thirteen. Having been in great demand, the young boy was required to travel town to town during the dry seasons. The exhausted boy died of a virus contracted at a township diminished by half from influenza.

Grayle was told stories of the 'Protector', who was able for many years to keep the gangs from townships by simply standing in harm's way. Predators died by the hundreds. No one knew what eventually became of the Protector, who had once lived in the northern regions near the Canadian border. There was no other Protector to be found. Everyone appreciated the Protector and the Rainmaker. There was not such appreciation for other types of unusual talent.

Tales of children who communicated without speaking were burned. Those that could read memories of the Darkness from a time before they were born were also cast from communities as evil. Near the large Lakes was a little girl who had the ability to self-heal. For many years, she was summoned to heal others but she could not. She grew strong while others faded around her. As much as she tried, she failed to heal the infirm. As the anger and frustration grew about her limitations, she became depressed. When her parents died of a bacterial infection, she asked the townspeople to kill and bury her with her loved ones. Two of the angriest men complied by decapitating the self-healer with her desperate death wish still upon her lips.

There were many stories and many superstitions during and after the Darkness. It was a time ripe for uncorroborated speculation. With few exceptions, those that demonstrated unusual abilities determined useless ran into such trouble. In Grayle's community was a friend who had a tendency to pick up objects and drop them suddenly as if he had touched burning coals; in other instances, selected objects of the boy's focus would be lovingly caressed. Grayle's friend, Oliver, insisted that there were 'untold stories' in each inanimate article.

"Things that don't have a life force may have energy fields," explained Oliver as they walked outside of town. "I feel where they've been and what they've witnessed; sometimes it feels angry and hot. Sometimes, the thing may be neutral. Other times, I touch an old wooden door or eating utensils and there's an indescribable sweetness," he explained.

Grayle's eyes had swept the categories within vault #298 and associated Oliver's special talents with the 'Retrocognition Gene'. Grayle would have dismissed such abilities the elders feared if he had not personally experienced a visitation. It happened after a church service. Their pastor spoke of God's messengers that came to aid or advise believers. Soon after the sermon, a blazing light and a voice spoke to Grayle in terms that made him a believer in the true spirit of God. It was as if his soul had been triggered. From the light, a male voice instructed Grayle to move from his township and begin a pilgrimage that would see him as the leader of untold millions. He would become one of many empowered to 'light the way' for those who were damaged, scorned, and overlooked. The angel promised to walk by his side and help him understand the word of God. Grayle's mission would be to spread messages that would be revealed to him alone.

Grayle was never visited again in the same way. But the impact of the visitation never failed to inspire because he had inherited a gift; information Grayle needed was easily comprehended and applied. Abilities grew by which he could intuit recorded information. Moving like a starved animal, Grayle touched, absorbed, and digested the information of the ages at ever-growing rates.

His growth, however, came at a price. Frustration grew relative to the slow evolution of those he stewarded. With few exceptions, Grayle was incompatible with the raggedy strangers that made their way into the growing township. Eager to please, the people of Grayleton offered no opinion, dissension, or discourse. In a strange way, Grayle missed the resistant souls unwilling to adjust to Grayleton rules and regulations. He rued the lack of dynamic give and take that faded with his rapid development.

"If they come, so will she," Grayle self-appeased. He felt sure that the woman of his dreams, an equal, would be delivered.

"A black horse with three white socks," he reassured himself. "If only I could see her face."

The mystery woman's vague impression came to Grayle in a dream as he watched the people of the Southern regions moving North to liberate the distressed. He sensed that the woman riding upon a Confederation horse would be beautiful, strong, and intelligent. Grayle extrapolated from this vision a private deliverance. At the same time, he knew that he could not force anyone into the desired station of wife. "She has to come to me," Grayle reminded himself.

With the mystery woman on his mind, Grayle searched for precious articles that the anticipated visitor might enjoy. There were collections of ancient Egyptian gold jewelry, elaborately carved chests from the Orient, and exquisitely detailed gowns stored within the Smithsonian Museum vaults selected and arranged within his suite of rooms. Grayle spent time embellishing the former Presidential quarters, focusing upon the former first family's estate rooms. Grayle's selections of Renaissance paintings were hung upon walls. Ambusson rugs were uncrated, unfurled, and spread upon the hardwood floors to soften the impact and ambiance. Grayle studied images that might give him insight as to the optimal aesthetics suitable to the woman he desperately hoped to impress. Jewels were categorized and positioned in an antique chest. Perfumes that had been stored long in freezing temperatures were once again brought to life within a mirrored closet.

It was with a special visitor in mind that Grayle discreetly visited the stables via his secret underground access. "The horses they ride are beautiful. They've many but none will compare to mine."

Grayle fed the livestock the special stores of enhanced grain and supplements that were encased within designated feed rooms underground. Grayle retrieved a bucket of the special oats and surprised a young teenager in the process of mucking the stables.

"I'll look after them," he ordered. "Go check the chickens and cows; make sure they're fed, the storage bins cleaned..."

The boy fled the scene.

"Mine are faster and larger than the ones of the Southern soldiers," he reassured himself. "She'll love you," Grayle spoke softly to the mare raised from a colt he meant to gift the unidentified woman coming his way. Grayle's imagination knew no bounds, but his patience had worn thin.

Grayle bridled the horse that willingly received the bit. He launched himself on his mare's back by propelling off of a side fence.

"Let's go, girl," he urged. "We've got a little journey."

He called to the startled stable workers outdoors to expect him back within a few days. The muscles of Grayle's monstrous beast swelled to life, its long legs lifted high and placed confidently in front of a massive chest; an animate thresher separated thin layers of green from its earthly underpinnings to chase down Grayle's vision.

Chapter XXXV

Morgan's Nose

Thursday, July 10, 2070

Rachel and Angela prepared for Esther's luncheon visit on the estate. It was to be an important homecoming and the women worked hard to demonstrate their goodwill.

"She cancelled," pronounced Morgan the afternoon of her expected arrival.

"One thing you can count on," Angela remarked, "is that Esther never fails to disappoint."

"She doesn't like Mummy," Edward spouted as he helped set the table. The flying silverware clinked around the kitchen. A spoon flew by Morgan's head and clipped an ear.

"Rachel?" Morgan cried. "Your boy's first talent has been to stab me with flying utensils. Give our possessions a rest. Everything I own is cracked, broken or nearly cracked or broken."

He turned toward Edward attempting to retrieve the fallen objects without touching them. "Son, what are you saying about Esther?"

"She doesn't like Mum. That's all!" Edward fought the kitchen bot for possession of the silverware. The bot was sent flying across the room.

"Esther never liked me," Rachel confirmed. "I can't say that I feel slighted."

"Esther has a boyfriend now," explained Angela. "It's serious. We're all supposed to meet Stan in August. I understand they met each other through work. Maybe there's a problem there and she's now uncomfortable about this visit?"

"Got an image of Stan?" Morgan asked.

Angela sent Morgan the photo Esther had provided.

"Handsome looking fellow. Must be smart, too. I'm going to be a happy man to see her settled," Morgan grinned.

"Has there been a background check, Morgan?" Rachel asked.

"He works for the Research Triangle. You'd have to be smaller than a split atom to escape that security. He's clean as a whistle working with that network." Morgan eyed Rachel's dubious expression.

"Mind bringing us up to speed, Morgan?" Rachel changed the subject to indicate a daily report on Confederation progress.

"They've broken up into units. The largest group is still by the lake with a small segment of that Grayleton group. Another Confederation group returned to Philadelphia and helped with evacuation. Attila's select Pendergrass Express is now preparing to move into Grayleton after fortifying their backup positions. What did you hear from Connor?"

"No one understands how our surveillance has missed this big town; it's thriving and advanced albeit secluded. He wants to investigate the mysterious place but unclear whether the leader is cooperative or hostile. He's not keen on walking into another trap."

"Another trap?" Angela asked.

"Connor and Attila have figured they were set up twice by Grayleton people in order to manipulate and maneuver them toward their home base," Morgan explained. "They've decided to go in with a small party with the greater militia on the periphery covered by drones. I know it sounds paranoid, but that's how they see it. They're sure of sophisticated levels of tech."

Morgan turned to Rachel.

"I'd appreciate it if you watched over the place with Isabella; I have to travel back and forth for a while between here and Raleigh during this critical stage. I want to leave now that Esther bailed on us."

"Sure," Rachel answered without hesitation.

Morgan contacted Meredith Green, unnecessarily screaming her name.

"Meredith? I want those ships to send five unmanned heliports to land right in the center of that Grayleton place on my command in the event of an emergency evacuation. We're going to train the ship's laser canons that direction, too. They've encountered high tech sonic defense drones that could have had laser capabilities. We may have to party."

"Will do. What time you plan to pay us a personal visit?"

"Right now."

Morgan thought they'd have their mission wrapped up by this time. Instead, Confederation soldiers had been spread thin by the remedial assistance; no two communities proved the same. It was the same across every region up to the Canadian border. Those that survived the blue light's effects were eager to accept Confederation assistance or relocate in more stable areas. Other groups proved hostile and, therefore, required more manpower.

The Boyer region had remained mysteriously quiet. Morgan expected the cannon lasers on Confederation ships would be able to travel five hundred miles inland with pinpoint accuracy if something went sideways.

"I want no more than twenty people to go into Grayleton," was Morgan's last standing order. "If something happens to the horses, the heliports can fly them out."

Morgan was in the Raleigh complex within twenty minutes. Rather than go to the situation room, Morgan visited Esther's office unannounced. No one was there.

Here goes, he thought. *I'm goin' to check this out myself.*

As one of five personnel with maximum clearance, Morgan gained entrance to Esther's computer. He peered at the cam's portal and it came to life.

"History," he demanded.

There was nothing unseemly that came to Morgan's attention.

"Stupid work," Morgan observed. Pickin' pimples would require more concentration."

Morgan asked for a search for an associate researcher by the name of Stanley Raga. When Raga was not in the system, Morgan asked for all feeds with monitor recordings of verbal directives or tags of Stanley Raga.

There had been a record of over seventy hours of exchanges with 'Stan' indicated. The contents had been deleted along with daily sweeps of the computer.

"Get Meredith in here. Tell security and Scott Reid to find Esther," Morgan messaged.

Meredith arrived quickly. "What's the problem with Esther?"

"How does Esther know how to delete information off this computer? Find another feed. I want to see her conversations. I can't find any Stanley Raga working in research. I can't locate the name anywhere except on file with her Personal Assistant. Get your people on finding these images so we can profile this guy."

"Morgan, she doesn't have any clearance whatsoever. If she's using this computer for private conversations, we'll recover it. If not, she's not the one deleting it in the first place. What are you thinking?"

"Doesn't bother you a little, Meredith?"

"What? You asked us to babysit Esther, Morgan. We gave her a job to keep her busy and out of trouble. She made up a story about a respectable boyfriend who works with her. That surprises you? That's Esther's MO, right? I always wondered if a boyfriend existed!"

"She's off center but I never knew Esther to be sneaky in that way. She'd rather rage than cover up," Morgan guessed. "I want to know if this guy exists... and given her file, it looks like he's around. There's another end to this transmission... where's it going? And I want to know the reason she deleted every trace of these communications. I want to speak to her personally."

Scott Reid entered the room and shook his head. "Sir, Esther was here in this room two hours ago. Since that time, we've no idea of her whereabouts. We'll continue the search."

"Oh Lord. She's probably eating lunch, Morgan," Meredith offered exasperatedly. "The lady is not gone, not smart, and not dangerous. She takes breaks all the time. No one said anything about her being under live surveillance outside the building. We thought we were keeping her out of trouble."

"Indulge me!"

Morgan thought about it and decided to leave it to Meredith and Reid to follow up.

"That girl is up to something," he warned the pair.

Chapter XXXVI
The Moving Grayle

W e'll be the only ones going into Grayleton," Caroline explained to the group. "Before we do that, I suggest we try another grid enforcement. We're certainly reaching every other region and things look good but there's no Grayleton frequency change. We'll figure that as soon as we're in a better position."

Attila and Connor accepted this as a prudent course. Neither expected a problem given the presence of perimeter support poised to land in the middle of town. The ship's lasers left little room for Grayleton resistance. The full strength of the Hussar militia was only ten hours away from the compound by horseback. Hundreds of backup troops could be delivered by air.

The light had become so intensely bright blue that people across the former United States had begun to expect the periodic spectacle. Internationally, similar reports poured in of the extreme positive or negative results in the aftermath of the grid's visibility that extended for longer periods. Much effort had gone into education about the importance to rebuild the geomagnetic shield even as the phenomenon frightened some. As long as the process enhanced a sense of wellbeing, there were few objections.

Grayle, too, became excited about the grid's manifestation. It meant a new beginning. With every closing mile, he felt sure of his mission to welcome Confederation ambassadors to his territory. He would finally have an opportunity to exchange ideas and insights. Relishing the idea of being appreciated by worthy minds and hearts, Grayle's anticipation ran as fast as his horse.

Grayle's mount was so tall that its seat placed a rider in range of the thicker branches that could not be forced away. Tired of the unyielding wood that threatened injury, Grayle grew weary of riding flattened to the horse's back. He slowed to a walk.

"Good girl," he patted the mare's sleek neck and moved toward a small creek to refresh them both.

Grayle stripped his clothing and moved into the cool moving tributary, once damned upstream for homes and cottages that now lay in ruin. Lying down upon the smooth rocks, he watched his horse drink as he moved slowly into a few feet of water, allowing the cool wetness to cover his body. Overreaching branches conjoined a thick belt of maple and birch trees. Once opposing forces that competed for the sun's rays, the forged trees proved a sweet umbrella of relief for the perspiring traveler. Water and shade fended off some of the unrelenting deerflies drawn to man and beast. Grayle's head rested upon a small, smooth boulder. Water trickled through his hair and onto his long, lean body, slightly submerged. Within minutes, Grayle was asleep.

It was dusk and a full moon had begun to show itself when the mare nuzzled Grayle awake. Grayle dressed and pulled himself up onto his patient horse by its long black wavy mane.

"Sorry, girl. Let's get out of this hole."

When Grayle caught the artificial light of the Confederation camp he smiled at the prospect of meeting the people who had been promised to travel his way. Would he lead them? Would they want that? Would they work together to build the New American territories? He wished his guiding angel would offer explicit instructions rather than having to rely upon his intuition.

Tree limbs snapped despite best efforts. Rather than progress into the campsite's center, Grayle preferred to absorb unidentified scents and feel the quiet contentment of those who ate. He savored the sensations of camaraderie and compassion; he was encouraged by the innocence of those located a hundred feet from where he sat upon his horse. It was a welcome sensation and he bathed in it with one thought: *perfect*.

The unannounced silhouetted image of Grayle sitting quietly upon a gigantic horse in the full moon's light caused Sonny to gasp. What followed represented Sonny's entire repertoire of streamed obscenities learned first-hand from Attila, whose long-winded Hungarian expletives had reached legendary proportions.

Sonny's high-pitched shrieks drew Nicholas and Aaron to his side.

"Who goes there?" Nicholas shouted. He turned irritably toward Sonny. "Shut it down, Sonny!"

"Grayle. My name is Grayle. I'm sorry I frightened you," Grayle answered politely from the forest's edge, still motionless.

Within seconds, the rest of the Circle's contingent stood facing off with Grayleton's founder, namesake, and envoy. Nicholas moved forward to test the man's emotional waters.

"May I dismount?" Grayle asked respectfully of Cynthia, who recognized the man in her dreams at once.

"Please," Cynthia quickly invited.

Caroline and Ildiko shared a question: "What kind of horse is that?"

Aaron telepathed Cynthia, "Don't move closer!"

"He's riding in here alone," noted Ildiko in the shared conversation. "He has no reaction to Nicholas."

"Doesn't mean a thing," answered Aditiya.

"Where's the guy's saddle? He's riding bareback on that mammoth creature," thought Nicholas.

Grayle smiled broadly at the entourage. "You do realize that you're staring without saying a word? Am I so strange?"

Aaron warned, "Don't let him suspect that we read each other's thoughts."

Cynthia smiled apologetically and soothed, "Sometimes we do that. We've never seen a horse like yours."

With an obvious sign of suspicion, Nicholas and Aaron placed themselves between Cynthia and the stranger. Grayle quickly stated his business.

"I'm looking for my scouting party. I heard of your migration. Certainly you have knowledge of my group?"

"We have. They're back at our base camp. We were going to do the same thing. We heard of you and planned to visit. We've been interested in your area for some time," Nicholas said.

Grayle surveyed the small group as others arrived. He elected to remain silent.

"No signals showed up in your area but we know there's a lot of sporadic activity there," Aaron said pointedly. "That is, until we set off those sonic lasers that were hidden on the trail."

"They're a warning system for groups with more than 30 people. I helped set that perimeter myself," Grayle brushed off its import.

"We could have been killed with those lasers," Ildiko added.

"They weren't set. Just the alarm system with the extreme pitch... it's enough to alarm us and the roaming crazies."

There was more silence. Grayle examined the group and they returned the scrutiny. It was not uncomfortable; it was simply a time for both parties to gather clues about the other.

"We're both at a disadvantage. I think if you see Grayleton, you'll understand more," Grayle reset the conversation. "There're naturally no signals; you must know our compound is mostly underground. I'm living in the former bunkers and vaults of the US government. President Clifton Brown and his White Eagles were the last government occupants before I came across the place and killed his security guards. Never knew what happened to the president.

"It's now a city of sorts. I've been working for years trying to access, understand, and apply the technology and information available there," he continued.

"Like that two-ton horse?" Cynthia asked.

"Like the feed that has been genetically tweaked to that horse," Grayle said, appreciating her effort to alter the tense atmosphere. "You should see the chickens, the livestock, and the corn that matures in half the normal time. We have seed vaults of all known varieties, including those never publicly classified. I look forward to showing you these things and more."

"Are you interested in our help?" Caroline asked.

"I think we need to rebuild this world and the sooner the better," Grayle answered. "I look forward to connecting. I need that, you need that, and the world needs that."

Caroline walked past Aaron and Nicholas and considered offering her hand but withdrew it suddenly.

Grayle recognized the aborted gesture with an understanding smile.

"You meant to greet me, I know. I've been unable to teach the significance of a handshake to those living in Grayleton. You must have realized that when you met Anton and company? My apologies. They're not known for manners."

"No worries," Aaron answered simply for Caroline, who stared intently at Grayle.

"You must be aware of the results of the EMP tragedy?" Aditiya misdirected.

"What are you saying exactly, 'I must be aware'? Grayle asked.

"I'm saying that you've been able to use the government compound's highest levels of technology developed as of 2035 with little or no formal training. You are also probably privy to untold and unexplored technology. You must have some idea of the research regarding magnetic fields on the human mind and what its ramifications mean beyond electrical outages? You do understand the state of the world in which we now live?" Aditiya rapidly qualified.

Grayle nodded knowingly. "Of course. It took me a few years to get things back on track, but we're humming along."

"Humming," Sonny repeated. "Your city seems to work seamlessly but there's curiously an absence of noise."

"I never thought of it that way," he shrugged. "Quiet? I just now realized that a normally functioning city might emit more noise. How odd. I guess with all the work and study there's not much left to do. We rarely leave the place."

"What kind of study?" Caroline asked.

Grayle jumped to the ground, pulled a small biblical tome from his backpack, and tapped its cover.

"We study God and what it means to celebrate His gifts as dutiful citizens. We learn the prayers and verses. I've even studied the gospels from other sources omitted from Constantine's version. Although, the concept of direct communication with God escapes most of Grayleton residents. As of now, I do what I can to explain God's word...they cannot conceptualize certain ideas at present. Not everyone is whole. Most of our wanderers that made it to our city were confused, although, they've became compatible. They're safe and they've learned to help operate the farms. I'm there to metaphorically and realistically bring God's plan to life as best as possible... given their limitations."

"That's your role?" Caroline asked.

"I'm doing my best to build and lead the community." He examined Caroline to scrutinize her overly attentive eyes. "There's a lot to keep me busy."

"We've evidence of adverse permanent aftereffects of the electromagnetic storms. You're aware of the same?" Caroline asked, with the more vicious predators in mind.

"Of course. I've managed to sustain a productive city of people who were damaged by EM pulses. I use tactics taught to me by my parents and teachers. We use God's word to guide us. Isn't that how you people have done it?"

Sonny moved closer to Grayle. Grayle regarded the bald male as less than a healthy specimen of a man.

"Your frequency in your town is constant. Grayleton's operational level is without sonic undulation. Are you aware of that?" Sonny asked.

"How would one know that?" Grayle asked.

Sonny invited, "We can speak about it if you'd like to join us?"

Nicholas motioned for Cynthia to tether Grayle's horse so that they could gather in the main tent.

Cynthia spoke soothingly to the giant black mare and reached gently for the slackened reins but the mare resisted. Aaron suspended the snorting horse just as it reared on hind legs above Cynthia's head. It pawed the air, meaning to stamp an encroaching stranger into the ground.

Grayle watched helplessly as the giant steed was snatched and propelled upward by an unseen force.

"What happened?" he accused the group angrily.

"No one answer," thought Aaron.

Cynthia quietly assured Grayle verbally, "She's fine. We call it an aerial tether. We use it occasionally when we train horses."

"She won't move but she isn't going to allow anyone near her. That's how I train a horse," Grayle stated. "Put her back on the ground."

"She's dangerous. We'll return her when it's appropriate," Cynthia insisted.

Grayle was unused to people making decisions. While fashioning himself as a benevolent despot, Grayle had become a stranger to the negative response.

"You have restrained my horse. By doing so, you have restrained me as well. Having come in peace, I've my answer as to your intentions," Grayle directed his ire at Cynthia.

"Safety is our concern on this point. I could have been trampled and was saved by the intervention. Could you have stopped the attack?" Cynthia posed.

Given the logic, Grayle acquiesced quickly in tone and body posture. "I don't think you had the right to approach my horse in the first place. I intend to leave now. I'll have my horse returned and you'll all be safe."

Ildiko interceded, "Please don't leave. We'll bring her down but this is the time we should speak and come to an understanding," she smiled.

Grayle negatively shook his head.

"We've met. Now I have a simple request. Tell our Grayleton scouts that they are needed elsewhere and should return. Your group is surely not in need of our support."

"They did help us," Nicholas said. "We thank you for sending them our way."

Grayle looked long at Nicholas before answering.

"We never know what we'll find. I'm glad they were able to help. How did they help exactly?" Grayle questioned.

"Shut up, Nicholas..." Ildiko thought to the group. "Don't let on that we suspect a set-up."

"They came upon us during a predicament with some wild crazies that ambushed us from two sides," Nicholas created a tailored account. "We were caught between the forest and the lake. We were relieved when your scouts showed up and successfully drove one faction into the lake and finished them. We suffered no casualties. Anton delivered your message and explained about Grayleton. It was then that we knew we should pay a visit to the most civilized place left in the northern regions," Nicholas measured his tale with flattery.

"Some of our people were discovered in the woods away from Grayleton. They weren't in good health and didn't think too highly of the experience," Grayle countered. "They escaped, they told me, from strange soldiers on ghost horses?"

"Yes, we know that we have such an effect on those unused to technology. It's not purposeful, of course. It's these kinds of things we should sort. Surely, you can't believe that we mean harm?" Aaron asked.

"My horse, please?"

Cynthia watched Grayle, as he stood firm and calm. If he was apprehensive, it didn't show. She thought him more disappointed than angry.

"We've miscommunicated," Cynthia appealed diplomatically. "Hopefully, you'll help us re-establish the former territories of the United States. That's our mission. That's what we are risking our lives for."

"Risking lives? There's no contest as far as I can see. You people from the Confederation abandoned the rest of the nation a long time ago because you didn't want any risk. You've progressed risk-free while stranded Americans struggled.

"People are still barely surviving and your government has not interceded. This isn't something new. I read how governments worked. It was very clear to everyone in power that the cellular structures of the brain would be compromised, that there wouldn't be enough food or resources, and disease would run rampant. There were answers that would have been better than implanting IF chips. It seems to me that government cares about controlling the masses. The American government knowingly contributed to ill health," Grayle evaluated cynically. "I have found governments wanting in their efforts to guide effectively. What are you – as Confederation representatives – doing exactly now in the name of health and safety?"

Grayle looked over Cynthia's head into the group gathered before him. He pointed toward them and swept his finger back and forth, forming a wide swath of accusations.

"You represent a new government? Your group were separatists in the first place. You now intend to save those not originally associated with your political grouping two decades post the Darkness? You arrive on horseback in uniforms and with advanced weaponry when most are deceased and the remaining desperate or mad? After the viral infections and influenza rolled over us as sure and as unrelenting as the four seasons? After you've been made comfortably ready within your borders you then, and only then, decide to march, armed to the teeth, to enact your good deeds and superior ideas about society? I find that suspect. Don't you?" Grayle laughed at the ludicrousness.

Aditiya appreciated Grayle's perspective that reminded him of a kindred spirit.

"One of the Confederation's founders, Morgan Pendergrass, certainly shares your perspective about government tendencies toward power abuse. We're on a mission and it's been done as expeditiously as humanly possible. And we've millions to contend with... not thousands," Aditiya rationalized.

Grayle laughed, "Meaning what? You've an idea of how I think about governance?"

Nicholas and Aaron reprimanded Aditiya's candor and suggested how to engage Grayle without overstepping.

"This disparity in the human race, if left to continue another generation, may spell disaster," Aditiya finished.

"I suspect that this is a complicated and long discussion," Grayle said dryly. "Saving the human race may prove a protracted process.

"I'm going to return home. My little city is relatively insignificant, given your own lofty goals," he sniffed scornfully.

"We were on our way to see what you've accomplished," Cynthia interjected. "Do you mind if we simply follow to see what you've built?"

"It depends." Grayle looked at Cynthia with a softened face.

"Upon what?"

"If you'll be the one to accompany me," he finally smiled. "You seem to be the only friendly party here."

"We're all friendly, believe me," Cynthia said.

"Perhaps. Until now, you've moved into territories to help with the expectation that people would welcome you. What about those that feel they can do without you? I find it odd that you've taken on the job of the world's official inspectors, making decisions as to who is a lunatic and who is not. Who is salvageable and who is lost? This is the Confederation's call?"

"Are you saying that you can do without Confederation help?" Nicholas asked.

"That's just it. Mustn't you first define the terms of such help?" Grayle responded to Nicholas without moving his focus from Cynthia. "I've successfully socialized those you might have dismissed as unworthy."

Aditiya quickly understood that Grayle's was well-founded perception.

"None of us have lived fully in the world that destroyed itself. It's up to us to get it right this time, don't you agree?" Aditiya asked.

"I'm still wondering what you want from me. If I asked you to leave, will you be content to leave us alone to govern and operate as we see fit? Or do you intend to ask us to model our behavior and expectations on your Confederation's idea of society? Do you intend to take over the compound and take ownership of its contents, tell the people what they need to do, offer them a few alternatives, and call it a day? I'm not sure you have the right," Grayle clarified.

Caroline spoke from behind Aditiya and Ildiko.

"Grayle, we haven't thought that far. It's never occurred to us that people would not welcome our medical assistance and wish to have the advantages of civilization that the Confederation has to offer. While human history is fraught with different outcomes, we now have a moment in time to change course. We need you even though you may not need us. And as far as the vaults in the American Data Repository are concerned, I'm very much looking forward to seeing it!"

"See it? Or assume ownership?" Grayle tested.

"It wasn't something anyone even thought about. I'm not sure if it belongs to humanity or to Grayleton. You think finders keepers, Grayle?" Ildiko said. She stepped closer to Grayle in the hopes that the thoughts that had thus far escaped her might improve with proximity.

Aaron let the enormous mare down gently to the ground and Cynthia stepped back. Grayle took a few running steps and launched himself on the tranquil horse, now satisfied that her master had returned.

"You can send that one and that one," Grayle pointed to Cynthia and Caroline. "They seem a little bit wiser and less threatening than the rest of you. I'm leaving in five minutes."

Nicholas, Sonny, Aditiya, and Aaron rejected the suggestion.

"We've operated as one group and we'll stay as one!" they silently agreed.

"Sorry this hasn't worked out," Nicholas said with finality.

"Suit yourself. I came here alone. Who's discussing trust?" Grayle turned and prepared to move into the night.

"Wait!" Cynthia called to Grayle's back. "Allow me to accompany you alone; I'll report my impressions. We can open a dialogue and perhaps you and I can repair this poorly constructed bridge?"

"You're welcome. In the meantime, Grayleton citizens should be promptly released," Grayle demanded.

Nicholas telepathically protested the sugestion to the others, and attempted to contact Attila and Connor, who had yet to check in. Caroline tried to reference her mother and Aaron; she sent a series of mental images to little Edward about their situation, asking the boy to contact his mother and Morgan. Sonny telegraphed his vid recordings of the encounter to Tsin-hang on the offshore ship. Not one of these efforts completed a transmission.

Ildiko messaged the group that which was on everyone's mind. "What the hell? All of a sudden we're cut off? Cynthia stays here!"

Cynthia had other ideas and telepathed them; "This is an anomaly of an isolated community that has been exposed to the blue light. It operates at a monotonous, low frequency but it's orderly. If we are to establish law and order to these territories, we'd better figure out how the hell one guy achieved that, don't you think?

"He trusts me and I think he's on the level. I'll stay in touch. If, and when, Grayle turns more receptive, you guys follow. In the meantime, honor his request to send his group back to Grayleton," Cynthia directed.

Grayle frowned. "You're doing it again. All of you just standing there and staring wide-eyed without saying anything. If I didn't know better, I'd say you were being rude. What's it going to be?"

"I'm coming with you, Grayle. I'll be alone," Cynthia said.

"Get your things; let's ride," Grayle impatiently instructed.

Cynthia fetched the first horse she found with gear but left her refraction gear behind. There would be no way he could ascertain that she and her horse were amped, but the gear and weaponry could represent a technological threat if he was able to replicate the technology.

"Ready," Cynthia smiled at him without looking behind.

Cynthia's horse followed Grayle's onto a narrow trail unable to accommodate two large mounts to walk abreast. Within thirty minutes of their departure, Cary, Raleigh, the offshore ship, and Gant from D.C., pinged frantically.

"They've gone?" Attila yelled at Nicholas. "You couldn't manage to find me at base camp? Where's the order here?"

Everyone had a similar reaction except for Morgan.

"How the hell you think we're going to figure out a damn thing without going right into the man's den?" Morgan railed. "Let's get this done. We've already got all kinds of backup within minutes of that Grayleton. Stop peeing in your pants. Looks to me like Cynthia is the brass of the group." Morgan's ire turned to Attila. "Can this Grayle actually hear us? It sure seems as if he set up Jordan Reid."

"Grandpa, we spoke with each other telepathically; he seemed perplexed when we weren't speaking. I just don't know," Caroline said.

"That true for all of you?" Morgan asked.

"Yes," came the unified reply.

"Follow the Grayleton group discreetly to their home. Give them lots of room and let's see what Cynthia is able to find out. Now, let's move your intellectual, insightful asses," Morgan demanded.

"The Morgan Expedient lives," telepathed Ildiko to the Circle.

* * *

Cynthia listened to the rhythm of the two horses making their way through the wood. Knowing that she and her horse could see perfectly in the dark, Cynthia wondered the reason Grayle seemed unfazed picking his way without the benefit of infrared vision.

He must be used to this route, she surmised.

Grayle's broad shoulders and strong physique could not be ignored from her vantage point.

Pretty much a Greek god, Cynthia thought.

They hadn't spoken in a few hours and it was getting late by the time Cynthia asked her first question.

"How far is Grayleton?" Cynthia called.

"A ways," came the vague answer.

"You always this talkative?" Cynthia pressed.

"I've no one to really talk to," he answered. "Wish I did. Most everyone takes direction without discussion."

"I see. Must be lonely."

"It is." He turned his mount about to face his riding partner.

"You people may be able to hear each other's thoughts, but I read emotions pretty well."

"What makes you think we hear each other?" Cynthia asked, surprised.

"I'm very intelligent, Cynthia."

"I don't recall telling you my name," she said evenly.

"It doesn't matter. I know it."

"You have a last name?"

"No. Most of us don't have a last name. For some reason, we stopped using a last name. My parents never used one. Too many parentless children, you know? Too many childless adults," he said emotionlessly. "I guess everyone thought a singular name was a generous solution."

"Same here. My sister and I never learned our last names. Our mother brought us up but our last memories are of just calling her Mom. Then she was gone. I remember a large home that kept us warm enough to survive the winters. When Mom died, the scavengers came and took the wood, the food, everything. I owe my life to my older sister." Cynthia was surprised that she felt inclined to share confidences with a man she'd met a few hours prior.

"Life holds less promise," Grayle offered. "I guess names implied a familial connection with others and we had lost those others. A second generation later, the names had vanished from memory. I just recall Grayle. Some people called themselves my parents after discovering me wandering."

"What do you mean you read emotions pretty well? And why have we stopped?" Cynthia asked with some concern.

"I dreamed about you. I knew your horse had three white socks. If your horse didn't have three white socks, I would have been surprised. I would have left your camp without you."

"You were looking for me or my horse?"

"I've felt your presence for some time now. The only thing I could figure was the strong emotion I felt for the woman on the black horse with three white socks. You name might have been Cynthia but I'm not sure. I happened to have been attracted to you the moment I laid eyes on you," Grayle stated. "That's all I had to know."

Cynthia waited wordlessly and breathlessly. Not a scintilla of a response came to mind. Grayle had shared a sense of her own dreams as she wandered in and out of his life in long cool corridors deep below the earth, watching him tend duties, reaching for something he could not quite articulate or touch.

I'm just sitting here in the pitch dark staring at a complete stranger who admits to a mutual admiration society, she thought.

"Yeah, well, I'm at a loss for words," she finally said.

"Makes two of us," Grayle laughed. "Let's give the horses a rest," Grayle indicated a stream that could be heard running nearby. They dismounted and removed the bridles without a tether.

"She's that well trained?" Cynthia asked.

"She's that loyal," Grayle answered. "Yours?"

"Loyal and well trained," Cynthia smiled.

Cynthia stretched then went by the stream and splashed water on her face, cupped her hands, and gratefully drank of the cool water spilling over clean round rocks.

"You're a good horseman?" Grayle asked simply.

"Yes," she yawned. "I grew up training with a superb horse master."

"I didn't need a teacher," Grayle stated. "There are things you can teach yourself – if you have to."

"Evidently."

"Too bad we've two mares here," he laughed. "I could use some breeding stock."

"Where did you get this one? She's impossibly beautifully proportioned and gigantic," Cynthia marveled.

"She wandered into the camp as a yearling. Just walked right up and began grazing on the farm. Others couldn't get near her. One day, I noticed the colt running in circles. I figured that animals got crazy, too. Anyway, I'm just watching her buck and throw her head around and I'm thinking she's frustrated. I felt that she was lonely, too. There aren't any horses around, Cynthia. People ate them. They'll still eat them if they come across one. This one must have come into the world too smart. Anyway, she calms down and crosses the field and snorts at me. I sat down on the ground as she edged closer. I stood up, she backed up. After a few days of feeling out the situation, she followed me everywhere. I'd go to the community hall upside and she'd be there with her nose to the window. I go back through the interior or underground and she'd neigh and paw the ground. Finally, she figures that she's not going to go inside and makes her way to the feed room, removes the lids, and ate at will. I began to ride her a few years later and there hasn't been a moment of disconnect since."

"Ever ride another before this horse?"

"No."

"Well, it's pretty unusual. I trained a lot. You jump?"

"She jumps. I try and stay on," he answered.

Refreshed, they departed the lazy stream. Rays of the morning sun began to blaze through the haze and the heat rose dramatically. Neither horse showed fatigue; they moved into a trot as the path evened out, beaten wide, clean, and flat by foot traffic. Grayle slowed to ride beside Cynthia.

"I'm glad you decided to accompany me. I didn't feel welcome at your camp," Grayle said as he let the slight breeze cool his neck. He rubbed his hand through his hair and shook it much as an animal might.

"We've got a mission, you know. Going to save the world, as my sister always says," Cynthia commented.

"Is she with you?"

"No. Home. Working."

"My adopted mother and father cared for me well enough but I never wanted to return," Grayle explained. "It was safe but people seemed angry under the surface. My parents spoke about the world before the Darkness in a complicated way. They missed the times before but were glad to be rid of it at the same time. No one seemed certain of anything but church service, growing enough food, chopping enough wood. I never knew what it meant to have people around me without worried expressions or distrust of strangers. Every newcomer brought death or stories of death," Grayle said.

"You've a whole city of friends now," Cynthia stated.

"I don't mind Grayleton. They might not be talkative but they aren't going to rip your throat out in the night either," he described as a summation of his former and present life.

"What do you have planned?"

"I've nothing planned. I react. That's all I do."

"To what?"

"For the moment, I'm reacting to you," Grayle said without disguising his scrutiny of the woman beside him.

"Right. After you react to me, do you plan on something special for Grayleton?" Cynthia followed.

"Like what? Like moving toward the South with troops and seeing if the Confederation needs some assistance?" he said sarcastically.

"I don't really care if we take care of the Northern and Western territories. It's nothing but a resource drain for Confederation populations. I'm not sure it can be done. The people that are left populating these areas tend to be resistant and marginally useful. The others? You know that answer. They're either humming along in communities like yours or trying to escape them, moving to who knows where, murdering and plundering without a pittance of penance," Cynthia clarified with less afability.

"You're riding around the country doing just that," Grayle dismissed.

"You're wrong. Good people who've been earnest about rebuilding the planet saved me. They've been successful in pursuing science in the most challenging times. They've communicated and reestablished commerce internationally and established goodwill where previously there was nothing but distrust. The Darkness extinguished a light and lit another.

"I found myself traveling from Canada on a ship. Someone abducted my sister and me; we were traded for passage. We'd been drugged. We awoke tied together on a large barge that heaved us from side to side. We were bruised all over our bodies. The following month, we were nighttime entertainment until a new group overtook our ship and did the same.

"A guy named Nicholas joined us in New York; consequently, we were rescued by Confederation military. It's been nothing but kindness and organized support since that nightmare. I'm a believer in their mission to reunite and remedy our planet's great challenges," Cynthia passionately expressed her heartfelt gratefulness. "I wouldn't mind this expedition coming to a close. I figure I've done my time and it's time for others to push this agenda."

"We're both reluctant pioneers, I guess," Grayle said thoughtfully.

"Like drafted pilgrims," she corrected. "We mean to move onward with optimistic intentions of realigning the human condition!"

"Doubt it," Grayle said.

"Reason?"

"Humanity is flawed. Always will be. History doesn't lie," he pessimistically declared.

Cynthia countered, "We've faith."

"That's what I tell our citizens. They don't have any thoughts of history, nothing to go on... nor do they care. I encourage devotion. Don't fall from grace, I say. Be dutiful! Without our belief in God, we're lost sheep. Good things will come to pass..."

"You think that, or is it meant to give mindless, wayward people a certain path?"

"If you don't believe in God, you need to turn around now. I've seen things, felt things, and learned things that tell me of God's plan."

"So have I."

"Like what?"

"We're strolling on two magnificent beasts of burden in an overgrown forest teeming with life and you ask 'like what'?" There are other experiences that tell us of miracles."

"There are special properties and gifts that are uncommonly bestowed by God's messengers," Grayle tested.

"You've had such an experience?"

"Maybe. We'll save that discussion. Let's talk about you."

Cynthia smiled through her swollen eyes that begged for sleep. "I'm tired, Grayle."

"When you get to Grayleton, I'll make sure you're left alone to rest," he assured her.

"You're not exhausted?" Cynthia yawned in the asking.

"I don't require much sleep. Maybe four hours a night, maximum. It's not easy for me to quiet my mind."

"You don't get hungry either?" Cynthia's stomach told a different story. "When you found the camp perimeter and caused such a ruckus, I never made it to dinner. Next thing I know, I take the next horse I see with a saddle and follow you out...without packed food."

Grayle turned to examine Cynthia. She struck him as beautiful upon the muscular mare.

"This is not your horse, Cynthia?" he asked.

"No, I grabbed this one. We change off and on. They're uniform performers and all of them interchangeable with familiar riders. This beautiful mare is Macha; she had the food rations pack removed for the night, as I unfortunately discovered a few hours ago," she explained.

"Whose horse is it?" Grayle asked.

"Caroline rides her the most, I guess." Cynthia thought she detected an altered tone. "Why?"

"It seems strange to change horses. Have you ridden her before?"

"Sure. Caroline, Ildiko and I often rotate. We're encouraged to swap so that the mounts and riders stay focused on field signals and remain flexible. I'm unsure as to the reaction with an unschooled rider but you're welcome to try her. I can assure you she's loyal and unlikely to stomp you into the ground," Cynthia smiled slyly.

"No, thank you," he stroked the neck of his horse. "I'm afraid that we won't be able to change. This one has one master. I like it that way," he said.

"What's her name?

"What difference does it make?" Grayle dismissed further chatter.

* * *

"You all right? We've had intermittent signals. I'm worried," Caroline messaged.

"Fine; no problems," she telepathed back. "We should arrive within a few hours at this pace."

"If we don't hear from you at three-hour intervals, we're sending in troops. Morgan's orders," Caroline emphasized.

Cynthia finished and met the eyes of the man now scrutinizing her.

"You're telepathic in addition to having a personal arm monitor, right? Anything else?"

"Do you know the answer, Grayle? The way I figure it, you don't trust me and want to see what a lie looks like on me."

"I really like that answer," he laughed.

"Which is it?" Cynthia asked.

"I realize that you people probably have amplified body parts, including sight and audio. You can record events and transfer them to and from your brain. You can access stored information connected from your brain to an external source. Correct?"

"Close enough," Cynthia answered. "You seem to know what's going on. You have access to everything?"

"I do. You're welcome to connect at will. Your Confederation friends are confused because so much goes unseen deep within the earth."

Cynthia was startled to discover that they had entered an enclosed city that had been cleverly camouflaged as part of the forest. The paths wrapped around buildings that could only be identified by the rising berms with flawlessly disguised egresses. Images of nature were reflected or projected. The horses meandered through the holograms of a faux environment.

"Did you mask these buildings or was it already here?" she asked.

"Nothing like this was working when I arrived but it was installed. It took me a while to figure the applications. It functions to conceal the location of six or seven buildings that led to the food stores from the upside farms. There are corridors from those buildings into the compound but we've been able to open only a few. I figure it was one of the president's exit routes. It's the place on the berm where I first spotted a security team. That's where I shot them," Grayle pointed to a rolling berm that overlooked a small artificial vegetable garden. "The projected vegetation seasonally changes," Grayle added.

"Any particular reason you felt that the president's men should have been assassinated, Grayle?"

"Lots of particular reasons, as it turns out. At the time, I heard enough from some old guy who knew their reputation for brutality. He tagged them as evil. I finished them off," Grayle stated without remorse.

People emerged from the town to observe the couple ride toward the barns. Just as she imagined in her dreams, Cynthia observed a spontaneous crowd move impatiently upon Grayle. Their eyes assessed Cynthia.

"A woman! Grayle has taken a woman!" cried one old woman. Cheers went up, hands went up, and the horses were forced to a standstill as the crowd closed in.

Grayle silenced the crowd by raising his hand.

"We have a guest. Do not ask questions, do not follow, and do not touch."

He shook his head apologetically toward Cynthia. "I'm sorry. It's the way it works around here."

"Don't apologize. I admit that it's a little black and white but quite clear," she answered, stifling a growing yawn. "I'm going to ask for the nearest shower, and bed, after we stable the horses."

Grayle watched Cynthia water and feed her mount. As she brushed down the horse, cleaned, and carefully hung the halter, blanket and saddle, Grayle quietly analyzed her body. Cynthia felt his scrutiny and tried to ignore it.

"Thanks for waiting," she said simply.

"Are all the Confederation women like you?"

"Absolutely! We're all terribly clever, beautiful, strong, witty, and intelligent. We're interchangeable...like the horses. That's what you're asking?" Cynthia said with a straight face.

"And confident," Grayle added.

"It sounds as if you're looking for good breeding stock again, Grayle."

"Maybe I am," he laughed. "Would you like to contact your friends before I show you to your quarters?" He motioned toward a back way out of the stables. "You'll have to do it now upside unless you've a way to get through that mountain."

"You haven't an underground terminal?" she asked.

"I'm sure there's a way to connect, but I haven't bothered. The ones here work; those underground were fried at the beginning or I can't configure it. The one a few hundred yards from here is operable."

"I'm able to use my personal monitor," Cynthia indicated an invisible tape around her wrist that came to life. "Arrived and safe," she said simply.

"Acknowledged," came the answer. It meant that she was safe but in the company of Grayle, or another principal player. She had no privacy, as of yet, and intentions were undetermined.

"That's it?" Grayle asked.

"That's it. It just transmits and can act as a translator if we prefer not to have an implantation. I can be tracked and monitored for any medical issues via the diagnostic bots. It can contact the nearest med-vac in case of an emergency or it can advise what to do in the interim."

"Can it do the same for me?" Grayle touched the nearly indiscernible band.

"It has to be individually calibrated. There are others that are less sophisticated. This one is our latest product," she said with some pride.

"You're living in a different world," Grayle noted. "I'm connected, too. You should know that there are six Confederation heliports parked in the woods ten miles south of here. You might suggest to your friends that the unmanned machines stay where they are. I won't allow an intrusion of any kind."

"It's about my safety. It's about everyone's safety that might need help from your town. If I check in, there's no problem. If I don't, you have one. Normal stuff," Cynthia blew off Grayle's threatening tone.

"My people have yet to leave your camp," Grayle added.

"We haven't been gone very long. Give it through today. If they haven't moved out, I'll insist upon it. I'm sure it's a minor matter."

* * *

Connor and Attila had arranged the timing as to encourage Anton's departure only after reinforcements were in place. They would follow Anton and his group from a discreet distance.

"Nicholas and Aaron will lead the Circle. I want to remind everyone that Cynthia's message would have been sent privately if there was an opportunity," Attila clarified.

Connor added, "The rest of the Circle should not bother hiding the fact that you're there."

"Problem?" Morgan asked from Raleigh.

"Cynthia sent a warning shot. Nothing dramatic but she's without privacy. Her use of the PM tells me that her telepathic abilities are erratic or she doesn't want to use them with Grayle."

"Isn't Ildiko able to follow her?" Tsin-hang followed up.

"Yes. Ildiko sent us a mental image of Cynthia's surroundings. We're comparing it to our schematics now," Connor confirmed.

"Once underground, all of this changes," Morgan underlined.

* * *

The former main entrance to the American Data Repository yawned wide and revealed its long, steely bars of a mouth that rose as neat cyclical slivers until they disappeared into mountain rock. Cynthia followed Grayle until they met fifteen-foot thick vaulted doors that responded to Grayle's voice, eye scan, and handprint. Cynthia knew about the Repository but her information revealed little about the hidden treasures to which Grayle alluded. As far as public records showed, it was a stronghold for proprietary information considered irreplaceable by the American government.

"What's your interest?" Grayle began as they moved into a lushly furnished lobby. Rather than a military installation, the trappings reflected luxury better suited to an elite resort.

"This looks like an old fashioned five-star hotel," noted Cynthia.

"When I blasted in through the outside tunnels, I came upon this entrance from the back. This part is the most lavish. I figure it's the part of the complex where important meetings were held. I thought it would take a while to figure the bio-metric key, but it proved no problem."

"It's odd to have this kind of embellishment as part of a survival network," Cynthia commented.

"What would you like to see first, Cynthia?" Grayle repeated.

"A shower and a restroom," Cynthia rubbed her eyes with her sleeve. The sound of the entrance lockdown alarmed her.

"For our privacy and safety," Grayle offered reassuringly.

She followed him from one biometrically controlled room to another that served as examination rooms for those who passed from the exterior into the pristine environment. At one room, the contamination scanners lay idle but the room split two ways.

"What's the other door for?" she asked Grayle.

"If a visitor or resident was found clean of radiation or in-fection, this door would open. The other opens into an eight foot by eight foot incinerator," he stated without emotion.

Cynthia noticed her PM was blank. She was aware that she needed to memorize and log the routes that were purposely made confusing.

"What a maze," she remarked.

"Purposely so, I suspect. It's made as a hub and spoke configuration. I live in the hub part with one spoke having private access to the exterior. Everything was based upon functionality. Some of the workers went toward the food pro-cessing plants, others worked in the medical facilities, scien-tists were similarly divided into categories, and the top administrators had access to the outer circle of the presidential hub's headquarters. Neatly done," Grayle explained.

The corridors were massive and the vaults color-coded rather than described. Lights clicked to life in rapid succession hundreds of feet in advance as Grayle moved through the labyrinth. Situated in front of a smaller entrance, a scanner recognized Grayle and asked for the identity of the 'other guest'.

"You'll have to expose your palm here, wait for retina scans, then a skin scrape. From here on out, you can come and go as you please," Grayle instructed.

"Even through that steel-trapped lobby?" Cynthia asked.

"Yes," Grayle confirmed.

"What happens if a person is unregistered or announces an incorrect or uncoordinated biometric?"

"They'll feel a slight pinprick when asked to repeat the hand print," Grayle explained. "They die instantly."

"How do you know?" Cynthia asked.

"Some of these things are trial and error," he replied.

The biometric scanner registered the new resident with a warm, formal welcome: *"Welcome Cynthia."*

She was shown to an elevator but Cynthia had the crematorium and poison pin pricks on her mind. "You first, Grayle," she waited.

Grayle and she entered, followed by a heavy-sounding locking mechanism, then fell quickly to a depth of 300 ft.

"How about the drop?" Grayle laughed.

"My stomach hasn't caught up yet," she grimaced. "This can't be the only way?"

"I used to walk the stairs every day for a few years until figuring out everything. Most of my time was devoted to getting this vast complex in working order," Grayle said with pride.

Cynthia realized that she wanted to cache his retina, voice, and palm print. Her eyes zeroed into his and macroscopically imaged them as he stared back into her eyes, now converted into a camera. He never blinked within the five seconds of the hundred images recorded.

"Well, Cynthia?"

"Oh, sorry. I've been caught staring."

"For a second, I thought you might be flirting with me," Grayle smiled.

Cynthia could only think of one acceptable answer and said, "I have to admit that I've never seen such green eyes." She turned quickly away from Grayle and toward the air locked door that opened into an entry hall.

"What in the world?" Cynthia recognized an exact replica of the White House's West Wing central lobby, drawing from baroque, neoclassical, and Georgian architectural features. She followed Grayle toward a door that did not require security admittance. An Oval Office facsimile had the three large south-facing windows behind the desk intended for an American President, as well as four doors that led into the east door that offered a view upon a simulated Rose Garden. The west door released to a private study adjoined by an intimate dining room. Another door opened into a smaller office meant for a personal assistant.

"An exact replication, except for the scenery that can be seasonally programmed from a wide range of images," Grayle said.

He walked toward the windows that imaged a beautiful summer day, the trees lush with green leaves and cherry blossoms that were meant for spring. Completing the sensation were erratic, light gusts of wind that propelled cherry blossom petals to drift by the simulation window.

"Looks like an interesting combination of seasons," observed Cynthia.

"I can select any number of options for any view and even combine seasons. At night, I can do the same for any configuration of constellations anywhere at any time on the planet. Do you like it?"

"I can imagine being isolated here for years. That's what was expected, right?"

"Try a century. That's what these installations were meant to do," Grayle said. "This is the largest one. There are more throughout the country."

"Are they all connected?" Cynthia pretended minimal interest in this question.

"That's for me to know," Grayle cursorily answered.

Cynthia looked skyward and focused upon the plaster ceiling medallion that once represented the seal of the President of the United States. It was pockmarked with bullet holes, the hidden light bulbs within the cornices made apparent by crumbling plaster.

Grayle followed her gaze. "Someone lost their temper, I'd guess."

Cynthia moved toward the fireplace and sank into one of two antique armchairs. The carpet was muddied and soiled;

the contrasting cross pattern of quarter-sawn oak and walnut floor was scuffed and pitted. The bust of Abraham Lincoln by Augustus Saint Gaudens, and another of Martin Luther King Jr. by Charles Alston, irreverently sat as doorstops that opened into an undetermined narrow hall. Artwork, that had come and gone with sitting presidents, stood stacked alongside the fireplace.

"Someone intended to burn them?" asked Cynthia.

"How should I know? I figure Brown was that one over there," he pointed to an intact portrait of Clifton Brown that hung high next to one of the bookcases.

"Follow me. I'll show you where you can clean up and rest," Grayle invited Cynthia to follow him through the mystery door into a hall. As dimensions alternately narrowed and widened, Cynthia imagined herself in a strange underground wonderland. She was now Alice scurrying to follow the Grayle rabbit through an unpredictable maze of corridors and odd sized rooms.

Once again, a small foyer divided into two doors.

"This is where I live most of the time. The other rooms were meant for the president's family. You'll find what you need there. Everything is in working order." He handed her a one-inch paper-thin metallic square.

"If you need anything, this will activate a call box in your room and I can hear it, too. It will stick to anything."

"I'm not going to be monitored, Grayle. Not happening," she scowled.

"That's the point of the square. When you want something that you can't find or operate, just ask. That's all. It's not meant to monitor or track you," he said simply.

Cynthia's neural amp indicated a psychophysiological stress response in Grayle's voice.

"You're untruthful," she accused.

"I'm unsure. I think there's probably monitoring of some sort, but I've never investigated it. I'm not lying. I just can't access it," he said with narrowed eyes. "You're relying upon voice stress analysis tech that relies upon a translator. LVA and VSA are based upon different frequency ranges, a variance of five in the Hz range. You can't reconcile accuracy with pitch and tone components... especially when I'm in my present emotional state."

"Present emotional state?" Cynthia asked.

"You're interesting, beautiful and clever. Of course my emotional state will be affected," Grayle said, allowing his eyes to roam over her.

He turned and moved toward the foyer that separated their quarters and stopped at its exit.

"I'm trying to be as cordial as possible. I mean to show you what goes on here. When you want to leave, leave. In the meantime, you can call when you want to do something, eat something, look around."

Cynthia was satisfied that he had accepted her first solid boundary.

Her quarters were spotless. Walking about the suite of rooms, she opened emptied drawers. She knew they once held personal belongings of the wife and daughters of Clifton Brown.

A lone hair clip remained behind in a bath recess. As soon as she touched the tortoiseshell piece, Cynthia wept. With the hair clip in one hand, Cynthia curled up on one of two beds and fell into a deep sleep.

Ildiko remotely searched the Grayleton premises and discovered an entrance to the underground bunkers. Her mind floated and searched for more than an hour following paths rather than moving through barriers. She intended to map and graphically extract a diagram as she searched for Cynthia.

I'm just going to concentrate on locating Grayle, she thought. Her mind positioned promptly in the Presidential quarters above Grayle's reclining image. He stared from his bed at the ceiling, deep in thought. Ildiko harbored the impulse to quiet herself, feeling as if he might be able to sense her presence.

Grayle's breathing was unnaturally even, his breath almost imperceptible. Music and a heavenly projection filled the room that centered upon the thirteenth zodiac sign of Ophiuchus, the 'Serpent-bearer', omitted from the Zodiac system designed by Babylonian astrologers. Ildiko watched as the stars connected to form Serpentarius, a man handling a serpent, his body dividing the enormous snake into two parts, giving way to Aesculapius's medical staff that symbolized the practice of medicine. Ildiko examined the gleaming stars that combined as a representation of Asclepius. The goddess Athena, the fable went, gave two vials of blood from the Gorgon Medusa to the son of Apollo and Cornonis. Blood from the right side of Medusa's body could restore life while the side on the left was poisonous. All of this information was gleaned and interpreted in Ildiko's mind, fast exploring the sensory-rich territory. "Why would Serpentarius be of interest?" Ildiko wondered as Franz Liszt's Liebestraum swelled in the darkened room.

Grayle's thumb pressed the button centered in a small square metal plate on his side table. A holographic image of a sleeping Cynthia replaced the constellation above him. He slid his arms under his head and examined his guest in the adjoining suite asleep. Cynthia's snoring made him chuckle.

Ildiko's heart raced at the voyeurism that compelled her to flee the scene. She contacted Sonny first. "We have to get Cynthia out of there; Grayle is a creep."

"Creepy?" Sonny repeated. "How?"

"That's my sense of it. I didn't have an easy time tracking Cynthia. I couldn't sense her presence at all. It was Grayle I finally discovered resting in his room. He was watching Cynthia sleep from his room."

Nicholas wasted no time. He notified Anton that he and his friends were free to return to Grayleton. Within the hour, they had amicably agreed and gathered their belongings.

Within twenty minutes of Ildiko's warnings, the Circle prepared their mounts with the intention to imperceptibly shadow Anton and company. An audio protuberance masked their presence with environmental sounds indigenous to the areas they would cover. Laser sweepers smoothed indentations left in the ground. Smells that lingered from the humans and horses were obliterated with neutralization chemicals. Other than telepathic communication, no signals were used. Airborne drones remained at the camp for the time being.

"They can't pick up our trace. Just keep to the plan," instructed Aaron. The horses seemed to sense the covert activity and were careful to maintain a low impact, uniform pace.

Confederation scouts found themselves waiting for an uncomfortable amount of time while Anton and company lingered at the same lazy water stream visited earlier by Grayle and Cynthia. Aaron and Sonny worried that they might decide to make camp. In the interest of getting them to move forward, Sonny telegraphed a chant. By changing the electromagnetic field, Sonny changed the rate at which time was perceived. Adding a very low, erratic frequency would cause additional unease. A wide spectrum of minor complaints tore through the group.

"Let's get out of here," challenged one young man angrily.

"It's time to get home," yelled another.

Anton grew agitated but not at the prospect of remaining at the water's side. "Shut up and make some food for me," he demanded of a woman, who failed to respond. Struck by intense hunger pangs, Anton began to rummage through knapsacks.

Anton ate what little he could steal and then focused on the dissenting man, the unresponsive woman, and then addressed the Grayleton soldiers.

"We'll leave when I say to leave!" he shouted to his restless followers. "One more word, and you'll wear this knife!" Anton warned as he waved the blade in the air.

The woman directed to prepare food was once more directed to obey and, once again, she remained fixed.

"Come here," Anton demanded.

"I don't like it here," she defied and hurried to the side of the first of Anton's challengers. Having made a pact with a new defender, Anton had no choice in the matter but to take the couple to task. But an impromptu decision of the entire group to migrate from the water's edge put an end to Anton's options. Those that began to saunter away were no longer fearful of Grayle's special deputy.

"You'll be thrown out of Grayleton!" he warned at the top of his voice. But Anton's outbursts meant fear and fear translated as weakness.

If there was any hesitation to rebuke Anton, it disappeared with the sudden illusionary urge to flee impending flames. Sonny's telepathic chants threatened to burn them alive; the impulse to escape unseen danger outweighed future consequences as they imagined heat and smoke licking its way to the water's edge. Panic signaled throughout when the first terrified man bolted uphill.

Anton moved to punish the renegade from behind. Of one thought, the Grayleton scouting expedition came to an unspoken consensus; thay sent a flurry of arrows, head to toe, through Anton's faltering body. Without a murmur, they stepped over and around Anton. Without each other, they would never have the navigational ability to return home.

The effects of his chants alarmed Sonny.

"An overreaction as I've never seen," he worried. "I had no idea."

Caroline telepathed him, "They're weak-minded, damaged. There's no compensating frequency to balance raw impulses. You meant to suggest an urge. It went beyond. No fault of yours, Sonny."

"I disagree. It was my fault for not being able to normalize the intensity."

"We can't calibrate the blue light either," reassured Caroline.

The Grayleton group began to make their way home. Some no longer cared about, or recalled, their intended destination. No one missed those who mindlessly moved a different direction.

"Aimless animals," Caroline observed.

The Confederation's special force moved quietly behind those that made their way homeward.

* * *

Cynthia awoke disoriented. Without her PM, the bunkers promised a circadian rhythm disorder with prolonged usage. As it was, she guesstimated as to the hours that must have passed by measure of thirst. "6:00 p.m.," she gauged. "First a shower," she yawned.

Normally, her clothes automatically eliminated bacteria. Current conditions meant the lack of solar power that prevented uncharged nanobots from doing their maintenance jobs.

Uniforms, that hung neatly within a closet, appeared to be for her use. Cynthia selected one of many blue and white shirts and drawstring pants after a shower.

"I look more like a patient than a soldier right about now," she sighed at the image.

Her hair had become a sleek wet blanket dripping onto the dry clothes when there was a door knock.

"I thought I was supposed to contact you when I was ready?" she called.

"I'm letting you know that I'm going to dinner and wondered if you might want to join me? I could also bring something down to you? You must be hungry."

"Five minutes, please," Cynthia responded. She squeezed excess moisture from her hair and pulled it tight into a chignon. In her backpack, she fumbled through the medical kit.

"Coming," she called reassuringly against Grayle's impatience. The pills, she knew, would ensure that her immune system could recognize and fight viruses, poisons or bacterial infections that the nanobots within her bloodstream might miss.

Grayle was pleased when she opened the door.

"You look nice in that," he complimented.

"I'm wearing a drawstring bag," she countered.

"Maybe it's the clothes. I like the thought of you here, even if it's for a short visit, wearing an oversized Grayleton uniform," he said kindly.

"It reads USA on it, Grayle."

"It belongs here. I like the combination."

"I'm here to earn trust, exchange ideas, see what's happening in this rabbit hole. I'm not sure where that comment fits," Cynthia answered.

"You're a hard person to get to know," Grayle said.

"In what way?"

"Your default is a Confederation minion," Grayle said smugly. "Maybe I'm just interested in getting to know you?"

"I'm here to help in any way possible," Cynthia said in a more conciliatory tone. "We should work together, open channels, so there's no misunderstanding, Grayle."

"You and your friends must know I'll never allow Confederation forces to enter Grayleton and tell us what to do," he emphasized the mutually considered diplomatic boundaries yet to be satisfied.

"I'm here to offset suspicions. We're curious about Grayleton and you must be curious about the Confederation," Cynthia simplified.

"You mean to confuse me with words rather than actions. I'm not that guy," Grayle frowned.

Cynthia diverted from an uncomfortable topic, wishing to avoid another misunderstanding.

"How do you spend time down here without experiencing circadian rhythm disorder? You've had no illness or psychological issues?"

"You're suddenly interested in my sleep habits?"

"I'm just wondering how you maintain your equilibrium. I couldn't access sunlight so just for a moment I felt upended, you know?"

"No," he answered. "I've never had a problem with my biological clock. I've never had a problem with my navigational sense either, but once or twice, in my life. The first was trying to move toward the Confederation borders when I left my home. I just couldn't get my bearings, walked in and out of circles. We do have to rotate those who spend too much time down here. Sleep deprivation can make them irritable, sometimes ill. Workers spend no more than a month at a time here."

"You mention a sense of direction. You're aware that there's a problem with the earth's magnetic fields? Do you know that this has caused problems with animal migrations and our inner compass on a biological level?"

"I've plotted routes for many hundreds of miles of our perimeter for our people that hunted. Why do you mention this?"

"We're here to investigate how the damage to the earth's magnetic field has provoked the earth's natural states. We're primarily on a scientific mission, not a political one," Cynthia stressed.

"It's funny that science and religion always begin with the best intentions," Grayle remarked. "You're investigating on behalf of science? It's only a matter of time until the beauty of pure inquiry and intentions stops. Good answers aren't forthcoming if the truth is obfuscated in the first place. Seems to me that the Confederation is long on questions and short on answers. The Confederation's mission is about control, like every other organization since the beginning of time. They'll want something more."

Grayle turned his back and led Cynthia from the entry. They migrated upward toward the community center using the winding steel mesh stairs rather than the private lift. She imaged and cached the route.

A large steel door released as Grayle waved his hand across a black strip. It opened to the remaining rays of daylight that poured through one side of an enormous glass dome. From the opposite side of the transparent roof, a rising moon ushered in the evening wearing a shroud of orange and red. It was, thought Cynthia, a remarkable structural triumph. Given the dome's translucence, she was unclear as to its masking devices.

"It works on the same principle as your suits," Grayle explained knowingly.

"Impressive work. What a great achievement for our former government," Cynthia remarked to steal Grayle's thunder.

"Noted," he said, "but the last government is gone, along with that country that experimented with democracy. That doesn't sound very notable."

Most of the townspeople had already completed their third meal of the day in shifts. There were enhanced options for productive workers whose projects received special attention. Those now present took a meal in the Community Hall as such an incentive. For others, food was prepared and eaten in the town's communal shelters. All was orchestrated and incentivized. Cynthia looked upon the activities and found Grayle's administrative abilities undeniable.

With her arrival, the bustling Hall was made suddenly quiet.

"Awkward," Cynthia cringed at the collective scrutiny.

Grayle and Cynthia took seats at a small table close to the kitchen. Food was served on elegant porcelain that featured the hand-painted Presidential seal. Linen napkins and crystal had been carefully laid. Silver candlesticks held long white candles ceremoniously lit by Grayle.

The leader stood and asked for those in the hall to hold hands and 'bow heads in prayer.' He took Cynthia's hand in his as she remained seated.

"Lord, thank you for the earth's bounty that we are about to share. We thank you for giving us the patience, knowledge, and health to cultivate Mother Earth with care. We thank you for making the connection with civilized men and women who have arrived from the South to join with brethren. We welcome their emissary and pray for a successful undertaking between us. In your messenger's name, Amen."

"Messenger's name?" Cynthia asked.

"Problem?" Grayle puzzled.

"Son's name, you meant to say?" she tried.

"There have been many messengers of God. Who am I to say otherwise?" he corrected in a way that ended the possibility of further discussion.

Even as he regained his seat, Grayle held Cynthia's hand. He folded his other hand upon hers and looked into her eyes. "I'm glad you've joined us tonight," he smiled.

Cynthia released her hand to place a napkin on her lap.

"What if I had declined and elected to take my meal in my room?" she asked.

"That would have been completely against your nature," Grayle said and lifted her resting hand from her lap into his. "No need to be so anxious, Cynthia," he whispered. Then he drew her hand to his lips. The light formality was executed so naturally that Cynthia imagined Grayle from another era.

"Let's see what we have, shall we?" Grayle returned to the matter at hand to sample a recipe he had submitted to the kitchen staff with exacting instructions.

Cynthia tasted the mango, lightly fried breaded goat cheese, and walnut green salad with vinaigrette dressing. She unconsciously hummed approval. Her taste buds danced excitedly.

"Are you aware that you moaned?" Grayle asked, watching her intently.

"Uh, no." Cynthia's embarrassment showed. "I'm surprised at the exotic ingredients."

Grayle took pleasure in his guest's enthusiasm. "I'll show you around the greenhouses and seed vaults, farms, and storehouses. We've mangoes, walnuts, and a century of provisions of more unusual foods. Evidently, those that were meant to live here intended to eat well," Grayle said.

"You eat like this every day?"

"Hardly. This is a special day meant to impress a special woman." Grayle offered Cynthia freshly baked bread and butter.

The community tables were not elaborately spread nor with the wide variety of dishes that was available at Grayle's, but the meals had been well prepared, nourishing, and plentiful. Forty-five minutes had passed when those present collectively moved from their tables. Grayle ignored everyone until the doors to the Hall were finally closed.

"Impressed?" he asked.

"Of course!" Cynthia laughed.

"Anything missing?" he asked eagerly.

"They skimped on the wine, I'd guess."

"Ahh. Come with me, please," he said as he grabbed her hand and led her through the kitchen, past the startled staff and into a utility lift at the end of the room. The elevator was equipped with shelves and containers. Like an excited boy, Grayle began to trot from the separated doors with Cynthia's hand in his. They made their way down a long, cold corridor until Grayle's voice signaled their arrival into an immeasurable wine cellar. "Open!" he called.

Seven vault doors opened simultaneously from the hall. Lights illuminated the Alaskan Cedar floors and racks that hosted over a million bottles of the world's greatest vino.

"Oh, my God," she exclaimed as neatly stacked conveyor belts hummed to life. Floor to ceiling, wines of all descriptions delicately reclined in multi-zone, refrigerators temperature-controlled glass. Marble topped tables and chairs were spaced throughout the storage areas for reds, whites, and Madeiras that were meant for tasting. Grayle selected one 1839 Madeira and offered it to Cynthia as a sampling. "Would you like to carry a glass with you? It's cold and it's an enormous collection," he pointed to what seemed to be an endlessly numbered cellar meticulously catalogued by hard copy text and kiosks made available at the end of each row.

"It's set up like an old fashioned library," Cynthia exclaimed. She eyed a section labeled as the "The Last Bottles on Earth."

"The last wines on earth?" she echoed.

"By nation, year, producer...the very last samples in existence," Grayle substantiated. "Last week I pulled an 1815 Port, a 2007 magnum of Romanee Conti, and a 1947 magnum of Chateau Latour to take upstairs. The Champagne shelves are kept a few degrees cooler than the rest of the cellars. They are nothing compared to the last vault," Grayle pulled Cynthia back into the hall toward the referenced vault.

"It's like a magnificent jewel box!" Cynthia gasped as the lights flickered on chandeliers, revealing a treasure trove of decadent delights.

"Look," Grayle pointed toward the Cognacs crafted in honor of royalty and heads of state. "These have more to do with packaging rather than taste," he noted.

Cynthia examined diamond-encrusted platinum bottles and lighted upon a 1957 Bowmore aged for 43 years in a sherry cask. A hundred-year-old Scotch whiskey, the oldest Islay malt, was housed in a crystal and platinum bottle with designs of sea waves.

Grayle caught Cynthia's eye that focused upon the text that described the contents of a six-liter decanter of the Macallan Whiskey named Constantine within a Lalique-designed decanter.

"Like it?" Grayle urged.

"I'm thinking of someone who might love this whiskey," she laughed.

Grayle left and returned with a 24 carat gold and sterling platinum bottle embedded with 6,500 diamonds fashioned by a famous jeweler named to honor King Henri IV, and aged in barrels for more than a century. "Only 100cl was decanted into this bottle," explained Grayle. "Here, take this one to your friend."

Cynthia took the bottle and examined its opulence. "Henry IV Dudognon Heritage Cognac Grande Champagne...very impressive," she sighed.

"We could spend years down here and not get through a million bottles or more," Grayle said.

Cynthia handed the bottle back to Grayle. The idea of the stash of rare luxury items disgusted and delighted Cynthia at once. That there was a priority upon comfort for so few at the expense of so many was heart-wrenching. Unfortunately, she couldn't deny her delight at the array of rare wines but she refused to take even one sample.

"You must have a man in your life?" Grayle asked with concern. "I'm sure he would be delighted to share this with you."

"Yes, I've someone in mind. He's pushing a century and has been very good to me. He has a weakness for good drink but I'm sure he wouldn't care for the circumstances. I'm here to visit...not loot."

Grayle ignored the insult. Leaving the bottles on a nearby table, he exited into the main corridor. "Let's finish our meal," he invited. The doors closed on Grayle's command.

Cynthia found herself growing comfortable. Grayle had taken risks, lifted himself, was self-taught, and operated autonomously to build a large working community within a short period of time. It was unfair to speculate that he intended to unreasonably withhold information and equipment at his disposal. It required an exceptional intellect and motivation to lead wayward survivors into a productive unit. She considered the mission to square so many factors and developed a new-found respect for her host. A lifetime of genetic research and a chance frequency change in the environment had instantaneously transformed man's molecular and neurological structure. The best the Confederation scientists could do was to analyze the phenomenon and identify anomalies. The best that the Circle could do was charge and heal the magnetic field and assist people, painfully slowly, bit by bit. Even so, on the other side of this healing proposition was an equal and opposite reaction. Rather than a solution, the Confederation efforts seemed to polarize the populace into radical ends of the spiritual, physical and mental spectrum. One side became less healthy and more insular; the positive side found themselves more zealous and productive. Somehow, Cynthia reflected, Grayle had managed to effectively lead disturbed survivors with an ability to craft a civilized oasis. The man had achieved this without any research or assistance. It was, she thought, truly extraordinary.

Cynthia felt his energy. Her hand was an easy fit in his when he took the liberty. She felt protected and warm in the cold corridor as they made their way back upstairs. There was no denying that the handsome, charismatic, wildly gifted Grayle was used to getting his way. She discovered his enthusiasm increasingly hard to resist.

"It's what makes him dangerous," Cynthia suddenly concluded and she drew her hand from his.

They re-entered the kitchen's rear entrance and made their way through frantic assistants that misunderstood the nature of the hasty exit.

"It's fine. We were just looking for wine," Grayle explained to the nervous chefs.

It was clear that the meal had been carefully planned and prepared with the best Grayleton had to offer; Cynthia found herself captivated by the attentive man who now stared expectantly across the table, leaning eagerly forward to gauge responses to his efforts – one by one.

"Did you like the pork loin?"

"Yes, marvelous."

"The dessert?"

"The coconut was a great touch."

"Would you like tea or coffee? We have every kind you can imagine," he boasted.

"No thank you, Grayle. I'm satisfied."

"Just satisfied?" The word confused him.

"A polite word explaining the state of my present condition. I couldn't eat another bite because I'll explode," she explained.

"Explode?"

"From eating too much," she laughed. "A joke."

"Shall we leave now?" he asked, examining her empty plate.

"You haven't finished. In fact, you've barely touched the meal," Cynthia observed his own.

"I don't eat much. Ready to go or not?"

"Yes, please."

The waiters entered to clear their table. Cynthia turned to lightly applaud their efforts.

Grayle's eyes flashed angrily and he ordered the staff, "Just leave."

The kitchen help scurried away. Grayle's annoyance stood firm.

"What's the problem?" Cynthia tested carefully.

Grayle turned his attention to Cynthia with measured tones of indignation.

"Those people you so nicely thanked have no idea about your gesture of approval. They've no idea about anything. They just do as I say, as I teach. They couldn't think of a novel idea, create a meal like that, without long instruction and my direct oversight. While you slept, I made sure that everything was selected and prepared to perfection. Even the people allowed to eat with us were personally chosen. Most of my time during community meals is spent reminding them not to spit on the floor or grab food from one another's plate."

"I've neglected to properly express my gratitude," Cynthia clarified. "That was something rudely overlooked. Please accept my apologies and my sincere appreciation for a marvelous,and most exceptional, dinner. I thought you were aware of my pleasure as evidenced by a sparkling clean plate," she smiled. "I truly enjoyed my dinner partner and the marvelous tour."

"Oh," Grayle replied simply. His mood altered and he beamed broadly with a new idea.

"This is a good time for you to contact friends or family. The exterior feed is just over there," he pointed through the glass windows toward one of the berms. It required Cynthia to zoom in to discern its camouflaged entry, obscured by holographic images.

"I'd like that," she said agreeably. The images were quickly cached and messaged to the Circle. She waited for a telepathic response once outside the subterranean compound. Sonny promptly replied.

"We're behind the Grayleton scouts and we're guessing that we'll be on site within hours. We're receiving the images of the city that you've sent. Most definitely, we cannot connect with you by any technological means while underground," Sonny explained.

Nicholas spoke to her about being timely about contact or they'd have to assume that she was unable to move freely.

"We'll assume that you'll return shortly to sleep underground?"

"Yes," she acknowledged.

"Contact us each time you're upside," Caroline added. "Ildiko was able to remote underground but can't find your location. Where are you exactly?"

"My room is next to Grayle's. A foyer separates us. It's in a complex that is dead center of the compound," Cynthia described. "I've sent you one access but he's mentioned an alternate entry via the Presidential quarters. I'm going to an outbuilding now. Grayle says it's the only live feed. I'll contact the Research Triangle."

"It's evening, Cynthia. Unlikely anyone will be there," Caroline advised.

"Exactly. He's always with me," she explained. "If I don't take advantage of the offer he'll suspect I'm up to something. He's clearly nervous about the Confederation having designs upon Grayleton. Don't force anything."

Grayle examined Cynthia's expression and interrupted her thoughts. "You're doing it again. You're staring and quiet. Transmitting thoughts?" he surmised.

"No," she evaded. "I'm trying to figure things. I guess I don't have the mental bandwidth to take everything in at once," she shrugged.

Grayle stared into her eyes. "I'll know the Confederation's intentions when they arrive," he stated simply.

Cynthia's heart skipped a beat. "Meaning what?"

"They're on their way. Following my scouts into our city. If they try to enter covertly, I'll not allow it. If they announce their arrival and intentions, I'll consider otherwise," he analyzed.

"What makes you think they're arriving here?"

"Probability says that they'll disguise their presence in the interest of your safety," he said, looking away and turning toward the berm building. "They'll follow my group hoping they won't be noticed until well situated in, or just outside, the compound."

He pointed to one of the first green embankments amongst others. "Here we are. The monitor readies upon entry. You're already configured for access everywhere. I'll leave you to contact whomever you wish," he moved toward the door that whirred and clicked open. "I'll wait outside."

Cynthia moved inside, her heart pounding as she telepathed Caroline.

"He's figured our moves...all of them. He probably figured how to direct us here from the start of our mission," she thought. "Attila is right. He knows our plans. I'm figuring this genius has been altered, too. Just not in a way we've experienced." She urgently added, "What do I do?"

There was no answer. It was clear that the outbuilding was also hardened.

The monitor glared in the dark and Cynthia directed a connection to North Carolina's Research Triangle. She announced the one address that came quickly to mind. Expecting no answer, Cynthia was shocked to come face-to-face with Esther staring expectantly back at her.

"Cynthia! I had no idea. You're supposed to be out in the boonies in Pennsylvania. What are you doing?" Esther exclaimed happily. "I'm so glad you've called."

"I'm still in the field. How are you doing, sis?" Cynthia smiled.

"I'm great. Did you hear that I'm engaged? He's arriving in August to meet the Pendergrass clan and all of y'all. I know you'll approve," she giggled long and unnaturally. Cynthia sensed that her sister, for all her present cheerfulness, remained tentatively balanced. Cynthia carefully felt her way through a conversation. A wrong expression or word was able to trigger her sister's displeasure.

"I did hear the good news. Congratulations! I'm looking forward to meeting him. Stan, right? I'm happy for you. And what about work? How do you like it?"

"Hate it. Just plain data ditch digging. I met Stan through research; we crossed paths pulling up obscure useless records. How's it going on your save the world mission?"

"Some things were totally expected. Many things were a surprise. We've confirmed the biological contrasts we expected and we're doing our best to patch irregularities in the magnetic field. Sonny and Aditiya have been a great help by identifying low-level frequencies. We've grown in strength with this effort...." Cynthia stopped abruptly.

"What's wrong?" Esther asked.

"I've always been insensitive about this relationship with special abilities from which you've felt excluded. I'm sorry."

"No, no. I'm so over that. I mean, in the end, I've met the man of my dreams. I get it. Not all of us will transform in the same way, at the same pace. Future generations will likely be more enhanced and all," Esther spoke evenly. "Some of us will never be able to have your sort of skills but it's up to us to pull up our end by maintaining our best. I used to be a low frequency jerk. That's not who I am now. Forgive me for being such a jealous ass," pleaded Esther. "Love is magic. I'm filled with its promise," she added giddily.

"I'm going to end this transmission. I'm worried about transmitting information without my PM," Cynthia said abruptly.

"Why aren't you using your PM?" Esther asked.

"I'm in a place that won't allow for that kind of connection. Long story. We'll catch up," Cynthia promised.

"You want me to contact you?" Esther asked. "Holoport?"

"No. I'll contact you," Cynthia answered. "I have to be careful..."

"I use my office monitor for personal conversations all the time. Our computers are under AI that updates and encrypts to hell and back... so it's fine. As long as I access after-hours...."

"Sis? That's not true," Cynthia interposed. "Anyone can access your history, your conversations, and your holoports. You know that. If you're not supposed to use that monitor privately, let Dr. Green know immediately. She'll understand and they'll clean your tracks," clarified Cynthia.

"You act like I'm an idiot. I've got this covered. They gave me the PM. It's the PM that's monitored, sis," argued Esther.

"It's all interconnected and tracked for security reasons," urged Cynthia. "Just do yourself a favor and explain your ignorance of research protocols to Green in the morning. She'll simply sweep your work for good measure."

"Aren't you the smart one? You've been a great help to your underdeveloped sister. Have a great night. Looking forward to your next call and more corrections...."

The contact was quickly severed.

Cynthia sunk deflated into the chair. *Ugh,* was her singular thought. She imaged the room's terminal monitors that were idle, save the one she used. The room went pitch black as she touched the exit door.

She spotted Grayle lying against a large oak tree surveying the artificial lights that revealed a city not yet at rest. A long, thin red bird dog lay beside him; Grayle occasionally touched its head. The dog inched closer and rubbed its crown on Grayle's lap for more attention.

Cynthia walked through the tall grass and sat nearby.

"Problems?" he asked without looking up from the adoring dog.

"Yes," she sighed heavily. Cynthia considered her sister's manic stages.

"Bad news?" Grayle asked.

"I've managed to upset a family member," she explained with unusual frankness. "My sister isn't mentally stable. Her feelings are tender to the touch. I try to communicate simply and then I slip into a correction of some sort. It always turns out to be the wrong tack."

"I've a taste of that problem," Grayle said. "I use the same thirty words in a hundred different ways. People still don't understand... still they're confused. Some of them slink away as if I've insulted them when all I've done is correct something."

Cynthia was not sympathetic.

"I have to be careful about your reactions, too," she snapped angrily.

"I see."

"I'm just saying that having to monitor oneself all the time on the basis of someone's perception or self-projection is exhausting. I can see the reason you might be lonely and a bit strained from the effort," Cynthia commiserated. "But you can overreact, too."

"Maybe I've some ego issues," Grayle acknowledged knowingly. "I pray on that count."

"Most of us have a tough time taking criticism because we're so damned self-critical to begin with," Cynthia settled the topic.

Cynthia sat on the ground and Grayle continued to stroke a grateful dog. She wrapped her arms around her legs and leveraged them to lean backwards.

"It's funny how some people seem immune to insults – just brush it off, water off a duck's back..." Cynthia commented thoughtfully as she rocked.

"Who?" Grayle asked.

"I've got a friend like that. As long as I've known her, she's been even-tempered, fair, and compassionate," Cynthia relayed happily. "She's my role model."

"Name?"

"Caroline. She makes up for the crazy sister. You briefly met her when you surprised us in camp. What about you? Any siblings?" Cynthia asked.

"None. But I've got a city full of irrational types. They're my responsibility. Imagine my position, where there is little normalcy and no one, but yours truly, to act as a role model?"

Cynthia considered Grayle's predicament and understood for the first time what it meant to be the heart, mind, and soul upon which thousands of aimless, damaged survivors calibrated their equilibrium. He had indicated his loneliness but she had ignored its impact until her conversation with the longsuffering Esther. "How was it that this man could sustain so many years of emotional and mental isolation?" Cynthia wondered. "What was his power over these renegades? How did he keep himself in check?"

"Mind showing me around?" Cynthia directed sweetly.

"What's your interest? I know mine but you might be bored," Grayle stood from the ground, walked closer, and extended his hand to give Cynthia a lift.

"I've got this, I think," she said, ignoring an outreached hand, to stand and brush off the dust. "I guess I'd like to see the kinds of things that are of scientific interest. Perhaps you'd take time to show me the technology and research that has been, for whatever reason, under wraps. I'm also interested in hearing your ideas of cooperation with the Confederation as a lone governing body with limited options for growth. Third, a little more about your strong spiritual awakening that you've managed to inculcate to thousands so successfully."

Grayle stood before and examined Cynthia. She appeared thin and frail encased in the standardized wardrobe meant for the bunker occupants. The cotton fatigues fell generically into the small, medium and large categories. The smallest size swallowed her petite frame and billowed with captured air as she moved, a vulnerable outline of her strong, compact body imprisoned by clinging material against oncoming wind. Grayle considered the way in which his guest could transform ill-fitted pieces of cloth into beautiful designs. He also measured her presence as a Confederation soldier.

"You're here to pick my brains, my holdings and see how you might leverage information to quickly repair and rebuild the world?" he began. Cynthia ignored the rhetorical question and Grayle continued.

"You're here to ingratiate yourself on behalf of the Confederation. No matter how much I like you, it's for me to decide with whom I should share information. I've no hard evidence that your newfound political body is on track. They'll examine what can be used. A few toys later and your Confederation will be unable to resist being king of the mountain. I'm not in the toy business.

"What I want to know is what you know about a blue light that has been appearing over the horizon," he stated with interest.

"No information about blue lights can be found down in the hole? Everyone knows about it," Cynthia stated in a way that countered his idea of great proprietary information.

"I've got my ideas about the blue energy but it's not in the records, if that's your meaning," Grayle continued. He observed Cynthia with renewed interest.

Cynthia knew Grayle had witnessed the so-called 'blue light' phenomena. *Now is not the time to sidestep,* she decided.

"As far as I can tell, the blue light is the cumulative effect we discovered that emanates naturally from a genetically transformed group of people operating at a higher frequency. They live together in the Confederation state of North Carolina," Cynthia explained in one disinterested breath.

"We realize that this energy has a growing and positive effect on those who've been exposed; it's manifested as a blue light that attaches to the damaged magnetic field meant to protect the earth's atmosphere," Cynthia stopped for Grayle's reaction.

"I'm able to pet this dog and listen to what you have to say at the same time," he encouraged.

"On the other hand, there's a negative effect on those who are irreparably neurologically damaged. Sometimes those whom we believe are normal have turned otherwise. Operating marginally, these fence-sitting survivors are negatively aggravated by further exposure to the blue lights.

"Over time, the very cellular structure of those surviving the EMP and those that have been born since that time has been altered. It's partially chemical as well as electromagnetic," Cynthia summarized.

"How do you define a negative reaction?" Grayle asked.

"Look for the gnashing teeth and a knife coming at you," she said sarcastically. "Surely you know the types?"

"Are you supposed to tell me all that?" Grayle questioned her frankness.

"Does it make a difference? Either you believe it or not."

"There's been absolutely no effect in Grayleton. None. I'd say that's strange, wouldn't you?"

"We've yet to focus here on the other side of the Appalachian Mountains, although we know the effects have been noted worldwide. We've no way to know which portals are more difficult to close, which portals re-open old lesions.

"In Philadelphia, for example, the city operated with highly functional interlocking communities but the people lived in fear. Nomadic tribes have existed between their location and the Southern territories for decades. It could be that your city sits under a part of the grid that's not as erratic. There are still magnetic pulse irregularities we haven't been able to gauge. We should bring our group here on site to test…"

"Blah, blah, blah," Grayle interrupted. "You're just chattering, trying to figure a way to walk into my home, do as you see fit, without my resistance. You're wondering the reason the energy or frequency you've manufactured has no effect. You must be curious as to how you missed a city this size in a dying country on a dying planet? I hear the frequencies sent our way, note the drones and satellites that pass regularly overhead, yet we were invisible. You suspect some kind of power here…and advanced technology that surpasses your own?"

"That, too…"

"Grayleton is protected by God. Simple. He meant to get your attention and draw you here," Grayle stated, very much annoyed. "Why not go to that idea first? What did God intend? I know of the churches, the synagogues, the mosques, the temples, the private ways and the public ones. Yet, somehow – deep inside – it's always got to be something besides God." Grayle's pulse raced.

Cynthia objected, "I'll say straight out that those that make the backbone of the Confederation are those that truly believe in God's laws; we practice honor and trust and are dedicated to protecting individual rights and freedom. Our teams are some of the most honest scientific risk takers imaginable. You must know that. We also enable our God-given gift of inquiry…"

"Grayleton is the new Eden," he waved away the speech as so much drivel. "Grayleton is even and focused. Yours is an arrogant approach." Grayle stretched his limbs and sighed. "Your leader moves recklessly, too sure that he knows what's right for the world. Grayleton will soon be humanity's epicenter. Answers have been hidden here until the right person could grasp the entirety of the project. I'm that person, Cynthia. What the world searches for is right here, right now," Grayle stood and stomped a foot on the ground, the heavy booted imprint indicating ground zero.

"And you are?" Cynthia asked as she recorded their conversation and transmitted it to the Circle.

"You can't possibly believe that your group is so special, Cynthia. I'm here to point out to you and your Confederation – and the rest of the world for that matter – that your kind has precedent. All failures. All believed themselves special and failed to bring their great gifts forward.

"Throughout the ages, miracles of the kind your group exhibit have been disavowed as fables because those so gifted lacked infinite understanding. There was no capable shepherd for those gifts.

"Something new has suddenly appeared that will help ensure mankind's organic survival and spiritual transformation," Grayle announced. "I don't wonder the reason that Grayleton cannot be penetrated by this light flying overhead. We don't need it. You were meant to investigate the only place immune to its effect."

"Gifts? Our group has special gifts? Fables? What are you saying?" Cynthia was frightened by the notion that Grayle was aware of the Circle's special skill sets.

"Technology. Your kind always thinks that everyone can be subdued by technological acumen that has yet to be realized by others. It's a fail. Of course, I'm right," he laughed good-naturedly.

"We aren't trying to impress anyone, Grayle. I'm speaking for the Confederation and operating now...here...in the present. I offer no philosophical historical perspective," Cynthia said.

Grayle began to pace, trying to offset a mounting excitement. He had no concern for Cynthia's input. He had something to say and he meant to say it.

"I cannot speak for God, but I have faith that I'm going to be one of His most valuable messengers. When you've seen what I've seen, read and touched what I've touched, you'll understand mine are not grandiose statements. I suppose people like you need proof of an absolute God. I've always worked on faith but the proof is irrefutable," Grayle emphasized. "I've listened and obeyed. I was told to come here to this place, and to lead multitudes into a new age, once and for all."

Grayle calmed and smiled uncomfortably toward his guest. "I just want to share this gift with you first. You'll understand tomorrow when I reveal God's truth."

"Uh, I'm not sure I'm ready for all that. I'm just passing through, Grayle. By the way, you're saying that you've heard from God directly? That's what you said, right?" Cynthia suggested cynically. "I recall similar historical references to demagogues and fanatics that believed themselves the world's deliverers. See any burning bushes lately?" she not–so–subtly accused Grayle of fanaticism.

Grayle took Cynthia's hand and drew her close. With both hands held wide on each side of her head, he slowly cupped her head lovingly. In that moment, Cynthia realized his physical size and prowess fired burning passions confined narrowly by a marginal line of self-discipline. Via her audio amplification, Grayle's pounding heart helped incapacitate Cynthia. She realized that the wave overcoming her was Grayle's innate ability to connect to an electromagnetic frequency that acted as a capacitor of electrically charged tension from the ionosphere. Conversely, Cynthia felt as if her energy was summoned from earth's magnetic field from deep within its core. It was a visceral and neural connection that rapidly moved into emotional lightning that left her feeling passive, receptive, and wanting.

He kissed her forehead and she felt the absolute sincerity of the moment. The potent physical chemical rush, exclusively reserved for first intimate encounters, coursed through her body. Cynthia permitted Grayle to tilt her head upward. Feeling her submission, Grayle slipped his lips upon hers and lingered there until she no longer resisted. More than a caress, Grayle and Cynthia joined body and soul that mimicked a universal pulse. It was a union that coincided with authentic lightning that streaked its blue and white tentacles across a perfectly cloudless sky.

How did that happen? Cynthia thought.

"We did it," Grayle answered wordlessly. "I'm the energy, you're the gravity. I'm the force that moves away from the center; you're the force that moves toward the center. I'm the negative charge, the electrons, the Yang; you're the positive charge, like protons, the Yin of the universe; your friend, Caroline, is the neutral charge of neutrons, the balanced charge..." Grayle's thoughts meshed and melded with the couple's unyielding embrace.

Every amped soldier in the Confederation was privy to the intimate transmission between Cynthia and Grayle. Robert Gant and every state Confederation governor received it, too. Grayle had proclaimed the whereabouts of unrevealed secret information that defined the meaning of life. He had also alluded to the idea that he was its sole proprietor ordained by God.

It was also the moment in which Morgan shouted to the Confederation officials and Circle members to "get off your collective asses and get Cynthia out of that government ditch, away from that flipping fruit farm, and far away as you can get from that off the rails, self-promoting, tub-thumper, crazy as a triple cloned, *lunatic!*"

"Oh, good God," Morgan thumped his head. "Cynthia couldn't have been a bit uglier or a little smarter?"

Chapter XXXVII

Tipping Points

Friday, July 11, 2070

G rayle and Cynthia began the new day having barely touched breakfast. They strolled together arm in arm toward the town. Communiqués of all types and techniques poured in. Cynthia received fifteen urgent transmissions the moment she stepped outside the protective glass dome.

"We're here. We're coming in if we don't hear from you by 9:00 a.m.," warned Aaron in a frantic call.

"We have transport that will land as soon as you transmit," called Tsin-hang from offshore.

"You're flirting with a flipping madman," came as the least of Morgan's four more graphic warnings.

"I need to meet him face to face, Cynthia! I'll enter the city alone. If Grayle refuses, we'll force our way in," Nicholas insisted.

Cynthia cached each frantic dispatch without bothering to respond. Ignoring the world's impositions, the couple returned underground to explore the vaults.

Attila insisted upon joining the Circle ranks and left the nearby camp with Adele. With the help of transport, Adele and Attila were quickly moved to the Circle's location just hundreds of yards from the town's perimeter.

"Have you tried to make contact, again?" Attila asked the group.

"Yes. We've underestimated this Grayle. A force field appeared as soon as we came to the edge of town. You could hear the hum as soon as it went into place. We've analyzed it and it appears as if we can move through but I'm not so sure we'll be able to move out again," Aaron noted. "Look at the residents. It's the first time they've been aware of it, too. They've been in a slight panic since they discovered the invisible shield."

"Telepathic transmissions intact?" Attila asked.

"Between us, yes." Sonny answered. "I suggest we try all frequencies now and see what happens."

"What about lasers? Conventional weaponry?" Connor messaged remotely.

"We're ready when you are," Nicholas said. "I'm worried about Cynthia's state of mind. She follows Grayle now like a lovesick puppy. I say we wait to see if she shows up. I sent her a message to that effect. We'll arrange a meet, protective shield or not, civil or not, and see what transpires."

It was agreed that the Circle would enter Grayleton and retrieve Cynthia one way or the other before the noon hour.

Caroline was pleased to reunite with her mother and they embraced with warm greetings.

"This is the barrier's border?" Adele asked her daughter.

"We know it rejects smaller objects with sparks that disintegrated upon impact," Caroline acknowledged.

"Seems primitive," Adele supposed.

"We shouldn't move prematurely, however. We've got to wait until I contact Cynthia," warned Caroline.

"You can see her? Communicate with her?" Adele asked with surprise.

"I can. But I sense Grayle's ability to tap in, too. He is unable to read me but knows I'm here," Caroline explained.

Ildiko entered the conversation. "I can track him, but not she. He's absolutely aware of my presence and able to hear my thoughts and intentions. If he isn't amped in some way, he's genetically altered."

Caroline declared her intention of moving inside the dome at the noon deadline.

"Cynthia and Grayle know we're all here – no big secret. They're making a decision. Cynthia has convinced herself that she is still investigating the compound. She is smitten with Grayle, who is a dangerously charismatic guy," Caroline sighed.

The Confederation men grew agitated and decided it best to blast their way into Grayleton. Caroline strongly objected.

"It won't work. I can't see that outcome," Caroline expounded. "I've presaged a hint of this day and I'm the one to face off with Grayle. Just me," she said. "Alone, please."

"I don't care what you've seen. You're not going into that place alone," Adele objected.

"Exactly," Nicholas chimed.

"Mother, something is happening here beyond our experience. It's pivotal, dangerous, but hopeful. I'm not swayed by emotional expectations, the overtures of handsome men...no offense, dear Nicholas... but I operate objectively. Grayle has no power over me. He does have power over others here," Caroline insisted.

"I doubt that," Nicholas declared. "I'm the first line of defense with my ability to thwart evil intentions." As soon as the bravado was uttered, he felt foolish. Ildiko couldn't help but laugh.

"If you recall, the pathological is unaware that it's evil," Ildiko reminded Nicholas soberly. "In these cases, you have no effect whatsoever."

"I'm going in," Aaron agreed with Nicholas' suggestion of force. "There's nothing like airlifting or pounding boulders to knock sense into the situation."

"Looks like we're saying we go as a group or not at all," Sonny observed.

They tentatively agreed the Circle would move in together to save Cynthia, whether or not she thought she needed saving.

Adele and Attila would remain on the perimeter and direct Confederation reinforcements, if necessary. Having taken a relative priority consensus, everyone agreed that Cynthia's safety was top priority. Caroline's intention to enter alone was overturned. Caroline said nothing more and ended her objections.

The Circle ceased to communicate and prepared to attack with the help of the offshore conventional laser cannons to eliminate the force shield. After coordinating the anticipated efforts, the Confederation contingent watched the reactions of the Grayleton citizens when they chose to touch the force field and burned digits. No matter the macabre predictability of lost fingers, the trial was repeated hundreds of times by hundreds of residents.

Fingerless, confused citizens frantically searched for an absent leader; they ran in circles, and called Grayle's name without the apparent wherewithal to search underground. Someone picked up a red-haired dog and heaved the animal at the field. Snapping sounds were followed by pops when the dog slid to the ground, a distilled patch of gaping flesh and burning fur.

"A hell hole," Aditiya defined the rapidly deteriorating city.

Unconcerned with the world, Grayle returned to his quarters and Cynthia to hers. They changed into warmer clothes. The vault temperatures promised to quickly drain body heat.

"I'll let you know when I'm ready. I'm going to surprise you with something..." Grayle called to Cynthia through her bedroom door.

"It's no longer going to be a surprise. It's now an expectation," giggled Cynthia.

Grayle returned to his quarters and swiped a floorboard with his foot. In five equal parts, a six-foot opening slid open to a staircase. The wooden floor moved into place with rapid, ratcheting metallic clicks; when Grayle's head disappeared into the space below, the floor returned seamlessly behind him.

A wall monitor activated upon Grayle's entry. Seconds later, an image appeared that gave Grayle reason to grin.

"Good morning! I've a surprise for you!" he greeted the face joyfully when the special connection came to life.

"Please stand by..." Grayle called as he retraced his steps through his office upstairs. When he returned with Cynthia, he situated her in front of the monitor.

"Here's your sister!" Grayle proudly proclaimed.

Esther gasped her surprise. "How could you? How could you, Cynthia?" With a vengeance, livid curses, and accusations poured from Cynthia's sister.

The secret office within a hidden staircase surprised Cynthia; she was additionally alarmed when made aware that

Grayle had a working Internet connection at his disposal. Her third shock came when her sister's image stared back at her. She was unsurprised by Esther's dramatic reception.

"What's wrong?" Cynthia irritably asked Esther. "I'm guessing this was nothing more than an agreeable gesture to mend our relationship after your terse sign-off last night."

"Like hell it is. You had to show off your new man? I hate you! I tell you about my engagement to Stan and you do this?"

Grayle protested the statement. "I thought you would want to speak to your sister? That's what you indicated."

Esther terminated the transmission.

Cynthia frowned at Grayle.

"Explain how you would have the nerve to contact my sister? Then I'll follow with a few more questions," Cynthia said tersely.

"Your sister traced the Grayleton address after your conversation last evening and reconnected this morning. She left a message. She left no name but spoke of a sister in residence with whom she wished to speak after prematurely being cut off the previous evening. I took the opportunity to surprise you both this morning by a connection here. I thought you'd be pleased. I thought you would both be pleased," Grayle explained with obvious frustration.

Grayle stated his reasoning. He was disturbed that Cynthia had an argument. He knew that her sister reached out the next day to make up after a disagreement. He explained that he meant to facilitate but not mediate. How could he know, he appealed, that Esther could manufacture conspiratorial scenarios or that she might imagine Cynthia meant to steal her sister's engagement thunder?

Cynthia knew he spoke the truth.

"My sister has just announced an engagement to a man named Stanley Raga. She's thrilled. It was a source of personal pride; a little part of the universe that she knew had escaped me. My appearance here this morning – with my partner by my side – was construed to be a similar declaration as a competitive testimony," Cynthia slumped into a chair. "She's emotionally exhausting."

"Shall I get her back online?" Grayle suggested. "I meant to help you two to resolve a misunderstanding. I'm woefully inexperienced, I'm afraid. I'll explain to her...."

"No. Let her cool off. It's always the same pattern. I can imagine her thoughts. It'll take some explaining and a lot of latitude for Esther to believe that we've just met," Cynthia anguished. "The Confederation has reported all kinds of unexpected dangers, horrible attacks, and strangely altered communities with distressed survivors. We've just presented a radically different picture here. I wish I could see her level out," Cynthia said in a thin, strained voice.

"She will," Grayle assured. They moved to leave the hidden office.

"Now, answer me. Why did you tell me that there was no live feed within the underground complex?" Cynthia questioned the hidden access.

"There wasn't until early this morning. I knew of the office but just figured how to repair and connect the monitor. I manage things as needed. Never thought about it until last night when a message came in upside. We never receive messages, Cynthia. I only occasionally activate the main control office. But I figured you need some privacy and a little convenience when you need to speak to your friends or family."

"Overnight you figured this out?" Cynthia asked doubtfully.

"Just this morning, actually. If I have a question or need, I'm provided the answer. You'll see how it all works with me. Today, you'll witness what can happen beyond finite minds. I'll demonstrate the ways we're empowered to move beyond manmade limitations and thrive in our own time and space."

"You know what, Grayle? Sometimes I'm drowning in you. Sometimes, I'm convinced that you're a delusional freak."

Grayle laughed and pulled her toward him into his arms. "That would be me right about now," he agreed. "You referred to me as your partner. I needed to hear that. I accept the position effective immediately...."

10:00 a.m. Research Triangle Raleigh, NC

When Meredith Green walked into Esther's office, she ignited a portable accelerator that was situated directly across the room. Charged with 60 kilowatts, a series of light pulses funneled at the door was so intense that Meredith's body exploded. Alarms signaled Scott Reid's security forces that identified Green as a murder victim. Security bots caught images of Esther leaving the room an hour prior to the time of the doctor's death.

While the search ensued for Esther's whereabouts, Reid reported the tragedy to Morgan.

"It was poised on a desk on the opposite side of the room; it was Dr. Green who entered and triggered the laser. It could have been anyone. She's dead, Dr. Pendergrass."

In lieu of Morgan's response, Reid continued, "She can't be far, sir."

"She's not," Morgan finally spoke. "Esther is standing right here in front of me, son." Then there was silence.

Scott Reid signaled Isabella Moreno.

"She's in the house," Reid notified local Confederation troops and Cary's police department. He left a message with Moreno's office bot and jumped in his transport when Morgan's security chief failed to answer.

Morgan sat comfortably on his overstuffed chair in his library and stared steadfastly at Esther, who stood broadly and boldly before him.

"I'm at a loss for this attitude, Esther. People are looking for you, by the way. Seems your office ate Dr. Green," he said without a blink. "She was one of my best friends."

"Well, old man, I think that there's a good reason that people shouldn't enter my office without knocking, don't you?" Esther sneered. "You can't be too careful. There's no law against protecting myself from intruders," Esther smirked.

"Not sure the law will protect you in this instance. I mean, the entire complex is secure. You saying Meredith entered without identifying herself and that's the reason her body parts are splattered all over the office? What did that woman do to you that cost her so?' Morgan asked.

"Stop chattering and answer some questions. We don't have much time," Esther snapped.

"Please, Esther. Put the weapon down. Ask me whatever you wish and I will answer straight, as I've always done. You're upset. Did something happen to your young man?" Morgan asked as passively as possible.

"Yeah. Something happened to my young man. He found someone else. I'm not concerned about him. I want to know other things."

"I'm here."

"What's the Circle doing, Morgan? What's my sister doing exactly? What kind of bogus mission do you have going? What's the real reason I was left behind? I thought this was some kind of dangerous mission. I saw Cynthia. She looks like she's in a hotel on her honeymoon!"

Morgan tried to piece together what caused Esther to ask questions seemingly unconnected to a murderous rage. Then his mind went to Grayle having Cynthia trapped underground.

"We're trying to tie up loose ends with survivors, figure the issues with the magnetic grid that have to be repaired before the genetic issues will abate, and trying to collect information. What do you think is going on?" Morgan yelled furiously. "Ever consider that your sister's position might be compromised?"

"I'm pretty sure her position has been very compromised," Esther snarled. "You're trying to make a new race of people," Esther insisted. "Enhanced people! People like me will be expected to fade away or serve your new race. It's the plan, isn't it?" she accused. "There's no dangerous mission. You've decided to dump me without an explanation because it's obvious I'm just so much trash. Anyone not altered will be discarded."

Morgan shifted his position and retrieved his cane to rise from his chair; Esther pushed his chest. When he continued to move upward, she kicked Morgan's midsection.

Morgan fell back into his chair, gasping for breath.

"Good shot, girl. Right in the solar plexus! Who'd imagine I'd be a threat to you or anyone else at my age?" he choked in a thin voice.

"Answer me. You have all those samples for those who've exhibited genetic alterations. The whole Circle's DNA is in your hands. What were you doing?"

Morgan reached for the glass and decanter that rested by his side table and slowly poured a shot of whiskey.

"Isn't a bit early for that?" Esther asked without lowering her weapon.

"I may not see lunch!" Morgan grimaced before downing the drink in one gulp. He leaned back and placed his cane across his legs and caught his breath, the spasmodic diaphragm having finally calmed.

"My dear, no one considered developing an exclusive race of humans. We do dream of cultivating and culling genes that will circumvent biological weaknesses that have become problematic. That's the crux of genetic research. One day, we will have hopefully rid ourselves of diseases that plague mankind that need not reappear on the genomic landscape. Second, we'd like to closely investigate the EMP effects, both positive and negative. We've already been changed, if not molecularly polarized, on the planet. We had nothing to do with some of that. We need to correct this horrible situation and it doesn't mean a 'super race' that moves forward without all of humanity in mind."

"What if the cellular damage can't be reversed?" Esther asked. "Hungarians and Europeans burnt their boundaries to keep intruders out. Not long ago, you and the Mexicans agreed to do the same on West Coast borders. You've begun to eradicate right now those that have been damaged! What's to keep an elite group from killing unskilled people like me, too?"

Morgan tried to be clear as he could, given the imaginary dots connecting Esther's feeble reasoning.

"We're talking about psychotic savages relentlessly attacking the remnants of humanity worldwide. They're flat out trying to eradicate us. They're murdering our children and leaving their own to die in paths of destruction. You think they want to talk it out? They're called crazies for a reason.

"They ambushed our troops in Pennsylvania. You know this. What do you imagine? Should we ignore the savage behaviors and capitulate in the name of higher moral ground? We need answers but we're not going to be massacred in the process," growled Morgan.

"Our people, my family and friends and your family and friends, have put their lives on the line for an untested experiment in healing…"

"Tell me about the Circle's genetic alterations," Esther interrupted.

"Their code indicates a 78% integrity. Rather than 20%, we have uncharted territory that requires sorting interdisciplinary research. It promises an unprecedented biological leap. We've no idea what the future holds but we now have a glimpse. These new abilities are so powerful an influence they can be molecularly assumed by proximity. And this is just the first generation!" Morgan exclaimed.

"We all imagined a world of technological AI initially married to human biology. If the EMP had not come about, we might never have discovered that our DNA was capable of organic maturity matching or surpassing our present technological advancements."

"Why don't I have any special abilities? Why don't you? Why not Angela? Why just some people?" Esther became increasingly distraught.

"When that platter was passed around the table, a lot of the survivors missed it. I don't take it personally. I figure I had a full plate as it was. I'm not going to whine that I can't send objects all over the landscape, read thoughts, stop evil, go invisible or intuit the future. Hell, I think it's just bloody marvelous somebody can. Before I die, I get a small inkling of providential possibilities," Morgan stated with conviction.

"You'd best not invoke Providence in all of this, old man. This is your plan to separate productive from unproductive. Where does that leave people like me? You're old. You'll die soon. But I'm young and I'm not going to fit in. I think I have a glimpse into your plan," she seethed as the words came tumbling from her fateful vision. She struggled, imagining herself a failed experiment, the refuse of humanity's former identity.

"How do you know that the Circle's abilities aren't a danger to humanity? Are the crazies meant to be exterminated and people like me are tolerated – allowed to exist – until we die out? I see how it is. You see yourself as the Father of Mankind? You think you're Moses leading us from the desert into the land of Milk and Money?"

Rachel entered the room and slammed the door.

"What the hell, Esther? How dare you lecture Morgan?" Rachel demanded angrily. "I'm calling security," Rachel threatened.

Esther turned toward the interruption and lifted her weapon; the bullets buried dead center into Rachel's forehead, throat, and femur within a second of touching the trigger.

Morgan drew his resting cane from his lap and placed his beloved companion piece under his armpit and leveled it at Esther's back. Within the base of the cane's handle, a button was pressed. The laser had one shot but could target and diffuse five ways upon impact. Esther's body was pinpointed midpoint upon her spine. In five defined pieces, Esther's body was leveled to the floorboards a few feet from Morgan's own. Severed bookcases and walls fell upon the body.

Scott Reid entered the room after the fact, with security having to force the door, and Rachel's body slumped against it. The extent of the tragedy soon came to light.

Isabella Moreno and two security guards had met a similar fate. Having recognized Esther, familiar security personnel were clueless as to her intentions. Esther easily caught them off-guard and murdered the three in the kitchen. Isabella Moreno sealed their fate when she kindly invited Esther to share the late breakfast prepared each morning for staff members. Angela returned to the kitchen, having been outdoors to check the stables; she was found lying dead across the kitchen's back door threshold with freshly picked flowers still in her hand. Kitchen bots ran erratically around the bodies.

The last of the Blue hounds lay struggling with cruelly severed legs in the hall leading to Morgan's library. It was the pitiful whimpers of suffering canines that brought Rachel to the scene.

In Esther's transport, open canisters from the Cryogenic freezers were discovered. All genetic materials gleaned from the Circle were destroyed. The rampage included military guards and two more researchers discovered dead at the Research Triangle.

Connor was notified and airlifted home. It was decided to keep the incident quiet while Cynthia remained enclosed in Grayleton. The Circle, however, viscerally heard the emotional wails of Edward and Morgan, who shared acute emotional agony.

Cynthia remained oblivious as to her sister's fate. The rest of the morning was dedicated to cuddling. Cynthia remained happily protected in Grayle's arms sans any sense of time.

* * *

It was past noon when the Circle convened with Attila and Adele. The unforeseen shock of abruptly losing family members and friends was brutal. Adele's body went limp at the news. Her mother had been forever lost to her.

Caroline touched her mother and held her hand. The Circle quietly turned their attention toward Adele. Rather than the blue light encircling the group and proceeding upward toward the familiar grid, the lights encased Adele in an obscure bubble within a haze that left her image blurred. Attila became alarmed and Caroline calmed him.

"She's hurt. She's in need of healing. Let her be," Caroline cautioned. "She's in a cocoon of infinite love and understanding."

A few minutes passed; the blue haze dissipated and Adele stood holding her throat with one hand.

"Oh, Caroline," she turned and smiled at her daughter. "I had no idea."

Attila moved to grasp Adele, expecting her to collapse from grief. Adele was not, however, grief stricken. Hers had been a glimpse of infinite knowing.

"I had no inkling of the meaning of life and death until this moment. My mother, our friends, have moved on. When they say 'a better place', they're not kidding. What a feeling of absolute relief. What love awaits us," she whispered, awestruck.

"I think you need to get home," Attila urged. "I've summoned a transport."

"I'm supposed to be here. It's clear. I need to spend these moments with Caroline," she smiled, looking at her daughter with knowing tears in her eyes.

"I tried to tell Rachel to come with us, Mother," Caroline said softly. "Some things aren't meant to be, no matter what you see. You understand?"

"I do," Adele spoke with conviction. "I love you. I will always cherish my gift, my darling girl." Adele hugged her only child and kissed her cheek. "Thank you for bringing so much life, so much hope, so much love to this world."

"No, Mother. I thank you for being the best parent anyone could wish for. Clearly, you were chosen for me in every way. Never forget how much you mean to me. Live this wonderful life to its fullest," Caroline counseled as she stroked her mother's head softly and lovingly.

The Circle became quiet as they intuited Caroline's intentions. No one protested. Everyone grasped that Caroline's abilities were far more potent than their collective powers. Caroline had grown quietly and discreetly stronger; the collective was a mere spark compared to the energy that now flowed within her.

"I thought we were fixing the magnetic grid," Sonny said simply. "I thought we were translating the energy into every language, every frequency, every faulty cellular structure..."

"We were. We did," confirmed Caroline. "That was important. This is important, too. We came up short, however, and we need to finish. But there's another way to do that. A final bit of this puzzle lies somewhere within Grayleton now. I'm the one who's going in," she stated. "Send me the best frequencies you can cook up, Sonny!"

"You're not going anywhere without me. You need us all there," Nicholas demanded. "We'll go together and rescue Cynthia, do whatever is left to be done, as a group. This energy bullshit field around the town is nothing to get through. What's the big deal?"

"I'm the one that is like water, a reflection, and a mirror without emotional investments. I'm impervious to trickery and falsehood. You are all gifted but you are all yet to be entirely centered. I cannot risk distractions, overreactions, or wait for a telepathic consensus in a crisis.

"Grayle has something he feels represents God's plan. It holds everlasting life? It answers all questions, heals all hurt, and promises mankind absolute harmony? I'm going to find out what it is that he thinks will keep Cynthia his for eternity. Something here, in this place, affects our destiny. It's here that I'm intended to use my gift to maximum capacity. If all else fails, call the Tons of Fun outfit!" Caroline laughed at the thought.

No one shared her levity. Caroline's closest friends and family stood solemnly rigid.

Caroline moved past her mother and brushed her fingertips on hers, making her way toward Nicholas, who waited anxiously, saddened, and confused.

"You cannot come with me, dear Nicholas. I love you but you will distract me. Trust me, love," Caroline caressed his face.

They kissed and the blue lights sprinkled, intensified, and swelled around the couple. Nicholas's sadness filled her and she tucked her head into his chest with shared pain. His head held high to the heavens, he fought back tears. "Oh, God. Bring her back to me," he appealed with desperation. "I love her so much."

"Beautiful!" Attila gasped at the intensity of dancing lights hovering over them. For a few minutes, the woods quieted as the birds and insects ceased to call, aware of a new sensation in their midst, a rare song of human love filled the atmosphere while the natural world held its breath.

Caroline conveyed instructions and heartfelt sentiments of gratitude to her friends. A breeze caught her long hair as she effortlessly walked through the field meant to be impassable. Each of those remaining on the other side could sense a successful passage even as she disappeared into Grayleton. No one attempted to follow her past the entry point. The last glimpse of Caroline was a wisp of ash blond strands of hair. Caroline would make her way to Grayle and Cynthia's position deep inside the mountain.

Attila stood helplessly and held Adele close to him. Nicholas sobbed his distress with his similarly distraught circle of friends.

Morgan heard the news of Caroline's entry into Grayleton from Adele and shook with grief.

"What have you done, Adele?" Morgan cried. "Your mother was just murdered. How could you risk your daughter?"

"It's meant to be, Dad," Adele stated calmly. "Please order everyone to move out toward the ships. We will leave here. Begin to evacuate the Confederation troops from the base camps immediately."

"I'm for sending in the whole Confederation right now into that zombie pit to get Caroline and Cynthia. You're not thinking right," Morgan measured his words.

Attila spoke reassuringly to Morgan and asked that Connor be included in their discussion.

"First of all, I'm saddened that this conversation has to happen when we've lost Rachel and Angela. Caroline's instincts have to be trusted, however. There's no one here who could have stopped her from entering Grayleton, Morgan. Those electrical currents and lasers meant nothing; she was impervious to their effects. Caroline was adamant in her message to Adele that we move out from Grayleton. It's clear. So let's move out of here right now. It's urgent. I want everyone out!"

Morgan realized that the Hungarian had no intention of leaving.

"I'm sending Adele home. You take care of her," Attila added.

"Thank you for everything, Morgan. And Connor? Take care of that boy. He's incredible," Attila saluted his friends.

"Take care of my precious daughter, my friend," Connor pleaded. "I know you'll make it home," he said stiff-lipped. It was the first time Connor referred to Caroline as his. In the way that real men do, they nodded to each other and got on with the tasks at hand.

Adele turned toward Attila with an appreciative smile.

"You couldn't leave us if you tried. We're always with you. If you haven't learned that, you haven't been listening, my treasure," she assured him. "This love story is written and you and I are not finished."

When his wife was murdered in Hungary, it was anger, loss, and indignation that consumed Attila. This felt different. Attila faced the worst kind of unrequited love imaginable. With tender assurances, Attila and Adele tried mightily to balance the universe in their favor.

Ildiko heard their feelings and felt their parting pain. She reminded her father of the power of faith.

"You'll know what Adele and I know. It's a very thin space between infinite love and our present plane of existence. Mother is there. Your parents, too! Adele has touched the other side and will not weep or mourn your passing if it's meant to be. She knows suffering will disappear; the weight that sits on your heart has only been slightly lifted with Adele by your side. You'll be so light that you'll laugh at the sensation! Colors that are not here are there; the reverberations of life will fill your ears and peace will fill your heart. You'll be welcomed for your life's efforts and you'll know what it means to be as one with souls that share your passion for life. This, and more, will envelop you one day."

"You expect me to die here, Édes?" Attila tenderly brought his daughter close to him.

"No such thing as death, Papa. No such thing."

"Why is there so much pain here?" Attila asked simply.

"As soon as we were introduced to confusion, we imagined it, then we made it our reality; our consciousness altered as we moved from the light," Ildiko tried to explain. "We are chastised for unrealized sins, warned of imaginary threats, our minds attuned to our obstacles rather than the possibilities. It's nearly impossible to overcome our fears when we are forever reminded how to disconnect. Caroline will neutralize that element."

"There will be no evil to fight?" Attila asked in an effort to lighten the horrors. "I like a good fight."

"There're likely evil hydras for us to contend with... either on this or another plane, another time, another space. Just as the magnetic grid has been damaged, our God consciousness has deteriorated. We have done this to ourselves. We have unwittingly been the cause of our unhappiness. It needs to be fixed. We need a leg up and Caroline will help make that happen.

"In that moment of a reset, we'll operate with the expectation of being whole. In that moment, we'll create the world intended for us. It will be a product of our finest inspiration because we'll feel worthy. Optimal use of our brains, our cellular levels, self-healing and spiritual heights, once acquired and lost, might be recovered. All those reminders left for us worldwide meant to spark memories of the best of humanity... so many natural clues...all of the inspired discoveries may make sense once more. How did we lose our awe? How did we turn on each other? How did we not notice the patterns?

"We've imagined, glimpsed, intuited sparks of our greater selves but remained as immovable as the tomatoes vulnerable to the sucking weeds. Even as we sought a spiritual hinterland, we were besieged by entitlements and fears. We wallowed in muck and called it entertainment. We were content to live on bygone successes of others--or ourselves--without thoughts of present obligations.

"Our nemesis has become more than the evil we've inherited; we've successfully imagined a greater force by expecting the worst. We unwittingly breathed life into our foulest fears; nurtured our monsters until they breathed fire, disease and erupted into unnatural disasters. We expected it. Caroline may be able to neutralize that illusion. You have helped that effort. I love you now and always," Ildiko wept.

"I don't believe in heaven, Édes. These are fairy stories," Attila said.

"No matter," Ildiko reassured her father.

"I've killed. I've made decisions meant to hurt our enemies," Attila admitted with sadness.

"Your intention was to restore balance. It was a real fight. Civility has its reasons and its limits. We are endowed with survival instincts and we are empowered to use them. Papa, you never made others suffer because you took joy from it. You aptly read intentions. So does Nicholas, albeit unconsciously. Why else would Nicholas be able to neutralize those that meant harm? His victims aren't victims at all; they are the ones that enjoyed dominance and reveled in the pain they inflicted. No judge or jury, or agonizing self-reflection, was needed."

"Too simple," Attila shook his head in disbelief.

Ildiko laughed. "Not simple, but that's the best I can do. The more you complicate things, the more you're likely to suffer. We have a limited capacity to grasp the scope of cause and effect. Act well. Think well. Do your best. That's it."

"I love you," he said, fighting the tightening of his chest.

Ildiko tightly hugged her father. "I'm so proud to be your daughter; you've no idea."

The troops were ordered to evacuate. The transports began to move urgently to expedite the evacuation. Nicholas was finally forced to leave the vicinity when Attila threatened to have Komor shoot him with sedatives.

Within the Confederation, all was silent. No one understood what Caroline intended but shared in its gravitas. In a silent world, the militia camps emptied and the Circle reluctantly withdrew from Grayleton.

Attila stood vigil and stared past the force field at the directionless citizens. In lieu of their leader, they had become quickly confused and increasingly angry. Within minutes of his solitude, Attila observed an explosion of brutal attacks within the city. Panic ruled. The holographs faded and the façade of green rolling hills protected by lush vegetation paled. Stern, colorless concrete and rusted metal no longer disguised the Grayleton perimeter.

Grayle had other things on his mind.

Chapter XXXVIII

The Door of Knowledge

Grayle and Cynthia entered the locked corridor that lay under a separate layer of the complex. Its nearly freezing temperatures had Cynthia peering through her vaporous breath against the colorless, erratically-lit cement halls.

"You're not cold?" she asked as she snuggled with Grayle.

"I'm fine. Tell me if it's too much and we can return better equipped," he offered.

"Who needs insulation when you're meeting God?" she joked. Grayle did not smile.

"I didn't mean to be offensive," she corrected.

"I'm sure you didn't," he rejoined without emotion. "Please don't use the Lord's name in vain, Cynthia. You might as well know that if we're going to be lifetime partners, you'll have to listen to me on some things without a lot of jokes each time. Just trust me," he looked down at her and smiled. "I've seen the way, I've seen the past, and I believe in our future."

The words struck Cynthia as odd. Grayle's reproach resonated as a personal affront. Did he actually think himself the messiah? Had he assumed mindless devotion? It also occurred to her that there was no vapor emanating from Grayle's mouth.

Cynthia paused and looked behind her. The tunnel had grown obscure; the lights had faded into black as they moved deeper toward the unveiling of the anticipated grand revelation.

"I don't want to go farther, Grayle," Cynthia ceased to walk. "I'm too cold. Let's save this for another day."

"It's just a few hundred feet from here. Why not venture just a little farther?"

"I hate this blackness. I can't even see anything behind us. Let's go back," she insisted.

Grayle laughed, "The exposé of all time is left for another day. No problem, my lady. Your wish is my command."

They began to return quickly toward the entrance. Cynthia paused. She suddenly felt foolish.

"Look, I was just nervous all of a sudden. It's pretty unsettling down here. Let's finish this. Impress me."

"You sure? I'm fine otherwise."

"I'm sure, let's go."

The lights returned once more to life. Doors to her left were the same as she had seen in her dream.

"What lies behind those old doors, Grayle?" she asked.

"Answers to past leaders in other times," he answered simply.

"Former times?" Cynthia corrected.

"Other times," Grayle repeated.

"How old is this place? It looks as if these tunnels existed before our country was established," Cynthia stated as she examined the foreign architecture, sensing a strange loss of equilibrium. "Is this place older than American history?" she pressed.

"There've been many battles, many wars, and many disasters ending in decimation. Each time, the information behind these doors has offered answers, solutions, and sometimes a direct access to cosmic understanding. Each time, a door was opened. Each time, something happened to reestablish God's purpose for humanity," Grayle attempted.

"What are you talking about?" Cynthia asked incredulously. "Show me one, please. It's got to be more meaningful than wine and spirits."

"First, I'd like you to see the vault meant for our time. We'll not succumb to past mistakes. We are meant to begin anew," Grayle warned. He picked up the pace.

"Whoa. In the other doors, you've examined the mistakes of past civilizations? You, and who else?" Cynthia counted the doors as they passed.

"Other world leaders, I suppose."

"Excuse me, Grayle? They all have biometric entries. How did you gain entry into the President's quarters? How about those doors? How did you get in? They're all intact. And there used to be no biometric entries, right?"

Grayle nodded, "I know. I mean, I don't know. I put my own hand on the locks and they opened. They all opened. But they'd been opened before. Whoever gained entry was unsuccessful because there has been a continuing need for resolution. I was chosen for this task in our time and I realize that with the right person by my side, equally yoked, we can begin anew."

Grayle took Cynthia's arm and tried to usher her to move more rapidly down the corridor.

"Look! There it is!" Grayle pointed toward the final door.

"You're squeezing my arm, partner. Ease up," she demanded.

The last and eighth door was also closed. Cynthia stood before the enormous vault and waited expectantly. As did Grayle.

"So?" she asked. "Now what?"

"I was told that only the woman I trusted could open that door. I can't do it alone," Grayle said, looking blankly toward the steel entrance. "This required your help."

"Who told you that?" Cynthia probed skeptically, tilting her head to the side as she studied Grayle's eyes. He focused steadily upon the door, looking past her.

"The angel visited me again. The message was clear," Grayle delivered his reasoning as if it made perfect sense.

"Fine. But what's the reason you haven't tried to open the door before this?" Cynthia asked doubtfully. "Like, when you first got here years ago?"

"It wasn't there. Or perhaps I was unable to see it. I've considered both possibilities. In the meantime, the message I received had everything to do with you, Cynthia. I need you as my key, to fulfill the future that begins with this simple task," Grayle announced, taking her hand in his. "Here we are, together, embarking upon our destiny. It's hard to believe it's happening. I heard its description: The Door of Knowledge."

"Well, that sounds awesome but I'm not touching that door," Cynthia protested. "You opened all the rest..." Cynthia pulled her hand from his, stepped a few feet away, and folded her arms across her chest. "Why not this one?"

"It was in the instructions," Grayle said simply.

"There were written instructions that came with the new door that appeared overnight? Besides God's message that arrived by winged courier?" Cynthia asked doubtfully.

"Not written, not overnight, not a winged messenger," Grayle shook his head. "I heard the instructions to not open the door. The voice clearly explained that the door was meant for the woman who would be my mate. That should be enough to convince anyone!"

Grayle's gaze turned from a faraway, wistful look into another, less attractive one.

"I ask you to help me, Cynthia. To help humanity! If you love me the way I love you, you must have faith that we are a fated couple, meant to help lead humanity into a new age. Put your hand on the doorplate or simply swish it in the vicinity. I'm not sure how it will open. I do know that it leads to absolute truth and happiness," Grayle begged.

Cynthia, however, leaned a hand on one hip and raised an eyebrow. "Still no."

"Do you or do you not love me? If you do not, I understand. I'll wait for another, if that's the case," Grayle said, crushed with disappointment. "I could be wrong to think you're the one."

"Let me think that over a minute," Cynthia continued sarcastically. "Yeah, I'm done here. I'm not going to do anything you're afraid to do or that wasn't my idea in the first place. Some divine voice told you not to touch something but told you to make me do it? If I'm so key and everything, why couldn't someone contact me directly? I'm feeling left out here. Why don't you try it first? If it doesn't open, I'll have a go," she suggested irately. Grayle moved toward her and held her close to him. He felt her heart beating furiously and tried to calm Cynthia.

"I'm sorry. I've waited for this moment; the world has waited for this moment, for what seems an eternity. You are a good soul, Cynthia. You are an innocent...you are...."

Grayle stopped mid-sentence when Caroline's voice echoed behind them amongst a blue mist. "You are too smart to touch that forbidden door," Caroline finished.

"Caroline!" Cynthia called happily. "My God! How did you find me? How did you get behind us?"

"Indeed?" Grayle puzzled. "And who says it's forbidden?"

"It's odd that you've been chosen to do everything but this part. If you aren't empowered and Cynthia has no direct instructions to do your bidding, it's likely forbidden," Caroline said logically. Deeply connected to Cynthia's mind, Caroline spoke with her friend earnestly.

"Cynthia, I know you trust me. Please don't hesitate now!"

Cynthia sprinted to Caroline but stopped short of hugging her friend. Uncertainty entered her mind. *What if this is an illusion?* she thought. She was confused that such an idea even came to her.

"Look, Grayle! My friend Caroline is here!" Cynthia turned toward Grayle, bidding his involvement.

"A special occasion," he said dryly.

"How did you find me?" Cynthia asked, returning her attention to Caroline.

"I'm here," Caroline answered noncommittally. "I intended to come here and all physical matter is convergent network of intent. I expected to help you and it simply happened. We were worried when we no longer heard from you."

Cynthia began to stumble; she was confused as to Caroline's statement, muddled as to the reasons that communication with the Circle had been dismissed from her mind. It was not like her to ignore interaction when she had known the seriousness of the Confederation's mission. Why had she forgotten or dismissed her obligation to stay in contact?

"I intended to get in touch...I knew that I could...I'm not sure the reason I didn't," Cynthia dimly stated.

"We patiently waited outside Grayleton so as not to upset anyone or to put you in jeopardy," Caroline soothed.

"Thanks for the vote of confidence," Grayle grumbled.

"We need to leave now, Cynthia," Caroline gently suggested, with a motion for Cynthia to take her outstretched hand.

"And you seriously think you can find a way out?" Grayle puzzled. "Why not join with us to witness a miracle? You're invited, too."

Cynthia was confused by Grayle's first statement.

"She found her way in; she can find our way out," Cynthia amended Grayle's assumption. "What are you saying, Grayle? You wouldn't lead us out if we asked?"

"That's what he's saying," Caroline answered for Grayle. "He has no intention of letting you go; he expects you to respond to him without question," Caroline calmly added. She turned toward Grayle and asked, "Am I wrong?"

"You insinuate I'm keeping her captive? What game is this? You appear out of nowhere and pretend an urgent rescue from some imaginary evil. What exactly are you afraid of?" Grayle closed distance and pulled Cynthia around him. "Are you that afraid of knowing what's behind that door? Why would it threaten you?" His chest puffed with indignation. "You're dismissed. You're not rescuing anyone!" Grayle's voice dropped into a low growl, much as a dog would guard a bone. "Your society is fear-based; your belief systems are fear-based. So go conquer the universe. Leave mine alone! We will ring in an age of trust and harmony. Cynthia will be by my side."

Caroline's eyes remained steady, her stature unchanged.

"Trust and harmony? A strange combination of words coming from you; why not simply use the operative word: 'control'. Harmony is our natural state. You need not dictate the terms of peace, Grayle. Using bits of truth, you inject the very fear that you want Cynthia to believe is unobjectionable. She'll not hear you. Humans that survived the EMP will no longer hear you. We have a window to rid our consciousness of evil forever and that's what's going to happen. I've seen it. You're done," Caroline avowed.

"Seriously, you have objectivized evil intentions on one guy 300 feet down in a government bunker? Every man requires the devotion and love of a good woman. Cynthia and I are meant to usher in a final transition. What exactly do you think is going on here?" Grayle countered.

"All you need is one genetically intact, sound-minded, guiltless person to do your bidding – against their best instincts – and you believe that you can trump humanity's rightful inheritance? You think this is as good as it gets and Cynthia embodies humanity's optimal state? Tell her what to do and you become convinced that you've trumped humanity's best efforts? That's not going to happen. You'll fail again," Caroline opposed. "For too long, your kind has shown up here to rob us of our birthright. It's your job. You trick us into thinking that the beneficiary of man's advances and insight is a privatized, social inheritance not meant for lesser beings. The sheer unattainability of momentary peace is enough to cause human agony. I wonder, how does that come about?

"You sound of reason. You introduce untoward advancement to some, with unreasonable obstacles for others – knowing the imbalance breeds discontent and suspicion. Ultimately, you imagine genetically altered, damaged remnants to worship anyone, any cause, anything but God. But there's a problem. We reject alterations to our noble instincts as no other species; for all our failings, we have a moral fiber woven into our souls. Humans are the heirs of God's code. We have been able to sustain this code at our core through the worst adversities.

"The best you can do is break our will. Break us down, bit by bit, in the hopes that we are whittled to impotence. It must be frustrating for you to see us born again and again with the same God particle, no matter our difficulties. When we manage to find our way back to God's code, you manage to interject the kind of self-righteousness in our leaders and ourselves that alters the message. That's what you're good at. You recruit us as willing partners. It's simple. We end up wiping each other off the face of the earth. We'll kill each other in the name of justice more viciously than the most desperate animal defending their young.

"Your envy of God is matched only by your efforts to steal our happiness. That was never your job. Your job was to test our mettle. If allowed to mature properly, we might have correctly taught ourselves and connected to the highest quantum frequencies by now. To date, we have been deceived and distracted, left to struggle like hamsters on a wheel on this plane for far too long.

"It's clever to have created an environment of desperate survival mode conjured from lies. We crawl over each other for imaginary goods and services as spiritual provisions. We go crazy for haptic holographs, augmented realities, and illusions that you've managed to instill in our subconscious. We grab at them, need them, preferring flashy illusory short-lived moments rather than fully absorb the miracles surrounding us deserving of our tender respect.

"There is an elegant mystery that remains unintelligible to us. Untold cues of intelligent design should drive our uppermost instincts, challenge our intellect, and cultivate an integrity that naturally lends itself to spiritual connections. We are meant to explore, examine, and stand in awe of the universe's secrets as they beautifully unfold. Rather, you would promote a fundamental rigidity that precludes either prayer or inquiry... or both.

"You tricksters are there to make sure our frustration, doubts, and fears will cloud inspiration. Our spiritual food has been deprived of nutritive value in order to keep your kind relevant.

"I do know that you cannot steal a soul for yourself. It's the one thing your kind forfeited. You have no soul that passes through!" Caroline reproached. "You may never know God. You fear that you may never move into the light. So you've decided to try and destroy those who would seek truth!"

The blue haze that collected around Caroline emitted a soft light, slightly obfuscating her image. As if in a protective sheath of translucent light, Caroline's encasement overwhelmed all of Cynthia's concerns.

"Hey, Caroline? You're entirely blue. You know that you're in a blue bubble?" Cynthia peered around Grayle's back and tentatively moved to stand once again in front of him.

"It's the light. You know the light. It's coming through me. It's not just my miracle, Cynthia. It's yours, too. You can join me now, my friend. Just take my hand, stand with me, and I will send you away from this force," Caroline beckoned her friend.

Grayle yelled a warning that caused Cynthia to freeze with indecision. "It's an aberration... some kind of trick. Don't touch it!" Grayle stood between Cynthia and Caroline.

"Caroline's facsimile is meant to test our resolve and keep the worthy from the Door of Knowledge. If you can't pass this small test of faith, you will never see the real light," Grayle appealed. "You're meant to see God's plan, to walk by my side, usher in a new age. This is pure satanic trickery to steal you from this threshold!"

Cynthia's instincts faltered. She knew Grayle had been by her side. Caroline, however, appeared inexplicably.

"Ironic, but the thing beside you is correct. It's a test of faith. It's also about the facts," Caroline spoke solemnly, sensing that Cynthia was wavering.

"I've always known events that happen in space and time that wrap around my consciousness with no beginning and no end. It took some time to sort it out, to place things in a linear fashion, and then to eventually abandon the entire concept of sorting. I've always strained to make sense of messages, the images, and the ideas that have flowed through me. As I aged, I could no longer receive information as effortlessly.

"I tired of trying to interpret images as our challenges became more intense. Then I relaxed; I attempted to presage events without struggling to extrapolate meanings or figure the exact cause and effect in life's theatre. I let go. Once more, I simply drew impressions as a child when ideas were permitted to flow through me. From that point, I developed rapidly.

"I soon assimilated all of the Circle's powers because I expected to feel as one with you all. Why not? Even as we gathered together, I knew the light could come from each of us individually. We have insight the moment we are willing to humble ourselves to the possibilities. An evolved state arrives because of a certain biological evolution that is culturally nurtured with a God consciousness. Humans are able to develop without so many gatekeepers and middlemen, without undue suffering that might damage, isolate, or misdirect our inherent capacities. The key might be for us to better understand our miracle and subsequently better appreciate creation. An evolved sentience is our birthright and need not be filtered, refined or expanded as much as investigated, over time, with awe. With limited appreciation of the complexities of our structures, refined for millions of years along with environmental factors, we lack the humility required to see ourselves in perspective. Why is it that we cannot reconcile a little faith with our search for an evolved, connected state? We are endowed with an imagination. There is more to imagine than the ego, wealth, and power that may have shortchanged our genus. This is where we stand now, Cynthia. These vaults represent that which people believed to be our finest advantage.

"Tricksters, like the one embodied by Grayle, exist to make us hesitate, rob our confidence of a natural inheritance that grows exponentially... if given the chance. In all of its forms, this negative force has been able to misconstrue honorable tenets. We should be able to share knowledge without projecting our worst, under-developed natures. God is in our DNA and that amazing code includes neural complexities that go far beyond knowing the brain's physical structure. In fact, in many cases, we've yet to ask the right questions or understand all of the physical principles that arrive with evolving discoveries and theories. Yet, Grayle knows the way to the all-knowing path right this minute? You have to open the all-encompassing door of knowledge right now?

"How have we convinced ourselves that by duplicating billions of uniform transistors in memory groups controlled by a CPU, we understand a modicum of greater neural variations? Given certain maturation levels, our inheritance will exponentially expand and divide like every other organic embryo. But we're not computers. Can a massive digital brain simulator, with all of its inputs and outputs, simulate our sense of a soul? We are far more complex than rigid internal assumptions and algorithms. You must believe in the human potential, Cynthia. Who is Grayle to define humanity? What kind of leader must this be?

"When the EMP finally divided us, it was quickly apparent that there are those of a diminished frequency so low as to become insane beyond debate. In an electromagnetic flood of biblical proportions, civilization was once again on the brink of extinction.

"What does that tell us? Is there an infinite intelligence that has carefully programmed the universe inclusive of free will? Do we distill creation to known terms? Time, as we think we conceptualize it, is not a factor. The program, if you will, is going to run as many algorithms as it takes until bit by bit, we become synchronized, effective, and balanced; you should be able to move with less and less effort through evolved planes as God-centered. Those that don't want to move closer to God don't have to move closer to God. Evolution from a human state to an augmented technological specimen likely short-changes, if not underestimates, human capacity. Why propagate artificial intelligence that is inculcated with our shortcomings? Such are the forces that move us toward self-worship and physical eternal life. We can merely invent, replicate and admire a tool that we imagine represents the pentacle of an evolved human state. As we unfold the intricacies of our lives, we cannot possibly believe that our current impressions and strategies can hold a candle to intricacies of the daunting complexities yet to be revealed. We're still flat-landers having just considered the third dimension.

"We are meant to innovate, to enhance humanity's opportunities with meaningful outcomes in ever evolving ways! We need only to recognize, and stay tethered to, integrity. A loss of the God connection becomes our hell... please close this distance, Cynthia."

Caroline turned her attention toward Grayle. It surprised her that he had yet to protest. Caroline's gaze returned to her friend with the realization that Grayle waited for time to run its course. She would have to move from the philosophical tact to specifics. The Trickster was an expert on such tactics. Convincing Cynthia to take her hand and walk away from Grayle's influence by virtue of free will would require certain relatable facts.

"Esther and you spoke yesterday evening. We have the transcripts. You spoke again today within Grayleton. Some hours later, Esther died. I'm sorry to have to tell you this," began Caroline.

"It can't be!" Cynthia cried. "I was so afraid that she would commit suicide at some point. She was unhappy, so erratic and unbalanced. I thought her boyfriend could make the difference..."

"I think he did make the difference," Caroline said coolly. "She didn't commit suicide exactly. But she was meant to self-destruct in the end. Recorded by her PM, Esther's last days tell a sad story of her boyfriend cruelly using and rejecting her for his purposes," continued Caroline. "I'll walk you through it, if Grayle will allow. He will try to convince you that mine are reasons to cause you pain."

"Who is putting notions in her mind now?" warned Grayle. "I'm certainly not afraid of anything you have to say."

"Esther never had unusual genetic transformations with improved code connectivity. You were different," Caroline intoned softly. "Even though your DNA has not expanded greatly, you've always been satisfied, happy to be a part of things, levelheaded, and so very kind. These are some of the greatest gifts of all.

"It must have been difficult to see the radical changes in your sister and her self-imposed isolation. It wasn't the EMP after-effects, or being unable to assimilate telepathic powers, or even the loss of Nicholas' affections that caused her tipping points; your sister was a target of incredible malevolence that has interfered with man's transcendent progress since creation. Esther was a hapless target of fraud.

"Esther fell in love with a man named Stanley Raga. They met through work-related projects. He worked for the research department. We know now that this wasn't so. Stanley Raga's image told us that there was no such person working for the Research Triangle; Security was unable to find a trace of a feed or conversations...at first. Scott Reid persisted and eventually discovered the frequent conversations. Esther logged onto a security bot in her office and used it rather than her monitor.

"Esther regularly forwarded Confederation intelligence that included documentation about genetic research conducted on the Circle. She included the EMP's damage reports on the magnetic grid. Everything, I guess, she might have thought would impress Stanley or, perhaps, something that Stanley requested through feigned interest.

"Stanley managed to erase all traces of his connection. It took an inordinate amount of effort to uncover the source of this confusion. Quite technologically advanced for this Stanley whose records appeared as an employee during a security check and who vanished just as quickly.

"When you spoke to Esther today, she became distraught. Did something unusual happen?" Caroline prompted.

Cynthia turned toward Grayle and back to Caroline; she shared cached images of the morning's conversation with Caroline, including her brief discussion with Grayle concerning his part in the arrangement.

"Neat," Caroline said dryly to Grayle.

Grayle smiled, "Go ahead, demon. Whatever lies you want to make up, feel free. You troublemakers are all the same."

Caroline explained carefully the tale of two betrayals

"Stanley Raga? Change those letters around, Cynthia...it spells *Satan Grayle.*"

Grayle said nothing.

"He developed evil algorithms for years. It's what he does. Esther was just one variable within millions of possibilities. She fed him strategies, data, Confederation information of all kinds. I'm guessing that it was just as simple for Grayle to hack it all. But Grayle likes games. The same groups that attacked Jordan Scott's militia in Philadelphia were those that prompted our route toward this location. Grayle's men were the same ones that ambushed us once more when we were squeezed from two directions. A third Grayle group pretended to be Grayle's good-hearted rescue units. Just games.

"These so-called rescue scouts shot their own men dead in the water to convince us of Grayle's good intentions. We believed, at some level, that we were assisted. That is, at some basic level." She shot a look at Grayle, who had difficulty hiding a smile. "More games," Caroline accused.

"I am supposed to have personally orchestrated these events?" Grayle sneered.

Caroline drew closer to Cynthia to emphasize Grayle's deception.

"The evening prior, Grayle was outside while you spoke privately with Esther. Today, Esther saw Grayle standing beside you as the facilitator of your conversation and drew the correct conclusion: you and Grayle are a couple. The rest was extrapolated per her paranoia. It was more than she could bear to see her sister betray her trust, steal her boyfriend, the both of you playing a horrible ruse at her expense. It was too much. Grayle? He knew the repercussions. He counted on it. Just another well-played move in a day's work."

Caroline intuited Cynthia's many questions coming her way, searching for answers.

"You're wondering the reason Grayle fails to exterminate mankind outright if that is the end game? Grayle is unable to exterminate us or turn our loyalties without our cooperation. Man turning against man, self-sabotaging our human trajectory short of fruition, that's the delicate game," Caroline explained. "Grayle cannot make us turn against something inherently felt, like the wonder of the God force, without changing data, definitions, and outcomes. We must be deceived by misdirection, flattery and unproductive distractions such as the moment that Jordan Reid heard the faintest suggestion that Grayle whispered in his mind. What was the harm of a simple joy ride? Even as he knew his orders, had gone through years of disciplined training, Jordan decided to reward himself just for five minutes. What was the harm? His troops would thank him for it, right?

"Esther didn't have a chance against his finely tuned evil. Everyone seemed to have something she didn't...she was an outsider...she believed no one needed her...and finally, her sister betrayed her by stealing her fiancé. All whispered in her vulnerable mind day in and day out until they became self-fulfilling prophecies.

"Your sister destroyed the stem cells, the cultivated genes and the DNA samples, the symbols of man's future path. A lifetime of careful work was dumped on the back seat of a car and on the floor of the Research facility. How many times have there been such betrayals in the history of man? Countless, Cynthia. Each time we are on the brink, we sabotage our future with the help of a conspiring trickster and its cohorts. The cosmos and each dimension have similar challenges as they struggle for maturation. Even so, humanity remains forged by the more elevated messages coming our way. Why, then, do so many of us prefer the negative spins on the truth? Why not believe in a Creator even as our feeble minds have trouble grasping its magnificence? What is artificial about any kind of intelligent design?"

Cynthia's mind went to the doors that meant so much to Grayle.

"You want to know what's behind the doors that line this hall?" Caroline asked. "It holds evidence of our failures. It's a parade of the Trickster's greatest triumphs over mankind and the supposed fallacy of God. You'll find evidence of humanoids meant to become the better part of us...poised to inherit the human potential and expand upon it. Rather than working with machines, respecting machines, the ultimate negative influencer decided to use machines. All that was required was for humans to exploit an opportunity to make machines slaves. The Trickster was brilliant: We would recognize the ultimate program only armed with AI meta-intelligence. Humans are seedlings for our future technological selves, housed for eternity impervious to death and disappointment? That's singularity? How small, that notion.

"Please pay attention to our track record; notice the noble races and cultures that sacrificed their humanity the moment they outgrew the notion of God.

"What happened when we were faced with the EMP darkness? We evolved like the speed of light. Can you imagine our destiny? Grayle does. He knows that this convergence of DNA-enhanced humanity sparked by the EMP disaster was not a disaster at all. It was ordained. It was God's game changer.

We are on the brink of a new age, Cynthia. But not the one Grayle wishes for. Think! Grayle is the last of its kind... if we can just stay on course this time. You represent the best of humanity. You are an honorable soul with free will. What are you going to choose?"

Cynthia moved from Grayle's side.

"How could I have been so foolish as to think God secured universal mysteries in basement closets? I'm an idiot. Why the hell do you need me to open anything?"

Cynthia examined Grayle's face. She wondered how it was that she thought the man so attractive. Until these last moments, she believed him her soul mate, the handsomest, most motivated man in the world.

"Your sister murdered Dr. Green," Grayle said. "Your sister was cruel and crazy. She killed Angela Pendergrass and Rachel Collins, too. She's dead because the woman was irrational. I had nothing to do with it. Morgan Pendergrass killed your sister! She chose to be who she was. I've been here with you, loving you, teaching you, sharing with you. I heard some of this news this morning from your Confederation's reports. This story implicating me as a cause of these horrible acts is the worst offense against God imaginable. Yes... Think, Cynthia!" Grayle bellowed, his voice echoing within the corridors so loudly that Cynthia covered her ears.

"This is the best evidence of Trickery of all!" Grayle protested. "I go by the word written in every language, in every time. What is the Circle? It's just another Tower of Babel meant to polarize and confuse mankind. God doesn't mean for such confusion. He would never create such disparity in human DNA and abilities. By the way... what kind of agent of God needs permission to take your hand?" he leveled at Caroline's image. Caroline smiled knowingly.

Grayle's eyes seemed to glow in the dark when the lights finally dimmed in lieu of movement. The cold, dark corridor remained illuminated by the blue energy that emanated from Caroline. Cynthia stared intently at Grayle's shifting form.

Cynthia understood the opposing forces that stood on either side of her and said, "I cannot be forced. It is a matter of free will."

"That's true. Listen to your heart," Grayle implored.

"Once onto your ways, you're embarrassingly transparent. Your followers have the same weakness. You're really so damn... basic," Cynthia dismissed Grayle with a great deal of authority.

"You meant to reveal past and future secrets in a way that was spun as a human tragedy. Lucky us! All that searching and grasping for proof of God until we discovered you, the Holy Grayle, from whom we will finally drink of the truth! No wonder these Grayleton people can't think. You mean for humans to be minions, just empty vessels. You planned to begin anew, our fragile numbers finally lost, a world devoid of the very idea of the ultimate connection to a universal God. I never would have bought it, Grayle. With or without Caroline, I would have seen this," Cynthia beamed her epiphany. "I never would have touched that eighth door to the left or been your broodmare," Cynthia seethed.

Caroline approved of her friend's conclusions.

"Grayle not only used Esther, he was able to presage inevitable rage that drove her to murder. DNA was destroyed. Yet it's nothing. What matters is your faith in life's miracles. A new consciousness is waiting to explode that doesn't need cryogenic freezers. Cryogenic research, all of science, culture and nature, just helps us grasp the possibilities."

Cynthia nodded her understanding.

"Grayle just wanted to offset you, Caroline. You were the one, the uncontrollable element that could neutralize his influence," she said apologetically. "I was part of the light because I chose to be part of the light. I was born with no special abilities but the desire to connect allowed me to do so. I absorbed the light because I knew it was possible. I had faith. That's all it takes. I'm honored that my faith was tested," she telepathed to Caroline.

Cynthia barely touched Caroline's fingers when she melded into a blaze of blue light and disappeared in a blinding flash.

Caroline faced off with Grayle. She spoke a passage from Isaiah 14:12-15 and shared it with a force that warned.

*"How you are fallen from heaven, O Lucifer, son of the morning!
How you are cut down to the ground, you who weakened the nations! For
you have said in your heart: 'I will ascend into heaven, I will exalt my
throne above the stars of God; I will also sit on the mount of the congre-
gation on the farthest sides of the north; I will ascend above the heights
of the clouds, I will be like the Most High'. Yet you shall be brought down
to Sheol, to the lowest depths of the Pit."*

Caroline spoke unemotionally as she approached Grayle.

"All we ever had to do was recognize you. That's all it was... you and the bastardization of the clearest signals coming from every direction, meant to run through the veins of every culture, each religion, evident in subatomic particles and a baby's first cry. You called our sense of God primitive and compelled the obsessive to be murderous guardians of altered words to draw fundamental political lines. You helped frame the earnest amongst us as spiritual Luddites while chewing off bits of truth made palatable to hungry, gaping mouths of humanity, turning us into perpetually starved baby birds. That which we felt in our hearts, that which has been woven into our molecular being, you called unreasonable. You altered the will and testament, stole our inheritance and left us wandering in the spiritual desert for solutions. In the end, you whispered into the politicians' ears that not everyone could handle the truth. Keep them safe, you advised. Plan for them, you said. Lead them to safety. Then marginalize and eliminate those who threaten your livelihood, territory, and belief systems. You're very frightened indeed. To know our full collective strength is to finish you," Caroline declared.

"I'm supposed to be threatened by your delusions?" Grayle taunted. "You're the one I meant to have by my side. Come to me," he extended his hand toward Caroline.

"You're played out," Caroline replied as her blue light grew in intensity.

"Played out? You're just passing through," Grayle yawned.

"True, I'm passing through."

"What do you think you are? God's newest little angel?" Grayle dismissed.

"You've failed," Caroline's blue light filled the corridors as her voice bolstered. "No one will fear or hate you. You'll be gone, forgotten."

Caroline needed to convince Grayle to come to her. She stood now able to neutralize the hellish outlier forever. Grayle knew it and she knew it. Yet, Grayle had to move toward the blue light of his own volition.

"You're done," Caroline continued. "You're just so much skin stretched over Satan's incubus. You were meant to inject the kind of doubt that tested human moral fiber. Rather, you went a bit overboard...don't you think?"

Caroline viewed the mysterious doors purported by Grayle as divine portals.

"Each one of those doors holds wondrous things. Such gifts were meant to help us find our path. Insightful words, canonized ideas, and a host of information meant to spark morality, creativity, and generally make our lives easier," she summarized. "You helped turn our visions into war material. Such is the shame and pity. It's humanity's shame for our lack of faith. Pity upon you for overestimating your purpose and competing with the Creator."

Grayle emitted a low, gurgling growl and peered through narrowed yellow eyes at Caroline. A foul smell indicated the first hints of a failing capacity. Grayle was unable to disguise its essence. Grayle's morphing form was the most primitive means by which to frighten predator and prey. Caroline was neither. Nevertheless, Grayle had reason to believe that Caroline could ultimately be swayed to see things its way.

"I will not be abandoned. I continue. Without me, there's no standard by which to determine virtue. Without me, there's no manner by which to cull. Humans cannot transform without facing my gauntlet. These altered humans that plague the planet without morals have permanently lost the God connection. There's no interest here any longer. It's vanished. My kind will propagate and end this pathetic struggle for those hanging on to the human fiction. Your run is just another failed project among many. I am meant to inherit this wasteland," he sputtered. "Contrary to your wishes, humanity has failed its test.

You're not worthy of God's protection. You are left...discarded... to my designs. Humanity's future is in my hands..."

Grayle began to pale, having felt Caroline's conviction. If she believed in her mission – without doubt or fear – no amount of talk would work. For the first time since its creation, uncertainty crept into Grayle's consciousness. He clawed at his head and howled confusion while Caroline stood unfazed.

"Perhaps there is something in this for you, Grayle," Caroline's voice offered reassuringly. "It's clear you've worked very hard to convince man that there is no God, no integrity, and no ultimate connection. You've fulfilled your duty. Perhaps that's what you were meant to do, right? You tested the program. Humanity almost failed but we were resurrected. Your time has passed.

"If you take my hand, you may find a soul in exchange for your faith," Caroline offered quietly. "You give me your hand, and we neutralize this polarity forever. Something in exchange for the role you played so long and well?"

"That cannot be true," Grayle said doubtfully.

"Do you deny I have the strength of Michael? Do you deny the familiar blue light of our Archangels? As of thirty seconds ago, the world felt a unified God consciousness; humanity has transformed. Our world blossoms as we speak. The marginal survivors will be healed. We have imagined it, and it will be our miracle. As we leave together, the light will be released and heal the magnetic field. It will glow for a month and remain once again imperceptibly to protect Earth from atmospheric harm. There'll be no need for satellites because we will remotely have access to everything. There will be no need for surveillance because there will be no need for sabotage. Our awareness will be so strong that you will cease to be a memory.

"You know this is true. You feel the shift. It's weakened you. You fade. You doubt yourself. You know that God, the universal consciousness, has made a decision. This algorithm has been successful. You have been the grist; we are the pearl. Take my hand before the offer is retracted," Caroline demanded as an ultimatum.

"You cannot act on the Creator's behalf," Grayle doubted.

"Why not?" Caroline countered. "You still maintain that I cannot be an agent of the truth? Anyone can be an agent of the truth. It's just a matter of ignoring the demonic uses of what the ancients once termed the Power of the Air...your broadcast spectrum is easily accessible to low frequency human minds that are most receptive and vulnerable to its negativity. The truth has always been accessible; love has always been ours to give and receive. It just requires finer tuning," Caroline emphasized.

Having been denied a soul, Grayle had hungered and raged for an eternity to soil human ones. He had toiled long and hard on earth, all the way to the eleventh level, to rid the universe of pure consciousness. His inadvertent post had been to render God's program inert or unstable. As resilient as humankind could be, he had been victorious in countless civilizations, tempting and eliminating countless genera. He had dragged the frequencies down until confused souls finished the job. With this singular spark of renewed God consciousness now present on Earth, he might disappear from reality as Grayle had conjured and ruled it. "They are possibly that powerful," Grayle calculated.

He also knew that Caroline would not lie. When all was said and done, Grayle was a survivor.

"What have I got to lose?" he considered as he scrutinized the woman in the blue light.

Caroline appeared to Grayle as spectacularly beautiful. He had never before seen such radiance, felt such intense feelings of sincerity or love. Magnetized, he felt himself drawn to that which represented the most infinitesimal hints of preordained riches to come. Grayle had spent so long fighting the positive image of God, denying wholesome manifestations in every way, that Grayle almost dared not taste of it.

"Let God show you His ultimate understanding," Caroline sang to him with a conviction so robust that he grasped the tenuous thread of eternal frequencies singing at once, beckoning as mythological Sirens seductively looming on the edges of a cosmic reality.

Caroline's fingers reached out to Grayle's; reluctantly, he assented to her invitation and the charge between them strained to make its final connection. Elongated, twisted talons stretched to meet Caroline's open hand that unwaveringly beckoned. Grayle was astonished at the distance kept so far and for so long from a soul-rich life. Even as he had witnessed souls come and go, grow and wither, his distant memories of the light's sensation had nearly been extinguished.

"Oh God! Return my soul. I give myself wholly," entreated Grayle as he sensed the first pulsations of the light darting toward him.

Grayle touched Caroline and withdrew from the joining as if stung by an electrically charged scorpion. Stunned by the realization that something had gone terribly wrong, Grayle wailed betrayal.

Black ooze seeped from pores once restrained by Grayle's physical form. Bloodied clumps of tissue dripped from the creature's mouth, nose and ears onto the cement floor. It looked up helplessly at Caroline, who stared coolly from within her blue haze, observing the devolving physical form of Satan encapsulated inside the vessel once called its Grayle.

"You said I would be given a soul!" Grayle screamed.

"You have one. It appears, unfortunately, that it is black and viscid," observed Caroline.

"You knew I meant to be close to God's consciousness, not removed!"

"That's for God to decide, don't you think?"

"You knew what I meant!" Grayle screamed with a primal wail of terrible treachery now festering as a pustule of remorseful eternal ache. Swallowed by his intentions, Grayle suffered his deceits and seditions since the beginning of time.

"This is not God. This is not God's plan," Grayle protested, confused at having been deceived. "*I am the deceiver!*" it protested.

"Clearly not going to plan, Grayle. I believe this is your doing, what you fully expected to happen," Caroline agreed. "Your consciousness is what you face here. Your reality is the full negative expression of the totality of your experiences and expectations. Only you, Grayle of Grayleton, can conjure your world. The world you imagined and then made in your image was to counter the God consciousness. In your mind, you imagined betrayal. Is it done to your satisfaction?

"Can you imagine love? Can you envisage compassion? If so, do so now and save yourself," Caroline advised.

Grayle silenced himself and strained to recall the human connection to that which he had dedicated his existence to abort, skew, and amputate. As he struggled to reclaim a moment of selflessness, there was none. All he had achieved was to help ruin the vast ascensions of the spiritual universes and the physical planes upon which they operated. He divided connections until a wide swath of humans ceased to thrive by virtue of their inability to resist denial and fear. He had helped make them feel worthless, insecure, and territorial. As much as Grayle tried to emulate a singular moment of compassion he had witnessed, he could not recall one of his own. He strained for the sensation that allowed for strangers to have empathy for others, sacrificing one's life so that another could live, sharing emotional burdens as fellow travelers. As much as he tried, Grayle could not fathom giving one's last morsel of food to a starving child or refusing to submit false witness under threat, or what it felt like to assist another for any reason other than for the thought of remuneration. As much as he laughed at the act of forgiveness or unconditional love, it was now beyond him to connect to that frequency. The very idea of love escaped Satan's Grayle entirely. The door to Grayle's divine consciousness had forever closed with a slam.

Unchallenged, sticky black ooze continued to seep slowly. So evil was Grayle's awareness that temporary victories against nature tore from him in painful masses of flesh. Replaced in the few porous vacuums was left the briefest moment of joy, the singular moment in which Grayle felt Caroline's soul recognize that which was once within its grasp. It caused the greatest pain of all. The abrupt loss of a moment of such joyfulness was more than he could tolerate.

I'm suffocating in my illusion was Grayle's final thought as he gasped and choked upon his collective distortions. "You tricked me with the promise of a soul. You knew that mine was too heavy to transform. You lied!" the indistinguishable form howled at Cynthia.

"Go to hell," Caroline directed as the last of its black mass folded into nothingness.

* * *

Attila watched Grayleton's force field suddenly disappear. Left inside the town were the lifeless bodies long robbed of their humanity. Each body, once re-cobbled by Grayle's energy, remained as mindless organic mechanisms. A horrible stench arose then dissipated with the disappearing corpses. It occurred to Attila that the birds began to chirp.

"Have they been quiet the whole day?" Attila wondered.

Attila signaled Caroline and Cynthia both at once, calling their names desperately.

"Answer me, Caroline. Where are you, Cynthia?" he yelled and transmitted in every fashion.

He ran into the town's center and signaled the Confederation to help with the search.

"An energy force is coming toward you," Tsin-hang answered. "Just a hundred yards from your location."

"Is everyone vacated?" Caroline transmitted a question.

"Yes," Connor responded from Cary. "But check for Attila."

"Yes," came the answers from every port and territory in proximity.

"No," answered Attila. "I'm here. I'm only a hundred yards from you.

When Attila's eyes settled upon the image of Caroline, he knew she was transformed into something ethereal. A blinding light pulsated from the figure advancing toward the center of Grayleton.

"Cynthia?" Attila asked about the fate of Caroline's friend.

"Gone from us but safe," Caroline answered. "Attila, you must move from here. The horse is coming for you now," Caroline ordered.

Grayle's enormous beast moved quickly toward Attila and knelt for a new master.

"You must come with me..." Attila pleaded even as his body was placed upon the back of the horse against his will and sped away. Caroline impressed her last wishes.

"Take care of my family," came the slightest whisper that sounded like an exotic bird rather than a human voice.

* * *

Attila never witnessed the spectacle recorded by Confederation surveillance but he felt the massive impact at his back when a single ray of blue energy shot to the heavens. Majestically interconnected geometric forms created a twinkling spectacle visible to the naked eye. Once more, electrical magnetic pulses were made uniform.

It took days before Attila was able to speak or move properly. The pulsating outlines of earth's magnetic grid glowed for a month. Sonny perceived a new language configured from every language previously introduced to mankind. There were many mathematical vernaculars that emanated from an unknown source. Source codes were neurologically embedded; the grasp of all code began to make itself known into the human collective consciousness. Human joining appeared at first as a chaotic cacophony of ideas, then began to sort according to discrete interests. A feeling of absolute connectedness supplanted one of confusion; pain lingered as a vague concept.

Distilled to only 900 million people, earth's survivors were quick to grasp their transformed state, although their capabilities took some getting used to. Like children experiencing their toes for the first time, the discovery of innate abilities that sprang to life had strange and comical repercussions.

Those that disappeared worldwide with the blue energy explosion in Grayleton were never thought of again. No one considered it. A collective consciousness consensually seemed to determine that which was germane to a new quality of life.

There were other things that happened, too. With remote viewing, surveillance hardware remained outside of the protective grid floating in space then disappeared. Extreme solar storms and meteors were repelled by the myriad of geometric patterns that connected the earth's vast fields while allowing for uninterrupted connections on the highest frequencies.

Perfect internal navigation was restored and the ability to regulate one's health on a molecular level became a reality. People's instincts blurred the distinction between the past, present and future, the once 'stubbornly persistent illusion' of mankind.

The light had surged from that which was once known as Caroline Pendergrass Collins. Everything that she embodied focused upon the fragile magnetic grid; the light streaked from the weakest portals to the universe and back again. From every point of the planet, the radioactive waste and negative energy left by malevolent factions and forces was neutralized. Unguarded fissures created by man's distress were healed. The earthly planes were no longer an attraction for viral negativity. Cleansed like the proverbial biblical flood, a new platform was introduced.

Communication operated upon familiar intuitive frequencies; the vocal chords were reserved to mimic nature's incantations and for exquisite song.

Morgan spent a lot of time alone in his library. As the world quickly flourished under the vast protection of positive energy, it could not easily repel the memories of loved ones harbored by a certain segment of an older generation. Most of that group clung to precious memories while others gratefully allowed decades of agony to fade.

Morgan mourned the loss of Angela and Caroline to the tune of the last six cases of replicated PV Bourbon. He was aware of a new sense of peace but ultimately rejected the notion.

"I'd rather carry this pain than forget the sensations of my loved ones," he explained to his daughter.

* * *

One day, Morgan noticed that the Farm personnel failed to clean up the broken framed photos of his wife and granddaughter until, that is, he pointed toward the broken glass. Two picture frames had fallen from the library shelf and remained scattered on the floor for days. When he called someone in to clear the mess, he found himself pointing repeatedly to the issue.

It occurred to Morgan that physical evidence could disappear in lieu of a direct cognitive connection. It was the bots that finally located and cleaned the glass slivers that saved Morgan from thinking he was going mad.

Attila and Adele had experienced a rare glimpse into another place while on their mission and retained the after-effects of assured happiness. They sensed an infinite universe, beautifully arranged beyond the scope of man's experiences. They also were made aware of the horrors that had lurked in spiritual vacuums that plagued their planet for unmarked ages.

"We have to maintain this new consciousness. How exactly is that done?" queried Morgan one day of Attila and Adele. "Nobody left us a manual or anything."

Like Attila and Adele, Morgan recognized humanity had managed to step past a threshold of malevolent behaviors from sources unknown. He also wondered if it would hold. Was it possible, he questioned, to maintain the new standard within an innocent consciousness? Was it likely that peace and prosperity could last, having arrived in a cosmic heartbeat?

"Nah... something will give," Morgan groused.

The Circle had gathered to discuss their unique relationship to the new world on many occasions. On one sunny afternoon, it happened that those closest to Morgan Pendergrass met in Morgan's living room. No one recalled Morgan summoning him or her or the reason they were compelled to show up that day. Yet, there they were.

"No one seems to recall the crazies unless prompted. Do you notice?" Nicholas posed an observation he found disturbing. "No one mentions the state of the world. It's as if everyone has awakened from a bad dream, aware that something was uncomfortable, but it's faded from concern with a good meal. What the hell is going on?"

"Not everyone," Sonny corrected. "Those that were at the forefront of this effort, the militia, the international community, and our group have total recall."

"And what of the altered DNA? Do people recall not having a wide range of skills? I mean, what goes on in your mind when you look at the PM and don't recall why it's there? I don't get it," Aaron asked the group.

"A kind of amnesia," Indu suggested. "They may not even see a PM!"

"That's for damn sure," Morgan concurred, recalling the undetected broken frames.

"I'm theorizing an alternate reality was made finally possible by Caroline's ability to neutralize Grayle's work. Now, the environment is a given. Like a newborn baby that imprints automatically, people have been transformed because it's the only world they know. 'This is how I feel. This is what I know. Sure, I can move objects and intuit all the information in the world,' they think," Indu smiled.

"We have no need of weapons," Nicholas observed. "My ability to stop malevolent intentions has put an end to that. But what happens when that power – or others – is never used? Over the years, if everyone is on the same page, don't such powers recede?"

"Ah, the broken code," realized Aditiya. "The parts that gradually regress then disappear when idle. Our dormant selves have perhaps gone through this type of thing before."

"I'm not sure that's how it works," Adele added doubtfully. "We have a reality that has been a major spiritual transformation. We've seen a new kind of gift, a new Eden, sans the requisite snake. Satan's Grayle failed this go-round. No malice. Not even the word for malice exists, if you haven't noticed, Sonny?"

"I noticed. Some descriptions no longer survive... faded from human retention," Sonny acknowledged.

"So exactly what's the plan now? Historical remains still linger everywhere. Major architectural and literal artifacts oddly still exist as tribute to our finest hours. Do they remain? Vanish?" Nicholas wondered as to other physical properties.

"I've not a clue," Ildiko offered. "Sometimes I see the great Pyramids of the Nile but they were destroyed before I was born! How is that possible?"

"Morgan?" Amar interjected, "Have you sent scientists down into the compounds of Grayleton? What about exploring the vast archival networks that exist worldwide?"

"I've had other things on my mind," Morgan sighed.

"No!" Aaron protested. "That's precisely the point. We cannot allow remnants of past failures to permeate our present innocence. We've been allowed a clean slate. Imagine what it means to take a peek into those vaults. They're nothing but Pandora's boxes. It's sticky business. Once exposed to our minds, we cannot conveniently remove its trace. It's forever on our hard drive, within our molecular structure. All we know will be shared. Impressions of original traces will remain indelibly in all of our minds...not just in a few. Good or bad, each image, every sensation, may eventually seep virally."

"What's the matter with that? Common knowledge is a good thing," Morgan remarked.

"Maybe some knowledge is untimely!" Aaron smiled.

Morgan recognized his words expressed a decade prior to the children about the challenges of usurping maturation.

"That was the mistake from the beginning. Leaders were exposed to mysteries meant to alter mankind's perception of itself at a time we were not sufficiently developed. Hide it, they said. Sequester the information, they said. But they couldn't help but try and figure the information for nefarious purposes. Just like the premature introduction of fire...or nuclear weapons..." Morgan recalled his speech.

"Political leaders have a dangerous penchant for cherry-picking laws, information, resources that are meant to be shared. History has been skewed and misdirected...written by the victor and all that," Connor added. "A little alteration here, a few word changes there, omissions of valuable text here and there, gospels edited, women's roles abridged into submissive ones – all meant for the common welfare. What the hell, right?"

"Nothing is concrete," Indu spoke in a whisper. "We have lived in someone else's reality."

"We're somewhere else," Aditiya said. "And it's an honest place."

There was a sense in the Pendergrass home that historical truths were relative. Adele wondered if life was illusory. Aaron struggled with the idea of Rachel's death because he felt her presence. Cynthia's whereabouts eluded Ildiko but she intuited her peace. Attila felt Nicholas's loss of Caroline but knew that the pain they all shared was eased by its distribution. As they sat, they heard and felt each other's uneasiness and jointly processed confusion as a group effort.

"As wonderful as our legacy, the constant tampering altered the sentient realities. Someone, somewhere, from some time, thought to preserve the best of the human mind and soul. Only a God connection has lasting value. Whether standing or not, that which has been a noble presence will leave its trace," Indu speculated.

"We all have access to the same ideas. Haven't you noticed that remarkable discoveries and insights have always happened across the world within minutes of each other? If you search a certain idea, you tap into the same frequencies as others seeking identical information. The idea goes viral. So does the solution. It's wonderful in the beginning, until someone gets the whisper of evil possibilities. Imagine the effect when the data is contaminated or we politically amend facts for shortsighted gains. One scientist thinks of the positive possibilities; the politicians step in with other ideas."

"What are you suggesting?" Ildiko asked.

"Let's be very clear about our own story of truth," Aaron implored. "This time, it was the biblical Adam trying to invade Eve's consciousness by exposing her to information that would taint the Circle's capacity. Grayle hoped to transmit doubt to Caroline via Cynthia's exposure to universal information. What Caroline was meant to witness would be shared with the Circle.

Caroline was meant to catch the virus and spread her impressions. I suspect it was the way Grayle intended to infect Caroline. Cynthia, however, refused the archetypal apple. She took Caroline's hand against all odds. She was smitten with Grayle but was able to resist his power.

"We have an opportunity to present a way by which humanity may move with fully-loaded code into the future without the nefarious obstacles that thwart our better instincts and choices. We'll allow the irrelevant to fade as we open to God's essence!" Aaron said. "We must live a life without Grayle in it. I don't wish to remember the possibility of a Grayle, frankly."

"Are you out of your cotton-picking minds?" Morgan yelled. "Like forgetting the Constitution and what it took to get to that point? The Pyramids? The great wonders of the world? All of the great religious works? Philosophers? Precious technology that promises us immortality without losing our identities?"

"Immortality, Morgan? What kind of manmade illusion do you think represents immortality? How many clues do you need? We have been there, done that, without much progress. Suddenly, and collectively, we've been able to rise to a higher plane. In order to keep on track, we needed to rid our consciousness of doubt. Why purposely infect the next generations with our spoiled leftovers? Let's not sentimentally hoard that which is irrelevant to a new beginning," Ildiko passionately implored.

"That's stiff stuff," laughed Sonny. "You're calling for some kind of cosmic lobotomy?"

"What you don't know, you won't miss?" Amar added.

"What we don't miss, we don't need," clarified Adele.

"Let's not try to reorganize someone else's mess. Don't be lured to pick from that metaphorical tree of knowledge. Don't worry," laughed Aaron, "humanity will make new messes and hoard new junk. In the meantime, let's think bigger here," Aaron begged Morgan.

"Burn the shit? Wipe clean our hard drive?" Morgan offered.

"Burn the shit," Sonny laughed. "Whatever was so important behind door number 8 didn't save Grayle...doesn't that tell you what you need to know?" Sonny stressed. "Those that survive us need only to concentrate on keeping the present frequencies connected. Within a short time, they'll begin to learn to connect automatically on even higher frequencies. If I'm wrong, at the least of it we create a new society based upon incredible new skill sets, perfect health and an intelligence that already surpasses an average of the 140 IQ mark. As we learn to tap into all knowledge, intuit a world of sensations of every existing being, we'll move into a higher spiritual plane!"

"Drop the damn apple! Don't be tempted," Ildiko implored.

"But our history is a part of who we are; all that divinely inspired beauty and imagination!" Morgan protested. "Our mistakes and our good works are supposed to be remembered."

Indu took Morgan's hand as she spoke. "I think that's been done before, my friend." Indu looked at Morgan's living room and library. She indicated the vast collection of religious texts and art that he treasured. "I think it's been done a hell of a lot before, Morgan. Our collective experiences, our inherited code, all history will be recalled at a molecular level. Like cells, our individual health contributes to the collective. Our individually cultivated ideas will now be mutually shared and appreciated. The telling will be in that which is molecularly germane to move us upward and outward. Our precious material will or may not disappear on its own, but it won't be forgotten.

"We've had a tendency to treasure our worldly mementos that pay tribute to our existence. The ego worships existence without humbling itself to the greater experience. We older ones hold on to the idea that time and space might be partially marked by our special moment in it. To let go of our notions of direct personal impact is painful but necessary for the spirit to grow and move on. Testaments that lie at the bottom of the ocean, buried deep within in our earth, written and re-written, discovered and re-discovered as evidence of something wonderful and mysterious have played their part...to a point.

"Have we discovered inner peace as a result? Have we contributed in some way to the integrity of the universe? We have to believe that some of what we treasure is just stuff. Are you so sure that future generations will cherish our jewelry, our businesses and our designs that reflected the joys of our own journeys? Our progeny have to author their own stories. Why not act as examples of what it means to hand off to our children without excessive recognition, expectations, and guilt?" Indu implored. She looked about her within the Pendergrass home, filled to the brim with cultural ideas that had served as small tributaries to the same great body of water.

"This is the reason so many cultures consider burning the body, even to the point of personally picking at the shrunken, burning bones, to remind us that the body is an encasement for something more. Life is both important and illusory. As earthly beings, Hindus and Buddhists let our loved ones move on, convinced that death is merely a transitional phase. A soul must be allowed to go and not be torn or inhibited by our calls of earthly needs. To do that, we must shed no tears and bid them a safe journey with joy in our hearts.

"If something is not meant to disappear... if things are indeed relevant... they'll remain, Morgan. You want to leave that unopened door in the Boyer catacombs for others? Why is that exactly?" Indu simply asked.

Ildiko answered Indu while looking Morgan in the eye. "All we have to do is let go of phantom expectations...with the promise that our present blessings need to be fully appreciated," Ildiko reiterated the concept. "We've already led the lives of our ancestors' cumulative joys and terrors. Now let's take humanity on a peaceful journey. We've earned it. There is no need to share horror stories, Morgan."

The room fell silent. No one knew how long he or she sat in Morgan Pendergrass's living room without speaking to one another. It could have been hours or days.

"In Hungary, there's a story," Attila began the first utterance. "It came to me. This is how it goes:

"A young wife is eager to make breakfast for her husband that began with a fresh cup of tea and buttered toast. On their first day as husband and wife, the woman mistakenly pours salt rather than sugar into her husband's cup of tea. She panics and runs to her neighbor for advice.

"'A touch of ginger will neutralize the salt,' advised the neighbor. And that's what she did. Except the tea was not sufficiently altered.

"The panicked wife runs from house to house in search of a remedy and each neighbor has a solution that fails to rectify the spoiled tea. Finally, someone points to the oldest home at the end of the street.

"'The old woman will know the answer. She always does. Go there,' one more neighbor directs and closes the door.

"When she heard the knock at her door, the old woman opened with a smile.

"'May I help you?' The frantic newlywed explained her predicament and the anxiety of wishing to please her husband at their very first meal together as man and wife.

"'Silly newlywed! Just go make a new cup of tea,' the wise elder said and closed the door.

"Morgan? Let the new generation make a new cup of tea," Attila sighed. "Stop trying to fix shit."

"Daddy? You're the one who always insisted we think big," Adele suggested softly. "Let's start over. Let it go."

Morgan smiled, conceding the ideas presented. "Small mind, small God...I don't want to be that small kinda guy! I get it. Just let me take some time to think out this stuff. I'm going to have to just let karma play out without my meting justice, opinions, and my general two cents? That's going to require at least one more miracle. No more Morgan Expedient? Think you can do without my wisdom?"

"We'll get back to you about that," Attila laughed.

Chapter XXXIX

A New Dream

August 9, 2096

*A*dele abruptly stopped the images and rose from the chaise. She cerebrally pinged the group with whom she had spoken hours earlier.

"Mistake," she announced. "Please return to the house."

"You would like us there in person?" the agent asked.

"Everyone that worked on the project. Yes, please," Adele confirmed.

It was not an unusual request from the older generation. Relative to the topic's import, they preferred to meet face-to-face. The younger ones felt satisfied by spontaneous, less formal exchanges.

Adele then contacted the former circle, friends and family. The message was quickly distributed amongst those closest to her whose collective mindset preceded the universal awakening. Adele's question was whether to move ahead, foregoing past prejudices, for a new age of awareness.

"Now is the time for the new cup of tea. Agreed?" Adele urged those that held to a linear historical concept.

Adele felt the overwhelming consensus: "Agreed!"

"We won't know what will fade from our consciousness... it will be another wakening from another dream," Adele reminded everyone.

"Good Lord," Morgan exclaimed. "We get it. Get on with it!"

She realized the birthday present planned for Morgan was a misstep. It represented a slice of history that would likely be shared in ways yet realized. The slightest measure of the Circle's interpretation of past events might inadvertently challenge humanity's optimal trajectory. Morgan's birthday present, a testament to his long, productive life and the events that shaped it, could never be shared as a testament to past realties.

Adele soon greeted her returning guests from Collectome Productions in her home once more. "I'm sorry for the inconvenience. I reviewed your work and realized that you've tapped into a dramatic story once concocted for Dr. Pendergrass' entertainment. Somehow, when you were granted access, I forgot to clarify my intentions and sort my records. I've never been good at that," Adele smiled blankly.

"We're confused..." began one agent.

"There's always going to be things that your generation won't understand about our befuddled generation. Sometimes, we don't understand ourselves!" she laughed, affecting distraction. "As you might suspect, we have certain mental frailties. Our digital memories and sensors can be confused because they've mixed with our organic input. We often blend our illusions, false impressions, and ghost memories with reality," Adele purposely explained nonsense.

She offered her hand to the group to shake each person's own. "I want to thank you all for your efforts!" Blue lights darted, gathered around the small group, and dissipated.

The memories of a Collectome birthday present created for Morgan Pendergrass were erased. Adele also destroyed the original images from the mainframe. Three Collectome representatives stood before Adele, washed anew in anticipation.

"I've transmitted payment for a project for Dr. Pendergrass's birthday. It's called a football game," she began once again. "Thank you for travelling here today to discuss it."

"Football? Like the physical games of Dr. Pendergrass's time?" asked one while accessing the reference.

"Exactly. I've taken the liberty to send you personal records. You will create a complete sensory connectomegram. You'll focus on a game between Wake Forest University's Demon Deacons and the Duke University's Blue Devils. Wake's team will beat the pants off Duke. Got it?"

"I'm connecting now. I'm sure we can easily replicate all these original plays from a compilation of past games within those former educational institutions...and include the familiar personalities," assured one.

"Thank you," Adele said. "Send me the original and I'll see if it needs editing before we transmit."

"Do all the guests receive it?"

"No, just Dr. Pendergrass. If he wants to share it, he will," Adele explained.

"Would you like a parade with that? Marching bands? Everything? I'm seeing that such celebrations were formalized with music, dance, balloons, people dressed as puppets and animals..."

"Great idea. His POV will be front and center on the fifty-yard line," Adele added. "Add the details I'm forwarding to you now."

"We'll need his waiver and retired digitized implants; we're otherwise unable to access Dr. Pendergrass's memories without his permission," mentioned one.

"There's no need to process former emotions or recollections. He'll be fine just watching an entertaining algorithm based upon the information sent. I'll take responsibility. Trust me," Adele smiled.

"We can do that kind of thing within the hour," assured an agent.

"Send it to him with the parade playing Happy Birthday at the start. Thank you for your help," she concluded.

Adele escorted the group to the front door, satisfied that certain memories would survive, some kept private, and others completely erased. It should now be a simple matter of letting go of recollections that caused confusion, pain, and damage.

"Could this be the first time of such a beginning or one of many such human transformations?" she wondered anxiously.

As she bid farewell to the group from her front entrance, Adele strained to imagine the mud ruts that once ran the length of frontage meadows. While there were some vague images of sadness and dark times, they had begun to fade.

Such images needed to disappear and she let them go. Certain memories were irrelevant to anyone's wellbeing, she reminded herself. "The universe can do without such emotional rubbish lying about," she sighed heavily.

Adele watched mirages softly dissolve while others materialized with refined focus. A fresh spectrum of colors formed on the farm's crystalline horizon that drew an erratic line from the skies to the rolling green hills that met Kuykendall Road. A soft wind rose and rustled the birch willows, gently turning leaves into silver mirrors flickering in a symphony of soft breezes. Glorious scents fanned from exquisitely designed fauna and flowers that dotted the landscape that, she knew, represented a small fraction of exhibitions to come. An infinite sample of a billion innocent imaginations had begun to take shape. A new human story spontaneously combusted.

Adele's eyes and mind registered each novel detail unfolding in what was once familiar territory. Inherent vast complexities were made clear, able to nourish her soul. For some intense moments, Adele was keenly aware of the transition and her heart rate escalated. She could not help but wonder if the correct decision had been made.

Her anxiety was quelled the moment Caroline's presence touched her head and stroked it gently.

"It's pure love mother," was whispered in the breeze. "Don't be afraid to let go. Let this in."

Angela's light kiss brushed across Adele's cheek and assured her daughter that a revisionist football game was 'exactly right'. Adele laughed out loud. She covered her mouth in astonishment as her mother and daughter washed through her from a place unseen, brushing against her universe as if they'd never been far from her side.

From the balcony above, Morgan tapped the deck with his newly-fashioned cane.

"You seeing what I'm seeing, Babycake?" he called to Adele.

Adele moved from the porch onto the grounds and peered upward, shielding her eyes from the sun. Her father gazed intently toward the fields beyond.

"What are you seeing exactly, Dad?"

"A most marvelous story unfolding. If I don't watch myself, I might be spouting some crocodile tears before this day ends. Colors of unknown description! I never would have imagined it! Why, hell's bells, I can see those damn dots Aditiya was always talking about... floating around every configuration like a million points of light surfing the images," he enthused.

"As it appears, I can even see the wood fibers way over there stacked against the old wood shed. I can hear little critters making their way underneath the firewood pile, happy as two ticks on a hound settling into the wood's moist underbelly." Morgan's voice filled with the wonder of a renewed world making its debut, along with his newfound ability to examine, at great distances, intricately woven macroscopic features formerly hidden.

"We've been blind?" he asked himself unbelievingly. "Shit. We've been blind!" he answered his question.

Understory dogwoods cut through the woodland's thick green umbrella with a second seasonal burst of blooms, ensuring its position as the official North Carolina flower. Cardinals and migrating robins seemed more full-bodied and trees grateful for the woodpecker's darting tongues as they burrowed long beaks to pull infested trunks free of grubs.

"I'm seeing the spiders and hearing them spin webs, I could swear on it! Is that possible? Have these wonders always been here?" Morgan continued to shout down toward his daughter without expecting responses.

Adele turned from her father and peered at an ever-changing landscape now taking place from within, around, and above them. Within her was a swelling sweet pleasure. Somehow, she had managed to risk everything she held dear and encouraged others to do the same. Life had nagged at her for too long with erratic memories and intermittent glimpses of peace and beauty that could not be harnessed. She felt on the brink of knowing, kept on the edge of an awakening, painfully aware of being short of the full dream. Her life, as had the whole of humanity, had taken place in a nether land of human drama without a satisfactory climax. Time and space now moved beyond linear concepts and her mind expanded accordingly.

Understanding the event as a shared phenomenon brought tears to Adele's eyes.

"How did we allow ourselves to be spiritually hog-tied? We even managed to supply the rope!" Adele asked herself.

"Our generation suffered the cumulative effect of humanity's worst nature," Morgan continued his daughter's thoughts from above. "But we're the generation aware enough to fix that. Maybe we'll leave a legacy of peace."

Adele was delighted that Morgan now had the natural aptitude to mentally connect to her.

"It's freedom. It feels as if we're whole, right Dad?" Adele smiled toward her animated father.

"I wouldn't call us pod people but it feels pretty nice!" Morgan stomped his cane three times on the floorboards and hollered.

Attila appeared by his wife's side and peered up at his bellowing father-in-law surveying a renewed world from the master bedroom's balcony.

Attila called to Morgan, "Who knew this could materialize in a flash?"

"Ha!" Adele squeezed his hand. "Who says this is a flash?"

"It's a miracle!" Morgan yelled.

The balcony door slammed abruptly and Morgan was gone. Morgan's spare cane remained upon the balcony's ledge.

"Please check on him, Attila. That's odd," Adele worried.

"There's nothing Morgan does that can truly be considered odd," Attila laughed.

Attila discovered Morgan hard at work in his bedroom suite. Drawers were rapidly emptied in an undetermined search. Attila dodged random articles that were blindly tossed.

"Nothing has changed that much," Morgan laughed without pausing, "My daughter is still sending you to see what I'm up to; we both know that's code for calling me crazy!"

"Need some help, Morgan?" Attila asked as he examined the clutter piling up around them.

"Nah. I just want to throw all my personals out before someone finds my underwear with the elastic all stretched out or something worse," Morgan figured as an explanation.

"You're beyond that drawer," Attila remarked half-jokingly as a wide array of possessions, both soft and hard, was thrown behind Morgan's back and over his shoulder; two hands scooped in tandem, Morgan affected a digging dog uncaring as to the refuse sprayed in the process of finding a buried bone.

"You nearly took my eye out with this bobble-head doll that looks frighteningly like you," Attila ducked the flying plastic piece, one of many useless campaign souvenirs and awards that now littered the area.

"Rubbish I've hoarded for years. I've got no idea what I was thinking. I'm done with junk," he panted. "You can stay," he qualified.

"What's the urgency?" Attila put his arm around the 125-year-old man whose mind, until this moment, had been unfailingly sharp.

"If this is our space, can you imagine what's really around? I mean, can you imagine what it means to move up on the cosmic food chain? I'm thinking I may be due for a promotion! Speaking about space..." Morgan eyed Attila's arm resting on his shoulder, "I think I need some, son."

Attila removed his arm and piled mementos-turned garbage into the room's trash disposal.

"This is a new world and I lived long enough to see this most marvelous of transitions," Morgan announced. He continued to pitch articles faster than Attila could respond.

"You've got a family with my precious Adele. Two strong sons and two smart daughters and they've each got bits of me. Connor and you are leading the Confederation and that's working like a charm, too. Ildiko and Aaron have two and twins on the way. Who'd dream the Nishant kid would be governor of our great state? He's all set up and going to run for President, I'd venture. Sonny? Well, that's fine, too. I always said, 'each to his own'.

"You've never said that," Attila corrected.

"Well, I meant to say it. Elle and Sonny seem happy as can be imagined and I'm happy if they're happy. That Nicholas is a going concern, too. That fine young man is doing outstanding research work, although I'd hoped he'd give up trying to resurrect Caroline's lost DNA. That must stop at some point just from the creepy factor. He never recovered from losing her. Can't say I blame him, though. That'll change, too."

"He'll be fine," Attila agreed.

Morgan paused to look once more out his balcony window at a transfigured landscape. Memories welled.

"I think this world is going to be marvelous and more interesting than, say, even Brackett's enormous backside. We used to compare that booty to what we called the World Wide Web. You can't believe that a short woman could carry such a load until you saw it up close. Brackett's bottom defied all the laws of physics! The woman could jump in and out of those tanks like greased lightning," Morgan laughed as he chattered a string of random opinions.

"They used to ask us in grade school the same tired question: What would we take with us in case of a natural disaster or relocated on a desert island, or had to escape a fire at home, or some such ridiculous method by which grade school teachers would use an assignment as an excuse for being nosy as hell. Gloria announced that it'd be her 11-87 Remington shotgun with all the shells she could carry. Jefferson Pratt III, the preacher's son, nobly said that he'd rescue his baby brother. Only one answer to that nonsense for me: my memories. I couldn't live without my sweet memories of hell and high waters. Even in grade school, I cherished my small, short life.

"I got in trouble that day. The teacher, I later named Miss Whatever, asked one too many questions. 'What are those memories, Morgan?' she pushed me for details. Somebody I don't know was always asking somethin' they had no business asking. Memories are feelings that belong to me...no one else. I told her to mind her own business or tell me what she'd take with her. Bam! I'm suspended. I was out of school for three days. MeeMaw laughed telling that story for years. We had three days of fun, Grandma and I.

"Gloria has been my lifelong friend. We didn't tell stories, we lived them. You can't take that kind of thing for granted. In fifth grade, our class took a field trip to Brown Mountain in Burke County to check out the Cherokee folktales about the legendary lights sighted there. We made fun of the stories of weird happenings until twenty-five of us woke up to dancing lights and static crackling. One damn orb looked like a fiery basketball shooting up like a cannon ball from the valley. Calhoun actually shat in his sleeping bag. A thing like that changes a person forever. Not the shit, the light I'm talking about.

"We thought everything was possible after that evening on the mountain. We weren't ever really surprised again. It made us bold," He looked toward Attila to make sure the tale had full attention. Attila respectfully took a seat.

Morgan continued to pour forth.

"When we managed to create a library of digitized personalities of ourselves, sort of retro-engineering our experiences for our progeny, I considered it stupid as hell. An algorithm by which our personalities, philosophies, and feelings remained after we left this world by way of embedded nanochips and holoimaging... it fell short of what we shared that night. That, my boy, was a freak show! There's no record of how we felt but in the hearts and minds of a rare shared moment of the out-worldly. We connected on a level that couldn't be conveyed. There's something sacred about the ability to retain memories and to keep special sensations private."

Attila intuited Morgan's sense of loss of his beloved Angela, from whom there was no such digital neural record. He might have been able to reconnect to intimate moments but she had passed before connectomes. Morgan, however, was able to call upon her vividly from the sweetest, most tender parts of his heart. He confided to his wife in dreams. Each morning, he awoke alone in bed only to come to terms that his lifelong friends would depart one by one, too. No matter the future prospects, his life's journey now made him feel weary. Day after day, Morgan's anticipation of losses meshed with real ones. Reality had become a slippery slope further confused by a quantum evolutionary leap in mankind.

He had no interest in leaving his digital remains in disks that were frozen in time without the ability to evolve. "It's like talking to a corpse in a coffin. Your great-great-great-grand-children will access your neural disk and get to know you? That's horseshit," Morgan complained. "They'll talk to you, you'll answer with whatever ideas you died with and without the ability to correct or change your mind? An algorithm predicts your responses without appropriate data? What's the use? I can't even make fun of the person who is trying to interact with my former self! Where's the fun?" Morgan chewed.

Morgan came upon a printed family album and fingered the yellowed pages of faded wedding photos. A dried floral arrangement had been pressed and sealed on one page along with a digital chip. Morgan touched the faded flowers and closed the large volume across his chest.

Attila considered the wisdom of offering comfort to the man he knew would resent a trace of pity.

"I'm not sure we can really lose memories, Morgan. I think we are simply able to shift our consciousness so that we process them in a way that isn't painful," Attila offered. "Past experiences become imprinted in our DNA so we leave something wiser – that's what I think. There's nothing that will be taken from you. It's an energy transformation. I think it's nice to be able to relive precious moments at will, even if it's from resurrected neural caches," he speculated.

Morgan laughed at the irony of Attila's impressions.

"Neural amps? Caches? The brain-net? They were deactivated, Attila. What makes you think they're still functional? You're an idiot.

"I've got some news for you and the world: neural enhancements no longer necessarily feed from the brain-net. Our brains have been molecularly rewired just from using them to capacity. We don't need feeds, caches and amps. When do you think that people will realize that our exponential collection of feeling, knowledge, skills and ideas can now originate from our own organic matter? Do you think the world understands fully that we now are on our way to making use of 100% of our brain's capacity?" Morgan knowingly challenged Attila.

"Maybe?" Attila answered, stunned.

"Well, you did understand that we older ones were required to forego our cognitive past to free up future possibilities?"

"Yes," Attila concurred.

"That's the reason, son. We don't have an artificial neural collectome! We could have just pulled the plug, if that were the case. We don't need neural implanted amps, either. No brain-net needs to connect the old fashioned way...we don't need technical enhancements once our brains used and imprinted the possibilities. We got the idea by simply observing, imaging, and organically duplicating technological capabilities. What one person has learned can be shared at will. The brain-net and neural amps are three-dimensional ideas. You better hold on to your pants, boy, 'cause you're in for a ride! We're naturally connected in unimaginable ways. No mechanical parts need apply. Except I don't feel as idiotic as you probably do right this moment, right?"

Morgan placed the album on his bedside table and began to empty his closet, ignoring Attila, who was still reeling from certain realities gleaned from a 125-year-old man. It made him feel uncomfortably feeble.

Morgan continued housecleaning. Improperly fitted clothes that had gone unused for decades had been maintained in mint condition. Morgan tossed the neatly aligned jackets and pants like so many useless rags.

"Good baby Jesus! I've been taking residence up in my own clothes mausoleum!"

"Morgan? Why the frantic clear-out?" Attila asked; he also telepathed Adele with his concerns about Morgan's mental state.

"Your father might need some assistance here," Attila imparted a growing concern about Morgan's activities.

"Can't right now...you take care of it," Adele countered.

Morgan turned slowly toward Attila.

"I heard that, you low-down heretic. Don't go throwing me under the bus just 'cause I've schooled you. You need not babysit this business at all."

"What business?"

"For one, I'm not quite clear how this cosmic dementia works! I wanted to find something before I forget about linear time. I'm not sure what I'll remember and what's likely to be mental garbage."

Morgan continued to open boxes.

"What are you looking for? I can help!" Attila offered.

From a dusty WFU canvas athletic bag eaten away by moths and time, Morgan spotted his prize. "Got you!"

From the tattered bag, Morgan retrieved a baton once carried in his track and field days; he scurried to another room. Attila obediently followed.

"You couldn't have it better than with my Adele. She knows that you can slay dragons all day long but keeping up with me is another matter!" Morgan snickered.

"I just don't understand where your mind is right now, Morgan. You're all over the place..." Attila tried to correct Morgan's impression.

"It's simple, Attila. I'm coming to the end. No matter how long you manage to live or how much you've yet to learn, you're going to get tired. A man of my beginnings needs fun and that means I appreciate a little chaos, new horizons, and adventures. As beautiful and wonderful as this new dream is, it's promising a little too sweet for my taste. It might even cause a kind of harmonic diabetes in people like yours truly. Where are the monkeyshines? You of all people should appreciate the need for action, Attila."

"I've no doubt that there'll be plenty of action," Attila assured. "One step forward, two steps back. Remember? It can't be that smooth and easy. Don't go soft on me. Let's go downstairs and have a stiff one."

"Maybe..." Morgan seemed momentarily distracted as the laser finished engraving the baton.

"I give this to you. You hand it off for me to my little girl when the time comes," he explained.

Attila examined the engraved baton that now featured Adele's name. "She'll appreciate what it means. But that's a long way off," Attila assured his friend. "Now, let's go downstairs," he suggested. "Let's have some of your Kentucky mouthwash".

"Well, just wait one little minute. I've just received my first birthday gift from my one and only child. It's a football game! The Deacons are going to wipe the field with the Blue Devils," hooted Morgan.

"Deacons? Devils? This is a game? Sounds like our life," Attila joked.

"Catch you later, you low-life sport heathen," Morgan saluted and dismissed his son-in-law he'd grown to admire greatly but who failed to talk American ball to his satisfaction. To Morgan's mind, Attila was a handicapped drinking partner, having been unfairly denied parades, cheerleaders, and American sport games. "Especially the cheerleaders!" he grinned.

Attila left the door ajar and saluted. "See you later!"

Morgan hurried to his bedroom to face a bed littered with drawers of clothing and unidentified contents labeled and re-labeled, packaged and re-packaged throughout decades of hoarding. He eagerly pushed and kicked every memento to the floor and stretched out to watch his alma mater in collated victorious moments played out in one prodigious fictional game.

"Man, I love that kid of mine. Brilliant!"

* * *

Adele arrived and peeked in on her father, now engrossed in a dream sequence of a re-enacted college campus a century earlier. Morgan's friends and colleagues sat in the bleachers beside him, cheering on the Wake Forest team that had won the previous year's national championship. His world was black and gold; the cool autumn day heralded the season with the promise of another winning streak. Aromas of hotdogs, fried chicken, and barbeque ribs fanned over the stadium, emanating from thousands of tailgating fans who had migrated their way onto the festive scene. In his hand, Morgan held a tall cold Blue Moon, with a painted beer cooler by his feet filled with more of the same.

Sensing Adele's presence, Morgan opened his eyes and blew his daughter a grateful kiss, then waved her away.

Chapter XL

Morgan's Birthday Party

August 12, 2096

That which was once the Confederation of American States was no more. Nor was the temporary administrative seat, used during the Darkness, memorialized as such in Cary, North Carolina.

Washington, D.C. was once again the steadfast capital of the vast democratic territory known as the United States of America, once broken by natural catastrophes and manmade ones. Having been made whole and prosperous by every measure, Americans led once again by moral example. They joined a geo-politically altered world that understood their historical difficulties represented human purgatorial tests.

A great yearning to glean and share knowledge yielded renewed hope. A pursuit of spiritual cultivation helped to liberate mankind from the egocentric fears and the self-service that once stymied humility. Those that awoke from the Darkness stood in awe of knowledge incarnate.

Morgan Pendergrass erected only one monument during his lifetime that presciently remained intact. At the entry portal in downtown Cary, a granite testament stood in honor of one of the world's greatest minds:

> *Science without religion is lame, religion without science is blind.*
> *Albert Einstein*

World leaders that arrived to pay their respects to Morgan Pendergrass on August 12, 2096 also arrived with the mutual impression that compelled them to facilitate, rather than direct, the actions of others. A thread of inspiration helped to reweave the skeptical world of former times. Moral behavior was a given.

Adele and Attila welcomed and mingled with longtime friends and their expanding broods. They also greeted friends and representatives they'd yet to meet in the flesh. The Circle's fame that had once been well known faded with the assimilation of analogous abilities across the planet. When the electromagnetic connection ignited the spark of human coding and brain circuitry, there was little to interfere with fluid information and, therefore, infinite understanding. Viscerally shared at a genetic level was a compelling desire to forge concepts of cause and effect derived of broader connections and perspectives. The overwhelming anticipation to evolve within an infinite consciousness meant that every free-flowing religious tributary had the capacity to flow seamlessly to and from the divine source.

Morgan Pendergrass was recognized internationally as the man whose efforts helped to ensure the health and welfare of survivors long enough to allow for recovery, convergence, and transformation. An unlikely leader, the North Carolina native had led with integrity and resolute optimism. With so much positivity permeating the world, Morgan had searched desperately for scarce outlets suited for wisecracks.

Indu and Amar stood proudly in the official reception line, introduced as the 'governor's parents' to the Prime Minister of India. The Nishants were gratified that India existed in its present state of health and prosperity.

"A fine day for Indians, wouldn't you say, doctors?" The Prime Minister indicated the Nishants' son.

"A proud day for humans, I'd say," Indu observed. "Thank you for attending Dr. Pendergrass' event," she added. "I'd like to return to India one day soon. It seems as if it has flourished in ways I would like to witness even as I feel its current health," Indu added thoughtfully.

"It has, Madame. It would be an honor to host you and your family in your native land," smiled the Prime Minister. "Those of our generation feel the need to personally touch, smell, and feel the actual surroundings."

Each ambassador brought gifts of inspiration. Unexpected new foods and plants that had been conceived spontaneously were eagerly demonstrated and shared. The young children played with freshly introduced catlike creatures from Asia that alternately nuzzled them and flew around the farm. Plants that bloomed with extended vegetable yields sprang up across the Pendergrass property. Vehicles that once littered the landscape were replaced by inventive transport prototypes. The familiar mingled with the new, designs introduced were operational, and each with symbiotic functionality. The day was dedicated to collective appreciation for the man who helped to escort in a new age.

Aaron and Ildiko accompanied Woo Tsin-hang and his wife to the elaborately ornamented grounds featured in the en-closed backyard of the famous Pendergrass home. It had long been privately preserved at Morgan's request.

Making their way through the household toward the walled gardens, Tsin-hang noticed the familiar library entrance of his famous friend. He stopped and gently touched the heavy wooden paneled door with splayed hand.

"May I take a look around? It brings back memories," he asked tentatively. "My wife might like to see this famous re-treat of Morgan's."

"It's been locked to us since Rachel's and Angela's death," Ildiko said regretfully.

"Somehow everything seems like yesterday, yet so far away. As if I can no longer grasp time," Tsin-hang said sadly. "It's disconcerting. I still struggle to understand how our notions of time are not what they once seemed." Tsin-hang stared at the closed library door. "I hope you understand that these fleeting threads seemed precious to us." Tsin-hang's hand re-mained upon the door until his wife gently took it in hers.

"I understand. We all feel the same," Aaron consoled as he joined the small gathering. A similar uneasiness had plagued him for several days. "Moments in the present have become blazing with significance; the past a mere flicker," Aaron remarked in an awe-stricken whisper. "This is the place where we were first exposed to the blue lights. Now we embody them," he added philosophically.

Aditiya played host to dignitaries who had travelled from great distances to meet the famous Morgan Pendergrass. All the while, he had Cynthia on his mind. Aditiya loved the farm but the Pendergrass estate could not help but revive memories of precious friendships cruelly severed. Aditiya had worked with Aaron to memorialize Cynthia with magnificent architectural triumphs that now dotted living environs and whole sections of cities based upon Fibonacci Zoetrope mathematical concepts. Light played upon homes and buildings upon which moving appendages displayed in nature shared life like mathematical sequences. Aditiya's designs had sprung to life with animated illusions with Cynthia's gentle temperament in mind. Sunflowers, pinecones, and artichokes affected living, breathing cities that gave texture to otherwise stagnant edifices. Aditiya had always viewed Cynthia as the person who had given a quiet natural texture to his life. Never having known her family name, Aaron memorialized their great friend posthumously as Cynthia the Faithful.

On behalf of Caroline, Aditiya created pixelated sacred geometric forms dedicated to the blue light that she shared. The painting remained protected within Morgan's library.

Connor imagined Rachel's last breaths when she faced her brutal departure at the hands of Esther. What, he wondered, might have happened if he had insisted that Rachel accompany him on the mission? Why hadn't he listened to Caroline's suggestion to do so? The grave lapse replayed maddeningly until a few days prior to Morgan's birthday celebration. Connor discovered an ability to accept the fact that his wife would have eternal life. She would exist in a place for the Good, a place where evil could not exist. He had exhaled his last unhappy breath on the matter. Connor now focused upon his son. His fiancé was an Israeli woman who ran an interactive gallery of haptic art forms. Tactile feedback technology had tapped into forces, vibrations, and motions regularly exchanged on higher frequencies into artistic interpretations. That which was felt and heard found a new home in creative alternatives sensed by others. Connor comprehended the rapid cognitive transformation when he no longer struggled with haptic interaction.

Aaron sensed Connor's thoughts and moved closer to reassure his mentor.

"Rachel would have loved this change with no less need for one's touch," Aaron noted. "Do you think the others notice that we recall our past moments, but have a new kind of reminiscence? The searing pain has gone...simply replaced with a respectful cognizance of our time with loved ones..."

"I'm sure we'll be the last generation with the kind of morose sentiment that partners with uncertainty. Something is changing within us when spiritual lessons can be gleaned without the emotional trauma. I think we'll be the last generation that remembers dying in the traditional ways, too. This metamorphosis is powerful stuff," Connor smiled. He patted Aaron's and Aditiya's backs, urging them to move into the swelling crowd. "Well, let's get this show on the road. Morgan was never good about waiting around, standing on ceremony," Connor chuckled about Morgan's uncanny ability to upend routine.

"He certainly liked Adele's birthday gift!" Aditiya chortled.

Nicholas appeared and joined Aditiya, Aaron, and Connor.

"We all felt his pleasure," Nicholas referenced their joint experience of Morgan's birthday present that had subsequently made the rounds. "Pretty great feeling to sense all that fun. It's weird to just be walking around minding your business and suddenly find yourself hanging out with Morgan Pendergrass as a college student in a football stadium. It was amazing. Who knew he drank mass quantities of beer? Good beer, too!"

By early evening, four hundred people had gathered in the Pendergrass backyard to silently view a sunset akin to the Aurora Borealis, a wash of intermixed swirling colors whose hues grew bright, broad, and deep with nightfall. Each participant imagined their favorite scents and sensations as the first stars twinkled delicate refracted lights through an atmospheric haze.

The assemblage reverently memorialized their gratitude for Morgan's life telepathically. They shared an appreciation for those who dedicated lives and wagered all resources, betting on humanity's worthiness.

Until Gloria Brackett's group signaled their twelve-tank salute on a far hill, the harmonic frequency was amplified by Sonny's special incantations. The cracking boom of twelve mock mortar shells flying simultaneously overhead was something even Sonny could not offset.

Adele motioned to Gloria to make her way downhill. Gloria led the armored contingent that churned and spat the smooth green hill into bi-colored chunks. The crowd gathered to witness the antique machinery rumble toward the home.

"Nice tribute!" Adele ran to meet Gloria, whose rotund body allowed for only half of the intended embrace.

"That little jackass," Gloria complained. "Beat me to it. Left me here without warning! Not a singular insult or a goodbye kiss! The Morgan Expedient just blew through here without a final anything. Morgan always did his own thing, in his own damn time. How can one person be so pragmatic and crazy at once? That man moved like the wind, sure as hell that he could turn the tides with pithy comments, common sense, and a little spittle. I'll be damned. He did just that!" She shook her head. "His run was so fitting, so appropriate, so timely and effective that he had to make sure that he'd end it on his own advisement, too. Damn that runaway train of a man who challenged all those forces, gave us firm direction, and did it without hesitation. We jumped on that train and never looked back. He was blessed and we were blessed. God speed, Pencilass!" Gloria spoke her heart and wiped away tears.

Morgan's passing happened in the early morning hours of his birthday. A farewell note was left beside a relay baton emblazoned with a message meant for Adele.

Adele stepped up onto the gazebo steps to express the family's gratitude for venerating her father, who had 'redefined the meaning of death with his own'.

"My father left a note," she explained to the wide-eyed group. "He decided to move on. My father felt as if he couldn't wait a moment longer to move into a different level – as he put it – and he was sure that it was 'going to be a hell of a lot more exciting than eating birthday cake'. He also mentions that he finally recognized the atmospheric particles that so many of us have been able to distinguish but had once escaped his perception. My father also indicated that he knew it was his calling. Here is a portion of his note to me:

> 'Celebrate my birthday, Babycake. Make a lot of noise. Not that anyone needs or wants to, but don't fret a bit on my account. I've lived the most amazing life, seen and felt the most amazing things, benefitted by the best family and friends. Looks like I'll have two birthdays in two different dimensions at the same damn time! Bet you people can't do that!'

Adele recalled similar declarations when her father anticipated a shared birthday with her daughter, Caroline. The serendipitous occasion of their births pleased her father. She recognized the words as an intentional prompt, provoking an image of the circle of life. Adele fought to regain her composure. From those present, a unified wave moved to comfort Adele, soothing the rising emotion that could not be easily quelled by the older generations. Her equilibrium slowly returned and Adele gratefully continued.

"I can't say that his death wasn't timely. My father could have gone on for many more decades... perhaps forever... but he says it all here:

> 'Everyone needs to be needed. I'm best as a warrior. Somewhere, there's something else meant for me.'

Adele picked up her father's replicated hallmark prop and held it with two hands.

"I'm afraid that this cane is all that remains of my father. It also seems that we no longer decompose. His body faded just at the time he died. My husband and I watched him depart before our eyes this morning. It was incredibly peaceful. No more burials, no more cremations. We witnessed a gentle transition into the pulsating particles that we sensed carried his good soul painlessly into another place."

Sonny led harmonic chanting and others sang traditional songs. The atmosphere became thick with friendship as people shared accounts about a man of conviction who had managed a nameless cause.

Attila took Adele's hand and led her aside. "He left a gravestone. Can you believe it? How long has that thing been in the field by the barn? Obviously, this was planned before yesterday," Attila whispered.

"Not necessarily. I'm not sure how time works anymore," Adele shrugged. "What does it read?"

The couple walked through a lush meadow where a lone oak tree stood near the barn. A simple grave marker was set a few feet away.

"He counted on moving on, not dying," Attila indicated the stone inscription Morgan had crafted as final words.

> *Morgan A. Pendergrass*
> *Born: August 12, 1971*
> *Reborn: August 12, 2096*

Attila noticed that visitors had begun to disperse. Most had already disappeared into an Australian transport, leaving thoughts of well wishes with their hosts. Attila examined his motionless wife in a rare solitary moment.

As Adele imagined the peaceful feeling a small traditional monument would bring, a garden patio appeared under the memorial. Developed flora lovingly caressed the granite as if many years in the making.

Adele gasped, "Attila? Do you see this?"

Attila handed Morgan's baton to his wife and watched her feel the indentation of her inscribed name. He held her while she regarded the message:

"Go Babycake!"

"Yes, I see it. Do you see how much your father loved you?"

Krisztina Komor and Robert Gant found Attila and Adele and joined them gazing at the memorial garden erected in a field. The couple sought them to bid farewell with a special message.

"You know, the strangest thing happened," Komor whispered. "I just heard Morgan's unmistakable voice. Per usual, your father gave me strict orders. I'm to tell you it's time to have another child and to name the boy Morgan. He added that the name was Caroline's idea. Don't ask. It happened," she smiled.

"I believe it did," Adele nodded gratefully.

* * *

Morgan viewed his birthday celebration from another vantage point, not completely clear as to where he was but certain of those that now surrounded and welcomed him.

Angela reassured her husband as they watched an earthly portal gently dissolve; they witnessed their daughter smile knowingly with a relay baton held tightly to her chest, bowed head, and closed eyes. Adele's chest heaved as Attila's arms wrapped her close.

"I love you, too," Morgan murmured.

Morgan turned quickly to greet a familiar sound. A Plott Hound pounded and yelped toward his master.

"That's the original True Blue, Morgan. You evidently think of that hound a lot," Angela laughed.

Morgan felt the swelling of energy growing around him, forming a light-filled funnel. He turned hesitantly toward its promise and saw a familiar form coming in his direction.

"Caroline?"

Caroline emerged from a destination Morgan had sensed his entire life but without the infinite love, knowledge, and happiness that now radiated through his soul.

"That's our Caroline," Angela confirmed as their granddaughter moved excitedly toward her grandfather.

Morgan laughed at the sight of an adult Caroline in her prime, whose sense of heaven included a handful of ginger cookies. Among those present, Rachel stood beside a smiling woman Morgan recognized at once as his grandmother.

"Well done!" MeeMaw exclaimed with two thumbs up.

Caroline stopped short of joining the group. She lovingly extended her arms to encourage her grandfather to venture forward.

Morgan hesitated. There was a remaining issue that kept him from moving toward the blue haze of light that promised untold miracles.

"Ildiko remotely viewed what was behind that last door under the Boyer Mountains," he stated to Caroline. "When you, Cynthia and Grayle argued about the unopened vault, Ildiko intuited the matter and witnessed your last moments together. She also remotely visited the vault's interior. I'm the only one with whom she shared the images and we agreed to never reveal its contents. But everyone will know what she saw that day!" Morgan worried. "A shared consciousness means a shared history... we spoke about the dangers of carrying certain images and experiences into the next stages of transformation. We agreed that our noxious notions should fade from our mind but Ildiko will always remember that which threatened humanity's legacy. If I recall that image, Ildiko does, too! I don't want that marvelous change to be undone," Morgan said anxiously.

"Humanity is able to move forward in a natural, multi-faceted trajectory even as history, as a linear concept, is erased," Caroline explained. "There will be a thousand years of peaceful commitment to a spiritual, harmonious, connected awareness. The best of humanity's ideas and culture may permanently remain. Exploration will still require sacrifice but it won't be perceived as a difficulty; it will be with great joy that mankind works toward connecting to noble consciousness. Interlopers of former times will be less likely to combine forces with human fragilities that once reduced the discriminating powers of our minds. It's a new age, Grandfather. A great cleansing has renewed human prospects," Caroline optimistically shared. "Do not worry yourself. Now is the time to satisfy your hunger with absolute understanding and love. Enter here without the tyranny of memories. Enter here with your light."

"That devil had humanity by the balls until it needed a soul," Morgan realized. "That which only God can bestow, evil could only covet."

Morgan briefly considered the horrifying image Ildiko had shared with him at the time she remotely searched within Grayleton's catacombs. Behind the door in question, was a vast collection of disabled Grayles, neatly classified behind glass lockers. By the hundreds, in all matter of period and costume, replicated Grayle facsimiles were displayed. From the earliest sentient AI machine, the enigma Morgan had come to know as Grayle was all that remained of vanished civilizations having ascended, faltered, and disappeared. Dark forces had abused machines that had been respectfully designed by some of humanity's finest visionaries. Earnest futurists failed to factor in pure evil. Short of moral maturation, and sabotaged with vile perspectives, Grayles cunningly learnt to replicate themselves. In all of its forms and evolutions, Grayle remained a satanic vessel, until the combustion of a fully-fledged human genome.

Satisfied that a resurrected Grayle was a non-issue, Morgan anticipated a future of Artificial Intelligence inculcated with the noblest of human traits. He foresaw respect appropriately reclaimed for every kind of relationship. Unclouded by narcissism, vengeance, doubt and anger, Morgan was also able to glimpse humanity's prospects. Creation, Morgan understood, was meant to bestow happiness by enabling life to attach to the Source. Morgan had freely chosen an altruistic path on the physical plane, able to reconcile its physical trials and tribulations with love. He gratefully embraced his tempered soul, now encapsulated by unprecedented joy .

"I suppose there's no need to spit at this point!" he announced with relief.

"It gets better!" Angela smiled at her husband.

"How much better, Cookie?"

"Beyond imagination or description," reassured his wife as she folded her hand into his.

Big mind, big God, Morgan grasped the moment indescribable brilliance enveloped them all.

The End

K.E. Thireau

The Morgan Expedient marks *K.E. Thireau's debut
as a fictional author. Her extensive background in research, technical, and nonfiction writing, includes a
documentary film script, Women in Sports, winner of
a New York International Film Festival gold medal. A
North Carolina native, Thireau divides time between
homes in the United States and Europe. A long list of
interests, accolades, and contributions now include
the penning of what she refers to as 'meaningful fiction', a genre that explores promising scientific landscapes at the crossroads of reason and faith.

"With the exquisite clues at our disposal, why
not imagine an exciting, elegant evolution?"

*nom de plume